PRAISE FOR TERRY W ERVIN II [illegible]

"The tech level premise is fascinating, but what rea[illegible] is the spirit of Krakista Keesay. Kra is a hero to root for—often underestimated, adept with brass knuckles, bayonet, shotgun, and all sorts of old style weaponry. He proves that, while technology matters, so do courage, intelligence, and daring."**—Tony Daniel, Hugo-finalist, author of *Metaplanetary* and *Guardian of Night***

"Relic Tech is a brilliant piece of science fiction space opera, with edge of your seat action, space battles, aliens, characters you can love (and hate) and a plot that catches you from the beginning and pulls you through to the end. You'll be cheering for Specialist Keesay all the way through this thrilling ride!"**—Angie Lofthouse, author of *Defenders of the Covenant***

"Blood Sword is a tremendous installment in one of the most inventive and compelling fantasy sagas I have read in years!"
-Stephen Zimmer, author of the Fires in Eden Series and The Rising Dawn Saga.

"Blood Sword continues the adventures started in Flank Hawk, in which Ervin created a unique and detailed post apocalyptic world where magic works but ancient technologies from the First Civilization--our world--still exist. You'll cheer as they face off against griffins, fallen angels, gargoyles, and worse, in a fun, engaging adventure filled with wall to wall action."
-David Forbes, author of the Osserian Saga

"A worthy successor to the original novel, packed with action and entertainment."
-Jim Bernheimer, author of the Dead Eye series and Confessions of a D-List Supervillain

"Grab hold! Ervin's got the magic!"
-C. Dean Andersson, author of the Bloodsong Trilogy

"A curious blend of epic fantasy, modern techno-thriller and non-stop action-adventure."
-Erica Hayes, author of the Shadowfae Chronicles

"Buy it or chalk it up on that long list of things you regret not doing!"
-Stephen Hines, author of Hocus Focus

BOOKS BY TERRY W ERVIN II

First Civilization's Legacy
Flank Hawk
Blood Sword
Soul Forge (Forthcoming)

Relic Tech

Genre Shotgun

RELIC TECH

Terry W. Ervin II

Gryphonwood Press

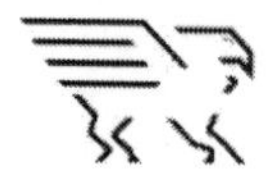

Published by Gryphonwood Press
www.gryphonwoodpress.com

Cover art by Christine Griffin

Printed in the United States of America

ISBN 13: 978-1-940095-10-3

ISBN 10: 1940095107

DEDICATION

This novel is dedicated to my friends William Justice and Darla Boram.

Bill and I attended BGSU together. There and beyond we shared both happy and difficult times. I served as his best man at his wedding and he stood as mine, before cancer took him.

Darla was a ball-of-energy coworker. We shared many laughs and began to share a mutual enjoyment of writing, before a heart attack took her.

Both Bill and Darla were fun-loving and filled with a sense of adventure, always eager to step out and take a chance, and I thank them for demonstrating that aspect of life. It's unfortunate my daughters didn't have the opportunity to know Bill and Darla. The lives of Genevieve and Mira would've been enriched.

ACKNOWLEDGEMENTS

I would like to express my appreciation to Bill Weldy, Jeff Koleno, Sibyl Brewster, Peggy Jester, David Tallman, Sandy Daily, and my wife, Kathy, for taking the time to read the manuscript, share their thoughts, and provide vital input. ***Relic Tech*** is a better novel because of their efforts.

With respect to the cover art, I am grateful for the opportunity to have worked with Christine Griffin yet again. You really captured Kra.

Finally, I'd like to thank David Wood and everyone associated with Gryphonwood Press for believing enough in my debut science fiction novel to publish it. I hope it's just the beginning of Security Specialist Keesay's adventures.

That leaves you, the reader. You're the reason I wrote ***Relic Tech***. Thank you for choosing my science fiction novel from the tens of thousands available. I truly hope you enjoy the story, and don't hesitate to let me know what you think by contacting me through my website or posting a review.

CHAPTER 1

I was on my back. Acid needles assaulted every nerve ending, and I knew the wracking pain was just the tip of the iceberg. Some folks say your first impression is the best one. If that's the case, instinct signaled I was in trouble...deep trouble.

I must have been on pain meds. They were keeping intolerable suffering at bay. With them I could handle it, just barely. Why did I need pain meds? The faint whir of small fans caught my ear. Probably cooling electronic equipment. I tried to open my eyes. Only the left responded. Blurred vision revealed a low, tiled ceiling. I made my first mistake when I tried to sit up. Straps held me down. Trying a little harder proved to be my second mistake. Searing pain shot from my stomach out to arms and legs. I fought against blacking out.

Just before losing consciousness I heard a man's voice. "He's awake."

When I came to, I was lying slightly elevated. Without moving my head, I observed my surroundings with my left eye. I was in a large one-door, sterile room. White walls with metallic accents suggested I was aboard a military vessel. A slight effort with my wrists indicated I wasn't going anywhere. I had pain to keep me company. Thin blankets matching the décor covered my legs. A lumpy inconsistency suggested a bandaged left leg. Tubes emerged from under the covers and swung around behind me, likely connected to computer monitoring equipment. Instead of an infirmary, I was in a conference room. My mind raced with questions. I wondered where I was and if I'd been caught up in some sort of accident. Where was my surgeon?

The door opened. In silence, military aides—low-ranking colonial marine officers—began setting up chairs and a long table. They placed computer clipboards on the table along with paper files. The aides filed out and a number of men and one woman entered. Suits and uniforms. From holo-news reports and my security training I surmised I was about to participate in a judicial pretrial proceeding. My vision still cloudy, I focused on listening.

A man seated at the left end of the table, tapping at a computer clipboard, cleared his throat. "Good to be alive?"

"Yeah," I responded in a dry whisper.

From behind, a man approached and held a clear cup of water with a white straw to my lips. I sipped. Moving my eye slowly, I found I could focus better. I took another drink. The water tasted metallic. My cup-bearing nurse retreated to his original position behind me, still in view of the assembled inquisitors.

I observed the seven men and one woman at the table. Their uniform medals and insignias of rank were impressive. The black suits looked tailored, with matching yellow and black patterned silk ties. Yellow and black meant corporate lawyers.

I looked down at my mangled left leg. It hurt marginally less than my face, and slightly more than my side. Maybe the tubes made a difference. Maybe seeing them made the perceived pain worse.

The nameless assembly waited a few minutes. There looked to be only two corporate lawyers, seated on the left end of the table. Next to them sat a colonial marine general. He was whispering to a fleet admiral with fewer medals and less gray in his mustache. The other three seated individuals included a rep from the criminal justice investigatory squad, a nondescript individual—probably an intelligence agency official, and the lady who wore the insignia of an intragalactic diplomat. An I-Tech technician stood at the end of the white table, readying some holographic recording equipment. Somewhere a judge would be observing the pretrial proceedings. Judges tended to be cold and anonymous, like all corporate actions they presided over.

This looked to be big, but how was I involved? I couldn't remember.

The lawyer who'd addressed me before cleared his throat again. "Krakista Keesay?"

I nodded ever so slightly. I recalled my name. Always a positive in a judicial hearing.

"Relic Tech, Class 4 Transport Security Specialist?"

I nodded again. I recognized the voice and looked closer. It was Falshire Hawks! He was the most prominent publicized corporate lawyer—always in the news. He stood perched, tall and angular with confident, cold blue eyes. He looked older than in the holo-newscasts. At least I knew one of my accusers, but why would he be attending a pretrial, addressing me?

Hawks feigned reading from a computer clipboard as he moved around the table. "Most recent assignment, Negral Corporation, aboard the civil transport *Kalavar*."

I recalled being assigned to the *Kalavar*. Had I boarded?

The lawyer cleared his throat impatiently and stepped closer. I nodded. It's not that I hate silk ties. I normally don't even despise those who can afford them. But Hawks's was an obnoxious yellow. I hated it with a surprising deep-rooted ferocity.

"Specialist Keesay, you have been accused of the following crimes." He held the computer clip up to my face.

My vision close up was still cloudy, but not as much as my memory. I couldn't make out the lines of script, and there were a lot of them.

"Please voice-acknowledge these indictments."

"I can't read them," I said.

"Are you illiterate? Should we add falsification of credentials to the list?"

"I request assistance of a corporate lawyer," I said in a steady but weak voice. "Negral Corp is my sponsor." Hawks wasn't impressed. I watched his smile broaden.

"That option is not available to you." He hardly waited for me to inhale before continuing. "Negral Corporation has been acquired by the Capital Galactic Investment Group, whom I represent. Thus, I represent you."

I didn't know precisely how, but I was about to be warp-screwed. A common occurrence when an I-Tech gets the upper hand.

"Specialist Keesay, *I*, as I said, represent Capital Galactic Investment. I represent you. I am the least of your problems. These individuals, however..." He scanned the long table. "They can speak for themselves."

They looked ready. But from my limited training in jurisdiction and the law, I guessed corporate-political protocol was keeping them at bay, for the moment.

My physical pain retreated to the background as concern over my situation grew. "Then whose side are you on? Theirs?"

"I am on the side of the investor. You are my client, as CGIG is now your sponsor." His musk-scented cologne mingled with his wintergreen breath mint. I found the combination repugnant.

Falshire Hawks stood with his chest puffed out and licked his teeth. "By default you are an investor, minor though it may be."

Maybe he could have put a little more sarcasm into his use of the word *minor.* "Could you please then read the list of accusations to me?" I asked. "I am having trouble focusing."

My lawyer sneered and tapped an activation region on the computer clipboard. The synthesized voice began as he tossed it on my lap. In my condition, even four ounces sent shockwaves of pain through my body. Still, I managed to listen.

"Krakista Keesay, R-Tech rated, Class 4 Transport Security Specialist, formerly endued service skilled investor of the Negral Corporation."

I fought bewilderment more than pain as it droned on.

"You are accused of the following crimes as described in common terms of understanding code, reference 44.6 section 119.4 subsection 2, under the joint jurisdiction of the corporate, civil and military codes. Aiding and abetting a non-human enemy, dereliction of duty, desertion, intragalactic espionage against the corporate state, abduction, planetary quarantine violation, sabotage of corporate property, two counts, subsequent destruction of corporate property, two counts, theft of corporate property, three counts, insurrection, and first degree treason."

"What?" I asked. "I don't remember any of that...I didn't do any..." Everyone was listening. The criminal justice official struggled to remain seated. The final charge, first degree treason, hit me the hardest. It meant my actions resulted in the deaths of over 100 military or corporate personnel! I couldn't even recall how I became injured. Something wasn't right. That yellow tie Hawks wore, I despised it. And it was coming closer.

"Well," said my lawyer, "you have heard the charges. Trust me, the evidence against you is overwhelming. As your representative I recommend you plead guilty to charges two, four, six, seven, eight and nine under the corporate code and accept your punishment. Don't you agree?" He leaned forward, pressing his hand on my mangled leg. "How do you plead?"

I gritted my teeth, struggling against the pain, hating that black and yellow tie and the torturing hand connected to it. Everything started to go black. Computer generated medical alarms sounded.

Falshire Hawks stepped back. "As the Capital Galactic Investment Group is currently represented by fifty-four percent of the Earth Alliance House of Corporate Representatives, our charges take precedence. Prodigious as your crimes are, as a rule we don't execute violators. However, the military does, after a satisfactory interrogation."

My mind spun. I needed time. Those crimes? What evidence? It took only a few seconds to finally realize that I was being set up. It was simple enough to frame someone, especially someone with no recollection of the facts. The last thing I recalled was boarding the shuttle to the space dock, from the Mavinrom 1 Colony in the Gliese 876 system. An I-Tech doctor or psychiatrist could wipe my memory. But why do that? And why would they send Falshire Hawks?

He wasn't going to give me time to think. "Well, Specialist Keesay?"

I stalled. "Could you repeat the charges?"

He frowned.

"Remove my straps," I said, "and I'll reactivate the clip."

The criminal justice official stood. "Absolutely not!" His eyes locked with Hawks's.

My lawyer raised an eyebrow in response to the CJO. "It is unlikely the…" Hawks started, but conceded the point. With an arcing motion he tapped the computer clipboard.

I ignored the synthesized voice repeating the charges. I had to think. I scanned the assembly. The general and the admiral displayed stern faces. The loud mouth CJO wore a frustrated expression. The diplomat was trying to appear disinterested and the intel man's face held no emotion at all. The other lawyer was shifting his attention between the recording technician and me.

All this top brass. War! Desertion and aiding the enemy, treason. The diplomat had to be attached to the Phibs. I examined the insignia more closely. It was mottled gray, green and brown. Correct, the Umbelgarri. Humanity was at war with the Crax and supporting our interstellar patron race. The Umbelgarri were A-Tech. I'd read volumes about them. That was the key.

The room fell silent, except for breathing and the cooling fans. They always underestimate us R-Techs. Contrary to common I-Tech belief, the R does not stand for retarded. Something was hiding behind that yellow tie. I might live if I plead guilty for CGIG, or at least until I encountered an industrial accident. The absolute best I could hope for would be permanent indenture if I agreed to even a fraction of the charges. Somehow I knew the truth was behind the tie.

"Well?" asked Falshire Hawks. "Clearly state your plea."

I'd never played Russian Roulette, and certainly not with five chambers loaded, but it was worth a shot. "I divest myself of all investment and interest in the Capital Galactic Investment Group."

The statement stunned Falshire Hawks along with the rest of the assembly. An R-Tech in the depths of space without substantial assets going independent? Charity being an antonym for corporation, under normal circumstances I'd just condemned myself to a decade of indentured servitude. Damn the legal consequences. It was my chance!

Without taking a breath I said to the lady diplomat, "As an autonomous individual, I formally request political association with the Umbelgarri and subsequent protection under such association."

Almost before I finished, the diplomat stood and replied, "As an official representative of the Umbelgarri, and vested with proper authority, I acknowledge your request and shall take it under consideration on their behalf."

I hoped this would hold the military at bay. Advanced military tech support and alliance matters should encourage them to proceed with caution. Capital Galactic, on the other hand, was a corporate organization and another matter. I'd managed to catch Hawks off guard. Everyone underestimates relic techs.

Falshire Hawks's partner whispered something into his ear. Calmly the senior corporate lawyer addressed the diplomat. "As you well know, it is against the Earth Alliance – Umbelgarri Treaty for you to offer political association to one under such charges. He must be tried, found innocent or guilty, and serve his punishment before he can be released to form any association."

With nods, everyone around the table leaned back, seeming to accept this without question.

A toothy smile spread across Hawks's face. "Further, as he has divested himself *after* having been informed of the accusations, he now lacks the ability to acquire legal representation." His eyes sparkled. "I can assure you that the Capital Galactic Investment Group will not allow this individual to avail himself of Umbelgarri or any other assistance."

I expected something like this as well. It appeared that the diplomat was interested in this case, and in me. Her quick action on my behalf, and the venomous look that she sent Hawks bolstered my resolve.

Hawks and his yellow tie faced me. "As his crimes against the Capital Galactic Investment Group supersede the others, as previously stated, he will be remanded to our custody pending judgment and assigned punishment by an appointed judiciary official."

I could see the diplomat expected this. She looked at me even as I stared at Hawks. I knew she was hoping I had something planned other than assuring my own execution. I really despised that yellow tie, but my emotions began to focus on the man behind it. I would try anything to get back at him.

"I acknowledge that as an independent, lacking a corporate sponsor, I cannot acquire legal counsel. Nor can I speak before a court with respect to the corporate code allegations, having divested myself of any corporate ties. However, it is also my understanding under the corporate code, any relevant evidence recorded prior to divestment indicating innocence of the accused, presented to the court by verifiable hard copy or a computer devoid of artificial intelligence programming, is permissible and may be submitted."

Hawks snorted. "You have no such evidence."

It was my turn to smile, but I didn't. With a straight face I said, "I do. I only require a computer to retrieve it and display it to the court."

He suspected something was behind my request. Now, I was the one who couldn't allow him time to think.

The Umbelgarri diplomat cut in, "If you deny the accused his legal request, the Umbelgarri will deem the Capital Galactic Investment Group to be acting in violation of the Earth Alliance – Umbelgarri Treaty and will immediately grant political association to the individual."

The two corporate lawyers began to confer. The diplomat apparently overheard. "This is pretrial. There is no appeal on this request. The Umbelgarri will grant immediate political association. You may appeal that if your corporation desires."

The diplomat, for the first time, viewed the holographic recorder. She addressed the judge on the other end. "May the Umbelgarri grant political association to the accused?"

A moment passed. Just before the small indication light flashed green, Falshire Hawks stepped forward. "The request of the accused is deemed admissible and granted."

All in the assembly looked relieved, except the diplomat, until I opened my mouth. "I request data retrieval and presentation via the Cranaltar IV."

CHAPTER 2

The Cranaltar IV is a 4th generation A-Tech or advanced technology brain-scanning device. It is being developed by several of the larger corporations with substantial Umbelgarri support. Some people consider A-Tech to stand for alien technology, which is in essence true, as humans are currently considered to be I-Tech or at the intermediate stage of technological advancement. Mankind probably would not have yet reached I-Tech if it were not for the Umbelgarri intervention during the Silicate War.

The previous Cranaltar prototypes were less than stellar successes. Any human hooked up to one came out somewhat addled at best. The ultimate purpose of the device is unclear, but it is purported to have the ability to draw information from an individual's memory and store it as any combination of audio, visual, or even text files. It has even been suggested that advancements in the Cranaltar Project could eventually lead to information retrieval from recently deceased individuals. It has been asserted that is how the Umbelgarri utilize their more advanced version of the device.

The Umbelgarri are amphibian and more cerebrally evolved. Their brain anatomy and chemistry differs substantially from a human's. Thus, adaptation for use on humans, or any lesser primate, has proven to be a real stumbling block.

The device poses obvious ethical issues, even if the mentally destructive risks are ignored.

Falshire Hawks swept his computer clipboard from my lap and stalked back to his seat. The assistant hastily pecked at his screen, calling up information on the Cranaltar IV. It wasn't a corporate or military black project. The Phibs are secretive, but general knowledge points to continued refusal in collaborative corporate black projects.

I watched as the diplomat attempted to suppress a smile. Hawks had never heard of the Cranaltar Project.

"Your request is out of order," said Hawks, still reading from his assistant's clip screen. "The device has not been proven. It is merely a prototype." He continued to scan the data now appearing on his clip.

The admiral, general and CJO sat, braced on the edge of their seats. Something other than my fate was in play.

The diplomat glanced down at her clip. "That is inaccurate. The Cranaltar III was used in two cases to successfully obtain information from unwilling convicted criminals. The information retrieved was deemed admissible as evidence to be used against those convicted and their accomplices."

Lawyer Hawks folded his arms. "But, Diplomat Silvre, it severely damaged the subjects' brains, rendering both virtually brain dead. Only the most basic autonomic functions remained intact."

"True, Mr. Hawks. However, vital information *was* obtained. Vital information in this case could also be obtained."

"What information would that be? Even if Specialist Keesay were by some miracle able to cast minimal doubt on even one of the charges, he would be rendered entirely unable to serve the punishment for his crimes."

"Your point is?" asked Diplomat Silvre, with eyebrows raised.

Hawks seemed puzzled or distracted by the continued, almost feverish activity of his assistant. Whatever it was, the information wasn't being transferred to his superior.

Hawks stood, then walked past the military officers and stopped in front of the diplomat. "My point, Diplomat Silvre, is that the accused's actions have resulted in substantial loss of life, capital, and future profits. Quite substantial in the view of the Capital Galactic Investment Group."

The diplomat turned her clip over so that Hawks couldn't view the screen's contents. "If he is indeed guilty of the crimes suggested, as a relic tech security specialist, the accused would never be able to repay the financial debt. And in essence, he would be calling a form of capital punishment upon himself."

"But over his lifetime the accused could repay some of the debt," Hawks' assistant stated as he made a final entry on his computer clipboard with a single thumb press.

A vicious glare from Hawks to his subordinate said it all.

Silvre leapt at the opening, re-engaging Hawks's attention. "The Umbelgarri will reimburse any potential income which could have been generated by Specialist Keesay. Assuming he is disabled and found guilty."

The military observers sat up, surprised by the assistant's improper initiative. Hawks stalked over to his subordinate. He gestured for a moment's delay in the debate before gripping his assistant's shoulder and whispering into his ear. The subordinate immediately deactivated his clip, removed his own yellow tie sporting four narrow black bands, and left the room. He'd be looking for a new sponsor without the benefit of a good reference.

Hawks turned and addressed those remaining at the table. "My assistant, Mr. Loams, no longer represents the Capital Galactic Investment Group. His statement had no standing in this proceeding. Any interjection or assertion is therefore nullified."

Miss Silvre's tenacity impressed me. "I was not referring to information with respect to Specialist Keesay's innocence," she said. "The evidence against him, though compelling, is incomplete. I believe that he had accomplices. If, in the effort to prove his innocence, he reveals other guilty parties, I believe that not only would the Capital Galactic Investment Group benefit, but so would the other plaintiffs." She leaned forward and looked down the table. "The intelligence, military and justice organizations represented at this table."

Everyone at the table nodded, even the recording technician. All eyes focused on the lone corporate lawyer.

Hawks was good, but I could see that he was mentally back pedaling. "Specialist Keesay's condition is critical and unstable at best," the lawyer said. "He may not survive the week let alone the device. Where is the nearest Cranaltar device?"

"The Cranaltar IV Project is located on Io," said the lady diplomat, "attached to the subsurface Umbelgarri outpost." She looked to the intelligence official.

He simply said, "Correct." His noncommittal voice matched his face.

She barely began to address the justice official when I started to feel nausea, followed by wracking pain.

Hawks finished tapping at his computer clip. "The Capital Galactic Investment Group moves immediately to freeze assets of the accused, as allowed under article 4, section 3 of the corporate code. And as he has no sponsor and no available assets, medical support is being terminated."

I had difficulty remaining composed as I felt the medical support shutting down. I knew I was in pain, but until Hawks's action, I didn't realize the severity of my condition.

Diplomat Silvre said, "The Umbelgarri will supply funding for the required medical support."

"Denied," replied Hawks. "This is a CGIG vessel. As the Umbelgarri are not a plaintiff in this case, they have no standing on this issue." I didn't have to see Hawks's smile to know it was there.

My vision began to blur and my heart thumped erratically. My leg, face and chest were on fire.

The diplomat stepped behind the intelligence man, who then leaned over toward the CJO. Hawks had unleashed his corporate 800-pound gorilla and it landed on my chest. I was dying. Dying fast!

My sight faded but I could still hear with remarkable clarity. The CJO quickly tapped some keys. "The Criminal Justice Investigatory Agency supports the desires of the Intelligence Agency to seek information on any of Specialist Keesay's conspirators with respect to his crimes against not only CGIG, but those which fall under military jurisdiction as well."

The medical machinery came back on line as the fast spoken words and keystrokes overrode the lawyer's cutoff effort. The pain receded. My heart settled back to a rhythm. I drew a breath, then two. Again, I struggled to remain conscious, and lost.

The last thing I heard was the low, calm voice of the intelligence man. "Prepare the suspect for transfer to the *Iron Armadillo*."

CHAPTER 3

The Iron Armadillo, *commissioned under the name of* Armadillo, *was a first series intragalactic military scout. Twenty years ago it was considered a very fast ship. It still is by today's I-Tech standards with a sub-condensed space speed of .38 percent the speed of light. It was the first vessel designed and built with direct Umbelgarri assistance and carried its own cascading atomic engine for initiating condensed space travel.*

The Armadillo *first saw action late in the Silicate War, eight years after the Phibs recruited humans in what was termed the Carbon Cause. She was one of the first human vessels sent into action against the Shards without Umbelgarri or other allied support. Until that time humanity had been restricted to a very miniscule corner of the Milky Way because humans were incapable of condensing space. Fortunately or unfortunately, depending on who is asked, the Umbelgarri contacted Earth through its Mars Colony and sponsored mankind into the Interstellar Society.*

Initially mankind was recruited for ground combat with human ships limited to rear echelon support. Humanity's violent history ever honed its combat resourcefulness and the Phibs directed it against the Shards. Human ships, like the Colonial Marines, bristled with effective weaponry. The Umbelgarri helped humans design the first series scout to add speed and mobility to humanity's arsenal.

After detecting a Silicate Fleet exiting a wormhole near the double star Capella, the Armadillo, *outfought two Shard frigates, destroying one, damaging and outrunning the second. The* Armadillo *escaped to warn a mixed Umbelgarri-Felgan fleet. The heroic action stalled a Silicate flanking maneuver. It also earned respect among several alien races.*

The combat damage sustained necessitated emergency patching over forty percent of the Armadillo*'s hull. The result wasn't pretty, with the dockworkers dubbing the hastily repaired ship the* Iron Armadillo. *The name stuck.*

I awoke with a splitting headache added to the pain brought on by my other injuries. It took my left eye a minute to focus on the tile ceiling, which was different. I cautiously moved my wrists. They weren't bound. I detected the familiar sound of the small electronic fans. I tried to recall my last moments of consciousness. "The *Iron Armadillo*," I whispered to myself.

"Yes," said a feminine voice. "Preparations are underway for transfer. It's en route, ETA thirty minutes." It was Diplomat Silvre. "Bed, raise front to thirty degrees, ten percent normal speed. Seems you have awakened just in time."

The bed elevated my head and torso, increasing my field of vision. I was in a small, rectangular room. Same décor as the last. My wrists were unmarked, so the restraints had been off for some time.

Diplomat Silvre stood on the left side of the bed where I could more easily see her. She was wearing a dark tan body suit under an olive jacket. It looked more like a sturdy, well-pocketed lab coat than anything else. Her new jacket bore the diplomatic insignia of the Umbelgarri.

My throat was dry. "Lost the fancy suit, huh?"

She nodded and offered me a cup.

My hand was a little shaky but it didn't hurt to move as much as I'd feared. The water still tasted metallic. "Thanks," I said and took another sip.

Silvre stood next to my bed a moment, waiting. She was short with dark hair, and moderately attractive despite the outfit. I knew intellectually I paled in comparison to her. The Umbelgarri recruited only the very brightest. She'd taken a weak hand and turned it into a winning one against Falshire Hawks, one of the best. I owed her.

"Thanks," I said, handing her the cup.

She took it and looked at me with her right eyebrow arched.

"For helping out with Hawks," I said. "By the way, where are we?"

"You might refrain from thanking me yet, and we're still aboard the *Pars Griffin*."

It took me a second to recall. The *Pars Griffin* was a heavy class passenger transport owned and operated by CGIG. I saw it launched on a holo-newscast less than a year ago. Or now, maybe more than a year ago.

She set the cup on a narrow table behind her. "We're orbiting Mars. Stationed 40,000 kilometers from Orbital Space-dock 4. The *Iron Armadillo* is en route from patrolling the Trojan Clusters near Jupiter." She crossed her arms. "Specialist Keesay, what exactly do you recall?"

I still had no idea how much time had passed since I'd boarded the *Kalavar,* until now. It was an easy question and might reveal my standing with the diplomat. "What day is it?"

She looked irritated. "Saturday."

Not the answer I wanted. "Good, I didn't miss church."

"Should it be my understanding that you intend to be uncooperative, Specialist?"

"I recall Hawks and his damn yellow tie if that's what you mean."

"Good." She shifted her weight to one leg and waited.

"Well, if you think," I started, but considered who else might be listening, or recording. "I don't recall any of the things I'm accused of."

She reached inside her jacket and produced a small metallic cube. She carefully touched three of the sides simultaneously before setting it on the bed. She confirmed what I already suspected. "This will foil any surveillance efforts."

"I still don't recall anything. I'm being set up."

"Maybe you should see this," she said as she walked across the small medical room and returned with a computer clip. "Here is a small cross section of the evidence aligned against you."

With a tap of her index finger, she activated the clip screen. A fuzzy and slightly distorted picture emerged. I could make out myself high up in some sort of balcony overlooking an internal space dock or hanger. The image wasn't steady but I saw that I was wearing full riot gear. I threw something, no two somethings in quick succession toward the recording device. The view shifted immediately toward the floor. I saw sparks that resembled muzzle flashes. Static followed.

I shrugged my shoulders, brining on a sharp stabbing pain.

She tapped the screen several more times. "That view was obtained from a colonial marine's helmet recorder, aboard the civil transport *Kalavar*. And those objects you threw at the marine have been identified as old-style grenades."

I thought a moment. "Maybe I was throwing them at something near the helmet. Recording can be initiated without being worn." I was grasping at straws while trying to figure why I might have lobbed grenades in a transport's hangar, at a colonial marine.

"Negative. Intelligence has determined from the angle and movement of the recording device, it was being worn." She stood with the clip held against her chest.

"Where's the audio?" I asked.

"Unrecoverable," she said. Then added, "According to technical experts provided by the Capital Galactic Investment Group."

"Was it tampered with?"

"Not according to intelligence."

"What else?" I asked, not really wanting to know. "Wait, what happened to the marine? What was going on—happened to the *Kalavar*?"

"The marine, Corporal Justice Smith, is presumed dead. His blood, mixed with Stegmar Mantis blood, was found on the helmet, floating in space near—"

I interrupted her. "Wait! Why has the date-time reference been left out? Stegmar Mantis?" I didn't want to get this piecemeal. "Why don't you just explain it to me?"

She finished, "Near Zeta Aquarius."

"That was the first scheduled destination of the *Kalavar*," I said.

She tapped the screen again. This time, angled from above and down a corridor, a recording showed me in full gear dragging a youth, probably male. Again, the time reference was missing. I shoved the youth ahead of me and motioning with my bayonet for him to move on, out of the camera's view. Was that blood on the bayonet? The audio consisted of crackling and hissing, with muffled explosions in the background.

"That was Maximar Drizdon Jr., son of Dr. Maximar Drizdon Sr."

"Maximar Drizdon?" I asked. "The famed military strategist? The Dr. Drizdon credited with every major success in the campaign against the Silicates?" I took a breath while Diplomat Silvre stared. "Is that who I supposedly abducted? His son?"

I mentally replayed the image. The boy wasn't wearing the garb of an I-

Tech. His clothes were baggier like an R-Tech's, and he wore a frumpy-brimmed hat.

She interrupted my thoughts. "What are the odds of someone carrying a pump-action shotgun with a bayonet? Other than you, Security Specialist Keesay."

My head suddenly throbbed a little more. "Where's the boy? Does anyone know? Will you explain it to me now?"

"No," she said, and deactivated the clip.

That seemed pretty final. "Then what was the little viewing for?"

"Just a little encouragement. Intelligence has authenticated the evidence."

"So I don't back out?"

She nodded and smiled, and it wasn't a friendly one. "There's a lot more, all authenticated." She returned the computer clip to the small table. "But for now, time is of the essence."

"You think I'm guilty! Then why help fend off Hawks?"

She waited, probably pondering how much to tell me. "If indeed you performed all of the actions of which you are accused, you must've had accomplices."

"And if I'm not guilty, then my evidence might reveal..." It was hard to think. I wished the pain meds worked better. "Might reveal something against Capital Galactic?"

She didn't respond.

"Are we at war?"

"We are," she replied.

"Crax?"

"Yes."

"Are we winning?"

"No," she said with scorn.

Now I knew why she was in such a bad mood. The Umbelgarri were tough. But after what the Shards did near the end of the Silicate War, they were a shadow of their former strength. News estimates indicated that the Umbelgarri would never recover. The Crax had moved to ensure that end. And we humans are allied with the Phibs.

I swallowed hard and thought a moment. Some corporations were rumored to be friendly with the Crax, most often Capital Galactic. Maybe not all humans are loyal to our galactic sponsors? "Is Capital Galactic helping the Crax?"

She shrugged.

"Was Negral Corp?"

Same response. Now I knew why she was less than friendly, even though she'd assisted me.

Silvre moved a hand to her ear and motioned for silence. She tapped the cube, deactivating it. After a few seconds she reactivated the security device. "Specialist Keesay, the *Iron Armadillo* will be docking in less than fifteen minutes."

As if on cue the room's single door opened. In walked the intelligence official from the pretrial. I caught a glimpse of at least one guard stationed outside. My single-eyed vision continued to improve. What happened to my other eye? I pushed that question aside to focus on the situation at hand.

The intel man looked plain, with a short, military cut hairstyle. He wore a charcoal-colored sport jacket over a lighter synthetic knit shirt.

A marine out there, I pondered. He wasn't posted there to keep me from escaping. A thought hit me. "Am I really in as bad of shape as Hawks indicated?"

Silvre adjusted the cube's settings. "Yes."

The intelligence official and the diplomat exchanged glances. The official introduced himself. "Specialist Keesay, I am Deputy Director Karlton Simms."

He offered his hand. I shook it. His grasp was firm, yet considerate of my condition. Director Simms and Diplomat Silvre were the closest things to friends I had. "Call me Kra."

Director Simms looked at the tubes and other apparatus running from under the blankets. "Would you like the details of your condition?"

"Not really. I can pretty much guess." Then I added, "What are the odds?"

He thought for a second. "I'd be stretching it if I said it was twenty-eighty."

"Any chance for a full recovery?"

He shook his head. "No." His eyes showed some sympathy, but not entirely sincere. I've always been pretty sharp when it comes to reading people. He'd been much better at keeping a blank expression during the pretrial. Nevertheless, I appreciated his effort.

"Well then," I said, "it doesn't really matter the results of the Cranaltar. If I am indeed guilty, the Cranaltar will wreck my brain, even if it doesn't kill me in proving it. I'll get mine and so will anybody else who helped. Right, Diplomat Silvre?"

She avoided my gaze by examining the support equipment monitors I figured were beyond the head of my bed.

"And if I am innocent," I said to Director Simms, "then whoever set me up and put me in this condition, you'll be sure to pay them back for me. Right?"

His gaze hardened. "That is correct."

"Well, it seems you can't lose."

"Yes, we can," Simms said. "We have to get you to Io and the research facilities there."

"You think Capital Galactic has something to do with the whole thing?"

Simms gave a non-committal look. For a fraction of a second he locked gazes with Diplomat Silvre.

"Anything is within the realm of possibility," she said.

"Some things appear more probable," he said, looking from her to me. "Kra, the *Iron Armadillo* will be docking shortly." He reached into his jacket and produced a small semi-automatic pistol. He checked the clip, chambered a round, uncocked it, and handed it to me.

My look must have betrayed my thoughts.

"Capital Galactic attempted to silence you once today already," he explained.

I examined the gun. It was old but well maintained. Twenty-two caliber, blued steel, rosewood grips.

Simms continued, "Not exactly heavy duty. I checked your file. I know you prefer old-style revolvers, but it should do."

The pistol was pretty light and would have little recoil. "In my condition, I think it'll be manageable. How many rounds?"

"Seven. I use it mostly for sport, sometimes as a backup. It's an antique. You're lucky I had it with me." He grinned. "I'll be sure to ask for it back."

"Thanks. It's in excellent condition. I'll try not to use it on Hawks should I see him in the next few minutes."

"Much appreciated."

I asked, "Do you really think they'll try something?"

"If they believe you have sufficient knowledge," said Silvre as she moved around the bed out of view. "Or information that could be damaging to their investors, or the investment group as a whole. We believe they'll try to eliminate the source."

"The captain of the *Pars Griffin* has denied personnel from the *Armadillo* boarding his ship, denied us escort off his vessel," said Simms as he retrieved the computer clip from the table. "Even though we're at war, military-corporate protocol dictates that under the circumstances, on this class vessel, it's his prerogative." He tapped a few spots, bringing up the *Pars Griffin*'s layout. "We're here," he pointed. "This is our route."

A red line traced a path left, down the hall about eighty yards, past one cross hall and another thirty yards, a short turn to the right to an elevator. Eight decks down and out. A straight shot, about thirty yards to the docking hitch and the *Iron Armadillo*. A yellow line began to trace another path five decks below that led to the hangar bay.

"The red line is our primary route," said Simms. "Keep that in mind if something happens. The yellow, don't worry about. It's our concern." He looked past me to Silvre.

I heard her working, opening up something. "What's she doing?"

"Preparing a little surprise for any would be assassins," said Simms. He was busy erasing the memory from the computer clip. He removed the memory plate and snapped it into quarters. He smiled. "Mind if I use your cup?"

"No," I said. "I'm finished."

He dropped the broken plate and a small tablet into the remaining water. It fizzed.

Silvre came back into view carrying a small mechanical device covered with lenses and fiber optic equipment. It was a holographic image projector of some sort, but far smaller than any I'd ever seen. It was so small it had to be A-Tech. Umbelgarri.

She set it under the sheets next to my side. "Try not to disturb it," she said almost reverently. Then she removed a small, faceted, rectangular box with a miniature power pack from one of her inner coat pockets. "It's not military issue, but it may make a difference should someone have ill intentions."

It was a defense screen. Advanced, A-Tech equipment as well. Doubtless her personal screen. "What about you?"

"CGIG, or your conspirators, won't be targeting me."

I watched Simms check and reholster his magnetic pulse pistol. Despite being R-Tech, I'd trained in the use of MP pistols. They can be quite effective, even one meant for concealed carrying like his. It held forty rounds about the size of BBs but with a phenomenal velocity compared to a .22 caliber round. I was willing to bet he had some of the chemically charged explosive rounds. Same size gun, about five times the firepower.

"So what does the diplomat bring to the occasion?" I asked.

"I plan on concealing myself behind you, and my screen if there's any trouble."

"She brought the marine outside." Simms winked. "Other than him and your nurse, basically we don't have a lot of friends on this vessel."

Silvre added, "If you have evidence against Capital Galactic somewhere within your cranium."

"Look, I really don't recall anything about any of the accusations. Even showing me the evidence hasn't rung a bell. Not even a jingle's worth." I looked at Simms. "You've seen my file. That's not me. I signed on with the Negral Corp to jumpstart my career. I want to join the R-Army GASF. But I needed experience to get noticed and recruited. I couldn't do that securing warehouses and storage depots. That was a dead end." I looked at Silvre. "Even if I could, I wouldn't undermine our alliance with the Umbelgarri, or turn traitor.

"Honest," I said to them both. "Fondness for reptiles has never been strong in my family."

I took a breath. Not too deep. "I'd like a drink. Alcoholic would be nice, but then it might deprive the Cranaltar of a few brain cells. Where's your—my trusty nurse?"

"Will water suffice?" Silvre asked. She offered me my cup and winked at Simms. "Freshly laced with?"

"Classified," Simms chuckled.

I held up my hand for her to keep it, and winced. "Wish it was morphine."

"Good," said Simms. "You might've spilled it on her holographic projector."

"That valuable huh? And I thought the screen was to ensure I didn't come to any harm."

Silvre smiled, then put her hand to her ear. She deactivated her cube. "The scout vessel just docked." After another second of concentration she reactivated the cube. "Escort again denied."

All emotion drained from Simms's face. "Let's be on our way." He went to the door and summoned in the marine and nurse.

The marine private had dark skin and wore a combat vest, stitched with the name Varney. He carried a magnetic pulse carbine with a light-duty laser module mounted beneath the barrel. A holstered standard issue MP pistol rested on his right hip. The white-clad nurse carried a medical kit and a portable diagnostic support kit slung over his shoulder, and a sizeable power pack in his arms.

The nurse moved behind my bed, made some adjustments and hooked up the diagnostic support kit.

Silvre picked up the cube and adjusted it, nodding to the nurse.

He engaged the bed's motor control. "Voice control override...on my voice."

Simms followed, "On my voice."

"On my voice," said Silvre.

Louder than necessary the marine chimed in, "On my voice."

It was either adrenaline or gung-ho. Good for him. I had neither at the moment. "On my voice," I said.

"Voice override locked," announced the nurse. The bed shifted as its wheels prepared to engage.

I said, "Bed, raise front to forty-five degrees, twenty-five percent normal speed." I knew it would hurt, but I wanted a better view.

Silvre deactivated the cube and stayed on my left. I looked at her questioningly. She looked back knowingly and slid it into an inner pocket. Simms moved to the right side of the bed. Private Varney led the way out the door while the nurse, monitoring my life support and directing the bed's path, brought up the rear.

CHAPTER 4

Twelve years after the establishment of the ground colonies on Mars and Io, and orbital colonies around Europa, Triton, and Titan, the cooperation of the participating Earth governments proved disastrous. The colonies' distance and isolation magnified the neglect, leading to increasingly critical shortages of supplies and equipment. Supply runs before the use of space-condensing engines were far slower and the colonies suffered greatly due to the delays.

In support with the then small colonial populations, several large corporations petitioned the involved Earth governments for control of the colonies. The governments granted control to the corporations after negotiating for reimbursement on expenditures.

The arrangement worked for the colonies. Many earthbound citizens began to demand similar representation. Several moderate-sized nations moved toward the model, meeting with unprecedented prosperity. More nations followed, some merging with others under corporate rule.

Unrest built between the non-corporate and corporate states until the appearance of the Umbelgarri and the onslaught of the Silicate War. During the crisis the corporate model merged with the parliamentary form of government into one entity, encompassing all citizens of Earth and established colonies. Within weeks new investments were made. Elections were held and appointments ratified. On this path mankind forged ahead into war and the future.

We entered the corridor and went left. The *Pars Griffin* was a luxury passenger transport mainly utilized for cruises and business travel. Although, like all interstellar vessels, space was allocated for interstellar freight. The corridor was eight feet wide and equally high. Unlike most interstellar ships, the usual exposed pipes and conduits weren't visible. The passage was clean and empty.

Private Varney set a brisk pace down the well-lit corridor. I had difficulty seeing what was going on but Silvre and Simms appeared alert. The sound of footfalls and the rhythmic breathing of my escorts mingled with the faint humming of the transport's engines preparing for departure. I set my hand on the pistol under the sheets. My heartbeat fell into cadence with the pace.

I heard the whirring noise of a supplemental security robot approach. Most are triangular in shape, squat, and maneuver on three wheels. Varney, carbine leveled, blocked my view. To my right Simms pulled what looked like a holo-display remote control from an inside pocket. It sported far more buttons and tiny screen icons than standard remotes. With his left-hand thumb he tapped in rapid succession. The whirring stopped.

"Deactivated," said the intelligence man to the marine. "Check it out."

Keeping his body between the robot and myself, Private Varney advanced. I scanned the walls, wondering if the nurse was watching our rear. I spotted a security camera recessed in a light casing. At the crack of MP gunfire I whipped my head to the front. Too fast. The pain rush brought on distorting, gray flashes.

After a few seconds my head cleared. Simms was pressing forward, calling the *Iron Armadillo*. "...terrorist robot, rally point red one! Yellow pass through!"

He didn't wait for the response that crackled from the remote, "Understood."

Varney was down. The sec-bot had deployed its stun net. Despite the electrical current coursing through the entangling mesh, the marine unsteadily maneuvered his carbine. Simms opened up on the sec-bot with his sidearm. The explosive rounds rocked the sec-bot, but only managed to make large pockmarks in what had to be a hardened armor casing. My old .22 caliber pistol wouldn't help.

I didn't know what the nurse was doing but Silvre was making hasty adjustments to a foot-long cylindrical object. In quick succession, two flashing blasts from Varney's laser burned into the armored menace.

I looked back up at the surveillance camera near the ceiling. I knew Hawks was watching. With effort I raised my pistol and fired two quick shots at it. Both painfully jarred my arm. The semi-auto's fire was considerably louder than the snapping crack of MP gunfire.

Varney's laser blasts must have penetrated as the security robot sat smoking and silent. Simms was lifting the stunned private to his feet when the faltering machine emitted a metallic click followed by an explosion. The flash temporarily blinded me.

Simms was down with Varney laying on him. The marine and my defense screen took most of the blast. Several thumb-sized metal fragments lay harmlessly on my bed sheets.

My nurse didn't wait to evaluate the situation. We rolled up to Simms, who pushed the dead marine aside. Blood flowed from the intel man's face and forearm. He tossed his remote to the nurse, waving us past. The nurse tossed Varney's wrecked carbine aside and snatched the dead marine's sidearm. The stench of scorched metal and singed flesh hung in the air. Anger overcame my rising nausea.

Silvre said, "Caylar, you take point. I'll bring Keesay. Simms, follow and watch our back."

We had twenty yards to go before the cross-hall with the turn to the elevator in sight. My nurse, Caylar, picked up the pace. When a door ahead to the left slid open, Caylar dropped to one knee, sending several cracking shots. A gray-clad man fell into the hallway along with a scope mounted MP assault rifle. Another door immediately to my right slid open. Without hesitation I raised my pistol and fired blindly at what should have been chest level. Two quick shots. If he was an innocent passenger, he should've stayed in his room. And if he'd had any type of synthetic armor I wouldn't have lived to confirm it. A brief, gurgling cry and thump said my second shot must've risen, or the target had been short.

"Good shot!" said Silvre from behind.

I couldn't respond. I was too busy fighting the pain in my chest those good shots had inflicted.

Caylar stopped near the crossway. Several cracks of MP gunfire sounded from behind followed by a return volley. Then shots from multiple calibers intermingled.

Caylar pulled out an old fashioned circular mirror used by R-Tech practitioners to examine teeth. He knelt, holding the mirror close to the floor and peered around the corner. He spun back just as parts of the wall buckled and shattered under impacting automatic fire. Caylar signaled Silvre to move up. Holding his hand a yard off the floor, he said, "Two each side, twelve to fifteen meters back. Heavily armed." Caylar produced a palm-grenade, winked at Silvre, and then tossed it around the corner. The fire abated. Nothing else happened.

Three clicks resembling marbles striking wet plexiglas, each followed by instantaneous cracks of MP fire, reverberated just behind my bed. Caylar rushed back and opened fire to my rear while Silvre made more adjustments to several washer-like disks at the base of her gray baton. In less than a second she finished. Only then I realized what she had. "Poor bastards," I whispered.

"The director is down," said Caylar, firing several more shots down the hall. "Good thing your screen's still up or you'd be dead."

"Feel free to use it for cover," I offered.

I'd seen holos of the beam weapons the Umbelgarri mounted on their combat vessels. I'd also read about the handheld version Silvre was about to use. She knelt and simply activated the baton while reaching her hand around the corner. A swift side-to-side flick proceeded brief cries of surprised terror.

Silvre looked around the corner, winced, and fought to keep her lunch down. Weakly she said to Caylar, "I have only eighty-two thousandths of a second left."

Caylar looked at the hand beam. "Keep it ready," he said over his shoulder as he trotted ahead.

"And pointed away from us," I added. Silvre forced a smile. She returned to the rear, commanding the bed forward.

I ventured a look down the cross hall and saw scarred walls and sliced, scattered bodies. I took as deep of a breath as I dared, and exhaled. "Where's our help?" I asked. "Didn't Simms contact them?"

Silvre had regained her composure. "They'll be at the first rally point. Bottom of the elevator."

That didn't make sense to me. We needed them here. "Who planned this?"

"Director Simms," said Caylar, slowing down. "It'll work. We'll make it as he planned."

Caylar stopped and knelt. First, he looked around the corner toward the elevator. Then he took aim at a surveillance camera. After one shot he signaled okay. We followed him around the corner and backed into the elevator.

It was a tight fit. Caylar had disabled the obvious monitoring devices before working the buttons on Simms's remote control device.

Silvre side-stepped up beside me. "Almost clear." She brought out and activated the little cube and set it on my bed. A little blood dampened her hair above the temple. She carefully reached under the covers and retrieved the Umbelgarri holographic device and began making adjustments while the elevator started its descent.

"I've overridden the controls," said Caylar. "Shouldn't be any more surprises."

"Does it have a warranty for manufacturer defects?" I said. "Or is there a security robot exclusionary clause?" I was nervous. A lot of bad things could happen in an elevator if somebody wanted them to. At the moment, that reality wasn't one I cared to ignore. The other elevator occupants must've been too busy to respond.

Caylar looked at the lady diplomat. She nodded, deactivated the cube, then reached across the bed, handing it to Caylar. Silvre made a final inspection of the faceted alien mechanism before a few precision finger taps brought it to life. She raised the alien device above her head and spun slowly around. For a fraction of a second, I saw double.

Caylar gently put his hand on my shoulder. "Don't move. Stay silent." He spoke into the remote, "We are preparing to exit the elevator. All clear?"

"Affirmative," crackled the device. "Rally point red one secure."

"Make way," said Caylar. "Yellow pass-through in effect."

"Acknowledged."

Diplomat Silvre looked down at me, still holding the holo-device above her head. Caylar activated the cube.

"I hope you are indeed innocent of the charges," she whispered.

The doors opened. With the holo-device held high, Silvre exited the elevator. Outside, lining the corridor, stood eight armed and ready marines.

Suddenly Diplomat Silvre flashed to a new position. She wasn't holding the holographic device. Rather, she was escorting me out of the elevator. Or my eye saw it happening, with Caylar maneuvering the bed from behind. The real Caylar placed a calming hand on my shoulder. I watched the image of us continue down the hall, flanked by the marines. I spotted a saucer-sized bloodstain spread across the diplomat's shoulder as the elevator door closed.

Caylar put his fingers to his lips, indicating silence, before activating the elevator with the remote. We descended further.

Caylar held Varney's pistol ready and tapped the remote a few times. I held Simms's pistol, knowing that if I discharged another round, I might not be able to endure the pain and remain conscious.

Caylar said, "You're on voice control if there's any trouble. Try to get to the yacht. The *Gilded Swan*. L-X-K, zero, zero, eight." He stopped. "You'll find it."

This didn't make sense. The *Iron Armadillo* was a sure thing. Whose yacht? Did he really think Silvre's holo would fool the surveillance? They have infrared and motion sensors. And if the *Armadillo*'s marines shot out the sensors, then why the holo-image?

Caylar stood, awaiting my response. "Right," I said. "The yacht."

"Let's go," Caylar said, opening the door with the remote. He stepped out, checking left and right. He signaled for me to follow.

"Bed, forward, one yard--damn, ummm, point nine meters per second, unless otherwise directed." I've always hated I-Tech metrics. The bed moved forward. Caylar used his boot to nudge a security specialist lying prone next to a control station. No response so he moved on.

I followed. "Bed, thirty degrees left…thirty degrees more left." I looked around, lowered my firearm. "Bed, thirty degrees left." I was falling behind. "Increase to two meters per second."

I followed Caylar past several shuttles and into a secondary hangar holding fewer than a dozen small vessels. Past a large corporate yacht, we came to a smaller one, maybe twenty yards long with at least two decks. The front ramp was down. The yacht's smooth, tinted gold exterior and had '*Gilded Swan*' scribed freehand in blood-red paint across its side. The vessel was even armed with a single-barreled pulse laser housed in a ventral ball turret. Impressive.

Caylar came around behind me while I scanned the deserted hangar, for what it was worth. Thankfully, Caylar guided me up the ramp and into the space-faring pleasure vessel.

The ramp retracted and the hatch slid closed. Lights switched on to reveal a spartan interior that included several fold down bunks, three padded reclining chairs, and a table. A storage area for cargo and supplies led back to a large door, probably to the engines and life support machinery.

"We're in," shouted Caylar as he maneuvered my bed to the port side and locked the wheel mechanism. "After I check your diagnostic support equipment, I'll have to strap you down." He looped the restraints to the wall. "You don't look so good."

He could have smiled while saying it. I took a breath and tried to ignore the splitting pain in my head, bad eye, and shoulder.

From above, near the starboard side lift came an announcement. "The *Armadillo* has just departed."

I knew that voice! I fumbled for my pistol but Caylar placed a hand on it. "Not necessary," he said.

From the lift, Hawks's former assistant, Mr. Loams, looked down. He appeared friendlier without his yellow tie. "No arm restraints for this trip, I hope?" He looked to Caylar. "I'll request departure momentarily." Mr. Loams disappeared after Caylar nodded in agreement.

Caylar set the safety and placed the pistol back within reach. "Mr. Loams is, as you might say, our ace in the hold."

I listened to my nurse hum a light tune as he manipulated my support equipment. "Hole," I corrected. I felt more pain meds entering my system. A good thing as my adrenaline was played out. "What was Silvre's holo all about?"

"Deception."

"It might fool the infrared. What about motion sensors?"

"It's A-Tech. I suspect it did, easily."

"Simms?" I asked.

"He went down." Any sign of mirth abandoned his voice. "Looked like he took a couple of shots to the legs, maybe one to the head." He paused. "Might be dead. If not, might wish he were."

"He's high-up intel. A Director?"

Caylar came around and began adjusting my straps. "You saw what happened back there. They were darn serious."

"They should've had us. Pretty disorganized."

"I agree," said Caylar. "Not professional."

From above Mr. Loams added, "They didn't have much time. Capital Galactic doesn't have a lot of contacts around Mars."

I asked Loams, "Did you take out the hanger security?"

"Yes," he replied. "They should still be seeing him standing guard. A loop of a prerecorded surveillance." He chuckled. "Even programmed in our departure. It should take them some time to find something amiss. Thirty minutes minimum."

"Still, won't they have to worry about Varney and Simms?"

"Director Simms radioed in indicating terrorist action," said Caylar. "That allowed the *Iron Armadillo*'s marines to board."

"And the captain of the *Pars Griffin* can use that to deflect any accusations against Capital Galactic?"

Caylar nodded while tightening a strap. "What's this?" He pulled from under the covers a small wooden carving. A four inch bust of someone wearing a hat.

I held out my unsteady hand. "Let me see." I examined carving. It looked like my work so I checked the bottom. "Read this."

"It has the initials KRKY," said Caylar. "Fancy script."

"This is my work! Diplomat Silvre must've put it there. Right where the holo-mechanism was."

Caylar looked at the small bust. "Not bad work. Authentic wood."

"I learned to carve before I was ten. Do it for bartering, extra credits." I looked at it closer. "I don't recall carving this. Does it look familiar to you?"

Caylar held it a moment. "Someone R-Tech, a youth. Buttoned shirt, floppy-brimmed hat. Looks like a fishing hat. That must've been difficult to carve."

"Hey! Is it that—you know—the one I was supposed to have abducted?"

"Maximar Drizdon Junior?" Caylar reappraised the bust. "Could be him."

I didn't bother questioning why my nurse knew the specifics of my supposed crimes. "What would Diplomat Silvre be doing with it? My carving?"

"Drizdon is married to her step sister, I think." He paused. "Yes, Maximar Junior must be her nephew with Maximar Senior her brother in law."

"What?" The pain meds made it increasingly difficult to think.

"I don't know. I saw them only once, briefly. I'm simply her personal assistant. A bodyguard." He scratched his head. "She didn't say a lot. I was assigned to her less than four months ago." He thought a moment. "Maybe your friend Mr. Loams knows more."

From above echoed, "We have clearance."

"No dawdling," suggested Caylar. "Let's put some distance between us."

"Agreed." After a moment Loams finished, "We're on our way."

I felt our acceleration before the yacht's gravity plates kicked in. "Where are we heading?"

"I'm not sure," said Caylar. "I think we're to meet up with another vessel shortly." He reviewed my vital signs. "Not good."

I already knew. In addition to my head, a throbbing in my chest had been growing along with a dull pain in my abdomen.

After a few minutes of intense work Caylar looked me in the eye. "Your internal bleeding has increased. I've made adjustments." He shook his head. "Your lungs are still in good condition, all things considered."

"I know. I'm in pretty bad shape."

He nodded sagely. "You should get some rest."

"But..." I began to argue, but knew he was correct.

Caylar continued to tap at the numerous icons and turn an occasional dial. I looked again. Dials meant the medical equipment was military. Hardened against electronic interference.

"I'm going to have to insist." He lowered the bed to fifteen degrees elevation. Then he went back to the engine room. With the door open the engine hum increased.

Five minutes passed. I examined the small carving more with my fingers than my eye. A woozy warmth crept over my thoughts and body. I was about to close my eye when the yacht surged and change direction.

Loams yelled down, "Mars tracking is on high alert! Planetary defense grid has been activated. There's a Crax vessel in the area!"

I almost sat up, except for the restraints. Pain hammered back the cozy warmth. I fought to remain conscious.

Caylar ran to the lift and looked up. "Where?"

"Logical guess," said Loams. "Opposite of where civilian traffic has been directed. Only slight alteration from our original course is required." He paused. "Reaching maximum speed. All combat ships in the area have been alerted and are converging."

This time I barely detected the buildup in speed. Fine workmanship in this vessel.

Caylar said, "Must have been hiding in the asteroid belt."

I stared at the metallic-paneled ceiling.

"What military ships are in the vicinity?" asked Caylar.

"Besides the *Armadillo*, I think there's a light cruiser, the *Red Bison*." The lights dimmed. "Powering down all non-critical equipment. The *Soul Scorcher* is still in space dock. Being patched up. She won't be any assistance."

"Any Umbelgarri?" asked Caylar.

"None that I am aware of," said Mr. Loams. "There are several police cutters, and three gunboats around Mars. Normally."

"Any idea what type of Crax vessel?"

"Sorry, my frequency isn't military. Sensors are picking up our ships. Not the enemy."

"The *Iron Armadillo*?"

"She's moving fast. Looks like she is trying to evade."

Five minutes passed. I was having trouble keeping awake. "Caylar, undo the sleep meds." He ignored me. "Caylar."

He looked back from the bottom of the lift. "You need to rest."

"Not until I know what happens." My eye closed. I strained to keep awake, keep focused. I faded in and out.

Loams's voice echoed. "The *Iron Armadillo*'s off the screen. Confirmed. The *Iron Armadillo* has been destroyed!"

That horrific statement carried over into troubled dreams.

CHAPTER 5

Contemporary theorists claim that if, on their own, humans ever managed to develop the ability to condense space with sufficient energy to maintain it, and the ability to provide energy for the necessary antigravity shell while generating adequate thrust to make the whole effort worthwhile, the current generation's great grandchildren might have been the ones accomplish it.

I endured troubled dreams about my older cousin, Oliver. He'd helped me get picked up by the Negral Corporation and signed on with the *Kalavar.* Oliver was organized, meticulous, and a decent guy. My older brother called him Spiffy. He called my brother Uncouth. Both nicknames fit.

Oliver's math aptitude and ability to interface with computers at a young age earned him notice. He was raised I-Tech. Scholarships and grants provided what his family couldn't toward remedial advanced technical education.

Later, the military recruited and trained Oliver as a gunner where he served aboard the destroyer escort, *Midnight Vigil.* There, for ten years he manned the dual beam laser housed in the forward turret, before transferring to the *Iron Armadillo.* After only six months Negral lured him from the prestigious assignment with a substantial contract to serve as chief gunner aboard an armed freighter.

In my dream, however, Oliver wasn't happily journeying to exotic outer colony ports. Rather, he was repeatedly dying along with the rest of the *Iron Armadillo*'s crew. Sometimes Oliver was trapped, burning alive while his shipmates struggled to reach him. Other times he was lost to the vacuum of space. In the last dream, his turret took a direct hit. The caustic bolt devoured the armored hull, only slowing when it reached my cousin's flesh.

I awoke, sweating. The *Iron Armadillo* was gone. I tried to sort things out. I knew Oliver wasn't on board when she went down.

I opened my eye. The pain had receded in my head, body and leg. That was good. The ceiling wasn't the same—grating instead of paneling, and that wasn't good. The hum of the engines was wrong. The sense of disconnection, of being slightly out of sync with my bed and everything around, added to the unfounded feeling of anticipation, told me I was no longer aboard the *Gilded Swan.* Space-faring yachts aren't built with the cascading atomic engines needed to initiate the condensation of space. The *Gilded Swan* wasn't large enough to harbor both condensing engines and the generation capacity to power an anti-gravity field. So, use of a con-gate was out.

I closed my eye again, and relaxed. No, the feeling was genuine and not drug induced. I felt to my left. The wooden carving was there. To my right Simms's pistol was missing. I suddenly felt vulnerable. Where was it? And where was I?

As if on cue, footsteps preceded a confident, feminine voice. "Good evening, Specialist Keesay."

I turned my head and looked toward the source. My mouth was dry. "Water, please."

The tall woman disappeared from view and returned with a large syringe without a needle. "This may be easier than a cup." She smiled and placed it in my mouth and slowly squirted a small amount of metallic-tasting water. "I was unsure whether using a straw would hurt."

I looked up and noticed she was tall, even for an I-Tech, unless my bed had been lowered. She wore a gray quasi-military uniform. Her hair was braided and wrapped into a large, tight bun. "What vessel am I aboard now?" I asked. "Where is Caylar?" That was the only name I had for my nurse.

She smiled. "He is not here."

"I guessed that, ma'am," I said after receiving the useless answer.

"How are you feeling, Specialist Keesay?"

"Confused and angry."

She frowned slightly. Her green eyes studied me.

"Ohh, you mean physically...Miss?" She looked young for an intel agent. But with I-Techs looks aren't always an accurate gauge.

"Special Agent Vingee," she said.

I was right. "Agent Vingee, you look like a bright girl. I should think astute observation on your part would lead you to the correct conclusion. That I happen to feel like I look. Like a chain saw, you know gas—fossil fuel powered, cuts down trees? Like one happened to dig into my intestines, maybe my spleen? After shaving my leg of course."

She took the syringe and walked away. After a moment she returned. "Will you require anything else?"

I already regretted my remark. "Yes, if you cannot answer my questions, just say so." I took a breath. "I'm sorry. I feel better than I did before my previous, medical provider put me to sleep."

"Apology accepted," she said curtly, then looked away. "I'll see if there is someone available who's authorized to answer at least some of your questions."

"Thank you."

She looked at the carving. "Excellent work. Done with a chain saw?"

I stared at her, unable to follow her last remark.

"At least," she said with a smile, "you know where *your* lower half is."

It hurt more to suppress laughter than to let it out. She turned away with a concerned look on her face before leaving.

I stared at the bust, wondering if I'd really carved it. I ran my fingers over the wood, sensing the cuts and the grain. I reexamined the signature mark. It didn't appear counterfeit. Other questions came to mind. Where are my tools, knife and gouges? My guns and equipment? I had them in the surveillance holos Silvre had shown me.

I set the bust down and pondered the face. Was there any resemblance to Diplomat Silvre? My talent wasn't that good. Did Silvre survive?

I thought about Simms and Private Varney. All dead. For what? Generals, admirals, directors, diplomats, high-powered lawyers at my pretrial. We're at war with the Crax. Was there a connection? Caylar wouldn't know but Loams might. And where were they?

All of this for a dying man. One demanding to have his brain scrambled to get at the truth, which he'll never know. Ironic—depressing and ironic.

Sleep, even a troubled sleep seemed preferable. It was.

Someone placed a hand on my shoulder. I looked up to see Agent Vingee. "Are you awake?"

"Yes, I am now."

"Good. Captain Hollaway will be here shortly."

"Will he answer my questions?" I asked.

"Some of them, depending on what you ask."

I figured that she wouldn't answer anything important. "How long have you been with intelligence?"

She thought a moment. "Longer than you've been in security."

She was being evasive. Or was it something else?

Vingee must have discerned my puzzlement. "I was a guest lecturer at the Rift Valley Finishing Academy. I spoke to your class on corporate-intelligence agency protocol. In reference to surveillance files."

My security training at the academy had consisted of nine weeks, twelve hour days. I squinted. Yes, I recalled her, vaguely. She'd ascended the stage in an unusual fashion. Two steps per stride up to the podium. It had been a less than stimulating lecture, as technical legal information usually is. "Yes, I recall now." Her lecture had been a bit condescending. Figured the R-Techs in attendance couldn't spell CPU correctly three out of four times. "You didn't seem too enthusiastic about being there."

She smiled, showing her flawless white teeth. "True. I was a last minute replacement. You earned a ninety-four percent evaluation over the material I presented. Second highest."

"Mostly from hitting the books. Your presentation wasn't riveting."

"True," she admitted, catching the archaic figure of speech. "I don't like lecturing. You prefer to read?"

It wasn't really a question. She'd certainly read my file. "It seems to be the most efficient way of gathering information, for me. Some security work requires a lot of sitting. Between rounds. Behind monitors...you know." Enough about me, so I asked, "Pretty good recall yourself, or did you look it up?"

"I have an exceptional memory for names, faces and figures. Riley earned the highest score, ninety-six percent."

"I remember Riley." I decided to test her. "Graduated top of our little class. Where is he now?"

"Security assistant, with Cardinal One Intrasolar Corp. First Lunar Weigh Station was his initial placement." She waited. "Have you kept track of him?"

"No," I said, recalling that Riley thought Vingee was pretty hot. Riley had a thing for tall women and he'd made a few lewd remarks within earshot. "More than just Riley's scores. He got your attention another way?"

She smiled. "I can assure you, Evan Riley's life has run into a few unexpected complications."

"He was kind of obnoxious," I said. "Smart but obnoxious. I'd like to hear about one of his complications some time."

She glanced at me before looking away. "Not much to tell." She paused and checked the medical monitors. "The captain should be here any moment. Can I get you anything?"

"No. No thank you. I'll just rest." I sighed. "My head still hurts."

"I will discuss it with your doctor while you meet with the captain."

"I could speak with the doctor myself, if he ever stops in."

"Oh, she has. Several times."

"While I was asleep?"

Vingee nodded once.

"Figures. Probably good foresight on her part."

We both chuckled. She longer than me.

An awkward silence followed. Vingee decided to double-check the monitors.

"Don't worry," I said, realizing she must have been concerned about my being hooked up to the Cranaltar. Capital Galactic had absorbed Cardinal One Corporation two years ago. "I'm sure Riley had it coming. My chips'll be cashed in soon enough, anyway." Suddenly, I liked Agent Vingee a whole lot more. "Do you have a first name?"

"Allison."

"Even acquaintances call me Kra, sometimes."

"I'll tell you what, Specialist Keesay. You pull through and I just might tell you a little story."

"Now I have something to live for." Then, a stabbing pain raced through my abdomen and faded. "Maybe," I finished.

Another awkward silence grew until the door opened. It was the captain. Agent Vingee said, "I'll talk to the doctor," and, acknowledging the captain, strode out.

Looking up at her, the captain had simply said, "Special Agent Vingee," before heading toward me.

The captain was stocky with short, peppered hair. Despite cosmetic surgery, his nose looked as if it had been broken several times, possibly explaining the nasal tone of his voice. Deep scars checkered his right hand. He offered it.

I shook it. "Captain." He was definitely a veteran of the Silicate War.

"I'm Captain Hollaway. I understand there's a few questions you want answered, young man."

"Class 4 Security Specialist. Yes I do, sir." I knew where to start. "What vessel is this?"

"*Evanescent Thunder*," he replied with evident pride.

I didn't recognize the name. "What kind of vessel is this?"

"A patrol gunboat."

Of course. I knew most gunboats had 'thunder' incorporated into their name. They're used for local patrol to police commerce and defend against occasional raiders. None that I'd ever heard of were equipped with condensing engines. If we were heading from Mars to Io, they'd have used a con-gate. "A gunboat?"

Captain Hollaway acknowledged my confusion. "This isn't exactly your standard gunboat." He relaxed a bit. "Deputy Director Simms called us in. We're to get you to Io safe and as soon as possible."

"Your ship's modified for interstellar travel?"

"Not exactly. We removed the part of the forward batteries and installed a small cascading atomic engine. Condenses only about a 5000-to-1 ratio. Good enough for local travel." He grinned. "We don't exactly advertise it. Is that all you wanted to know?"

"No, sir."

"I thought not." He eyed his watch. "Ask away. Dr. Goldsen will be here shortly."

"Well, where are Mr. Loams and Caylar?"

"Mr. Loams and Mr. Guymin went to look for Diplomat Silvre."

I must have looked hopeful.

"Odds are pretty slim for their success, son." He sat on the edge of my bed with hands resting on his knee. "The *Iron Armadillo* ran for an interdiction minefield. Newly laid, with the war on. She led the enemy in, turned and made a stand."

"What was she up against?"

"Selgum-Crax frigate. She was so intent on getting the *Armadillo* she followed her right in. That old scout was no match for a Crax ship. When we got there, the *Red Bison* had engaged along with three other gunboats. Two cutters were already destroyed, and a gunboat crippled."

His hands tightened, emphasizing their scars as he spoke. "The Crax frigate had been damaged, a proximity mine. Hemmed in, she couldn't maneuver. The *Bison* got her with a canister nuke. We lost the damaged gunboat before it was over and the *Bison* is going in for repairs." He shook his head. "With the radiation and mine explosions, it's doubtful any of the escape pods made it."

He thought a moment. "Getting back to your first question. Rumor has it the Crax frigate targeted an escape pod during the fight. I can't confirm that. We got there near the end of the engagement, just before two destroyers." He looked a little put out. "We did manage one long range shot, glancing hit with negligible damage. Still top of the line gunnery." He looked from me to the monitors. "More than you probably wanted to know."

"No. Actually if the records aren't classified, yet, I'd like to review the action." I figured combat data of the surviving ships would've been downloaded to create a holographic display. I figured the captain had already downloaded it to a personal file. "Loss of the *Iron Armadillo*. It'll be one for the history books." That's if humans ended up on the winning side, I thought. A Crax frigate, undetected, this close to the center of humanity?

Captain Hollaway seemed distracted. Maybe he was having the same thoughts. "Yes," he agreed. "She went down fighting." He shook his head. "I've got something you'd probably rather see. After the physician has her time with you."

"What is it?" I asked. "Also, Director Simms lent me a semi-automatic pistol. His personal one, pretty old and valuable. While I was out, it disappeared. It was my responsibility."

"No, it's not missing. I have it and will entrust it to Agent Vingee, to return to Director Simms."

"Is he alive?"

"I read Mr. Guymin's report. I'd like to think so." He didn't sound encouraged. "Guymin left a message for you. It's short and that's good. We're nearing Io and will be shutting down the condensing engines." He looked at me with penetrating eyes. "Son, I understand you've got quite an ordeal ahead of you. Looks like you've already been through hell. I'm told a lot of people'd like to see you euthanized in some pretty nasty ways. Director Simms isn't one of them. I respect his opinion more than most." He stood. "Good luck, Specialist Keesay."

"Thank you, sir."

As if rehearsed a thousand times, Captain Hollaway exited just as the doctor entered. She was an aging woman with short gray hair. She wore wire-framed bifocals, but all other evidence indicated she was I-Tech.

"I spoke briefly with Agent Vingee," she said without introduction. "Not surprising. I have tried to keep the pain medication to a minimum." With apparent deliberateness, she continued more slowly. "The Cranaltar IV will be more effective that way."

Then I recalled Dr. Marjoree Goldsen was attached to the Cranaltar Project. I'd read about her heading up a number of projects in conjunction with the Umbelgarri.

Dr. Goldsen stepped around the bed and examined the monitors. "You are quite fortunate to have survived thus far. You were lucky to have had A-

Tech medical assistance. Your internal injuries would have been beyond our ability to temporarily mend. As it is, your recent activity nearly caused fatal hemorrhaging."

She was trying to be very simple in her explanations. I replied, "Couldn't be helped, really." Then I caught what she had said. "A-Tech?"

"Yes, A-Tech. Still, your long term prognosis, or outlook, is very poor." She hesitated, and pursed her lips. "The cellular regeneration process does not appear to have been aimed at recovery."

I slowly nodded. "I've read about your work, Dr. Goldsen. On the Cranaltar Project, and also your dissent to the Kipper-Hammer Study." My last statement seemed to break her concentration. "Took a lot of convincing to get the corporate heads to agree that the Blaytech's Longevity Serum did indeed have deleterious consequences. Your expertise is still in neural electrochemistry?"

"That was a long time ago, early in my career."

The Blaytech's Longevity Serum was a sore point for any I-Tech. Every I-Tech man, woman and child with the surname Blaytech, changed it. I figured that there was no sense pushing the issue, especially with a physician who was against it from the start—and who was taking care of me. "I understand you've been part of the Cranaltar Project since its inception."

Her eyes widened as she nodded and continued her examination. She folded back the covers and removed some of the wrappings over my chest and abdomen. "They told me you read a lot." She checked the tubes running in and out of my body. "You requested use of the memory replication application specifically?"

It was the first time I'd been able to see some of my injuries. Pink tendril scars radiated from a large mottled mass of scar tissue located over my ribcage, primarily on the lower right side. The seeping viscous fluid didn't look healthy. "How long have I got?"

"I would estimate no longer than three to four weeks. The stabilizing measures will likely begin to fail within two weeks."

"What did it?"

"I am not well versed in wound analysis," she prefaced. "Appears to have been a Crax weapon. One of their multitude of caustic chemical rounds." She replaced the bandages. "Curiously, it seems the Crax were also the ones who treated the wound to your chest. It should have been fatal. They would be the most adept in counteracting their weaponry."

I winced when she removed the bandages over my bad eye. Giving a cursory exam she remarked, "Physical trauma damaged your eye, appears beyond repair, although it appears unusual."

Dr. Goldsen seemed to be holding back something in her last statement. I didn't say anything while she replaced the eye covering. I was trying to correlate the charges against me and being wounded by Crax weapons.

Without an inspection she concluded, "Your leg has received multiple injuries. Some more recent than others."

"Is there any chance of surviving the Cranaltar?" I asked. "I can't recall how I got this way. Who is responsible? I'd like to know before I give up the ghost."

"We have never had a volunteer subject. It may make a difference. We have improved our accuracy of transcribing the electrochemical signatures, memory, to virtually one-hundred percent."

"So I understand," I said. "It's an intrusive process. How much of my brain, my cognitive functions will be scrambled?"

"You have done your homework." She began thoughtfully, "Well, in layman's terms, in transcribing, the Cranaltar takes an imprint of a memory. Normally the pathway to that individual memory is connected to many others. With each connection an additional transcription must be made. Even the simplest of memories can require thousands upon thousands of pathways to be followed and copied." She stopped to see if I followed.

I nodded. "Like writing my name. The Cranaltar would have to trace back to the memory, recalling the formation of each letter, possibly the root of learning that letter. The skill to hold a pencil and the muscle control to use the instrument. Also the knowledge of paper could be tapped into. Recognition of color of the paper, pencil?"

"You are correct. And that is for a simple action," she said with enthusiasm reflected in her voice. "And on very, very rare occasions the process slightly alters a chemical sequence or a synaptic connection, altering the memory. We have figured out how to recognize and correct the altered memory if the same pathway is crossed again. On the transcription," she frowned. "Not in the brain."

I didn't need to do the math in my head. With the time frame I'd be exposed to the Cranaltar's processing, statistically speaking it was obvious. "Odds are I won't exactly be wired to code anymore?"

She looked at me questioningly.

"I won't come out even remotely the same person I went in?"

"The anticipated required length and depth of the procedure. The complications associated virtually guarantee it."

"Will I be effectively brain dead?"

"In all probability. And if you are fortunate," she stated grimly.

"Do you know why I can't remember what happened? Was it the Crax?"

She thought a moment as if weighing what to say. "Quite possibly. There is evidence of a...reconstructive procedure, that has altered some of your neural connections. Minor, delicate, but noticeable."

"So maybe the whole thing won't work?"

"Yes. That is a possibility."

"Will the Umbelgarri assist you?" I was hoping. They'd already demonstrated an interest in me.

"I believe so. If needed, they might," she said. "At least to reverse the tampering with your frontal lobe."

"Dr. Goldsen, will you do me one favor?"

"If I am able," she said warily.

"Can you implant a memory into my brain? Even if it's scrambled, one that would tell me I was innocent? Or guilty?"

"Either way?" she asked.

I nodded

"I will try," she promised.

It sounded sincere. I noticed a difference in the background noise. The disconnected feeling ceased as the condensing engines and the antigravity field shut down.

"We must be nearing Io," said Dr. Goldsen. "I will leave you now to make final arrangements for your transfer."

"I hope it's less eventful than the last."

With a serious look she responded, "It will be."

As she turned to go, I asked, "Dr. Goldsen, can I have anything to put me to sleep? If it's all the same to you, I'd rather spend my remaining time that way."

"Unfortunately, I cannot give you anything. If you can manage to sleep on your own, you are welcome to. Agent Vingee is waiting outside." She turned and hurried out.

There was no way I was going to be able to put my mind at ease. Not enough to doze off. Maybe it was for the best. My mind and I were scheduled for departure soon enough.

CHAPTER 6

Identifying an individual as I-Tech can be as simple as knowing their occupation. Programming analyst, electrical engineer, and ship's navigator are excellent examples. However, occupations such as corporate executive, physician, or security specialist require closer examination of their clientele, responsibilities and education.

Identification of I-Techs through physical appearance is possible as I-Techs engage in limited genetic selection for their offspring if they can afford it. Traits such as eye and hair color can be reliably manipulated. Another common, but more difficult, characteristic to manipulate is stature. I-Tech parents value above-average height for their children as it is considered socially and professionally advantageous. As a result, I-Techs tend to have similar traits, distinguishing them from the more varied R-*Techs.*

Unfortunately, genetic engineering isn't an exact science. Commissioning a reputable corrections lab to modify genes after fertilization is expensive. Altering the male genetic code after conception leads to infertility. Females, their gametes having developed at an early fetal stage, are less likely to encounter such risks. As adults, astronomically wealthy women use this to their cosmetic advantage.

Altering intelligence through genetic engineering turned out to be so risky that such efforts were abandoned. It has always been far more reliable to provide the proper learning environment. Thus, contrary to popular belief, high intelligence is not necessarily an I-Tech trait.

Other clues can be found in dress, accessories, and sometimes wealth. The most identifiable factor to a security specialist is attitude. It's difficult to explain, but one knows it when one encounters it.

I did my absolute best to relax. I tried to clear my mind of thoughts on what was to come. I'd never been much for holo-cast programs, but any distraction would've been appreciated.

I never considered myself a coward, but I was getting mighty anxious. I'd made a choice. Inspired by confusion, desperation, and spurred on by hatred of a yellow tie and the man behind it, I was about to follow the narrow path my choice at pretrial had forged. Maybe I wouldn't even make it to Io. I felt like a hapless guppy riding the currents in a piranha-filled river. Even if I made it to the end, all that awaited me there was a steep waterfall. One which fell upon jagged rocks, certain to ensure a tragic end. Sleep would have been nice.

"Specialist Keesay, your message."

Startled, I looked in the direction of Agent Vingee's voice. I stared at her blankly. "Sorry."

She smiled. "I brought your message. Captain Hollaway told you about it? From Mr. Guymin."

"Oh. Thank you."

She handed me a computer clip. "Just tap the flashing red icon. I'll be outside."

"No. That's Okay," I said. "The captain said it was short." Agent Vingee was still wearing her gray uniform, but had added a matching jacket. I spotted a bulge underneath, an MP pistol. "Expecting trouble?"

"No." She smiled and stepped back from the bed.

I tapped the icon, hoping the message was indeed short. I lacked the strength to hold the clip long and I didn't dare rest it on my chest. Agent Vingee's hand appeared and steadied the clip.

The screen filled with what must have been the bridge of Loams's yacht. I spotted him moving in the background as Caylar spoke. "Greetings, Specialist Keesay. My apologies for abandoning you but circumstances require it. I am traveling with Special Agent Loams to what remains of the *Iron Armadillo*. Available evidence indicates all crew and passengers were lost. As Diplomat Silvre's personal assistant, I must be sure. I leave you in the capable hands of Captain Hollaway and his crew. They will get you to Io as Director Simms intended." He paused. "We have faith that those who sacrificed will be vindicated. Agent Loams assured me of that. If you survive." Caylar ran his hand across his chin. "You really have, guts. Good luck." In the background Mr. Loams nodded in agreement as the entry ended.

Vingee took the computer clip. "Would you like it replayed?"

"No, no thank you. Just erase it." I thought a moment while she tapped at the screen. "Mr. Loams was a mole?"

"Apparently," she responded.

"Did you know of him?" I asked.

"No, my area isn't corporate espionage. I specialize in records and information."

"Can you use that firearm under your jacket?"

"I am very proficient," she said, somewhat offended.

"Of course you can. In the back of my mind I guess I was hoping you couldn't."

Agent Vingee glared at me. Her head tipped and her jaw clenched.

"It seems," I said, "that a number of people don't want me to make it to Io, and get hooked up to the Cranaltar. As it gets closer, I'm tending more and more to side with them, but for different reasons."

Anger and contempt spread rampant across Agent Vingee's face. Even with my less than stellar vision, I viewed it more plainly than a local sun gone supernova.

"Oh, don't worry," I explained. "I have no intention other than to follow through."

She just looked down at me in disgust.

I was getting a bit angry. "You don't seem to get it. I'm no coward. I've faced rioting mobs, but this is worse!" My throat burned as my voice rose. "This is the hardest thing I've ever had to do. Than you've ever had to do. Have you faced death?" I didn't wait for a response. "I don't care if you have, this is worse. It isn't like facing a firing squad or a lethal injection. I don't even have a fighting chance." My thoughts were all jumbled. I knew I wasn't making sense. I felt my chest thumping.

I took several shallow breaths. Her hard face showed a small fracture. She shifted her stance, while I continued. "Do you know what the Cranaltar is? What it does? It won't just kill me. It may not even kill me!" Breathing was harder. My chest was heavy.

Her eyes flashed to the monitors. I didn't care. "Look at me!" I said. "I'm scared. You bet I am. That thing won't kill me. It'll take away who I am. It'll grind up who I am like hamburger."

Vingee called into her collar for Dr. Goldsen. I was sure the monitors had already done that. She looked back at me. Any accusation had abandoned on her face.

"They say I've committed appalling crimes, done terrible things. And I'll never know!" I struggled for a labored breath. "I asked Dr. Goldsen to let me know. But even if she does, I won't even...be." I laid back and looked at the ceiling and fought the pain, realizing my own end.

The door opened and the captain rushed in followed by Dr. Goldsen. I looked at all three. "You don't even know."

Dr. Goldsen stood by the bed. She took my hand and held it a moment. "I know," she assured me. She pointed to her head. "All we are is up here. You're risking it. And you don't know for who, or why."

I slowly nodded. The pain had spiked and was receding.

"I am sorry for my failing," said the doctor. "I know what it will do to you."

"Son," said the captain. "You're a man of character. That's evident. I wouldn't just say that. Of course you didn't do those things. I know it. Karlton Simms knew it. You know it too."

I said to Vingee, "I never intended to back out."

"You were right," she whispered. "I didn't understand. Not fully."

The monitors fell silent. My chest lightened, although the throbbing in my head didn't abate much. "That little episode probably whittled a week off of my life expectancy, Dr. Goldsen." Then I asked Captain Hollaway, "When do we visit Io?"

"Shuttle's ready," he said. "As soon as you show up. Sorry, I won't be able to accompany you. But these two ladies will escort you."

"And two of your most violent marines, I'm told," said Dr. Goldsen.

"Affirmative."

"They're welcome, of course," I said. "But I've got Agent Vingee. If she's half as good as Director Simms, they won't be necessary."

Vingee placed her right hand over her pistol and winked. "Time to go."

She moved behind the bed.

Dr. Goldsen prepared my bed for travel by making quick disconnections and reattachments.

Captain Hollaway spoke into his watch. "Fitch, Neville get in here." Two fully armed marines entered. "Don't worry, Specialist," said the captain. "The *Evanescent Thunder* will keep her guns ready on your way down."

"I suspect the Umbelgarri might have a few nasties ready," I said, "for any inquisitive vessels in the area. Only for back up, of course."

Captain Hollaway laughed but gently shook my hand. "Let's be about it, marines," he said. "The ever popular Falshire Hawks is waiting."

"Yes, sir," the marines said in unison, and led me out.

"Hawks is down there?" I asked.

"He is," said Vingee.

"I bet he'll be glad to see me."

Vingee snorted a laugh. After that, everyone was silent on the way to the shuttle.

Patrol gunboats are less than ninety yards in length and we started amidship, moving aft. We spent half the travel time in the elevator. It took two trips to get everyone down to the shuttle bay.

The aging military ground assault shuttle sat ready to go. While the nose remained smooth and polished, the boxy body displayed multiple battle scars and patching. The interior had been prepared for my bed and needs. Dr. Goldsen looked out of place in the military atmosphere, with laser carbines and armored vests secured to the walls.

Sergeant Fitch and the doctor spread a sturdy gauze netting over my legs and torso, leaving my head and arms free. They attached the netting to the bed. The locking mechanism's *clack* signaled Neville had immobilized my bed.

Sergeant Fitch checked to see that everyone was properly strapped in their seat. "No grav plates in this old bird," he remarked while tightening his own straps.

From his perch in the dorsal turret, the pulse laser gunner focused a roving eye on Agent Vingee, which she worked to ignore. I tapped Fitch and motioned, indicating the situation. The sergeant's threatening glare encouraged the gunner to focus his attention elsewhere.

My mind wandered as we traveled to the Io Colony. What is it about tall women? I'd read about the economic success of a booming resort business. Some nameless entrepreneur had set up an orbiting space dock in the 70 Virginis system almost twelve years ago and named it the Celestial Unicorn Palace. Some men, enough men, have been willing to travel dozens of light years to vacation with seven foot blondes built like exotic dancers. Frequent holo-cast advertisements show dozens of enormous, voluptuous blondes chanting the slogan, 'Come be a stallion on our range.' Agent Vingee was attractive, but she wasn't that tall or even blond. Maybe I'd travel out that way someday, if I ever won a share of the intra-colonial lottery.

We struck Io's thin atmosphere. The jarring brought me back to reality, but I continued my wandering line of thought. That is, if I ever won the lottery and survived the next twenty hours. Both registered equivalent odds. Right, must be an I-Tech thing. No, that little adventure was pretty near the bottom of my list should I survive the Cranaltar. I'd never spoken with anyone who'd actually visited the Celestial Palace. My limited social circle? I'd have bet that old Falshire Hawks had spent a little time there.

"Ever been on Io?" I asked Agent Vingee.

"No. Is this your first time?"

"Yes. I hear it's cold. Probably bad as Pluto or Charon. I was never out on the surface while assigned there. Even all geared up, still frigid. Is that correct Dr. Goldsen?"

"Well," said the doctor, "the moon's surface certainly is inhospitably cold without proper equipment. Except for the few volcanic hot spots, of course. But, in the few surface complexes and large underground areas, they have tapped into the thermal vents to supplement the heating. More energy efficient. The surface radiation from Jupiter is more dangerous than the cold." She paused during a bit of turbulence. "The Umbelgarri colony on Io, near my lab, keeps it very warm. They have set up immense towers to generate electricity from Jupiter's magnetic field."

"You've been in there?" I asked. The Umbelgarri have always been very secretive. Isolationist in many ways. The amphibian aliens were rarely seen during the Silicate War. And since then almost never. Their crab-like thralls have always been more common, but still infrequently encountered. This line of conversation seemed to have caught everyone's attention.

"I really cannot say much," said Dr. Goldsen. "But from time to time it has been necessary to consult with them on the project. They are not exactly what you would expect."

Dr. Goldsen's statement ended the conversation. I guessed that everybody was content to ponder the mystery of the Umbelgarri until we landed. The touchdown was smooth and the landing pad immediately lowered the shuttle into the underground portion of the colony.

The marines checked their gear and became attentive to everything about them. Fitch assisted everyone in freeing themselves before removing my retaining net and releasing my bed. Agent Vingee spoke briefly with the pilot and then asked, "Ready?"

I nodded. The marines lowered the ramp and led the way. A number of shuttles and small interplanetary vessels sat silently in the cavernous hangar bay. My marine escorts' boots echoed. The faint humming and calliope of other electronic support equipment provided the background music. One of the wheels on my bed had developed a squeak.

We exited the hangar and took several turns down long corridors. Each appeared similar to the previous. Numbers identifying location were carved into the gray stone walls. The tunneled complex and lighting reminded me more of an ancient earth cave than a modern space colony. The place seemed deserted. I guessed we were following an ancient lava tube. I wondered how they kept the complex intact with the gravitational forces of the nearby gas giant, Jupiter.

The marines escorted with automatic MP rifles held ready. Dr. Goldsen strove to keep pace. "Can we slow down just a little?" I asked.

Sergeant Fitch nodded and slowed our march. Soon we entered a large freight elevator.

"Normally," said Dr. Goldsen, "we use electric carts to move about. But Captain Hollaway did not think it was wise. Not much further to my laboratory facilities." She sounded a little winded, but more agitated by the silence. "This route is seldom used and more secure."

About fifty paces from the elevator we came to a set of double doors guarded by two alert marines. They were almost as intimidating as Fitch and Neville. It was warm, but the two guards showed no discomfort.

With a nod the guards stepped aside and the steel doors slid open.

Dr. Goldsen's laboratory facility was a stark contrast to the dark, endless corridors. It was large, two-tiered, with an arched ceiling. Lights and computers filled every nook and cranny. Some areas had been partitioned off, but for the most part it was open. At least two dozen men and women in white lab coats, with computer clips in hand, moved swiftly about. Several looked up to see who'd entered before refocusing on their assigned task. Specialized sound dampeners kept the noise level far lower than it would have been.

Dr. Goldsen directed Agent Vingee to wheel my bed into a small alcove. Even its walls were lined with computer hardware and other equipment. Fitch and Neville stood at attention just outside the small area while Vingee remained next to me. I felt the wooden carving under the blankets. I thought about giving it to Vingee. She could get it to Silvre's family. What they might do with it was unknown. After reconsidering why the Umbelgarri representative gave it to me, I decided to try something else.

I was getting warm. "Agent Vingee, could you please fold down one of my blankets?"

She was observing the activity in the lab. "Sure." She folded one down to the foot of the bed without disturbing my tubing or my bandaged leg.

Some people entered the lab that I recognized from my pretrial. An anxious looking Mr. Hawks was first. A new assistant wearing a matching yellow tie with more black in it than Loams's followed him. Behind came the admiral, general, and CJO, followed by an older man with a thick gray mustache, an intelligence official. The last two were discussing some matter. I didn't see an Umbelgarri representative.

"Do you know the intelligence man?"

"Yes," said Agent Vingee. "Deputy Director Cavelvar. He doesn't travel willingly or often."

"An associate?"

"Hardly. He is number three."

"And what are you ranked?" I asked.

"About forty-thousand."

"Really? Did you actually look that up?"

"Recently?" she said. "Would you like an exact figure?"

"Do you have time?"

"Do you?"

"That depends," I said. "But first I need to know something."

She looked at me with head tilted and one eye squinted. "And what would that be?"

"How fast can you count?"

She suppressed a grin.

"I know, that was a little anemic," I admitted. "But hey, I'm under a little pressure."

Her mirth faded.

"Glad you didn't have to use your pistol," I said. "Of course, the evening is still young."

"It's midmorning on this region of Io," she corrected.

"Thanks for the tip. And thanks for taking responsibility for Director Simms' semi-automatic antique."

"No problem," she said. "I cleaned it for you. But that's okay, you'd had a long day."

"It was night, but who's watching the clock?"

She laughed. "I think you might've gotten a smile out of Sergeant Fitch."

A quick glance and a wink from the marine indicated it was true.

"Sergeant Fitch," I asked. "Did you see a representative of the Umbelgarri enter?"

"Affirmative," he said quietly. "He was already here. Near the back of the lab."

"Thank you," I said. "And thank you, Special Agent Vingee. I wanted to sleep away my last hours. I am glad I didn't."

"Chin up, Security Specialist 4th Class Keesay. Remember, get through this and I'll have a story for you."

Dr. Goldsen and two assistants approached our alcove.

I sighed. "Looks like it's about time." I knew that if I survived, memory wouldn't be my strong suit. But there was no sense rubbing that in. "Think I'll get a chance to say anything to Hawks?"

"Possibly," Vingee replied.

The two assistants started to move my bed.

"I know, you're information and records, not legal affairs." My wide smile increased the pain around my injured eye, but I held it.

She responded with a weak grin and concerned eyes.

All things considered, I was feeling pretty confident. For some reason,

Hawks and his yellow tie inspired me.

The assistants wheeled me to a side area where a large lift that looked like a giant pancake flipper hung attached to the wall. Sergeant Fitch followed.

"We have to switch you to another platform," apologized Dr. Goldsen. "It won't be as comfortable, at first. It will undoubtedly hurt to be moved."

"I think I'm beginning to form bed sores," I said as I motioned for Dr. Goldsen. "Will that make a difference?"

When she stepped near me, I discretely handed her the little carving. "Would you pass this on to the Umbelgarri?" I whispered, "They can forward it to Diplomat Silvre's family."

Not looking at it, she slipped the bust into a lab coat pocket. "I'll see what I can do about those bed sores after the procedure."

I was right. There was some form of surveillance. Not surprising, but whose? Possibly the sound dampeners helped. If there were the cameras I hoped they didn't have a good angle. I was sure Fitch had observed the handoff.

Dr. Goldsen was correct. The switching didn't take long, and it was exceptionally painful. My new bed, if it could be called that, was hard. And I did have a few bedsores forming.

My new mode of transportation didn't have wheels. It used a reverse gravity plate, offering a far smoother ride.

Dr. Goldsen had gone on ahead. Sergeant Fitch nodded and remained behind. I couldn't see Allison Vingee. Besides Dr. Goldsen, his would be the last friendly face I'd ever see.

CHAPTER 7

In the age of interstellar space travel communication is much akin to the American West's 1860's Pony Express. Information distribution is limited to the routes and timing of vessels traveling to and from a world, space colony, or outpost. Electronic transmission remains limited to the speed of light and is acceptable within a solar system. But the vast distance between the interstellar colonies means reception of a radio transmission could take decades or longer. Utilizing the condensation of space circumvents the speed of light limitation, keeping distant colonies reasonably informed, if they are common destinations. If not, message rockets launched through a con-gate are used to transmit vital information.

Dr. Goldsen explained the details of the Cranaltar and what to expect. To the best of my understanding, my memories and associated knowledge would be delivered to the Cranaltar IV along the lines of a class-one message rocket: expensive to me, not totally reliable, and definitely one way. My intellect would be expended like so much rocket fuel.

The Cranaltar didn't look technologically impressive. Most of its functioning and hardware was housed behind walls, out of sight. All I saw was a small, well-lit area with a large silvery parabolic overhead dome. A thick cable extended down and divided into several hundred somewhat frayed endings, each tipped with a long slender needle. Dr. Goldsen explained that once in the brain each needle would further divide much like the needles on a pine tree's branch. Those would split off multiple times as well, seeking prearranged destinations before the actual operation would commence.

While a med tech shaved my scalp with a sonic depilator, Dr. Goldsen traveled in and out, giving assistants whispered directives. I would've preferred my straight razor but, like everything else, that too was lost.

At last Dr. Goldsen walked back to me. "Mr. Keesay, we are going to perform a brain scan now."

I gave her a puzzled look. She caught on that it had been a long time since I'd been addressed as Mister.

"You are under my care now. No formal, militaristic titles or classifications are necessary." She smiled and read the monitors. "You will be presented images, pictures, words and other sensations such as cold and warmth. You will be asked to perform some simple mental tasks. During this time your brain will be monitored and mapped. After that is finished, you will feel a tingling sensation. Once that ends, your cranium will have been marked for insertion by the Cranaltar probes."

"You mean the needles over there?" I asked, pointing at the apparatus under the silver dome.

"Yes. It won't hurt. We will see to that. Before the actual scanning and recording begins you will be partially submerged in a gel to keep you from moving, and to insulate you from outside interference." Dr. Goldsen continued explaining while checking my tubes. "The brain lacks nerve cells to indicate pain. When the Cranaltar receptor probes radiate through your cerebral cortex, and to a lesser extent the cerebellum, you won't feel it." She checked some readings while an assistant moved me toward the scanning tube. "Do you understand?"

I wanted to ask her about the tampering with my brain and if they had figured out how to deal with that, but I didn't. I figured everything was being recorded for my trial, so I simply answered, "I do."

The med tech replaced my eye bandaging with a thin patch that itched. Even though I was getting used to the pain, I was thankful for the added distraction as the grav-bed slowly traversed the tube.

Just before reaching the end of the tube, the bed stopped. Holographic images began to appear in front of me. At first they were simple shapes like squares, triangles, and cubes with solid colors followed by varying patterns. This went on for several minutes. Next, I was shown multiple shapes. A synthesized voice asked me to picture each in my mind after they were taken away.

Soon I graduated to pictures. At first simple ones, like a ball, a dog, a building, a space dock while visualization and verbal tasks were asked of me. Later, letters, words, sentences, and numbers were presented. I was asked to read silently. Then, I was asked to recite from memory and read orally. I was asked to perform simple and complex math problems. I'd never studied much beyond algebra and trigonometry, so that section of mapping took much less time than the reading and verbal.

I was asked to move certain parts of my body, to focus on breathing, and to listen to various words, sounds and tones. I was asked to identify verbally and mentally some of them. The process became tedious. At least two hours must have passed, maybe more.

Whenever I asked a question, I was directed by the synthetic voice to refocus and perform as requested. A short section introduced cold, warm, hot, tickling and painful sensations. I wondered how they intended to accomplish taste until the voice directed me to imagine the taste of common foods while presented with an array of scents and odors.

Next, I was shown images of familiar people. They must have really gone back into my file. I saw my mother's and father's images at various ages along with their voices. An image of our old apartment flashed past. Famous generals, political figures and alien species paraded by. I recognized many of them. Then some images of my equipment were brought to my attention. Boots, revolver, helmet, my bayonet. Surveillance recordings of me on duty, moving about in the warehouse on Pluto. I was really becoming fatigued.

The scanner or the operator must have sensed this as I was given a break. Maybe he simply scanned normal brain activity because the harmonic humming sounds continued. I almost fell asleep.

Finally, I was shown images of unfamiliar people. One I recognized as the *Kalavar*'s captain. I'd seen her image prior to boarding. Images zipped in and out in rapid succession with little time to focus or comprehend, including corridors, people, a moon and planets. I saw an image of Maximar Jr., possibly from the evidence Silvre had shown me. They presented random snippets of voices and sounds. Most were unrecognizable, especially in isolation. I lost all track of time.

The grav-bed shifted back slightly and I felt the tingling begin. It reminded me of flimsy wires brushing across my scalp. I felt a small prick under the skin. Then another, and more. As the pricking sensation became more frequent, the brushing sensation lessened, until only pricking occurred, which abruptly ended. I rested for several minutes until my bed exited.

I was just beginning to relax again when I heard a clicking and scraping noise on the hard floor. I tilted my head and looked toward the source. It was a Bahklack! An Umbelgarri thrall. I'd never actually seen one, only holographic images.

The alien, less than ten feet away, approached Dr. Goldsen. It resembled a fiddler crab except that it was as tall as the doctor's waist. The thrall's exoskeleton was a dull blue color, speckled with greens and browns. Its eerie black eyes rested on the end of 12-inch stalks that independently surveyed the room. The three-foot claw was the alien's most notable feature. Unlike the rest the Bahklack's body, the oversized appendage appeared to shift in coloration. I'd read changing color patterns are a major communication component between the Umbelgarri and their thralls. They use chromatophores much like squid native to Earth's oceans.

I watched the complex patterns of stripes, blotches and mosaic patterns form and reform.

In addition to its oversized claw and its smaller counterpart, the Bahklack had two small grasping appendages, each with three prongs. It used them to communicate with Dr. Goldsen. Without an appropriate computer to translate, gesturing with hand-like appendages is how many aliens converse with other intelligent species. I recalled my sketchy training in the Official Galactic Sign Language, but my angle was poor and each alien species tends to have a unique gesturing dialect. Some aliens are said to communicate through outright bizarre thought patterns. Galactic signing is a very complex skill to master and I was definitely a neophyte.

Dr. Goldsen was facing away, so I couldn't view her initiations and responses. The conversation lasted about a minute. "Done, good, and go," were the only words I managed to pick out with some measure of certainty.

The Bahklack clattered toward me. Although I'd never encountered an alien species before, I couldn't imagine how an intelligent creature could be more odd. It examined me with its stalked eyes. I followed suit. I wanted to reach out and touch the large claw even though it had taken on a pattern matching the rest of its exoskeleton. Instead, I signed, "All good?" flinching at the painful movements.

The Bahklack rose to present its motioning arms. I think it responded, "Yes." Then it clicked its way out of the room, through a concealed exit. It was fortunate the creature walked sideways, as the opening wasn't very wide.

Dr. Goldsen stepped closer. "We are confident that all will proceed without hindrance."

"That's good," I said. "The less trouble the better."

"We are almost ready to begin."

"Where are my inquisitors?" I asked, hoping I'd still get a chance to address them.

"They're in a room nearby," she said. "One level up. From there they will be able to view the initial results of the Cranaltar procedure almost as fast as the transcribed information can be processed. Initially there should be less than a minute delay."

"Nobody has been willing to tell me the extent of my memory lapse."

Dr. Goldsen looked at me over the rims of her glasses.

"You know," I said. "How long?"

"Well, I can't state it exactly. I do not know all of the facts. And the less said to influence any memories the better. Let's just say that viewers will require more than one restroom break."

"Thanks for your honesty. I've been able to piece together through clues, distances, the war, scars and healing, the fact that my fingernails have been trimmed, that it's been several months at least." I nodded and licked my lips. "Will I survive that long? It'd be pointless to die of my injuries half way through the procedure."

"As the Cranaltar interacts with your memories, it should become more and more familiar with your pathways. We have never tested it that extensively." She glanced up as if calculating in her head. "I estimate that at top efficiency, ten hours of conscious memories can be transcribed in a little less than twenty minutes."

I did the math in my head. "Are they going to watch in shifts or what?"

"That is up to them. Complete copies of the transcription will be made available to the relevant parties after completion. They will see it in sequence, without leaps. The intelligence agency insisted every concerned party be on equal footing."

"I'd imagine that Hawks will have somebody watching at all times. Will my dreams be recorded?"

"No, only your conscious memories will be accessed."

I could guess why. Instead I asked Dr. Goldsen, "What will the presentation look like? I read that the Cranaltar's transcription was best suited for a flat screen monitor."

"It will definitely be first person point of view. They will see and hear what you saw and heard. In most cases even your thoughts will be added. It will be set up on a large sphere screen. The presentation will be limited to just under 180 degrees horizontally and less vertically. One of my assistants has the exact figures, but equal to your field of vision."

I smiled. "Good thing I'm not a Bahklack. With those stalk eyes, everyone would get sick after five minutes."

Dr. Goldsen nodded with eyebrows raised before checking the monitors. "True. The perspective of a horse was disorienting enough. Nearly 360 degrees vision. Except directly to the front and rear."

"Do I get copyrights to the transcription?"

"I do not know if that is possible with court materials."

"Will I get to address the admirals, generals and others before it begins?"

"Yes, you will," she said. "In fact, Mr. Hawks has requested it."

"Really? When?"

"Quite soon."

"Where is Agent Vingee?"

"She has left the area. I do not know if her assignment is to remain on Io."

"Up to her superiors," I agreed. "How about Sergeant Fitch?"

"I believe he returned to his ship." She turned from the monitors and looked directly at me. "I will be back before the procedure starts. If you have not noticed, the grav-bed will not allow you to get up and wander around."

"Or leave?"

"Or leave." She rechecked the equipment and left.

I closed my eye and listened. The sound dampeners muffled already distant conversations and the hum of cooling fans. I was very fatigued and eventually dozed off.

A technician disrupted my slumber, setting up three recording cameras, some transmitting equipment, and a large holographic display.

"Almost show time," I remarked.

The technician smiled and went about her work. It looked like top of the line equipment. It was a modular setup so she completed her task and tested the equipment within four minutes.

She spoke into her collar. "All set up in here." She must've heard a response through an imbedded chip in her ear. Most I-Tech had them. She cupped her hand while listening to the reply. She nodded. "Okay."

"Do the dampeners interfere with your communications implant?" I asked.

"Only marginally," she said, refocusing on activating the equipment.

After a moment the technician stood off to the right. One of Dr. Goldsen's assistants came into the area and stood next to her. Except for their chins, they could have been siblings. Maybe they were, but more likely their parents had selected similar genetic characteristics for them.

The holographic display flashed to life, bringing a three-dimensional image of the inquisitors into view. Each sat in a comfortable chair behind a small table. Each table held a computer clip among other small electronic devices. The group was arranged exactly as it had been at my pretrial with three different faces. Hawks wore the same agitating yellow tie.

The grav-bed elevated me to a forty-five degree angle while its internal gravity plates held me in place. The images were about eighteen inches tall and close enough that my functioning eye could pick out reasonable detail.

Deputy Director Cavelvar stood first to speak. In response, the holo-program enlarged his image. "Security Specialist Keesay, the transcription procedure utilizing the Cranaltar IV, as you requested, is ready to commence." He spoke in a low, gritty voice. "Do you have anything to say?"

"Yes," I said. "But before I do, it is my understanding that Mr. Hawks requested a chance to speak. I would like to hear what he has to say before I make a statement."

The intelligence director looked to Falshire Hawks before reseating himself.

Mr. Hawks stood, straightened his black suit jacket, and adjusted his yellow tie. "First, I should correct you. I did not request to speak. The Capital Galactic Investment Group, whom I represent, desired to give you the chance to reconsider your decision. It is our belief that you were not fully informed as to the consequences of your decision."

"You are correct, Mr. Hawks. I did not realize that so many people would die as a result of my decision. Did Capital Galactic?"

"That is absurd."

"Remember," I said, "this is a legal proceeding. You are being truthful?" Hawks stood as if relaxed but his jaw tensed. I doubted that this was a course he'd anticipated the proceedings would take. I decided to spend my last moments having a little vindictive fun at Hawks's expense. "You're a good lawyer. Will I have copyrights to the transcriptions the Cranaltar IV makes of my brain?"

"I am not your representative," he said smugly. "If you recall, you divested yourself. You are currently without legal representation."

I suppressed a grin. "In that case I would like it to be known that should I become incapacitated, that any transcriptions be made part of the public domain. Except, of course, any of my transcribed recollections which are determined to be inappropriate for public knowledge by the Department of Intelligence, Director Cavelvar."

Hawks tapped at his computer clipboard and shuffled a few papers. "Then it is to be understood that you desire to follow through with the procedure?"

"That is correct, Mr. Hawks. But I just wanted to be clear. You see, I've viewed a certain surveillance recording. Even R-Techs run across interesting recordings. I'm hoping that during the Cranaltar's delvings, the one I am thinking of becomes part of the transcription. Part of the official record."

Director Cavelvar stood. Both images of Hawks and Cavelvar grew prominent. "What are you getting at, Specialist Keesay?" asked the Director. "Are you referring to evidence in this case?" He looked more puzzled than angry.

"No. I just wanted to indicate to Mr. Hawks that he might be featured in a bit part. Definitely not a starring role. You are quite the stallion." I smiled as Hawks's cheek involuntarily twitched. I was right. "I'm ready."

Hawks stepped before the group. "It is clear that Specialist Keesay is not taking the continuation of this pretrial hearing seriously."

"Not as seriously as you take your vacation pleasures." I noted raised eyebrows on the admiral and general. Hawks continued to play it cool, but I had him worried. He had no idea that everything I implied about his vacations at the Celestial Unicorn Palace was complete fabrication. Even though it would never show in the Cranaltar transcription, I hoped he'd spend time and resources seeking an imaginary recording. At least I'd have a lasting impression on somebody's life. "Unless there are any other questions for me, I'm ready to prove my innocence."

Director Cavelvar waited for the remote judge's green light and then spoke into his collar, "The defendant is ready. Let's get underway."

The holographic images disappeared. The lab assistant came forward as the grav-bed returned to horizontal. She worked some of the controls, elevating my body several inches above the bed. It felt like zero gravity.

"Is what you said about Lawyer Hawks true?" whispered the assistant. "There's a recording of him?"

I didn't want to lie, but why not take the chance to embarrass the esteemed Mr. Hawks further. The more outlets for a rumor the better. "What would be the point of someone about to have their brain transcribed making things up?" Let her interpret that however she liked.

Dr. Goldsen entered the room and the assistant returned to business. "We are about to begin, Mr. Keesay," the doctor said.

"Call me Kra."

"If you prefer. Kra, maybe you would like to take a moment for prayer?"

Dr. Goldsen must've been working on her bedside manner. I-Techs aren't known for their religious beliefs, especially scientists. "It's getting close," I said. "I think I will." She nodded and went about her work.

I'd never been a religious zealot, but I attended services when I found the place and time. Sporadic would be a better term. But in my situation a little praying couldn't hurt, so I did. It actually felt warmer, more practiced and positive than I'd ever experienced. I wondered if it was a good or a bad omen. To let her know I was ready I asked Dr. Goldsen, "What will it feel like?"

She stopped next to me. Her eyes looked away for a second as she thought. "The best description would be as if you were dreaming. But it will seem more real. You will feel pain, or pleasure, more intensely than if you were dreaming. To counteract, the Cranaltar inhibits the brain's interaction with the central nervous system. Safer for the subject—patient."

The assistant positioned my bed under the large metallic parabola. Dr. Goldsen stepped to a keyboard and began entering instructions. The needle-bearing cable came to life and slowly stationed itself above my head.

The assistant attached clear plastic sides to the grav-bed, forming a box.

"What are those for?" I asked.

"To hold the immobilization gel," explained the assistant. "Less chance for interference."

Made sense, I thought. Hadn't somebody already mentioned the gel? At this point I figured it didn't matter. The assistant continued to work, but didn't look too involved, so I asked, "I'm likely to be here a while?"

"You'll be continuously monitored. You'll be provided nutrients through your support tubes during the procedure, if necessary."

Dr. Goldsen walked over and leaned close. "Are you ready, Kra?"

"Let's get this over with." My voice cracked just a little.

Dr. Goldsen took my hand. "Things might turn out better than you expect."

I heard the assistant adding liquid below my suspended body.

"You might want to close your eye." Dr. Goldsen squeezed my hand and let go. "Relax."

"Sure thing." But before relaxing, I added, "Innocent or not, learn something from this. So the next person has a better chance."

She met my gaze and nodded. I closed my eye, determined to keep it shut. I didn't want to see the Cranaltar begin its work.

Almost immediately I sensed more than heard movement of the needle-filled cable. Warm solidifying liquid flowed around me. I couldn't move. All at once hundreds of pinpricks radiated across my scalp and forehead. There was definitely no going back now.

I wondered if my scalp was bleeding, but that question was lost. Something intruded into my thoughts. I began to see flashing images from my past. Oliver. Tending bees, collecting honey. My mother's drawing room. One of her political cartoons.

It became difficult to concentrate, as if I was fighting for control. I tried to stay focused on a thought, but more persistent ones kept intruding. It was the Cranaltar taking over. I tried not to resist, but couldn't. Eventually, the device became more established, more dominant. My thoughts became more random, weak, retreating. I clenched my teeth as I fought to hang on.

Suddenly, I was preparing to board a shuttle from the Mavinrom 1 Colony to the space dock in the Gliese 876 system. I knew it wasn't real. I wasn't really there. I was lying, mortally wounded, in a grav-bed on Io. But I felt so healthy. I was walking and excited. I was there.

CHAPTER 8

Although deadly infectious diseases are not entirely a thing of the past, for humans at least, the threat isn't a major concern. The human immune system, as compared to most alien species, is highly effective. There hasn't been an alien-born plague inflicted upon a major human population. The same cannot be said about every alien species that has encountered humans.

One of the reasons this is true is the government mandated vaccination program. From birth, every infant begins a strict inoculation regimen until the age of four. Each individual is marked with a tattoo-like geometric pattern located just beneath the left ear. When further vaccinations are administered, the half-inch pattern is modified, indicating the sum of protections received.

Over time the vaccination identification mark, or V-ID, has evolved into more than a medical records marking. Because each individual's V-ID has an identification sequence they are also used to restrict travel. Some colonies require supplemental inoculations based upon needs, environment, and expected alien contact.

Strictly enforced protection is vital to the overall health and safety of the expanding population. Corporate use of the protective health policy to deny travel by colonial citizens is not unheard of. There are appeal processes, but they are lengthy and heavily weighted in a corporate entity's favor. Freedom of travel isn't a luxury held by all.

I scratched at the V-ID just above my collar. They always itch after modification. I was glad to be leaving the Mavinrom 1 Colony. It was a small, very poor and densely populated mining colony, located on a very large and desolate planet. The frequent power shortages didn't inspire confidence. If the grav plates counteracting the planet's immense gravity ever failed, few areas of the mining colony would survive.

The local security checked my V-ID. With it, I was now permitted to travel among the border and even to some of the outer colonies. The woman checking me over was I-Tech. She wore a grayish green uniform with a lettered patch of metallic green outlined in black on her sleeve, spelling out 'Negral'. My uniform was the same color with the same Negral Corp logo, except hers was a snug-fitting body suit while, like most R-Techs, I preferred loose coveralls. Her uniform still showed the outline of a previous logo's removal. The rating patch above her right breast pocket indicated she was a Class 3 Security Specialist.

I was a C4 Sec-Spec. Only R-Techs like me are initially assigned a class 4 rating. I smiled. She sneered. I wouldn't be happy either if I were assigned to this dismal planet.

I pulled my equipment cart along. During my weeklong layover, I rarely left it, or anything I valued, unattended. I never ventured about unarmed and

I didn't stick to a set pattern or daily routine. No sense being an easy mark. Poverty necessitated theft for some, but I wasn't in a charitable mood. Whenever I was feeling charitable, I gave extra at the collection plate.

Negral Corp had recently purchased the rights to and the facilities on this planet. Negral Corp wasn't like most corporations; it balanced investments between people and equipment. The policy was self-serving in its goal to obtain more votes for its citizenry in the House of Commons. Negral was too small and financially weak to secure even marginal influence in the House of Investors. Negral Corp's unorthodox strategy was an unreliable method of securing votes, but one of the few viable options for an upstart company. I was betting on Negral's success. I'd just divested myself from the Primus Resource Transport Group.

I unlocked my possession cart, allowing the other C3 Sec-Spec to review its contents. I was wearing my body armor vest over my uniform coveralls. In addition to my holstered revolver, I showed him my concealed backup on my leg. The male C3 eyed them with passing concern. He was more interested in the cart's contents than my archaic weaponry. He performed a cursory inspection of my modern titanium-alloy shotgun and the two other stored archaic firearms. He largely ignored my small stockpile of ammunition. My clothing and other personal effects weren't even touched. Being R-Tech has its advantages.

These guys weren't on the ball. If I hadn't been harboring a few questionable items, I would've reported them on the spot. The only thing that caught the C3's eye was my small stash of authentic wood. I'd neatly sealed each four-inch block in clear plastic wrap. My attentiveness ensured nothing disappeared.

"You're clear, Specialist Keesay."

I caught his ID patch under his rating. "Thank you, Specialist Nitchumn." I ignored his smirk as I closed my cart and secured it with an old-style padlock before pulling it through the main passage toward my transport. I intended to see my possessions securely stowed on the shuttle before boarding. My cart lacked modern automated drive and reverse gravity plates. Instead, it sported two wheels and a handle. Upon inspection of the cart lineup, I ventured to guess mine was the most secure.

The cargo handlers were busy, but smiled when I approached. "Afternoon," the older of the two said.

I nodded. "Can you find a nice place where this won't bump into any of those fancy rigs and damage them?" From my pocket I produced two small wraps of chewing gum.

The older cargo handler scratched his shoulder as I handed him the candy. He tossed one to his partner. "No problem, Specialist. The other passengers are sure to be grateful for your concern."

I politely stepped back and let them work. The tip was good quality, some genuine sugar. Odds were I'd be back this way. I'd seen the two workers around the colony and they seemed to know some of its ins and outs. I read the name patches on their steel gray coveralls. I'd remember them, hoping they'd remember me.

The launching bay construction appeared structurally sound to my untrained eye, but it was in need of routine maintenance. Several rows of computer terminals sat covered and unmanned. Beyond them rested heavy robotic equipment with simple 'Out of Order' signs affixed. As a newly endued investor, I hoped my sponsor didn't pay too much for this place.

Negral Corp owned the planetary colony, not the orbiting space dock. I didn't look forward to the standard cost-cutting 1.8 by 2.8 meter room. Such was the life of a lowly space-faring security man. I wondered what my quartering aboard the *Kalavar* would be like.

I noticed a middle-aged woman also observing the area. Although she was dressed business travel casual, her stance and awareness indicated something else. She scanned the loading and the mingling passengers heading toward the transport shuttle's ramp. The woman definitely had military training. Odds were she was a corporate bounty hunter...maybe.

I waved to the handlers as they closed and sealed the external access cargo hatch. Both nodded while I moved toward the boarding ramp. There appeared to be few passengers leaving the planet's surface today. I fell in line behind a taller man in a business suit. He turned and noticed my sidearm before spotting my rating and company logo. He sported a red tie riddled with random black geometric shapes. The large amount of black on his red tie identified him as a low-ranking political bureaucrat, probably an assistant to an assistant sent to visit the Mavinrom 1 Colony. I nodded politely, "Good morning."

He must've taken it as some sort of cue. "Good morning to you, Specialist Keesay," he said with enthusiasm. "Traveling on business for Negral Corporation?"

I politely responded, "Correct." In my experience some bureaucrats can be very long winded despite having nothing of relevance to say. Oh well, I thought. "And you are?"

His grin revealed more teeth than the average dental commercial. "Garnose Linnuhey, Secretarial Assistant to Nephron Jones, Corporate Advisor to Representative Vorishnov." He extended his hand. "Mind if I ask you a few questions on the way up?"

Although he looked a little disheveled and overworked, his handshake was firm and confident. "Sure." I nodded, seeing the short line had disappeared. "We're next."

He turned and proceeded through the scanning arch. I followed him toward the ramp. The observant brunette had quietly maneuvered in line behind us. I kept an eye over my shoulder as she passed through the arch. Assistant Linnuhey seemed oblivious as he shifted a palm-sized computer clip from an inner breast pocket to an outside one.

The sleek, modern transport shuttle looked to be in excellent condition. For its size it had to be. Few small transports could generate sufficient thrust to escape Mavinrom's gravitational pull without antigravity assistance. Moving toward the standard portside ramp, I spied evidence of the necessary plates near the hull's aft section. I followed Linnuhey in, observing the interior. There were 42 high-backed seats arranged in eight rows of six with an aisle splitting them down the middle. There would have been 48 except the mid-entry ramp necessitated the removal of six for passenger loading. Negral Corp's logo was prominently displayed on the forward section wall, leading to the pilot compartment. I listened to the bounty hunter stride up the ramp.

A third of the seats contained stacked packages held in place by netting. Passengers occupied about half of the remaining seats. I stopped in the aisle, politely blocking the way aft, pretending to search for someone. Bounty hunters often made a security specialist's life difficult. Why not return the favor while I had the chance? With most of the midsection seating occupied, lingering seemed a reasonable ploy to force the bounty hunter to select a seat forward.

Too quickly Garnose Linnuhey stopped and turned. "Back here." He pointed. "More room."

I couldn't come up with a response to stall. A bounty hunter wouldn't want to draw attention to herself, but Linnuhey had solved that dilemma for her. "Sounds good."

Several passengers watched as we passed open seats on our way to an isolated corner. He selected the furthest seat starboard.

"I kind of like aisle seats," I said.

Unfazed he grinned. "Corner's better."

I shrugged my shoulders and tried to remember why I started talking to this guy.

Linnuhey glanced at the trailing brunette. Until now I hadn't scrutinized her appearance. Her attractiveness probably caught the bureaucrat's eye. She took a seat on the back row as well, across the aisle.

Linnuhey's voice interrupted my observation. "Better strap in, Specialist Keesay."

"Good idea." I secured the leg and ankle restraints. Then I buckled and adjusted the shoulder harness, making sure my sidearm wasn't unnecessarily bound. I hadn't loaded it with armor-piercing rounds that could compromise the hull. Getting off Mavinrom put me in a better mood. "Just call me Kra."

Linnuhey fidgeted with the seat's lumbar adjustment. "Most of my friends call me Garney."

Friends, I thought. Acquaintances maybe. He acted more than a bit odd.

"Nice vessel," he commented.

"Hope it's as comfortable as it looks. The transport I took down didn't compensate for the planet's gravity very well."

ss shuttle before. It'll be just fine."
ie brunette. She was tying her hair back before
e other passengers sat ready and waiting. Nothing
vonder at the delay. I figured Linnuhey's lack of
was at a loss as well. I heard some commotion near

innuhey.
ad an aisle seat I could see." He appeared oblivious
I released my harness and stood. "A security
noting his body armor, helmet and medium-duty
dolly-bot with a fancy crate." I couldn't be sure, but
red security version. The security man glared at me
his rating, Supervisor 2. None of my business so I sat
akeoff.
nning behind," said Linnuhey.
s, the ramp retracted and the hatch sealed. "Guess
or grav plates activate. They were less noticeable than
den down. Linnuhey was probably right.
"

"No. This is my first time out of the solar system. I was stationed on Pluto for about a year."

"Doing what?"

I was trying to review the details of the C2 and dolly-bot but answered anyway. "Warehouse security. Pretty boring."

"Not much activity on Pluto, or Charon?"

"Some ethane collection on Pluto. Except for the ice harvesting transports working the Kupier Belt, not many layovers. They sometimes need supplies." I craned my neck a little to see between the seats. "Parts, a little entertainment." I heard and felt the engines fire up. "I was there to ensure nothing left unaccounted for."

Linnuhey grinned. "Makes sense—what's so interesting?"

Through the ceiling-mounted speakers a voice announced, "We have clearance. Secure for takeoff." Everything from my vantage seemed okay. A few seconds later I felt a minor shift, much weaker than I'd expected.

"Anti-gravity sled," Linnuhey said. "Maneuvering us out of the holding bay."

I nodded as if appreciative, then flicked a glance at the bounty hunter. She appeared to be staring off into space, or listening.

"See," said Linnuhey, "what did I tell you?"

"We haven't left the colony's influence yet," I said, although I knew he was right.

Passing through the launch bay's integrity barrier sent a wave of energized pressure through my body. The increased engine noise made our neighbor's eavesdropping a little more difficult. I wondered how a low-level bureaucrat repeatedly secured transport on top of the line shuttles like this. "You travel often?"

"Why yes. More than most." He inspected and deftly adjusted his harness. "Mostly on business."

"Gathering statistics?"

"Yes, that and other things for Mr. Jones."

"Really, what else?"

"Oh, meeting with supervisors, local governors. You know."

His responses struck me as a bit vague. Maybe he was distracted by the brunette. "Meet with anybody interesting?"

"Not really," he said with a sigh.

"What do you think of Negral Corp?"

He paused. "Surprising company. Has secured the rights to two planets." He pressed his tongue against his upper teeth. "Bold, or risky considering Negral's limited assets."

"Bold." I rubbed my chin. "After I transfer to the *Kalavar*, I believe my final destination will be Tallavaster."

Linnuhey's eyebrows rose. "Do you know much about Tallavaster?"

"A little," I said. "Do you?"

Linnuhey nodded. "Pretty desolate place. Not much has evolved there. Bacteria, algae, some lichens." He reached into his pocket and pulled out his palm clip. Faster than most programming engineers he brought up information. "Says here that frequent impacts by meteorites have hampered its ecological development."

"Well, I doubt I'll be stationed there. Might be a good thing."

"Negral Corp has transported a heavily armed monitor to Tallavaster. They plan to use it to intercept and destroy any celestial threats." He scratched his head. "If I recall, the *Kalavar* will be transporting R-Tech farming equipment."

He seemed to know an awful lot about Negral Corp's plans. I looked at the bounty hunter, then back at Linnuhey.

"Attractive women make you nervous?" he whispered.

She did, but it wasn't her looks and I wasn't going to tell him. "How long will our flight be?"

"Not long, maybe another five minutes to reach orbit, then fifteen to the space dock."

I looked at his red and black tie.

He set aside his clip. "I should be up for promotion, soon."

I was really beginning to dislike his toothy grin.

"Negral Corp doesn't own anything on Pluto, do they?"

"No," I said. "I was working for Primus Transport Interest. Negral Corp picked up my contract as a skilled service investor."

"Security," he acknowledged. He returned to his clip. "Quinn and Negral agreed to keep the dock and colony names linked. Mavinrom." He grinned.

"What did you think of Mavinrom 1?"

"Poor," I said, picking my words carefully. "I was hoping Negral didn't pay too much for the place. I read they outbid CGIG."

"Surprising," he agreed. "Capital Galactic Investment is used to getting its way."

"Quinn Mining really made out?" I needed a little time to think. I offered Linnuhey a gum wrap.

"No thanks. Hurts my teeth." He fished around in his left pocket. "You know, I think you're right. They probably did, considering the difficulties mining on high gravity planets." He produced a thick, plastic wrapped stick. "Here, try this."

"Jerky?" Real beef, I thought. Out here?

"It's a little old, but still edible."

"Thanks, but I can't accept." Candy was one thing, but preserved beef.

"Sure you can. This stuff lasts for years." He moved awkwardly, attempting to place it into one of my pockets.

I caught his hand. "Really, I cannot accept." Out of the corner of my eye I spotted the bounty hunter shift in her seat. "I have no way of repaying you."

"You offered first and I cannot chew gum or jerky."

I wanted to ask him how he came across it. Why he had it? I released his hand and accepted it. "No sense eating it now. I'm too nervous to enjoy it."

He relaxed, retrieved his clip, and began pecking away as I tucked the rare foodstuff in a thigh pocket.

"What did you think of security?" Linnuhey asked.

"Hmm?"

"You're a security specialist. What did you think of it on Mavinrom?"

Well, if he did travel a lot, I wouldn't be revealing anything. "Pretty lax."

"Doesn't that bother you?"

"Yes, it did. I noticed it most while boarding." We'd escaped Mavinrom's oppressive gravitational reach so I loosened my harness and leaned closer. "I'll report it, but not down on Mavinrom."

"Why not?"

"The two checking the carts and luggage, they're not original Negral hires. Didn't look too happy with their job. Probably had their contract bought out. I figured it could be the same with their immediate superior."

"How do you know that?"

"Their uniforms. I saw where the Quinn logo had been removed."

"I hadn't noticed."

I didn't believe Linnuhey. He was up to something.

"Guess it doesn't matter," he said. "Mavinrom's not exactly a prime site for smuggling."

"True, but if so, what's in the fancy crate up front?"

"They mine some pretty rare elements here," Linnuhey said matter-of-factly. "Unusual isotopes. The pressure and all."

"It would be easier to...standard to send up quantities like that in a return-duty rocket?"

"Not if it's really valuable," he said, "or maybe it's just that this shuttle was going anyway."

I nodded. This guy knew an awful lot for a low-rung bureaucrat. He was interested in security and what I knew. I pondered while he tapped away at his clip. If he was a corporate spy he didn't seem like a very good one. Pretty chatty. Did he offer the jerky as a bribe?

Linnuhey interrupted my thoughts. "Was smuggling a problem on Pluto?"

"No, why would it be? Not much traffic, especially without a space dock."

"Maybe they were just lax because you're one of their own."

"Not likely. I'm an R-Tech, class 4. Even lazy, they were less than polite."

"Agreed. Most I-Techs don't think much of relics."

Did he really think I'd fall for that sympathetic-heart line? Maybe I could play off it and confirm something. I deliberately placed my right hand on my .357 magnum revolver. "What do you think of us relic techs?"

I ignored his answer and instead focused on the bounty hunter. I sensed her tensing up. I glanced over and suppressed a smiled. She appeared calm except for her eyes. Intense. Linnuhey was some sort of spy and she was his lookout or bodyguard.

Whatever Linnuhey had said, I was sure it was apologetic. "I didn't think you cared one way or another," I responded, sliding my hand to my thigh. "So what market is there for those rare isotopes?"

Unfazed by the abrupt topic switch, he answered, "Most of the elements mined are useful to alien races, A-Techs."

"Like the Crax?"

"Well...yes," he said, licking his lips. "But the Umbelgarri would seem a more suitable trade partner."

"True, humans are on better terms with them." Somehow, he seemed too easily intimidated to be a corporate spy. Unless that was an act as well. I wasn't up to speed on the espionage business, but whoever Linnuhey was, he rated a bodyguard. Either they were amateurs or I was out of my league.

Linnuhey continued tapping away at his clip. "Marginal last three years running."

"What?" I asked.

"Profits, for Quinn Mining Interest on Mavinrom."

That did it for me. Sure, he could have looked it up on some standard published corporate reports, but something just wasn't adding up. "Mr. Linnuhey—"

"Garney," he cheerily interrupted.

"Mr. Linnuhey," I said in a low voice, "or whoever you are. Look, in addition to those C3s, I plan to inform my superiors of your suspicious activities."

He wasn't fazed. His mirthful eyes matched his grin.

"You may be a secretarial assistant," I said. "I doubt it. More like a corporate spy. I don't have the time or the authority to look into it. But I know who can and will. You and your lady friend.

He looked past me, still grinning.

"You might think this is some type of game, or that you've compromised me." I held out the jerky wrap, and reminded myself to keep my voice down. "Bribe? Try to press it on me. You've got a lot more to lose than I do. Either you're not too bright or are in it for the long run, thinking I'd be a useful contact. That proves you're not too smart." I leaned closer. "I recommend you steer clear of Negral Corp operations...say, for the rest of your life?"

"I'm glad to hear that!"

I expected denial or ignorance. Where was this going?

"Prepare for bay landing," the intercom voice announced.

My mind raced. Was he some sort of company plant? Was this a test? "Explain."

"Better tighten your harness," he said. "Just in case."

I adjusted my straps and I considered the brunette. How much had she heard?

Clunk. "Not the softest of landings," said Linnuhey, releasing his harness. "I'm glad you're an honest man. Integrity is sometimes hard to find."

"Thanks. I am sure you won't mind then, if I follow you both out."

The questionable bureaucrat stepped past me. "After you," I gestured to the brunette.

Linnuhey looked back. "It's okay, Miss Brown."

Her threatening glare didn't bother me. I responded with a Linnuhey-like grin.

By now most of the passengers had exited. Linnuhey waited for his protection before strolling down the ramp. Brown was on his tail, doing her best scan the bay while keeping track of me.

The bay was large and well lit. Some of the passengers had moved off to the left to retrieve their carts. The S2 and the dolly-bot had halted a short distance away. It struck me as odd.

"Down, Vorishnov!" ordered Brown as she ran, pulling him off the ramp.

I went for my sidearm. My training indicated robbery, but my instincts cried, *Hit*! The cracking of MP fire echoed. The S2's laser carbine flashed. I looked down. Brown was on top of Linnuhey—Representative Vorishnov—with an MP pistol in hand. Her attention was still split between the erupting chaos and me.

I wouldn't shoot her. I was hoping she went for the chest where my armor might protect me. Bold movement to the left caught my attention. Everyone around the carts was down or fleeing except one handler who'd leveled a large laser pistol at Vorishnov.

Brown sensed it, too. She spun in front of Vorishnov, taking the searing blast in the back.

I took cover in the shuttle entrance as I thumbed back my single-action revolver's hammer. *Crack*! My shot went wide, rocking the nearest cart. I cocked again as the assassin fired off a second shot at the representative.

He missed. Sporadic fire continued across the bay. Ignoring it, I took aim. The handler fired off a third shot just as I pulled the trigger. I hit him and he staggered back a step when a grunt sounded from below.

Vorishnov had been hit in the shoulder while reaching for Brown's gun. Rounds ricocheted off the ramp. Vorishnov huddled behind the fallen woman as I ran down the ramp. "Damn." I'd have to complete her assignment.

I let loose with a shot forcing the assassin behind a cart. With his body armor, success required a headshot. His laser capacitor would recycle in seconds and my armor couldn't handle a fully charged blast. I fired again, impacting the top of the cart forcing the assassin to seek complete cover.

Grabbing the representative by the collar, I yanked him beneath the ramp. A set of teeth clattered across the floor. Shouts echoed in the distance above the gunfire and lingering civilian screams.

"Hope that's the cavalry," I muttered.

Despite the pain, he chuckled. "It'd better be."

"Two rounds left." I cocked back the hammer again. No time to load AP rounds. No sense going for my backup. "Next time, screw regulations."

Linn—Vorishnov responded, "Next time, how about a *modern* weapon—here he comes!"

The baggage assassin charged, firing.

I took aim as his shots went high then wide. Mine struck him high in the shoulder.

He kept coming. Firing again, he returned the favor into my left shoulder.

"Ahhgh!" I grunted, letting go with my last round. My bullet shattered the assassin's right shin in mid stride. As he crashed onto the ramp, I leapt up and slammed my revolver down on his skull—twice.

I examined Miss Brown. Her spine had been severed and half of her internal organs were cooked. Seared metal mingled with burned flesh isn't a pleasant odor.

Pounding footsteps approached. "Drop it. Down now!"

I rolled away from Brown after discarding my empty revolver. Before my hand could reach Brown's dropped pistol a boot stomped on it. I looked up to see the S2 and a few pals.

I moved to the prone position and spread my arms and legs. My shoulder wound didn't hurt much.

The representative was on his back with someone attending him. Blood flowed from a gash across his cheek. He looked my way. "Delighted to see you found the most effective method to employ your weapon."

"I think they stepped on your teeth."

He returned a grin with his authentic, smaller set.

"Shut up!" came from above. "Hands behind your back, Relic."

"What for?"

"Do it, now!"

"Hey, I just saved his life, Chip. Where were you?"

Several boots and a stun baton later I was unconscious.

CHAPTER 9

Shortly after the Silicate War an official nomenclature was established for navigational software incorporating a trinomial system similar to the standard biological taxa of three terms. Thus genus, species and subspecies for biological identification corresponded to celestial identification as stellar system, planet and moons.

Human nature was anticipated in this venture. First, common names have always been more easily recalled. Just as a great percentage of people would be able to conceptualize a specific fresh water turtle when given the common name, red-eared slider, a precipitously low number would accurately identify it when provided with its scientific name, Trachemys scripta elegans.

Secondly, stellar and planetary identification has remained a hodge-podge of historic, scientific, and corporate naming. Political sponsored renaming has added further complexity.

All of that being said, it can be argued that more people have a greater interest in colony locations than freshwater turtles. And despite the whims of current influential officials, human navigational programmers wrote code and initiated artificial intelligence programs anticipating such factors.

I awoke to the taste of blood. It took a second to recall that I was on the space dock, orbiting Mavinrom in the Gliese 876 system. With my wrists and ankles cuffed, two men hauled me face down. I knew where I was, but not my situation. I decided to remain quiet until I knew more, other than the fact that my dragging boots would require polishing.

After about twenty seconds a youthful voice from the warder on my left commented, "Some mess." He shifted his hold. "A lot of blood. Especially the bureaucrat's."

"And his," replied a husky voice on my right.

Their jovial attitude did little to help my injured shoulder. Complaining would've made it worse. Four pairs of feet and maybe my cart escorted me down the corridor.

"Put him in there. His stuff in there." It was the S2's harsh voice.

"Sure thing, sir," promised a voice with my trailing cart. "Break it open?"

"No," said the S2. "Use the key. Here. Wait for the inspector."

Metallic clatter, followed by laughs echoed in the corridor. "Nice catch, Dosser," said the right porter. "Don't lose it."

"I'll just have maintenance cut it off."

I almost snickered at the thought. A door slid open to my rear and the S2 departed. The porter shifted as he tapped the door code. I didn't bother lifting my head to look.

The left warder asked, "On the bed?"

"Sure, why not," said the right porter. "He'll be sore enough. Gaverall sure don't seem to like R-Techs. I don't blame 'em."

"Some are okay," responded the left, his voice lacking confidence.

They lifted me onto the bed. The process was too painful to continue my ruse. "Ugh." I rolled my head and opened my eyes.

"Hey there, fella," said the right warder. "Up for another go round?" His nametag read, Dribbs. He looked a little old to still be a Class 3 Sec-Spec. His C3 partner, at least twenty years younger, frowned at the remark.

"Didn't think so," Dribbs said. "C'mon, O'Vorley."

I shifted to a more comfortable position and watched them exit. I didn't bother to request removal of my cuffs. The bed was hardly more than a table with a couple of blankets. A stool sat in a corner and an obvious security camera hung recessed in the single intense light. No doubt, the door was locked.

I examined my shoulder as best I could. The laser blast had burned through my protective vest and uniform. I rolled my shoulder. The wound felt superficial and someone had taken the time to slap on some ointment. My lower lip was split and swollen. I tasted fresh blood and medication on it so I hadn't been out long.

I rolled onto my right shoulder and got comfortable. It could be a long wait, and I knew better than to try and slip my arms under my legs. Magnetic locking cuffs had a tendency to further activate when the wrist and ankle versions came in close proximity. Things were bad enough.

I closed my eyes and waited. Although the hit attempt had been quick, I vividly recalled it. Instead of replaying the event, my mind wandered to broader questions. Why was Representative Vorishnov traveling in disguise? I thought about corporate news editorials denouncing his populist voting record. Was it enough for some CEO to order his assassination? Apparently so.

I was getting stiff. Stun batons were bad, but better than a complete boot bruising. I got up, and in three hops, reached the stool. Sitting, I took a new line of thought. Why was Vorishnov here? Was he working with Negral Corp? My sponsor was more inclined to favor his policies. A successful political hit was rare away from Earth, unless there was an itinerary leak. Tough questions. Somebody knew, of course, but not anyone who'd confide in me.

Without a ship chronometer in the room and unable to see my watch, I guessed two hours had passed. I wasn't closer to any answers. I began to wonder if the *Kalavar* would arrive on time, and if this mess would be sorted out before its scheduled departure. If not, I could be in a bit of trouble.

Startled, I looked toward the open door. A plain-faced man dressed in casual business attire walked in. No tie to identify standing. Definitely intelligence.

"Good afternoon, Specialist Keesay," he began. "I am Field Director Karlton Simms." He pulled a small cylindrical object from a jacket pocket. "Would you like those removed?"

"Actually, yes. That would be nice." I turned on the stool.

Director Simms removed my manacles and placed them in their case before tossing it on the bed. His face remained emotionless even while he spoke. "Quite a morning." He reached into an inner pocket and pulled out a small remote control device. He pointed it at the light and tapped an icon, dimming it.

Not exactly how I expected an interrogation to start. "Yes. Quite a morning."

Director Simms put the remote away and pulled out a small clamshell computer clip. "Want to tell me about it?" he asked, leaning a hip against the table.

"Not really. What's the clip for? Aren't you recording this anyway?"

"Specialist, I'm busy and you have a transport to catch." After tapping a few keys he pulled some small metallic disks from his jacket's inner pocket.

I knew what they were so I unbuttoned my collar. "Has it arrived?"

"It's not due yet and I expect it to be delayed," said Simms as he approached. He placed one of the disks over my left carotid artery, one on my right temple, another at the base of my skull, two across my forehead and last on my right palm.

"How would you know that?"

"Common occurrence." He tapped away at the clip. "Now, Specialist, this isn't the first time you've been debriefed by our agency, so let's get to it."

He knew about my involvement in Earth's Colonization Riots, probably from records on his clip. I didn't think a Field Director would have such access. So much for promises. "What do you want to know?"

"Do you know who you were sitting next to on the shuttle?"

"I do, now."

He stared at me a moment. "This is going to take a long time unless you're a little more forthcoming, Specialist."

"Let it. I see no reason to confide in you."

"Why would that be? I'm only asking simple questions. I've already interviewed other witnesses." He moved a step closer.

"I've been debriefed only one other time in my life. You shouldn't know that unless you're other than who you claim to be, Field Director." I decided to stand before continuing. "And if you do, and you are who you say, then someone further up has been dishonest, giving me even less reason to comply with your request."

He was several inches taller than me and stood his ground. "This is the way it is, Specialist. I've got a very important job. Occasionally my superiors do send subordinates to do work in the field. And they don't generally send us out ill informed. You have security training. Think about it. Think about who's involved and what you've seen." His stare intensified before refocusing his gaze on his computer. "This incident is peripheral compared to the big game."

I sat back down and thought about the S2 on the shuttle ride up, with a box and heavily armed. A controversial representative in disguise in an out-of-the-way place, and an assassination attempt. Was Director Simms telling the truth? My guts said, 'Trust him.' My training said, 'Make him work for it.'

I decided to play it by ear and see what happened. "Well, you're here right on schedule so intel must've been doing more than trailing a cold scent."

After thirty seconds of silence I continued. "He was Vorishnov. I didn't know it—until after someone tried to kill him."

"Thank you." He returned to the table. "Now why did you sit next to him on the way up?"

"He approached me. He seemed annoying but otherwise...I was glad I did." The director split his attention between the readouts and me. Verifying truthful statements is usually a two-person job, unless the operator is exceptionally good. "At the time."

Director Simms concentrated on his readings. "Why?"

"Because," I said, "after a while I figured something wasn't right." I knew it wasn't possible, but I could almost feel the receptor-transmitters monitoring my brain activity, my vital signs, my reactions. "I thought he was a corporate spy and I told him I was going to report him to my superiors."

"What made you suspect?"

"He knew an awful lot. About Negral's activities. Asking questions about security. Certainly more than a bureaucrat the level of his cover would." I thought a second or two. "He seemed more accustomed to luxury. You might tell him that."

Simms smiled. "He was complimentary toward you. Why did Special Agent Brown think you might have been part of the attempt on Representative Vorishnov's life?"

"What do you mean?"

"She turned her firearm on you?"

"Correct. During the trip, she seemed suspicious. I thought she was a bounty hunter. Then I pegged her as a bodyguard." I figured Simms already had this information from the representative. "My actions in determining this might have alarmed her. She wasn't very covert."

"No," agreed Simms. "Her specialty is combat tactics and weaponry. You're lucky she was unsure about you." He pointed between my eyes. "Top five in the agency."

I didn't bother to point out Simms's lack of past tense. He tapped at the small screen. Did he detect me holding back a foremost thought. Was he that good?

"Why did you intervene on Representative Vorishnov's behalf?" he asked patiently. "You didn't know who he was at the time. Why defend a corporate spy working against your sponsor?"

"Good questions," I said, stalling. "He was still on the ramp of the shuttle, Negral Corp's property. I work for Negral Corp as security." It wasn't exactly the whole truth, but I hoped he'd buy it. "He was under our protection."

The field director simply raised an eyebrow. He knew what he was about.

"...And I felt responsible. His bodyguard took a hit for him. If she hadn't been distracted, maybe she would've gotten the baggage handler."

He nodded absently.

"Mind if I ask a question?"

"Will you trust my answer?" he asked, again leaning against the table.

"That depends. Was the dolly-bot carrying anything valuable? Or is that S2 part of your operation?"

He thought for a few seconds before answering, "Well, the cargo is valuable, and it is part of the *Kalavar*'s scheduled cargo. Security Supervisor Gaverall is an expert marksman as well. He took out four to your one."

"Marksmanship isn't everything," I said. "Proper training. Brown was a poor choice. And an S2 in charge of local security that has five plants on his team?"

"Six," Simms corrected. "Specialist Dribbs winged one. And the Representative insisted upon Agent Brown."

He was using names around me. He either planned on letting me go, figuring I would look into it anyhow. Or he was up to something else?

"Speaking of poor choice," said Simms, "why would you arm yourself with a single-action revolver?"

"I didn't exactly expect to be in a crossfire." Talking irritated my split lip, but I ignored it. "Normally, I'd have my shotgun when on duty or in a high-risk area. But carrying without cause tends to upset civilian travelers. You know, shotguns are mainly used in penal colonies. I'm new to Negral. Didn't want to make an unfavorable impression."

He nodded. "That didn't exactly answer my question. With available equipment, why even carry a thumb-buster?"

He used the old-time reference for my revolver. He had some knowledge of archaic firearms. A little confused, I continued, "A few reasons." This didn't seem like a logical line of interrogation, but I went on anyway. "First, if my sidearm were taken, how many I-Techs would know to cock the hammer? While they're fiddling with the trigger or even looking for a safety, I might have a chance to go for my backup, hit him, run, whatever. Second, a .357 has some knockdown without being too cumbersome. A variety of rounds are available. Plus, it's an antique, handed down by my great grandfather."

Simms reached to the small of his back and pulled a small sidearm. "It's a late 20th century .22 semi-auto. My father was a collector so I know something about antique firearms."

"Have you had work done to yours? Mine's no longer all original parts."

He handed the pistol to me. "Unfortunately, yes. After a century, wouldn't be safe to fire otherwise."

"You sure are the trusting type." I looked it over. "Nice condition. I prefer revolvers." I handed it back. "You've seen my backup, a double-action revolver. With a semi-auto, if you're down to one arm, like I almost was, can't reload and fire."

"That's one way to look at it. A standard MP pistol would solve that dilemma. Your shotgun has a mounting for a bayonet?" he asked with a puzzled or amused look.

"More intimidating," I assured him. "Even makes an A-Tech wonder."

"How many aliens have you employed this 'fixed bayonet theory' on?"

"None." I smiled. "But seems logical. And why not?"

Simms reholstered his pistol. "Maybe, but don't try it on a Coregar Crax. They prefer blade combat."

"Their size and training?" I shook my head and laughed. "Compared to me...but if one's that close no sense trying to outrun it. Pretty slim odds running into an elite Coregar warrior."

"You didn't expect to get shot this morning either." He closed his clip and began removing the metallic receptor-transmitters. He'd gotten me so off guard I'd forgotten he was monitoring me. "Speaking of your arm," he said, gesturing. "I was informed you received only minor second degree burns. You're lucky your opposition was trigger-happy. One full blast would've seared right through your vest."

I shrugged. The medication in the salve was working.

"Look," he said, "I don't have a lot of time. You were cleared for duty on the *Kalavar* a long time ago."

"What do you mean? It's only a civil transport less than two years out of mothballs."

"Your involvement in the Colonization Riots got you more than just an out-of-the-way posting on Pluto. I was just reconfirming the decision."

"What's on board the *Kalavar*?" I asked, scratching my head. "Rare elements?"

"Some, but that's not it. Security Chief Corbin will inform you if he deems it appropriate. Don't bother to ask."

"But why me, a Class 4 Relic Tech?"

"Do you think a Relic isn't up to the task?"

"Are you kidding?"

"Just do as you're ordered," he said. "Here, this ought to add to the mystery." He pulled out a small syringe and bottle.

"What's that, truth serum? Test's over, isn't it?"

"Actually, quite the opposite." He couldn't have been more serious as he drew a small amount of the clear liquid. "You are not to divulge to anyone the events that occurred. If asked, it was an organized attempted theft.

Bureaucrat Linnuhey was simply caught in the crossfire, and you were doing your job as security in foiling the attempt. You know of nothing exceptional on board the *Kalavar.*"

"That won't be a stretch."

"This is serious." He reached for a vein in my forearm. "What I am giving you will foil attempts to use drugs in obtaining answers which you're unwilling to divulge."

I was trying to decide if I really trusted him to put the needle into me. In the end I didn't really have a choice. "Do you have a countermeasure drug?"

"That, like this, is classified."

"Okay, you do. I won't tell anybody."

He finally smiled. "We have arranged for a new uniform and some replacement body armor." He handed me two magnetic keys and the case. "If you return the manacles, you can have the deposit. It's been cleared. Just mention my name, Corporate Investigator Simms." He thought a moment. "The armory here is well stocked and you may be out a while. Chances of coming across R-Tech ammunition are pretty slim."

"Thank you," I said, recalling this had been an important military base during the war. Knowing travel schedules often suffered delays, I asked, "When might the *Kalavar* arrive?"

He offered me his hand. "I would expect it to arrive tomorrow at the latest." We shook hands. "And keep those popcorn nukes of yours out of sight."

I grimaced. He was sharp. "They're not illegal. They're of pre-ban civilian manufacture."

"Stick with that line, Specialist Keesay, and they're sure to be confiscated." His face went blank before he exited. "O'Vorley," he called, "Specialist Keesay needs to clean up and requires a meal. We owe him that much."

"Yes, sir, Investigator," O'Vorley replied in his youthful voice.

CHAPTER 10

News. Reliable, accurate, timely, and unbiased information is difficult to come by. Most sources are corporate with releases issued to suit their specific needs. The same is true of information from military and government sources. Intelligence, generally considered an independent arm of the government, is the best informed, yet the least likely to distribute.

Actual eyewitnesses in positions to distribute uncensored, or unvetted, information are rare. The best an interested individual can do is to gather information from multiple sources and, through careful evaluation, hope to find a sliver of truth.

I stretched my joints as the anxious guard, O'Vorley, peered in. I tucked the case under my arm and headed out. "Which way?" Technically he was my superior, being a C3. But he worked for a different company and I wasn't on duty.

I met O'Vorley's blank stared. Young with short, light brown hair. He was trying to grow a mustache. "Clean up?" I asked. "Meal?" I looked both ways down the dimly lit corridor. Access grates ran down the center of the floor. Conduits covered much of the ceiling and the tops of the walls, so I wasn't in a fancy civilian section. No sign of Simms.

It took O'Vorley a second to snap out of it. "Sure, this way." He wanted to say something as we walked but didn't know where to begin.

If he wanted to ask something he'd have to muster the courage. I licked my swollen lip and wondered how messed up I looked. "Before we go, where's my cart and equipment?" I pointed. "Possibly that way?"

He looked surprised. "Ah, no, they were...the corporate investigator moved them."

We just stood there. "Well, who knows? The investigator is gone."

"Did he say it was to be released to you?" asked O'Vorley. "I wasn't informed."

"He said as much, but didn't he give me a signed permission slip."

"Signed?"

"Coded authorization, then."

"Then I cannot allow you access to your equipment," he replied without confidence.

I was growing impatient. "Then let's go see someone who will." I didn't have much by some standards, but I didn't want any of it to disappear. "How about Supervisor Gaverall? Where's he?"

I stepped aside as a tan uniformed maintenance woman and her utility work-bot passed down the hall. She glanced over her shoulder but said nothing.

Finally, O'Vorley spoke into his collar. "Supervisor Gaverall, sir,

Specialist Keesay would like access to his equipment." He nodded. "Where is it, sir? Okay, sir, Investigator Simms instructed me to allow Specialist Keesay to clean up and to provide him with a meal."

My young escort was getting an earful through his imbedded chip. When O'Vorley was refocused on me I asked, "How long have you been onboard?"

"Twenty-eight hours," he offered.

I struggled not to roll my eyes. "First posting?"

He nodded. "I'm still getting to know my way around."

"You don't know where my equipment is?"

His gaze fell to the floor. "I was told the location."

"Follow me," I said, leading him in our original direction, toward a major intersection. After about twenty strides I was loosening up. "Any voice terminals in this area I could access?" We slowed. "You know, one for civilians?"

"Why?" he asked.

"Because, if you tell me the location, I can relay it to the terminal and it can tell us how to get to my equipment." We stopped. "Get rid of the middle man. Your boss."

He looked confused but hopeful. "This way," I said, "you won't have to bother anyone and your voice imprint won't be logged requesting the information. That's what you're worried about."

"I'm on my probationary period," he agreed. "It might look bad."

"I doubt it, but this'll be just one less worry. Which way?"

He indicated the same direction and we were off.

"They been giving you a rough time?" I asked.

He rubbed his hands together. "Sort of. I really don't know too much."

I realized it wouldn't do any good to tell him to make their lives just as difficult. I would, but O'Vorley just didn't have it in him. We approached a cross section. "Where to?"

"Two decks up there's one, I think."

"Let's try. Makes sense there aren't many. This was constructed as a military space dock." I looked around. "Elevator is right over there."

We waited until it arrived. One marine and two engineering techs were already inside. The marine ignored me, but the red-clad technicians glanced a little longer than was polite. The elevator stopped and we exited.

O'Vorley led me about twenty feet down a more lavish corridor. It was painted a faded green with fewer exposed pipes. We approached a terminal.

"Do I look that bad?"

"Well," he said, "your lip is split, you have an abrasion across your cheek and your right eye is blackened."

"Well, your supervisor and his assistants were less than cordial upon our meeting." My hand explored my face. "I'm surprised there isn't a boot imprint. I've run into worse crowds."

"Plus your shoulder," said O'Vorley.

"Good point. Where did they say my equipment was?"

"Green Storage, locker 478, bay 2."

"Green Storage," I said. "That's probably near the armory. Do you know where that is?"

He shook his head. "Not from here. If I go back to Security HQ or my quarters and start, I could find it."

"Your first time out in space?" There was more to this kid's story. Kid, I thought. I'm not much older.

"It's pretty obvious, isn't it, sir."

"Yes, it is. And I'm a Security Specialist 4th Class, certainly not sir to you." I stepped in front of the terminal and surveyed the screen when it activated. I tapped the icon for tourist information requests. Giving it a second, I said, "Diagram route to Green Storage."

A synthesized voice replied, "That area is restricted. No civilian admittance."

I looked at O'Vorley, then continued, "Just because I request information does not mean I intend to follow up on it. Diagram route to Green Storage."

"Request is for information to a restricted area. Your voice imprint does not match proper admittance records."

I care very little for artificial intelligence programs. "Is the deck level of Green Storage classified?"

"No, it is not."

I watched O'Vorley frown as I spoke. "Terminal, what deck is Green Storage on?"

"Deck Twelve."

"Omitting the restricted areas, display layout for Deck Twelve." If it did this, it wasn't too bright of a program or what I was seeking wasn't restricted enough to alert monitoring programs. Or security would arrive and rough me up again.

I pointed to the screen. "I'd guess there." O'Vorley nodded in agreement.

I leaned back and looked near the elevator. "Display layout Deck Eight." We studied the screen. "Can you find it now?"

"Yes, I can," O'Vorley said, turning toward the elevators. "You're R-Tech?"

"Correct."

"You use an information terminal pretty well."

"Correct, I do." I knew where this was going. "Just because I choose not to have various implants or advanced technical training, or become hooked on electronic gadgetry, doesn't mean I'm totally ignorant of computer functions and use."

"Oh," he said sheepishly.

"Contrary to popular I-Tech belief, most relic techs aren't morons."

Maybe I was overdoing it. "A common misconception. No harm, no foul."

"What?"

"It's just an archaic sporting reference—means don't worry about it." Although I knew the route, I asked, "Which way, Specialist?"

"This way, back to the lift." As we fell in stride, he tensed up. "Specialist Dribbs said you killed one of the offenders by clubbing his skull with your old-style steel gun."

The corridor was empty, as was elevator when it arrived. "I figured the second blow might have finished him. He was down in front of me with laser in hand and I was out of rounds." I shrugged. The elevator ascended. "He tried to kill me. I responded."

O'Vorley looked at my shoulder. "Him or you?"

"Pretty much. I'd have shot him in the head if I could've."

The door opened. My companion looked a little pale. "I don't think I could've done that."

"You might be surprised," I said. "When someone's shooting at you, your adrenaline—instincts take over." I watched him ponder as we walked. "It's kind of like in training, but more intense. You just react."

O'Vorley said, "I didn't have much training."

"What do you mean?"

"You know how things are on Earth—the recruiting."

"Wait!" I grabbed his shoulder. "Slow down. You just came from Earth?" Of course he did, I thought. Pay attention!

"Yeah. Straight to here. Got my training en route."

"What's going on? What do you mean?" He didn't follow. "Who's doing the recruiting? When I was stationed on Pluto, there was news about the Colonial Marines stepping up efforts. Is that it?"

"Yeah. The recruiters came to my career tech center and everything. Checking records and testing. My dad said not to sign up. I had several months before draft eligibility." He thought a moment. "My dad got me a contract with Quinn Mining. They told us that I'd complete my study in planetary geology and work for them."

"I didn't know the draft had been reinstated. You did this to avoid the draft? And now you're out here?"

"Uh huh." He frowned. "The contract's fine print said that if required, my original assignment could be deferred."

"How bad is it?" I was anxious. "Where are you from?"

"Security?"

"No," I said and led O'Vorley past several technicians repairing a heating transfer. "I've read sketchy reports that the Crax are gearing up for war." We almost missed a turn. "Reception on Pluto isn't much."

"There was a lot of talk about it in Rio de Janeiro, but hardly any holo-casts."

"You're from Rio de Janeiro?" I asked. "When did you leave?"

"I left a week after signing with Quinn. They transferred me to Cairo and enrolled me in tier two geology classes. Then they reassigned me here, around Gliese 876—as security."

"What do they say about the Umbelgarri? Is that why the Marines are recruiting?" I led the way while O'Vorley searched for an answer. We had a distance to go.

He shrugged his shoulders. "Nobody knows."

You don't know, I thought. But now I have something to think over. Damn! I'm missing my chance for the Relic Army's GASF.

I felt bad for the kid, but I had one more question before I let him relate his ordeal. "You probably didn't hear if the Relic Army is recruiting for its Ground Assault Support Force." It was a long shot, but even among I-Techs they're respected.

"I don't know for sure, but I wouldn't doubt it."

He must've seen my disappointment. "Did you want to be recruited? Can you get out of your contract?"

"Mine would be even harder than yours." I looked around. "And I bet you and your father tried."

"We did." O'Vorley sighed. "But young bodies are hard to come by it seems." He stared ahead. "I got six weeks training. I don't think it was very good. Supervisor Gaverall won't even issue me a sidearm. Says maybe in a few weeks." He put his hand on his equipment belt. "Issued me a stun baton."

"They can be pretty handy," I said.

"If you know how to use it. I got about four hours of weapons training. Most of my work was online. Law, regulations and customs." He unhooked and extended his telescoping baton. "For this, a thirty minute holo-instruction on its use, care and maintenance." He looked down. "Maybe you could show me?"

"Sorry." I disappointed him. "My transport, the *Kalavar*, should be in tomorrow at the latest." I gave him the name. If he looked it up, he'd know it was the truth. "But, I might be able to tell you how to obtain proper training."

He looked hopeful.

"Marines are stationed here. Others passing through. Some stay a week or more?"

Confused, he nodded as we moved to the side for an orange-clad engineer and several assistant technicians. Seeing their red uniforms gave me an idea.

"Do you have anything to trade—skills?"

"Like what?" he asked.

"I carve small wooden busts for barter. You know anything unusual like that?"

As we neared Green Sector I spotted an armed marine. "You aren't going to get much help from Dribbs or his pals," I explained. "They're probably shorthanded and mad all they got was you. Young, and untrained.

"Most marines live to demonstrate their skills," I said. "If you had something to trade. I know your disbursement after company support allocations is nothing to speak of." I was thinking as we approached the marine. "It might be demeaning, but you might offer to clean and polish boots or..." I pondered out loud. O'Vorley was new, less experienced than me, and unlikely to take the initiative. "Something, and maybe they would help you out. Maybe."

"I can't think of anything."

"Put some thought into it," I urged. "Could save your life." He sent a quizzical glance before we passed a wide cross corridor. "Look at me. I didn't expect to be shot by some criminals while getting off a shuttle." O'Vorley would be an easy mark. "Said you studied mostly regulations, rules, company policies?"

He nodded, "Sometimes fourteen hours a day."

"I'll see what I can do for you. No promises."

I looked ahead at the marine to avoid seeing the kernel of hope I'd just planted. I recalled my cousin, Oliver. He'd always been far more worldly than me. I smiled to myself thinking that could change. As we neared the guard I got a sick feeling. I hated making promises I couldn't be sure of keeping.

The marine's challenge interrupted my thoughts. "This is a restricted area."

Not looking the marine in the eye, O'Vorley replied, "We are here to retrieve Specialist Keesay's equipment."

The marine's haughty gaze shifted. "You're Keesay?"

"That's what my uniform reads." I pointed carefully to each letter on my patch.

"I can read, R-Tech." He sneered, noting my battered appearance. "Read better than you can fight."

I couldn't believe I was trying to get on a marine's bad side. "Look," I said, "if you've been on duty here in the last four hours, you probably saw the one who roughed me up, on a gurney. He was the one with the caved-in skull." I grinned wide enough to encourage my split lip to flow. "I may not be as good as you, but I get the job done."

He spoke into his collar. "Security Specialist Class 4 Keesay is here for his equipment. Do we have it?" He directed his gaze at the security camera.

He looked at me. "You have permission to enter."

I pointed to O'Vorley. "You still owe me that meal. I'll get my equipment, find a place to clean up, and meet you at the cafeteria near the main docking bay." I raised an eyebrow and smiled. "I can find it no problem, okay?"

O'Vorley looked relieved. "Three hours?"

"Can you make it two? It's been a while."

O'Vorley nodded. "It'll be close but I'll see you there." He turned and strode back down the corridor.

The door buzzed and the marine commented while stepping aside. "Strange kid."

"Just a little green," I said.

"Straight down to the desk behind the bullet-proof plastic."

"Right. Thanks." The door closed behind me. I wiped the blood from my lip and began to consider as I walked. Me, referring to O'Vorley as green? That gunman wasn't the first person I'd killed as a security specialist. I'd have to take a careful look in the mirror someday soon.

Passing a number of doors on each side, I walked up to the desk at the end of the short corridor. A clear wall extended from floor to ceiling. A cute blonde with wide green eyes looked up from behind the barrier. Crow's feet framed them as she smiled. Inoffensive as she appeared, I knew with a few finger taps she could trigger the automated defenses. I'd treat her better than the marine outside.

"I am Security Specialist 4th Class Krakista Keesay. I'm here to retrieve my equipment."

"Yes," she responded. "It has been arranged." A door to my left slid open. "Locker 478, bay 2. You have the key."

I almost questioned her. Then I recalled the magnetic keys I'd absent-mindedly slid into my pocket. Simms didn't say more than he had to.

Locker 478 was easy to find. My equipment was in the second of five bays. I examined my cart and found nothing wrong. On top rested both keys to the padlock. I looked inside, unpacked, and checked every item: clothes, wood, tools, ammunition, firearms, Bible, and personal papers. Everything was in order, even my popcorn nukes. They sat neatly concealed within a box of 12-gauge shells. I'd carefully painted over the warning and codes on them so that they resembled standard slugs. Simms was the first to catch it, but not many people ever had reason to look closely. I gave them no more notice than was due normal ammunition as there was bound to be surveillance. I placed the manacle case with key in a pouch next to a water bottle, after taking a swig.

I examined the contents of the shelf above. Freshly cleaned, my revolver rested in its belt holster. Next to it was a small plastic box. Inside were my backup .38 and the contents of my pockets, including the beef jerky from the representative.

Everything seemed in order. I loaded my revolvers with standard jacketed lead rounds and reorganized my pockets and belt pouches. I strapped on my wristwatch and the attached automatic sound dampener.

I paused, then retrieved my bayonet and sheath and hooked them on my belt. Maybe I'd purchase something other than a blade for unexpected trouble. Pondering this, I locked up, took hold of my cart's handle, and exited the bay. My left shoulder reminded me of its injury. I approached the desk and held out the locker's magnetic key.

A panel at my feet slid open. "Place it in there," she said.

"Could you tell me the way to the Corporate Quartermaster?"

"You're R-Tech, right?" she asked politely.

Although she already knew I answered, "That is correct, ma'am."

"Then I'll show you." The transparent wall became a localized map of the space dock. I looked at my current location and the yellow path. A synthesized voice read the subtitles explaining the route.

"Do you need to view it again, Specialist?"

"No. I believe I can find my way. Thank you." She didn't appear putout at having to call up the display. Normally she would've relayed a temporary auditory sequence to a receiver chip implant, if I were I-Tech. My stomached reminded me that it was hungry as I nodded to the marine guard while exiting the Green Sector.

Stares from technicians and civilian travelers, reminded me of my need to get cleaned up. Field Director Simms probably wouldn't approve of me drawing unnecessary attention and raising questions.

I reached the corporate quartermaster station just before the shift change, so I was able to go right up to the counter. I opened my cart and set the manacles, key and case on the counter. "I'd like to return these for the deposit."

The attendant tapped a screen just out of view. The counter scanned what I'd placed there. "It shows here that there is also a security uniform requisitioned for you." The information readout scrolled across the counter. The attendant eyed my shoulder. "Have you seen a doctor?"

"Briefly," I said. "Could you apply the deposit credit toward a stun baton?"

"Type?" he inquired.

"Medium duty use, retractable, extended charge."

He tapped in my request. "I could give you light duty, standard charge, and retractable, in exchange."

"No," I said, making a fist. "I prefer one with a little duration...and more oomph."

"Don't intend to have another rough morning?"

We both laughed. "That's the idea. I should have sufficient funds on account with Negral Corp. You can access my account?"

"Yes, just set it up six months ago," he explained as he tapped a few keys. "With Negral on the planet below, we administer most of their local accounting."

I showed him my left thumb. The attendant caught on. "R-Tech," he said. "No chip access. This will take a moment." He worked diligently through the directories.

"Not a lot of us out here?" I asked, knowing the answer.

"Very few, at least who visit the quartermaster." He continued tapping.

"Why not get an account chip? Faster and hurts less."

"This is more reliable. Tough to fool a DNA reading."

"True," he agreed, "but you pay three percent on the transaction cost for the inconvenience."

"Hey, while you're at it, can you access the armory's inventory?"

"I can. Is there something specific?"

"As long as I'm giving blood, may as well only do it once." I looked around. "Slow time of day?"

"For about another twenty minutes." He relaxed. "Okay, what were you looking for?"

"Any old-style ammunition? Thirty-eight Special and .357 Magnum caliber rounds. Also any 12-gauge?" I smiled. "I know it's kind of a long shot out here, but I was told you might have something."

"We do," he said with raised eyebrows. He looked closer and punched up something from his screen to the counter. "You're name is Keesay?"

"Correct." I said, surprised at the question.

"Shows here that you have a package, some of the ammunition you requested."

"Really?" It seemed odd, but I wanted to be careful of what I said. Maybe it was from Simms.

"You'll have to pay the storage fee, and pick it up."

"I'll do that. Where?"

"At the range, near Green Sector."

"I know where that is," I assured him. "Anything else of interest?" Maybe there was another surprise. "Any gunpowder? Old-style firearms?" It was worth a shot.

"Gunpowder, no. Firearms, nothing you're looking for."

I watched as the inventory scrolled by. "There!" I pointed. "Old-style grenades."

He keyed up the information. "Those have been in stock here since...since the Silicate War. You want'em?"

"Maybe. What kind, what'll they cost?" Did Simms know these were here?

"Well, if they can be found...hold on." He accessed other files. "Just sent an inquiry." He kept reading, going through codes. Finally, he came up with something meaningful. "Fragmentation, flash-stun, concussion." He looked up. "Mean anything to you?"

I nodded. "How many?"

"One case of each, holding nine."

Less than I'd hoped for. An electrical engineering technician came up behind me.

"It'll be a moment," the supply attendant said to him.

The technician said to me, "Nice cart." I was too excited to worry about his opinions.

"If you're rated to dispose of them, they're yours. Inquiry sent back that their recommended date has expired." He tapped a few icons. Waited for a reply.

"Okay," he continued. "A section in front of the counter opened and extended. "You know the routine."

I placed my thumb on it, stated my name and classification, and waited.

"How long is this going to take?" complained the technician. He was only four inches taller than me.

"I've had a difficult morning," I said. "Would you like to schedule your visit to the infirmary now?" I felt the prick as a minute sample of blood was taken. "Or would you prefer to arrive unannounced." I squared off, knowing I shouldn't have let the first comment go by.

"You sure look intimidating," he said with a sneer.

"Most of this blood isn't mine, and I can still report for duty." I licked my lips. "They won't for a few days."

"Gentlemen," warned the attendant, "I don't want to have to call security."

If we'd been alone, I'd have nailed the technician right there. Maybe he was as relieved as me that the attendant had intervened.

My adversary pointed at the counter. "C4," he said, "your request's been authorized. I've got things to do."

"Me too, thanks for your patience, Technician." Then I looked at the account information. All seemed in order. It'd cost only 40 credits.

The attendant appeared anything but pleased. "Process the transaction?" he asked.

"Yes," I said. "I appreciate your time and efficient service." I grabbed my cart. "Just because I had a bad day doesn't mean everyone else should." I stepped aside. "I'll wait for my order over here."

The tech requested a few components for some personal project. He was gone before a dolly-bot arrived with my packages and set them on the counter for scanning.

"One security uniform with vest," said the attendant. "High grade, with proper insignia and identifications attached. One stun-baton medium duty, extended use, retractable." He looked up and handed me a small account chit. "You'll have to pick up your ammunition and other equipment at the armory."

"Thank you," I said while slipping the chit into a hip pocket. "Again, sorry about the trouble."

"I'm sure you get it all the time."

"It depends." I licked a blood bead from my thumb. "Hey, is there a place to change? Maybe I'd get less flack if I looked a little more respectable."

"Flack? Probably true." He pointed. "There's a common area down the corridor about forty meters, to your left. You should be able to clean up. For two credits I can enable water access." His eyes held some concern.

"Specialist, shouldn't you have requisitioned some medical equipment?"

"I have water, and a first aid kit in my cart. Just haven't had the time to use it."

"We just stocked a large medical shipment. Medical kits, good ones. Usually they're in demand." He prepared to enter the request. "I have some older ones that are still good. Won't cost much."

"Sorry, but you've seen my account. I really can't afford a new first aid kit." It was true, for that account. Nice try on dumping more outdated equipment. "My transport will be in soon. I hope to avoid needing one." I laughed.

"I do too," he joked, "but if you can't, don't come around here!" He went back to work, sorting data files, or whatever he was assigned when not filling orders.

I hurried down the corridor and into the common area. It was corporate, but open to the public. I lacked water rights, but needed the space and privacy.

Two full engineers, wearing the standard dull orange bodysuits and leaving the restroom for the lounge, ignored me. I went into a stall area and unlocked my cart before unfolding and examining the uniform. It was the correct size. It wasn't labeled as such, but I could tell that it was a high-grade resist synthetic fiber. It offered at least twice the protection against blades and projectile penetration than my current uniform. Negral never would've supplied me with this.

The protective vest was military issue in corporate dress and a little bulky to wear beneath my uniform. I mentally thanked Simms as I stuffed it into my already full cart.

Before changing uniforms, I pulled out my small first aid kit. I cleaned my cuts and abrasions and wiped around my shoulder's burn wound, being careful to avoid removal of the ointment. I taped a protective patch over the burn.

My new uniform fit well. The loose fitting legs covered most of my boots' laces. There was plenty of room in the arms and shoulders. Simms knew what an R-Tech preferred.

I left the stall and checked out my uniform in a mirror. It was fine, but I looked pretty bad. The white of my right eye was red. Crusted blood covered small gashes beneath my black eye and my bottom lip. I combed my short hair and used an antiseptic cloth to wipe down my neck, arms and hands. Putting everything away, I headed off for my meal.

CHAPTER 11

Finding life in the Milky Way Galaxy above the microbial level is an infrequent occurrence. Intelligent life, especially that which survived long enough to achieve interstellar travel, is extraordinary by any measure. The only factor that favors such unbelievable odds is the vastness of the universe itself.

Fortunately, or unfortunately, humanity overcame such odds and reached the stars at a time when a fair number of intelligent species roamed the Orion Arm of the Milky Way. Some are civil and hospitable. Others are not. But not by any stretch of the imagination are any, even remotely, human.

I checked my cart into Negral Corp's temporary storage outside the hangar bay and glanced at my watch. I hoped O'Vorley was on time as I hustled past the bay toward the dining area.

The cafeteria had a customary two-line setup. The one for expensive gourmet food was empty. The other line, which featured standard processed food selections, had a few customers. Dock personnel comprised the majority of patrons but a fair number of travelers on layover sat disbursed among the long tables. The attached seats were uncomfortable and discouraged loitering. Few of those not eating were engaged in conversation. Rather, they sat occupied with their computer clips and personal entertainment systems.

Movement near the left entrance caught my attention. It was O'Vorley, beckoning, so I headed that way.

O'Vorley said, "You made it on time, Specialist Keesay."

"You seem surprised. And call me Kra, if you like." A pair of engineering techs, one heavy set, crowded past. "We're in the way here. Let's sit down." I took the nearest empty wall seat.

O'Vorley sat across from me. "You can call me Kent." He handed me a small transparent card with an imbedded microchip. "I picked up your chit at HQ. Investigator Simms must have thought a lot of your effort."

"Why do you say that?" This chit appeared identical to any other. "How much is on it?"

"Enough for you to try the gourmet line and then some."

"Is it limited?" I asked.

"What do you mean?"

"Is it only good for meals?" I tapped it on the table. "Or can I use it elsewhere on the station?"

"It's a voucher for food, and lodging. You've got an upgraded room for the evening. I just didn't get around to telling you that. It might be transferable to medical." After I didn't comment he turned and looked at the lines. "Are you hungry? I can meet you back here."

My shoulder felt pretty good; the ointment was working wonders. I'd wait to see the medic onboard the *Kalavar*. "We'll both go for the usual. My treat." I stood, waiting for O'Vorley. "Don't look puzzled. If I try the good stuff, I'll end up missing it later."

He frowned. "I know what you mean. I miss my mom's cooking."

"I'm sure what they have here's better than what they served on Pluto." I grabbed a tray and followed O'Vorley. "I know it's synthesized protein, but you'd think they could conceal it."

"I've only eaten at the company cafeteria," O'Vorley said, letting a lady tourist ahead of us. "I hear it's better here. But Quinn only covers seventy percent."

He moved to the first station. I handed him my card before he ran the back of his hand over the scanner. "I said it's on me. Keep the thirty percent in your account."

"Okay," he smiled back, "just didn't want to be presumptuous." He ran my card and handed it back. "Avoid the pork."

"Good," I said, "I prefer chicken."

We moved through the line, stopping at each automated station and tapped in our order from the limited selection. Simulated ground beef, chicken patty, or pork chop for the main course with instant potatoes, rice or synthesized carrot sticks for the vegetable, and a variety of gelatin deserts.

I ordered rice and red gelatin with my chicken. O'Vorley had skipped the main course and ordered rice with double carrots.

"How's the water?" I asked. "Metallic?"

"Yeah, I'd recommend the juice."

I took the orange juice with the standard vitamin supplement added and followed O'Vorley back to our seats. I wasn't paying attention and almost tripped over a Chicher. Luckily it scurried out of the way. "Oops," I said automatically, trying to keep my tray's contents onboard.

The rat-like alien chattered while an awkward translator device attached to an equipment harness replied, after a second's delay, "Yes, my near tumble as well."

It would have been an excellent chance to try my limited sign language skills, but my hands were occupied with a tray. Besides, the Chicher had already scampered off toward the line.

"I see you nearly stepped on our newest ally," O'Vorley said.

"What?" I sat down. "We're teaming up with those guys?" I looked over O'Vorley's shoulder toward the line. "For trade? Exploration?"

"Maybe military," O'Vorley said. "It was on the holo-news this morning before I went on shift." He picked up his fork, preparing to dig in. "Said the government is working for cooperative efforts on all fronts."

I thought a moment as I tried the chicken. It wasn't bad for artificial rations. The Chicher had disappeared from view. That wasn't surprising considering the alien's small size.

"But they're high R-Tech at best," commented O'Vorley, after swallowing. "What can they offer?" He pierced another carrot with his narrow fork.

"We humans don't exactly have a lot of allies," I said. "Just the Umbelgarri."

"Good point," he agreed. "Safety in numbers."

"Plus," I added, "they've been out in space for decades. A lot longer than us." Technically, humans have probably been in space longer, but not beyond our own solar system. O'Vorley knew what I meant.

"I'd like to know how they did that, being only R-Tech and all." O'Vorley stifled a laugh. "I heard they still use vacuum tubes."

"Their computers probably are bigger and slower. Main systems certainly aren't quantum. It takes them longer to get anywhere. But somehow they figured it out on their own." I pointed at my tray. "This food isn't too bad."

"They didn't have anyone sponsor them," said O'Vorley. "Or not directly. The Felgans were the first to encounter them—tried to conquer them two centuries ago. The Chicher were only exploring their own little solar system at the time." The young security specialist paused to look around and took a drink before continuing. "Somehow ran the invading Felgans off."

"You know a bit about the Rats," I said. "You like'em?"

O'Vorley was a fast eater. "No. My senior cultural thesis was on them." He shook his head after taking another drink of his pink juice. "Assigned to me—but it could've been worse."

"They certainly look like giant rats," I said. "Maybe a little squirrelish."

"Yeah. They sound like squirrels more than a squeaking rat." Waving his arm like a snake, O'Vorley added, "You know they have prehensile tails."

"No," I admitted, "never studied up on them. Maybe I should have." A crowd poured into the cafeteria. "A big shuttle must've landed. Anyway, what grade did you get?"

"I got a passing score, let's leave it at that. At least there was some data on them."

"True," I said. "You could've been assigned the Umbelgarri. Who knows much about them?" I shook my head. "I've read in depth about the Silicate War. Studied the battles and all. The Umbelgarri are really our only ally and we know hardly anything about them."

"I'm like everybody else on that one." He got serious. "Kra, you think the Crax are..."

I cut him off with a quick hand gesture. "Speaking of friends..."

The Chicher approached our table. Its high-pitched chattering was translated, "Do you humans mind if I nibble in your company?"

O'Vorley looked to me. I said, "Sure, but we're almost finished."

The Chicher's ears shot back for a fraction of a second, nearly knocking its earpiece out. "No intention to disturb you," it said, turning awkwardly on its hind legs. "Delight in the orb passing." The translation device finished a second after the fur-covered alien began moving away in its bipedal gate.

"I think I insulted it—him. Do you think?"

"Kind of hard to tell," O'Vorley said. "His translator was hard to follow."

I reviewed the brief conversation, then got up. "I'll be right back. No sense insulting our newest ally."

The skittish, or at least wary, rodent was trying to make its way through the moving crowd. Being just over three feet tall while upright wasn't helping. Few people bothered to look down or pay attention. Kind of funny, I thought. If they actually looked down, they might step far around a forty-pound rat. And the fact the Chicher wasn't a natural biped added further difficulty. Still, with utmost patience, he was doing his best to balance his tray and make it to an open seat across the main walkway.

Hurrying ahead, I ran interference for him. When we got to his targeted table I made my apology. "Sir, forgive my unclear statement." I helped with his tray as he climbed onto the seat. "In a direct translation, my response to your direct question was ambiguous." I waited a second for the translation device to catch up. The alien received the interpretation by means of a thin wire that ran along the harness up to a small earpiece. "In normal human conversation, my response was one of welcome, but simply informing you that we were nearing the end of our meal."

The alien's narrow face observed me for a second before chattering a response. "Your effort is seen. My errant sound snatch." He tapped his saucer-shaped translator hanging across his chest. "It must have better input sorting and reporting. Good you spoke to me as a surrogate pack member."

The Chicher sat on his haunches and placed his paw, or hand, on his plate filled with a real fish and several nuts from the gourmet line. "You are done nibbling," the alien continued after scrutinizing my uniform. "You have tasks, Security Man. Maybe a different orb passing we nibble?"

"Maybe," I replied. With a simple sign language gesture, I said, "Good bye." I must have been successful, as his response was the same. With a measure of satisfaction I returned to my seat.

O'Vorley asked, "What'd he say?"

"Not much." I sat down and finished my drink. "Seems friendly enough. I wonder why other races avoid them?"

"Maybe they steal technology. Could be that's how they're at such a low tech level and still travel across space."

"Maybe," I said. "But it's possible that they're just advanced in some areas and behind in others." I lightly rubbed my injured shoulder. "The medical technology of the V'Gun far surpasses most races from what I've read. But they still can't figure out how to build a fusion reactor, let alone a cascading atomic engine."

"Yeah," agreed O'Vorley, "but neither could we until the Umbelgarri gave us technical support."

"That's my point. The Crax are supposed to have been sponsors of the V'Gun for decades, but the V'Gun still can't build a space-faring ship." I leaned closer, pointing to my head. "Don't you see? Different aliens are wired up here differently." I tried to think of a reasonable analogy. "Just like some people make better artists and others make better engineers. Maybe their whole race is hooked up to be artists and not engineers."

"But they know medicine."

"You're missing my point," I said. "Having an innate ability or a high level of knowledge in biochemistry doesn't necessarily translate to same—equivalent technical ability in quantum mechanics or astrophysics." I leaned back. "Or not at least by our standards."

"I think I understand," he said. "Speaking of the Crax and the Umbelgarri." He leaned closer and finished, "Do you think they'll go to war?"

He'd started this topic before. I didn't know why he thought I'd have any special knowledge, but I'd read a lot on it. More than most. Certainly more than I had on the Chicher. I leaned a little closer as well. "Seems likely. The Umbelgarri took a real beating in the war. They've been holding their own, but with their homeworld destroyed, they're at a big disadvantage."

"But they had time. They could have gotten stuff off, evacuated."

My look of amazement must've stunned O'Vorley because he leaned back. "Kent, maybe if they hadn't spent twenty-some years in a war and weren't scattered across the galaxy they could've done better." I had his attention again. "If the moon were to crash into the Earth in less than a month, how much or how many could we save?"

"But they're A-Tech."

"You put too much faith in technology," I countered. "Even so, don't forget their homeworld was a moon.

"Look at the Chicher," I said, and paused while he glanced over his shoulder. "They're probably no further along in most aspects than we were during latter half of the 1900s. Yet they managed to fend off an advanced race. And achieve interstellar travel."

"How would we fare against the Crax?" he asked. "I know you're R-Tech, but if we go up against them, even with our best technology, we'll get slaughtered."

"Maybe," I said before adding a thought that had just occurred to me. "And maybe that's why we're allying with the Chicher."

A couple sat down near us. I picked up my tray and signaled for O'Vorley to follow. We took them to the disposal area. "You up for any target practice?" I asked.

"Sure, but I haven't been issued a sidearm."

"We'll see what we can do." A brisk pace brought us through the crowds toward storage. "Besides, you can help me carry some things back to my room."

I returned with my cart. "Which way?"

"You trust me to find it?" asked O'Vorley.

"I'm guessing that you took the time to at least figure out a route from the bay cafeteria to my room." His nod and grin told me I was correct. "But the question is, once we find our way to the range, will you remember the way back?"

"I hope so," he replied as we made our way.

"You'll have incentive," I said. "You'll be lugging the heavy stuff."

O'Vorley looked and stopped. "What did you buy?"

I urged him on. "You'll see. Come on, mule."

"What?"

"Come on, organic dolly-bot," I corrected.

We found my room with little trouble. I unpacked some equipment before taking out my pump-action shotgun and my old-style double-barrel shotgun. O'Vorley looked at them resting against the narrow fold-down bed.

"I have a special slot in my cart for them," I explained. "Had one more made should I ever need it. Right now it's filled with water bottles." I dug around to the bottom and pulled out an old replica Dragoon and opened its plastic case.

O'Vorley was amazed. "Kra, is this stuff ever old. Can I hold it?" he asked, pointing at the Dragoon.

"Sure, but it's heavy," I warned. "Want to try it out?"

He picked it up. "That'd be great. What's it shoot?" He tried holding it steady with one arm extended.

"Lead balls." I tossed him a small box. "It isn't an original. If it were, it'd have been sold to a museum long ago. But it's old enough, a replica made in 1992."

"It's still well over a hundred years old."

"Correct. It's valuable, and functioning. So's this," I said, drawing my old single-action duty revolver. "This one's less complicated to load and fire." I opened the loading gate and ejected the cartridges. "Much more modern—in comparison. Here, let me show you a little about this before we get down to the range. You said you had some basic training in firearms?" I asked before handing him the empty firearm.

"Yes." He took the revolver. "I viewed some holo-casts, mainly on safety." He looked it over.

"Get a feel for it," I said, moving back a step while he held it in several standard firing positions. "It's a .357 magnum, stainless steel single-action revolver," I explained. "That means that you must thumb back the hammer before it'll fire. Just pulling the trigger won't work."

"Is this a gun of the old American West? I saw them on old flat screencasts."

I shook my head. "No, this is a more modern version, if you want to call a 140-or-so-year-old gun modern. It's a few years newer than the Dragoon and about twenty years older than the double-barrel."

He seemed comfortable enough handling a gun. "It has a transfer bar." I took it back, cocked the hammer and showed him. "Safer. You can load all six chambers without worrying about shooting your foot off when it's holstered." I handed it back. "Here, try to get a feel for it. Dry fire a few times."

O'Vorley awkwardly pulled back the hammer with his thumb and depressed the trigger. *Click*. He flinched a little and blushed. Then he stiffened. "Is this what you used to kill the offender?"

"Yes, it is," I said. "Struck him twice."

Breaking the awkward silence, I lifted the revolver from his hand. "Let me show you how to load and unload it." I watched to see if he followed each step. "Got it so far?"

"I even got the clockwise part," he smiled. "Will it rotate counterclockwise?"

"Studied history I see. Do you know where those terms come from?" His blank expression told me he missed that part. "Later with that."

"Looks pretty awkward and slow," O'Vorley said. "Couldn't that be dangerous?"

"Well, you're right. But remember I'm R-Tech. Now watch." I picked up the pace and loaded the remaining chambers and snapped shut the loading gate. "All ready." I cocked back the hammer. "Pull the trigger to shoot. If you don't want to shoot, hold the hammer with your thumb and depress the trigger. Slowly lower the hammer."

"I should probably try that unloaded?"

"Correct, unless you want to ventilate a wall." I reopened the gate and reviewed how to unload unspent and spent cartridges. "You practice a time or two."

O'Vorley was cautious, but a quick learner. After he'd done it several times, I showed him my watch. "You know that the old-style guns are loud, especially in an enclosed area?"

"I've heard...well, not exactly." He forced an uneasy laugh.

"I have a sound dampener on my watch band. It's keyed for old-style firearms." I pointed to it. "Without this your ears would be ringing after a round or two. Although sometimes there are advantages to firing without one."

"How loud without your dampener?" he asked, carefully returning the revolver.

"Like I said, it'll leave your ears ringing." I checked the gun and holstered it. "May cause some ear damage. Should draw attention—near and far."

"Now I remember!" he said, looking at my watch. "Those old-style watches had three hands and they all went around positive degrees."

"Clockwise," I winked. "And they still make them, if you know where to special order."

He examined my watch. "And those are Roman Numerals."

"Can you read them?"

"No," he admitted. "Never needed to. Why do you have that type anyway? Doesn't look like it'll tie into a ship's chronometer." He picked up my double-barrel shotgun. "I've seen other R-Techs who wear advanced digital."

"It keeps accurate time. Even in space." I picked up my duty shotgun. "And as you might have guessed, I kind of like old things. Old ways." I pumped it. *Ca-chunk*. "Recognize that sound?"

O'Vorley nodded. He set the double-barrel down.

"Everyone does," I said, handing over. "It's a little slow, but effective. Variety of rounds available. Don't have to worry much about punching through vital equipment in a warehouse or onboard a ship. Titanium, light. Still not modern, but you asked about danger. I count on this when I expect trouble."

"They still use them on penal colonies, I think."

"Correct. This is one of their standard riot control models, modified."

"What's this?" he asked pointing near the end of the muzzle. "A modification?"

"That's where I mount my bayonet," I said with a wink. It's not often people ask me about my equipment. "I also added a perforated titanium alloy jacket over the barrel. In essence, a ventilated hand-guard."

He handed the shotgun back. "I know you want me to ask, so tell me why?"

"I know you want to know, so I will." I set it down and began to rummage through my cart for target ammunition. "The bayonet is for intimidation, and an additional line of self-defense. The jacket is for when the barrel heats up after firing a number of rounds. Too hot to properly handle in hand-to-hand. And in some atmospheres heat is even less likely to dissipate."

"How likely are you to be in a long firefight or in one of those atmospheres?"

"Do I detect skepticism?" I asked with a playfully raised eyebrow. "Truthfully, I don't expect to. And the titanium alloy jacket includes some Phib components. Expensive, but nothing's going to damage that barrel."

O'Vorley nodded as I continued. "Actually, I did some research on trench warfare during World War I. Believe it or not, some soldiers thought the trench shotgun should be banned." I laughed. "All the while they were using chemical weapons on each other. That got my interest."

O'Vorley scrutinized the weapon up and down. "That's why you picked and modified that shotgun?"

"I figured riots resembled some of the old-style warfare, even trench warfare. Back then they fought and learned tough lessons. Similar models were used in subsequent wars, decades later. Gave me a few ideas about effective uses of a shotgun." I stacked several boxes of .357 and 12-gauge shells on the bed. "I was right."

"What do you mean? You helped put down a prison riot?"

Angry with myself for getting carried away, I answered his question. "Wasn't a prison riot, and surviving it wasn't a cheerful experience." Before he asked more, I finished, "It's not something I care to talk about." Or could talk about, I thought to myself.

I threw the shells into a sack and then slipped the pump shotgun back into the cart. "Watch," I said, picking up the double-barrel and showing him how to load and fire it safely. He watched intently.

I handed him the shotgun and picked up the shells. "It's a replica of a Coach Gun," I said. "Of the Old American West around the late 1800's. Not a hundred percent authentic but close. I had a relative way back—great great grandfather, who was into Old West Reenactment." I paused while O'Vorley went through the loading and unloading procedure.

"Its barrels are a lot shorter than your pump shotgun's," he said.

"Correct, and it'll have a lot of kick." I tapped my shoulder. "That's why I won't be shooting it, even if my off shoulder is the hurt one."

I held open a cloth carrying case and he slid the old-style side-by-side into it. "You carry this double-barrel. I'll get the rest of the shells and the materials to load the Dragoon." I didn't want to take the time to explain, so I picked up about my deceased relations. "I had another relative, my great great uncle, who did American Civil War Reenactments. Must have been popular in the late 1900s." I shook my head. "But it kind of makes sense."

"That's where you got the Dragoon," O'Vorley said. A confused expression emerged. "I've never heard of anyone wanting to reenact the Silicate War, Kra. Have you?"

"No. But I think what they were trying to do was to relive the history. Understand the past. I don't think we do that enough."

"You seem pretty intelligent," O'Vorley said cautiously. "So, is your view on reliving, or holding onto the past why you're an R-Tech?"

I looked at O'Vorley and decided to skip the lecture about the fact that retardation isn't a prerequisite for relic tech status. "No." Then I thought a bit. "Well, maybe a little. Maybe I have a little too much of my relatives in me."

Knowing he was on thin ice with his last statement, Kent seemed a bit relieved when I didn't take him to task. "Maybe we can discuss my philosophy some other time," I suggested, knowing I'd probably leave before we got the chance.

I finished packing the grease, powder, and lead balls and other shells into another sack before putting it into a satchel. I slid my brass powder measure and some percussion caps into my pocket.

O'Vorley looked at my cart. "You keep a lot in there."

"Efficient packing, and a lot of stuffing," I assured him. "I think we have everything. Cart's locked. You know the way?"

"I'm fairly sure of that," he said, grinning and heading for the door.

"We'll see."

Even though O'Vorley knew the way, I paid close attention, occasionally looking stiffly over my shoulder. Most ships, bases and docks are set up with right angle turns and a logical pattern.

The halls were moderately busy, initially with visitor traffic and later with station personnel. During a lull waiting for an elevator I interrupted our silence. "Kent, you wouldn't mind taking on a little extra clerical work, would you?"

"No. Why, you need some done?"

"No. But I was thinking we might run into some marines stationed here who would."

"What for?"

The elevator opened. Three marines occupied it. "I'll explain later, but if I don't have time, just follow my lead." I stood next to the burly marines. "Deck twelve."

O'Vorley appeared perplexed as the elevator descended. He'd lost some of his spunk and newfound confidence. I leaned over toward him. "Training, bartering, remember?"

He smiled, looking a little relieved as the doors opened. We followed the marines to the practice range.

CHAPTER 12

The Corporate House consists of 500 seats, each having a ten standard-year term of office. Silent bidding for half of the Corporate House seats occurs every five years. The risks are great concerning potential benefits vital to a corporation's long-term growth and stability. In addition to jostling for power and influence, the bidding results also provide the government revenue to fund communications, intragalactic diplomacy, judicial oversight, and the defense of humanity as it expands into the Orion Arm of the Milky Way.

"Not quite what you expected?" asked Kent.

"You're on the mark there. In the war this was a major staging area." We stood in the observation area above the main range, and to the right of the secondary one. "There must have been five times the facilities."

"That is correct, Specialist," agreed a coarse, throaty voice.

I turned to see a marine looking over my head into the range area. I tried to disguise my surprise. "Looks slow tonight."

"Usually is," said the marine, "with too many security types about these days." He stepped between O'Vorley and me. "No need for the advanced targeting routines or extensive combat maneuver facilities." He glanced down at the quiet scene. "Hmmmph."

The marine's name patch was parallel to my line of sight. His obvious intimidation effort wasn't going to succeed if I could help it. "Are you looking for anyone in particular, Private Ringsar?"

"Real company," he said, intentionally bumping into me on his way out. "Not a Class 4 Security, R-Tech."

O'Vorley looked anxious until the marine exited. "Don't worry, O'Vorley," I said, "I've already been unlucky once this week."

"Good thing. I don't want to end up looking like you."

"Yeah. But he would've ended up in the infirmary, too."

"You really think we could take him? He's big as us both."

"No," I said, "but surely he would've needed some bandages...for his severely bruised knuckles." I grabbed O'Vorley by the arm and angled him toward the Ordinance and Equipment Station one level below. "You already know my head's hard."

"So I've heard," he said, looking to see if the hulking marine had really left.

"Maybe you could lead me to the O&E station." I gestured and gave him a curt bow. "Oh, experienced and wise."

"At least I know how to avoid a stern bruising. Calling an S2 a chip is anything but wise," O'Vorley said, slowing the pace. "Especially Supervisor Gaverall. He's anything but neurologically impaired."

"Where'd you hear about that?"

"From Dribbs," O'Vorley said. "He was there. He wouldn't lie about that—especially if he thought it might get back to Gaverall."

"Dribbs. Wasn't he that older guy teamed with you?"

"Yeah. And another thing he said was—"

I cut O'Vorley off. "I know what happened, and can guess what he said." I hadn't reflected much upon the event. "What do they say about Supervisor Gaverall?"

"Well," O'Vorley began as we entered the local elevator to the O&E station below, "I guess he used to work for Quinn, but your sponsor acquired his contract when they bought the rights to Mavinrom 1." The door closed. "Down to O and E's level," he commanded the lift before continuing. "Part of the deal for the colony. From what I've heard, most of the security down there was scheduled to transfer up here, but CGIG came in and offered substantial incentives. So they left."

"And you were transferred here. That explains a lot."

"Explains what?"

I picked my words carefully. "I noticed lax security down on Mavinrom. Maybe the best were offered contracts, leaving a shorthanded, weak team. I'd never thought about Gaverall being dealt a bad crew."

Then it occurred to me. Maybe Capital Galactic had something to do with the attempted hit. I couldn't mention my thoughts to O'Vorley.

Bidding for the Corporate House was a year away. Vorishnov might have been here to bolster Negral Corp somehow. But, if CGIG could cause instability, weaken investor confidence in Quinn or Negral, it could affect stock value and future profit margins. They'd have less available to invest in the process. It didn't all quite seem to fit. Simms probably knew all of this, and more. Maybe Gaverall knew something of it. I pondered the connection between Simms and Gaverall. Now, at least the security supervisor's hostile attitude in the bay made sense. Gaverall provoked me so that he could shut me up. He didn't want me to reveal an attempted hit had just occurred.

O'Vorley tapped me on the shoulder before stepping out of the elevator. "Hey, did you hear anything I just said?"

I'd only half heard how Gaverall was pulling double duty with the space dock and the colony and would have things running smoothly down there in a few months. "Sorry, just a few random thoughts I had to sort out." I scratched my head. "Extended warehouse duty can dull one's conversational ability. Hope you never experience it."

"I can tell you about Gaverall some other time. Rest assured, he shows no signs of suffering from Post Implant Neural Atrophy. I'm surprised he didn't let Dribbs do permanent damage."

"Well, nobody likes to get roughed up without reason. My adrenaline was running pretty high, and Gaverall laid into me first. Bet Dribbs forgot that part." I placed an index finger on my split lip and grinned. "In retrospect, accusing this particular supervisor of being a chip was a mistake."

"We're almost there," he said, nodding in agreement. "What was it you were going to pick up?"

The area looked militaristic with no attempt to disguise support beams and conduits. "You'll see in a second," I said, stepping up to the counter and presenting my left thumb. "I have some equipment to examine and pick up. Also, I'd like to know what ammunition inventory you have for old-style firearms. Shotguns and revolvers."

The attendant responded and the countertop lit up. Inventory records showed three cases of 12-gauge shells, 00 buckshot. Nothing for my duty revolver. Maybe Simms was in error. I tapped through a few more screens. The assistant, lending a hand in my search, turned up several boxes of regular lead target .38 specials.

I had no room in my cart for a case of shotgun shells. But they were pretty inexpensive. So were the 38's. "How long have the .38 specials been in stock?"

Almost instantly the attendant responded. "Fourteen years. They were ordered and never retrieved."

"Two good reasons for their bargain basement cost."

"If you mean to say their low credit cost, yes."

The attendant seemed polite enough. "That's what I meant. Same with the shotgun shells?"

He was ready with a reply. "No, we go through six or seven cases a year. Occasionally penal colony personnel pass through and visit the range."

I thought a moment. "Can you have a case of the shotgun shells transferred over to the transport *Kalavar* when she docks?"

After a moment delay. "That would not be a problem. Two percent fee."

"Would that be before or after the three percent markup for the blood work?" Again, I presented my thumb.

"If you mean a blood DNA check for access to your account, it would be before. The markup is strictly for the difficulty in verifying the correct account for the transaction."

"You mean inconvenience in verifying the account." I smiled. "You know it also verifies through my unique thumb print." I placed my thumb and felt the prick.

"Aren't we all unique, Security Specialist 4th Class Krakista Keesay?" He hesitated a moment. "It seems you are quite special...at least today. There is a package waiting for you."

"Really?" It was the one I learned about at the quartermaster's. I was betting it was from Simms. "Who is it from?"

"Records indicate it is from a chief gunner aboard the," he sounded it out, "*Peripatetic Boxcar*?"

"That would be my cousin, Oliver. Interesting ship name, eh?" Both O'Vorley and the attendant nodded. "The entrepreneur who commissioned his ship's construction was a bit eccentric. Or so I've heard."

"The name confirms it," agreed the attendant. "Must be a philosopher." He continued checking his files.

I watched the counter while several screens flicked by. "Maybe, but I'd take it more to mean a wandering freighter. She travels the outer colonies. Maybe further."

I gave up trying to follow screens when the attendant stopped. "You had an additional order?" he asked.

"Correct." I looked at O'Vorley who was taking this all in. "Some might accuse me of being a packrat, but who knows when I'll have access to equipment again?"

"If by packrat you mean—" O'Vorley began.

I elbowed him in the ribs and said to the attendant. "Three cases of old-style grenades."

"Please confirm, Specialist Keesay. Three cases of grenades. One case of fragmentation, one case of flash-stun, and one case of concussion. All old-style, each case holding nine?"

"That is correct."

"What are you going to do with those?" asked O'Vorley.

"Like any packrat, store them away for future need." I considered commenting on using them on those with signs of Neural Atrophy, but with the present company and the marines nearby, thought better of it. "You never know."

"Specialist Keesay, you are rated to dispose of them if necessary?" questioned the attendant. "They are beyond expiration due to lack of inspection and maintenance."

"Yes, I am. You can check."

"I already did. I simply needed verbal confirmation. I need to remind you that they all need to be properly inspected before use or proper disposal."

"Acknowledged."

He continued, "You have already picked up one medium-duty, retractable, extended charge, stun baton and," he paused, "a replacement duty uniform. Correct, Specialist Keesay?"

"That is correct."

The attendant nodded. "Would you like the remaining items all transferred to the civil transport *Kalavar*? Again there is a minimal storage fee for the package from, the *Boxcar*." He smirked.

I was eager to see what my cousin had sent but really didn't have room to cart it and the grenades about. Besides, there could be less hassle boarding without them. The fewer questions about my possessions the better. "Just send it all over when the *Kalavar* arrives. Except for the .38 shells. We'll use them here."

He tapped a few screen commands. The invoice appeared on the counter screen. "Please place your thumb there to acknowledge."

I reviewed the acquisition and transfer information before completing the transaction. "We'll be over at the range. How long will it take for your robot to retrieve the shells?"

"Less than four minutes."

"Thank you. I'll be back to pick them up. Or possibly Specialist O'Vorley here. Will that be okay?"

"I'll be on duty for another six hours. They've been here for fourteen years. Shouldn't be any difficulty with those arrangements."

I gave him a thumbs up, left-handed, of course. I liked his deadpan sense of humor. We headed back toward the preparation area and the range master. "They certainly have unusual duty hours here."

"The dock captain apparently agrees with the company," said O'Vorley. "They stagger all duties so that there's a constant flow of activity. Never a rush."

We approached the range master's station. Instead of unfinished metallic and cream-colored conduit, shades of green and brown dominated. A marine lieutenant stood up. "Specialists."

"Lieutenant," I said, "we would like to schedule some range time."

"Purpose?"

"Firearms training."

He looked at me, then at my rating and my company logo. Then he eyed O'Vorley. "Who is to perform the instruction?"

"I am, Lieutenant, sir." I knew Negral Corp had an agreement with Quinn Mining, as there were no facilities on the colony below. "I would like to request an hour on range two. Beginner and intermediate target programming."

He began tapping away. "Type of firearms?"

"Old-style revolvers and shotgun."

He looked over O'Vorley. "Specialist, will you require loan of a firearm?"

Taking my lead, O'Vorley spoke with measured authority. "Thank you, not today, Lieutenant, sir."

Before the lieutenant made final arrangements, I asked, "Could we have fifteen minutes before our range time commences?"

He tapped a few strokes. "Not a problem, Specialist. You are authorized for 14:30 Earth standard."

I looked at my watch just as O'Vorley checked the station chronometer over the lieutenant's shoulder. Only 2:15 pm, I thought. What a long day. I knew I'd sleep well tonight. Still, it beat the long hours on duty in a cavernous warehouse.

"Let's go," I said. "Remember about following my lead, bartering." I led O'Vorley to a bench and table in the prep area. Private Ringsar stood among one of several groups of marines. His great size set him apart even among his peers. No one appeared to notice us, which was fine for now.

As I unpacked the loading supplies, I took note of several security cameras. "Don't try to hide them in here," I said, looking up. O'Vorley nodded in agreement while I listened in on some of the local conversation. The most prevalent were stories about training, combat, and women, focusing on expertise and subsequent exploits. I didn't see any female marines. Standard routine, as the military generally kept male and female units segregated.

I didn't have a stand for loading the Dragoon, so I signaled to O'Vorley and we pulled the bench out and straddled it. "Quick lesson, O'Vorley. How to prepare and load one of these old, old-style revolvers. Always check to make sure it's clean and clear." O'Vorley was attentive, so I continued my instruction.

Half way through we'd attracted some attention, so I spoke a little louder. "See how I've set it on half-cock so that I can rotate the cylinder?" I then adjusted my wrist dampener to absorb most of the sound before firing off all six caps in rapid succession. "Even with just caps, make sure it is pointed away from anyone or anything you care about."

A couple of marines led by the guard outside the storage bays moved our way. I continued with my explanation after removing the spent caps. "Next, you add the powder. For this percussion revolver?" I looked up at O'Vorley.

"Fifty grains," he said without hesitation.

O'Vorley absorbed information. I stood up and removed the powder measure from my pocket, and attached it to the small powder flask. "Preset to fifty grains."

"Security Specialist Keesay, right?" interrupted one of the marines.

I recognized the voice as that of the marine guard in Green Sector. "Correct, that's me," I said, looking at his patch, "Private Yizardo."

"What kind of archaic piece are you fooling with there?"

"It's a century-old replica of a Colt Dragoon. A percussion revolver."

"Black powder?" asked Yizardo.

I nodded. "I was just instructing Specialist O'Vorley here in its loading before we try some target practice."

"What's it fire?" asked another marine. He was on the thin side with dark hair and blue eyes.

I reached over and tossed him a lead ball. "A .45 caliber round."

"Is that old thing safe to fire?" asked Yizardo.

"He's R-Tech. I'm sure he knows his stuff," said the marine with the lead ball. "If it's unsafe, it'll be his friend, O'Vorley, who shoots it first."

"You're right there, Corporal Smith," said Yizardo to his fellow marine. "We might just hang around to see who fires first."

I smiled, sat at the bench with the Dragoon, and began pouring powder into one of its chambers. "Probably not another one of these within fifteen light years."

"Probably true," Smith agreed. "You'll need to seat this next." He tossed me the ball.

"You ever fired one of these?"

"Nothing exactly that old." He laughed. "Took an ancient weaponry course. We learned about medieval crossbows, flintlocks and muzzle loading rifles." He pointed. "Same principle as your revolver."

"Correct," I said, beginning to seat the balls. I looked back at O'Vorley. "You place one of these over each chamber. Rotate it under the loading plunger here. Pull this lever here from under the barrel and seat the ball. They're a little oversized, so some shavings may peel off. See?"

I handed the Dragoon to O'Vorley and set five other balls on the table next to him. "You try it." He was nervous but eager and went right at it. As he worked I got out a tub of grease. "Smith, you know what this is for?"

"To lubricate the bore and chamber and to keep the powder fouling soft."

He knew his stuff. "And," I said, "since this isn't a perfect procedure, to avoid chain firing."

Yizardo and a very young marine standing to his left, Private DeLark, looked puzzled until Smith clarified it for them. "See, if you shoot and a spark catches some stray powder in one or more of the other loaded chambers, it could cause them to fire."

"Correct," I agreed. "Doesn't matter how old the gun is, you won't like the results."

DeLark, looking at his right hand, said, "Cut down on pleasurable activities other than combat." His voice was higher pitched than I expected from his muscular frame.

"You could get a cybernetic replacement," Smith said.

"I wouldn't want that! What good is that—and what woman would want an artificial hand caressing her?"

"Good point," said Yizardo, "or before long all men would have at least one appendage replaced with an artificial one, if women had their way."

A good round of chuckling ensued while O'Vorley finished. Then, using a pocketknife I showed him how to seal the chambers with grease. Setting the tub down and pocketing my knife, I added, "And it's edible in a pinch. Barely, except for you tough guys. Of course, it may have other potential uses," I added, winking to Private DeLark.

Yizardo laughed, then asked, "Isn't all that stuff expensive?"

"Lead isn't. Out here the powder and caps are unheard of. The grease can be too, depending. It all could be fabricated, but..." I checked my watch and looked around. Ringsar and his three pals were still busy near range one. "But if you know where to shop it isn't too bad. Still, on my compensation I don't bring it out too often."

I started gathering my equipment. "O'Vorley, can you get the shotgun? You gentlemen are welcome to share the range with us. Smith seems to be knowledgeable enough, so after we've fired off this set, you're welcome to give it a try."

O'Vorley looked a little disappointed, but said nothing as I continued. "You might want to check with the range master to see if he has a sound dampener and some eye protection."

"Thanks," said Yizardo, "I wouldn't mind giving it a try."

"I've got thirty-six caps and balls. I'll probably be busy, so let Smith inspect before reloading. I didn't bring everything down to clean it, but you should be able to fire thirty-six rounds before powder fouling gets too bad."

"DeLark," said Smith, "go check on the dampener and eye gear."

"That relic firearm may be interesting but not much use out here in space," Yizardo said. "Thirty-six rounds before cleaning wouldn't last long in a firefight."

"It was state of the art two-hundred and fifty years ago and wasn't built with a four-hundred pound charging Crax in mind. Your MP pistol will be equally obsolete soon enough," I said. "And although not recommended, just like your pistol, this baby could fire in space. The powder and caps contain oxygen enough for the chemical reaction. The cold and the recoil could be a problem."

"Never thought of that," said Smith. "But you're probably right. I don't think the metal would hold up."

We headed for the range. O'Vorley asked, "Don't we need to put on the percussion caps?"

"I figured it'd be better to do that just before firing. Standard safety," I assured him.

The area lit up as we entered. It was small, but had room for four people on the line. The range extended for only forty or so yards, but the computer generated holographic targets simulated greater distance.

O'Vorley sat at the computer console. "What would you like me to program, Kra?"

"Standard round target, non-moving, fifteen yards, O'Vorley." I hoped he caught onto the appropriate use of last names in present company."

"Is that all?"

I held up the Dragoon. "This isn't a precision instrument. Iron sites. No scopes, lasers or passive targeting assistance."

"Good point, Keesay," said O'Vorley.

Smith asked me, "How well can you shoot?"

"Well enough. I'm accurate, but not fast."

Yizardo whispered something into Smith's ear, which evoked a snicker.

"What's so funny?" I asked.

"Yizardo here says that you're better at pounding targets with your gun than shooting them with it."

"Very funny. I'm sure you could've done better, but I haven't had the privilege of Colonial Marine training. And since you weren't there, I had to manage despite the handicap."

My tone must have signaled to Smith that he'd struck a chord. "You got the job done," he said. "Something we're all expected to do." He looked over his shoulder, through the transparent wall. "Here comes DeLark." The door slid open. "Did you get the gear?"

"Yes, I did, Corporal." He handed each marine a dampener chip and miniature power source. He brought one over to O'Vorley. "Just stick it on your sleeve. Adjust it by tapping here." Then he looked at me. "Figured you had one." He looked around tossed a set of eye visors to everyone except me, seeing I had my own.

I handed O'Vorley the Dragoon and the tin. "Half cock and place the caps."

O'Vorley's nimble fingered worked fast. After we advanced to the line, I drew and held my duty revolver in a two handed stance. "Thumb the hammer back and hold it out like this." He did. "Next, line up your target. The V notch on the hammer should be lined up with the sight blade at the end of the barrel. Align them so that the point of aim is just above. Exhale and slowly depress the trigger. There'll be recoil, but the gun's heavy and will absorb most of it."

I stepped back. His first shot was stiff and wide, but he handled the recoil. Standard MP firearms have little recoil in comparison. His second attempt was smoother but still off.

Smith approached. "Do you mind?"

"Not at all, Corporal. My next bit of advice was on how to clobber your target with the butt."

"As heavy as this thing is," O'Vorley said, "I'm sure it'd be enough."

While Smith instructed O'Vorley, I returned to the bench and pulled out the old double-barrel. "Ever seen one of these, Yizardo?" I tossed it to him.

"On flat-screen westerns. Doc Holiday had one." He broke it open and peered down the barrels. "Is this what you carry on duty?"

"No. I'm a little more modern than that." I winked, handing him two boxes of 12-gauge shells. "Fifty number four shot. Good for small game, and okay for target." I stood up and caught a glimpse of Ringsar watching from a distance. "Yizardo, do you think you and your friend can figure it out while I check to see how much Smith has screwed up my trainee?"

"We're Marines," Yizardo said, turning to DeLark. "Punch up some small game targets."

"What kind?"

"I don't know. I've never hunted small game with a shotgun before. How 'bout a duck?"

"Is that small enough?" asked DeLark. "Says quail on the screen. What's quail?"

I ignored their little debate. Smith was supervising O'Vorley in reloading the Dragoon. "How'd he do?"

"Pretty rough. Maybe above average for a security specialist."

"Does he have potential, Corporal?"

"Not as an expert marksman, but with training and practice, and a real weapon, he'd be competent."

I looked at Smith. "Problem is, his corporation sent him here with no training. From what I've seen he isn't likely to get it. You can learn only so much from holographic instruction." I shook my head. "It's the best he's likely to get. You've seen things around here."

"Not really. I'm on a short layover. Been assigned with DeLark and a few other marines for a transport coming in tomorrow."

"The *Kalavar*?"

"Yes," said Smith. He examined my company logo. "You mean I'm going to have to share air with a true hard-core R-Tech?"

"That could be the case." I watched DeLark and Yizardo blasting away. Shifting my focus down range, I spotted a holographic pile of birds and other vermin. "Good shots," I said to no one in particular before looking back at Smith. "I saw Yizardo on duty in Green Sector. Like all Marines, I'm sure he's good man. You think he might be willing to work with O'Vorley here?"

"Maybe," said Smith. "What's in it for you?"

"Nothing really. I nearly got killed in a crossfire today." I nodded toward the listening O'Vorley. "If he'd been in my place, he'd be dead. His sponsor won't even issue him a sidearm yet."

Smith leaned back, evaluating what I'd said.

"I'd train him myself," I explained, "if I had time. But I have orders like you."

"So all this old firearm demonstration and friendliness was meant to sucker us in?"

"Corporal," I said, "do you really believe I think that little of the Colonial Marines?" I pointed to the Dragoon and looked over at the other two marines having a good time. "But if I hadn't caught your interest with this stuff, would you have even exchanged pleasantries with us?" I pressed on before Smith could respond. "And even if nobody was here, or interested, O'Vorley would've gotten some range time under his belt."

"No," agreed Smith, "we'd never have learned what wonderful fellows you two security types are." Then he shook his head, grinning. "Well, maybe you, Keesay. Yizardo told us about your morning."

I looked to O'Vorley with eyebrows raised.

"Do you think," O'Vorley asked, "maybe Private Yizardo would take the time to train me in firearm proficiency?" His voice was quiet. "Our current schedules would seem to permit it. I couldn't pay him much—but I'm well trained in routine network systems and report filing. Our duty report formatting is almost identical."

"You'll have to speak up if you ever want to get noticed," Smith said. "It ain't up to me, but you guessed it, O'Vorley. Yizardo hates report filing. Maybe despises."

"If you're just passing through here, how do you know him?" I asked.

"We came up through basic together," Smith replied before looking back at O'Vorley. "Kid, I'll soften him up for you, but you'll have to make your own pitch." He took the Dragoon from O'Vorley's hand. "And if you screw up his reports, my fellow marine will let you know it."

"In other words, it'll take weeks before O'Vorley's face gets back to looking as good as mine?" I asked, turning to present a profile view.

Smith patted O'Vorley on the shoulder. "Your friend's got the gist of it." He prepared to join his friends.

"Smith, before you have your fun," I interrupted, "do you know anything about that marine, Ringsar out there. Seems like someone stitched his undershorts a little tight."

Smith glanced through the barrier. "Don't know him. Looks pretty big. I'd avoid letting him work out his problem on me."

"Thanks for the helpful advice." I turned back to O'Vorley and handed him my duty revolver. "Let's see what you can do."

After thirty rounds, O'Vorley showed some progress. After a dozen more, I gave O'Vorley my backup .38 and a box of shells. "See what you can do with Yizardo. And make sure there aren't any shotgun shells to carry back."

"Thanks, Kra," he said quietly before heading over.

I reloaded my duty revolver and holstered it before leaning back on a bench to relax. My eyes hadn't closed for more than thirty seconds when I felt a thumping on the transparent barrier behind my head. Ringsar stood looming with a less than delighted look on his face. I checked my watch. We still had at least ten minutes on the range. He signaled me to step out. Not good, but I didn't seem to have much choice. My lip began to throb as my heart rate stepped up, just a bit.

CHAPTER 13

Shortly after the Silicate War ended, humanity negotiated its way into the Intragalactic Frontier. As with all interstellar species, a treaty zone was established around the homeworld. The purpose is to provide a secured area of expansion, ensuring an initial buffer from the more advanced, aggressive interstellar explorers. Just before negotiations commenced, the Umbelgarri shared surveys that indicated a comparatively large number of potentially habitable planets and moons existing near the outer edges of a 100 light year radius from Earth. This was especially pertinent due to the sparse potential identified closer to Earth.

Regrettably for humanity, the diplomats sent to negotiate were intragalactically inexperienced and overconfident. Prideful in the belief that humanity did not need to hold the hand of another species to find its way, they brashly rebuffed Umbelgarri assistance. And forgetting to dispense with humanity's egocentric view, they hastily signed the finalized version of the treaty. To their credit, the human representatives did establish 102 light years radiating from Earth's sun as sovereign territory. Citing historical precedent they boasted over a third of a million cubic light years better than the average negotiated treaty. Unfortunately, the treaty arbitrators were the Troh-gots, and the arbiters were the Primus Crax. Each of their primary manipulative appendages has only four digits. They count in base 8.

I stepped out to confront Private Ringsar. His three companions stood a short way off, watching with interest as the door slid closed behind me. "We've still got fifteen minutes scheduled," I said, looking up into his narrowing glare.

"I'm not interested in range time," he said, moving closer. "I want to know why you're putting on a good time for those marines and not for me and my friends?"

Ringsar was so close his muscular frame blocked my view of his friends, but I stood my ground knowing where this was going. I couldn't afford being laid up in the infirmary with the *Kalavar* due to arrive. It could void my contract, leaving me stranded and without a corporate sponsor. "If you recall, Private Ringsar," I said calmly, "it was you who clearly pointed out you did not desire my company."

"It was a joke, Specialist."

"It didn't sound like one to me and it's been my experience to give a marine his space if he requests it."

"Are you saying that I don't have a sense of humor, R-Tech?"

While looking for some sign that Smith, Yizardo, or even O'Vorley had taken notice of my predicament, I kept my voice even. "I'm saying that I take a Colonial Marine at his word." I felt his breath. Maybe they'd pull him off while I was still in one piece.

"Pardon me, Marine," came a voice from behind Ringsar. "I would— "

The marine half turned to scrutinize the speaker. It was the attendant holding two boxes. He apparently didn't realize I was talking to the huge marine. "You would what?" Ringsar said with a snarl.

"I ahh..." said the attendant. Looking quickly, he handed me the two boxes of .38s. "I brought you these. Thought you might want them." Without glancing up he retreated.

"Thanks," I said, setting the boxes on a ledge behind me.

"Pillar," called one of the observing marines, "what's the relic got to say for himself?"

With nonchalance Ringsar turned his head. "Nothing intelligent. I think his intention is to insult my honor."

It was my chance to get in a first, and probably only, shot. I passed it up. My chances against a marine nicknamed Pillar weren't good.

Ringsar looked back, surprise I didn't try anything. His ears turned red. "You sure are cowardly, boy."

"Let's just say that if I'm going to get roughed up by a marine, the reason should be clear ahead of time."

"I'd say I'm gonna more than rough your ass up," he said, squaring up. "And the reason is you pissed me off."

"And exactly how did I manage that, Marine?" I asked, trying to keep him talking. "By agreeing with you and doing as you requested?" He was going to have to throw the first punch. If I could make him miss, I might get to counter. At least it'd be on record. "I wouldn't want to make the same mistake again."

"Your mistake'll be—"

"Private Ringsar," barked an authoritative voice.

My adversary relaxed for a fraction of a second, then turned and stood at attention. "Sir."

The range master, standing several paces back, asked, "Is there a problem?"

"No, sir, Lieutenant."

"Of course not, Private. Specialist, is there a problem?"

"There might have been," I replied. "I was just asking Private Ringsar what rule of etiquette I broke, sir."

"Looking to bloody your knuckles again, Marine? How did the security specialist manage to offend you?" The lieutenant didn't wait for an answer. "If you gentlemen have a dispute, settle it on the target range or take it elsewhere."

Ringsar saluted as the lieutenant turned and left. Then he looked at me. His companions approached as the door behind me slid open. "How would you recommend we settle this, R-Tech?"

"I'm still unclear on how I managed to offend you," I said and glanced over my shoulder. Smith, and DeLark were right behind me. A little late. I didn't figure they'd back me, but maybe they could've cooled him off. "But you apparently wanted a chance to fire my old-style weapons. Why not settle it with them?"

"What are you getting at?" he asked with a skeptical glare.

"I'm simply saying that we settle our dispute as the lieutenant suggested, with a little competition using the exact firearms you're implying I snubbed you with."

"I told you earlier, R-Tech. Due to your presence, advanced targeting and combat programming is no longer supported."

Ringsar's associates crowded up behind him. I stood aside as Smith and his friends stepped out of the range, followed by O'Vorley.

"I wouldn't expect you to compete with me on a security training program," I said as Ringsar's arms dropped to his hips. "It comes down to training. A colonial marine is trained to hunt and kill. A security specialist is trained to observe and react."

"So what're you getting at, R-Tech?"

If he was expecting his repeated use of R-Tech to get under my skin, he was wrong. But I could also see his mind was at work. "What I am saying, Marine, is that with my old-style firearms we should compete on a neutral targeting program."

"You pick the weapons," he said. "I pick the program." One of his buddies tapped his shoulder. "Yeah, and my friends here wanted to shoot, too."

"Okay," I agreed. "Two shooters. We'll use my revolver and the double-barrel."

"Good, you and your fellow Sec-Spec."

Nice try, I thought. "You indicated the dispute is between you and me…"

"Backin' out?" he interrupted.

"As I said, the dispute is between you and me. I'd say that one marine for you and one shooting with me wouldn't tip the scales. Unless you need someone to pick up your slack." I again observed his ears reddening. "And you can choose the targeting program, if my shooting partner agrees that it's neutral." I glanced quickly at Smith, hoping it was a smile that he was working to suppress. I figured on asking him. He knew about old-style weapons. Yizardo was stationed with Ringsar and his pals and his eyes were wide during the exchange so I didn't know how that would play out. DeLark was a good shot, young and brash enough. But I trusted Smith more.

"You think there's a marine on this dock that'll shoot with you, R-Tech?"

Smith stepped forward. "I know of one. Choose a targeting routine."

"What do I get when I win?" asked Ringsar.

"Respect, *if* you win," said Smith. "Quit stalling."

"What do you got to put up when you lose?" I asked.

Ringsar's cohorts laughed. "What have you got to put up, Relic?" said the towering marine, again beginning to fume.

"Since you're so fond of my old-style firearms, let's say if you win you can have the double-barrel."

"What about your revolver?" he taunted.

"It is my duty firearm. I could relinquish it no more than you could your marine-issued sidearm." Ringsar seemed unfazed. "Okay then, if you—"

Corporal Smith cut me off. "It's against regulations."

I had to keep the pressure up. "Then what do you have to put up of equal value?"

"What's that old hunk of steel worth?" he asked. "A week's worth of field rations?"

"Obviously, you're ignorant of antique firearm values. It's probably worth two or three month's pay for a Colonial Marine private. When you lose, I can arrange to have your wages transferred directly to my account."

"What? For that?"

"Come on, Private," said Smith. "Let's get on with it. Come to terms and choose."

The focus of Ringsar's ire shifted. Two of his friends grabbed his shoulders. DeLark stepped up as Smith's face released a long-retained smile.

I thought of O'Vorley stuck on this dock with Ringsar. "Loser pays for two Gourmet Line meals. I'll settle for that. How about you, Smith?"

"Fine with me," said Smith. "Now select if you can afford that, Private."

"Fine," growled Ringsar.

I saw Ringsar's mind shifting gears. I handed O'Vorley my duty revolver. "Run a brush through this," I said. "It's loaded." He took it. "And the shotgun too. There's a brush with a telescopic rod in the bag." I looked at Smith and then to Ringsar.

"Crax Com-Tower Approach," said Ringsar. "Stegmar Mantis Primary Defense."

Smith shook his head. "Requires assault tactics, demolition knowledge to complete. Remember, Private, neutral parameters."

"You didn't let me finish," replied Ringsar. "Diversion, Damaged Bunker Defense."

I knew what the Stegmar Mantis were, but I hadn't read much on them. They're two-foot high aliens resembling a praying mantis. Small but strong enough to tear a man's arm from its socket. Fortunately, the holographic programming couldn't simulate that.

"Score based on targets eliminated and duration of diversion," Ringsar said. "Good enough for you, Corporal?" The big marine seemed to be getting his head about him.

"DeLark, what's left to shoot in my bag?" I asked.

"About a hundred 12-gauge shells," he replied. "Three boxes of .357 shells."

"Plus these .38s," I said, grabbing the boxes from the ledge. "We'll split them evenly. Who's your shooter?"

"Hiroyuki is," Ringsar said, mirroring Smith's smile.

"Fine, but no advanced gear," I said, tossing Hiroyuki the boxes of .38 specials. "Just what we're wearing."

"Program options allow for field equipment selection," Ringsar said. "Whatever you take is deducted from your final score."

"Defensive, fine." I looked at DeLark. "Will you split up the ammo?" As he nodded I looked up. "You need any firearms instruction on these simple old relics, Colonial Marine Ringsar? I'll be more than happy to provide it."

DeLark went to get O'Vorley along with the firearms and ammunition. Yizardo volunteered to see the range master about the programming.

"Yizardo," Smith said as he turned, "tell the range master to set programming to Marine Training Protocol with an additional four minutes between competition rounds to clean and prepare the old-style arms." Then he looked at Ringsar. "Well, Private, Keesay here offered you remedial training. You need it or are you stalling again? I'm hungry for a gourmet meal."

Ringsar considered.

"It is R-Tech equipment after all," I said, hoping to keep every advantage possible. "It may be too complex for him to figure out."

"I ain't no retard, Relic!"

Ringsar was on the edge. Good. "Then you decline. That's okay." DeLark and O'Vorley returned from Range Two. "Everything ready and divided up?"

DeLark nodded. "One box of .357 target, one box of .38 specials each holding fifty rounds. Forty-nine 12-gauge shells, size four shot. Range will simulate as size four buck shot."

Yizardo returned and announced, "Range One is set up. Diversion Damaged Bunker Defense for Crax Com-Tower Approach, Stegmar Mantis Primary Defense. Scoring based on targets eliminated and duration of diversion." He took a breath and looked around then at the chronometer. "Program commences in 45 seconds."

"Sounds good," I said. "Private Ringsar, you selected the program, you go first."

"Fine," he said, searching for something to add. "But you can't watch my round."

"O'Vorley, give him the revolver," I said. "It's even loaded for you."

"Ninety second prep time and simulation starts," Smith said, looking at his watch. "Marine training protocol. Thirty seconds to start."

Ringsar didn't have time to object. Stuffing rounds in their pockets the two shooters moved efficiently toward the range entrance. Each hastily examined the workings of their firearm.

"You break my guns, you pay for them," I shouted. It was understood range etiquette but why not remind them. Everyone but Smith moved toward the elevated viewing area. I spotted the attendant heading our way.

"Okay, Keesay," Smith said, "here's what you need to know. After we enter we'll have ninety seconds to select bunker dimensions and special defenses. Our job is to hold out as long as we can. Assaults will come mainly from Stegmar Mantis."

"I know a little about them and something about the Crax," I interjected.

"Good. There'll be few Gar-Crax and they'll probably have defense screens of unknown strength. Hopefully, not too much. We'll have to lay in concentrated fire. Also, there'll be Bulldog Beetles." My expression told him I needed an explanation. "They're trained animals, kind of like military attack dogs but smaller. They fly and their pinchers inject a numbing toxin. Weak, but effective on humans."

"They'd be taken with the shot gun," I suggested. "Best range would be forty yards or less unless they're hard to penetrate."

"Right," Smith said. "Now, the Stegmar fire high-speed needle projectiles with various toxins. From the computerized defense options, I recommend we select the antitoxin inoculation."

"Doesn't it detract from our score?"

"It does, Keesay, but if you're hit early you're out."

"Stegmar. They're R-Tech, correct?"

"Right," said Smith.

"How are the needles fired, propelled?"

"Compressed gasses, CO_2 I believe."

"Can I use riot gear in place of inoculations?"

"Sure," said Smith, "but why?"

I turned to the attendant. "Can you get a riot control shield?"

He looked a little taken aback to be addressed. "Sure."

"Get it fast!" I urged. "I'll make it worth your while."

Fortunately, for his own reasons, the attendant took off running. I looked at the chronometer. "Simulation should be starting within fifteen seconds. I'm figuring they won't last long."

"We may not either, but it's your game," Smith said. "Anyhow, something else. You know anything about the Stegmar's predatory sounding?"

Puzzled, I said, "No."

Smith looked a little troubled. "It's loud and can be unnerving." He paused. "Best I can describe it would be an agitating, clicking sound. They use it to panic prey, flush them. And when there's a group sounding, it's worse." He thought a second. "Penetrates right to the bone, like nails scratching a chalkboard to a factor of ten. You'd have to deaden all hearing to negate it."

"Nice analogy with the chalk," I said, hoping the sounding wouldn't distract me too much. "Eliminating all verbal communication between us, correct?"

"When they get close enough," he said. "That'll be in the simulation. I bet Ringsar hopes it'll unnerve you."

"I'm pretty steady," I said. "Let me warn you, I'm not a fast shot, but I'm accurate. You take the shotgun?"

"That's what I figured," Smith agreed. "Just wanted to prepare you. Trust me to make the bunker selections?"

"I trust your judgment. And I'm glad you're willing to shoot with me."

"Pillar, I think they call him," Smith said, glancing over my shoulder. "You took my advice. He was spoiling for a fight and you avoided it."

"He'd have made quick work of me. But maybe we can make quick work on terrain of my choosing."

"You pushed him pretty hard. Shooting with you is one thing..."

"I know, but I needed an edge in negotiating terms of the match."

"Here comes your friend, Keesay. So what's your plan?"

The attendant hustled over. "Here. I checked it out for an hour."

"Plenty of time, thanks." I handed him two gum wraps. "Real cane sugar in them."

Looking pleased, he said, "May as well go watch, what's left. The lieutenant's recording it."

Interesting, I thought. Maybe the lieutenant doesn't care for Ringsar. I unfolded the clear reinforced duro-plastic shield before adjusting the braces and arm sling. Smith watched. "This should protect me from the needles," I said. "If scoring is similar to security scenarios, then using R-Tech equipment in lieu of I-Tech injections will decrease point deduction before the time factor." I demonstrated by hunkering down with the tall convex shield over my left shoulder. "I can curl in behind this while reloading."

"I'll keep that in mind when I select the defensive setup." He pointed toward the range. "Must be over. Short like you expected. All we have to do is to last longer and kill a few more." He patted me on the shoulder. "Let's go."

Infuriated, Ringsar emerged from the range. "Worthless piece of crap," he yelled. "Here take it, Sec-Spec."

O'Vorley cringed when Ringsar slammed the revolver into his hand. The young security specialist shifted his grip to a safer one and moved to the table with Yizardo who'd retrieved the shotgun. Ringsar stomped our way. His action was over, so there was no reason to rile him further.

"You little..." began the fuming marine, but he was too angry to finish, his hands balled into fists. "If I ever," he started before lunging.

I wasn't surprised and deflected his bulk with my shield. Still, he knocked me off balance. If he got a hold of me, the shield would be useless, so I discarded it before he came at me again.

I thought I was ready, but with near perfect execution he stopped, pivoted, and came around with a kick, striking my right leg. The blow hurt, but I kept my footing and came back with a punch to his kidney. Little effect. I backed off, blocking a blow to my head. Even that staggered me. If he got hold of me I was done for.

Seeing that I had no desire to engage him and probably recalling the lieutenant's recommendation, two of Ringsar's buddies tried to restrain him. He threw them off and charged again. That delay gave me time to retrieve a little relic technology to help my cause. I was going to lose, but he'd pay a price. This in mind, I slipped on my brass knuckles and made ready.

This time my foe directed his assault with more cunning than rage. I dodged and swung, but before I knew what was happening he knocked me to the ground. I sent two brass reinforced jabs to his face. He snared my jabbing arm in an iron grip. I tried to roll him off as he landed a crushing blow to my chest.

I gasped, trying to refill my lungs while his massive hand palmed my face. I pried at his grip with my free hand to no avail, then braced myself as he drew my head up and prepared to slam it against the floor. I bit at his palm before he thrust my skull downward.

My head never struck. Someone rammed into Ringsar and knocked him off of me. I rolled away, still gasping for air. More surprised than stunned, Ringsar rolled to his feet while O'Vorley scrambled to his, and backed away.

"Halt!" O'Vorley shouted in a shaky, adrenaline-charged voice. "Or you'll be detained and charged with assault."

I struggled for air, not expecting help from the any of the marines. They watched with interest as Ringsar grinned.

Wiping blood from a gash above his eye, he laughed. "Back off, kid, or you're next." He started toward me, but hesitated at O'Vorley's next move.

With stun baton in hand, O'Vorley stated with a measure of authority, "Marine Private, I said stop!"

One of Ringsar's buddies started to make a move, but Smith grabbed him and mumbled into his ear.

Ringsar turned on O'Vorley. "Then I'll take you first!"

I reacted, but not fast enough.

O'Vorley stepped back and swung his baton. The marine easily blocked the strike and caught Kent across the chin with a right. He was even less of a match for the hulking marine than me. Before I could get there, O'Vorley was down. But I saw my chance.

Just as Ringsar turned to face me, I came in low and plowed my shoulder into his knee. It popped as we went down. Grabbing O'Vorley's baton, I rolled away before the marine got hold of me again.

Ringsar bellowed, grabbing his knee, "Get him!"

Two of his fellow marines responded before a commanding voice behind me ordered, "Marines, halt!" Silence followed. Behind me stood the lieutenant and three Marine MPs. "What's the matter, Private?" asked the lieutenant. "Pick a fight and lost this time?" He glared at me. "What caused this incident, Specialist?"

I knew it was all recorded. "I am not sure, sir. Private Ringsar came out of the range and charged me."

"And what about him?" he asked, pointing at the unconscious O'Vorley.

"Specialist O'Vorley ordered Private Ringsar to restrain himself and threatened him with detainment if he didn't." I thought quickly. "Specialist O'Vorley was within his rights, even in Green Sector, as the altercation involved a fellow security specialist."

"I know the regulations, Specialist. He was out of line."

I wanted to keep O'Vorley and myself out of trouble. "Technically, sir, we are under the same authority through corporate agreement between Negral Corp and Quinn Mining." I looked at Ringsar. "I would like to keep this incident off the record. Even if the situation would warrant it, I have no intention of filing any charges against anyone, sir. I can speak for Specialist O'Vorley. He doesn't either."

The lieutenant looked skeptical. "Corporal Smith, is what the specialist said occurred here, accurate?"

"Yes, it is, sir."

"Could he file charges against Private Ringsar?"

"I couldn't say for sure, sir," Smith said, catching a glimpse of a surveillance camera.

While the lieutenant pondered the situation, two Quinn security personnel entered the range area. "Specialist Dribbs," said the lieutenant, "you have a man down. Take him to the infirmary."

"What happened here, Lieutenant, sir?" Dribbs asked.

"Specialist O'Vorley has declined to file charges, so it's out of your jurisdiction."

Dribbs looked around and took in the scene. "Yes, sir."

I handed Dribbs the stun baton. "This is O'Vorley's."

He grunted, inspecting the welt rising under Kent's left eye. Blood trickled from Kent's mouth, down his cheek. "Wake up, kid."

O'Vorley stirred and then awoke with a jolt. "It's all right, kid." The older Sec-Spec helped Kent to his feet and provided support.

As they went past, I winked. "Thanks, O'Vorley. Now you look like me."

"Just what he needs," Dribbs mumbled. Still unfocused, Kent grinned.

"Get moving," said the lieutenant. "You, Keesay, get your gear. You are prohibited use of this range and associated facilities until further notice. Yizardo, assist him."

I could live with that and moved to follow his directive fast as my aching body allowed.

Not looking happy, Yizardo said, "I'll gather the spent casings for recycling and the unused shells."

"Just toss them together," I replied while inspecting my duty revolver.

"I'll sort it out later." I heard the lieutenant speaking harshly, but in muffled tones, to Ringsar. "What do you think'll happen to Private Ringsar?"

"He'll go on report," Yizardo said crossly. "Depends on how long he's off duty."

I didn't feel guilty in the least. "If he didn't have such a hot head."

"If you hadn't set him up."

"I know you have to stick up for a fellow marine," I said. "He wanted a fight and I tried to avoid it. He got what he wanted, just not what he expected."

"That kid stuck up for you," Yizardo said with measured respect. "Surprised the hell out of me."

"We're not as highly trained as you marines, but the same type of blood flows through our veins. Just a different vintage." I put the shotgun in its sack. "If he'd had some training, he wouldn't have been dropped so easily."

"Give me those brass knuckles," replied Yizardo, "and I'll make sure he can shoot straight."

I pulled them out of my pocket. "What'll I do next time I run across an angry marine?"

"Get your ass kicked just like today."

I reached into another pocket. "Tell you what. You give those to O'Vorley and I'll give you this instead." I handed him the beef jerky.

"Where'd you get this?"

I grinned. "Us R-Techs have our sources. Do we have a deal?"

"Sure thing," he said. "Got everything?"

I placed my .38 in its ankle holster. "Yes."

"You'd better get out of here before the lieutenant changes his mind."

The lieutenant continued chewing out Ringsar and his pals even as they loaded the injured marine onto a stretcher. "Right. My transport comes in tomorrow, but maybe our paths will cross again."

Yizardo smirked.

I made it back to my quarters, earning a few stares but without incident. I was too sore to go out and find a meal, so instead I scribbled a note to O'Vorley, personally thanking him. I cleaned my guns and sorted shells before making arrangements to be notified when the *Kalavar* made contact with the dock.

After that, I packed everything for travel and prepared for bed. As I relaxed my battered body, I thought back on the past day. The image of fallen Agent Brown brought a tear as I said a prayer for her, and for the soul of the gunman I'd killed that day. I didn't have the strength that night to pray for the others.

CHAPTER 14

An inner colony is defined as one established within the negotiated security zone. During the Silicate War the military, supported by corporations, established a number of outposts with con-gates inside the security zone. Immediately after the war, corporations forged their way further into the stars seeking planets, moons and asteroids to exploit and settle.

With few habitable planets discovered within the security zone, efforts focused on the relatively large number of planets, moons and asteroid belts offering mineral wealth, despite their otherwise inhospitable characteristics.

Exploiting the mineral wealth in the inner colonies, corporations, with military support, leapfrogged to establish border and even some outer colonies. It is a difficult and dangerous, yet profitable, enterprise.

I awoke to shrill beeps sounding off at two-second intervals. Using the illumination from the flashing wall screen, I activated the lights and tapped the red section of the screen.

"Patron computer request has monitored an incoming message from the civil transport *Kalavar*," said a sharp, synthesized voice. "You have been notified per your request." After a pause, it continued, "May I be of further assistance?"

Who authorized artificial intelligence programs to refer to themselves as 'I'? "Yes, you can," I said, being very concise. "When is the civil transport *Kalavar* scheduled to dock with this, the Mavinrom Space Dock?"

"The transport is scheduled to dock at 05:26 Earth standard time. One hour and twenty-nine minutes from now. Will that be all this morning, Specialist Keesay?"

Its syntax impressed me, but I didn't care for the familiarity. Some I-Techs feel more at ease conversing with a computer than a person. Not me. "No. I have another question. At which docking bay is the civil transport *Kalavar* scheduled to be received?"

"The transport *Kalavar* is expected to dock at Bay Four. May I be of further assistance to you this morning?"

"That is all."

"Thank you," it replied before the computer screen flashed to the Quinn logo, a bold, blue 'Q' emblazoned upon a pitted asteroid.

I performed my morning regimen of stretches, sit-ups, and pushups. I did pretty well considering my battered condition. I hopped in the shower to take full advantage of water rights provided by Field Director Simms. My shoulder was tender but healing. My lip and eye needed some time, too. Using my straight razor, I shaved before brushing my teeth, running a comb through my hair, and placing ointment on my injuries.

Fortunately, the room had a cleaning chamber. Many I-Tech inventions are annoying, but this one is handy, despite the fact that Capital Galactic Investment holds the patent. The night before I'd placed my uniform in the rectangular wall panel and activated the chemical cleaning sequence. As usual, it did an excellent job.

Last, I dressed, including my new, pocketed duty vest before strapping on my duty sidearm and backup. I missed my brass knuckles. I had an hour before docking so I rechecked my cart and refilled my water bottles before hurrying to the central transport hub to take an internal shuttle.

I was correct in my assumption that the shuttle wouldn't be crowded, nor was the bay area when I checked my cart. For breakfast I selected a double order of toast, synthetic eggs and orange juice along with a vitamin supplement. Bread was the only authentic item available in the standard processed food line.

After breakfast, I stopped at a patron service station to confirm my ordered equipment was scheduled for transfer to the *Kalavar.* I then commissioned a courier-bot to deliver my note to O'Vorley and transferred what was left on my chit to my personal account. I could've sent Kent's note electronically, but those are impersonal.

I made my way to the lounge area and sat in one of their meagerly padded chairs. I spotted Smith and his squad heading for a meal before forming up. I also saw a Chicher, possibly the one from the day before, scamper to the gourmet line.

With nothing else to do but wait, I pulled down the overhead computer clip and set it to inform me when the *Kalavar* arrived. I spent the rest of my time reading the *InterStellar Times News Update.* Computer magazines, still called ezines by most, and made available compliments of space docks, are usually more advertisements and propaganda than hard news, but they're better than nothing.

While skimming an article on an attempted hostile takeover of 14th Venture Travels by CGIG, the preset docking indicator flashed. I switched the screen over to watch the docking approach. The *Kalavar* wasn't large by today's standards, being about the size of a World War II era battleship. Today, anything built under a kilometer in length is considered, at best, medium class.

I'd researched the *Kalavar.* Originally her exterior had been sleek. But her modernization included a series of armor plates patched over most of the hull. It made the transport appear boxier than her designers ever intended. Since the vessel no longer served as a high-class transport catering to the wealthy, fashion was no longer a consideration. The patchwork reminded me of the *Iron Armadillo*'s exterior. A tingle of excitement ran down my spine.

I retrieved my cart and waited in the contract employee section along with a few technicians and their automated carts. I'd dined next to one tech planetside; she had nothing to say to me then. I knew better than trying to start a conversation then, and now. They felt the same about me. Still, I gathered from their whispers that they were new hires as well.

Shortly after the ship docked, a cross-looking class 2 Sec-Spec by the name of Club, sporting an Emigration Official patch, scanned our V-ID and checked us in. Upon closer observation, she appeared more exhausted than angry.

"Specialist Keesay," she said, "report immediately to Security Chief Brold. Your possessions will be delivered to your quarters." Before I could ask, she finished. "Deck Three, below aft-observation."

The C2 didn't appear open to questions. "Thank you, Specialist Club," I said. I'd studied a basic layout of the old civil transports and modernization upgrades for interstellar travel. If there was an aft-observation located above the engines, then there must be some sort of weapons mount on Deck 1. Interesting, I thought, as I boarded.

The vessel retained much of its old design as evidenced by the low ceilings and numerous pipes and conduits. A few new lines had been added. As on freighters or military vessels, placing them out of sight wasn't a priority. I moved from portside, aft and upward, observing that the *Kalavar* had received more than one round of upgrades. Medium transports normally have a minimum crew of 50 technicians and engineers, in addition to general maintenance, service, and support staff. I had no idea the complement of security personnel on board. I passed only one person, wearing soiled, tan coveralls. Apparently they kept maintenance techs busy.

Hesitating only once or twice to get my bearings, I thought about the name of the chief. Simms said his name was Corbin. Maybe a change in personnel or an unlikely error on Simms's part.

I arrived just as a pilot in a flight suit exited the security chief's office. No one was in the outer office. Before I announced myself to the monitor, the door opened. "Enter, Specialist Keesay," ordered a deep, gruff voice.

Behind a broad desk sat a man with gray eyes and even grayer hair. His crew cut suggested a military background. Despite the gray, his build and attitude indicated anything but elderly. I took in all of this, including the nameplate, while coming to attention. It read 'Security Chief Corbin Brold.'

He pulled a small reddish stick from the corner of his mouth before addressing me. "Specialist Keesay, it seems you had a little action before we arrived. Quite a shiner." He smiled. "Do you know why you're here, Specialist?"

His insignia identified him as a C1. "To serve aboard the *Kalavar* as a security specialist."

"Do you know why they hired you?"

"My training and experience qualified me for the position." He sat stone-faced. "And I understand that there is a shortage of security specialists currently available." No response. "And that as a C4 I could do the same job for less, meaning more profit for Negral Corp." I didn't even think he was breathing. "Random luck, Chief?"

"Don't know, do you, Keesay?" he said. "They didn't exactly consult me either. Any or all of your reasons may be correct." He leaned back. "Fact is, you're here." He quickly sat forward. "Damn. Step around here, Keesay."

I did, and looked down at his desk and followed his finger. One of the multiple surveillance screens showed a man in uniform heading down a corridor.

"That's the executive officer, Lieutenant Commander Carlos Devans. A company man. Smart, but a pain in the ass." With a tap he enlarged the screen. "See that weasel-eatin' grin?"

"Yes, Chief."

"That means he's got an idea." He switched screens as the lieutenant commander turned a corner. "And he's heading this way."

The chief slid the red toothpick back into the corner of his mouth. "Your first assignment is to stall him. Then, your second assignment is to familiarize yourself with the ship." He finished with a business-like tone. "Report back here in three hours."

"Sure thing, Chief," I said, studying the screen.

"Turn right on your way out," Chief Brold suggested. "You've got about ninety seconds."

I turned and checked my watch. Three hours. Now to stall. I left the chief, turned right and strode down the corridor with a purpose.

This was a test to be sure. Of what? Ingenuity? The ability to respond? Maybe the chief wanted to finish a cup of coffee. I'd heard rumors that Negral supplied unusual fare, on occasion, to its crew.

I trotted down the corridor, refocusing on the task at hand. I didn't want to foster a bad first impression with the XO, nor did I want to tinker with any of equipment in the halls, which might ultimately cause somebody grief. Ahead I saw an old man moving with a bow-legged shuffle, examining the walls, pipes and grating. He had thinning, gray hair and a well-manicured mustache.

The man had to be a centenarian, or older. He wore an aging leather tool belt carrying wrenches, pliers, and other old-style tools. A loose-fitting, faded black uniform draped his wiry frame. The color black didn't conform to standard ID of a specific specialization.

As I approached, he smiled. "You look to be in a hurry there." He eyed my healing cuts and bruises through a set of half glasses.

"I am just that..." There wasn't an ID tag on his coveralls. "Maintenance Specialist?"

"No," he said. "I'm not a part of any specialist conglomeration."

"You're right, I am in a hurry." Viewing his tool belt, I asked, "Say, do you have anything that I can borrow to reach down through a floor grating access port?"

"Sure do," he said, pulling out a flexible rod with a small claw-like tip.

"Just grip it like this, and use your thumb on the plunger to open it."

"Great! Exactly what I need. I'll get it back to you in about ten minutes?"

"No need rushin'. I'll be around."

"Thank You, Mr..."

"Just Elmer, but my friends call me Mer."

"Thanks, Mer. Just call me Kra. Love to chat, but I've got to go!"

He shuffled aside and chuckled. "No problem."

I hustled down the corridor, scanning the floor for an access hole in the grating. I came across one along the wall. It had a five-inch diameter. I reached into my pocket and produced an ever-handy gum-wrap. Looking through the grate, I lowered the candy through the unused port, and flipped it toward the center of the floor. It landed just beyond some conduits about three feet away. They conveniently obstructed a floor level view of the candy. Perfect, just in time.

Around a corner strode the executive officer. He spotted me on the floor with my arm in the access hole. I looked up with a surprised expression before removing my arm and standing at attention. I saw more clearly what the chief meant by the XO's smile. It was serious, whetted with a hint of wiliness.

He stopped and appraised me. "At ease, Specialist." His voice wasn't deep, but it resonated. A contrast to my initial assessment. He caught my eyes darting a glance through the grating as I relaxed.

Looking at my hand and then my ID patch, he continued, "What have you got there, Security Specialist Keesay?"

I didn't know the term for the tool. "A tubular grasping device, sir."

"And what are you attempting to do with your, grasping device?" He scrutinized my sleeve. "You're not auxiliary maintenance."

Reestablishing eye contact, I said, "I was just leaving Chief Brold's office, and preparing for my ordered tour of the *Kalavar*." I looked around and didn't spot the old fellow. "I was considering celebrating my new assignment with a gum-wrap, authentic sugar. As you can see, it ended up under the grating. Out of reach."

"Chief Brold's office." He nodded. "Where did you obtain the device?"

"I came across what appeared to be a maintenance technician. He calls himself Mer." The XO didn't respond, so I continued. "I borrowed this from him. I should have requested his assistance." He seemed to be taking all of this in. I hoped he responded to my leading statement.

"And why would you need his assistance?"

"The gum-wrap is too far to reach by hand a find by touch, sir. When on the floor, the view is obstructed by the conduit piping."

"Do you have a solution to this dilemma?"

"Actually, I do, sir. If you would be willing to direct me as I attempt to reach the wrap, we could commemorate the occasion." It was worth a shot. The XO seemed friendly enough. "I would be willing to split it with you, sir.

"Is this how you mark your experience aboard each new vessel, Specialist?"

I detected a hint of skepticism. "Actually, sir, this is my first assignment aboard an interstellar vessel. My other assignments were in the Solar System."

"I cannot chew gum while on duty, Specialist."

"I understand, sir. Sorry to have detained you from your business." I stepped out of his path and waited for him to pass.

"Can you be quick about it, Specialist? Wouldn't want any rats, or crew with better equipment to run off with your valuable prize while you're off seeking assistance. Would we?" He winked.

I smiled back. "No, sir."

I bent down and went to work, not wasting any time. I'd played my hand as best I could. Besides, Lt. Commander Devans was very adept at providing directions. Appearing inept at following them didn't seem wise. Within twenty seconds I'd retrieved the candy and stood at attention. "Thank you, sir." I held out the gum wrap.

"You are welcome, Specialist," he said before turning to leave. "Now I am off to see the security chief."

I acted surprised at his statement, unsure how convincing I was. As soon as he was out of sight, I went looking for Mer. I checked my watch and estimated the XO's delay to be almost four minutes. I hoped it was enough.

Ten minutes later I located the old maintenance worker inspecting a series of rivets along the wall. "Elmer," I said, holding out the tool. "Thanks for the loan."

"Mer," he said. "Remember?" He replaced the tool in his belt and looked me over. "An R-Tech, and space faring too."

"Not that unusual," I said.

"What ships you been on?"

"Not many. What about you? Those don't appear to be the accessories of your average computer engineer."

"Hee Hee," he laughed. "No, they ain't." He put a calloused hand on my shoulder. "It's just you and me, Kra. The only R-Techs, 'till the passengers board."

"We're hauling R-Techs?" I asked.

He nodded. "That's what I hear. I'm sure your boss'll fill you in."

"You're not an official part of the crew. What are you? A passenger working off debt?"

"Something like that, but the other way around." He pulled a rag and wiped the rivet. "It'd take a long time to explain."

"You know this vessel," I said. "Pretty well I bet."

He puffed out his chest. "Sure do."

"If you're not part of the crew, then you're not on duty."

"That's right."

"Maybe you could help me out. Chief Brold suggested I take some time to get the *Kalavar*'s layout. I've studied the diagrams and blueprints, but I'll still be stumbling around." His face lit up. "Would you mind?"

"Not at all, there," he said, removing his glasses. "Looks like you've had a rough time, and about due for a good turn."

"That's a long story, too," I said. "I've got about two hours to get the layout. Whatever time you can spare."

"That should be just enough time, and maybe get your story in. This way, Kra. We'll start at the beginning." He led me down the corridor. "The *Kalavar* is now classified as a medium class transport because she's less than two-hundred and fifty meters long." The word meter rolled stiffly off his tongue. "Still," he continued, "she displaces over two-hundred thousand cubic meters. In her day, she was a top-of-the-line transport, ferrying important businessmen and the rich from Earth to Mars, and back."

His voice had taken on a distant tone, but seemed to snap back. "That was before the war, and before the Phibs taught us to condense space. Nothing fancy anymore, especially after the armor plating." He pointed and gestured as we continued. "We're heading to the front of the ship. See these new conduits? The metallic red ones?"

"Yes, I noticed them earlier."

"They run to the outer hull and power the anti-grav panels. They put in a space-condensing engine too. So now she's interstellar."

"Wasn't the *Kalavar* in mothballs?" I asked.

"Yep," he acknowledged. "During the Silicate War the *Kalavar* was converted. Part of her ventral section was gutted and turned into a cargo hold. Some of the passenger compartments were knocked out and turned into freight areas. Then, after the war, she was mothballed. Set in orbit around Venus." He sighed. "That was a long dark time for me."

I looked at him, but before I could say anything, he cut in, "We'll get to that some other time. Anyways, she was set to orbiting Venus with all of the other obsoletes. Everything of value'd been stripped. Just a few controls for the secondary engines." He looked to see if I was following. "They tore out the main, center engine."

He seemed pretty spry, and walked at a decent pace. I wanted to ask how old he was, and why he was so familiar with the *Kalavar*'s history, but didn't and, instead, kept looking around, familiarizing myself as much as I could. We passed few crewmen. Occasionally, I spotted recessed security cameras. "Why didn't they take them all out?"

He looked at me blankly.

"The engines, I mean."

"In case the military wanted to use her for target practice," he said with muffled ire. "But the *Kalavar* got a second lease on life. About four years ago Negral Corp bought her, and rebuilt her. Like I said, made her interstellar."

"Must've been expensive."

"Sure was, but the shipyards are running full capacity. Years behind on their contracts."

"Negral probably didn't have the pull," I agreed.

"True, but they got a deal. They don't make them like this anymore." We were past mid-ship and nearing the front of the vessel. He shifted to a business tone. "Like I said, start at the beginning."

I was about to ask his connection to the *Kalavar* when a small hand-held radio hanging from his belt crackled. "Mer, this is Chief Brold."

He grabbed the radio and held it close to his mouth. "Yes, Chief."

"Send Specialist Keesay to Medical, immediately. I mean now! Understood?"

"Sure thing, Chief. Pronto." Mer looked at me. "Sounds like he wants you there yesterday." He signaled to me follow him. I jogged to keep up with his shuffling gait.

"I'll show you the short cut," he said, leading me toward the outer hull. "All of these red lines run together. Some places there are powered maintenance sleds along them. Faster than by foot and lifts." He wasn't losing his breath.

"The chief sounded a bit excited," I said. "Out of character isn't it?"

"Yep."

CHAPTER 15

Companies have tripped over themselves to explore and establish a presence just outside the relatively barren security zone. As the border region of space is not under explicit treaty restrictions, interstellar vessels of other races have been spotted and may be establishing a presence. Not all races are friendly to humans, and some are not hospitable toward other regional alien explorers. Galactic colonization is a dangerous game and humans are new to it.

We stopped under merging red conduits that carried power for the anti-gravity plates. "Up here," urged Mer, climbing a recessed ladder with a penlight clamped between his teeth. "It's cramped."

I crawled after him between the deck levels, following the conduits. I focused my own pocket flashlight and watched him tap keys on a panel. He whispered, and the cramped section lit up.

"We ain't supposed to use these except for emergencies," he said. "And the chief sounded pretty urgent to me." He pocketed his penlight.

There was a two-foot clearance. "They built this to maintain the anti-gravity system?" I asked, before sliding under paired, red power conduits, and moving up.

"Guess so," he said. "They say failure of anti-gravity in condensed space can be a problem."

"Fatal," I agreed, happy I wasn't claustrophobic. Mer stared down a recessed track running parallel to us, waiting for something. "Hey," I said, "both of these conduits split off, but always into pairs, and run to the outer hull." I shined my light. "See? If it's a backup system, it doesn't make sense to have them running parallel."

"You're right," he said. "But engineers don't get contracts for being stupid."

"What does that mean?" He didn't answer.

A humming announced two flat sleds approaching. He climbed onto one. "Get on, Kra. Strap yourself in good, and I'll get us there."

I was having second thoughts about the legitimacy of Mer's route. I signaled and said, "Ready." How much time were we really saving?

"Might want to turn off your light and hold your stomach," Mer said while pecking at the control panel.

We shot off. Powered by a magnetic pulse, the ride was smooth, except for a section where we slowed, switched tracks, and sped a different direction. In thirty seconds we were at the other end of the *Kalavar.*

Mer muttered and tapped at a panel, providing lights. "Unbuckle yourself and hop down. Medical will be straight ahead a bit, to your right."

As I slid down the ladder, I spotted Chief Brold standing outside Medical. I trotted up to him. "Chief?"

"Keesay," he said with arms crossed, "just what the hell did you booby-trap your cart with?"

"A lock, Chief. Did somebody try to pick it?"

"Apparently. Explain."

"It's rigged to spray blue dye on anyone who tries to pick it," I replied, in an even tone. "It also acts as a numbing agent." I took a breath. "Who tried it?"

He ignored my question. "What if the lock is cut?"

I didn't know if I should be angry or worried. "If it's cut, Chief, an interior tube was installed in the loop. To deter the trespasser." I wanted to say, nail the crook. "Severing the lock releases an aerosol containing a visual irritant, and a nauseating inhalant."

"Is it lethal?"

"No. The airborne chemicals are extremely short lived." I flexed my fingers. "Who broke into my cart?"

Before he could answer, a medical technician ran out of the lab. "Security Chief, get in here!"

I followed my boss and the white-garbed med tech through a small reception area to the treatment center. Med techs moved in all directions, but generally away from one of the rooms. A vaporous cloud hung outside the closed door, and from it a powerful acidic odor assaulted my eyes and nose. No Biohazard alarms had been triggered. A med-bot sped around, spraying a neutralizing agent. Still, I wasn't too confident.

Chief Brold grabbed a med tech's arm. "What's going on?"

Before the tech could answer, a doctor stepped away from two assistants in protective gear. "Well, Chief," he said, "our patient expired. Took part of my examination room with him."

"Dr. Sevanto, what happened?"

Despite the commotion, the doctor remained calm. With an air of authority he directed the chief away from the traffic. "We had alleviated the respiratory distress and flushed out the visual irritant. The patient was still visibly agitated. Readouts indicated unidentified chemicals in his system. The patient sat up just after I suggested to Tech Gorborski that you might be interested in interviewing our patient."

Dr. Sevanto halted his story for a second and spoke into his collar. "That will be sufficient." He looked back at Chief Brold. "The room has been emptied of all potential hazards, and is safe."

"What happened?" repeated the chief.

"Let's take a look." Dr. Sevanto led us into the room. It was small, plain and antiseptic, like any other medical examination room—except for the pitted remains of an examination bed with the emergency filtration system drawing in the remaining fumes.

"As I was saying, Chief, after your name was mentioned, the patient laid back down and closed his eyes. Within seconds, what I suspect to be an internal acid, began to dissolve his body." He stepped closer, gesturing despite the ruined equipment's lingering odor. "It stopped halfway through my examination table."

My eyes would've been wide as dinner plates, if they hadn't been watering. The chief seemed immune. "Did the decomposing begin in the torso?" he asked.

"Not exactly. The entire body came under the effect. At least to the ankles and wrists. All organic matter was consumed. It should have been recorded on your security network." Dr. Sevanto looked around. "Know what caused this, Chief?"

"Possibly. Some aliens are known to have capsules imbedded in their bodies. Usually near a main circulatory artery. The capsule's contents can be activated by a chemical entering the body." Chief Brold scratched his head. "The Crax are reported to have a set up with a delayed onset that allows an inert acid to circulate though the body before a released enzyme activates it." He maneuvered closer and examined the area. "Did a thorough job." He retraced his steps. "Could've been worse."

Dr. Sevanto asked, "Do you think Tech Stardz was connected to the Crax?"

"I wouldn't rule anything out, yet." The chief reached into a pocket and produced a small clip. "Specialist, do you recognize this man?"

I looked at the flat-screen picture. "No, Chief."

"Doctor," said Chief Brold. "Collect samples of the acid and anything else. Or at least have the xeno guy look over what's left. See how it reacted to whatever it came into contact with."

"Already requested, Chief."

Chief Brold spoke into his collar. "Specialist Club, get to Medical and assist the xenobiologist in collecting samples." He nodded his head. "Dr. Sevanto will bring you up to speed." He glared at me. "Come on, Specialist. We need to talk."

The silent trek to the chief's office gave me time to wonder if any of the chemicals from my lock had triggered the deadly reaction. It didn't seem to fit the pattern Chief Brold had laid out. But I was neither a chemist, nor an expert in human physiology.

I sat patiently while the chief reviewed surveillance recordings. Half of my thoughts wondered what had happened and why. The other half focused on why my equipment had been tampered with, and why security had allowed it. After several minutes, I relaxed, figuring I'd know soon enough. Instead, I tried to identify the security measures the chief had installed on his desk screen and around his office. The method and setup could say a lot about a person.

From my vantage, I couldn't see precisely what the chief had running on his desk screens, but a small readout to the right of the screens flashed a verification, indicating he used fingerprint and retinal verification. Looking around wasn't exactly proper etiquette, but at this point, if the chief had a problem with it, he could say something.

Several Silicate War vintage pictures of the chief in Colonial Marine garb rested on a shelf. One showed Chief Brold and several other marines outfitted in servo-armor. It looked like the type designed for hand-to-hand combat with the Shards. The picture was fancy, but outdated. The trees in the background waved in the breeze, while everything about the primary figures remained stationary.

I spotted several recesses above the entry door. One probably housed a verification device, keyed to the chief's iris or facial features. I'd have been willing to bet he had voice security as well. Layered security, various levels and complexity; the chief knew his business.

Chief Brold invited me to the other side of his desk. "Here's Tech Stardz." I watched the engineering tech lingering outside a hallway, looking around. Then, he turned a corner. "There," interrupted Chief Brold. With a touch of his finger, the action stopped. From this vantage, I confirmed that the desk screen's security was coded to the chief's fingerprint with the flashing green light above the door confirming a secondary long range optical scanning device.

I refocused on the screen as he replayed the sequence in slow motion. "Yes," I said, "he just pulled something from his pocket."

"See how it's concealed?" Chief Brold said, magnifying the area around the hand. "No help there. Now watch." The tech continued around the corner. "This monitor should have picked him up." The screen displayed an empty corridor.

"Pretty handy device," I said.

"We didn't find it after Specialist Club apprehended him." The chief tapped the screen again. "See how he just appears?" A few seconds later the chief commented, "Here's Club finding Stardz doubled over, just outside the area."

I noted the elapsed time was just under four minutes. "How far away is that from my equipment?"

"One deck down," he said, leaning back. "Specialist Club is what you might say, quite knowledgeable. She pegged your set up earlier, and put two and two together."

Chief Brold sat forward again and indicated I take a seat. "I've got a couple questions for you, Keesay." Brold's demeanor appeared relaxed, except for his eyes. "I'd like you to speculate what happened during the time Tech Stardz activated his screening device. And, I'd like to know why he had an interest in your equipment."

I wondered why the chief didn't show me the storage surveillance, but it wasn't time for my questions. "Chief, I would guess that Tech Stardz simply entered the storage area, and attempted to pick the lock. Apparently, he wasn't as observant or knowledgeable as Specialist Club. He may have used some simple, or even electronic picks to open the lock. Didn't find any on him?"

The chief shook his head, so I continued. "Well, the lock was set to spray a contact dye containing a weak corrosive and nerve agent. The corrosive to penetrate hand protections and assist the numbing agent in deterring further lock picking efforts. Apparently, Tech Stardz wasn't deterred, because the lock released the aerosol I told you about. That's why Specialist Club found him doubled over."

The chief seemed interested. "See," I explained, "most thieves are careful not to leave much evidence behind. But if they vomit, then a whole array of traceable evidence, including cells from the stomach's lining, is left behind."

The chief cracked a half smile. "Not bad. It might even catch a few professionals."

Did the chief think Tech Stardz was a professional? "Tech Stardz tried to pick it," I said, "and probably was unsuccessful. Panicked and tried to cut the lock and fled." Now, was my turn. "I'd like to examine my equipment and determine if anything was taken."

"We'll get to that later."

"If Specialist Club didn't find tools or the screening device on Stardz, then he had an accomplice. Maybe a review of all the recent surveillance could catch someone else being screened?"

"Already being done, Specialist. It may narrow the list. But anybody walking in range of the scrambler would be screened."

"How many crewmen would wander past a vomiting technician without assisting or reporting?" His smile indicated he'd thought of that. And that he was holding back.

The next part would be tricky. I hated to lie to my boss. Worse yet, getting caught lying. A shift in his eyebrows indicated I'd better finish.

"Why Tech Stardz had an interest in my equipment? He figured it an easy theft opportunity?" I shrugged. "Normally, there'd be little reason for an I-Tech to steal from an R-Tech cart." I took a thoughtful breath. "There was an incident on the dock, prior to my boarding. That may be connected, but I don't know how."

"What incident would that be?"

"Well, there were actually two, Chief." I was sure he knew of them. "I don't think the incident with the marine would connect." He gave an ever so slight acknowledgement. He knew, but how much? Hadn't Simms referred to the chief by his first name? "If you were to contact Investigator Simms, he might have more information on any possible connection."

Hiding any reaction, the chief said, "I'd like to hear what you have to say before I make any effort to contact him."

"Apparently, there was an inside job attempted on the dock. Some baggage handlers, who weren't company loyal, attempted a theft, or something. It didn't work out as planned. I got caught in the crossfire and killed one of them." Certainly, he knew that much. I scratched my head as if in thought. My bruised face made prolonged, thoughtful squinting a bit more painful than it was worth. "If Stardz was part of that organization, then there might be a connection." A thought hit me. "Maybe he wasn't trying to steal, but maybe plant something."

"He was," replied Chief Brold. "Senior Engineer McAllister is trying to identify it. Maybe after this interview we can consult her and figure out a bit more."

Interview? Try interrogation. "I'm not sure there's much more to tell. Other than maybe payback, for whatever I helped foil." Was it something illegal Stardz tried to plant? The obvious break-in would quash any frame-up job.

The chief saw my mind racing. "Is there anything you'd like to add, Specialist?"

"I don't think there is anything else I can add." It was vague but let him take it however he would.

"What do you mean by, 'can'?"

I sat up even straighter. "Exactly what it means, sir." I knew that answer would delight him almost as much as being called sir. In the back of my mind, the image of water swirling down a drain formed.

"That's good to hear, Keesay."

"Chief?"

"I'm not going to compel you to lie. Too much file work involved in that. Karlton gave me enough details.

Was that Simms's first name? It seemed so long ago. Chief Brold must've correctly interpreted my expression.

"Your Corporate Inspector Simms." He chuckled. "Maybe I'll tell you about him sometime. But while I've got you here, let me go over your duty assignment." He checked the chronometer above the door. "And give McAllister a little more time to report."

His tone said we were following his agenda. I was interested in my new assignment, but more interested in what Stardz had been up to, and what Field Director Simms had told my boss.

CHAPTER 16

None of the five reported outer colonies are located on habitable planets. Two are large space docks located in asteroid belts. Two orbit different planets in the same binary system. The final one, located on a moon orbiting a Jupiter sized gas giant, is shared with the Chicher.

Located over 300 light years away, the joint colony functions as a hub for the other outer colonies. It is one of the few ventures where multiple corporations have acted in unison for the benefit of mankind. It is also one of the few large-scale, far-seeing operations where the Capital Galactic Investment Group has been shut out. It is believed the Chicher wanted it that way. Some say it takes one rat to sniff out another rat.

The *Kalavar* was short of security with several auxiliary team members having primary duties in other areas. In addition, the marines were to assist during transit, but only if necessary. I got the impression the chief wanted to avoid involving them. The only other thing I learned, before we were interrupted, was that a delayed shipment included my company communications gear.

"Understood," Chief Brold answered into his collar. A hint of surprise passed over his face before fading into concern. "I agree, Senior Engineer McAllister. Specialist Keesay and I will await your arrival." He nodded again. "Contact Specialist Club. Have her change the entry code before you leave." His brow furrowed. "It doesn't matter. Security is responsible for any access code changes."

He wasn't happy with the response. "You wait there," he said. "I'll send Specialist Liu to secure your lab until Club gets there. Then report here immediately. Out." He shook his head and held up a finger before returning to our conversation.

He tapped a corner of his desk screen. A class 2 administrative specialist entered from the adjoining room. She wore a navy blue jumpsuit with a gray-green armband indicating a secondary duty assignment as a security specialist.

I stood as did Chief Brold. "Specialist Krakista Keesay, this is Admin Specialist Li Liu, who serves as my assistant."

Liu's physical features reconfirmed her name's Asian ancestry. Sometimes people change their name, or even their outward appearance. It didn't appear that Specialist Liu did either. I waited, on the off chance that she might offer her hand. She didn't.

"Welcome aboard, Specialist," she said, before turning back to the chief.

"Liu, contact Club and have her change the access code to the engineering research lab. But it might be a while. She's in Medical with the cleanup crew. I want you to post outside the lab until she completes her task and relieves you." He paused. "Use communication protocol Prime Two."

Liu frowned. Her eye shifted to me, then back to the chief. "Understood,

Chief."

"Good. Prevent access to the lab, except for McAllister and myself. And Club, of course." He checked the chronometer. "Contact me if Club hasn't reported to you within the hour."

"If any of the engineering or tech staff should desire entrance?"

"They can contact me or McAllister."

"I'm sure they'll contact you, Chief," she said before returning to her office.

"Keesay, pull over another chair for Engineer McAllister when she arrives."

I did and sat down while he tapped past a few screens on his desk. "Keesay, your file says you're adequate in the use of computers." He pulled a pen from his desk and scribbled something on a slip of paper. "Here's the access code and password to your onboard account."

Chief Brold's handwriting was small and precise. I placed the paper in my breast pocket and looked up, waiting for him to continue.

"You have Level D clearance for access to information and records. When you log in, you can set your own password as well as secondary security. For you, finger print, voice, or iris scan."

"Can I set additional parameters? Like a minimum time frame between keystrokes?"

"That's possible." He leaned back and smiled. "Not the trusting sort."

"Not exactly, Chief."

"Just what do you know about computers?"

"Not much. I've had some basic programming, but very little in hardware support."

He nodded and skimmed a few more files. "While we have a few minutes, are there any other surprises that I should know about?"

I thought a moment. Surely Specialist Club found the popcorn nukes. "You mean like the lock?" When he nodded, I tugged at my belt buckle. "I have this buckle blade. I had some brass knuckles, and will try to replace them." I sheathed the blade. "I recently picked up some old-style grenades, and I have advanced AP rounds for my duty revolver." I scratched my head to cover my nervousness. "A vial of potent muscle relaxant. I also have two .002 kiloton cased fusion explosives." He didn't seem surprised. "Their configuration focus is to emit a high powered electro-magnetic pulse for communications disruption."

"I didn't know about the blade, and Club sent the vial to Medical for analysis. She located the devices you mentioned, along with the AP rounds. She actually might've missed the nukes, except for the need to re-inspect your cart."

"Will my popcorn nukes be confiscated, Chief?"

"Is there any reason you should have them aboard the *Kalavar*?"

"They're personal property. Obtained legally. I am trained and certified in their use." I looked around. "Obviously their use aboard a vessel would be of limited value. But—"

The chief cut in, "Catastrophic is the term I'd suggest, if detonated onboard."

"I can think of several situations where they could be utilized effectively and safely."

"So can I. And they're a stretch, Specialist. I'll consider it, but I doubt you'll retain possession."

He didn't dismiss retention right out of hand. "If you do choose to take them, I would like to request compensation."

"Exactly how did you come by them? Certainly out of a C4's salary range."

"Honestly, I am not at liberty to say, other than they are of pre-ban manufacture and legally obtained."

"I don't doubt that." He glanced down at his desk. "I'll inform you of my decision. You can keep the AP rounds. Little chance they'll penetrate the outer hull. You'll have to speak with Dr. Sevanto about the drugs."

He tapped a few more screens. "You've got a false screen, just after your record of graduation until your duty on Pluto. Bet you a buffalo nickel that's when you got your nukes."

How could he tell it was a false record? "Sorry, Chief, I don't own a buffalo nickel. I do have a Queen Elizabeth head penny."

"I have a Lincoln head, Keesay, and I wouldn't wager either lightly."

"Neither would I, Chief."

"Whatever you were into back then, it's what got you assigned to the *Kalavar*." I wasn't sure what he was getting at. There wasn't much to say as he scanned my files. "How much more trouble are you going to stir up?"

"None that I know of."

He didn't look convinced. "In my experience, Keesay, some people just attract trouble, intentional or not."

"I'll do my best to avoid it, Chief."

"I'm sure you will. But like I said, with some people it's just natural." The chief rested his hand on the edge of his desk. "Kind of like a raccoon."

"A raccoon? I've been called a lot of things. Never a raccoon."

"Not an insult. Just an observation."

"I don't see the connection."

Chief Brold leaned back and slid his red toothpick back into his mouth. "See, raccoons are pretty smart as far as animals go. But sometimes they get into places they don't belong. Get into mischief, intentional or not. Sometimes a lucky raccoon's activity goes unnoticed, or ignored. But, eventually, every raccoon gets the hounds set on him and he's in for a scrap. A raccoon's long-term survival depends on resourcefulness. And luck."

"And the determination of the hounds," I added. Maybe the chief had hunted raccoons, but I didn't see where he was going.

"So, Keesay, why would an R-Tech head out into space?"

"Restlessness. Adventure." Maybe the raccoon skin fit a little. "I'd like to be recruited by the R-Army GASF."

"This is one route," he said thoughtfully. "Believe it or not, this assignment just might increase your prospects." He glanced at his desk. "Senior Engineer McAllister's coming down the hall." He sat up, removed the toothpick. "Our little discussion before, Keesay. She's one hound you don't want on your trail."

"Noted, Chief." I stood and turned as the door slid open. In walked a slender girl, or woman, brimming with energy. Senior Engineer McAllister, or that's what her dull orange coveralls and nametag read, along with her shoulder stripes indicating specialties in software, hardware and electrical engineering. What surprised me was that a medium class transport would have a senior engineer competent in multiple areas. That paled, when it registered that such a qualified engineer appeared to be years younger than me.

Luckily she didn't take notice of my expression. Instead, she began to tear into the chief. "Security Chief Brold, did I not make it clear that the lab was to be secured?"

The chief replied in a laidback voice, "Yes, you did, Senior Engineer McAllister. That's why I directed Specialist Liu to stand guard until Specialist Club arrived."

"You sent your secretary! How marginally efficient of you." McAllister's small frame seemed barely capable of containing her emotions. On the other hand, her wild red braids were right on target. She might even be cute, when not spouting off.

Chief Brold sat down, and indicated for Engineer McAllister and me to do the same. "Engineer McAllister, Specialist Liu is up to the assignment. I appreciate your concern." He nodded toward me. "Specialist Keesay has been brought on to bolster our understaffed department."

I looked at her and said in a neutral voice, "Good to meet you, Senior Engineer." When she turned my way, I noticed that her eyes differed. The left was green, the right blue. The second thing I spotted was an immediate pupil contraction.

"You!" she accused.

Several long seconds passed. I unsuccessfully tried to recall ever meeting Engineer McAllister. With my recent run of luck, I prepared for a physical assault.

"Brold, you hired this man?" Her knuckles whitened as she gripped the chair.

"The company did, and I approved."

"Since when did Negral make it policy to hire murderers?"

Well, that narrowed it for me. Must have been the Colonization Riots.

Chief Brold said, "I'm not aware that Negral Corp supports a policy of hiring convicted felons for security positions." He leaned forward. "If you would like a transfer to personnel, McAllister, I can arrange it." His voice was low, and menacing. "Now, I believe you graced us with your presence because you had something to report? Get with it or get out."

She shot me an icy stare. "The newest member of your security staff had an advanced technology explosive device attached beneath his possession cart. Superficially, it appears of Chicher design, but the sensing mechanisms and inner components are more advanced. Not Umbelgarri or Crax caliber." Talking technology calmed her. "Information's sketchy on the V'Gun, but the sensors might be their design. The micro-explosive fusion device appears to be Felgan, at least superficially. No human components."

"Rare, smuggled parts," said the chief. "More difficult to trace."

But could narrow the field of suspect organizations. I started to express that observation, but thought better of it. The chief would realize it. Stardz must have planted it.

With a searing glance my way, McAllister continued. "Strong enough to blow through this transport's decks, and maybe breach the hull, if detonated close enough." She sat back and began to pick at her fingernails. "The reason I decided to confer with you here is the fact that the sensors, almost certainly set for partial facial scan, can penetrate most walls standard to transports." Her eyebrows furrowed. "Extremely low energy emission. Hardly registers, and I knew what to look for."

"What you're saying," said Chief Brold, "is that Specialist Keesay could trigger the device even by passing a deck below it?"

"Possibly. If it's set to scan for his image. It may have passive voice sensors. It may be set for more than just him." McAllister sat up straight again. "It's beyond my ability to analyze further with the resources available on the *Kalavar*."

Chief Brold nodded. "I'd imagine you took quite a risk determining that much."

"Limited," she said. "I recognized the potential hazard immediately, and relied exclusively on optical scans for my initial assessment. Some passive analysis devices, checking for radiation and various spectra information ruled out known corporate manufacturers. It's not configured for remote detonation." She leaned forward and placed a hand on the chief's desk. "In essence, the device and its components haven't been tampered with. And should remain intact."

"Agreed," the security chief said. "We can reasonably assume it's not set for you, Specialist Club and Specialist Liu."

"And the captain and Technician Schultz," said McAllister with a smile. "I tapped into the surveillance records to identify who walked by the lab before I had secured the device."

"Thank you for informing me of your unauthorized access."

"You're welcome. And, I also established a random distortion of all communications incoming to the lab facility. Set on my voice lock."

"Any recommendations before I inform the captain?"

"Yes, Chief. Either immediately detonate it or export it to a better equipped facility. Whoever ordered it planted is well connected, and financed." She glanced my way with a smirk. "If it had detonated, all we'd have found is fragments of Chicher components." She leaned forward to stand. "I'll send you the detailed report?"

"Good enough," said the chief. "Thank you for your expertise, Engineer McAllister."

Chief Brold and I stood as Engineer McAllister prepared to leave. "As for you, Specialist Keesay," she said. "I can see you have difficulty making friends. Not surprising. Whoever did over your face didn't do enough."

I shrugged.

"Just keep away from me." She turned to leave. "I hope no one else pays the price when they manage to finish the job."

As soon as the door closed, the chief pulled out a small plastic box with various wires and gyros. He plugged it into a power outlet, activating it.

"This," he said, "along with the regular security, should disrupt external surveillance." He checked the scrambler's settings. "Okay, Senior Engineer McAllister appears to be acquainted with you. Believes you're a murderer. Care to explain?"

"I don't recall ever meeting her, Chief. Given time I might." I'd confided quite a bit in Chief Brold. Might as well go a little further. He'd get the information from McAllister, if what I suspected was true. "I have never murdered anybody. It is possible that Senior Engineer McAllister made a recent reference to the Colonization Riots."

"You were involved in that incident?"

"I cannot confirm, nor will I deny your assertion, Chief. However, I would not be surprised if Engineer McAllister was a participant in some capacity."

"That explains a lot."

"Explains what?"

"I currently cannot explain anything. But I will confirm that you may not have been the target of an assassination attempt."

I could puzzle it out later. "Understood, Chief."

"So far today, Keesay, I've been two for two on hunches."

"My hiring by Negral and penchant for attracting hounds?"

"Affirmative, Specialist. Care to venture a guess as to Senior McAllister's first name?"

I looked to see if the scrambling device was still operating. "Maddog?"

He laughed. "Good guess. Try Nova."

"Fits. I'll do you a favor and try to avoid her."

"Do yourself a favor. One less hound, remember?"

"Right, Chief."

"Mer's outside. He'll escort you to your quarters. Stay there until instructed otherwise. I've got an urgent meeting to schedule with the captain." He escorted me to the door. "Your new communications gear will be sent there. Contact Specialist Liu in her office if you have any questions."

"Understood, Chief."

"Glad to have you aboard," he said, offering his hand.

CHAPTER 17

Like all R and I-Tech species, human efforts to obtain A-Tech designs and equipment are a high priority. Sometimes corporations and the government cooperate, but even such efforts are normally in vain. Even if a rare and long sought after piece of equipment is obtained, it is unlikely that it will be understood or even replicated by human engineers. As a matter of public record, unlike most corporate acquisitions, there are some weapon components acquired during the Silicate War that the brightest military engineers are still struggling to understand.

Mer led me to my quarters a few decks below. He was quiet, which seemed out of character for him. Maybe we both had a lot on our minds. He said that he'd stop back with a late lunch if I was still confined to quarters. Mer knew about my restricted movement. I made it a point to find out about him.

A simple thumbprint scan provided access to my quarters. Armor plating and inward construction reduced what had once been spacious travel accommodations, leaving them small and cramped. Parallel red conduits ran overhead. Maybe one of the maintenance tracks ran along the other side of the wall.

Mer had mentioned my roommate's name, Benjamin Cox. From what I could tell, Tech Cox either had few possessions or he'd stowed them. I couldn't even tell whether he used the top or bottom foldout bunk. One computer terminal rested behind a worn padded chair. A larger metallic recliner with patched cushions was the only other piece of furniture. I looked a little closer. Duct tape, freshly applied. My roommate just jumped up a notch.

I logged into my account, disabled the voice interaction, and immediately changed my password to 14~greengun-onE with a minimum three-second delay after the hyphen. It wouldn't foil a determined hacker, but included some annoying parameters. Most I-Techs don't have the patience for code-entering delays. Next, I added an iris scan for access to my quarters. I always avoided voice access, as serious throat infections could cause a glitch. With nothing else to do, I fumbled around in the system a bit. After about an hour, I had the basics down.

I had Level F clearance to all systems, except for Information and Records. My Level D security clearance in I&R allowed me access to crewmen's and passengers' front page files. I could then request more detailed information. Exactly what a C4 could expect.

I keyed in Stardz to find his file flashing, 'currently restricted.' I looked up manifests and transfer information. Everything on him was blocked. I was curious about Engineer McAllister, but thought better of even superficially exploring her file until I had a better handle on things. She'd certainly note my attempt and no sense in getting her even more riled for nothing.

I keyed in Elmer, and got a blank screen. I retyped Elmer and then tried Mer with the same result. I was beginning to wonder about my access, so I keyed in Chief Brold. A screen appeared with a picture and text identifying him as security chief of the *Kalavar*, along with inconsequential corporate information. At least I could access someone's file. I keyed in Benjamin Cox. His picture revealed a middle-aged Class 3 Maintenance Technician with short hair, big ears and a genuine smile. The text indicated he was on disability recovery, meaning our financial compensation was equally meager.

Finally, I brought up my file. I looked over what the chief had said was a false record. In reality, it was a fictitious interview and trial work record. It started several weeks prior to my early graduation and the Riots, until I was transferred to permanent stationing on Pluto two months later. What tipped him off?

As I read, my duty info file flashed green, hinting that I should attend to it, but numerous other questions pressed foremost in my mind.

I opened my duty file and scanned the routine section on general regulations and responsibilities. My duties included ship-wide roving patrols and security station monitoring as needed. My primary responsibly was to provide security and assistance support for a group of R-Tech colonists. Why they brought me aboard made a little more sense. What didn't make sense was a separate section that indicated I'd be paired with a sec-bot, if it arrived prior to departure. I couldn't locate any data on my primary responsibility. Not even one file on any of the colonists, just that there were eighty-nine. This part of my duty was either poorly planned or a last minute booking by Negral.

I rubbed my eyes. Since I'd need to study the regulations in detail, I sent Specialist Liu a request to borrow a hard copy. All ships normally kept one on hand. I doubted any I-Tech would want it.

I took a pen and a small pad from my pocket and jotted down questions for my immediate supervisor, Specialist Club. A breakdown of the colonists? Were they family units, individuals, mixed? Where would they be housed and what monitoring resources would I have available? Training and background would be helpful.

The list went on for two sheets, front and back. For decades before my birth they'd been calling for a paperless society. I did my best to undermine the effort. I'd stored fifteen pads of various sizes and several pens in my cart. I didn't consider using them for duty a waste of resources, but maybe I'd break down and get one of the electronic note pads. Some battles were too expensive to fight.

I logged off and looked around the austere room. I should've asked Mer to swing by the lavatory before dropping me off. Instead of focusing on that, I stretched out on the old recliner for a nap.

A determined buzz followed by Mer's voice interrupted my slumber. "You in there? Lunch time."

I checked my watch. Almost 1:00. It took me a second to get to my feet and open the door. "Just catching a nap," I said, stretching my bruised body. "More comfortable than it looks."

"I know," said the old maintenance worker, stepping in. "Benny keeps his place tidy."

"My roommate?" I asked. "Almost barren."

"Nah, Benny's okay. I just think he wanted to make a good impression."

"Or wanted to be sure I didn't steal anything."

"I'm sure that wasn't it." Mer winked, before stepping back out into the corridor. "He's pretty trusting. I kind of watch out for him. Lunch is in my room."

"Before we go anywhere, I need to hit the head."

"Thought you might," he said, pointing down the hall. "Twenty paces that way. Door's marked. I'm next door to you. But don't go anywhere else."

"Thanks." I hurried down the hall.

The facilities were divided for men and women. A scan of my V-ID provided access. There were three showers and sinks along with two urinals and toilets. The sinks didn't have timed shutoffs, but I was sure they were monitored. Despite the fact that all water was captured and recycled aboard an interstellar ship, it's still standard policy to conserve. The alternative risks overburdening the system.

Mer sat, waiting in his cluttered quarters. The room was twice the size of mine, and looked like he'd lived in it for decades. Memorabilia and knickknacks lined upper shelves. The lower tiers were laden with books. A standalone computer sat in one corner next to a pile of manuals, and below another full bookshelf. Six lit tanks set into a side wall caught my attention.

I strode over to them. "Wow, they let you keep fish? These are guppies, right?"

"Yep," Mer said, resting in a chair and eating a cold-cut sandwich.

"They're not fluorescent," I said, staring at the black-spotted males with sporadic coloring and the plain females. "What kind are they?"

He swallowed before answering. "Just plain old common guppies." He pointed to a tray and chair. "Sit on down and eat."

"Thanks. I don't believe I've seen that type before."

"Wouldn't doubt it. They're probably rarer than any fancy type you can name."

"I thought interstellar transport of animals, pets especially, was restricted?"

"It is."

I knew he was baiting me. "Are they sterile?" I didn't think they were with the different sizes swimming about.

"Nope."

"You have a permit?"

"Yep. Wouldn't want to break any law or regulation."

"You must have some pull, Mer."

He shrugged his shoulders. "More than some, less than others."

"More than most." I stared into the tanks, considering water I hauled in my cart. "Those tanks, that's a lot of water."

"Yep. Aren't you hungry, Kra?"

"Yeah, but it looks like you've got young fry *and* adults."

Mer set his tray aside and stood next to me. "The top two tanks hold males and females, separately. The middle two are for breeding pairs. See the dividers?"

I nodded. "You're breeding them now?"

He nodded. "And the bottom two are for fry and juveniles."

"They're live bearers right?"

"You know something about raising tropical fish?"

"Not really. I had a few goldfish as a kid. But I read about guppies in science." I walked back to my seat and picked up my sandwich. "Guppies were used to control aquatic parasites around the Glasgow Colony." I searched my memory. I'd inspected a wheeled transport with guppies on its manifest just before the Riots. "They were common guppies. Now I remember where I've seen them."

"In your science book?"

I took a bite of the sandwich. It was synthetic chicken salad. After a second, I nodded. "How do the developing young survive traveling in condensed space?"

"Actually, mostly in the wash," he corrected. "And not very well, but better than humans."

"Then why are you breeding them now?"

"Breeding them for our final destination."

"Then," I said, "those that do survive would be more apt to produce offspring resistant to the effects of condensed space?"

"Could be. I've just been picking the healthiest. The rest go into cold storage."

"Are there parasites on Tallavaster, like the Glasgow Colony's?"

"Something like that," he said, gazing at the fish. "We'll need as many as can be raised between now and our arrival."

"Still, you're selectively breeding them, right?"

"Seems so," he said. "Avoid inbreeding as much as possible." He shook his head. "But the facilities, as you can see, are limited."

"A few tank-fulls won't be much help, will they?"

"No, a few tank-fulls won't." He sat back down. "We've been putting them in cold sleep for quite some time."

"Oh," I said, thinking about what he meant by 'we.' I finished half my sandwich and dug into the red gelatin. Six tanks couldn't amount to much, unless it was a localized problem. “Do they do well in cold sleep?”

“Tested it once. Near one-hundred percent.”

“About the same as humans. Not bad.”

“It’s pretty good,” he said, “considering humans receive better treatment than these little critters.”

“So, common guppies are pretty hardy.”

“A lot more than their fancy glowing cousins.”

Something nagged at me. “Common guppies saved the Glasgow Colony, right?”

“Well,” said Mer, “at least its profitability.”

“Yeah, that’s where CGIG got its big start.”

Mer frowned. “Yep.”

He set his gelatin aside. I finished mine. After a moment I asked, “Must be decent profit in breeding the fish?” I gestured toward the wall. “A lot of water to be maintained. Kind of a joint venture between you and Negral Corp?”

“Hmmm. Yes, Kra, you might say that.”

“You’ve been on this vessel a while, and you have this big cabin,” I said, looking around.

“Actually, I was on this ship’s maiden voyage.” Mer’s voice trailed off. He looked at the floor and sighed. “Seems more than ten lifetimes ago.”

Most R-Techs are, to some extent, nostalgic. “It seems you’ve done well for yourself. Fish breeding must pay well.” Mer’s thoughts seemed to be elsewhere. “Confirms my belief that you don’t have to be an I-Tech genius to make it.” I finished the second half of my sandwich, sipped my juice, and relaxed watching the fish.

Finally, Mer snapped out of it. After rubbing his hands and clapping them once, he levered himself out of his chair. “Picked up some of your equipment.” He shuffled over to a small shoulder sack hanging next to his tool belt.

Just as he got there, the hand-held radio in his belt crackled. “Mer, this is Brold. Are you with Keesay?”

Mer picked up the set and winked. “As a matter of fact, Chief, I am. We’re just finishing lunch.”

“Did you pick up his communications equipment?”

“As a matter of fact, I did.”

“Have you delivered it to him?”

“As a matter of fact, Chief, I haven’t. Have you been attempting to contact him?”

“As a matter of fact, Mer, I have.”

“Thought so.” Mer cackled. “Anything you’d like me to relay?”

“Yes. After you hand over his communications equipment, tell him that all is clear. And that he’s to report to Specialist Club in the Control Room.”

“Mind if we finish lunch, Chief?”

"Doesn't matter to me. But it might to Keesay, if he keeps Specialist Club waiting."

"Gotcha." Mer replaced the hand radio and reached into the sack. "Here you go, Kra. One old-fashioned communication head set with belt attached light-weight power pack with send and receive booster adjustments." He pointed to a wall terminal obscured by clutter. "Instructions are on line."

It was standard issue equipment to R-Techs. "I've had training on these." I slipped it on my head, adjusted the earpiece and the mic around my cheek. "Has it been calibrated?"

"Yep. All the frequencies set. Just state the name of who you desire to contact in your call. The communications network will do the rest." Mer pulled out a security cap, an old-style baseball hat with the Negral Logo across the front. "Here, this will help hold it in place."

"Thanks," I said, slipping on the cap. "Sturdy, hard wired. Secure, I assume."

"Secure? Yes. And it'll get better reception than those microchip implants, and stronger broadcast than the collar mics."

"I'm sure of that. Let me try it out." I clicked it on. "Mer? Can you read me?"

He grabbed his radio. "Affirmative."

I adjusted the volume and gave him a thumbs-up. "Specialist Club, this is Specialist Keesay. I just received my communications equipment and will be reporting to you right away."

An immediate reply shot back. "Acknowledged."

"I'd better get moving, Mer. Don't want to keep Specialist Club waiting."

"No, you wouldn't," he said, shaking his head and shuffling back to his chair. "Think I'll catch a nap."

I had a hunch, so I asked, "Would you?"

"What?" he said, turning back. "Keep Club waiting?" He chuckled. "Have you met her?"

"Yes." I had a better question. "Could you?"

"What do you mean?" Mer asked, rummaging through his bag, apparently without success.

I tried a different track. "What's your assignment on this ship?"

"I told you before. I just go around and fix what needs fixing."

"But you said you were on this ship's maiden voyage. Are you a part owner?"

"Me, part owner? Nah." He tapped at his breast pocket before gently directing me toward the exit with his other hand. "You really want to keep Club waiting?"

"Not really," I said, turning. "Control is right next to the chief's office?"

"Yep," he said, extending his hand. "Here, you might want these back."

"What?" I asked, as he slapped a pair of 12-gauge shells into my hand.

"Now, time for my nap." The door slid shut.

I looked at the shells and headed toward the elevator. Twelve-gauge slugs. I looked closer. They were my popcorn nukes. How had Mer gotten them? How did he get authorization to return them? Maybe he was the owner of this transport? Maybe he was an associate of Field Director Simms? I was missing something. It was possible I'd been hit one too many times in the head. I pondered that as I hustled to meet with Specialist Club.

Before reaching Security Control, I attributed Mer's position on the *Kalavar* to three possibilities. He could be a relative of a Negral Corp board member. But that seemed less likely when his attendance on the maiden voyage was taken into consideration. He could be a retired officer of some sort, but that didn't seem to fit. The last solution, that he worked for intelligence, seemed remote. His age weighed heavily against it. On the other hand, it'd be an excellent cover, and reason for access to the maintenance sleds and ability to return my popcorn nukes. After all, Chief Brold seemed to approve the sled use at least. A mystery that had to wait.

The heavy-duty door opened after I nodded to the camera outside Security Control. Inside the deep, rectangular room sat Specialist Club, wearing what seemed to be her perpetual frown. The circles under her eyes had grown even deeper. I stepped in and she tapped a key, closing the door. She finished dictating log information into the nearest of the three computer consoles, summarizing the findings of the medical staff and clean-up crew. Basically, she established a hypothesis that supported Chief Brold's suggested cause.

Flat-screen security monitors covered every inch of wall space. Two stand-alone quantum computers covered the far wall opposite the door. Club swiveled her chair in my direction, briefly glancing at some of the monitoring screens before giving me a more studied appraisal than when I boarded.

"Reporting as requested, Specialist Club."

"Club will do in here." She pointed to a chair. "I see you have established security codes for your account."

"That is correct." I figured to stay formal until common sense dictated otherwise.

"The system rated them satisfactory. Better than I thought you'd come up with."

"Your point being?" I asked.

"Maybe my expectations aren't high, Keesay. But I'll give you a fair shake."

"That is appreciated," I said evenly. "I know how to competently implement proper security procedures."

"So it seems. That's good," she added. "With the shortage of personnel in our field, I had concerns the company might be less meticulous in recruiting."

"Maybe they were," I suggested, "but even a fisherman with low standards occasionally adds a fine catch to his stringer." She didn't seem to follow. "You've never been fishing?"

"Nope," said Club. "But I think I followed your idiom."

"Idiom?"

"Do you know what an idiom is, Keesay?"

"Yes, Club. Like scraping the bottom of the barrel."

"Excellent." She almost cracked a smile. "Seems we might have gotten a good catch."

"What do you mean?"

"Well, you came recommended. The chief and the XO seem to agree with the assessment. Your response just indicated that you're educated and that you're willing to question any statement which is less than accurate." She spun toward the console, tapped a key, and scanned several of the monitors as they switched views. "Think you'll be able to learn this monitoring system?"

"I believe so, with a little instruction. Looks similar to what I worked with on Pluto." I inspected the terminals and readouts. "Maybe a little more up to date." I scanned the walls. "More monitoring stations." I reexamined the controls and readouts, before looking back into her fatigued eyes. "Basic trouble shooting if there's a problem."

"We wouldn't expect you to do any of the technical work and you won't be spending that much time in here anyway. Negral contracted you to spend more time on the beat. Also, I requisitioned an ocular receiver-transmitter. It should mount on the brim of your cap just fine but we might get a more advanced one." She glanced down. "Those leather boots comfortable? You'll be logging a lot of kilometers."

"I'm up to the task, and so are they. You know, I have a second pair…somewhere."

She ignored the comment and instead followed a quick-moving figure across two screens. It resembled a kid in a brown jacket.

"Let's see what you know," she said, spinning around and cracking her knuckles. Again, she surveyed the monitors. "Roll your chair on over."

CHAPTER 18

Most alien races despise and avoid the Chicher, with similar sentiments accorded to the Umbelgarri. As such, the established relationship with the Umbelgarri and the growing contact with the Chicher makes a statement about the human race and its increasingly pariah status in the galaxy.

My meeting with Specialist Club lasted thirty minutes. I'm not a computer genius, but her overview of the security monitoring system was a whirlwind. Fortunately, I had experience on an antiquated version of the system. I was also provided with files on each of the eighty-nine R-Tech colonists. They were scheduled for recovery from cold sleep prior to transfer. Finally, Club gave me a user manual, an actual hard copy, of the standard grade security-bot that would accompany me on my rounds. She assured me it had arrived and was being assembled as we spoke.

We barely touched my list of questions. My request for an electronic note pad, and not a clam-shelled computer clip, wasn't taken well. Club dismissed me to determine any special arrangements I deemed necessary for the colonists.

After returning to my quarters to drop off the sec-bot manual, I discovered my cart resting inside. I snatched the keys hanging from the new padlock and checked my watch before leaving.

As I strode out, I nearly tripped over a small figure hurrying by. The brown fur and chatter of surprise left no doubt it was a Chicher. "Pardon me for our near collision." I said, before looking closer. "We have met before."

"Yes, Security Man," the Chicher said through its translator. "Our relocation trails have crossed."

I tried to recall the phrasing. "We shall have to take the time to nibble together on this long trip."

"Your company will be welcome as a surrogate pack member on this journey."

It took me a second to interpret. "You are the only Chicher aboard?"

"Yes. I will be without a pack member or a diplomatic counterpart."

"Well, you know where I am quartered when off duty," I said, pointing at my door. "You are welcome to stop by." I hadn't thought how my roommate would feel about this, but the words were already out.

Staring at my ID tag, he said, "I will transfer electrically to you my temporary nesting location."

"Good," I said, holding still and wondering if he could read my name. "I must be on my way, Diplomat."

"Your chatter is welcome, Security Man," the Chicher said before scampering away on all fours.

I made my way to the converted cargo area slated for colonist housing. Along the way I thought about the Chicher diplomat. He must have pull to obtain boarding permission so soon after docking. I wished I'd read more on the Chicher. But I'd never had an interest, before.

I made it to the upper decks, just below the current cargo bay where a section had been converted for temporary habitation. It looked dismal with a crude, low ceiling and dingy walls that reminded me of an old city parking garage. I explored further to learn it even spiraled into two levels, mimicking one of the old structures. Whatever I-Tech designed it was either ignorant or sadistic.

The setup lacked individual, or even family, privacy. Only two small sections had been walled off for men's and women's facilities. I'd have wagered as an afterthought because half the bolts anchoring the walls were loose or missing. The water hadn't been turned on, but the piping was poorly installed and bound to leak.

Maintenance had stacked old cots with crates on seven of the tables and associated benches. Piles of ash-brown clothing, and gray sheets and blankets sat organized on several tarps.

I pulled out my notepad and jotted down what had to be done. Weeks, let alone months, under such conditions guaranteed unruly behavior leading to trouble.

I'd bring my concerns to Club. I didn't know what type of pull she had, even if she cared. Maybe Mer, or my roommate, Tech Cox, could advise me on whom I might consult if Club didn't assist.

Next, I needed to determine a time frame for colonist boarding. I figured Medical would know the colonists' cold sleep recovery schedule. Besides, I wanted to pick up my impounded muscle relaxant.

All was quiet in Medical, so I moved to the nearest medical clerk. "Excuse me, is Dr. Sevanto available?"

The young lady looked up from her terminal to my ID tag, and politely smiled. "May I ask what it is about, Specialist Keesay?"

The navy blue bodysuit identified her as an administrative specialist. She probably knew I was connected to the earlier emergency in the lab. "Mainly about the colonists."

"Maybe I can help you?"

"You might, Specialist Tahgs," I said, leaning on the counter. "I'd like to know when the colonists are scheduled to board."

Specialist Tahgs smiled and entered the request. She pursed her lips before answering, "The eighty-nine R-Tech colonists are scheduled to be brought out of cold sleep in seventy-two hours. They will be monitored during recovery at the space dock's facilities." She stopped and read further before adding, "Those that survive will be transferred to us shortly thereafter."

"Those that survive?" I asked. "Do you expect there to be trouble?" Odds were, one or two might have a severe reaction to the chemicals used in recovery. *Maybe* one might die.

"I'm sorry, Specialist, but all I have is an addendum indicating an expected higher-than-normal level of fatalities in recovery."

"What does that mean?"

She consulted several more screens. "I'm not sure. It could mean any number of things."

"I understand, Specialist Tahgs." I jotted down her statement. "Is Dr. Sevanto available? He might have access to the information I need."

"If you will have a seat, I'll let him know."

I sat down and reviewed my notes. Ten minutes later Tahgs ushered me into Dr. Sevanto's lab. He sat perched on a tall stool, dictating information into a wall terminal. "How can I help you, Specialist Keesay?"

"In two, maybe three ways, Dr. Sevanto." I flipped through my notes. "It shouldn't take long."

Dr. Sevanto closed the file he was working on and gave me his undivided attention. I took advantage of it. "First, the eighty-nine R-Tech colonists are to be brought out of cold sleep within seventy-two hours. Working with them is one of my primary responsibilities. I've been informed of a higher than normal fatality rate expected in recovery. As a security official, is there anything that I should be made aware of?"

He gave me a sideways glance while thinking. "Some technical problems were detected after cold sleep was initiated."

"Technical problems?" He didn't answer. "Malfunctions in equipment? Improper preparation for cold sleep? Drug contamination?" I'd casted a wide net with no response. Not even a blink or flinch. "Should I discuss this issue with Chief Brold?"

"What I do know isn't much, Specialist. Speak with your superiors in Security."

I checked off some information. "Okay," I said evenly. "I have looked over the quartering area for the colonists. I believe that unless some modifications are made, there will be many justifiably unhappy R-Techs. Who on your staff could I consult with respect to this?"

"That depends, Specialist. What do you believe is wrong with the quartering?"

"It's not my intention to go through Medical with the issue. I'm new on board and just wanted to know who to consult, should the need arise."

"Understood. What do you see as problematic?"

"Unsanitary conditions," I said. "Lack of privacy. If they want to warehouse the colonists, they should just keep them in cold sleep."

"I believe they are to undergo some sort of agricultural training en route."

"Well, that's good. The less time they spend in their housing area, the better. But still."

"I get your point, Specialist. If you require, I will direct my opinion to your superiors." He got up from his perch. "Is that all?"

"Two more." I scratched my head. "I'm quartered with Maintenance Technician Benjamin Cox. A cursory check of his file indicated disability rehabilitation?"

"You haven't met Benny?"

"We haven't crossed paths yet. Is there anything I should be aware of?"

"Tech Cox was in a decompression accident." He paused. "And suffered a severe head trauma. He had neural and other reconstructive surgery, followed by rehabilitation."

"Okay. So there is nothing to watch for?"

"Well, Tech Cox appears a bit slow, and his gross and fine motor skills are somewhat impaired. It's likely he's already reported to the Mavinrom Dock Medical for evaluation, so you won't see him around for a few days."

"So his mental processes function just a little slower because they've been," I searched for a word, "rerouted?"

"Yes, that is one way to look at it." He shot a glance at the ship's chronometer.

"Last item, Dr. Sevanto." I slipped my notepad into a vest pocket. "I had a liquid drug compound impounded when my possessions were searched."

"You did," he said, nodding. "It was turned over to Medical for identification."

I waited. "I would like it returned."

"I see no reason for a Class 4 Security Specialist to have in his possession such a potent neuron inhibitor."

"It's not a controlled substance."

"It is a dangerous substance."

I placed my hand on my duty revolver. "This is dangerous as well. Negral Corp allows me to carry it."

"You have been trained and authorized to carry a sidearm. You do not have medical training."

"Isn't that the point of categorizing a substance as controlled?" I began to have doubts of winning this round. "Regulations allow financial reimbursement for confiscations of this nature."

"That can be arranged."

I wasn't going to make this easy. "I expect reimbursement equal to the cost at which the confiscated substance was purchased." I stared at him. "I purchased the concentrated Triskiseral while stationed on Pluto."

"You have a record of the purchase, Specialist?"

"As I said, Dr. Sevanto, it was legally obtained for 393 credits. I assure you, I have a verifiable record of its purchase price."

"I am unable to authorize reimbursement for three times the value of a medication."

"You can." I was sure that Dr. Sevanto ran a clean shop, but nobody likes investigators checking into files. "It will send up a red flag calling for an explanation to corporate HQ."

"Security Specialist," he said, "do you consider it wise to press such an issue with the head of Medical on a ship to which you're assigned?" He sat back on his stool, confident he'd just uttered checkmate.

"Medical Director, do you consider it wise to cheat the security specialist responsible for eighty-nine R-Tech colonists?" I let it sink in a fraction of a second. "Colonists who will likely be less than cooperative after weeks of substandard living conditions?" I could live with a stalemate.

"I am confident you will see to the correction of those unsatisfactory conditions."

"I will do my best." I measured my words. "Medical appears well staffed. Security is not. Like you, I have a large number of duties. Unlike you and your staff, however, I'd bet that many of the colonists likely to visit Medical are less than model citizens."

"You wouldn't be threatening negligence of duty?"

"I am neither a moron nor an incompetent, Doctor," I said flatly. "Yet you deem to treat me as one. I assure you, in my list of duties, the priority of escorting colonists to Medical and waiting while they are treated isn't high."

"I could speak with Chief Brold on this issue. I think you know those results." He waited a few seconds. "But I'll give you a chance. Convince me. Why do you need the Triskiseral?"

"If you insist," I said, preparing to unbuckle my belt. "But this will take a second."

"I've already given you more time than I intended." He crossed his arms. "But even if you don't convince me, I'm confident it'll be interesting."

I loosened my belt that held my holster and equipment, before reaching down my coveralls. I pulled out my protective cup. "See, I can tell by your expression your last statement has been confirmed." I disassembled the backing and handed it to Dr. Sevanto. "Note the micro-syringe loaded in the shallow area. That holds Triskiseral. If I get kneed or punched in the groin, a magnetic pulse propels it forward through the small hole, injecting the striking appendage."

"Does it work?"

"It did, once." I smiled. "Except the nerve agent wasn't fast-acting enough."

He looked more closely. "Is it patented?"

"Yes," I said. "Just not a common item."

He handed it back. "So what you are saying, Specialist Keesay, is that the concentrated Triskiseral is for use in duties directly related to your corporate assignment?"

"That is how it should be interpreted," I said while replacing the cup.

"And why didn't you indicate this when you requested the return of the Triskiseral?"

I adjusted my belt. "It shouldn't have been necessary."

"I don't know you well enough to make that judgment."

"But you know Chief Brold," I said. "If he thought I was incompetent, would he have allowed me on board? And if Negral Corp overruled him, I'm confident that as head of Medical, you would've been informed." I checked my gear. "If not by him, then by the XO."

"And if I question your competence, I am in fact questioning his?"

"That's how I interpret it."

"Interesting line of thought," Dr. Sevanto said. "Although, whenever possible, I prefer to make my own judgments. Don't you?"

"I do."

"I don't hold the incident with Tech Stardz against you. But the abrasions and contusions around your face and hands I question." He crossed his arms and waited.

"Fair enough. Some were received in the aftermath of an attempted theft. They were mistakenly inflicted by over-zealous security, who also preferred to make their own judgments." He raised an eyebrow and nodded. "The others," I continued, "were delivered by a colonial marine nicknamed Pillar." His smile followed mine. "You have the transferred medical reports which can confirm this. The first bruising was in the line of duty. I will defer to your judgment on the second."

He grabbed a nearby computer clip. "You may pick up the Triskiseral tomorrow. See Administrative Specialist Tahgs." He placed his arm on my shoulder and led me out. "And try to avoid running into bulkheads, or pillars."

It was a lame joke, but I laughed anyway.

CHAPTER 19

While many languages remain in use on Earth, especially in R-Tech dominated pockets, English prevailed as the dominant corporate and, by default, intra-colonial language. This is because the majority of scientific research continues to be recorded and published in English. Although not easy to learn and comprehend, especially by alien diplomats, corporations determined retaining it more practical than implementing change.

My alarm startled me from a troubled sleep. Normally I dreaded dreams that recounted my participation in the Colonization Riots. This morning was an exception. The first thing I did was enter in my electronic notebook a reminder to mention it to the chief.

The last three days had passed quickly. I checked the rest of my schedule. A morning security meeting; the first one with the entire staff. Next, I was to accompany Dr. Sevanto to the dock while the colonists were brought out of cold sleep. After that, I was to check on the modifications to the colonists' area.

I wasn't the only one getting an early start so I skipped most of my exercise routine. I could work out later. After a hurried breakfast I arrived five minutes early and took a seat in Specialist Liu's office. She smiled politely and went back to work. Club entered with a tall, lean man a little older than me. His ID tag read Frost. He carried a military issue MP pistol, stun baton and a light-duty hand laser that was good for maybe three close-range shots.

Before they sat down I got up. "Good morning."

Frost said nothing. Club replied with a nod, then sat, leaned back, and closed her eyes. Frost took out a palm computer clip and tapped away. I pulled my pocketknife and cleaned my fingernails.

A moment later a muscular, heavy browed man wearing tan coveralls sauntered in and sat next to me. His gray-green armband identified him as auxiliary security.

"Greetings, Keesay," he said. "Anatol Gudkov. Glad to have you on board."

"Nice to meet you, Maintenance Tech Gudkov." I offered my hand.

He shook and chuckled. "The more Sec-Specs they hire, the less I have to cover."

"Prefer your other duties?"

"Only an aux because of a stint at a penal colony, and failure not to volunteer." He grinned at the admin specialist. "Liu, heard they might bring another sec-spec on. You know anything?"

"Can't confirm that one, Gudkov," she said, still engrossed in her work.

"You, Club?"

Eyes still closed she shook her head.

"You just came from the dock, Keesay?"

"Correct. But I wasn't impressed with what I saw."

Frost chimed in. "Shortage everywhere. Give it up, Gudkov. You're stuck."

"What do you know, Frost?"

Frost went back to his clip without response.

Gudkov opened his mouth to say something more when the door slid open. A woman and two men entered. All three were armed like Frost, but the lean, dark-skinned man's coveralls were creased and worn across his right shoulder. It mimicked my coverall's telltale sign of a rifle sling. The rifleman stood next to me. "Hey, Keesay," he said, looking down at my fading bruises.

I stood, read his tag and offered my hand. "That's correct, Nist."

"Go in for that old stuff I see." We shook briefly and he slapped my shoulder. "Heard about you."

Gudkov cut in, "Nist, you know anything about new sec-spec hires?"

"Now, why would I know anything about that? I was on leave." He turned his back to Gudkov and said to me, "We'll talk later."

I sat down, adjusted my gear, and began to ponder how Specialist Club armed herself. Specialist Liu stopped her work. The door to the adjoining office opened. "Come on in, team." We all moved at Chief Brold's order. Six folding chairs supplemented the two cushioned, resulting in cramped conditions. Liu and Club took the good chairs. I sat between Frost and Club.

The chief tapped a key on his desk, closing the door. He tapped another. "Let's get started." Liu pulled out a large clip and began recording.

"We have one new member. Class 4 Security Specialist Krakista Keesay, stand up." Chief Brold began to his right. Each nodded as they were introduced. "Zabden Frost, Dorian Ross. You know Li Liu and Joyce Club. Anatol Gudkov, Faxtinian Muller and Larcher Nist." He paused and I sat down. "Keesay comes to us from stationing on Pluto. And for those of you who're interested, the XO rated him a 6.4 on his diversion assignment. That tops everybody but Club. And doubles Gudkov."

It took me a half a second to recall my meeting with Lt. Commander Devans. It *had* been planned. Whatever the measuring criteria, I did well enough.

Slipping a red toothpick from his mouth's corner, Chief Brold glanced at his agenda. "You all can get acquainted on your own time. On to business." He paused. "Hope those who had leave enjoyed it. Those still scheduled, it'll be just as short. Soon enough we'll be several months hurtling through space in this steel can."

Several groans followed but it couldn't be worse than warehouse duty.

"Club and I've worked out a tentative duty schedule. Nist, you're our liaison with the marines. Keesay, you're assigned to the colonists. Gudkov, sec-bot maintenance and relief duty in the Control Room. Frost and Ross, passenger support. Muller and Club are primaries in Control. Liu, administrative. Everyone but Liu will be on roving patrol, especially around engineering." He paused. "Any questions thus far?"

Gudkov stood. "Chief, I heard that the company might provide more assistance."

"Still angling?" The chief shot a glance over to Club.

"Mer's gone planetside," she said, standing to address us, "and came up empty. Maybe on the dock, but even if he does, you'll still be part of the team."

She continued in a low tone. "I know we're short. Everybody is. Negral is doing the best they can. We've got the marines to take some stationary watch, if needed." She looked over at Gudkov before sitting. "We have sec-bots to supplement our efforts."

"How is that project going?" asked the chief.

"Slow," said Gudkov. "The three we got were less than preassembled. And the reprogramming protocol established by Senior Engineer McAllister is, well, time consuming."

"I'm sure it is. When will you be finished?"

"They're assembled, Chief. The first has been programmed and I'm awaiting evaluation from the engineering department."

The chief glanced toward Liu. "Chief," she said, "the engineering department has placed priority on the special maintenance project."

He acknowledged her statement with a nod. "Gudkov, you may have a forty-eight hour leave after this meeting, provided your primary supervisor approves." Everyone but Gudkov frowned, or held a straight face.

"Liu, recheck the passenger list. Make sure we have all available background downloaded. Ross, check the manifest and monitor the loading of the corridor cargo pallets. Muller, inspect the scientific survey vessel loaded in the cargo hold. Then go on leave. Forty-eight hours." Some activity on his desk distracted the chief. "Keesay, you're to meet Dr. Sevanto at the main docking hatch. Accompany him while he monitors the colonists' cold sleep recovery." Brold surveyed us. "Any questions? Those on duty, same time tomorrow. Dismissed."

Everyone filed out except for Liu, who gathered the folding chairs. Club stood aside, waiting to speak with the chief.

"You're keeping the doc waiting, Keesay."

"I know, Chief, but I think you might want to hear this." I glanced at Club and Liu.

"Club, assist Liu and report back in five." They exited. "Okay, Keesay," he said, sitting down. "What's burning your tail?"

"Well, Chief, I recall where I encountered Engineer McAllister."

"This better be good to keep Dr. Sevanto waiting."

"If my memory is accurate, she remembers me from an action I took while assigned to, a duty." I awaited acknowledgement before I continued.

"It was during a confrontation with a hostile mob. I was part of a small security contingent and we were forced to engage. I recall clubbing her with the butt of my shotgun. Mismatched eyes, red hair, same face."

"Hardly qualifies you as a murderer."

"I bayoneted a young man next to her when he pulled a sonic blade. She went to him, then for the blade." Chief Brold frowned as I continued. "I was in full riot gear, but close enough to be identified."

The chief ran his hand from his chin to the back of his neck. "You certain of this?"

I thought back hard, reviewing the unpleasant experience. "It was chaos," I said, placing a hand on the cushioned chair. "We'd been ordered to hold. They'd sniped our C1 along with two others. We were on high ground, no cover." I took a steadying breath. "We were there for show. I took command. We couldn't retreat so I ordered us to close." I saw it all again. "They fell back, then surged."

"I read the reports," the chief said. "Viewed the holos. It was bad."

"We all," I started. "We were a diversion. A sacrifice to pull the ire of the mob. Of the public." My back stiffened. "I put down at least fourteen rioters. Wounded dozens. It could've been any one of them. But I think it was." I paused. "The bayonet wound took him square in the chest. He was one of the fourteen. She was next to him."

"Understood, Specialist." He tapped at his desk and spoke into his collar. "Dr. Sevanto, I have detained Specialist Keesay. He will be there shortly."

I forced the images back into their dark corner. "That is all to report, Chief."

"Gives me something to chew on," he said. "She's a little older than you'd guess." I turned to go but he signaled. "Keesay, speculate for me. Is McAllister anti-Phib?"

An odd question, I thought, but answered anyway. "Hard to tell, Chief. Factions were there for half a dozen reasons." I scratched my head. "She was among one of the more militant. Could be." Maybe not so odd of a question. "Definitely anti-ME though."

He nodded. "Steer clear of Senior Engineer McAllister."

"The *Kalavar* is barely medium class, Chief. But I'll do my best."

"You'd better, or your pelt may be tacked up on her wall."

I nodded once, recalling our past conversation. Wasn't cornering a raccoon risky business?

He guessed my thoughts. "That wasn't a suggestion." He tapped the door open. "Now get to Dr. Sevanto, like yesterday."

After adjusting my communications gear for full capacity send and receive, I sent an electronic message to O'Vorley, informing him that a *Kalavar* representative might be on board recruiting. It took me several minutes longer than it should have, so I double-timed it.

Dr. Sevanto dragged his eyes from me to the chronometer. "We're on a schedule. Theirs, not ours."

"Understood, Doctor." Dock security waved us through. I fell into step. "Security Control."

"This is Control," Club answered.

"Just checking my gear, *Kalavar*. I'm onboard the Mavinrom Dock."

"Signal's strong. Shouldn't require dock relay."

"Acknowledged, *Kalavar*. Out." Dr. Sevanto's set a brisk pace so no need to workout later. We headed to the lower decks. "We're not going to Medical?"

"No, Specialist. The recovery area is elsewhere." We turned. "I sent Administrative Specialist Tahgs ahead to check on Maintenance Tech Cox before coordinating with the recovery staff." After a few more steps he asked, "What do you know about cold sleep?"

"Very little, Doctor. I know that chemicals are injected to affect the cell metabolism. Complex sugars too? Alters the cellular fluid."

"Cytoplasm. Go on."

"Cytoplasm. So that when put to sleep and the temperature is lowered, the cell structure isn't damaged."

"Is that all?"

"I hear it makes you ill."

"In recovery," he said. "Actually the catalyst which initiates and accelerates, thawing, has several side effects." He pointed. "Turn here. Once activated, its residual components cause fever and severe muscle ache. Some nausea."

"My knowledge comes from reading journals and viewing still photos." He nodded. I asked, "What are the tubes in the stomach, nasal cavity and colon for?"

"They're inflated after induced sleep, but prior to cold sleep," he said flatly. "So that activators can be pumped in and released to the body core and vital areas more rapidly."

"That simple?"

"Actually, no. You received the layman rendition."

"Why aren't there holos of the procedure?"

"Because, as you're about to see, recovery is, shall we say, unpleasant." We stopped at an elevator. "It isn't advertised because full knowledge might discourage its use."

"So, there are few repeat customers." If they can afford it, I assessed silently.

"Actually, once in the system, the chemicals remain for months. And after the first reaction, antibodies reduce the catalyst's side effects."

"The colonists shouldn't be able to cause trouble in their condition. Correct?" He nodded once. Maybe now was my chance to get some answers.

"So, what am I there for?"

He lowered his voice. "Recall our previous conversation?"

"I brought it up with Specialist Club when discussing the colonists' quartering. She said she'd forward the query to Chief Brold. I'm confident she did."

"As before, I cannot discuss it." I noted his casual glance around.

"Understood."

"I expect there to be severe reactions to the catalyst, especially with this group."

"Understood," I said, looking him in the eye. "The colonists are my assignment. I will watch the proceedings carefully."

We worked our way down. Dr. Sevanto was sure in his route. I commented, "Very little foot traffic down here."

"We're almost there," he said, before speaking into his collar. "Specialist Tahgs." He slowed. "Specialist Tahgs." After about ten more steps he stopped. "You try."

"Specialist Tahgs." I changed settings, patching through the dock's communication network. "Specialist Tahgs." I looked at him. "Must be a malfunction." I went to maximum boost, send and receive. "Specialist Tahgs." I shook my head and keyed a diagnostic. "They assured me this set is superior to implanted chips."

We continued walking. I tried, "Maintenance Tech Cox," and shrugged. "Maybe you could contact Medical or the recovery area?"

Before he could, I grabbed his shoulder. "I'm getting something." I listened, readjusting. "Thought I heard something."

"Can you replay?"

I grabbed my com-set and set it to replay the last ten seconds. I heard a faint sound. "Maybe nothing, let's go." We moved on.

"Mavinrom Dock Medical, this is Dr. Sevanto of the *Kalavar*." He listened. "Has Administrative Specialist Tahgs reported in?" He slowed. "Your signal's weak. Acknowledged." He looked at me. "About thirty minutes ago."

I held up a finger and motioned for silence. I heard a faint, female voice. "Help...no." Then, a deeper muffled voice growled, "Shut up. No one can hear you. Now talk." A muted scream followed.

I kept my voice low. "*Kalavar* Security. Priority one." Dr. Sevanto looked at me. I waved him off.

"Priority one acknowledged."

"Club, run this message. What do you make of it?" I keyed the command to replay the faint message.

"Received, Keesay, stand by." Five long seconds passed. "That's Admin Tahgs! What's your location?"

"On the dock with Dr. Sevanto." I looked around. "Deck thirty-nine, yellow sector. Approaching recovery area for the colonists." I looked to the doctor who nodded affirmative. He started to say something but I raised my index finger.

"Computer says it's her signal," Club said. "Electronic interference. You must be close."

"Acknowledged."

Chief Brold cut in. "We're coordinating with dock security. Keep moving, Keesay. Keep sending."

"Understood." I released the holding strap for my revolver and signaled Dr. Sevanto to follow. I picked up the signal again.

"I don't know," Tahgs said, distraught, maybe crying.

"Signal's stronger, Keesay. Keep going."

"Understood, Chief." I looked to Dr. Sevanto. "It's Tahgs. She's nearby and in trouble." I grabbed and extended my stun baton. "You know how to use this?"

He shook his head so I explained. "Stun baton. Push here to activate. Top two-thirds, anything you smack will get a charge." I handed it to him. He was wide-eyed, but steady when he took it.

"Nooo."

"Signal's fading, Keesay. You passed it."

I looked down the corridor, hoping we were on the correct level. We'd only gone about twenty yards. "Acknowledged," I whispered. Dr. Sevanto took the hint, his jaw clenched. I checked my com-set's readout and noted a rise in interference, a drop in reception. I pointed at the door, then waved Dr. Sevanto back.

"I think I found it, Chief. Door code is level thirty-nine, access door Y one zero zero eight."

"Some strong signal dampener, Keesay. We've coordinated with dock security. Their signal may be compromised. Will explain later. Expect to move faster than instructed. You have Full Corporate Authority."

"Class 4 Specialist, this is Mavinrom Dock Security."

"Receiving, dock security."

"Be advised, we are dispatching a patrol to investigate communication anomaly. ETA fourteen minutes. We have jurisdiction. Proceed to original destination without delay."

"Acknowledged. On the way." I looked at the doctor. "We've got twelve seconds. Stand there." I pointed about five feet to the right of the door. "Tahgs is in trouble. We have Full Corporate Authority, so set the baton on full." I drew my revolver and cocked it. "I'll go in. Anyone comes out you don't recognize, take them down."

I crouched on the left side, zeroed out my wrist dampener, and tapped my com-set selecting alternate transmission scramble. "*Kalavar*, I'll be going in." It would've been nice to know the dimension or room type but if transmissions were compromised, any communication could be a tip-off. "Will provide continuous transmission."

"Still receiving, Keesay," Chief Brold said. "Acknowledged and good luck."

The door began to cycle open, then slid shut. Damn, so much for surprise, I thought. No time to go through the *Kalavar*. "Dock Security, boost signal or something, the door tried to open then closed!"

"Right! Help is on the way!"

Move or Tahgs is finished, pounded in my thoughts. Three seconds later the door slid open, followed by MP fire pelting the opposite wall.

Despite this, I popped a quick look inside and pulled back. A second burst clipped the doorframe and opposite wall. Half a second later I'd analyzed. Small room. One man shielded behind Tahgs, next to a prone man. One standing to the right of the entrance. No time. I hoped my new vest and armored uniform worked.

I stood, spun in, and fired on the man near the door. He opened up on me, clipping my right shoulder, maybe penetrating my uniform. My round took him in the neck. Ears ringing from firing my revolver, I knelt and thumbed back its hammer. Tahgs struggled with a large man in a security uniform holding an MP Pistol. I recognized him. "Freeze, Dribbs!"

Tahgs tried to break away but was no match for the turncoat. Dribbs shot her in the midsection. Before he could shoot again, I leveled my revolver and fired. His head snapped. Blood plumed from his temple as he staggered back, dropping the slumping Tahgs. I cocked again and took aim while the dazed Dribbs instinctively squeezed off rounds. One whizzed past my ear. My bullet took him in the face, bringing him down hard.

I leapt forward and examined the prone man with a Negral Logo on his tan uniform. "Dr. Sevanto! In here!" I pointed to Tahgs while scanning the room. The first man I'd shot lost his struggle to stem the blood flowing from his neck. "Dock Security, send medical assistance immediately. Two friendlies, two bad guys down." I couldn't hear an acknowledgment because my ears were still ringing. It'd been a long time since I fired without a dampener.

Dr. Sevanto tossed my baton aside and rushed to Specialist Tahgs while I checked out the maintenance man. I called to Dr. Sevanto, "Tech Cox has a pulse, lump on the back of his head. Looks like a flesh wound to the right calf."

The doctor hardly looked up. "Keesay, I can't get through to the *Kalavar*. Check out those clips on the crate." It was a good thing he yelled.

"Right," I said, and moved to the crate. "*Kalavar*, bad guys eliminated. Tahgs is down. Cox is down. Sevanto administering aid." A cord ran from a larger computer clip to a smaller one stamped with the Negral Logo. Programming gibberish flashed across both blood-spattered screens. "*Kalavar*, send a software engineer. They're trying to access Specialist Tahgs's computer clip. Please advise."

"Your signal is still weak. Nist and Muller are on the way. Dr. Miller and a med team are right behind." In the background Club called for McAllister and Gudkov to report.

Dr. Sevanto had rolled Tahgs on her side before tearing open her vest and jumpsuit, trying to examine the exit wound. She was cooperative but grimacing. "Where's that medical team?" he asked.

I took my bayonet and sliced through Tahgs' garments. "Reportedly on the way."

"Thanks. Clean exit."

"Here." I offered him my handkerchief. "It's clean."

He pressed it into the bleeding exit hole and rolled her back over.

"Report, Keesay," came through my headset about the same time as dock communication chatter broke in.

I adjusted my set to ignore the chatter. "*Kalavar*, Dr. Sevanto has stabilized Tahgs. No backup yet. Dock or ours."

"They've got other troubles," the chief said. "How about the computers?"

I walked back over. "Bad guy's larger one displays an error message. Tahgs's screen keeps flashing in pulsating red and orange, 'I Super Nova. You Super Loser.'"

Chief Brold could hardly keep from laughing. "That's Engineer McAllister's work."

Dr. Sevanto commenced communication with the dispatched med team as a dock C3 Sec-Spec and Private Yizardo rushed in. "Report, Specialist," ordered the anxious sec-spec.

"All secure," I said to the muscular C3. "Two captives injured. Two offenders eliminated, including Specialist Dribbs." The single curl of blonde, almost white, hair on the C3's forehead bounced as he looked where I pointed. "Quite a delay."

"We had three sec-bots go rogue just after you called in." He stepped toward the computers.

"Do not disturb the evidence," I said, blocking his path.

"This is Mavinrom Dock jurisdiction, Class 4 Specialist."

"Individuals employed by Quinn Mining abducted and assaulted Negral Corp personnel assigned to the *Kalavar*." I placed my hand on my revolver. "I have been granted Full Corporate Authority."

"Listen, Relic, I— "

Before he finished, I had my revolver drawn and cocked. "Do not disturb the crime scene, Chip." His MP pistol hadn't cleared its holster. We locked eyes.

Private Yizardo warned, "He'll kill you, Specialist Haxon."

The C3 risked a glance. "Whose side are you on?"

"Neither, I'm simply military support," said the marine. "This relic here is O'Vorley's friend. Didn't you watch the security holo of him caving in someone's skull?" Haxon's pupils widened. Yizardo added, "He wasn't scared of Pillar. What makes you think he's scared of you?"

Haxon stepped back, lifting his hand from his pistol. I kept mine drawn. "Negral Corp appreciates your cooperation." Dr. Sevanto and Specialist Tahgs began to breathe again just as Nist and Muller arrived.

"Keesay, report," said Nist.

"Area secured. Crime scene integrity maintained. Dr. Sevanto is awaiting medical support."

"Why is your firearm still drawn then?"

Yizardo cut in, "He doesn't seem to trust local security, or..."

"Not now, Yizardo," said Nist. "Keesay?"

"I was granted Full Corporate Authority. An abduction and assault was perpetrated on Maintenance Tech Cox and Admin Specialist Tahgs." I pointed at the two corpses with my revolver while watching Haxon. "By individuals employed by Quinn Mining. Specialist Haxon moved toward the computer clips, possible motivation for the crime, and risked disturbing the crime scene." Holstering my revolver, I glared at Haxon. "I stopped him."

"Understood, Specialist. I request transfer of Corporate Authority to me."

"I transfer Full Corporate Authority to you, Security Specialist Nist."

Four med techs from the *Kalavar* entered with two grav beds in tow. "Dr. Miller," said Dr. Sevanto, "proceed to the cold sleep recovery and observe. I'll take care of Janice and Benny."

"Keesay," said Nist. "Accompany Dr. Miller. Relieve Specialist Club and inform her I need her expertise here. Muller, escort Dr. Sevanto and his patients as soon as they're ready. Specialist Haxon, stand over there," he pointed. "Observe, if you desire."

"I protest," he said.

"I don't care," said Nist.

Dr. Miller took that cue to exit. I followed, shutting down my com-set's continuous send. "Next time, I am going to carry more than just a revolver." Dr. Miller looked at me quizzically as I replaced the three spent rounds.

We reached the recovery area in less than two minutes. A posted marine leveled his carbine. "This area is closed. Turn around and leave."

"We're from the *Kalavar*," started Dr. Miller.

"Specialist Club," I called into my set. "There's a colonial marine barring our entrance. I am here to relieve you and Dr. Miller is here to assist in recovery."

"You're not with Dr. Sevanto?"

"No. I'm accompanying Dr. Miller per Dr. Sevanto's directive."

A second later the marine stepped aside and we entered the low-ceilinged, well-lit room. Three med techs from the *Kalavar* tended to five colonists, four men and one woman. The pale colonists sat on cots, wrapped in loose garments, sweating and shaking. One male colonist began dry heaving. The heavy, average-looking woman peered at me before falling into another fit of tremors. I'd expected five times the medical staff on hand.

"This way, Specialist," directed Dr. Miller. He approached an occupied restoration table. Two techs were preparing to pump fluid into a thin, ten or eleven year-old boy. "Any difficulties?" asked Dr. Miller.

The oldest technician, wearing a white smock and plastic gloves, replied. "The *inhibiting* agent has nearly neutralized the contaminant." He seemed to wait for a reaction. None came. "The initial seizures are less than twenty seconds in duration. Subsequent seizures continue to diminish in duration and intensity."

"Stop," said Dr. Miller. "Why wasn't the recovery procedure held until Dr. Sevanto's arrival? Where are the dock medical support personnel?"

The med tech stammered, "I, I got here after, the step down had already been—"

Specialist Club strode over from a monitoring console and took Dr. Miller aside. Although she wasn't winded, perspiration said Club had made quick work to get down here. Dr. Miller returned and said, "Continue recovery procedure."

Observing, I moved toward the holding area where I watched two dock med techs unseal a metallic environmental control tube and place a ghostly-white body onto a grav bed. The burly colonist lay on his back, arms and legs slightly spread with slick jell over his closed eyes. The same jell covered his eyebrows, short brown hair, beard, and fingernails. Even in sleep the man projected a disgruntled, if not foul, disposition. They moved him on the table next to the boy.

It took me a second to connect the face with the file. Carver Potts. I'd scanned all of the files, but hadn't found the time to review each in its entirety. His I recalled. The file indicated previous experience in citrus fruit, mainly in manual pruning and harvesting. Potts lost his position when the corporate farm folded. If the colonists were to work in agriculture, he had reasonable qualifications. Portions of his corporate interview indicated Potts was a chronic complainer with several minor corporate law infractions. He applied to Negral as a colonist shortly after his job had been eliminated. Like most colonists, he wanted a new start, but he also wanted to avoid a substantial fine for theft of corporate property. Negral pulled some strings for him. I knew he wouldn't appreciate it.

"Keesay," called Specialist Club. "Chief Brold just requested your presence on the *Kalavar.*"

I raised an eyebrow.

"Senior Engineer McAllister is assisting Nist. I'll take care of things here." I whistled at her heavy-duty laser pistol and shouldered power cell. She smiled. "I only wear this on special occasions. And if you don't report to medical and speak with the chief, the next special occasion will be your flogging."

"Is it the sidearm or the thought of my pain that made you smile?"

"With you onboard, Keesay," she said, "I suspect I'll be smiling a lot."

"I hope it's the firearm," I said, reevaluating the high-powered weapon. "That cost would be less burdensome, at least for me." I held up both hands. "I'm on my way."

I turned and strode toward the door. To my left, supported by Dr. Miller, the female colonist stood over the recovering boy. They began pumping fluids into both ends. I said a quick prayer and exited.

Corporal Smith leaned against the hatch, feigning relaxation. "Found trouble again?"

It was hardly a question. "Correct."

Smith noted the condition of my duty coveralls. "Lucky again? What's the password?" Before I could say anything he stepped aside. "Get your ass onboard."

Once onboard the *Kalavar*, my adrenaline shut down. I adjusted my com-set's send and receive strength. I slowed, replaying events. "Specialist Nist." I waited.

"Keesay, this is Nist."

"Could you pick up my stun baton? I lent it to Dr. Sevanto."

"We scanned it in as yours. Already taken care of. Out."

Chief Brold stood waiting outside Control. "Follow me, Specialist." He spoke into the surveillance camera. "J-J-2-9-4-falsestart two." The door opened. Inside a marine sat at the monitoring station. "Private Slavkonski, report."

"All quiet, Chief. No one has boarded except *Kalavar* personnel. Specialist Muller escorted Dr. Sevanto and the medical team along with two patients. The only other," he said nodding to me, "Specialist Keesay. All monitoring stations remain clear and normal."

"Thank you, Private. You are relieved. Report to forward engineering. Assist Private Mohammin and Parks."

"Right, Chief." He grabbed his carbine and left.

Chief Brold took a seat and began to monitor. "Report, Keesay."

I described the sequence of events, answering a few questions.

"Why did you pull your gun on Specialist Haxon?"

"As I indicated, Chief, an abduction and assault had been perpetrated on—"

He cut me off. "I know that, but why pull your gun?"

"I had Full Corporate Authority."

"And that went to your head?" he asked, ignoring the monitors.

"No, Chief. I assessed the situation. I had two Negral personnel down, one treating. I'd lent my stun baton to Dr. Sevanto. If it came to unarmed combat, even if I prevailed, the crime scene would've been disturbed. In addition, both perpetrators wore Quinn Mining attire. Dribbs, I knew was with dock security. I'd encountered him twice on the dock while he was on official duty, so at least his uniform was authentic. Transmissions were suspect so it was possible the conspiracy, if you want to call it that, extended further than Dribbs and the other downed perpetrator. Therefore, I trusted no one but Negral personnel."

"There was the marine," said Brold.

"In theory, he'd be neutral. I didn't know if Negral personnel would arrive before anyone else. I deemed it necessary to retain complete control of the situation."

"Would you have shot Specialist Haxon?"

"Yes, Chief."

"Where?" he asked with a raised eyebrow.

"In the chest."

"What if he was wearing above C-Grade body armor?"

"At that range, it would've knocked him down. I would have then shot him in the head."

"What if the marine took you out first?"

"I had my weapon drawn, Chief. It would have been forty-sixty." Against a colonial marine, I was being optimistic.

He shook his head smiling, and scanned the monitors.

"What would you have done, Chief?"

"Exactly what you did. Except I would've had an MP pistol."

"Then why did you question my actions?"

"Because, Keesay," he said, while adjusting the view around engineering, "I wanted to know why you did what you did."

I nodded. "How are Specialist Tahgs and Tech Cox?"

He shot me a glance and continued scanning the monitors. "They'll recover."

"Do you know what is, or was happening on the dock?"

"Nothing firm. Specialist Liu will organize a report as soon as I have command of all the facts."

I knew he was holding back but maybe he'd answer this. "What was the significance of the message on Tahgs computer clip?"

The chief couldn't help but grin. "The two perpetrators questioned Specialist Tahgs about the colonists' files. When she wouldn't talk they tried forcing her to access the information. She refused. They tried to hack the files." He scanned the monitors showing the Chicher moving about.

I'd already figured something was important about the colonists' files as I had limited access, and the chief was too astute to reveal unauthorized information. Informing me of the effort to hack the files was an indirect hint at some importance. More was going on than was apparent. I took the puzzle piece and let him continue.

"I don't especially like Senior Engineer McAllister," leveled the chief, "but, I respect her." He followed the Chicher's movements. "Did you know she has written at least fourteen encryption codes of various classified applications for the military?" He leaned back. "How many aren't documented?" The Chicher returned to its quarters. "She was Earthside Code Wars Champion three years standing, before retiring to freelance for the military."

Impressive. She was at least a year or two younger than me. "Freelance?"

"That's right. She wouldn't join up." He leaned forward. "Take note. Tahgs's clip has one-eighth the processing power. Yet, McAllister's code not only fended off the hack attempt, but defeated the perpetrator's defensive codes. Hacked and isolated their clip's memory. She's top of the line, Keesay. Handpicked."

"By Mer?"

"Indirectly. He okayed you, too."

"I can see why she was hired. But what about Gudkov? He seems unmotivated and not," I wanted to say 'well respected,' but settled on, "a team player."

"He's not popular, but he is one of the few people who can work with Engineer McAllister. And he has experience in security, and worked as a diplomatic bodyguard."

"Really?"

"Yes. Spent nine months aboard a Chicher transport." The chief scanned the monitors again. "Don't be fooled, Keesay. He was a light heavy-weight kickboxing champ. Three Intra-Colony Platinum Rings."

"And," I added, "he's friendly with Engineer McAllister. The ship just keeps getting smaller."

A wicked grin crossed the chief's face. "Ready for some bad news?"

I held back a sigh, and straightened. "Sure, Chief."

"Negral just bought Security Specialist Haxon's contract."

CHAPTER 20

Onboard space docks, interstellar vessels, orbiting colonies and on otherwise uninhabitable planets, food is derived from artificial, sometimes referred to as synthetic, sources.

Genetically engineered bacteria, algae, and fungi are utilized to create protein, carbohydrate, and amino acid supplements. Dispensed vitamins and minerals are suspended in juices to fill in the gaps. Much of the basic genetic manipulation was developed prior to the Silicate War, but the more efficient strains are of alien import.

I spent a long night filing an official incident report. The rest of the time I spent combing the colonist files. The female colonist I encountered in recovery was Lori Watts and the boy was her son, Michael. Her duty assignment as youth educator was to provide schooling to the nine colonist children en route and to provide adult remediation at the Tallavaster Colony.

About half of the colonists had suffered through a long night in recovery. A father and his son had died, with several other close calls. Dr. Miller reported it as an unforeseen genetic predisposition to the procedure. Now, only eight children for Watts to educate.

I showered and dressed, thinking about the colonists and the contamination. Who'd want to kill off a group of R-Tech colonists? Was it tied to the incident with Representative Vorishnov?

If there was a puzzle, I didn't have enough pieces to answer, so I checked my electronic messages. No more colonists had died. A continued 'stay of leave notice' preceded a meeting reminder. That would be popular but the abduction of Tahgs and Cox, and the trouble on the dock, cancelled all leave.

I responded to a query about the sec-bot and a forwarded confirmation on the partition installation in the colonist housing area. I finally made it to the one nonessential message from Specialist O'Vorley and called it up.

Kra,

Thank you for the notice. There has already been a hire. Specialist Gable Haxon had his contract bought out. I find it very unusual considering circumstances and the short handedness. Corporations. I do not know him well. He is quiet and observant and has only been around about six months. He treated me OK. He asked me about you. I said you were rugged and knowledgeable, and not to let the C4 rating fool him. You will like him.

Private Yizardo is taking me up on a barter of services you suggested. He said he ran into you yesterday. Said you were your typical self. I can only guess. Hope you didn't need your steel knuckles.

Time is short. My hours have been increased. Send back if you can.

Kent

I replied with a similar text-only message:

Kent O'Vorley:

I ran into Specialist Haxon already, along with Yizardo, and a fellow who had inflicted a particular bruising. Interesting meeting. I have duties to attend to. Do not know when the Kalavar is scheduled for departure. Take advantage of your training opportunity. Private Yizardo is one to respect. May our paths cross again.

Krakista Keesay

I grabbed a packaged breakfast so I could swing by medical before the meeting. I wondered if my message to Kent would get through dock security intact. Maybe not, if the artificial intelligence program was awake.

Medical was slow this early. Fortunately, a technician noticed me just after entering. "Can I assist you, Specialist?"

"Yes. Is Maintenance Technician Cox or Administrative Specialist Tahgs available for a brief visit?"

"Is it official business?"

I figured the less information he had to work with, the less chance of visitation denial. "No."

After a pause he said, "I'll check," and moved to the back area.

A moment passed. Dr. Sevanto's appearance surprised me. "Specialist Keesay, I was told you were here." He came around the desk. "Excellent performance yesterday."

"Thank you, Doctor."

"Interesting combination of weaponry you carry."

"Gets the job done."

"So I noticed," he said, leading me around the desk. "Consider having your hearing checked. Your firearm is potentially deafening."

"That was intentional," I said, pointing. "I have a dampener, but I thought the noise would provide distraction."

"I believe it did. I had my hearing checked along with Specialist Tahgs and Tech Cox."

"Everyone check out satisfactory?"

"Miraculously, yes."

"What?" I smiled.

"I am quite serious, Specialist Keesay."

"Understood, Doctor. I'll try to schedule a time."

"I will schedule one for you, whether your superiors find it convenient or not."

We approached the patient care area. "That wasn't the intended message, Doctor. I have free time and will arrange it today."

"If you don't follow through, I will."

"Understood." We stopped. "I came by to see Tech Cox and Specialist Tahgs."

"I released Tech Cox for light duty less than ten minutes ago." Dr.

Sevanto shook his head. "He has a limp, but didn't want to be off the job too long."

"Imagine I'll see enough of him during the voyage."

"You'll like Benny." Dr. Sevanto thought a moment. "Remember, he may appear slow, but don't let that fool you. He has regained ninety-seven percent of his mental capacity." He watched to see if I followed. "It sometimes takes him a while to retrieve it."

"Don't worry, Doctor. I'm patient and easy to get along with." He looked less than convinced. "Let me amend that. If the individual doesn't unjustly treat me as inferior, or doesn't cause me to enforce corporate regulations."

"Benny won't do either." He checked the monitor and then led me to Tahgs's room. "Make this short. Specialist Tahgs has taken the incident fairly well." He paused again. "The round perforated her small intestine. It's been repaired and the potential for infection has been treated." He knocked on the door. "Specialist Tahgs? You have a visitor."

"No problem. I'm awake, Doctor," she responded.

I stepped into the sterile room. Standard white bedding covered her, drawing attention up to her violet eyes. Her face erupted in a wide grin.

"Three minutes," warned Dr. Sevanto.

I checked my watch. "Honestly, that's all the time I have."

Specialist Tahgs waved me over. "I was hoping to see you." She started to sit up, but her face showed pain.

"Wait," I said, examining the bed controls.

She blushed and slid her fingers over the panel, directed the bed to elevate her while rolling her eyes. "I only work in medical." With a big grin she added, "I just wanted to say *thank you*."

"You're welcome. I was simply doing my duty. Following orders."

"That's not the way Dr. Sevanto told it."

"Dr. Sevanto may be knowledgeable about medical procedures, but I suspect he's lacking in the area of security procedures."

"What about Chief Brold?"

I wanted to move on. Visiting may have been an error, but it would've been awkward if Specialist Tahgs learned I tried to look in on Tech Cox and ignored her. "I'm sorry you took a round to your abdomen."

"I'll heal. And don't downplay your part. I was there, remember?"

"Understood. I'm also glad that Tech Cox will fully recover."

"Benny and I go way back. He's anxious to meet you. That's why he checked out early."

"I guess we were thinking along the same lines." I glanced at my watch.

"Before you leave, I have something that's yours." She pulled a pale pink handkerchief from under the covers. "Stained, sorry." Her smile disappeared. "Med Tech Merriam says it's all natural cotton."

She was a little hesitant to give it up. "You're welcome to hold onto it," I said. "Maybe as a good luck charm? If you believe in such things." She offered it again. I held up my hand. "I know how to get the stains out. I'll relay the information to you."

"Thank you. Would you?"

I looked at my watch again. "Chief Brold wouldn't look kindly upon a late arrival."

"Please, stop in again."

I slid toward the door. "When are you expected to be back on duty?"

"Two days."

"Dr. Sevanto insisted I have my hearing checked," I said.

She flipped her hair revealing an ear. "He did mine."

"I'll try to schedule it for two days from now. And I'll send the cleaning instructions."

"This place is very boring."

"Well, maybe it is where you are, now," I said, standing in the doorway, "but I have about nineteen hundred and thirty-seven things to accomplish in the next forty-eight hours."

She waved. I gave her a thumbs-up.

I recorded in my electronic notebook a reminder to schedule an appointment, and then double-timed it to the meeting. Even though I was two minutes early, everyone was waiting.

Gudkov looked unhappiest of them all. "About time, C4."

I considered responding to Gudkov's remark, but didn't.

"I better get my leave," he continued. "That's all I have to say."

"That's all you've *had* to say," said Nist.

"I heard we bought the contract of a sec-spec," Frost said. "You should be happy about that."

"Keesay here said he wasn't impressed with them," Gudkov said. "Undoubtedly about as worthless as you."

"Enough," warned Club.

"Too bad," said Nist. "Not often you hear Gudkov saying anything positive about anyone's opinion."

"But his own," Frost muttered.

"Frost," said Gudkov, looking from him to me, "I care about his opinion just above yours. His ranks just below your average blood-maggot."

Enough is right, I thought, before saying, "I'm devastated, Specialist Gudkov. Wait." I feigned thought by rubbing my chin. "I would be, if I cared about your opinion. May I retract my previous statement?"

"Who here knows what *enough* means?" asked Specialist Club, standing up. "Nist, wipe that smile off your face. Gudkov, taking out your frustration on everyone else won't encourage the chief to reinstate leave." She crossed her arms. "I've got more file work than I can handle. Open your mouth again and I'll consider it a formal request to be my assistant on your off-duty hours." She glared at me, "Same for you, Keesay."

Time itself must have been intimidated by Club's speech as the next thirty seconds seemed unwilling to pass. Eventually, the door opened, right on time. We filed in. Standing next to the chief was Specialist Haxon.

"There's your man, quick-draw," chided Gudkov.

"Thank you for volunteering," Club said. "Report to me after the meeting. We'll coordinate your additional duty."

She shot a glance at me while Gudkov took in a sharp breath and turned red. I took the nearest seat, remaining oblivious to either's stare.

"This is the newest member to our team," started the chief. "Class 3 Security Specialist Gable Haxon comes to us from Quinn Mining." After the chief had introduced each of us, Haxon sat down and the chief continued. "Specialist Haxon will be our floater. Assigned depending upon need, by either Club or myself."

Chief Brold covered routine information, progress reports and updates. Replacing his toothpick, he looked to the new man. "Specialist Haxon, everyone here has reviewed the recordings and read the incident reports. Would you update us on what you know of the incident, and any connection with the rogue sec-bots on the Mavinrom Dock?"

Haxon stood. "Well, Chief, I was able to briefly review the *Kalavar*'s material prior to this meeting. The follow-up investigation concurs with Specialist Nist's findings." He sounded less than eager to endorse Nist's competence. "As you know, Chief, Supervisor Gaverall believes the attempted abduction was tied to the three sec-bots detaching from security override. They fired on both passengers and station personnel. Gaverall believes the maintenance technician and the security specialist didn't have the programming skills to accomplish it. Dock Security is following up on several leads. But with the two known individuals dead, it's difficult."

Haxon looked at me. I withheld a shrug. He continued. "It is believed that the offenders were attempting to gain information on relic tech colonists. The rogue sec-bots drew security resources. Twenty-seven wounded and fourteen killed. Medical response to the emergency reduced support for cold sleep recovery."

"Two of the dead are colonial marines who responded to the crisis." It was Corporal Smith's voice.

"Thank you, Corporal Smith," interrupted Chief Brold. "I have invited the corporal to listen in from the monitoring station while he covers." He set the toothpick on his desk. "Continue."

"He is correct," said Haxon. "Along with one security." He paused. "It is believed that if they had been successful, the two offenders would've moved on their target."

"Thank you, Specialist," said Chief Brold. "Now, a few of you might be wondering, R-Tech colonists, a target?" He scanned his security team.

"Someone is serious. The cold sleep drugs were tampered with prior to the colonists taking the final preparatory regimen. According to Dr. Sevanto, our med team back on Earth was sharp. Identified the problem, and introduced a countering medication that saved all but two colonists. They're all sicker than dogs." He tapped a few times on his desk while he finished. "And none too happy." He looked to me. "Keesay, I'd like to hear your opinion. Speculate."

I stood, gathered my thoughts, and said to Haxon, "Apologies for killing the two offenders, and thus making the investigation more difficult. I'm now even more convinced that there was little choice. It's apparent that the two offenders lacked any inhibition with respect to killing, if they were related to the rogues."

I looked at the chief. "It's possible that one of the colonists is a target of a crime syndicate," I lied. "Going underground into R-Tech communities isn't unheard of, especially in larger cities." I looked at the others. "I can think of three syndicates which would have the resources to infiltrate medical facilities on Earth, and would have the funds to entice otherwise loyal company personnel to illegal action." I licked my lips. "Specialist Dribbs seemed advanced in age to be a C3 and he lacked the temperament to be a good sec-spec. Possibly that's why he hadn't advanced. It's more likely he transferred from a different career track. I haven't seen his file." Everyone but Gudkov appeared to be listening. "Either would make him more susceptible to influence by unsavory individuals."

Gudkov stood. "I would like to make a comment or two, Chief."

The chief squinted just a bit, "Okay, Gudkov. Stay on topic."

"All Keesay has spouted is unfounded fantasy." Gudkov looked at his peers then back to me. "Chief, this Relic Tech is a liability. He didn't even know what was happening when the offenders were attempting to access Specialist Tahgs's clip. The company had to get a sec-bot to back him up."

The chief nodded toward me.

"Auxiliary Security Specialist Gudkov," I said, "I appreciate your candor. But you are allowing personal views to interfere with your reasoning. I suspect it never occurred to you that I just might have access to information not available to you."

"Anything of importance anybody shares with you is a mistake, Relic."

"Let's get this aired out now," said Chief Brold. He looked from Gudkov to me, and then the rest of the group. "What's said in here, stays in here. Ends in here."

This emboldened Gudkov, but I was ready. "Surely," I said, facing Gudkov, "your assertion is based on more than your revered opinion—and by the way Negral acquired three sec-bots. What other two incompetents are they teamed with?" I knew one had been assigned to Club, and the other to standing patrol around engineering.

"You want facts?" asked Gudkov, reddening. "How about two Negral Corp personnel wounded in your botched rescue effort? If you had training with modern communications equipment and didn't carry outdated firearms, you might be useful."

Chief Brold acted as a gatekeeper, indicating my turn with a nod.

"Ignore the fact that I'm fully trained and competent with the model MP pistol you carry. Please clarify. How would you have done better?"

"First, I have an ocular." He pointed to the contact lens in his left eye.

"Very advanced," I said. "I am impressed."

"I could've called up a schematic on the room to be entered. Second, your vast and in-depth training should allow you to know that the rate of fire of my medium duty MP pistol far exceeds that slab of steel you carry. I would've taken out both offenders in half the time it took you."

"Is that a fact?"

"Are you calling me a liar?"

"No, I am stopping just short of calling you ignorant."

"Would you like to see just how fast I am?"

"Gentlemen," warned the chief.

I took a breath. "I have little doubt that you're fast. And you may even be more accurate than me, but both of those points are irrelevant."

"How could accuracy and firepower be irrelevant in a rescue situation?"

"They're not," I said. "Your equipment is the issue. If you'd been the one escorting Dr. Sevanto, you would have wandered past the abduction area without even knowing there was a problem. My communications gear isn't implanted." I pointed to the set on my belt. "It is larger and less modern, but even more pertinent to this incident, affords vastly superior reception." I let it sink in. "I was barely able to receive Specialist Tahgs' distress call. You, with your modern I-Tech equipment," I said, tugging at my ear, "would have missed it. Am I correct?"

His eyes darted to Brold, then Club then Nist and Frost. He clenched his jaw.

"If you recall," I continued, "my report stated Maintenance Tech Cox had been shot prior to my intervention. Interviews with Administrative Specialist Tahgs confirmed this." I saw his mind racing to recall the details of my report. "And it's not always how many rounds you fire, but where you place them."

He gave up. "You were lucky."

"Quite possible." I figured I had better soften the landing. "You were correct about the ocular. Negral has one, less advanced to be sure, on order."

"Don't patronize me, Relic." He clenched his hands into fists and sat down.

I stared at him. "You were a champion kick boxer. You didn't achieve that by allowing emotions to run your thoughts and actions. Nobody can remain long in your career track who lacks above standard intelligence."

"I'm tired of your lips flapping," he said, again standing. "I was calm and focused enough to kill two opponents in the ring." His grin was mildly intimidating. "I sparred with your pal, Pillar, last time we docked. He was almost challenging." Gudkov cracked his knuckles. "Care to go a round or two with me?"

"When your body count is up to seventeen," I said, resting my hand on my sheathed bayonet, "let me know."

"Are you gentlemen done?" asked the chief. It wasn't a question. "If I didn't know any better, I'd have thought you two didn't like each other." He stood and addressed the room. "On behalf of everyone, I would like to thank you for your first and final performance. If you gentlemen get into it, it'll be more than the end of your careers."

He looked at the chronometer, then scanned a file on his desk. "Well, Keesay, you were close."

I felt Gudkov's gaze and heard Nist suppress a snicker. The chief shot him a glance. Nist sat up, expressionless.

Complete order restored, the chief continued. "To end the mystery, the apparent target among the R-Tech colonists was eliminated. He'd been a whistle blower in a patent dispute and was in a witness protection program. They got a lead on him, possibly through a communication made by his son. According to medical, the chemical agent placed in the cold sleep drugs was genetically targeted." He scanned the assemblage. "One for the bad guys."

He tapped at his desk a few more times. "Anything else to add, Specialist Club?"

She stood. "No, Chief."

"Good. Assignments are posted. Those scheduled for leave, forty-seven hours. Enjoy." The door opened. "Welcome aboard, Haxon." Chief Brold clenched the red stick between his teeth.

Everyone filed out except me.

"Keesay," questioned the chief, "should I schedule time after each meeting especially for you?" He closed the door.

"Your call, Chief."

"Let's hear it, Specialist."

"Your account of the slain R-Tech colonist was accurate?"

"About as accurate as your rendition. I just took what you had to say and gave it my own touch."

"Would I be out of bounds to ask why, Chief?"

"Yes."

Nothing more? I tried a different approach. "It's just that there's an awful lot of…activity. The incident exiting the shuttle, the planting of the A-Tech explosive, poisoned colonists and now the attempt to obtain files on the colonists."

"Your point being, Keesay?"

"Although I have no evidence, I suspect there's a connection." I also suspected Chief Brold did as well.

The chief leaned back. "How do you figure?"

I recounted my conversation with Field Director Simms. "Dribbs was involved twice. He tried to kill the only surviving offender outside the shuttle, after wounding him. And of course, he abducted Tahgs and Cox." No sense tipping my hand any more than necessary. "Can you tell me if the chemical agent planted in the cold sleep drugs was DNA specific?"

"I will not deny it."

Interesting choice of words, I thought. "Was it targeted at the dead colonists?"

"I will not confirm that."

"So, whoever was targeted is still alive."

"It's possible," said the chief. "If you figure it out, Keesay, let me know."

Either the chief didn't know and, if I figured it out, he wanted to know. Or he knew and simply wanted to be informed when, and if, I figured it out. I suspected the latter. "Understood, Chief." Was it that he didn't trust me, or that I was only a C4?

"Keesay," he said with a smile, "I understand that you've talked one of the maintenance techs into making a set of brass knuckles."

The chief impressed me with knowledge of something so minor. "That is correct. I bartered away my other set."

"These are titanium?"

I hadn't received them yet, but titanium would do. "I traded a few gum wraps. Asked a maintenance tech to use whatever scrap he could find."

"They won't make a difference with Gudkov."

"That wasn't my intention." I scratched my head. "Why does he put up with Nist?"

"Gudkov? I'm not sure. If you figure that one out, let me know as well. Dismissed."

With a third of the *Kalavar*'s crew on leave, it was easy to find a seat for the evening meal. I recognized some of the maintenance techs, including Benjamin Cox.

"Chicken patty again, Keesay?" asked Maintenance Tech Segreti.

"Seemed safest." I sat down next to him and across from Cox and Minapp.

"You don't act like one who takes the safe route."

"Only when it comes to my stomach, Segreti." Benjamin Cox remained focused on his meal. "How's your leg, Technician Cox?"

He looked up and stared at me a second. "Just fine. Call me Benny." He went back to eating.

"Benny likes to savor the fine cuisine," said Minapp. "He'll talk after he's done."

"Have you gentlemen completed the colonist quartering?"

"Are you kidding?" asked Segreti. "Give us two more days." He rummaged through a pocket. "Here." He slid a bundled shop rag next to my tray.

"That's all the time you have," I said, before folding open the rag. "The chief informed me that you were working on these. Said they're titanium."

"Wouldn't doubt it. Those cameras are everywhere." He took a drink. "Say, Keesay, I was wondering. You're having us install those security cameras and sound monitoring devices. But you only want half of them dropped and activated?"

"Some questionable individuals signed on as colonists." They nodded, knowing I meant criminals who had their sentence commuted for volunteering to colonize. "They'll figure on being monitored. First opportunity they get, they'll attempt to locate and identify them."

"So," said Segreti, "after they think they've got the system mapped, you add to it."

"Correct. Might catch them off guard."

"Think it'll work?" asked Minapp.

"They were caught at least once," I said. "Proves they're not infallible."

"That's why you wanted the more advanced units held back," said Segreti. "It'll be tougher to access and install them later on."

I spied Haxon heading from the line, looking for a seat. I thought it might be good to find where he stands. "Specialist Haxon, you're welcome to join us."

He looked our way just as Gudkov's voice echoed, "Over here, Haxon." He was still fuming that he'd volunteered to assist Club.

Haxon was closer to our table. "Your choice," I offered.

Gudkov bellowed above the room's chatter, "How do you expect to soar like an eagle, Haxon, if you sit around with a bunch of turkeys?"

Segreti and Minapp looked at each other. Minapp shook his head, signaling 'no' to his friend who'd started to get up. Then, like Cox, they focused on their meals.

"Correct me if I'm wrong, Gudkov," I replied. "But is not each and every remaining species of eagle endangered?"

"Yes. They are each a rare and majestic species, Keesay."

"Quite true," I said as the cafeteria conversation began to subside. "And the few that survive owe their continued existence to the vigilant protection of others, in isolated sanctuaries."

"Are you insinuating that eagles are weak and unable to—?"

I cut in. "Wild turkeys on the other hand continue to flourish where eagles have not."

"I've heard that hunting wild turkeys is an interesting and satisfying sport. They squawk a lot before they meet their end."

"That's not been my experience. It could be you're more knowledgeable about squawking than me." I took a bite of chicken.

He stood. "I'll make you eat those words."

"What? I am simply comparing one species of bird to another. What are you talking about?"

"There will be a Christian missionary on board," announced Benjamin Cox, looking at me in earnest.

"I think even Benny knows what's best for you," laughed Gudkov and waved Haxon over.

The newly assigned security specialist turned his back on me, and sat down with Gudkov and several engineering techs. I wasn't surprised. The exchange reminded me of two middle schoolers posturing in front of their peers. I decided to avoid his game in the future.

"I saw the Bible on your shelf," Cox said. He held my gaze with a serious expression.

"Correct. A King James version." I took a drink. "You're welcome to read it. My mother got it for me when I was a kid. Had to memorize verses. Still read it on occasion."

"...Thank you. I have a twenty-first century revised. It might be interesting to compare."

"I find the older language more challenging to follow. Makes me think about each passage."

"...Yes, that makes sense."

The brief delay before each of Benny's responses was like communicating through a com-link a quarter million miles away. "I read less often than I should. Too much file work."

"...Would you like to set aside some time tonight?"

"Depends on how fast I read files, Cox. The colonists are boarding in two days. I need to be on top of things."

"...Benny. If you get the time."

I finished my drink. "I must be about my duties, gentlemen."

Segreti looked up, wiping his mustache. "You're okay, Keesay."

"We turkeys have to stick together."

"...Gobble gobble." Benny grinned with a wink.

It's always nice to end a meal with a good laugh.

I made it back to my quarters late that night. Mer and I exchanged neighborly waves before he shuffled to his room.

Benny was on the bottom bunk, pecking away at an electronic device. "Hello," he said, sitting up.

"Hello, Benjamin," I said offering my hand. "We haven't really had a chance to introduce ourselves. Krakista Keesay. Call me Kra."

"...Kra it is. Benny will do." We shook. "Mer just left."

"Saw him."

"...We were admiring your carving." He pointed toward the unfinished work on my cart. "Fish?"

"Correct," I said. "I started it after I came on board but haven't had much time to work on it." I picked up the pair of guppies I'd started to whittle out of the block. "Usually I carve people. Busts. This is proving a quite challenge for me." I set it down.

"...Looks good to me. Do you like fish, or is it for Mer?"

I nodded. "For Mer. What are you working on there?"

He lifted the small device. "Therapy. I practice responding to its visual and auditory cues."

"Oh." I emptied my pockets. "I've been sleeping on the top bunk."

"...That is alright," said Benny. "I hope you did not mind my intervening earlier."

"Is Gudkov always spoiling for a fight?"

"...He is very good at his job." Benny searched for words. "But his interpersonal skills are not the best." He pointed to my Bible on the shelf. "I think the missionary is a priest."

"Not very common." I organized my equipment, and slid my revolver into a padded sheath before slipping it under my pillow.

"...Specialist Tahgs and I are very thankful for your rescue."

"It was nothing, Benny. Breakfast tomorrow?"

"...Sure."

"Keep working on your therapy." I keyed in the computer to wake me at 5:15 am. "I can sleep through anything."

"...Okay. Let me know."

I was asleep three minutes after climbing into bed.

CHAPTER 21

To achieve a balance of power, the government retained control of military forces, while corporate entities took control of purse strings and military equipment production. Corporations are limited to security forces equivalent to municipal police forces. Prisons and penal colonies are manned with more heavily armed security teams due to potential violent uprisings and the risk of escape with outside support.

After a penal colony, the only place a criminal, or even a suspected criminal, has fewer rights and greater risk of summary execution is under corporate authority during interstellar transit. In those instances, the training required to carry out the execution of sentence is as legally straight forward as the task itself.

Twice, I rolled over and fell back asleep while Benny moved about. The cramped area made even the most subtle maneuvering noticeable. I sat up.

"Sorry, Kra," Benny said, staring my direction. "I guess I am used to being alone." He got up from the wall console and set a memory chip on my cart. "I programmed a series of verbal command options for the computer."

I was still waking up. "Pardon? Commands?"

"...Yes, for lights, the alarm, even some music."

"You did that this morning?"

Benny nodded. "After I showered." He sat on the edge of his chair. "Tried not to disturb you."

"That's okay." I hopped down and stretched. "Small quarters. I could've done the programming." Opening my closet storage, I grabbed my shower bag. "You're pretty handy with computers?"

"...I am proficient. Just not as fast as I used to be."

"It would've taken me at least an hour to do it."

"...You are trained in programming?"

"Minimal. R-Tech." I smiled, checking the computer for messages. "I can usually figure things out."

"...The systems are user friendly. I will wait for you for breakfast?"

"Sure thing. Be ready to tell me what you think about the Chicher." I moved on, allowing the door to close before he could respond.

I was fifteen minutes ahead of the crowd, so getting ready wasn't a problem. Benny sat, manipulating his therapy device. "You about ready?" When he nodded, I grabbed the rest of my gear and followed him out. Benny's leg wound made his awkward gait more noticeable. We passed two technicians monitoring several large dolly-bots securing box pallets to wall mounts. "Sure cuts down on the corridor space."

Benny nodded. "…Every bit of cargo counts. The *Kalavar* was not designed as a freighter."

We passed two more pallet crews. "The brackets aren't in all of the corridors."

"...Mainly in the crew areas. None near high-priced passenger cabins or where wide access is needed."

Passengers. That reminded me. "Do you have anything against the Chicher?"

"...They seem okay for big rodents." Benny scratched the base of his neck. "Why?"

"They're our newest ally. Wonder if they consider us revolting?"

"...The Crax do not seem to care for our species." We waited for an elevator. Benny pondered the question. "I believe I prefer big rats to giant lizards. We have one on board."

"I know," I said as we stepped into the elevator. "I invited him to stop by some time."

"...You have a hard time making friends among your own kind?" His delayed wink and grin contrasted the serious tone.

We exited the elevator and made our way toward the cafeteria. "I'll probably get along better with the rat than with McAllister," I said. "And definitely better than Gudkov."

"...Mer seems to like you," he said. "Janice Tahgs does. They are good judges of character." We entered the cafeteria. "I can tolerate chattering rodents, but I draw the line at Crax and Gudkov."

"McAllister?" I asked quietly.

"...She can be difficult," he said, "but brilliant. I respect her, and she has always treated me fairly.

"Understood." Nobody was in line. I didn't consider anything about Senior Engineer Nova McAllister fair minded. Brilliant, yes. No sense debating, so I handed Benny a tray and changed the subject. "Any recommendations?"

"...Keep away from the synthetic bacon."

"Really? I had a serving yesterday and it seemed good enough. Better than the ham." We moved through the line. I ordered bacon.

We sat alone. As we ate, Benny said, "After the real stuff, the synthetic is less appealing." Benny noticed my startled expression. "Last transport run we had authentic bacon."

I waited for him to smile or wink. "How did you manage that?"

"...The company manages it. Not an advertised perk, but once a week Negral serves the crew something special. Last run we had cotton candy, meatloaf, calamari, pears, sauerkraut, bacon, and clam chowder soup." His fingers crisscrossed his heart. "Starts first Thursday out of port."

We chatted, but everything else was anticlimactic. He left to visit Specialist Tahgs while I attended my meeting.

The chief was agitated and terse during the brief meeting. He assigned me to accompany Gudkov to pick up the sec-bot, and have him adjust my com-set. I'd already fulfilled my quota of questions this week and just went along.

Gudkov's work area, near engineering, was small with tools and diagnostic equipment scattered in a semi-organized fashion. Gudkov received a transmission and responded into his collar, "Yes, I'll be there right away." He looked up. "I'll be back in a moment. Don't touch anything."

He was daring me. He'd have his station monitored, so I just looked around at his half a dozen projects going at once. Those, plus his duties in security would keep anyone occupied. The busier he was, the better I felt. I sat on his work stool while updating my electronic notebook. I'd be tied up most of the day with colonist issues. Club had requested my assistance tomorrow in monitoring passenger boarding which was more interesting than final freight inspection, or screening passenger carts.

Tech Gudkov returned, giving me an annoyed look. "Your sec-bot is ready. Tech Schultz will bring it over in a minute."

I got up and offered him his stool.

He responded with a lightning jab at my chin. My reflexes kicked in and I attempted to duck, knowing he'd caught me off guard. I felt my microphone jerk away with Gudkov's right hand firmly grasping it.

My hat fell to the floor as he stepped back. With deft movements, he detached the audio sensing tip. "Almost quick." He grinned. "I've got orders to replace this part." He reached onto his desk without taking his eyes off me, and replaced the microphone. "Incorporates visual reception and transmission. Not as good as an ocular, but more than sufficient for an R-Tech." He tossed the replaced part on his workbench before speaking into his collar. "Specialist Club, I've installed Keesay's visual relay."

He flung my headgear at me. I snatched and examined it before sliding it on.

"Acknowledged," Club responded on both our links. "Keesay, initiate visual and audio transmission."

I worked to adjust my com-set.

Gudkov chuckled. "Need any help with the I-Tech equipment?"

Ignoring him, I activated the proper settings and looked around the room.

"Checking transmission now," she responded. "Gudkov, whistle, or slam your head against the wall."

He responded by snapping his fingers in rapid succession while I panned his way.

"Up and running," Club said. "Prepare for incoming visual transmission."

"Acknowledged." A narrow beam of light shot into my left eye.

Gudkov manipulated a hand-held remote device. "In case you're wondering," said Gudkov with a hint of sarcasm, "I'm adjusting the beam so that it bends properly when it hits your cornea. Close your right eye. Look ahead. Let me know when it's centered and in focus."

As I followed his instructions, a shifting circle of light centered in my left eye's field of vision. "Centered." Then, I saw a blurred image that formed into Specialist Club wheeling around in front of her monitors. "Focused...now."

I opened both eyes and looked at Gudkov. Club's shadowy image remained in the background. If I paid attention to it, I could see her. A little awkward, but with practice I'd adjust.

Gudkov smirked while sorting his tools.

"You can shut her down," Club said. "Out."

"Just like modern equipment," said Gudkov. "You don't trust, or like me very much?"

"Dislike? No," I said flatly. "Trust? I'm confident you carry out assignments efficiently."

He sat on his stool. "Would you like to go a few rounds in the gym?"

"The chief made that clear," I said, picking up my hat. "Afraid not. I like my current assignment."

"True. Might have your contract cancelled." He feigned thought. "I might, too. But I have real, marketable skills."

The door opened before I could reply. A squat triangular sec-bot preceded Tech Schultz through the door. Schultz's stained tan uniform indicated a long shift. "Everything is ready, Senior Tech Gudkov. Awaiting final security initialization input."

"Thank you, Tech Schultz." Gudkov checked the ship's chronometer. "Send a memo to Senior Engineer McAllister that the first sec-bot's been delivered. Then get some shuteye."

Tech Schultz shot me a glance and departed. Gudkov spun around to his workstation and accessed his computer. "This sec-bot will respond to your voice commands," he said. "They can be overridden by all superior ranking security personnel." His back was to me, but I sensed his gleeful grin.

"This is the sec-bot assigned to me?"

He spun around and slapped his thighs. "That is correct, Specialist Keesay."

"That being the case," I said, "protocol indicates that only Specialist Club and Chief Brold could countermand. All others should have emergency deactivation command."

"Those are the parameters set by Senior Engineer McAllister. Take it up with her." He turned around. "Are we ready for final initialization?"

I searched my memory but I lacked experience in this area of regulations. Technically, McAllister was probably authorized to establish those settings, initially. "I request the necessary access codes to adjust the parameters."

"Are you up to the task, C4?" Before I could answer, he continued. "Regulations stipulate you must personally program the protocol, or an authorized member of security."

"That would be you, if I am correct?"

"You are. And as you can see," he said with a sweep of his hand, "I have more pressing maintenance duties to perform."

If I could get a little help, I knew I could get around the regulation without breaking it. "The codes?"

"I'll send them in a secured file to your account," he said, a bit surprised.

I considered reminding him never to underestimate an R-Tech. No sense giving him sound advice. "By this evening if possible. Can we get on with the initialization?" I scanned the room. "Like you, I have other duties to perform."

He turned around and began tapping at screens. "Stand in front of the bot." He tapped a screen and the sensors activated. "Identify yourself to the bot, and then assign it a working designation."

"I am Class 4 Security Specialist Krakista Keesay." I paused while I read the assigned code on the sec-bot's front panel. "Security robot model C-19.4, series D, serial number 122166-D, will respond to Lefty."

"Interesting," said Gudkov. "From you I expected Nanny."

"Specialist Gudkov, I strive not to impose my needs or desires upon you. Please grant the same courtesy to me."

"Get out of here, Keesay."

"Thank you for your time, Technician," I said, heading toward the door. "Lefty, wave goodbye and follow. We have work to do." The wheeled robot's manipulative appendage emerged to swing twice as it followed.

"Lefty, stop," ordered Gudkov. The robot halted. "I almost forgot something." He took a scanning tool and ran it over several of the sensing panels. "Just double-checking calibrations." He looked at the read out. "Everything's fine." He turned back to his workstation. "Lefty, follow Specialist Keesay."

The sec-bot joined me in the hall. The door slid shut, muffling Gudkov's laugh. I'd hoped to finish Mer's carving but changing command parameters was this evening's first order of business. My appointment with the colonists in their holding area was next.

Prior to our tour, Dr. Sevanto informed me that most of the colonists were fully recovered, and bored. The retaining area was biologically and intellectually sterile. A few entertainment holos were playing, and colonists occupied three of the five available computer consoles. I made the rounds with Dr. Sevanto and took the opportunity to introduce myself. The majority accepted my presence with a few pretending to. Six openly resented my presence and took to my sec-bot even less.

The young boy, Michael Watts, stopped me as I followed Dr. Sevanto out. His mother, Instructor Watts, had keenly avoided me. "Doctor," I said,

"I'll see you in Medical." He waved in acknowledgment as I turned to the youth.

"Sir," the boy asked. "What model of security robot is that?"

I recalled his file. He could read, and the model was clearly printed on the robot. "You're, Michael Watts, correct?"

"Yes, ahhh...sir."

"Specialist is fine, Michael. That's Lefty. His model number is printed on the front plate."

"I don't like that name."

"Lefty? Seems sufficient for a robot."

"No, Michael!" said the boy as his mother approached. "I don't like it."

"Oh," I said. "Mike then?" He frowned. A questioning glance to his mother got no response. "I think it's a fine name. Did you know one of the greatest of God's angels is named Michael? As a general, he defeated the armies of Satan." The boy shrugged, emphasizing his temporary garments' poor fit.

Michael's mother rested a hand on the boy's shoulder. "I'm Lori Watts."

"You'll be providing academic instruction during transport." I held out my hand. "I'm Security Specialist Krakista Keesay."

She was slow to respond with a shake, which turned out to be cold and weak. "Negral Corp hasn't assigned me an official classification."

"Class 4 Primary and Intermediate Level Instructor," I informed her. "During the voyage."

"That's not a magnetic pulse pistol," Michael said, pointing and continuing to eye my holstered sidearm, "or a laser."

"No, it's an old-style revolver." His eyebrows rose. "You know," I said, "propels lead or other metallic bullets by gunpowder?"

"Don't ask so many questions," interjected his mother. "Specialist Keesay has other duties to attend. Am I right?"

"That is correct, Instructor Watts. See you later, Michael." His gaze fell to the floor. "Maybe we can come up with a suitable nickname." His mother smiled and nodded at my suggestion. "Lefty, come on."

"Is that the gun you shot the kidnappers with?" Michael asked.

I stopped and looked at the boy, then his mother.

She squeezed his shoulder, saying, "Some of the med techs discussed it while Michael was in recovery. Specialist Club reprimanded them."

Not fast enough, I thought. In a place this isolated and boring, any news or gossip would spread. "Yes, it is," I said, looking Michael in the eye. "Not all duties are pleasant. One performs them anyway."

"Why?" he asked.

His mother said, "That is enough, Michael."

"No, I can answer this one, last question." She took in an apprehensive breath. I measured my words, trying to keep it simple and avoid interfering with family authority. "Because, Michael, within any structure or organization, whether it's corporate like with me, family like you, or even military, everyone has a part to play. A responsibility to the others and to themselves. Occasionally, we must do what isn't the easiest or most enjoyable." I leaned closer. "I don't always have access to complete information. My superiors have more. Thus, I count on them to provide me with appropriate duties, and I carry them out." I paused. "My family runs the same way."

He started to ask another question. "Your mother is correct." I checked my gear before asserting, "I have other duties." Instructor Watts nodded but it was unclear if the approval referred to my assertion of duties, or to my explanation of duty. Several other colonists had been listening. Less than a day and they'd be out of this mind-numbing area. I waved, turned, and departed. Carver Potts began grumbling to some of his pals.

I whispered, "Lefty, initiate a recording of conversations in the area we are exiting and do not acknowledge the order." We didn't slow down. Lefty recorded less than ten seconds of hopefully revealing conversation.

As soon as we made it back to the *Kalavar*, I instructed the sec-bot to transmit the recording to my com-set. I listened and, after several directives, was able to isolate Potts's voice and those of his fellows. Nothing other than suggesting I prefer little boys to women. Their tone indicated they had little regard for Instructor Watts, with Potts the main instigator. Although he was rated with above-average intelligence, I made a note to review Potts's educational record. "Cunning and dislike of authority," I said to myself.

"Profile entry?" queried the sec-bot in a hollow, synthetic voice.

I jumped. That was the first time it had responded verbally. "Negative." We passed Maintenance Techs Segreti and Minapp mounting pallets, and exchanged nods. I directed the sec-bot, "Initiate a file on Agricultural Laborer Carver Potts. Attach and date the recorded conversation."

"Directive completed."

I checked my watch. Almost time for lunch. "Lefty, proceed to the colonists' quartering area. Scan and attempt to locate any surveillance devices. Do not hinder maintenance crews. Remain in the area. Wait for my arrival near the lower entrance."

"Enacting directive." The sec-bot wheeled away at a brisk pace.

I hurried to my quarters to review programming security regulations and policy before lunch. If I consulted the printed hardcopy, Gudkov couldn't trace my inquiry and efforts. And if Benny was willing to provide indirect assistance, I might be able to accomplish my goal.

At the end of my duty hours I picked up an evening meal, returned to my quarters, and ate while working. As anticipated, Gudkov had sent the file, simple code without documentation. I instructed my sec-bot to shut down before I took out a pen and notebook, and began transcribing from the screen. My programming knowledge allowed me to understand bits and a few consecutive parts. This helped the process. I finished and set the quarter-filled notebook aside just as the door slid open. I cleared the screen before Benny entered with Specialist Tahgs.

She smiled sheepishly. "Hello, Specialist Keesay."

Hiding my disappointment, I offered her my chair. "I bet you didn't expect to see me hovering over a computer screen."

"...I have seen the way you study the colonist files," said Benny. "Does not surprise me."

"Actually, later, I'd like your computer assistance, Benny, with a couple of things."

"...Janice is very proficient. She might be able to help."

Tahgs looked hopeful. "I wouldn't mind."

"Doesn't matter to me." I thought quickly. "You could help me with one, Specialist Tahgs. And maybe Benny could the other?"

"Janice," she said, trying to disguise her disappointment.

"Sorry, habit from being on duty. Were you able to remove your handkerchief's stains?"

"I received the instructions but haven't had a chance to try them."

Benny was busy gathering fresh clothes. "I should have changed too," I said, looking at my duty coveralls. "But I don't work up a sweat like Benny."

"Not every day," Janice teased.

"That's true," I said. "I should work out this evening."

Janice rubbed her abdomen. "I haven't been released for strenuous activity, but if you need to."

"No," I said. "Maybe while Benny is cleaning up, you can help me schedule the downloading of my journals." She looked at me skeptically. "I generally wait until the last minute," I said. "One can never be positive when the latest updates may arrive." I waved to Benny as he headed to the showers. "I'm not accustomed to this system yet."

"It's not that difficult, even for," she paused, "someone with your background."

"True," I admitted. "But my request won't be a priority. I have little knowledge on the customary volume of data transfer prior to departure. Too soon, and I may not get the latest update. Too late, and I get nothing." She caught my meaning. "This should be right up your alley."

"Alley?" she giggled. "Haven't heard that one before."

"Means, you should be very familiar with this routine's parameters." I pulled out my electronic notebook and brought up the file. "The six journals I want downloaded."

"Interesting, varied reading topics," she said, looking it over. "And these are the dates of the last update you downloaded?"

"Correct." I opened my cart while Janice began a mixture of tapping and voice commands.

"If they don't have any updates, do you want to download an alternate journal?"

"No," I said. "I can always reread what I have. Oh, and if possible text files with flat screen pictures and diagrams."

That raised an eyebrow. "If you're looking to save credits, the *Kalavar* has a reading library. Although I don't recall any of these titles."

"Already checked. I couldn't find info on any scheduled updates."

Janice finished before I located one of my decks of cards. "All you need to do is access the file, 'Journaldown1' and enter your account authorization." She rolled the chair away from the computer. "You might consider donating the files once you're finished. That's where most of the library selections come from."

"I'll consider it." I sat down on Benny's duct tape chair.

"What are those?" she asked, getting up.

I dumped them out of the tin box into my left hand. "Cards. Ever played euchre?"

"Yes, but not with cards." She held out her hand and I gave them to her. She flipped through them carefully. "They're not marked, are they?"

"No, the design is just a steam-driven paddleboat." She smiled playfully and I laughed, telling her, "I think you've seen too many old flat-screen shows." I glanced at the sec-bot. "Benny will probably join us. Maybe he can talk Mer into playing. If not, I may have to partner with my robotic counterpart."

"I'll be your partner," she volunteered. "Mer won't pass up anything as old-style as a real card game."

The door opened, and Benny poked his head in before marching across the room to put his soiled uniform into the cleaning compartment. He grabbed his therapy device and turned toward the door.

"Kra suggested an old-style card game." Janice waved the cards and inexpertly fanned the deck. "Think you and Mer are up to the challenge?"

It turned out to be an enjoyable evening. Mer proved to be well versed in euchre and hearts. Janice was inexperienced in both, but a fast learner, and prone to taking long shots. Benny was competent and conservative. I shared some gum wraps. The conversation remained light, except the few times it focused on intragalactic politics. Mer seemed very insightful and far more knowledgeable than anyone else around the table. He was also the one who desired to turn in early, and it was his portable table.

I offered to clean up while Benny escorted Janice to her quarters. She looked disappointed while Benny seemed resigned. Being my first day on duty with Lefty, I explained, I also had some file work to coordinate. A recalled thought struck Benny after my comment, and he offered to assist me upon his return. I eagerly agreed.

I'd just completed reviewing Lefty's inspection of the colonist area when Benny returned. "Pretty fast."

"...Figured you had a lot to do before tomorrow. I explained it to Janice. I think she likes you, Kra."

"I noticed," I said, expecting this conversation. "Two problems." I stood up from my perch over the robot. "One, duty requirements take precedence. And two, it may be more the fact that I saved her life in the line of duty than my charming personality."

"...You may be right, Kra. I am not so sure." He walked over and inspected Lefty. "Is that what you needed assistance with?"

"Kind of. It's a decent model," I said, rolling it off to the side. "It did locate all the active monitoring equipment in the colonist area." I made sure my com-set was off. "What I intend to ask you to do is more letter of the law than intent of the law."

"...Skirting regulations? It has been done, more than once."

"Successfully, I hope. If you turn me down, I won't take offense."

"...Let me hear it," Benny said, sitting close.

"The problem is, Gudkov programmed the sec-bot based on a technicality. Because of this, every other security person, and I haven't calculated what other *Kalavar* personnel, can countermand any directive I give to my assigned sec-bot."

"...You are the lowest ranking security official on board."

"Correct. But standard protocol allows for only the chief and my direct supervisor, Specialist Club, authorization to countermand or even nullify an order."

"...If he did it by the book, Senior Engineer McAllister would have approved it."

"Correct. But also by the book, I can establish the standard protocol. The difficulty being my programming skills may be inferior to the task." I knew what he was going to say. "And it must be done by hand. No voice-programming interface, which would have simplified the task."

He nodded. "That helps to assure integrity of the sec-bot's systems."

I handed him the notebook with the transcribed code. "I considered asking Nist for assistance, but I don't know him. Everyone else, except Specialist Club and the chief, are intimidated by Gudkov."

"...There are parts missing, Kra," said Benny, scanning my transcription.

"I know. I omitted the security sensitive areas. I will actually do all of the inputting. I will do all of the security sensitive sections alone. The rest, as much as you're willing to assist."

He mulled it over. I brought him the hardcopy of the regulation and flipped to the pertinent documentation. "Read this before you decide. I wouldn't want you to agree blindly."

"...I will take your word on the regulations. I was just weighing the possibility of crossing Senior Engineer McAllister."

"She could make your life difficult?"

"...If I am not connected, and if it will frustrate Gudkov," he contemplated, "I will do it."

"Affirmative, on both counts."

We went to work. What would've been a twenty or thirty-minute job for Benny, turned out to be a three-hour effort for me. He was in bed long before I finished my part. Fortunately, Benny instructed me on how to loop the online diagnostic program to a secured area. That assisted greatly in debugging errors. Before hitting the hay for two hours, I isolated one unidentified non-standard program file on the robot's drive. I was unable to ascertain its purpose, but Gudkov's fingerprints were on it. I doubted I could outwit him in this arena. So rather than mess with it, I purged the file from the system. But first, I downloaded it to a portable storage chip, just to be safe.

CHAPTER 22

Corporations are limited to paramilitary equipment when arming security teams. Even if equal in firepower, the equipment is inferior in some fashion, usually in its inability to withstand intense electronic warfare. Military-grade production facilities are subject to random inspection with stiff fines and assured incarceration for any individual knowledgeable of unauthorized production or post-manufacture alteration of equipment.

Retired military personnel, especially those who served twenty or more years in good standing, are occasionally granted limited waivers. Sometimes outdated, yet still effective, equipment is available to those highly sought after personnel who opt for security as a second career. This usually includes civilian ship command staffs, who often keep their official military rank in reserve status.

Frost met up with me after breakfast. "On your way to the chief's meeting, Keesay?"

"Figured it'd be wise to be extra early today."

"True, everyone'll be there," Frost said, picking up the pace. "Tough to find good seats."

"Everyone trying to snuggle next to Gudkov?"

"Bah," he said. "Didn't he issue your sec-bot?"

"Yes. I have it on a mission."

"So, what do you think of your partner?" he asked, suppressing a grin.

I didn't play into it. "Lefty? Seems efficient. Was able to locate all of the surveillance monitors installed in the colonist area."

"Those weren't exactly state of the art. But I heard the sec-bots are decent quality. Negral doesn't issue bottom of the line equipment, if they can help it."

"That's what I read before signing on."

"Read, huh?" We waited at an elevator. "You read a lot?"

"I used to. Not a lot of action with my previous assignment."

"On Pluto, right?" Frost led the way in. "Less time onboard the *Kalavar*." He shook his head. "We'll get by, but could use a few more. What do you think of the new guy, Haxon?"

I hesitated as we passed through the main gravity plate. Elevators switching directional gravity and orientation takes getting used to. "I haven't run into him except at meetings."

Frost ignored my discomfort. "You probably wouldn't," admitted Frost. "Seen him working out and eating with your pals Gudkov and McAllister."

McAllister's dislike of me had to be common knowledge. I wondered if Frost knew why. I was silent, so he continued. "Haxon politely avoids contact with me, too." The elevator door slid open. Frost slapped me on the shoulder. "His loss, right?"

"Correct," I replied, and led the way down the pallet-narrowed corridor past two maintenance and one engineering tech. "I pulled duty with Club. What about you?"

"Have to monitor a team of exploration scientists as they load the rest of their equipment. Then liaison with dock security before departure." He paused. "Did you see their fancy exploration shuttle?"

"From a distance. Why?"

"A lot of what you'd call bells and whistles. Maybe even some A-Tech," he whispered, and nodded once.

Interesting, I thought, but sloughed it off. "All the same to me."

"You're a lot more up to speed than you pretend. You and your archaic firearm there."

"Thanks for the vote of confidence." I leaned close. "I won't let it get around."

Specialist Club stood waiting in the doorway. "Glad to see you gentlemen are early. Not a lot to cover, but a lot to do after." She ushered us, the last to arrive, in.

The meeting lasted four minutes. We reviewed assignments with a lot of nodding and no questions. As soon as it was over I crowded next to Specialist Club. "Meet you at the main docking hatch in twenty minutes?"

"Keesay, where's your sec-bot?"

I surveyed the room and didn't see her assigned sec-bot. "Lefty is on a mission. Should be at my quarters in five minutes."

She said, "I sent Rusty to ensure no errant passengers wander near the forward engine room."

"Rusty?" I licked my teeth to suppress a smile.

"By your schedule, you have nineteen minutes to meet me at the hatch, Specialist. You and your robotic assistant."

I stood at attention, nodded and shot off. En route, I contacted my sec-bot and met it at my quarters. I grabbed my cleaned pump shotgun, and slid eight extra shells in my belt loops and a half-dozen slug rounds in an empty thigh pocket. My robot already had a box of fifty revolver rounds in its storage compartment. Recalling the incident in the med lab, and the explosive device on my cart, I attached a flash-stun grenade to my belt. It was one of two I'd inspected.

I pondered the robot. It had a teargas canister, so I exchanged my teargas shotgun shells for three light shot. Along with my flare rounds, they'd be firepower without lethality. I buttoned the vest pocket. "Lefty, follow me to the main docking hatch."

Overnight the *Kalavar* had aligned with one of the passenger loading bays. Specialist Club stood at the hatch with her heavy-duty laser pistol and shoulder power pack. She eyed my slung shotgun, then shifted to my bayonet. "Are we expecting trouble?"

"No. But recently I've experienced situations where a little more firepower would've been handy." I dropped my gaze to her power pack. "Should I be expecting trouble?" Maybe she knew something I didn't.

"You? No," she said, stifling a yawn before pointing to her patch. "You're not the emigration official." She looked down the corridor. "Medical will supply personnel to scan V-IDs and engineering a few techs to scan and monitor passengers and carry-ons. First Class, then standard passage."

"The colonists will board last," I added. "Already been scanned. Their gear," what there is of it, I thought, before finishing, "has been checked and loaded."

Club looked impatient. "They're being held in a waiting area adjoining the passenger bay." She indicated a closed doorway to the left.

I looked in. "Did we upset somebody?"

"Middle of renovation." She eyed the unfinished walls and high ceiling. "Acceptable. Acoustical tiling and lighting. Just not the final touches."

I frowned at the temporary rows of seats. "Doesn't look very efficient."

"It'll double as a multipurpose auditorium. Concerts, catering hall, conference center."

Near the docking hatch, two long folding tables had been set up with a red line indicating the proper path to each. About halfway across the bay, maintenance had placed chairs in two columns, three rows deep. Plush padded chairs for first class passengers lined the facing front rows. Bolted down behind them were more rustic versions with flip down seats.

Passengers filled a dozen of the seats. "Three times as many seats as we'll need," I said, knowing passengers would continue to arrive during the boarding process.

"After we depart, a larger transport's scheduled to dock. They'll be short." Club completed a visual inspection of the area as well. "You plan on fixing that bayonet?"

"With your sidearm, I'm confident our minimum intimidation requirement has been met." She cracked a smile, but it faded, adding annoyance to signs of fatigue. Not a good combination.

"Maybe your associate, Anatol Gudkov, will weld some charioteer spikes on Lefty?" She nudged the sec-bot with her boot. I was unsure how to respond. Humor might alleviate the situation now, but the potential long-term consequences with Gudkov were unknown. She observed my silence and stared ahead. "First class are the worst."

I double-checked my gear. "Really?"

"The *Kalavar*'s a fine ship, but not top of the luxury line. If they really had credits—"

"I know the type," I cut in. "Like to posture for all to see." And prone to look even further down their nose at an R-Tech. I thought better of verbalizing the second opinion.

"Usually, not even big fish in a small pond." She looked around again, checked her watch and flexed her fingers.

It'd be a long morning if Specialist Club became really irritated. "More like a mid-growth mackerel in a tidal pool?"

My last comment interrupted her thoughts. "You have the situation. No need to explain the standard passengers." Several medical and administrative personnel rounded a corner. Club signaled to the senior med tech.

Janice Tahgs was part of the team. I nodded when she winked. She'd added a light violet nail polish to match her eyes. Janice looked around, oblivious to Club's muffled verbal lashing of her superior.

"Come on, Keesay," said Club. "We've got a duty to perform. Let's do it efficiently." We walked in, followed by the administrative team. Two engineering techs arrived to assist. They avoided Club by tying the portable computers to the scanning equipment.

"We'll have Lefty remain in view off to the side." She led me away from the crew. "They've tried adjusting the scanners to pick up equipment similar to the explosive device set by Tech Stardz."

I'd been intentionally left out of that ongoing investigation, so I didn't ask any questions, but hoped Club would clue me in. She didn't.

"Senior Engineer McAllister finished this morning and thinks it'll work."

"I understand she is very good." I tried to erase the image of a bull's-eye painted on my forehead. Even so, a thought recurred several times...would McAllister do her best, knowing her efforts might prevent my suffering and demise?

"Okay, Keesay," Club said. "They're about set up. We'll have two scanners running. Two lines." We walked over to the tables. "You take station at the front. Direct and kind of loiter in between, keeping an eye on things. Keep it moving." She looked over her shoulder. "I'll be monitoring the scanning of the carry-on possessions." She observed the growing crowd seated about twenty yards away. "No assistance from dock security today. Anyone suspicious, signal me and be sure they go to the right-hand scanner." She seemed a little tense for routine boarding duty. "I'll take it from there."

I checked my watch and scanned the crowd. "Two minutes," I said. "The teams look ready. We could start early."

"No sense giving passengers the idea we don't stick to a posted schedule." Club cracked her knuckles. "You look a little edgy. What kind of a grenade is that?"

I put my hand on it. "Flash-stun."

"Not fragmentation? They don't know that." She smiled, eyeing the first class crowd. "They should be the edgy ones." She checked the chronometer above the hatch. "Minute and a half and you can get them started." She moved behind the two tables, hands on her hips, and waited.

Janice caught my attention, so I walked over. "Expecting trouble?" she asked.

I ran my thumb under the rifle sling to adjust my shotgun. "Expecting? No. Better to be prepared." I stood next to the table and evaluated the crowd. Some were chronometer watching. The majority sat engrossed in their computer clips while the rest wore entertainment headgear. Most had the goggles, but a few sported the more advanced glasses. Very modern and very expensive. "Your team was running behind?"

"Technical trouble," she said. "Think any of them are terrorists?"

"About as likely as shooting the moon with no face cards." I tapped my watch. "As the chief would say, time to earn our keep."

With a mild sense of urgency she asked, "Will you have time for dinner? Benny says that they're working you pretty hard."

"We're short of personnel, but if things run smoothly, I should be able to meet you at eighteen-hundred hours." Specialist Club signaled the go ahead. "Duty calls."

I walked forward about ten paces and centered myself between the red lines. In front of me was a four-foot diameter red circle. As soon as I began to speak, the holding circle and lines shifted to glow an emerald green. "First class may begin boarding." I didn't bother tying into the speaker system. "Advance to the check-in stations along the green lines."

Most of the first class passengers acted as if they had all the time in the world. I was tempted to issue the last call for first class, but knew better.

Several had advanced through when an older couple leading two muscular canines caught my eye. Once they'd crossed the bay the graying man said, "Good morning, Specialist Keesay," after reading my tag. His pet awkwardly sat when he stopped to talk. His wife followed, and smiled. She wore an imitation straw-weave hat with a long white and red-tipped feather. Her dog sat and began to pant.

"Bulldogs?" I asked, already knowing the answer.

"Very perceptive, young man," the gentleman said. "Natural conception, purebred English Bulldogs." He stooped to pat the canine. "Both champions."

"And they're certified for condensed space travel," boasted the woman.

I knew they desired to chat about their pets, but I had to keep alert and the line moving. "Exceptional canine specimens," I said, looking over my shoulder. "I believe the left scanner is open." The red section of the line in front of the couple leading to Specialist Club changed to green.

"Thank you, young man," said the gentleman. Without urging, his dog led the way.

"Come on, Daisy," said the woman. The dog ambled ahead. "See you on board, young man."

First class and R-Tech, I thought. The old couple should vex some of the passengers. Maybe some of the crew. I signaled the next passenger from the padded seating. The mid-level, well dressed, businessman had anticipated and deactivated a belt-mounted relay and pocketed his entertainment glasses. Waiting about fifteen seconds, he pretended he'd decided to enter the holding circle on his own initiative.

That gave me an instant to think. The models of entertainment glasses I'd read about always advertised the fact that they didn't require a bulky support box. The older model goggles did. Something about his stare before he got up. I decided to send him to Specialist Club's post.

The line to the left switched green. "Excuse me, sir," I said, halting the man's progress. "Please wait for the right line to open."

The passenger feigned politeness. "Is there any particular reason?"

"Sir, you may wait here until the right line opens. Or you may return to your seat and I will signal you directly when it does."

"I do not appreciate this delay, Specialist 4th Class."

I glanced at the sec-bot, then back at the man. "On behalf of Negral Corporation, I apologize for the inconvenience."

The right lane's red faded and emitted green. Before I could say anything, the businessman moved on, muttering about being forced to travel on second-rate ships. "Club," I whispered into my headset. "Special attention to the belt relay."

Two more passengers advanced through the left line before I heard a disagreement over my shoulder. "Sir," Club said, "we will hold this device for further examination."

The man shouted, "May I have an explanation for depriving me of my property?"

Hostile arrogance wouldn't get him far with Specialist Club. "Sir, I believe your entertainment device contains questionable components."

I moved a passenger to the left line and signaled to a bearded, casually dressed vacationer. He seemed interested in the disagreement, and didn't immediately respond. An anxious woman pretended I had signaled her and rushed forward.

Club and the businessman continued the heated conversation off to the side. I sent the woman down the right line. The bearded man came forward. He acted extremely uptight for a vacationer. "Is there something I could help you with, sir?"

I interrupted his concentration on Club's diplomatic efforts. "No."

My idle sec-bot might be useful. "Lefty, go to Specialist Club and await any directives she might provide." The little robot circled around the lines and took up station behind the irate businessman.

The vacationer's shoulders drooped slightly. "What is the problem?" His wording was smooth, but he continued shifting weight from foot to foot, ever so lightly.

"I am not sure, sir, but I am confident it will be worked out."

"Didn't you send the man down the right line intentionally?"

"That is correct, sir." I scrutinized his unusually fresh and crisp traveling attire. He waited, but I didn't elaborate while formulating a hunch.

The left line returned to green. The vacationer released a small breath. "May I, Specialist?" he asked, stepping forward.

"Negative, sir," I said, taking a step back to keep parallel, "I believe my superior would prefer you advance through the right line."

"This line is open," he said with a tinge of frustration, or restrained anger.

I looked back at Specialist Tahgs waiting. Our eyes met. The line reverted to red.

The vacationer looked at the line, to Tahgs, then to me. "Why are you intentionally delaying my passage? I paid for first class. I expect appropriate treatment."

Tahgs hadn't been quick enough, but I held my left hand to my ear and pretended to listen anyway. "Sir, the operator is running a diagnostic and recalibrating the system. It will only take a moment. Please return to the holding circle."

A tall olive-skinned woman came striding toward the holding circle. Her low cut, silver bodysuit could've been painted on, straining to contain her genetically enhanced chest. The matching satchel held closely against her hip was the only thing not responding to the rhythm of her determined step.

The vacationer turned as the woman neared. He angled back, out of the holding circle.

She halted inches from collision, but I held my ground and shot a glance to the gawking vacationer. "You, sir, do not leave." I swung my vision directly into the tall brunette's green eyes, something with which she was certainly unfamiliar. "Is there a problem, ma'am?"

"Indeed there is," she said, with what might have been an exotic Latin American accent. "Why do you insist on unnecessary delays? The left line is open." She pointed before shifting her stance with a jolt, sending waves of movement through her upper torso. Her right hand rested on her hip, but her eyes remained locked with mine. They were far older than her skin and figure suggested.

"Ma'am," I began.

"Ms. Jamayka Jazarine to you, Specialist."

Something clicked. These two were a working pair. The vacationer was probably the mule carrying some sort of contraband and the exotic dancer was the interference. "Ms. Jazarine, thank you for your concern over the boarding schedule. However, I suggest you return to the seating area, or your passage aboard the *Kalavar* will be revoked."

With a huff, she spun, slapping me with her satchel and stepped into her partner, bumping him aside. "Excuse me," he said. She didn't bother to acknowledge and stomped away.

"The right line is now clear for advance, sir," I said to the vacationer as he turned his attention back to me.

"Might be an enjoyable trip," he said, grinning and scratching his beard.

"Club," I whispered into my com-set. "Sending a possible mule working with the exotic dancer in silver."

"Acknowledged. The last fellow appears to have unauthorized V'Gun components running his entertainment system."

"Lefty," I whispered. "Monitor and record the female who just departed the holding circle. Let me know if she passes anything to another passenger."

"Directive enacted," responded the sec-bot as it edged toward the passengers.

Banned black market parts, I thought. The V'Gun are highly advanced in biotechnology. Reportedly, components incorporated with their knowledge offer greatly enhanced sensory interaction. Research also indicates their use leads to mental addiction, unless used in extreme moderation, which was a possible explanation for the businessman's stare and subsequent irate behavior. The offender's equipment had already been confiscated and a substantial fine would follow, if the initial readings proved accurate. Maybe the fine would actually be enough to hurt. I waved forward an executive toting a large briefcase.

"Smooth talking with the dancer," teased Tahgs over my com-set. "So I guess we're still on for dinner?"

"Remain alert, Specialist Tahgs," I said. "She and the man who advanced along the other line are questionable." She responded by switching her line to green.

The lean executive stepped into the green circle. "Interesting morning already."

"Preferable to monotony, sir," I said. His orange tie had only a few black splotches. "The left line is open to advance."

"Contraband?" he asked.

"I have not been informed as to the results of the scanning."

"Good security work." He winked. "What did you use to spot him?"

"As I said, sir, I am not privy to the results."

He looked me up and down. "Any special equipment?"

I pointed to my head. "Only what God has provided. Sir, the line is green."

"Chokks Habbuk, Senior Vice President of Recruiting for the Chiagerall Institute." He looked at my ID tag and pulled out a small clip. "Keesay?"

"Correct, sir. I am satisfied with my current contract." I looked past him. "Mr. Habbuk, I must insist you advance. I wouldn't want to offer credence to the lady's suggestion that my actions are impeding passenger boarding."

"Are you aware of the Chiagerall Institute?"

"Yes, I am, Mr. Habbuk. Military think tank, research on extraordinary mental abilities, pioneering work on the Cranaltar Project."

"Impressive, Specialist Keesay. Observant, and knowledgeable for an R-Tech." Without warning, a surprised, panicked look washed over his face.

Concern filled his eyes as he looked past me, toward the right line. "Specialist, prepare for trouble."

His tone jabbed at my instincts. "Clarify, from where?" A cry from behind drowned his response. Spinning, I unslung my shotgun and chambered a slug round. *Ca-Chunk.*

"Take him out!" Club shouted aloud and over her com-set. "Emergency Code Red 5."

I leveled my shotgun and fired on the vacationer. Lefty wheeled toward the back-pedaling target who was holding a pointed finger toward the downed engineering tech. My round was on target but failed to impact. Lefty deployed its stun net which discharged against an invisible barrier. I pumped and sent another slug as Club's laser blast fizzled before impact. The man backed toward the wall, while attempting to manipulate a palm clip.

"Crax shield!" yelled Club over the rising cries of the passengers. "Only defends from the front!"

Lefty moved to flank as the vacationer pointed his finger and returned fire on Club. I shot again while Club kicked over the table and dove for cover. Lucky for Club his palm clip seemed more important, causing him to be off target. Still, nickel-sized holes erupted in the table, before expanding tenfold as the metal dissolved.

A med tech screamed. Club popped up and sent two blasts into the shield. Then everything went black. That, and the emergency hatches slamming down, stunned the passengers into silence. The backup lighting failed to kick in and only the fading glow of the holding circle and lines remained. "Energy disruptor," Club yelled.

A-Tech! I waited for the gravity to fade before remembering the Mavinrom Dock, at its core, was military construct. I took a chance and sent a slug where I thought the bad guy should be. *Blam!* My dampener was dead. The area's tiling absorbed most of the shot's echo. Knowing the muzzle flash revealed my position, I dove left and came up kneeling. Clicking impacts, followed by fizzing, emanated from my previous position. "He lacks night vision gear," I shouted over the again rising clamor.

I unbuttoned a breast pocket where I kept my special shells. Three flares. Too late to consider packing teargas or chemical shells. I loaded the multiple colored flare shells, swung to the left, and fired the first high above the main dock entrance. On the move, the remaining two were sent high across the hall. Each flare round slammed into a wall and cast eerie green, red, and yellow surges that intertwined with layered shadows.

I spotted the silhouetted bad guy hunched over and backing along the far wall. I pulled the pin on my grenade and yelled, "Fire in the hole," hoping at least Club would react. The flash-stun grenade arced behind what had to be a terrorist. I fired a round from my shotgun just to cover the noise of the landing grenade, then rolled, covered my ears and closed my eyes while praying the disruptor had no effect on old-style grenades.

After the concussive blast I ran toward the terrorist. He was on the ground but getting to his knees. I fired my last loaded round at him. His shield was still up.

Above the ringing in my ears, I thought I heard Club yelling, "Shoot from the hip!"

Interpreting what she said, I moved closer, sliding several more shells from my vest pocket into my gun. The terrorist began to scramble forward. Less than ten paces away from him I spied the clip's glowing keypad. *Blam!* It skidded across the floor. I put another round of #8 shot into it, and the third at the terrorist who was glaring at me in anger. He didn't even flinch.

A brave civilian charged the terrorist and paid the price, falling away, clutching his dissolving abdomen. The passengers sheltering on that side of the room, blinded or not, fled. I backed away, drawing my revolver. Maybe I could deflect a round off the floor and circumvent the shield. We exchanged fire. His went wide and high, mine struck the shield.

The emergency lights flickered to life. Out of the corner of my eye I caught Club toting part of a table while advancing along the wall. Her laser was holstered with its power cord dragging behind. I sprinted to the left to draw attention, and if not, flank him.

The terrorist backed against the wall and opened fire on Club. The floor and wall each took a round before he hit the table. Club backed away, then broke and slid behind the downed passenger. Before the terrorist-vacationer turned to me, the silver-clad exotic dancer emerged from the chairs behind the terrorist and threw a thin knife. It wasn't balanced for throwing but still managed to pierce his thigh.

She hurdled into the seats and disappeared as he pointed his lethal hand and sent several rounds. The dancer screamed. I emptied my revolver into his facing shield, failing to distract him. How many rounds could his shield stop? Satisfied, the terrorist hobbled to the far corner.

I took position behind the front row of cushioned seats, holstered my revolver, and reloaded my shotgun. Movement on the other side of the chairs caught my attention. I peered underneath and spotted the silver-clad dancer awkwardly crawling along the floor.

"Move as quickly as you can," I urged. "I'll wait until you pass before I fire on him."

She rolled onto her side to see under the chairs. She clutched a maimed left hand below where the terrorist's weapon had burned away part of her little and most of her ring finger. She breathed steadily despite the pain. "Do me a favor," she said without accent. "Don't wait. Just kill that bastard!"

Above the ringing in my ears, I heard distant sizzling of metal followed by renewed screaming. "That's the plan," I said. "Keep moving." I peered over a row of the chairs. The terrorist had hunkered down in a corner. With obvious deliberation, he was pointing above the main docking hatch. I spied a large area of corroded metal near the ceiling. His goal was to burn through the outer hull.

I stood and fired at the terrorist. He ignored me, his shield absorbing everything. His long-range fire proved accurate. I slid in my last load of shells, wondering if he was almost out. I pulled my bayonet. "If he burns through, we're all dead anyway," I mumbled, fixing the blade to the end of my shotgun.

I hopped over the first row of chairs. The dancer turned and looked at me from a distance. I shrugged and hopped over the second row before moving toward the end of the row. Some of the passengers had managed to pry up the hatch leading to the colonists an inch or two. I couldn't hear the hull sizzling over the pounding and screams, but my eyes confirmed continued progress. I steeled myself. "Be seeing you soon," I whispered to God.

Flashes sped by. I glanced over the row to see Club standing about twenty yards away, laying into him with her heavy laser. If her recovered firepower couldn't burn through the Crax shield, my shotgun never would. But my bayonet might penetrate. Club's fire would cover my final move. Oblivious to me and ignoring her, he continued his assault on the hull.

Just after I spun around and charged with bayonet raised, Club's blast burned through, taking the man in the chest. With a grunt of surprise, he collapsed.

I looked over my shoulder at Club who simply shook her head and laughed. The engineering tech next to her stood, puzzled.

The terrorist's body began frothing from within. I maneuvered my bayonet and stabbed at the right hand of the terrorist, detaching the little finger before it was consumed. My eyes began watering as I flicked the severed digit across the floor before backing away from the gruesome sight.

I coughed and blinked, attempting to clear my eyes. Club barked orders to the engineering tech, who ran toward the hatch. The dancer was standing, holding her injured hand. Tahgs ran toward me, while the fearful clamor subsided.

"Kra!" cried Tahgs. "Are you okay?" She pulled up short.

"I am." My throat stung but my vision was better. "You are, too?"

She nodded. I surveyed the scene. "Tahgs, I have to secure the area and see to the passengers." I spotted the approaching dancer.

"Right," Tahgs agreed, still trying to catch up with events.

"Escort Ms. Jazarine to Medical," I said. "Report the incident. Remain with her until relieved or directed otherwise by Security."

"Who?" Then she turned to see the dancer. At first Tahgs looked upset until she spotted the dancer's hand. She bit her lower lip. "Please follow me, Ms. Jazarine."

The dancer was stiff with pain, but still gazed at me, and then along my shotgun to the bayonet. Her eyes sparkled. "Thanks for trying, Specialist," she said, reviving her accent. "But your superior got him first."

CHAPTER 23

Mankind's knowledge base increased exponentially early into the 21st century, but the learning curve wasn't able to keep pace. Efforts to overcome this with artificial intelligence, including neural assisting microchip implants, ended in dismal failure. As a result, the knowledge curve leveled to a slow, steady climb, with occasional sporadic increases. This appears to be the model for all intragalactic species.

I finished dictating my incident report and waited while Specialist Club completed her debriefing in the captain's office. Ensign Selvooh, working at his desk, ensured no one disturbed me. He was the only other crewmember besides the captain, her XO, and the navigator who'd retained their active military rank. In a crisis, would he be fourth in the chain of command after the chief navigator? Or would Chief Brold or the chief engineer? I refocused and re-ran the violent sequence through my head, straining to recall any unrecorded detail.

The door opened and Specialist Club strode past, exiting without acknowledging Ensign Selvooh or myself. I stood. Selvooh advised, "Captain Tilayvaux will signal when she is ready for you, Specialist Keesay."

I sat back down, knowing that at least I was second. Tahgs, and the rest of the involved crew were waiting in isolation. Ensign Selvooh kept his dark, freckled face straight as he worked. "Routine work, Ensign?"

"Not exactly, Specialist. I'm organizing the crew's individual incident reports into one summary brief."

"For the lawyers?" Two passengers killed by the offender and fourteen injured, the majority being sprains or light contusions brought on by panic.

"Among others." He sighed. "You know the procedure."

"Correct." I knew the lawyers wouldn't want any corporate representative to influence recollections. "How long will this delay departure?"

"The departure schedule hasn't changed." He held a hand up to his ear. "They are ready for you." He went back to work.

I wiped the surprise from my face before the door slid open. I halted next to a hard plastic seat, across the desk from Chief Brold, Captain Tilayvaux, and a yellow-tied lawyer. The polished mahogany desk looked old but well maintained and its inset computer was deactivated. Specialist Liu sat to my right, recording.

The captain's face was round and soft, almost puffy. But her eyes were hard, framed by blonde bangs cut straight across the brow. "Nice to meet you, Specialist Keesay. Be seated." Her voice was scratchy. Despite that, she spoke with precise enunciation. On the wall behind her hung an oil painting depicting a pack of wolves bringing down a bull moose.

Captain Tilayvaux glanced at the chief to her right, then the lawyer on her left. "We have reviewed portions of the confrontation provided by security monitors, until they were interrupted by the offender's device. We have reviewed your report. It matches the security recordings and Specialist Club's observations." She leaned forward. "Do you have anything to add?"

"No, Captain," I said evenly. "I do not."

She nodded to the chief. "Relax, Keesay," he said. "We find no fault with your actions. As a matter of fact, we had one gentleman involved who offered to buy out your contract." He waited for a response.

Was there a question? I looked at the lawyer. The tie's yellow was largely masked by black designs. Probably the best they could get on short notice.

"Conversing is part of a debriefing, Keesay," said the chief. "Don't fret. Anything said here remains with the company. It'll never see the light of day in a courtroom." I knew the chief approved of my caution. "Do you know to whom I am referring, Specialist?"

"I believe you would be referring to Mr. Habbuk of the Chiagerall Institute."

"Yes, and what did he say just prior to the incident?"

"He indicated that there was going to be trouble."

"And how did he know this?"

"I do not know, Chief."

"Speculate," Chief Brold said, leaning back in his lightly padded chair. "Could he have been associated with the offender?"

"He could have been, but I don't believe so," I answered, confirming the orientation in my head. "Mr. Habbuk is taller and was facing the scanning stations. I was facing away. He may have detected some suspicious movement or action by the offender. That may have tipped him off."

"We reviewed the images," stated the captain. "He warned you prior to any overt action taken by the offender."

I remained cautious in answering. "That may be true. I cannot attest to that. I was not facing the offender."

"Is it possible he utilized precognition?" asked the lawyer.

I almost snickered. "I don't believe in seers or fortune tellers."

"Then how do you explain his foreknowledge of events?"

I considered a moment before responding. The Chiagerall Institute is well respected in many circles and its personnel, resources, and research are sought after, especially by corporations with substantial assets. But some of the articles published by its research staff are highly speculative with little foundation and outside collaborative support. Most notably, the speculative studies involving foreseeing an event's occurrence. "He may have seen an expression or subtle movement which tipped him off."

"Your supervisor did not recognize whatever Mr. Habbuk might have seen."

He was a true believer. "Mr...?"

"Mr. Elzo Boyden," the lawyer informed me, "Fourth Class Security Specialist Keesay." He ended with a tone of dismissal.

"Mr. Boyden, I cannot speak to the observations or actions of Specialist Club. Or any of the medical or tech staff. My back was to the situation." I reminded myself not to automatically despise a lawyer. This one was on Negral's side, but what was his angle? Was he looking to be recruited by Mr. Habbuk?

Before the lawyer could respond, the chief cut in. "Why did you order the offender to advance on the right line?"

It was in my report but I restated it anyway. I'd have to thank the chief for redirecting the conversation. It rarely pays to upset a lawyer, especially one on your side. "Because he appeared apprehensive. I believed he was concerned with Specialist Club's identification of potential unauthorized components. I felt he might have contraband items as well."

"Did you direct the sec-bot to monitor a woman?" asked Mr. Boyden. "A Ms. Jazarine?"

Again, reported. "Yes, I did."

"Why did you give this directive?"

"She approached while I was confronting the offender. I was suspicious of the timing." I considered ending with that, but I knew Mr. Boyden would follow up. "I believed it was an effort to distract me. Also, her actions, striking me with her satchel and bumping the apparent vacationer who was under question, led me to believe that they were working as a team." I took a breath before finishing. "I believed that he may have transferred something to her."

The chief asked, "What was it that the offender handed to the woman?"

It was a softball question. "I did not observe an exchange. I suspected, so I assigned the sec-bot to monitor."

Mr. Boyden followed up. "Did you direct Specialist Tahgs to take this woman, Ms. Jazarine, to Medical on the *Kalavar*?"

"I did."

"Why, if you *suspected* her as an associate of the offender or possibly carrying contraband items?" accused Mr. Boyden. "She was *not* subject to search."

Maybe the lawyer was seeking to determine if my actions could stand up in court. "Five reasons," I said. "One, she had assisted in dispatching the offender. Two, the offender fired on her with lethal force. Three, she was a potential witness. Four, she would be in the company of a *Kalavar* crewmember." He could jump on the fact that Tahgs wasn't trained in security, but I continued before he cut in. "Finally, she was going into shock. Despite the fact that her wounds did not appear life threatening, they might very well have been."

"How did you come to this conclusion?" asked Mr. Boyden, continuing to see a problem with my action.

"Specialist Club identified the offender's shield as Crax," I said. "I am not sure how, but I trusted her assessment. The offender's ammunition was caustic, much like standard Crax weaponry. The residual components of Crax ammunition can get into the blood and if untreated, it's known to cause severe and possibly fatal damage to vital organs, such as the liver." I stared at Mr. Boyden. "My assessment of Ms. Jazarine was one of a proactive individual who wouldn't hesitate in locating a lawyer to recover damages for failure of Negral personnel to act in a timely manner." I looked at the chief and the captain. "Considering her positive actions, and the injury she sustained, she might have had a case."

"Relax, Keesay," said Chief Brold. "You're not on trial."

"I wouldn't rule the possibility out," warned Mr. Boyden.

"Right," laughed the chief. "Three passengers threatened to retain Falshire Hawks. Nobody boarding has that stature, money, or connections to CGIG." He looked back at me. "You performed well, Keesay. And Club identified it as Crax by the way the sec-bot's stun-net outlined the shield when it discharged." The chief stared directly at Mr. Boyden. "And lopping that cybernetic finger was fast thinking."

"I agree with the assessment," the captain stated. "Do you recall how the safety door came to be elevated?"

"The one leading to the colonists?" I asked, trying to recall. She nodded, so I continued. "It appeared the locking mechanism failed and the passengers somehow pried it up." The trio's faces indicated my assumption was incorrect. "As I stated in the incident report, I saw the passengers seeking a means of escape."

"That will suffice," said the captain. "In retrospect, is there any action you would have omitted or performed differently?"

"Only one," I said, watching Mr. Boyden's eager reaction. "I would have carried teargas rounds for my shotgun instead of counting on a sec-bot for deployment."

"Hell, Keesay," said the chief. "I'm damn glad you were lugging flare rounds."

After a long moment of silence, Captain Tilayvaux said, "Your com-set will be returned within the hour. Your sec-bot is being checked out and should be ready in two days." She leaned back in her chair, revealing an unusually snug uniform fit. That brought my attention to the Fire-wings patch, designating her as a fighter pilot for the Red Phoenix Wing. After that I noticed the large number of combat ribbons below the patch.

Chief Brold added, "Maintenance and engineering techs are busy repairing or replacing passenger equipment damaged during the incident."

"Understood," I said.

"Right now resources are tight," he continued. "Captain Tilayvaux intends to depart on schedule. Will it be a problem to load the colonists without assistance?"

I stood, giving the only answer. "Not a problem, Chief."

He stood and offered a hand radio. "Borrowed this from Mer. Circumstances have allowed us to requisition some military equipment hardened against electronic warfare. It'll be installed in your com-equipment, and some in your sec-bot."

That would give Gudkov another round programming my sec-bot. "Does that upset you, Keesay?" asked the chief.

I must have frowned. "No, Chief. Just prioritizing all the duties yet to carry out before departure."

"Well, get on them. Maybe I can scrounge you up some help. Dismissed."

I grabbed a nutrition bar on the way to my quarters. Everyone onboard the *Kalavar* was running full speed. Although I didn't expect real trouble from the colonists, I was out of shells. I cleaned up reloaded, and hurried to the main docking hatch. There, Corporal Smith leaned against a bulkhead.

"I hear you need help herding some colonists." His casual grin slowed my tempo.

"I wouldn't turn down assistance," I said. "Know anybody competent for such an arduous task?"

"Using big words won't impress me. I know your assigned duties." He shifted his slung MP carbine and slapped me on the back. "Heard you had a rough morning." He looked me over. "No new black eyes or split lips?"

I led him through the hatch to the dock. "Not yet." Repairs to the damaged walls and floors were underway. "Is the Mavinrom Dock always such a dangerous place?"

He shrugged. "Heard you bayonet charged that fellow with the shield."

News travels fast. "Not exactly, but if that's what people want to believe."

"You're a nut, Keesay."

"Is that your professional opinion?" We angled through the busy repairmen to the colonist holding area. "I'll request its inclusion in my personnel file."

He laughed. "Hey, got a recording of Pillar with your archaic firearms on the shooting range. Care to view it some time?"

"I assume you'd rate its entertainment value high?"

"That depends," said Smith, "on who you're rooting for."

I entered the room and pulled out a printed list. The colonists sat, agitated and bored. Before they could voice complaint, I ordered, "Everyone line up as I call your name. If you are unable to follow that simple directive, Corporal Smith will be forced to assist you."

I ran down the alphabetical listing and most fell in line without delay.

Fortunately, I'd committed most of the names and faces to memory. "I will lead the way to your quartering. Corporal Smith will bring up the rear. Follow single file. Move quickly and avoid interfering with dock or transport personnel." I eyed the line. "Any questions?" I expected Carver Potts or his associates to speak up. They didn't. "Excellent."

When we finally reached the relatively open recreation area inside their quartering area, the colonists stood or took seats on the benches that lined several tables. I glanced at the temporary walling and the heavy curtains that covered the entry to each divided sleeping area. I waited for silence. "I have assigned quartering arrangements. You will find your name and the names of any roommates posted next to the entry. Inside, you will find a cot, storage trunk, and three changes of clothing, including boots, socks and undergarments. Your personal possessions will be distributed later."

"Spared no expense," muttered a man nearby.

I agreed it was substandard but couldn't verbalize it. "You will spend the majority of your day in training during transport to Tallavaster."

Carver Potts edged his way to the front. "Why can't we pick our own bunkmates?"

"To keep families together and for organizational purposes."

He placed his hands on his hips. "And if we decide to switch?"

"You will take your rest in the assigned quartering, Agricultural Laborer Potts."

"And if I choose not to?"

"I will install floor rings and handcuff you there each and every night." I looked at the other colonists. "Does any colonist besides Laborer Potts have a question?"

There was silence until Potts whispered something into the man's ear next to him. The man raised his hand.

I eased my right hand into my pocket and into my brass knuckles. "Yes, Laborer Custer Simon." I maneuvered my right hand behind my back while pointing with my left. "You have a question?"

"Will you be wiping us after we crap?" He grinned proudly.

I walked up to him and locked eyes and waited. When Potts's eyes shifted from me to his friend, I brought my right fist up into his jaw. Potts staggered back into the crowd. The grin disappeared from Simon's face. Potts didn't get up.

"That was Laborer Potts's question. What was yours?"

"What did you do that for?"

"Is that your question? Or would you care to stand by Labor Potts's query?"

"You don't know—it was his question," Simon said. "You can't prove it."

"Under the terms of Laborer Potts's contract, proof is not a requirement for action I deem appropriate." I spoke to the group. "Most of you probably have never been aboard an interstellar ship. The rules of evidence and actions taken by authorities are quite different than planetside. I will post a copy for you." I lowered my voice as some of the colonists began muttering among themselves. "According to your file, Laborer Simon, your record is fairly clean. I would recommend you disassociate yourself from Laborer Potts."

I stepped back. "I suggest you all find your quartering. Your instructors will arrive shortly to get things started." The colonists dispersed. "Remain in this area until directed otherwise."

I signaled to Corporal Smith and we examined the unconscious Potts. I wiped up some of the blood from the gash my brass knuckles had made and tied my blue bandana under his jaw. "Can you get him to Medical while I finish up here?"

"Made another friend I see." He hoisted Carver Potts over his shoulder.

"You might be surprised," I said. "How many friends did I make by taking on the local bully?"

"Need training in non-lethal takedowns?"

"No. I'm competent in several. When the situation calls for them." I smiled. "I didn't think marines specialized in non-lethal combat."

"We don't," Smith answered, shifting the unconscious colonist to a better position. "See, my dad worked security. Taught me a few, so I could win fights without being brought up on charges. But if you ask nicely, maybe I'll show you a few."

"Point out Private Nicely, and I might." He laughed while I spoke into the hand radio. "Medical, this is Specialist Keesay. I'm sending a colonist with a possible fractured jaw."

CHAPTER 24

As humanity traveled to the stars a single time standard for all docks, space vessels, and colonies was established. Although planetary rotation and orbits differ, the standard 24-hour day and 365 1/4 day year remained in place. It is one of the threads that tied mankind together as it spread across the galaxy.

I stood outside the cafeteria, checking my watch and comparing it to the chronometer above the entrance. My watch remained accurate, but the mundane components kept it from tying into the ship's system. After my trip to the Mavinrom 1 Colony, I had to reset it. A second here and there generally doesn't matter, but no reason to be off.

I checked the corridor once more. Ten minutes late; Tahgs wasn't coming. I considered contacting her with my rebuilt com-set, but if she wasn't here, she was engaged in required duties. That was fine. With less than three hours before departure, I had plenty to do.

Movement through the cafeteria line was brisk and most company personnel wasted little time socializing. A few passengers, mainly standard class, were dining. I received more than my fair share of stares with whispers, "That's him," and nods in agreement.

I steered my chicken patty and carrot slices to an open table. Several bites into my meal a couple came up and thanked me for stopping the terrorist. I smiled and pointed out it was my superior, Specialist Club, who should be credited with ending the violence. This sequence transpired a half dozen times before a young man wearing black and a priest's collar sat down. His long hooked nose overshadowed his bushy mustache.

I stood. "Reverend."

"Father Cufter," he said, sitting down. His voice was deeper than expected. "Marcus Cufter."

"Specialist Krakista Keesay," I said, following his lead. He didn't have a tray. "Have you dined?"

"Not yet, Mr. Keesay. But I can tell that you're in a hurry."

"It's been a while since being addressed as Mister. You are welcome to call me that or simply Krakista."

"Don't let me interrupt your dining," said the priest with his hands folded on the table. "I witnessed your efforts in the loading area. And I've been told that you have recently found yourself thrust into other violent confrontations."

I wondered as to his source. Maybe Benny. "Performing my duty as trained." I took a drink and another bite.

"I understand. I just wanted to invite you to services."

"Thank you, Father. Have you spoken with Benjamin Cox?"

"I can't say that I have. Is he a crewmember or passenger?"

"A friend of mine. He was very excited to learn that a missionary was on the passenger list. You might look him up."

"You could bring him with you to services."

I finished my last bite. "More likely it'll be the other way around." It's always difficult to turn down a preacher. "I'll make the effort."

He stood. "If not, maybe we could just dine together on occasion? From what I hear, you're a very interesting person."

Was it okay to ask a priest his source? I was getting up when I noticed the Chicher diplomat approaching. His high pitched chattering translated, "Greetings, Security Man, I see I am delayed to nibble with you."

"You are correct, Diplomat. I must get back to my duties."

"Agreeable." The Chicher's brown eyes darted to Father Cufter. "Spirit Man," he bowed, shifting his tail to the right. "Delight in the orb passing." His translator had just finished when he scampered away toward the line.

"Your source, as to my being an interesting person, has just been verified."

"I have only one source," he said, smiling broadly. "But many brothers. Talk with you later, Krakista."

I stopped by Security. "Specialist Club, any orders before I proceed to the colonist area and await departure?"

"Yes, Keesay," she said, watching the monitors. "Stop by Medical."

"Dr. Sevanto has a question about the patient I sent?"

"Affirmative." She pointed at a screen. "Seems the missionary is working on a new convert. Dining with the Chicher ambassador."

"There's worse company he could keep." I observed the two monitors dedicated to the colonist area. Most were clearing their trays and returning them to the delivery carts. "Did they like their meal?"

"You suggested the chicken patty?"

"A personal favorite. What's good for one R-Tech should satisfy another."

"To tell the truth, most were pleased," she said. "Better than what the dock served them."

I tapped one monitor screen. "The maintenance tech by the two catering dolly-bots looks ill at ease."

"Right. He contacted me twice, wondering where you were." She switched views on several monitors. "He'll get over it."

"Maybe, you could add catering to his duty skills?" After Club snorted, stifling laughter, I asked, "Any incidents I should know about?"

"Breaking that colonist's jaw made an impression." She wheeled over to her main console. "Would you like to see it?"

"No, thank you."

"The chief thinks you went a little hard on the fellow."

"He publicly challenged my authority. I determined it was better to provide a public lesson."

"You don't have to convince me. Better they learn the rules before crossing a line with permanent consequences." She was even more serious than usual. "There are some bad characters among them."

"I know. Carver Potts is the loudest, but not the worst. Vyctor Putin, Stosh Meadows."

"I don't know why, Keesay, but the company really turned over some rocks to fill out the complement of agricultural laborers."

"According to the reports, Negral screeners and recruiters felt they'd benefit the company. Sometimes people simply need a break." I caught my pun with respect to Potts, but it went right by Club.

"Never pegged you for an optimist," she said. "Thanks for your assistance earlier."

"Just performing my assigned duty."

"Well, I'm glad I brought you along." She cocked her head. "Do you always carry flare rounds?"

"What better way to break up unruly crowds. Other than chemicals?"

"Unconventional," she said, reaching into a drawer. "Here. The chief wanted this returned to the dancer." She handed me a knife. "It was coated with a potent narcotic."

"Really?" I examined the slender steel blade.

"She has a carry permit," Club explained. "Short duration. It should've knocked the offender out fifteen seconds after entering his blood stream." She shrugged and reviewed the monitors. "Dancer's still in Medical. Stop by on your way."

"It is clean now?" I clarified, before securing it to my belt.

"That's right." She tapped a screen and the door opened.

I waved to Benny on the way to medical. He was part of a team inspecting the wall-mounted pallets. Specialist Tahgs sat at the reception desk, dictating and tapping away when I entered. "Dr. Sevanto wanted to see me."

She tapped a few screens. "He has been notified." She nodded. "He will be with you in a moment."

"Missed you at supper."

She didn't look up. "Couldn't get away."

"Understood." I stepped back to let her concentrate. I updated my electronic notebook, and then adjusted my com-set. Using the ocular, I brought into focus a current security view in the colonist area. All was quiet with most milling about. I made a note to acquire entertainment other than holo-casts.

It took my eyes a second to refocus after Dr. Sevanto approached. He looked fatigued. "Sorry, Doctor. I need more experience with this ocular."

"This way, Specialist." He led me to a wall computer and offered a stool. "Agricultural Laborer Potts. How was the injury inflicted?"

"A set of brass knuckles." He looked puzzled so I pulled them out.

"You believe in the direct approach."

"When it's called for, Doctor."

"Recent track record indicates your methodology's success." He tapped up a screen showing the fracture. "Hairline here," he said, pointing. "I've immobilized the jaw and administered a growth stimulant to the damaged area." He tapped to a diagnostic screen. "Should be fully healed within a week."

"Will it affect his ability to attend assigned agricultural training?"

"No, he'll be ready tomorrow morning. He will have difficulty participating verbally." Dr. Sevanto switched screens for a rotating view. "I've scheduled a liquid diet."

"Do you want me to take him tonight?"

He looked down a corridor. "No, we had to sedate him. Thank you for sending a marine escort."

"When do you want me to pick up Laborer Potts?"

"When do you come on duty?"

"Never pays to upset the doctor. When do you open for business?"

"Just arrive after breakfast. We can keep him tied down until then, if necessary."

I eyed my watch. "I have a delivery for Ms. Jazarine." I drew her knife. "She has a carry permit." I offered it to him. "Can you see that she receives it?"

"Although I prefer my patients unarmed, you may deliver it."

"Say the word, Doctor, and I can withhold it."

"No, I've seen her file. She applied through Negral for the permit. And in her line of work…"

I suspected but hadn't checked her file. "Exotic dancer?"

"Among other things, Specialist. You don't have access to her file?"

"I've been concentrating on the likes of Carver Potts."

"Ms. Jazarine is quite successful. Worked at the Celestial Unicorn Palace."

"I thought the Palace only employed blondes?"

"Maybe that's why she no longer works there. You can ask her."

"In your professional opinion, should I do that before I hand her the blade?"

He pointed down a hallway. "Room two. She's a pleasant lady, but I guess that's part of her job." We stood. "Remember, Keesay, first thing in the morning."

"Thanks," I said, before proceeding to Room 2, past the examination room Tech Stardz destroyed. Recalling the grotesque demise recently witnessed, I overrode the urge to give it a wide berth. I pressed the com-button and spoke. "Ms. Jazarine, this is Security Specialist Keesay. I am here to return one of your possessions."

The door slid open. "Enter, Specialist Keesay," she said in her flowing accent.

I looked around as she deactivated a holo-cast entertainment file. Her injured hand rested on an elevated cushion. An IV drained into her other wrist that rested on the white sheets.

"The reckless Keesay of Security," she said. "Come to visit?"

"No," I said. "Actually, I was directed to return your knife." I held it out for her to see.

"Kind of your superiors." Her eyes appeared glassy as she shifted them from her elevated left arm to her right. "Possibly you would be so helpful as to place it in my bag." She nodded toward a wall panel.

It was unlocked. "The narcotic has been removed." I lifted the glittering satchel. "Is there a sheath?"

"There is. It slides into a concealing fold."

I was familiar with the setup. I replaced the knife and closed panel. "Would you like me to activate the lock?"

She shook her head and sighed. "Hardly a nurse or technician enters."

I stepped toward the door. "Thank you for your assistance. I hope you recover quickly."

"It was an ordeal," she started. "But do I appear so horrid that your compulsion to depart cannot be overridden?"

"That's hardly the case, Ms. Jazarine," I said, not playing into her game. "I'm sure you know it." I glanced over my shoulder to the chronometer above the door. "Our departure time will soon arrive, and I have duties to attend."

"All duty and business," she said, losing her accent. "Well, that's better than leering and drooling." She looked around. "Have you ever been in one of these little rooms?" She took a deep, sheet-raising breath. Still playing the game. At least she was versatile.

"I've been lucky in that respect, Ms. Jazarine." I pointed to her bandaged hand. "It could've been much worse."

"He should've been knocked out."

I shrugged. "He had access to A-Tech equipment." I knew Security already interviewed her. "Why did you do it?"

"I saw the opportunity to put an end to the situation."

"How did you know to get behind Mr...?"

"Mr. Haggins," she said. "Amateurish effort. Your superior shouted the shield's weakness. I've been around, Keesay." She looked at the bed sheets. "With a body like this, a lot of men introduce themselves."

"And Mr. Haggins was one of them," I said. "Understood. I can relate from personal experience, people underestimating one's intelligence. As far as bodies go," I said, looking from her to myself, "life deals us each a different hand to play."

"You don't trust me, do you?"

"It's my job to be suspicious." I edged toward the door. "I gambled that the pain meds might cause you to slip up."

"If there was anything to learn, it might have worked."

"I have eighty or so R-Tech colonists to attend to. I doubt any have experienced interstellar travel."

"They're monitoring my blood chemistry. Dr. Sevanto said he'd attach semi-permanent prosthetics." She moved her hand and winced. "I'll be here a few days. A visitor, as opposed to an interrogator, or spectator, would be nice."

"If duty allows," I said, leaving.

Before the door slid closed, she said, "I'll take that as a no."

Tahgs was gone when I left medical. I passed Mer on the way to the colonist area. He gave me a thumbs-up, congratulating me on my efforts against the offender. He had a spare radio hanging from his belt. Even so, I informed him his hand radio was in my quarters.

I entered my room and picked up my tarred canvas satchel and loaded it with cards, dominoes, and a small checker-backgammon set. I topped it off with my carving tools, the unfinished project for Mer, and a fresh woodblock.

I arrived at my duty area and assessed the situation. Most of the colonists were nervous, avoiding conversation. I selected a seat in the common area that provided a good view, and began carving. Eventually, some of the children came around and inquired what I was doing. The first was Michael. Until then he'd been running and sliding across the smooth plated floor sections, attempting to get his floppy hat to fly off.

"Sit right there, Skids," I urged.

"Skids?" he asked, taking a seat.

I set aside Mer's completed fish and pulled out the fresh block. "Better than Michael?"

"Sure is. Who taught you to do that?"

"Hold still, Skids, and I'll tell you." I continued cutting away with my knife and wood gouges. "A neighbor we called Old Man Miller. Some called him Crazy Man Miller. Those that didn't call him crazy he took hiking and camping."

"Does that glove protect your hand?"

"Correct." Some of the other children watched with their parents hovering nearby, unsure as to my intentions. "Where are you from, Skids?" The question alarmed him.

A young boy said, "His name is Michael, not Skids."

"I know," I said. "It's a nickname."

"I want a nickname, too," said the boy. He had short, black hair and was under ten years. Several others nodded in agreement.

I stopped carving. "Vargus, correct?"

"Vargus Idaduhut," he said proudly.

"Well, Master Idaduhut, I can't just assign a nickname. It has to fit."

"When will you have one for me?"

"First, your father has to approve." I looked at the other six youths. "Or mother or guardian. Then it will come to me."

"I want an old-time one," said Vargus.

"We'll see." I shrugged, and looked back to Michael. "Skids, look this way." He grinned as I continued carving. The children began getting restless.

"Do you know any stories?" asked a woman. I looked up to see it was Michael's mother.

I thought a moment. Maybe she wanted something educational. "How many of you have heard of the *Iron Armadillo*?" Several said yes, but with little conviction. Twenty minutes later I finished the background on the Silicate War and the *Iron Armadillo*'s contribution. Several adults joined the group.

"Have you ever seen a Shard?" asked a girl named Sallie. Her hair was braided like McAllister's but it was dark, matching her complexion.

"No, I'm too young to have fought in the war."

"Maybe that marine that was with you has."

"Sallie," I said, "I don't believe Corporal Smith is old enough to have fought the Shards. But I think he'd have done a good job."

An elderly colonist named Lowell Owen spoke up. "I worked in a lab that housed one of their offshoots, a Flake."

Everyone looked his direction. He regretted speaking up. "What did it look like?" I encouraged. "I've only seen pictures and holos."

"Well." He stood up scratching his head. "It didn't look like a Shard. They're big. Eight foot masses of jagged crystals." He stared ahead, recalling the memory. "No, the Flake was about this big around." He held his hands eighteen inches apart. "Maybe it was a small one. Frosty white and fragile, like a three dimensional snowflake. Wouldn't want to touch it. Or them touch you. But this one was dead."

"Why not?" asked Michael.

Colonist Owen's confidence grew. "Scientists in the lab were studying it. Said if parts of it got under your skin, it would rupture the cell structure. Get into the blood stream causing hemorrhaging. Internal bleeding."

"How'd they move?" asked Sallie. "I seen a picture, and they don't have legs, or wings."

"They flew, but I don't know how." He looked toward me.

"You're the expert on this one," I said.

"Scientists said they manipulated micro gravities." Colonist Owen shrugged. "That's what I gathered. They're rigid and can't move like us." He sat down. "That's all I know."

"My grandpa told me the Crax are going to start a war," voiced an older child named Arden. His wide brown eyes shifted from Owen to me. "Is that true?"

"The only ones who know that," I said, "other than the Crax and their allies, would be our generals and admirals. And they don't consult with me." A few of the nearby adults chuckled while the children looked confused. "The answer is, I don't know." I checked my watch, then set down my completed carving and pulled out the games. "We have about an hour before departure, and then another thirty minutes before passage through the con-gate." I looked to Instructor Watts and the small assemblage of adults. "Last night of freedom. Schooling starts tomorrow." I pointed to the games and the children scattered. "Make sure I get them back." I tossed a deck of cards to Colonist Owen. "Maybe you can put these to use. I have to make my rounds."

I got up and started putting away my carving equipment. "Here, Instructor Watts." I finished carving my mark on the bottom of the completed bust.

She took it. "It looks just like Ma-ichel, Specialist Keesay."

I ignored her stutter. "I'll call him Skids. Unless you object."

She was tongue-tied. "You really have talent."

"My mother had artistic talent," I said. "A political cartoonist. Marlene Keesay." She didn't recognize the name. "I have to make my rounds."

She intercepted. "This was very kind. Wood out here must be extremely expensive."

"It is if you don't bring your own." I winked. "I do."

"How can I repay you?"

"I needed to build rapport with the colonists. Carving was one way to get their attention." For some reason I didn't classify Instructor Watts as a colonist. I looked around, finally seeing a few smiles. "But if you could help ensure return of all the parts to my games, that will be appreciated."

"I believe that can be arranged," she said, turning to look for her son, cradling the wooden bust.

I wandered and chatted with the colonists. Most were friendly enough. Vyctor Putin, Stosh Meadows and Custer Simon made a show of avoiding me.

Lowell Owen was an amateur historian and we discussed aspects of the Silicate War. Colonist Owen said he'd worked for a military contractor bought out by Capital Galactic Investments. They non-renewed his contract. With no family or friends tying him down, he signed on with the first company that hired him.

"It's almost time, Colonist Owen," I said, and walked over to the floor-mounted holo-projector. While adjusting it, I received a call through my com-set.

"Specialist Keesay, this is Club. All in order for departure?"

"Affirmative. Everything is in order."

She wasted little time. "Acknowledged, out."

I adjusted my com-set to receive launch information before returning my focus to the holo-projector and tapped into a local satellite feed. "For those of you who are interested, you can watch our departure and movement through the con-gate." About forty colonists gathered around. Those in front sat so the others could see the three-dimensional view of the *Kalavar.* Two other ships docked alongside dwarfed the *Kalavar.*

"Which is ours?" asked a colonist.

"The smallest of the three." I examined the ship outlines. All were long, rectangular, and boxy in shape. "The largest is an interstellar freighter. The other appears to be a military troop transport." I looked closer. "Orbiting in the distance there's a large transport."

"Where's the con-gate?" asked the same colonist.

I examined the projector's menu, tapped several directives, then sat back. "Projector, switch to view local con-gate." The holographic image flickered to show the distant gate. "Enlarge image." The con-gate, a series of five enormous hoops tethered by a skeletal superstructure, zoomed into focus.

"What are those four big boxes on each circle?" asked Vargus.

"Those are power generators," answered Lowell Owen. "The more condenser rings a gate has, the more it can condense space. Generator sizes are pretty standard for maintenance reasons, so if you count the rings, you can tell the strength of the con-gate."

I didn't point out that a lot depended upon the gate builder's tech level.

"Why is it moving?" asked a young lady colonist.

I waited for Colonist Owen to answer, but he didn't. "It shifts orientation," I said. "So when a ship passes through, it enters condensed space with proper trajectory."

"What's that mean?" asked Sallie, looking to her mother and father.

"Going the right direction," her father replied. "You can't turn very well in space moving so fast."

Her father had the gist of it. "The *Kalavar,*" I added, "will maneuver for the correct approach. She has a cascading atomic engine and could condense space independently. But it's more efficient to use a gate."

"Why?" asked Sallie.

Michael began to speak, but his mother grabbed his shoulder and whispered in his ear.

"With all of those generators on the con-gate," I said, "it takes less time to build up the energy needed."

"Also less strain on a ship's engines," added Colonist Owen.

"All systems check, Captain," came over my com-set. "Ready to detach from the Mavinrom Dock."

"Projector, return to view of Mavinrom Dock," I commanded. As it switched, I announced, "The *Kalavar* is preparing to depart. Every colonist except Instructor Watts and Colonist Owen braced themselves. I found myself with the majority. A small metallic vibration ran through the hull. On the screen the *Kalavar*'s docking thrusters flared.

Vargus said, "That was boring."

"I'm glad it was," said Willie Beddow, Sallie's father.

"It'll take about thirty minutes to reach the gate," I said, getting up.

"What does it feel like going into condensed space?" asked an unseen colonist.

I looked around. "I'm hardly an expert," I said. But many worried expressions beckoned for an answer. "Ships really don't enter condensed space. They ride just ahead of the wash. The anti-gravity field generated protects the ship." I was unsure of the actual physics behind the phenomenon and the physiological consequences. Still, I tried to come up with an adequate analogy. "Scientists say it's easier to enter condensed space than exit. They describe it like running into a soft foam barrier. But if you come out too abruptly it can damage your organs and tissues, mind and body. Like ocean diving. You come up from the pressure too fast and it causes internal chemical imbalances." My explanation clarified little, and only heightened anxiety.

"It will feel like you're accelerating in a fast rocket," said Colonist Owen. "But you don't experience the gravitational forces. And once we're traveling, you'll feel unusual. Kind of disconnected." He strained for the right words. "Almost like you're waiting for something to happen."

"You'll hardly notice it by morning," I said. "I recommend, after we pass through the gate, you turn in for the evening. Breakfast arrives at 7:00 a.m. Your instructors will be awaiting you."

"Prepare to fire main engines," came the order from the captain over my com-set.

"Projector, switch view to departing medium transport *Kalavar*," I ordered. As the engines blazed to life, I felt the change in inertia. Most of the colonists noticed it as well. "At least that orients you as to the fore and aft of the ship," I said. The almost inaudible hum of the main engines added their voice to the mingling background sound of the lights and other machinery.

The colonists didn't notice or care. The main center engine's exhaust glowed a whiter color than the two secondary. I recalled Mer stating that the main engine had been torn out before mothballing. The replacement had to be more advanced and powerful.

"Prepare to fire auxiliary engines," the captain ordered. The two temporary rockets packed with liquid hydrogen fired. A second shift in inertia ran through the hull.

"Wow, look at those engines!" Sallie pointed. "They're brighter." She tugged at Colonist Owen's brown shirt. "See?"

He nodded. "Yes, they'll get us moving faster before we enter the con-gate." He looked toward her father. "Once we're through we'll count on the ship's main engines."

Again, Colonist Owen looked nervous but continued since all eyes were on him. "The temporary engines will be jettisoned once the more volatile liquid hydrogen is burned. We'll count on our main engines burning metallic hydrogen." I didn't add what I suspected, that our main engine was a hybrid capable of ion drive thrust. Pretty advanced, and expensive.

I stepped close to Colonist Owen, who was watching a game of dominoes from afar. "You're not R-Tech, are you?"

He experienced an internal debate. We stepped out of earshot of the other colonists. "No, Specialist," he said with a little disgust. "I figured talking would give it away."

"Did you really work maintenance for a military contractor?"

"Yes—yes I did." He chuckled to himself. "Guess it really doesn't matter now."

"Your skills always matter," I said.

"No, that's not it. See, I worked for Blue Star Industries, a subsidiary of Capital Galactic." He ground his teeth in thought, and looked around. "Let's just say that Blue Star was involved in questionable acquisitions." He paused. "I blew the whistle." He slid to a bench, but changed his mind about sitting. "To make a long story short, my contract was non-renewed. Somehow my benefits were forfeit. My local representative, who was supposed to look out for me, was less than helpful."

"Not all politicians respond to their constituent's needs," I agreed.

"Bought, would be more accurate." He shook his head. "Government work was out. I took the first thing I found."

"I recently signed on with Negral," I said. "Its future seems bright."

"Yeah, I was desperate and sold myself cheap. And after that cold sleep transport. These facilities." He looked around. "A few of the maintenance crew were here earlier. Said you petitioned Negral to improve the place."

"Negral is a new corporation," I said. "It'll cut corners where it can."

We sat in silence for quite a while. I checked several security views through my ocular and sound through my com-set. All appeared in order.

"Approaching con-gate, Captain," came over my com-set.

"Jettison auxiliary engines," ordered Captain Tilayvaux. The two lifeless rockets catapulted way. "Initiate sequence to enter condensed space travel."

Almost on cue, Instructor Watts handed me the domino and checker set. "They're finishing up their card game."

I stood and led Instructor Watts toward the holo-projector. Looking back, "Colonist Owen," I said, and signaled him to join us. Grudgingly, he did.

The *Kalavar*'s constant acceleration propelled us toward the con-gate. The view from the satellite was imperfectly angled, but reasonable. I set my com-set for broadcast, but with a two-second delay for security purposes.

"Establish anti-gravity field," ordered the captain. Her measured and precise voice gathered colonists' attention.

"Established," responded the navigator.

"Mavinrom Dock," called the captain. "Is the gate aligned?"

"Affirmative," answered the dock controller. "Transport *Kalavar*. Con-gate is aligned for transport from Gliese 876, the Mavinrom Colony to Zeta Aquarius en route to HD 222582, the Tallavaster Colonies."

"Acknowledged," said the captain. "Destination, Zeta Aquarius." She paused. "Request activation of con-gate."

"Request received, transport *Kalavar*. Activation sequence engaged."

The *Kalavar* continued its approach. The angled view into the con-gate revealed a five-stage distortion within the enormous rings.

"All readings are stable," stated the controller. "Condensation ratio 51.375K."

"Acknowledged" said Captain Tilayvaux. "C.R. is 51,375 to 1. Estimated arrival to initial destination, five months, eighteen days."

"Good luck, *Kalavar*. Mavinrom Dock, out."

Every colonist held his breath as the *Kalavar* accelerated into the gate. I found myself holding, too, while a sensation, like a thin film of water washing over and through my body, preceded a feeling of being pulled without movement. The anticipatory anxious feeling followed.

Smiles, hugs and backslaps ended with a few cheers and shouts. Then the crowd, taking my advice, dispersed to their rooms. I loitered a few minutes, gathering my playing cards before departing.

I caught up with Mer as he shuffled down the pallet-narrowed corridor leading to our rooms. "Mer, give me a second and I'll return your hand radio."

"Sure thing, Kra. Just come on over."

Benny wasn't in. I pulled the finished carving of two guppies from the canvas sack and grabbed the hand radio. I tapped lightly on Mer's door. It slid open. The old man stood in front of this fish tanks.

"How are they adjusting to the travel?" I walked over to see. Most were swimming normally. A few younger ones darted about erratically, while three or four corkscrewed through the water. "Will those make it?"

"They might adjust," he said. "Just set the radio on the bed."

"I brought this, too," I said, handing him the finished carving. "I don't have any paints, nor am I very talented when it comes to their application."

"This looks finer than anything I've seen in a long time. No need for paint." He shuffled over to his shelf and slid other knickknacks aside. "Ever since I saw you working on it, I've been anxious to see it finished."

"Carving gives me something to do," I said. "Relaxes me."

"Playing cards was relaxing, too," Mer said, yawning. "Maybe we'll do it again sometime?"

"Anytime I'm not on duty. I'll leave a deck under my pillow if I'm not available." I edged toward the door. "I have a full schedule tomorrow so I'll take my leave." I turned to go and felt my balance shift. "What was that?" His expression indicated it wasn't my imagination.

"Felt like something shoved her in the side," Mer said. "There she goes again."

"A disruption in the anti-grav field?"

"Don't know, Kra. Hold on." Mer shuffled over to his wall computer and activated it.

Captain Tilayvaux's face appeared. "You felt it, too," she said.

Mer asked, "Well, what was it?"

"We're checking." She moved to peer over the navigator's shoulder. The camera view followed.

I started to ask a question, but Mer signaled for my silence. Why would the captain discuss the malfunction, or anomaly, with Mer?

With a grim look the captain stated, "Readings are consistent with the near passage of two message rockets. One may be parallel to our trajectory. The other along a similar, but not parallel, vector." She looked back to the navigator. "We can't be sure."

"The dock wouldn't have sent something our direction through the con-gate so soon."

"I agree," said the captain. She looked back at the navigator. "Lieutenant Pidsadaki believes they were ship launched and entered condensed space independently."

Mer scratched his head. "Could've been the military transport sending an update on the Crax invasion of Felgan space."

Mer didn't sound convinced of his last statement. Crax invasion? I struggled to remain silent. A message rocket with internal cascading atomic engine? It would be hard to imagine what could justify such an astronomical expense with a con-gate available.

"The *Pars Griffin*," said Captain Tilayvaux.

Mer nodded. "Do you recommend bringing the main thrust engine to emergency acceleration?"

"If the cascading atomic engine can accommodate it," she said. "Chief Engineer Harkins and Security Chief Brold have been monitoring. We'll get on the calculations and risk analysis. Keep you advised. Out."

Mer switched off his computer and stiffly settled into his chair. After a second he slammed his fist against the armrest. "Them devils," he seethed. He hissed, releasing a pent up breath before glancing at me calm as ever. "Maybe you heard more than you should've." He didn't wait for a response. "Wondering why the captain consulted me?"

My mind was in full gear. "That," I agreed, "among other things."

"You'd have figured it out soon enough," he said. "The captain, she commands the *Kalavar*. But I own her." He held up a finger. "The other things...don't forget'em. But don't ask or talk about'em."

It'd be hard. "Understood." I stepped smoothly out as Mer reclined and stared at the ceiling.

Two hours later I finally dozed off.

CHAPTER 25

All interstellar ships simulate Earth's twenty-four hour cycle. Appropriate UV radiation is provided during daylight hours. After nightfall the lights are dimmed, the temperature is lowered by several degrees Celsius, and UV emissions are significantly reduced. Mission critical areas are exempt.

Such implementations have been standard practice since the inception of interstellar flight. When such a regimen was absent, psychological factors including stress, fatigue, and irritability increased, leading to disruptive and dangerous consequences.

"This corn is excellent," I said before gnawing another bite from the cob.

"The authentic butter is the real treat," decided Security Specialist Frost.

"...I liked last week's black raspberry yogurt better," said Benny, despite the fact he'd already finished his corn.

I conjured the yogurt memory and compared it to tonight's experience. "I agree with you, Benny. Even better than the first week's treat, authentic maple syrup."

"Nawh," said Frost. "It tasted the same as synthetic yogurt."

"Not quite," I disagreed. "The texture, that's the difference. Mixing chemicals to fool the taste buds is easier than concocting the proper texture."

"...Does not matter," Benny said, wiping his hands on his cloth napkin square. "It is better than standard food."

"How often do the first classers dine like this?" I asked.

"More than us," said Frost. "But less than they'd like."

I didn't want to dwell on the fact that my meal was almost finished. "Frost, how goes roving patrol?"

"Spend most of my time assigned to engineering. Either aft near the thrust engines or forward around the cascading. Lot of activity there." Frost tossed his barren cob onto his tray. "How about the colonists?"

"They've located the security cameras and recording devices." I moved my cleaned cob aside and searched for butter to sop up with my bread. "The few I've identified as probable transgressors avoid the monitored areas."

"Does your sec-bot help out?"

"Lefty's there twenty-four hours a day, except for maintenance and recharge. They like the sec-bot less than me." I finished my juice. "I'm in contact with their instructors. Diesel mechanics, agriculture and livestock management. They keep the adults busy with training and after hour assignments."

"You're helping out the youth instructor, too." Frost grinned and shook his head. "Seen you and Corporal Smith in the shuttle bay playing ballgames with the colonist kids."

"Yeah, sometimes I cover their recreation time in the marine training area. Only open place available except for the first class ballroom."

"Saw that Chicher with you," said Frost. "What's it there for?"

I smiled. "Umpire."

"What's it know of—what's that ballgame?"

"Whiffle ball. Can you think of a more impartial umpire?"

"It's a diplomat. Hasn't it got anything better to do?"

"That's the point, a diplomat. Apparently not." Frost looked puzzled. "The missionary suggested him," I said. "Don't ask me. I've had a few meals with the diplomat. Chicher are used to running in packs, so I suppose any interaction keeps him occupied." I watched for Frost's reaction. "And he's a good ump."

Frost squinted, saying, "I don't know. What do the colonists think of their kids running with an overgrown rat?"

"It's good for them. They need to get used to aliens if they're going to be light years from Earth."

"From where does this wisdom rise?" Frost grinned again. "Personal experience?"

I shook my head. "No. Common sense. Heard of it?"

"Yeah, unfortunately I left it under my pillow the day I signed on."

Before I could respond, Benny said, "We have your marbles and leaping cords in Maintenance."

"Jump ropes, thanks," I said. "And I'll need to speak with your maintenance buddies about activating some of the dormant security monitors."

"...You will need to schedule it with Gudkov," Benny said without emotion. "We are working with engineering on several projects."

I wasn't thrilled to work with Gudkov. "I'll speak with him at our next security meeting."

We stared at our empty plates. I was about to get up when Frost looked around and signaled me closer. "I wouldn't doubt that Gudkov and his pals have something brewing, if you know what I mean."

I nodded. "I've done my best to avoid Gudkov, Haxon and Senior Engineer McAllister." Benny could hear so I kept formal when naming McAllister. "Occasionally, I check under my pillow."

"I don't know about McAllister," Frost said, "but your avoidance has irked Gudkov. If Haxon didn't have separate duties, I'd mistake him for Gudkov's shadow."

Frost probably knew more than he let on, but any information was helpful. No sense pushing. "His choice," I said.

Frost scanned the area and gathered his tray. "Gentlemen."

Benny watched him leave. "He is hoping for trouble between you and Gudkov."

"I know. He may not be completely looking out for my interests, but he certainly isn't for Gudkov." I finished my drink and checked my watch. I still had a few minutes. "Mer mentioned getting together for cards."

"...I am free. Any suggestions for a fourth?"

"I could get Lowell Owen, one of the colonists," I said, "or maybe Corporal Smith again."

I saw the look in Benny's eye as he formed the words. "...What about Janice?"

"She's your friend, Benny. If you want her to play, you can ask her."

"...She won't show unless you ask."

"Janice is a very nice lady," I said. "And I'm sorry if my quartering assignment has disrupted your friendship."

"...I know last time you asked—"

"Yes, last time I asked, Administrative Specialist Tahgs said she refused to fill in until Dancer Jazarine received her temporary prosthetics."

"...I know," he said, looking away. "She really had fun when we played."

"So did I. Tell you what, after I make my rounds I'll track Specialist Tahgs down and ask her, one more time. After that, it's up to you."

About a half hour later I contacted Benny over my com-set. "Sorry, she has other, indefinite plans. Let me know if you find a fourth. I'll be in the gym working out."

"...Guess you were right, Kra."

"You can always get her and someone else. Cards are under my pillow."

"...No. Mer and I will probably watch an old flat screener. You can join us."

"Maybe later, thanks. Out."

"Who you talking to, Keesay?" asked Smith, slapping me on the shoulder. "Getting used to that modern hardware?"

"Benny. I was just heading to the gym to work out. Need to improve my athletic prowess if we're going to beat your team."

"Those kids really get into that whiffle ball don't they? Where'd you come up with those nicknames?"

"Came up with what seemed to fit."

Smith checked his watch. "About three days from now, I have you scheduled for another trouncing." He stopped and motioned the other direction. "Hey, if you got a few minutes to kill we can check out that recording."

"I'm not sure. It might invoke flashbacks and nightmares."

"What, of Pillar kicking your ass?" He shook his head. "If you suffered a nightmare every time you were reminded of a sound thumping."

"What makes you think I get thumped on a regular basis?"

"Remind me. Is this the second full week I haven't seen you with a black eye or a fat lip?"

"And how many weeks have you known me?"

"Too many. Now let's go relive some fond memories."

I followed him to the marine quartering that consisted of a large barracks area with equipment stored every, and anywhere. Several marines were sleeping. Training holos occupied the others. After rummaging through his duffle bag Smith called, "DeLark."

The young marine hopped off his bunk and trotted over. I recognized him from the dock shooting range. "Yes, Corporal," he said in his uncharacteristically high voice.

"Keesay here is interested in viewing a target shooting competition." Smith grinned. "You haven't seen it either?"

DeLark split a wide smile and slapped me on the shoulder. "Yeah, I'd be interested."

"Here," said Smith. "See if you can load this memory chip into the mini-simulator."

"Right away, Corporal."

We followed Private DeLark at a leisurely pace. "A large transport full of marines docked just before we departed. You know anything about it, Keesay?"

I shook my head. "No." Maybe it had to do with the Crax invasion of Felgan space, but I said nothing. "Saw one docked when we departed."

"The *Iron Wagon*," he said. "Fast transport. Carries the Third Colonial Marines, the Scrap-Iron Division." He waited for a response.

"I know of them. Best trained. Toughest of the elite."

He stepped a little closer and lowered his voice. "Did you know a battle group including the *Spine Crusher* and *Hornet Nest* was stationed on the other side of Mavinrom?"

"A battle cruiser and heavy carrier behind the planet? Orbiting opposite the dock? No."

"You do now," Smith said. "Heard they were waiting for reinforcements."

"That would eliminate any training exercise theories," I said.

"That firepower could eliminate a lot more than theories." We approached the simulator. "Your captain probably knows. Just hasn't mentioned it to you." He rapped on the metal door. "Ready yet?"

DeLark stuck his head out. "What?"

"Is the program loaded?"

"Yes, Corporal." He swung the door open and stepped aside. "Enter at your leisure."

"After you, Specialist Keesay," offered Smith. "Remember what I told you about the Stegmar Mantis?"

The simulator was roughly four yards wide and deep, and at least three and a half high. "The predatory sounding? I remember." I continued to examine the interior. A myriad of projection lenses and speakers were lodged along the walls, floor and ceiling.

"He hasn't heard it before?" DeLark asked. "Hope his bladder ain't full."

"He can handle it," Smith said with a warning glance my direction. "Start the program."

I stood along the back wall between the two observing marines. DeLark held a remote, controlling the simulation. A location, date and time image hovered before the scene set itself. Privates Ringsar and Hiroyuki appeared and began selecting their defensive setup and equipment. DeLark adjusted our view so that we were slightly elevated to the scene.

"They took the simulated injections to ward off the toxin," Smith said.

The targeting program loaded terrain features. Ringsar and his partner took up positions behind a four-foot crumbling concrete wall. In the distance, to the right of a pale, red setting sun, a large communication tower stretched skyward from a rubble-strewn landscape.

"You fire on any fliers," ordered Ringsar. "I'll target ground runners. Concentrated fire on any shielded Crax."

Then it started. The noise, a combination of harsh clicking and screeching chirps, rose before movement could be spotted. Involuntarily, I gritted my teeth. Corporal Smith watched my reaction out of the corner of his eye. "It gets worse," he said, "but doesn't last long."

I spotted the movement just after the shooters. "Keep down," urged Hiroyuki. "Their weapons have better range." A barrage of projectiles clattered against and over the wall, interrupting his orders.

Ringsar and Hiroyuki struggled to shake off the sounding's effects as it intensified. "Here they come," grunted Ringsar. I struggled to focus through the nerve-wracking noise as well. "Three bulldogs," shouted Ringsar, "three o'clock coming in low."

A trio of basketball-sized beetles, each with a double set of pinching jaws, flew awkwardly in. "Diversion," said Hiroyuki.

"I know," said Ringsar. "I'll take the lead, then repel the left." He popped up and fired. One beetle staggered in flight before crashing. Hiroyuki popped around the side taking the other two.

Ringsar pulled the trigger at another target. I smiled inwardly as he spun back to cover, thumbed the hammer. "Damn," he cursed at wasting the vital second.

The double-barrel shotgun sounded twice as Hiroyuki brought down two Stegmar. He caught one firing and the other while it leapt forward, toward cover. Ringsar's quick aim nailed three of four advancing Stegmar.

"We won't hold'em for long with this equipment," shouted Hiroyuki, reloading. He spun and emptied both barrels on target, taking a needle in the leg. "I've taken one," he said. "Perimeter, twenty-five meters."

Ringsar had removed my revolver's cylinder and was attempting to extract the empty casings. "Cover while I reload!"

Hiroyuki popped up, taking a low approaching beetle and forcing a mantis on the left to duck behind a pile of cinder blocks. "Took another in the arm," he said.

"Argh," grunted Ringsar as he dropped a fresh round trying to load.

Another double-barreled blast. "Perimeter fifteen meters," announced Hiroyuki. The sounding's ferocity climbed to new heights causing me to break into a cold sweat. "They're coming!" he shouted.

Muttering what must have been curses, Ringsar slid the cylinder in place, slid the pin and locked it in. "Ready, NOW!" he shouted.

The marines turned and opened up on the encircling swarm. Their horribly inadequate firepower allowed Ringsar to only get three rounds off, taking out two and wounding one. His partner managed to unload both barrels once more before the simulation announced, "Disabling damage sustained by both defenders."

"Lights," commanded Smith. A little stain hung in his voice.

After taking a deep breath, DeLark said, "Pretty low score."

Smith grinned, watching me wipe my brow. "Cut off the ending," he said. "Didn't think you'd care to hear Pillar's choice words about you and your equipment."

I tilted my head and stretched my neck. "I know his opinion of me. Guess my old-style guns aren't up to modern combat."

"We'd have done better, but still would've been fast overrun," Smith said. "Really, against the Stegmar and the bulldogs a shotgun is okay. If you go up against a screen in combat." He stopped. "Right, you know the consequences first hand."

Before I commented, DeLark spoke up. "At least you didn't puddle."

Smith laughed. "DeLark, Keesay here bayonet charged an armed terrorist sheltering behind a Crax shield." He opened the door. "Keesay, you do look a little tense."

"That battle call really gets under the skin," I said. "Do you get used to it?" I rotated my jaw, trying to release some of the built up tension.

"A little. But you can turn the tables on them."

"Is that all, Corporal?" interrupted DeLark, offering him the memory chip.

"Sure, thanks," Smith said before leading me toward his bunk. "Said you were going to work out?"

"Correct. A little exercise to work off the day's frustrations, and the simulation."

"Mind if I join you?"

"Be my guest." I watched while he grabbed some sweats. "What were you saying about turning the tables?" I led the way out of the barracks.

"Oh, right." He swung his garment sack over his shoulder. "If you have enough men who won't falter, and can keep a steady beat, you can turn the tables."

"Drown out the sounding?" I asked skeptically.

"No. But instruments or a song with a strong rhythm can unnerve the bugs, throws off their sounding." Hand gestures emphasized Smith's points. "See, they originally used sounding to panic prey into flight. But organized resistance seems to get under their...ahh, exoskeleton. Breaks their confidence."

"Why not arm each combatant with sound recordings?"

"Doesn't work. Scientists don't know why. Just doesn't."

"How many voices are required?"

"Six to eight," he said. "Might need more if their numbers are excessive."

"Doesn't it bother the bulldog beetles or the Crax?"

"The bulldogs are probably immune. Maybe like a hunting dog getting used to his master's gunfire. The Crax?" He shrugged his shoulders. We walked a moment. "You know," he started, but squinted his eyes and switched topics. "How goes your fourteen-hour days?"

"Only five days a week. Half duty on two."

"Should've signed on with the Marines. At least you'd get a decent uniform."

"Do they issue bayonets?"

We laughed and joked the rest of the way to the gym.

Smith went over to chat with a few marines while I stretched. Gudkov and Haxon stood, joking around near the free weights. They lost their smiles when I began my laps. Before I knew it, they were gone. So much the better.

After three miles and a breather, I wandered over to Smith at the wrestling mats as he talked to a stocky, angry looking marine. The angry marine shot me a glance and departed. "Smith, you want to show me that takedown you've been talking about?"

He looked distracted. "Sure, Keesay." We walked to an open mat and leaned close. "You know anything about Thrust?"

His question took me by surprise. "Thrust?"

"Combat enhancement drug," he whispered. "Triples strength. Doubles reflexes. Masks pain."

"I've heard of it. Isn't it restricted to front line combat units?"

"According to regulations, yes. Ever see anyone on it?"

"No, why?"

"Let's practice some simple takedowns. You listen."

"Okay." We went through some basic moves and throws.

"You're about to be set up." We went through several holds. "Someone on the stuff." He reversed a hold. "Going to want to spar with you."

"My friend Gudkov?"

"Don't know," he said. "Maybe."

"You sure about this?"

"He led me off the mat. Best we shower-up."

"Think I should duck him?" I grabbed a towel. "It can become a bad habit." His jaw almost dropped as he stared at me. "Would you?" I asked.

"It ain't me. Just my sound advice, Keesay."

Nobody would know if I simply left now, I thought. "How'd you know?"

We turned to leave. "I just do."

"Keesay!" boomed Gudkov's voice across the gym.

"Always a second late and a credit short," I said to Smith.

"What?" Smith asked me as we turned and watched Gudkov and Haxon swagger across the gym. "Smith, how do I spot someone on it?"

"Their eyes," he whispered. "Narrow pupils. Constant movement, even when staring ahead."

Gudkov and his shadow approached. Gudkov's eyes appeared intense but normal. "You called my name, Tech Gudkov?"

He ignored Smith's presence. "You up for some sparring?"

I stared at Haxon. "Not with you, Gudkov." Haxon's eyes held steady, unmoving.

Gudkov feigned disappointment. "Too bad. But no, not with me. One of my friends."

"Sure, I'll go a few rounds with Haxon."

Haxon smiled and brushed aside a curl of blonde hair.

"Glad you're interested in going a few rounds," said Gudkov. "But not with him."

"Then I'm not interested."

"Sure you are, Keesay. Consider a trained sec-spec ducking a match with a woman?"

His minor etiquette breech, referring to a fellow security specialist as a sec-spec outside our circle, was meant to get attention. "I'm sure you're aware a woman can become an expert in unarmed combat. Just like any man."

Gudkov crossed his arms. "There're separate divisions for men and women at the top levels because physically they can't compete. Trust me, Keesay, I've watched. I'll give that you're competent. If you weren't, the company wouldn't have hired you."

Much of the gymnasium activity had slowed. "I was preparing to leave, so get to your point."

"McAllister would like to go a round or two with you." He projected the challenge just loud enough for all to hear. "Unless you're afraid." He leaned in. "Word like that gets around. And sticks."

"I'll go with Haxon. Not McAllister." I scanned the area not spotting her.

"Why not?"

"He's trained," I guessed. "She's not."

His grin widened. "Check her file, Keesay. I trained her." He leaned closer. "So when she kicks your ass, it'll be like part of me doing it."

I took a chance. "Who'd ref?"

"No need. Just a friendly match."

I refrained from looking at Smith. It was a set up, but maybe I could turn the tables. I spotted McAllister over his shoulder. Too far away to be sure if she was on anything, but her movements seemed jerky and restrained. "Like I said, Gudkov, I was getting ready to shower. She wants a piece of me, try tomorrow."

"She's here and ready. You're here and running. How's that going to look to your colonists?"

I couldn't lose face with some in that crowd or I'd be up against it for weeks. "Give me a minute to hit the head." I turned and hoped Smith would follow. He did. We made it to the lockers. I looked and listened. Nobody around. "I've got a plan, Smith. You in?"

He shook his head. "She's on it. You won't win."

"Maybe not. She may not either." I retrieved my com-set from my locker and made a few adjustments. "Here. You familiar with this set?"

He looked it over. "Simple."

"Good. I've set it to record. Will relay it to my personal file and my sec-bot. All you have to do is record."

"Won't be the first time I watch you get slammed."

I reached into my locker and traded cups. Then went to relieve myself. "Right, and maybe we can view it with DeLark. I might lose, but that doesn't mean I'll let them win."

"It's your body. You've no comprehension of Thrust's effects."

"How does it react with other drugs?"

"Not well, why?"

"That's too bad." I winked, and led him out.

He grabbed a towel and tossed it over my com-set and joined the stocky marine on the sidelines.

A dozen spectators, including Nist and Frost stood around. McAllister walked out toward the central mat. I moved to the far left one and waited while she stiffly crossed over.

She was barefoot and wearing a white martial arts robe with a brown and green sash-like belt. Her eyes twitched ever so slightly and her pupils were constricted. "Anatol put you up to this, or was it your idea?"

"Listen up, smart ass," she hissed. "When I've finished with you, if you aren't dead you'll be permanently disabled."

"I probably should be scared, but in the big picture I've got a lot less to lose."

"Don't worry, Killer. Unlike you, I'm capable of making it look accidental." Her drug-crazed grin had to be hell-spawned. "And if I don't, what's a career compared to a life?"

Up until that moment I hadn't considered the situation life and death. I'd take Corporal Smith's advice without question in the future. Maybe I should mutter it so he could make it my epitaph.

No sense playing on the up and up. I shifted my eyes over her shoulder and feigned surprise. "Think the captain will appreciate your handiwork?" I didn't wait to see if she fell for it. She did because my right connected with her chin, staggering her. I ducked, anticipating McAllister's response. Still, her swing clipped my scalp. My left jab took her in the midsection, knocking some of the wind out of her.

McAllister hopped back and smiled but I closed, unwilling to give up any advantage gained. She met me with a hail of kicks and blows, about a half of which I blocked. My nose and mouth were bleeding and I was sure I had several cracked ribs. She was too fast and her blows might well have been Kickboxing Champ Gudkov's. Through it all, I glimpsed her maniacal grin.

I snagged one of her arms and yanked her close. She spun to throw me. With my free arm I snatched a handful of her wildly braided hair and when she flipped me, and I clung to the red braids, yanking her to the ground after me. Then I felt it, a crushing knee to the groin. Her face, dripping blood from my initial punch, hung close to mine as I fought to remain conscious. A sudden fear registered—what if Dr. Sevanto switched the Triskiseral for something inert?

McAllister's smile faltered. I snapped my forehead into her face and rolled her off. Her nose spouted blood. She tried to stand but her right leg collapsed. I couldn't stand erect and could hardly walk, but it was my turn to smile. She looked from her leg to me. I met her bewildered gaze with the strongest right cross I could muster.

A body hit me from the side and I found Gudkov on top of me. Before he could do anything someone barreled into him. I watched but couldn't get up. Smith and Gudkov were going at it with several others joining the fray. I think Haxon landed on me.

The thirty-six hours following the incident dragged as I was confined to quarters except for testimony and medical care. I was less than confident of the results.

"They are ready for you," droned Ensign Selvooh.

I didn't bother to acknowledge. Instead, I proceeded through the door. The captain sat stiffly behind her desk. To her left was Mer. To her right, the chief. No lawyers for this internal corporate matter.

"Be seated, Specialist Keesay," ordered Captain Tilayvaux. She nodded to Chief Brold.

"We have reviewed your claim," he said. "Surveillance monitoring doesn't support your version of events, which precipitated the incident. That includes recordings from the main network, and those directed to your personal account and to your assigned sec-bot."

He feigned reviewing notes on a computer clip. "Interviews of witnesses neither bolster your claim nor contradict the recorded evidence. And there is no trace of any restricted substance in Senior Engineer McAllister's blood or tissue samples." He looked back to the captain.

"These findings," she stated precisely, "investigated by Chief Engineer Harkins and Dr. Sevanto contradict your claim. Senior Engineer McAllister's account of the incident is fully supported by the evidence."

I looked to Brold and then to Mer. Their view concurred with the captain's.

The captain sat up straighter. "You have been found guilty of a class-two assault upon a superior endued service skilled investor of Negral Corporation. Do you have an official statement before your sentence is handed down?"

"I do."

Unfazed, she leaned back. "You may make it."

"I request that all forensic evidence of this incident be secured and isolated from possible tampering or manipulation. To include all security and recorded files of the incident, any records or interviews of witnesses, and personal clothing and equipment of all involved personnel examined as evidence for this case, including blood and tissue samples. And that the evidence be secured in storage such that access is not routed through any manner of ship-wide computer network. Accessible only through direct and simultaneous action by any two of the three individuals present at this judgment and sentencing."

Only the captain appeared surprised. "And the purpose for this stated request?"

"To insure integrity of the evidence as I intend to appeal."

She looked to her associates. Distracted, Mer nodded. The chief followed suit. "Chief Brold," said the captain. "You handle the details."

I knew she was about to pass sentence, so I stood.

"Security Specialist 4th Class Krakista Keesay, the penalty imposed for your class-two assault upon a superior Negral Corp service investor is as follows." She read from a clip. "Three weeks of solitary confinement in the brig. All contract compensation from the time of the incident until this transport reaches Tallavaster shall be transferred to the personal account of the assailed individual. All opportunities for promotions or other advancement within Negral Corporation will be denied for four years from this date. This binding recommendation will be attached to transfer of contracted services to any other organization including but not limited to corporate, governmental, or military. All privileges onboard the *Kalavar* are revoked. Upon release from solitary confinement, two months of confinement to assigned quarters except when on official duty will follow." She looked to her right. "Any additional comments?"

Chief Brold cleared his throat. "Specialist Keesay, your sentence is lenient, owing to your recent action in putting down the terrorist. Any further infractions, major or minor, will result in long term incarceration."

"Understood, Security Chief."

"You have," said the captain, eyeing the ship's chronometer, "twenty minutes to report to the brig. From that moment you have four weeks, two days to petition for an appeal, should sufficient cause or evidence be brought to this judging council's attention. Dismissed."

Anticipating a result involving the brig, I'd locked down my equipment and prepared a satchel of approved items for confinement. I ignored the stares and hisses of fellow crewmembers along the way. Gudkov's echoing laugh found me at the last turn. My regulation 1.1 by 2.5 meter cell awaited. Refuge to plot revenge, or redemption, or both.

CHAPTER 26

Corporations go to great lengths to ensure that ample security is onboard interstellar vessels. The primary reason is to keep order and enforce civility while traversing vast interstellar distances.

The second reason is to safeguard the ship and corporate property. Security is entrusted to deter and foil hijack attempts and to repel external boarding efforts aimed at wresting control of the ship. A vigilant security presence substantially decreases onboard incidents and the potential unlawful acquisition of a ship.

Metallic water is nasty stuff. I swilled some around in my cup. Any time now.

The door opened. "Keesay," droned the chief.

I stood, turned toward the voice, but didn't grab my bag.

His gaze narrowed. "Time's served."

Silence reigned all the way to his office. Liu nodded to the chief, but ignored me as I passed. The door slid closed. "Sit."

I waited while he tapped away at his desk. The office's recycled air was refreshing. He slid a file of papers toward me. "Had two visitors and a stack of letters." He waited. "Visitors were turned away. Letters held."

I nodded and remained silent.

He flipped the folder open, revealing a stack of crinkled, handwritten letters. Authentic paper. The top one was in carefully blocked manuscript. "Bullfrog?" He flipped to the next. "Athena." And the next, "Skids, Little Elvis, Chopper, Spinner?" He flipped to the last. "Slugger." He closed the file. "Certainly not code names."

"Nicknames, Chief Brold."

"Does this have anything to do with the Chicher?"

"The letters? I do not know their contents."

He sat back. "What's your game, Keesay?"

I suspected what he was after, but I was going to make him spell it out. "The Chicher diplomat served as umpire during recess time. I approved and monitored."

"Did you issue alternate names to the colonist kids for the benefit of the diplomat?"

"No, Chief Brold. I provided a nickname to Michael Watts who indicated he did not like Michael or Mike. The other children desired nicknames. I cleared it with the parents."

"Just a convenience for the diplomat?"

"I don't follow."

"Sure you do, Keesay. Don't play dumb."

Sure I followed, but pretended it just struck me. It wouldn't fool the chief, but if he wasn't going to be straight up with me. "You're referring to the fact that Chicher do not call by name anyone outside their pack?"

"Right, Keesay. Like I'm, 'Top Security Man.'"

"And I am, 'Security Man.' I learned of that practice while reading up." I figured Specialist Liu had retrieved all accessed files for him, so I added a little to the pot. "I discussed the nuances with Father Cufter. Like the diplomat will not give out his name to anyone outside his pack."

"Yes, and Cufter was one of your visitors." He leaned in again, closing the file. "Did you pass something on to the preacher?"

"Did I give the missionary something before my confinement?"

"Let's cut to it, Keesay. Did you pass information to the Chicher?"

I did and he knew it. "Affirmative. Regulations were not violated."

"What was it?"

"A probable lead for my appeal."

"I advise you to give it up. I warned you to steer clear of McAllister."

"Chief, I intend no offense, but the warning was equivalent to telling the proverbial fish in the barrel to watch out for snipers."

"I instructed you how to turn the tables on your accusers." He slid a cinnamon toothpick into the corner of his mouth. "If your assertions were true. You rejected it."

I looked around. "Is this room secure?"

"Would I tolerate it otherwise?" he huffed.

"Are you sure? I'm not."

He bit into his toothpick. "It is."

"I'll trust you on that," I said, and went on before he could vent. "If you really know Corporate Inspector Karlton Simms, you might realize why I refused the injection." I leaned back and let that sink in. "Protocol dictates that I would have to be questioned under truth drugs to show plausibility for my claim, before McAllister could be forced to."

"Why didn't you say something about that?"

"Because you already threw the towel in on me. Don't worry, Chief. I won't bring you in on this." I looked around. "Now consider the implications if even part of my assertions are accurate."

"You're a real turd-stirrer, even if you're right."

"Chief, I've already lost. That doesn't mean there has to be a winner." I stood. "When do I go back on duty?"

"You have an hour to shower and eat." I grabbed the file and made it to the door. "And, Keesay, your second visitor was that exotic dancer, Ms. Jazarine."

My return to duty was one of the worst experiences I'd ever encountered. I immediately sought out Security Specialist Frost, and found him outside of Medical. "Specialist Frost."

He continued on his way, pretending he didn't hear me. The hitch in his step gave him away, and he knew it. Or maybe he thought something else, but he turned. "What is it, Keesay?"

"Inaccurate duty reports, that's what."

He checked his watch. "Aren't you confined to quarters when off duty?"

I stopped less than two feet away, looking him in the eye. "Follow up on reports is considered part of my duty."

"What problem do you have with my reports?" Frost asked, examining his fingernails.

"They indicate all is running smoothly with the colonists."

"Everything was fine up until this morning, when you took over."

I spotted an almost instantaneous rise and fall of his eyebrows. He wasn't a good liar. "I've received complaints of seven reported assaults not followed up on, and one possible rape." I took a calming breath. "And that doesn't include the minor incidents."

"I properly followed up on every incident reported to me."

"You did nothing. What about the incidents reported through the sec-bot? What about the injuries treated in Medical?"

"They're R-Tech. Probably too incompetent to interface with a sec-bot." He leaned against the wall while suppressing a grin. "I did all that was required. I've been reassigned now that you're out of lockup." He glanced at the ship's chronometer.

"I know," I said, "that Colonist Lowell Owen can properly interface with a sec-bot. The incidents reported through the sec-bot were deleted, without follow up. That is against regulations and will be reported."

He checked the chronometer one more time. "Well, Specialist Keesay, I'm off duty now. Therefore, this conversation is no longer considered in line with your assigned duty. I suggest you scuttle off to your quarters." He started to walk away but turned. "Report whatever you like. Your opinions and assessments mean nothing."

I filed my report from my quarters anyway. And I placed a formal request to alter my duty hours to coincide when Potts, Putin, and the ring leader, Stosh Meadows, had been allowed to regularly harass and have their way with the other colonists.

Benny hadn't much to say to me that night, and was up and gone before I awoke. I checked my electronic messages and pulled the one from Medical marked urgent. I washed up, dressed, and ate a breakfast packet on the way to Medical where I found Specialist Tahgs on duty. "I would like to see Colonist Owens."

She looked up, frowned, and said, "One moment."

"May I access the terminal?" I pointed to the public wall-mounted version. She activated it. "Thank you."

It took a little longer to access my account than usual, or maybe I was simply impatient. Several general information messages appeared, but nothing about my request. I'd finished scanning when a nurse approached.

"You are here to see Colonist Lowell Owen?" she asked.

"Correct."

"He has already been interviewed by Security Specialist Haxon."

"I would like to speak with him." If she wanted more she could ask.

"Is this a personal or an official visit?"

"It is related to my assigned duty."

She spoke into her collar. "Dr. Miller, Security Specialist Keesay desires an interview with the colonist in Room Four." She nodded. "Understood, Doctor." She eyed me. "Three minutes."

"I cannot perform a proper interview in that amount of time."

"A security interview has already occurred. Dr. Miller considers this a follow-up."

My only contact with Dr. Miller had been brief, during Benny's and Tahgs's abduction on the Mavinrom Dock, so I was in no position to call in favors. Maybe our lack of contact was the only reason I was being admitted. "Understood."

The nurse led me down several short hallways. She tapped the door access. "Three minutes."

I checked my watch. "Thank you."

I didn't need to see Owen's chart. Bruises and contusions covered his face and his right arm resting on the bedcover. I knew the white blankets concealed similar injuries.

Lowell Owen looked up, smiled and winced, showing at least one front tooth had been broken off. "Specialist Keesay," he said with distorted speech due to his swollen lips and damaged tooth.

"I am short of time," I said. "Who did this?"

He thought a moment. "Take care of your problems first."

"Your problem is my problem," I said. His eyebrows rose in momentary surprise. "What?"

His eyes flashed to the monitor. "I don't know who." He closed his eyes, maybe suppressing a tear. "Parallels."

I waited a moment while his eyes remained closed. He'd say nothing else. "Heal quickly. I'll send Father Cufter." He nodded before I left.

I strode up to Specialist Tahgs. "I would like access to the terminal again." She tapped in the code without acknowledging. "Thank you."

I gained access, this time without delay. I ordered an immediate download of my sec-bot. I reviewed his surveillance files. Nothing of value, only the aftermath. It showed Instructor Watts contacting Medical upon finding Lowell injured outside the shared public facilities shortly after midnight. Why was Watts there at that time? Why was Owen?

I called up surveillance of the area during the estimated time of the assault. There appeared to be a camera malfunction. I fast-forwarded through the time frame. No picture. No sound.

I checked the log. Specialist Muller reported the malfunction at 1:00 am. At least he was on the job. I attempted to access his incident report but was denied, which was odd. Nevertheless, I forwarded a request for access to Specialist Club.

While the morning security meeting was cold as expected, the colonist interaction was even colder. A belligerent colonist forced me to cuff and detain him after I spotted him in a restricted area. I discovered sensitive scanning equipment from the restricted area in his possession. This particular colonist had never shown signs of criminal behavior. The subversive element had surged in my absence.

I decided to take an early lunch and was heading down the hall when I heard a trio of footsteps on the grating moving up behind me.

"Specialist Keesay," called an unfamiliar voice.

I stopped and pivoted, expecting the worst. It happened to be the combat shuttle pilots who flew the *Kalavar*'s antiquated attack shuttle and fighter craft. The pilots were corporate hires and not on reserve status, and thus not considered officers. However, the civilian generic term ship's specialist or shuttle pilot didn't seem appropriate. I settled on, "Gentlemen?"

The three appeared an odd combination. One, wearing the markings of an attack shuttle pilot, was very dark-skinned with short curly hair. His partner, the weapons and ordinance operator, was taller and of Asian descent. By far the oldest, the fighter pilot was of mixed, possibly Middle Eastern, heritage. He was the one who'd addressed me.

"Are you available for a security consultation?" He smiled knowingly.

I hesitated. "I was going to take my lunch."

"We'll take it with you." His associates nodded. "If you don't mind."

"I will be dining in my quarters."

"That would even be better," the fighter pilot said.

"Let's be on with it then." I checked my watch. "My time allotment is short." They matched my pace and followed me through the line.

Veteran fighter and attack pilots are afforded a lofty status compared to others of their rank. The expense and training provided, and the rare combination of intelligence, reaction and bravery, makes pilots a valuable commodity. In their presence, stares and muttered insults were absent. I wasn't sure of their motive, but I welcomed the temporary status elevation lent by their company.

They joked and discussed combat scenarios as we walked. I listened until we entered my room. The pilots referred to each other by their call names, and encouraged me to do the same.

I offered the console chair to the ordinance controller, Howler, and

Benny's duct tape chair to his pilot partner, Bolt. The fighter pilot, Griffin or Graying Griffin as they referred to him, I offered a seat on my bed. They rested their trays and began to eat. I followed suit.

I checked my watch and then to the trio said, "Gentlemen?"

Griffin held up a finger and withdrew a small device from his flight suit pocket. He held it partially concealed, still I noted that it was small, gray, and the controls appeared awkward for his fingers. It flashed red once, then hummed. Griffin smiled and continued to manipulate the controls. It flashed white and began to screech. Painfully, I watched the pilot continue to manipulate the device.

He frowned and then placed his hand over his mouth. "This will be awkward, Keesay. You certainly realize your room is monitored."

I nodded but said nothing.

"My electronic device is able to scramble any audio recordings, but it cannot do anything about the visual. I was warned of this and recommend you cover your mouth before speaking."

I did. "Understood. So that the movements of our lips cannot be translated. I shall strive to keep as straight of face as possible." I looked to the others. They looked back to Griffin.

"I'll keep this short. Your friend, the Chicher diplomat, completed a task for you. He passed the pertinent information on to us just prior to his quarters being searched and scanned by members of your security department."

"Understood. And the results?"

"Did you know that prior to his assignment as diplomat, he was in intelligence, a code breaker?"

I wanted to say yes to impress the pilots. "No, I didn't."

I saw the smile in his eyes. "Prior to that he was a pilot. A fighter pilot, or as close as they come."

"One of their midget frigates?" I asked.

"Right, Keesay," said Griffin. "You seem to know a little about everything."

"But not enough about anything, or I wouldn't be in this predicament."

"We care for that red-braided bitch almost as much as you," Howler said, mouth barely concealed. "You're the only one who's had the," he paused, "mettle, to stand up to her. Heard you roughed her up in a disturbance some years ago."

I didn't care to go down that path. "How did you all get involved?"

"The diplomat is a fellow combat pilot," Griffin said matter-of-factly. His gaze tightened, then relaxed. "We've spent many hours in the simulators teaching him a thing or two, and picking up pointers on Chicher tactics."

Howler suggested, "You should join us some time in the simulators."

"Thanks, not in the cards, now." I looked at my watch. "Let's make this fast, okay?"

Griffin nodded. "Attached to the bottom of my tray is the original programming code you passed on to the diplomat. He broke it down and translated it. Seems it was some sort of program written to automatically download and transmit files. The first time it would have been activated, it would have imbedded itself into the normal code and been undetectable to most programmers. That information is included as well."

I refrained from looking at the food tray. "I was lucky then. McAllister and Gudkov miscalculated when they loaded it in my sec-bot."

"Luckier than you think. If it would have been brought up on any ship-standard operating system for examination, it would've erased itself."

"Lucky nothing. I identified something, but lacked knowledge how to go at it. Ignorance kept me from triggering erasure." I thought for a second. "No sense handing it off to me. If they can get at the diplomat's quarters, they'll have no problem getting at me."

"What would you like us to do?" asked Griffin.

"Can you pass it directly on to the chief? If he won't back me, and the truth, I'm done for anyway."

"Can do, Keesay." They got up and prepared to leave. "Anything else?"

"Yes. Hand me something from your pocket as we shake hands. Anything."

He lowered his hand from his mouth and smiled. After reaching into his pocket, he offered his hand. I shook as smoothly as possible and palmed a memory chip. Trying to look nonchalant, I slipped it into a pocket before retrieving my tray.

Griffin deactivated the device. "Good luck, Keesay."

"Luck has nothing to do with it," I said. "Could you return my tray? I'm almost late for duty."

We exited my quarters and parted ways. They laughed and carried on as usual. I rounded several corners but made it no further. I expected Gudkov and McAllister to move on me. Still, they caught me unprepared.

CHAPTER 27

It is pointless to transmit electronic messages while in condensed space. They are invariable garbled due to condensed space distortions and active cascading atomic engines. Besides, the sending ship will arrive before the message.

While it is difficult to receive transmissions when traveling between the stars, some computer programs have been written to unscramble such messages. Quantum computers, even those with the latest artificial intelligence programming, are unable to fully compensate. Since artificial intelligence programs lack intuition, they are miserably inaccurate at inference and guesswork. Even under favorable conditions with twenty percent of a message getting through intact, it will likely be misinterpreted.

I heard a voice far off, mumbling. It neared as I gathered strands of recollection. Meeting three combat pilots and going for lunch. Then what? What did I order? Didn't they tell me something important?

I shook my head to clear my thoughts. It was a good thing I was lying down, because it just made me dizzy. The cool, antiseptic smell meant I was in Medical. I forced my eyes open, just a slit. I tried to sit up and became nauseous.

"Lie still. Focus," ordered a voice. "Try to recall what happened."

It was the chief, right next to me. I closed my eyes and obeyed. I replayed events to no avail. I swallowed hard, noted my throat was dry, and tried recalling again. Chicken patties too regularly, came to mind. "Too predictable," I said. "Someone drugged my lunch?" I opened my eyes.

"Half right, Keesay," said the chief. "What do you recall?"

"The combat pilots...escorting me to lunch..." I searched my memory a third time. Nothing after the pilots." I shook my head, gingerly. "Anything on surveillance?"

The chief rubbed his chin and frowned. "Malfunction."

My head was clearing as Dr. Sevanto approached. "Same thing when a colonist," I paused, "when Colonist Owen was assaulted."

"Saw Muller's file work on that."

Dr. Sevanto stepped in front of the chief before he could continue. "They got you with a contact tranquilizer. A fast one." He flashed a penlight into my eyes. "We're examining the trace components of the compound now. Definitely nonstandard. I suspect one of the intended effects, besides unconsciousness, is memory loss."

"Permanent damage?" I asked.

"Doesn't appear so," Doctor Sevanto said, examining several monitors before checking my reflexes. "Scans and our monitoring indicate a loss of memory limited around the time of the assault." He checked his computer clip. "I administered several agents to bring you around and counter any other effects." He tapped an entry into his clip. "You may come to recall some events since I administered treatment shortly after the assault."

I considered that possibly a blow to the head was adding to the ache. I wasn't happy about their shooting drugs into me without full knowledge but maybe there wasn't time. Dr. Sevanto was good, and things appeared to have worked out. "Thanks."

"You're welcome, Specialist." Dr. Sevanto moved toward the door, but looked up from his clip before exiting. "Specialist Tahgs will be glad to know you'll recover."

"Two women in your life, Keesay?" chuckled Chief Brold.

"What?" I didn't know I even had one.

"That exotic dancer, and one of her escorts found you," said Chief Brold. "You might recall her escort. A Mr. Chokks Habbuk, Senior Recruiting VP for the Chiagerall Institute?"

I recalled him from the boarding incident. "Yeah, did you ever determine if he had any link to the terrorist?"

"No, he appears clean. However, you might thank him if you see him." The chief scratched the back of his neck. "Seems he redirected Ms. Jazarine from their intended route, taking a longer passage. They came upon you. Interrupted your assailant."

"Why? How'd he do that?"

The chief shrugged. "Because you're a lucky SOB, and backlogged on a bit of good karma?"

Again, I closed my eyes, trying to recall details of the assault upon me. Nothing, but I could guess who was behind it.

"I had visitors," said the chief. He waited until I opened my eyes. "Some pilots completed your business." He waited for a response. Seeing one wasn't coming, he continued, "You'll want to press for an appeal."

It was a statement, not a question. "I will, when I have the necessary information."

"Keesay, you do." The chief held his hand to his ear, then spoke into his collar. "I don't care how much or how long she yells." He paused. "If she gets violent, immobilize her. Same with Gudkov."

Gudkov? I grinned.

"I see I made your decade." Chief Brold sat on the edge of my bed, and plucked two cinnamon toothpicks from a breast pocket. "Try one?"

"Sure, Chief. I can guess some, but details would be nice."

"Well, Senior Engineer McAllister and Specialist Gudkov are being detained. Chief Engineer Harkins is investigating any tampering with ship security systems. And files and programming in Medical." He shifted his toothpick. "As we sit, McAllister's blood samples, the original ones, are being run. But with a software package from the exploration shuttle. In addition, the backup program from Medical is running a sample on one of the quantum computers isolated from the distributed net. If it turns up what I suspect."

"That I was right," I said, guessing my actions must have triggered a mistake on McAllister's part.

"Maybe, Keesay. Don't go counting your chickens just yet."

The cinnamon reached my tongue. "What about Haxon?"

"Specialist Haxon? For now he's Club's shadow. They'll be best buddies until things are cleared up."

I didn't like the sound of that and was about to protest when the chief put a hand to his ear. I waited, tried to recall with new vigor recent events. Still no luck.

"Yes, Dr. Sevanto," the chief nodded. "Is that a fact? Hmmm. I suggest you have the exploration shuttle crew make an additional backup of their program. Then have Chief Engineer Harkins run a comparison of the ship's version, and the archived backup." He nodded some more. "I know she's been trained to avoid repetitive code, but there might be some common sequences." He shifted his toothpick. "Yes, I'll have Club release computer access to your staff. No, you'll have to clear each with her. Acknowledged. Out."

"I was correct," I said, sitting up, ignoring the dizziness.

"Seems so," agreed the chief. "To what extent will have to be seen." He held up a finger. "Club, contact Dr. Sevanto about computer access. Seems McAllister has altered the archived medical programs as well. She didn't get to the shuttle's files." He listened. "Good idea. Do that and report. Out."

I followed the conversation but was tired of waiting. "The charges against me? My record?"

"It'll be up to the captain and Mer."

No sense being diplomatic and holding back. "Shouldn't Haxon be detained?"

"He's been placed on restricted duty. Like I said, with Club. And confined to quarters."

"Am I still restricted?"

"Until this is resolved, yes. And you'll have an escort."

"To watch me, or to secure me?"

"Both. Corporal Smith and anyone he designates."

I pointed to the wall storage. "May I have my sidearm until I'm released from Medical?"

"Sure thing." He retrieved my revolver and com-set. "Trusting sort." He handed me the former and hung the latter over the bed railing.

I checked my duty revolver. "Thanks, Chief."

He nodded. "Medical is busy so it may be a while." He activated his ocular. "Smith's outside. I suggest you rest." He shook his head as he strode to the door. "Bet what's really got McAllister's craw is that she tangled with a relic and lost."

"*Nemo me impune lacessit*," I said.

He halted just as the door opened. "You are full of surprises, Keesay."

"Never underestimate an R-Tech," I assured him.

CHAPTER 28

Using wireless signals to alter transmissions, and intercept others, one organization finally stepped over the line, triggering the Information War. Exactly what line was crossed and by which government or corporation depends on the historian utilized as a primary source. Nevertheless, applications used in times of peace lent themselves to direct military application. Tanks, ships, and aircraft, all unmanned and automated by various artificial intelligence programs, had been the military wave of the future, until the impossible. Friendly units accepted commands from the enemy! Unbeatable codes were broken.

Before it was over, man again found himself thrust bodily into machines of destruction. The human mind was again meshed upfront with military hardware. One of the outgrowths of this realization led to the vital, and highly competitive, game known as Code Wars.

"...How did it go today, Kra?" Benny asked when I returned from the showers. He was resting on his bunk.

"It's getting better. No fights. No instructors reported insubordination. But tomorrow Carver Potts and Stosh Meadows are due for release."

"...Detention," Benny acknowledged. "I heard you have been riding them pretty hard."

I examined my new dress uniform. "That's right," I said, buckling on my sidearm. "They were behind the assaults while I was locked up. Among other things. I know, I can't prove it, but I've got eyes and ears other than surveillance." And Benny knew the malfunctions had subsided since Gudkov and McAllister had been caught altering medical and security programs. "Most of the colonists were good hires. Even the thugs are smart." I examined my uniform fit in the mirror. "At least they have potential."

"...Been easier since that situation with Engineer McAllister was cleared up." He pulled out his electronic therapy device, and began tapping. "More work for all of us until they can return to unrestricted duty."

"Three weeks of solitary confinement wasn't long enough if you ask me."

"...Their skills are vital," Benny trailed off. He looked away, then concentrated on his device.

I wasn't offended. A senior engineer with multiple areas of expertise and a quality maintenance tech coupled with security training made my contributions seem small. "Well, Benny, at least I get a slice of their company pay. Compensates a little for my deflated ego." I went over and patted his shoulder. "Paid for my new uniform. And it's paying for my evening out." I felt uncomfortable about dropping so many credits, but Gudkov and McAllister would hear about it. Petty, but I was getting two for one with the investment.

He responded with a thumbs-up. "What are you going to see?"

"Shakespeare's *Othello.* Preceded by a cocktail dinner party."

"...I hear they have some authentic juices in them."

"Hey, I'll be rubbing shoulders with most of the first classers." I fingered my security specialist 4th class patch. "Some real wine and nothing on the menu is synthesized."

"...Promise me you won't get into a fight."

"I promise, Benny. Unless someone insults my date."

Benny checked the chronometer. "If you are late, you will have a fight on your hands before you even get to dinner."

I clipped one of Mer's hand radios onto my belt. Next to it I dropped an ear receiver in a snap pouch. "Understood." I waited, debating if I should carry any additional equipment. I was off duty. Still, I had my stun baton and my duty sidearm with spare ammunition, including six of the silver bullets my cousin, Oliver, had given me. They looked nice resting in the bullet loops on my belt. I reached into my pocket and tossed my brass knuckles to Benny. "There, that should discourage me."

When I arrived, Specialist Tahgs's roommate, Med Tech Merriam, had just exited. She brushed her red hair aside and gave me a friendly wave over her shoulder. Janice answered the door wearing a long purple dress with shimmering vertical stripes. Over it she sported a yellow mesh blouse. Its looseness contrasted the fit of the dress.

She caught me looking. "Some duty assignments," I explained, "aren't on call twenty-four hours a day." I caught the fragrance of her perfume. Flowery, maybe lilac.

"I'd hoped you were thinking something else." She offered me a seat. "Would you like to relax a few minutes?"

"I wasn't imagining Specialist Club in that outfit, if that's what you're getting at." She giggled. I checked my watch. "Maybe we'd better just head on over. Spent too much time on file work and chatting with Benny." I offered her my arm and she accepted. "He suggested I avoid engaging in fisticuffs if at all possible."

"That would be nice," she said. "Unless Joyce Club comes looking for a dress I borrowed." She adjusted and smoothed her outfit. "You look nice this evening."

I hoped Club wasn't monitoring the conversation. "Thanks. Had fabrication services put it together. I bet they had to pull some old programs to incorporate the buttons."

She smiled and shook her head. "Hey, did you read all your journal articles we downloaded?"

"Not much to do in isolation. Glad I had them. Thanks."

"I thought you might've. I ran across and downloaded a flat screen comedy routine. Thought you might like it."

"Really?" I led her into an empty elevator.

"Yes, it's an old, old-time comedy act called, *Who's on First*." She saw I didn't recognize it. "It's about baseball."

"That's right." I paused while we passed through the main gravity plate. "You came down and saw the colonist kids playing."

"Them, you, the pilots and a marine." She smiled and winked, ignoring my gravitational discomfort. "I'm not sure who was more competitive."

We exited the elevator. "Don't forget the Chicher umpire." We were almost to the first class entertainment hall, or ballroom. "You should've joined in."

"No," Tahgs said. "Enjoyed watching and talking to Instructor Watts. Not what you'd expect for an R-Tech instructor."

"True. She picks up on computers and other tech stuff pretty fast." I recalled several times simply nodding as she went on about tech details I couldn't follow. "Extremely fast."

"I know you're friends with the marines. How'd you get the combat pilots to play?"

"Some marines," I corrected. "I've expanded my circle of associates since confinement. Beyond you, Mer, Benny and a few odd maintenance techs."

"Heard the pilots helped you implicate McAllister."

"No, not exactly." We were approaching our destination.

"So you've recovered your memory?" She slowed. "Dr. Sevanto was concerned when they brought you in."

"Bits and pieces. It's like snippets from a dream."

We stopped in front of the door. Janice ran the back of her hand over the scanning console. I had to call up a thumb print scan for admittance. A middle-aged couple in fine, gray eveningwear came up behind. "Relic," the man mumbled.

"Thank you for inviting me," Tahgs said, hoping to distract me.

I wasn't looking for a brawl. "You're welcome, Janice. Let's go on in."

Soft golden light emanated from ballroom's ceiling for the evening meal. There were fourteen round tables of various sizes set at the far end. White cloths covered all of them but the larger were set with eight chairs. Ours, a private with only two, sat couched in the center. As we strolled to our table, a small lamp rose from the center to reveal silverware, crystal flutes, plates, cloth napkins, and a bottle of sparkling wine resting in an ice bucket.

I pulled out Janice's seat. "There you go."

"Thank you, Kra." She looked around. "We're early."

"No," I said, "we're on time. Not fashionably late." Then my heart sank when I spotted Ms. Jamayka Jazarine enter. Her sleek black gown had caught more than my attention. Her escort, a tall businessman, grinned. I looked to Janice who hadn't noticed yet, so I continued the conversation. "Have you met the Chicher diplomat?"

"Other than at your game where I exchanged greetings, no." She squinted a bit, but continued the topic. "How did you meet it?"

"I nearly tripped over him during my layover on the Mavinrom Dock. Almost lost my tray of food." I observed a few more passengers enter before Ms. Jazarine and her escort moved toward our table, as did the couple in gray. "The Chicher spends a lot of time with the missionary."

"That's what Benny said," agreed Janice. "He said you've been to a couple of church services."

"Three." I tried to avoid eye contact with the approaching diners. "My duty schedule conflicts, although..."

Ms. Jazarine and her escort stopped at our table. "Good evening, Specialist Keesay."

I stood, "Good evening, Ms. Jazarine."

"Glad to see that you have recovered, Specialist," she said, revealing a warm smile.

I'd only sent her a message by courier thanking her for finding me and reporting the assault. "Thank you." I didn't know what else to say, knowing I should have done more. "I see that you have recovered as well." She flexed her prosthetic fingers. Maybe it was the lighting, but I couldn't tell.

"Yes," she said. "Thanks to Dr. Sevanto and his skilled staff."

"Where are my manners?" I moved around the table behind my date. "Have you met Specialist Janice Tahgs?"

She nodded. "Yes, we met in Medical. And this is Mr. Dabbit B'down." She presented her escort. "Of Cardinal One Intrasolar Corporation."

Mr. B'down stepped forward and confidently shook my hand. "Yes," he said, "we are looking to work with Negral Corp on several small projects." His orange tie was heavily marked with black pinwheel designs. Barely a midlevel executive.

"That'd be good," I said. "I know someone from security with Cardinal One. Said it was a first order company." It must be, I thought, if someone his level had an expense account to afford evenings such as this, and could attract the company of a quality exotic dancer.

There was a long pause. Ms. Jazarine leaned toward Janice. "You're lucky to have the companionship of Specialist Keesay. He has politely avoided me most of the cruise."

Janice smiled, not knowing what to say. Then simply responded, "Thank you."

"Come, Jamayka, it's time to be seated," said Mr. B'down. "Nice meeting you."

"Nice to meet you," I replied as they moved to the next table. The rude gentleman in gray sat with them. He glanced over his shoulder with a sneer while Mr. B'down seated Ms. Jazarine next to his elegant companion. Eight seats, and they had to select the ones closest to us.

I examined the wine. It was a Cava from Mexico. Champagne wasn't appropriate for a dinner, and I couldn't afford real French Champagne. But the Cava was close, and this was an event, at least for me. "I haven't had a sparkling wine since my cousin Oliver was recruited by Fleet Military."

"Really?" Janice said. "Are you worried about him?"

"The war? I don't know for sure if we're at war. More rumors than anything else." I sat back. "He did serve on the *Iron Armadillo*, but now serves on an armed freighter to the outer colonies."

"You're right. A lot of rumors. What do the marines say?"

"Anything of interest is classified. They're tight-lipped." I unfolded my napkin. "If Chief Brold knows anything, he won't tell us until we prepare to drop out of condensed space, if we are at war." I refolded the napkin and watched the gentleman in gray. He was sitting at an odd angle to his companions and out of their conversation. "If he or the captain knows. The *Kalavar* is only a medium class civilian transport."

"You're probably right. But people are saying that's why McAllister got such a light sentence." She took a sharp breath and gauged my reaction. I kept it straight. "They'd need her to keep intact computer command and control integrity."

"She is top notch when it comes to that," I agreed. It also meant that my stay onboard the *Kalavar* would be short. One of us would be dropped as soon as convenient. I didn't mention that. "Heard she was banned from the onboard Code Wars competition."

Janice nodded eagerly. "That really altered the odds. Have you wagered any credits?"

"Actually, yes. On Benny to place in the top five." I heard a few corks pop, and reached into our bucket. "I like long odds and he's sharper than others might suspect."

"You're right," she said. "Last I looked there were only two who've placed anything on him."

I waved off the waiter. I wouldn't need a corkscrew. Janice squinted. I was very careful not to waste any. I poured. The wine sparkled and fizzled. "So you're the other," I said. She nodded and sipped. "Want another tip?"

"You never seem to go out on a beam without an edge." She leaned in. "Let's hear it."

"Colonist Owen. He'll place far better than his ranking." I could see her recalling the list. "Third from the bottom," I offered. "Two behind Benny."

"I'll look into it," she said. "Anyway, the contract on the code variations has been doubled. McAllister's status and all."

"Hah," came from the other table. "What would a Relic know of codes?" The man in gray turned his chair. "His associate must be equally ignorant."

Janice looked stunned; I wasn't. I suspected he was following our discussion. "Sir, listening in on a private conversation is ill mannered. Interjecting yourself into one is doubly so." I felt for my brass knuckles and recalled giving them to Benny. "I would ask that you refrain from doing so."

He turned his chair fully around and flipped his orange tie forward.

"Specialist 4th Class, what would you know of class and social manners?"

His companion, his wife based on the elaborate wedding band, tugged at his arm to hush him. He brushed her off. "Well, Relic?"

Janice's expression had shifted to embarrassment. His mistake for publicly insulting my date. I wouldn't stoop to degrading his wife, but he was fair game. "I don't claim to be an expert, but even a lowly primate is cognizant of proper etiquette. You, sir, are apparently still working your way up." Red rose in his face. "All in attendance understand that evolution takes time. When you reach the proper stage, I will accept your apology. Until then, I will understand."

Janice was now showing anger, hands clenched, shoulders tense. I caught Ms. Jazarine whispering into the wife's ear.

"A craven man you are," boasted the loudmouth, "to utter such, hiding behind your weapons and position as a security official. Bottom rung I might add."

"Sir, it is my position that has allowed this conversation to continue this far. Everyone in attendance would be best served if we simply went back to our meals."

His wife tugged at his shoulder. He spurned her again. "Ha!" he said. "I have studied martial arts extensively, and hold a second degree black belt in Karate, not to mention my study of Judo."

I knew the moment I stood, it would be over. I forced my legs to relax. "Sir, I believe you have let the alcohol do your talking. We would both benefit if this moment were allowed to pass."

"Coward, as we all knew." He nodded looking around. "Why don't you just shut up and slink away? You don't belong here."

"I should inform you, sir, I collect belts, too. I've a half dozen tacked up in my quarters—those of morons who let their mouth say what their ass couldn't back up." I pointed at him. "One more word out of you, and I guarantee the rest of your trip'll be spent in Medical. Recovering."

He stood, and removed his coat. "Step over here, Relic, so I can shut you up and send you back where you belong." His orange and black speckled tie landed on his wife.

I looked to Janice. "You'd better get out of the way. This Chip's blood might ruin your dress." I stood and removed my gun belt. My stun baton was in my thigh pocket if things got out of hand. I was sure they would. Janice came over beside me, and started to say something. My eyes were locked with the loudmouth's and I didn't have time for it. I handed her my equipment. "Hold this a moment."

I started to step forward when Mr. B'down slipped between us. Two of the loudmouth's friends pulled him back down into his seat. I couldn't hear what they said to him with Mr. B'down, hands raised, urgently talking to me. "Specialist Keesay, you've been more than reasonable. Mr. Kolber was out of line. There's no need to take this any further."

My adrenaline was running, but I took a step back. I kept my eye on Kolber.

"That's him," said one if his friends, pointing to me.

Kolber's staring eyes widened. He looked around and grabbed his coat from an associate. "My mistake," he said, before turning to his wife. "We'll...let's go." She scanned her peers, and, humiliated, followed her husband out.

Not caring to acknowledge the eyes on me, I turned to Janice. "My belt?" She stiffly handed it back and began talking. I strapped it on and swung around to her seat. I offered it to her. I hadn't caught what she said and whispered as she sat, "Sorry for ruining the evening."

She surveyed the room. "Not ruined, just reminded a few passengers that wealth isn't everything." She must have read my puzzled expression. "Never mind."

I rearranged the silverware. "I shouldn't have let him get under my skin."

She slid her chair next to mine. "You get this all the time? Relic tech training?"

I shrugged. "Occasionally."

She smiled. "Didn't you board with a black eye and cut lip?"

I recalled my run-in with Pillar. And with Mavinrom security before that. "Yes, and those were on top of yellowing bruises." She snorted, trying to hold in a sip of water. "What's so funny?" I asked.

"Nothing, Kra. Why don't you pour more champagne and examine the menu." She nodded as the waiter came around.

I did as Janice requested. I took the large clip from the waiter and ran my finger down the items. A description appeared for each I touched. The price wasn't listed. "I don't recall goat being on the list of fine dining cuisine."

"I don't think it is," answered Janice. "It's one of the original species exported to Tallavaster."

I looked over the menu with an eyebrow raised.

"Dr. Sevanto says it isn't too bad," she said.

"Well, if that's the case, then I think I'm going to try the broiled goat-chops on cheddar stuffed tomatoes." I looked further. "With buttered garlic sauce."

"I think I'll have the same, but with lemon juice."

"I'd suggest the biscuits with honey."

"Honey?"

"Sure," I urged. "Maybe it'll be as good as the honey my uncle collected."

"Your uncle collected?"

"I doubt it," I said. "Yeah. When I was a kid I helped him some with his bee stock. A risky business. So dependent on the weather. But some years my uncle banked a lot."

"Aren't bees dangerous?"

I watched the waiter return. "Not the domestic strains." I'd learned proper dining etiquette through formal dinners my mother hosted. I ordered for both of us, before requesting a new pitcher of water and fresh ice for the wine bucket. An awkward silence followed.

Janice began thinking aloud. "I wonder what made his friends pull him back?" She was less used to confrontations than me. "And why he left?"

"Maybe Specialist Club communicated to them," I said, touching my ear, simulating reception through a fictitious com-chip implant. "She wouldn't tolerate my blood spoiling her stunning dress?"

Janice laughed and we continued with small talk while the oblique glances our direction tapered off and meals began to arrive. "You've been restricted from the Thursday dining specials."

"Correct," I said. "Imposed after the trouble with McAllister."

"I also heard that you managed to have your portion given to the colonist children?"

I nodded. "Depending on who Instructor Watts identifies as the top student for the week. Her son Michael won this week." I spotted our waiter with tray and stand approaching. "What did they serve yesterday?"

"Vanilla ice cream with chocolate sauce." Her eyes looked down, then shot back up grinning. "I was hesitant to bring it up. But you deserve to be told how kind it was to put in such a request."

"Thank you," I said, despite the fact that many of the colonists, especially those with children, had done so. "I figured that the colonist children would enjoy the treat even more than I would've, and it was pointless having my portion divided among the crew." I nodded as the waiter set the tray and began serving.

"This looks delicious," said Janice. "I'll need to concentrate on our meal. But I still want you to tell me more about the combat shuttle simulations."

I refilled our flutes before tasting my goat-chop and nodded. "Agreed. More so than the Thursday special."

The meat was a little tough but the garlic sauce added the necessary zest. Maybe it was the fact that I hadn't tasted authentic meat in so long. Maybe it was that I'd never dined on goat. I debated this while eating. Janice smiled, sighing between bites. Until then I hadn't noticed the holographic musicians were playing. A harp, violin and oboe. Their accompaniment made the experience even more satisfying.

Swallowing the last bite, I harkened back to the dinners organized by my mother. They normally included an appetizer, but interstellar travel had its way of impacting all events. I continued to observe others dining. Most were half through their meals. Ms. Jazarine was smiling and nodding to her escort. The opposite table speculated on the threat posed by the Crax. The waiters perched nearby. One moved our direction.

Janice finished just as he arrived. "Will that be all, sir?" he asked.

"Additional water, please." Janice nodded approval, and he was off.

"Why do you carry your weapon on your opposite hip?"

Janice caught me off guard. I ran the question through my head for a second hearing. "Oh. Easier to sit." I shifted positions. "Not in these chairs. But the barrel being five and a half inches," I did the mental conversion, "fourteen centimeters, causes problems in some. This cross-draw changes the angle." I reached across with my right hand. "Also," I said, pretending to draw, "I can bring it out and around like this and strike someone."

"You could use..." she started, before switching her approach. "I've seen you work with your sec-bot and on the ship's systems. I'm sure you could advance to I-Tech."

"Advance?" I chided. I'd been down this line of questioning before. But she appeared puzzled. "I-Tech is more than simply computer interface and application of technology. It's a belief system." She leaned away, eyebrows furrowed. I leaned closer. "Our jobs are different. We work with people all day. What will most of these people do when they finish tonight?" I didn't wait for a reply. "Go back to their cabins. Interact with their computers? Pull up a holo-cast? Program?

"The standard class passengers. How many do you see out and about? Ninety percent of their time spent in cabin? Granted, a number are engaged in various forms of computer facilitated education or training. But meals ordered in? How much human interaction?"

Janice raised an eyebrow. "Is that it? Interaction?"

"Partly." I pointed to my ear. "Implants." Pointed to my eye. "Oculars."

"They make communication more efficient."

"With computers," I said.

"With people too."

"Correct, but not completely—and without physical connection." I nodded and she followed my glance. "See that woman sporting the holographic tattoo?" I'd seen it earlier. A small waterfall scene on her shoulder. "Genetic manipulation to achieve it."

Janice looked down, and I knew what she was thinking. Her purple eyes. "It's not just the manipulation," I said. "That woman. Odds are she had it done simply because it was the newest advance. The thing to do, if you can afford it."

Janice replied, "Technological advances in artificial intelligence, space travel, genetics. They're all important." She scratched her neck beneath her V-ID. "If you didn't mingle with the Chicher, I'd have guessed you remain R-Tech because you're anti-alien."

"Correct. I'm not, even though they are in essence an R-Tech species."

"I think it's because you're," she hesitated, "you're concerned you might lose your individuality."

I considered it. "It's not so black and white." The waiter filled our glasses. "See, society needs variety. Software engineers are important. But where would they be without doctors?" I thought of the colonists. "What about agricultural laborers?"

"They aren't necessary, but I get your point."

"No, they aren't necessary, but we wouldn't be dining here if they didn't exist. Think of your office. You aren't necessary, but things sure wouldn't be the same there without someone, a person, to fulfill your duties." I could see her mind racing. "A valet-bot could be modified to do what you do. Or even an access terminal with holographic interface. But would it be as effective?"

"So, what you're saying is, a balance between man and technology. A slot for everyone in society."

I hesitated. "You could look at it that way. And my niche happens to be a class 4 security specialist. Yours happens to be a class 3 administrative specialist."

"I think..." She smiled, and fingered one of my uniform buttons. "You just like the attention drawn by your relic equipment and dress."

"Some of the attention it draws, I could do without. Like tonight."

"But you're too stubborn to change."

"I shouldn't have to change. He should have accepted me for who I am, just as I accepted him for who he was."

"Did you accept him?" She looked over at the lady with the tattoo. "So, you accept her?" She sipped her wine to disguise a smug grin.

"It depends," I said, "on what you mean by accept. Would I live the life he does, or get a tattoo like hers, if I could afford it?" I shook my head. "But as long as they break no regulations or laws." I tapped the table with a finger. "Maybe the better term would be, tolerate."

"What about respect? Do you want I-Techs to respect your decision to be, to remain R-Tech?"

"Interesting question," I said, thinking. "No. Respect me, for who I am. Don't be close-minded. Get to know me."

"But you don't respect that lady for getting her tattoo."

"No, but I tolerate it. Later, if I get to know her, I may respect her, and her decision." I looked around. "How many others would afford me the same courtesy?" I scanned the room. "Strike that. Tainted by socio-economic condition. But even wealthy R-Techs are looked down upon. I don't see that older couple with the bulldogs. Virtually every other first class passenger is present."

"Was," she said. The waiter approached and began to clear our table. "I get your point, Kra. I don't agree one-hundred percent. And I'm glad you tolerate my violet eyes." She winked.

We stood and moved to the side while the waiters and maintenance-bots took down the tables and erected seating for the play.

"I still haven't heard about the combat shuttle simulations."

"Not much to say, really." I took her arm and guided us out of the middle of the growing crowd. I couldn't observe from in there. "Anyway, Howler, the weapons and ordinance operator, invited me to try the onboard simulations. How could I pass that up?"

"What's it like?" she asked.

"Different than the standard programmed simulations found on most systems. Maybe for security reasons. I was allowed to man the pulse lasers and some of the other weapon systems. Like the missiles and explosive caltrops."

"How'd you do?"

She seemed interested, so I continued. "I wasn't very fast or efficient interfacing with the combat assistance computer. But on manual, which still provides some targeting assistance, I almost scored average rating." No one was listening to us. Still, I maneuvered to a better vantage. "Against the Crax, where computer lock-on is iffy, I fended off the bandits only two of eleven runs. One launch, our missile got a near miss on a frigate. The other time all four were destroyed after launch." I shrugged.

"So if we go up against the Crax, we don't stand a chance?"

"Howler says when he began new recruit training, they didn't even use combat shuttles. Their first simulations were in old tech air combat craft. He flew things like World War II fighters. Propeller driven Spitfires or Mustangs with machineguns, against jet fighters with rapid-fire cannons and missiles."

"Why?" she asked, showing the same puzzled look I had when I phrased the same question.

"He said they were being screened for aptitude and the ability to engage despite being at a severe disadvantage. The fighter and attack shuttles on the *Kalavar* are obsolete, but Earth's top of the line equipment is equivalent to a Spitfire against, I think he called it, an F-16 Falcon." I wondered if that was why the combat pilots retained the clock face designations in combat.

I could tell Janice wasn't clear. I said, "Remember the computer clips your parents used in their primary schooling?" She nodded. "It'd be like using one of those against a state of the art one, in a Code Wars competition."

She paled. "We haven't a chance?"

"Not exactly." I held her arm tightly. "Two things. It isn't all hardware and software. The pilots, or as you I-Techs might call it, organic factor, plays a role." She didn't look convinced. "Hey, I did okay against two I-Techs." I patted my revolver. "And, we're allied with the Umbelgarri."

She was silent before asking, "Howler. Why do they call him Howler?"

"He plays old and classical music, when in combat. You know, Wagner, Mozart. The pilot claims his weapons officer hums along, until things get intense. Then sounds more like a baying wolf." I shrugged. "His favorite is *O Fortuna* by Orff. Maybe it confuses intercepted communication between pilot and weapons officer, or between shuttles?"

Janice smiled and ran her fingers through her dark hair.

"Actually, the attack shuttle kind of looks like an ancient torpedo-bomber from World War Two."

Janice politely took a drink to hide her smile.

"Really," I said. "Superficially. No propeller, more aerodynamic and comparatively oversized. It's weapon systems, with dual fusion reactors for power."

Janice nodded and added, "And packed with metallic hydrogen. But I only know that because my roommate was hot on the trail of the attack-shuttle pilot. All I heard about for a month."

"So you already knew about this?"

Janice took my hand and cut me off. "No. I never really listened to Genni. But I'll listen to you."

I spotted the Chiagerall Institute recruiter. He was moving our way. Janice turned and smiled.

"Good evening, Specialist Keesay and Specialist Tahgs, if I correctly recall."

"Good evening," I responded before turning to Janice. "This is Mr. Chokks Habbuk, Senior Vice President of Recruiting for the Chiagerall Institute." I wasn't sure Janice knew about the Institute, but she nodded.

"It seems you are always finding trouble," said Mr. Habbuk.

"Life has never been so exciting," I agreed.

"Have you considered my offer, Specialist?"

"Yes, I received your electronic message. I do not believe I would function as an efficient personal bodyguard." Janice's eyes widened. Her eyes would have widened further had she witnessed the vision that haunted me. Special Agent Brown, lying dead on a shuttle ramp.

"You might be surprised," said Mr. Habbuk. "And I am confident it would result in an increased rate of compensation."

I thought of Agent Brown, trained in weapons and tactics, not as a bodyguard. It got her killed. It jeopardized Representative Vorishnov, whom she was assigned to protect. "I'm not trained for the position."

"Training can be taken care of. You have the instincts."

I didn't want to be rude. "Thank you for the compliment. I will reconsider your offer, but I don't believe I will change my mind."

He held out his hand. "That is all that I can ask. The offer will hold until we reach the Zeta Aquarius Space Dock." He nodded to Janice. "Madam."

Janice watched Mr. Habbuk blend back into the waiting crowd, only to appear next to an elegant businesswoman sporting an orange dress scarf, with few, very narrow black pinstripes. "Did you see his tie? He's pretty far up, Kra." Janice measured his companion. "Do you think you should turn him down?"

"I'm under contract to Negral." Janice looked uncomfortable. I relieved her by stating what she was thinking. "I know that I may not be retained on the *Kalavar*. McAllister and I will never mix. But Negral is up and coming. There are other opportunities."

"The best you could expect would be a lateral move within Negral. Mr. Habbuk indicated an increase in pay."

"But I'd stagnate in the position. I wouldn't, couldn't move up. My current position with Negral offers vertical mobility, hopefully ascending." I took her hand. "Besides, I like the current company."

She blushed. Staring me in the eye she said, "Flattering, but do consider it."

"I will," I said, snapping my attention. "Mr. B'down."

"Am I interrupting?"

"No. Of course not," said Janice. "Where is your companion?"

"Ms. Jazarine," he said, grinning. "Momentarily indisposed. She will be back shortly."

Janice said, "Sounds like a good idea. Please, excuse me."

Mr. B'down watched Janice flow through the crowd. "Fine looking young lady."

"Yes, she is. I'm proud to be her escort."

"You should be, although I don't think she likes Ms. Jazarine."

"Oh?" I lied, but he saw through it. I shrugged. "Ms. Jazarine has my respect. Correct me if I'm wrong, but was it she who got me out of tonight's situation?"

"You are quite correct. She apparently respects you as well." He stepped closer. "I'm not clear on the specifics, but she warned Mr. Kolber's associates. Said you had been banned from the Mavinrom Dock after crippling a marine. Crushed the skull of a lunatic assassin, and killed two renegade security in a shootout. All in the week prior to departure." He chuckled. "They scoffed until she pointed out you were the one who bayonet-charged the terrorist during boarding." He scratched behind his ear. "Is all that true?"

"More or less. Mainly less. I'll have to thank her."

"Actually, you'll get the chance," he said hesitantly. "That's why I slipped over. Our seats are adjacent." He looked around. "Your companion may not enjoy the play as much sitting next to mine. We've been assigned seats 6G and 6H."

"We're 6I and 6J," I said.

"Make sure you sit in 6I?"

"Thank you for the heads-up." I caught him eyeing my equipment. "I left my brass knuckles at home."

"Always a good decision for formal dinners."

"It almost wasn't." We laughed. I reached into a breast pocket. "Gum wrap, Mr. B'down?"

"Thank you, Specialist Keesay." He eyed the wrapper as he began to chew. "Authentic sugar. Very kind of you."

"No problem," I said, before engaging in small talk. To our surprise, approaching together were Ms. Jazarine striding and Janice bounding.

"How fortunate, Kra," said Janice. "We have adjacent seating. Jamayka has seen holo-plays by this troupe before. They're excellent!"

Ms. Jazarine nodded. "I've attended one of their live presentations. A different Shakespearean tragedy, *Hamlet*."

Janice and the exotic dancer continued to chat until the crowd began moving toward the seating. "I see," I whispered to B'down, "that you're an expert on women. At least in this area I'm your equal." Our muffled laughs went unnoticed. I wondered if Janice recognized Jamayka's accent was fake.

I was familiar with *Othello*, as was Ms. Jazarine, who whispered brief commentary on plot points to Janice during the play. I was more impressed with the holographic presentation than the acting. The number of feeds and angles of projection created the illusion of a live performance. The fact that I heard no complaints by the other spectators cemented my opinion that the *Kalavar*'s technicians were top notch. Momentary churning of bile ensued as I did my best to ignore the certainty of Senior Engineer McAllister and Tech Gudkov's contribution. Overall, I was able to enjoy the production. The treachery and machinations of the villain, Iago, and his compatriot, Roderigo, hit close to home. It almost left me in a sour mood when the final curtain fell.

Everyone applauded. I followed suit. Clapping for holo-casts didn't make sense, but some actions to blend in never hurt. Janice sat erect, clapping with mixed emotions. The sad ending, and the fact that the performance was over, blended with the experience of the event. Ms. Jazarine was the first to rise and Mr. B'down rose quickly, in response to her agitated stare. I took Janice's hand and cleared the aisle for them.

Mr. B'down motioned for us to follow. "They will be serving carbonated waters and sardines. Care to join us?"

I looked to Janice. "It's late, but I can catch up on the sleep some other time. You?"

Janice grinned. "Without a doubt." She leaned close my ear. "What are sardines?"

"Just a moment," I said. "Need to check in." Janice waited next to me while Mr. B'down and Ms. Jazarine joined arms and moved on. I pulled the hand radio, adjusted it, and inserted the ear receiver. "Sec-bot Lefty, this is Specialist Keesay. Report." There was no answer. I repeated to no avail. "Security, this is Keesay."

"Yes, Keesay, this is Muller."

"I was unable to make contact with my sec-bot in the colonist area."

"We're experiencing some minor communication difficulties. You're pal McAllister is on it. Let me check the monitors."

"Acknowledged."

"The sec-bot doesn't respond to my communication either. But all looks clear. No one up and about. The sec-bot is moving through the dining area.

"Acknowledged."

"Hey, Keesay, what are you doing checking in? Aren't you in the middle of viewing a performance?"

"Just ended. I need to make rounds before I turn in tonight, but thought I'd stay for a few of the after-performance festivities."

"I would," said Muller. "Will keep you advised."

"Thank you, out." I turned back to Janice. "Sardines," I whispered, before leading her toward the crowd, "are salty preserved fish. If you don't like them, that's what the carbonated water's for. You wouldn't be any different from the upper crust."

"Upper crust?" She shook her head. "Maybe later."

As we approached the standing tables, Mr. B'down waved us over. I directed our path so that Janice would stand next to Ms. Jazarine and I would be next to Mr. Habbuk who, along with his executive companion, stood at the table.

"Decrease table elevation, ten centimeters," the Chiagerall Institute recruiter whispered before he directed his attention to us. "Greetings again, Specialist Keesay. I hope you and Specialist Tahgs enjoyed the performance."

Lowering the table was a courteous gesture by Mr. Habbuk. With her heels, Janice was several inches taller than me. He could have done it on her behalf, as everyone around the table was taller than she was, but I doubted it. I looked to Janice. "I believe we both enjoyed it."

"Let me introduce Ms. Zelenda Kneft. She represents Tri-Star Horizon Investment Group."

"A pleasure to meet you," I replied. Janice held my hand under the table. It was cold and sweaty. "Have you ordered?"

"No, we have not," said Mr. Habbuk. "We were awaiting your arrival."

"Extremely kind." I placed my gum on the edge of my small white ceramic plate. I flipped the shallow matching cup in an away-motion before returning it to the center of the plate with both hands. Janice mimicked my move. It was kind of like holding out your little finger when drinking tea in society years ago, or so my mother had said. "What would you recommend?"

"The black raspberry?" suggested Ms. Kneft. All nodded, and I followed suit. "Mustard, tomato, or oil?" She looked across to Mr. B'down's companion.

"Mustard sauce?" offered Ms. Jazarine. All nodded. "Salted or spiced crackers?"

I tapped Janice's foot, and she took her cue. "Salted, lightly?" All nodded.

Mr. Habbuk, who was senior in rank, tapped the table screen, sending the order. "An excellent combination."

Ms. Jazarine seemed to be in an uncharacteristic dark mood, and Janice was very quiet, possibly feeling out of her element, but the other three continued to chat. I utilized my skill at keeping abreast of the current conversation while monitoring those around us. The food and drink was an additional distraction but manageable.

A table behind was discussing war with the Crax, the potential implications to commerce, and which corporations were best situated to take advantage. Some felt Negral would survive, but all agreed that Capital

Galactic was well positioned, considering its diversified assets in multiple planetary resource bases, and connections as a favored military contractor.

The table to the left was discussing the racial aspect of *Othello* and if it still had relevance today. One businessman was arguing that individuals, when they work or are in social situations, prefer those who look and act like they do. He was arguing basic human nature, and pointing out examples of company boards and their composition. His associates were scoring points indicating the weakness of allowing this in a company, holding up highly successful corporations known to bring aboard the best person for the job, regardless of economic origin, race, or gender.

"What about you, Keesay?" asked Mr. Habbuk.

I shifted back to our table's line of conversation. "Me, if I were Othello and discovered the treachery? Translated to a similar offense today? I'd run him through with my bayonet. Wouldn't even waste a shell."

"Wouldn't apprehend him for trial and conviction, eh?" said Mr. B'down.

"No," said Ms. Jazarine, monotone. "He wouldn't."

Mr. Habbuk opened his mouth to speak, but instead looked at me then reached for his drink. He almost toppled it.

"Keesay," crackled my ear receiver.

Mr. Habbuk's hand shook slightly as he sipped his water.

"Keesay here, Muller."

"Report to the colonist area immediately. Will advise en route."

"Acknowledged." I replaced the radio. "Sorry, ladies and gentlemen."

"Specialist Keesay," Mr. Habbuk interrupted. He looked pale. "Could I trouble you for an escort back to my cabin?"

"Are you ill?" asked Ms. Kneft.

"My apologies, Mr. Habbuk. I have been ordered elsewhere." I turned. "Specialist Tahgs could contact, or escort you to Medical." Looking at the man, I knew it was fear. Recent experience suggested the recruiter's instincts were not to be ignored. "Muller," I called into the radio. "Dispatch Dorian Ross to the ballroom."

"She's assisting engineering. What's the problem?"

I refrained from clutching the radio. "How urgent is my presence required in the colonist area?"

"There's been an assault and possible homicide."

Mr. Habbuk gripped the table. "It is not a problem, Specialist."

I stared at him. "If no one else is available, Muller, assign a marine. Have him report to Mr. Habbuk, Senior Vice President of Recruiting for the Chiagerall Institute." A few of the nearby diners had noted my extended conversation into the hand radio.

"Is it necessary?" asked Muller.

"Affirmative." I surveyed my party. Janice and Ms. Kneft looked as confused as Mr. Habbuk did worried. Ms. Jazarine and B'down stared into their drinks. "Duty requires my immediate departure. Mr. B'down, could you see that Specialist Tahgs is escorted to her quarters?" A sharp look silenced Janice. He nodded. "Mr. Habbuk, there will be an escort momentarily. Again, I apologize for being unable to fulfill your request."

"Thank you for your efforts," he said. "You have more important escort duties yet to perform."

Not knowing how to respond, I turned on my heels and strode out.

CHAPTER 29

One thing mankind learned was to avoid scrapping obsolete equipment during intervals between wars. Vast inventories of combat vehicles rest in under-ocean storage and on otherwise barren moons. Mothballed fleets of military and discarded civilian vessels silently orbit planets and moons. Because military planners required vessels designed with oversized standard modular systems, the decommissioned ships can be recovered and brought to serviceable duty within weeks. Military planners put stock in the theory that "Quantity has a quality of its own," which mirrors the Chicher's translated belief, "Swarming inferiors smother superiors."

I stepped off the ladder access between decks when a marine spotted me over his shoulder and doubled back. "Keesay," he called. "Communications are down. I have your new orders."

Explains why I didn't hear from Muller, I thought as the marine halted. "Private Fleishman?" I'd never spoken to this marine. I recognized him by his large hooked nose, even more prominent than Father Cufter's.

"Specialist, you are to immediately report to Medical. And avoid the lifts."

"Why?" I asked.

"Comm's not the only system experiencing outages." His tone was composed and direct.

"Private, do you know if anyone has been assigned to escort one of the passengers, a Mr. Habbuk, back to his cabin?"

"Negative, Specialist. I do not."

"What are your orders?"

"To locate you. Direct you immediately to Medical."

"Then?"

"Report back to the colonist area. Corporal Smith ordered me to assist Specialist Club. Help secure the area."

"Are you the only marine assigned?"

"No, Private Joachim." Agitation crept into his voice. "Specialist Club is on site investigating." He looked at me hard. "Your superior wanted me to find you yesterday, and for you to be at Medical the day before."

"Understood." Joachim was the stocky, angry marine who'd tipped Smith about the Thrust, before McAllister and Gudkov set me up. "What's she investigating?"

"Specialist, the word *immediately* is part of your orders."

Maybe there was a reason Private Fleishman hadn't informed me of the colonist situation and avoided my question. I'd know soon enough. Mr. Habbuk still required an escort. As Private Fleishman was working under

Security, technically I was his superior. "Private, return to Specialist Club. Inform her that I assigned you to report to the first class ballroom to escort Mr. Chokks Habbuk, Senior Vice President of Recruiting for the Chiagerall Institute, to his cabin. It is imperative and he is waiting."

"There's an awful lot going on, Keesay."

"Tell Club she can countermand my directive, but I would NOT recommend it."

"Will do, Keesay," the marine said, turning on his heel and trotting off.

I descended the ladder, and hustled toward Medical. I sidestepped several technicians tearing open access panels before I crossed paths with Mer and Benny, both faces weighted with concern. Mer pressed the maximum from his shuffling gait. Our eyes met. I knew whatever the situation, it wasn't good.

Twice I attempted to contact Security. Before giving up on the hand radio, I scanned broadcast frequencies and came across a scrambled communication. After calling on it, Corporal Smith acknowledged and ordered me to abandon the frequency. Mer's hand radio wasn't programmed for Marine encryption. By then I spotted a marine posted outside Medical. It was Smith's pal, Private DeLark, armed to the teeth. He stepped aside.

"Specialist Keesay," sobbed a child's voice. A nurse held Michael.

I looked from boy to nurse. She motioned with her eyes, followed with a flick of her head. I nodded, acknowledging the direction to take.

"My mommy!" Michael broke from the nurse and clutched my arm. "I wanna see her."

I stooped, eye to eye. "Skids, I'll check into it." I looked up. "Dr. Sevanto?"

"Yes," replied the nurse. "Room One."

"Skids, Dr. Sevanto and I are close associates. I'll speak with him." The boy wiped his eyes, looking hopeful. I handed him my bandana handkerchief. "Here. No promises."

He bunched it in his right hand. "The med techs took Mr. Owen, too." The nurse nodded affirmative as she pulled the boy back to a seat.

In Room 1, Dr. Sevanto stepped away from Instructor Watts. A seeping abrasion ran across her right cheek. Hers distant eyes held a mixture of concern and fright.

"Specialist Keesay," directed Dr. Sevanto, "step next door."

"Doctor?" I asked.

"Colonist Lowell Owen is in Room Two." He looked back to Instructor Watts before continuing. "His injuries are extensive. He wants to speak with you."

"How is Instructor Watts? Her son—"

"Can wait," Dr. Sevanto said, cutting me off. "As can Instructor Watts."

His meaning was evident. I turned and strode next door. Dr. Miller, a nurse, and a med tech crowded around the bed, manipulating respiratory and surgical equipment. Their actions were just short of frantic. Blood covered their surgical gloves. The med tech looked up. "Dr. Miller."

Dr. Miller passed a surgical device to the nurse. "Do what you can. Focus on the lungs."

"Why isn't he in the operating room?" I didn't yell but got my point across. "And why isn't Dr. Sevanto in here?"

"Main medical systems are down. Even if they weren't, it wouldn't matter for this colonist."

"What happened?" I moved closer. Lowell Owen was stretched across the table with his tattered clothes cut away. Gaping abrasive lacerations crisscrossed his body while under the skin, red welts, some seeping, covered his torso and arms. Tubes, one from the nose, two from the chest and abdomen ran to a portable support machine. Blood coated two of the three.

"He was attacked with a sonic blade," explained Dr. Miller. "Moderate intensity one. Not well focused. Still, his internal organs have suffered massive damage. Internal hemorrhaging. Damage to his lungs, liver, heart, arteries, intestines, and one kidney. His spinal cord. There's more." He licked his lips. "And an unidentified toxin."

I mouthed the words, "I should have been there." The nurse worked quickly, staunching some of the bleeding. The ministration was impossibly slow. In a grim voice, the med tech monitored and relayed information the support computers provided. The miniature fans cooling the equipment hummed incredibly loud.

Beeps erupted from the monitors. "Doctor!" called the technician. "Anti-toxin measures failing!"

Dr. Miller pointed with a blood-covered rubber glove to a shelf. "The colonist left a message for you, in transit. Or so I was told." He slid back into place. I moved around, next to the technician.

Lowell's breathing began to sputter and blood welled from his mouth. They applied suction. His eyes began to flutter. I looked up toward the doctor, who was sidestepping to allow Father Cufter room. When did he enter? The med tech slipped a rubber glove over my right hand and urged me closer. I gripped Lowell's gashed and swollen hand and his eyes opened. Blood had pooled in their corners. Still, he spotted me and tried to speak. The tubes. Desperate.

I leaned close. "Your message, received," I articulated, nodding sharply. "Understood." His grip tightened then relaxed. I placed my left hand on his forehead, wiping cold beads of sweat. A spasm, followed by gurgling coughs that wracked his body. Blood erupted around the chest and abdomen tubes and his gaze drifted, unfocused.

Father Cufter leaned close. He placed a hand upon the dying man and began to speak. I couldn't hear how the priest started; the support equipment drowned him out. I could guess. This wasn't the first time I'd seen Last Rites given. The technician shut off the medical alarms. "Your sins are forgiven,

Lowell Owen." The priest's words were measured but hurried. He'd ministered to the dying before. I stepped back to offer the two men privacy in one's final moment. "Rest in peace," the priest said, and helped the dying man cross.

Lowell gasped and relaxed. Where some lights and screens had been yellow, they flashed red before fading to gray. My guts turned. I should have been there. I struggled to keep my lavish supper down if for no other reason than I still had my duty to perform. Guilt could wait. "Thank you, Father," I said. "Lowell was a good man."

"Indeed, he was."

I said to Dr. Miller and his staff, "Thank you for trying. Did he say anything? Of his assailant?"

"No," said Dr. Miller. "He was unconscious upon arrival."

I took the micro recorder from the shelf. It was a sleeve attachment model. "Who was with him when he recorded?"

"We were," said the nurse, pointing to himself and the med tech. "When we got there Specialist Club was in charge. It's her micro recorder."

"The colonist might've said something to her," added the med tech.

"If there's anything I can do," offered Father Cufter.

"Thank you, Father," I said. "Not at the moment. Dr. Miller, preserve the body and any evidence. I'm sure Chief Brold—who ordered the marine posted outside?"

Dr. Miller and the two assistants looked surprised. Father Cufter nodded, affirming my statement. "Thank you," I said, turning to leave. I heard Dr. Miller ordering blood and tissue samples, as preservation of the body might not be possible if med systems remained down.

In the hall I adjusted the recorder for direct audio and held it to my ear. There was a lot of noise and confusion but I could discern Club barking directives, fading away in the background. The nurse and the technician each tried to contact Medical. Then the tech directed Lowell to speak. His weak, raspy voice whispered, "Kra, ward and ware." A gurgling cough and groan followed. Then, "The boy...his mother...you must."

Nothing else except the nurse and med tech for another twenty seconds. The nurse finally said, "He's lost consciousness." I pocketed the micro recorder and again sought to speak with Instructor Lori Watts with renewed urgency. Room 1's external monitor was down so I prepared to knock when the posted marine stepped inside Medical and called, "Specialist Keesay, Chief Brold requests your presence in his office."

"Understood. Will comply momentarily." I watched the marine return to his post. The nurse and Michael weren't in the lobby. I knocked, then entered. Inside, Dr. Sevanto and the nurse who'd been with Michael continued to examine Instructor Watts. I spotted Michael on a stool in the corner watching, pale and quiet. I signaled him to me, and picked him up. He gave me a hug and a load of snot on my collar. "I've only one minute twenty seconds, Skids. You okay?" He nodded, untruthfully.

I carried him toward the bed. Dr. Sevanto began to protest, but changed his mind. The nurse continued to draw blood. "I've been recalled to Security. Be sure the marine remains posted outside."

Dr. Sevanto's eyes flashed the direction of Lowell Owen's room. I shook my head once, but it was enough to get Michael's attention. "Mr. Owen?" the boy asked.

"Didn't make it," I replied, setting him down. Instructor Watts gasped. I took my bandana from Michael's hand and wiped my collar before adjusting the fold, exposing a clean area. I spotted tears welling anew. "Blow. Harder." He did. I checked my watch. "Fifty seconds, report."

Having been under my instruction, Michael knew what that meant. He sucked in and began. "Mom was sick. She went to the bathroom. Mr. Owen came over and took me to his room. I took my bedroll and went under his cot." He saw my eyebrows rise. "Mr. Owen put his cot up on blocks so I can camp there some nights." Michael went silent, knowing he'd admitted to breaking a posted habitation rule.

Elevating cots was common, but usually to level it and to increase storage space. "Minor infraction," I said. "It will be overlooked. Continue your report."

"Mr. Owen said it was okay, to give Mom a break." He took a breath. "He went to check on Mom. Someone came to the room. I saw boots and tan pants. I didn't say anything and he left. It was a long time. Then the C2 security woman and a nurse came and she ordered the nurse and a marine to take me here. They looked me over. I was okay but Mom and Mr. Owen aren't."

I looked from Dr. Sevanto to Instructor Watts and back. "She'll make it," Dr. Sevanto said.

"Top notch report, Skids." I checked my watch. "I've duties to perform. You do, too." I reached in my pocket and handed him my whistle. "See this?"

He nodded. "You use it at recess games."

"You keep it. Use it if someone other than a marine, security or medical enters. Understood?"

He sniffled and nodded. I gave him a thumbs-up. Dr. Sevanto and the nurse took a second to do the same. His mother looked pretty bad, so if they had Michael in the room then the rest of the medical staff must've been on emergency calls.

I left and took the initiative to retrieve my com-set and shotgun. On instinct I grabbed my brass knuckles from my pillow, then activated my com-set's ocular. Nothing. Corporal Smith had enabled my com-set for Marine encryption so I switched to it.

"DeLark reporting," called the marine. "All clear."

"Acknowledged," said Corporal Smith.

I felt better until I recalled Mer's expression, and broke into a trot. An unnecessary delay was the last thing the chief needed.

I arrived at Security to find the door wedged open. The chief looked from the monitors. "Keesay, stay here and monitor until relieved." He shoved a clipboard in my hands and strode past.

"Not much to monitor," I muttered. All but two screens were blank. And the working two faded in and out, providing brief instances of digitized distortion. The auxiliary lighting flickered. Hurry up and wait here while events happened elsewhere. I checked my sidearm, then moved the rolling chair to a spot near the back of the narrow room. I watched the monitors and entrance, while flipping through the clipboard's two pages of handwritten notes and directives.

Thirty-two minutes later, some of the screens came on line. A cursory examination told me other systems were being restored. The frequency of ungarbled communications increased. Fourteen minutes later all but five of the monitors were up and I'd just finished jotting my third page of observation notes when the chief returned.

"Report, Keesay."

I handed him the clipboard. "Eighty-seven percent of security functions appear to be back online. I was unable to detect any anomalies. Only *Kalavar* personnel and marines observed in the corridors. Prioritized for isolation and recovery, three suspect or important transmissions as requested in your written directives."

He flipped through my notes. "Interrupted call from marine at 01:08?" He glanced up at the now-functioning chronometer.

"Correct," I said. "My watch is independent of the ship's chronometer. It was a marine frequency transmission. Sounded like a shout or yell. Couldn't make it out. It may have been an order, but sounded more urgent." I handed him Club's micro recorder. "It's on here. If you check setting two point three-three, there is the recording from Colonist Owen also referred to in my notes. In the middle, set off by brackets, is information obtained from child colonist, Michael Watts."

The chief immediately moved to a console. "Keesay," he said without looking up, "patrol the colonist area. Return and report in forty minutes. Keep'em locked down."

"Understood," I said, knowing that he meant to restrict the colonists to their room as all had canvas curtains for doors. I heard the chief calling McAllister as I marched down the hallway.

All remained quiet in the colonist area. Any evidence of Lowell Owen's struggle had been removed. Many colonists were awake and whispering to spouses, children, or bunkmates. A few ventured, with permission, to the lavatory. The sec-bot continued its back-and-forth patrol. I checked my watch. "Lefty, continue patrol. Report any disturbances."

"Order acknowledged," replied the sec-bot.

I passed four *Kalavar* personnel in the corridors, and was nearly trampled by two marines before I made it back to Security. Specialist Liu, dark circles forming under her eyes, sat dictating and tapping away at her screen. I interrupted her. "The chief directed me to return and report."

She stifled a yawn and nodded before speaking into her collar. "Chief Brold, Keesay is here." She tapped a spot on her desk. Not bothering to see the door slide open, she said, "He'll see you."

The chief, writing on his clipboard, pulled the nub of a toothpick from his mouth. "Report, Keesay."

"All quiet in the colonist area. A few *Kalavar* personnel in the corridors. No one else spotted except two agitated marines."

"Agitated?" the chief asked. "Understood." He flipped the clipboard facedown and tore a sheet from the middle. "Keesay, your watch isn't over. Patrol aft of Medical. Lower decks for another two hours." He folded the sheet in quarters and handed it to me. "Any trouble, report and respond."

"Understood, Chief." I pulled a pen from my thigh pocket. "If systems fail I'll record observations." I slid the paper and pen into a breast pocket before leaving, knowing my effort provided inadequate deception if the chief's security systems were compromised. But his predicating action was even worse.

Two levels below I approached an alcove formed by two wall-mounted pallets. I examined their locking mechanism and the brackets. Nobody was in view and the security monitors would prove ineffective. While between the pallets I pulled the note and read the chief's single scribbled order. It simply read, 'Pick a fight with Gudkov. He's ready, Raccoon.' I read the directive again before pocketing it. I moved several pallets down and repeated the procedure. While doing so I tore out the written section of orders, chewed and swallowed. Repeated another inspection and hid the remaining paper in a crevice.

I was confident Gudkov was in my assigned patrol area. Rather than try to determine the reason for the chief's nonstandard, aberrant directive, I strode toward the assigned patrol area pondering an equally elusive answer—how to defeat the holder of three Kickboxing Intra-Colony Platinum Rings.

My jaw began to ache. Nothing in my security training would help. I considered the tactics Smith had taught me. Not likely. I'd witnessed Gudkov take down half the marines onboard in the rec area. I clutched my brass knuckles. There was one tactic that might render Gudkov less potent and shorten my stay in Medical.

My ocular provided no views of the assigned area. I slowed my pace to organize a strategy, but around the next corner stood three tan-clad maintenance techs. "Specialist Gudkov, I've been assigned this area. Report."

"Systems are coming back on line, no thanks to you."

"That is correct. *My* assignment doesn't involve maintenance of the currently failing systems."

Gudkov took a squared-off stance. "Whose fault is it? That I and McAllister were barred from system monitoring and maintenance?"

"Excellent question, Specialist Gudkov," I said, feigning thought. "Just whose arrogance and stupidity landed themselves in confinement?"

"Listen, Relic," he growled.

"I'm all ears, Chip." I reached into my breast pocket for pen and the paper. I forgot I'd disposed of the leftover paper from the chief. Oh well, I thought, no signaling to Gudkov that I was following the chief's orders. "Sorry. No paper. Guess I'll just have to focus real hard and hope to retain those bits of your endless wisdom."

Gudkov dropped his equipment belt. "Too bad, Keesay," he said, looking up. "Surveillance is down. But I'm sure you'll recall this lesson."

Tech Schultz moved to step between us and received Gudkov's sharp elbow to his chest. Schultz fell back struggling for breath.

I slid my shotgun to the floor. "Tech Segreti, with surveillance out, you might want to keep track of your supervisor's teeth."

"You sure, Keesay?" Tech Segreti asked.

I unbuckled my belt and smiled, giving my best performance. After I said, "I am," the maintenance tech nodded once and stepped back. Segreti was a brawler and knew some karate, but not in Gudkov's league. It was good to know at least one crew member was willing to stick up for me. Gudkov said he'd taken out Pillar, who cleaned my clock back on the Mavinrom Dock, meaning I wasn't in his league either. Not even close.

I slid my brass knuckles onto my right hand. They hadn't helped then and probably wouldn't help now. But everyone knew I carried and used them. Segreti made them, so if I didn't use them now someone might see through the ruse. I just hoped Gudkov really got the chief's message.

Gudkov stepped forward in a loose fighting stance. Nevertheless, he was like a compressed spring. I watched, gambled, waited for his leading right-foot kick. Even anticipating it, I wasn't fast enough to sidestep and catch it fully in the crook of my arm. Somehow Gudkov managed to twist and spin, and was bringing his left leg around. I gripped his right leg, shifted, and landed my brass knuckles against his shin. His strike glanced off my shoulder and we both hit the ground.

We rolled and came to our feet about three yards apart. He was up before me, favoring his right leg but not enough. I shrugged. Gudkov smiled. I'd hurt his leg but not enough to hinder him. I let him close on it anyway. He snapped a jab at my face. I flicked my head down. His knuckles impacted on the curve of my forehead. A thud resounded through my skull and masked what I hoped to hear—his knuckles splintering.

Gudkov's jab staggered me. I shifted and tried a right uppercut. I saw his right too late and paid for it. Did he swipe my feet from under me? Would Tech Segreti keep track of *my* teeth?

CHAPTER 30

Bacterial genes have long been a part of the human genome with approximately 120 of the 30,000 human genes being bacterial in origin. Additional bacterial genes have been inserted through the use of retroviruses during vaccinations. Colonial Marines reportedly receive the strongest measures, enabling them to better withstand hazards related to chemical and biological warfare.

Smelling salts. Somehow they got past the clotted blood. The chief pulled the salts away. "Don't think it's broken."

I squinted and took in my surroundings. I was slouched in a padded chair in the chief's office with Gudkov to my left. I tried to sit up straight but gave up, for the moment.

Gudkov grinned. "Got all of my teeth."

"Gudkov," the chief barked across his desk. I was slow to turn his way. "Corral your marbles, Keesay. We've got urgent business."

I probed with my tongue. Some of my teeth were loose, but no gaps. How many times did Gudkov hammer me before I went down? Or after. Someone else sat to my right. When I realized it was Specialist Haxon, Gudkov's pal, I suppressed a groan. At least Gudkov's right hand was wrapped.

"Not bad, Keesay," Gudkov said. "Faster than I thought. Must sandbag when you work out with Smith." He mimicked a kick with his right foot. "Only two people have ever countered that move."

I forced myself up from slouching. "I know."

"Really." It wasn't a question. "Know your enemy."

"Opponent, and correct." I nodded. The motion broke the clotting. Haxon shoved a bloody rag into my hand. "Thanks." I dabbed my nose and winced. The pain cleared my head, somewhat. "Reviewed every one of your recorded matches," I said between dabs. "Not much else to do in confinement." I looked to the chief. He said nothing, so I continued. "Against opponents who were of significant inferior skill, you opened with the right kick forty percent of the time."

Gudkov chuckled. "You've been thumped one—make that two—too many times."

"Keesay, you coherent?" asked the chief.

"I am," I said, noting my sore jaw. "Mostly."

"Mostly, eh? What's the first thing Maintenance Tech Gudkov said?"

"He...pointed out he still had every one of his pearly whites?"

"What is your current assignment?"

"Security specialist 4th class aboard the civil transport *Kalavar.* Operated by Negral Corp. Main duty is the colonist area."

The chief slipped a toothpick into his mouth. "Who handed you that rag and why?"

"Gudkov's sidekick, to mop up his handiwork?"

Chief Brold tapped several times on his desktop console. "Guess you'd never have survived to adulthood without a thick skull. Right, Anatol?"

"For the record, Chief," said Gudkov. "If Keesay pulls those brass knuckles on me again, you'll be plucking ribs from his lungs."

Despite my sore neck I looked over my shoulder and around at the monitors before responding.

"This room has been secured," said the chief. "Go ahead, Keesay. I stirred the pot this time. We've got a few minutes, so let's get it out in the open." He glared at all three of us. "Anything said here stays."

"We're such good buddies," I said, looking from Gudkov to Chief Brold. "Even if the fight was staged, I had to try to win or whoever the show was for would've been suspicious. You expected a punching bag. Instead you're pissed you got a little hurt."

"Gudkov," said the chief.

"Keesay, you're lucky I held back. Call it my internal thespian."

I started to respond, but instead addressed the chief. "Who was the fight for if the monitors were down?"

"We're waiting for someone. I'll get to that soon enough. In the meantime, Gudkov, you know most of this, but Keesay and Haxon need to get up to speed. There was an attack on the ship's systems. That's obvious. But there's a lot more to it."

I wanted to ask who else, but figured I'd know by meeting's end. Hopefully it wasn't McAllister. She'd get too much pleasure seeing me roughed up by her loyal associate.

"You with me, Keesay?"

"Yes, Chief, I am."

"Good." His tongue slid the toothpick across his teeth. "Not all systems were attacked. But security, medical, communications, inventory and weapons were. The primary systems, backup and even archived."

Haxon asked, "Including the remote secondary?"

"Affirmative. Some of the personnel and accounting files have been damaged as well as company files. Navigation, engineering and life support were untouched except for one targeted area." He was silent while the information sank in. "Engineering is scrambling to salvage what was lost, and using isolated backups as patches." He shook his head and gnawed his toothpick. "When we tried an immediate reinstallation from memory plates, a dormant program delayed four minutes, then launched a new virus attack, corrupting them." The chief threw his toothpick down.

"Lucky as to the infiltrator's target?" said Haxon, rubbing his cheek. "Although the coding and protections are different, if they could've attacked selectively along such routes even into archive, they could've targeted engine control, or navigation. Could have radically altered condensed space trajectory." He didn't have to explain the catastrophic results. "And I say infiltrator, as we are agreed it was an inside job?"

Gudkov grunted. "Whoever was behind it knew their business. Engineer McAllister isolated parts of the program before it self-destructed. Crax. Advanced, possibly Primus Crax. We were lucky." He shook his head. "Especially for the assistance that exploration shuttle crew gave us. Powerful system onboard. I'd wager there's some Umbelgarri software, maybe hardware." Gudkov's hands became animated, emphasizing his explanation. "Coordinated by McAllister, a two-pronged counter-attack was launched against the multiple imbedded virus programs. The attacking program had harnessed eighty-seven percent of the ship-wide CPU before McAllister launched an offline secondary defense program in conjunction with the exploration shuttle's system. The culprit or culprits definitely knew our system, and had some grasp of McAllister's primary security programs.

The chief held up his finger. He spoke into his collar. "Send him in." He tapped the desktop and admitted the executive officer. He looked angry, embarrassed and frustrated.

The door slid shut. "Lt. Commander Devans," said the chief. "I'm sure your ass chewing was none less delicate than mine." Haxon brought him a chair. "I've been catching Keesay and Haxon up on the targeted systems assault. Anything to add?"

"Only that Mer estimated a twenty percent loss in stock." He opened the folding chair. "I'll get to that."

I flicked my head a little too quickly to catch the chief's expression. Instead of dull headache, a throbbing started, but I ignored it. Stock? Negral stock? How could Mer or anyone know? How did events on the *Kalavar* tie in?

"Why don't you take over, Commander?" suggested the chief.

The XO nodded and shifted his seat to face Gudkov, Haxon and myself. "You three are here for various reasons. Some specific knowledge or skill for the issues at hand. I'll clarify as much as I can."

He licked his teeth. "First and most obvious, we have at least two saboteur-assassins on board. At least one is a crewmember. Placement of the advanced explosive device on Specialist Keesay's cart, the advanced non-detection device Maintenance Tech Stardz had and presumably handed off to an accomplice. Keesay and Club stopped one of their number before boarding or we'd have even bigger trouble, as evidenced by having similar A-Tech equipment and method of self-immolation. And a security recording you'll see shortly."

"Why the *Kalavar*?" interrupted Gudkov. "Mer's important, but it doesn't appear he's the target."

"Good question," said the Executive Officer. "I'll get to that in good time." While the XO's voice was conciliatory, his sharp gaze was not. Gudkov took the hint and leaned back in his chair.

"Prior to departure, the captain received a hand-delivered message. The Crax have attacked a number of Umbelgarri installations and outposts. Initial enemy actions were largely successful. The government, backed by a unanimous vote of all major corporate executive boards, has declared our intention to oppose the Crax in defense of our ally."

No one in the room was surprised, least of all myself, having overheard part of it while Mer conferred with the captain. But to actually hear it confirmed. What about the Chicher?

Looking at me, the XO continued. "Captain Tilayvaux, as you may know, was a highly decorated fighter pilot and is well respected. But despite Mer's influence, she commands the *Kalavar*, an aging civil transport. Do you have anything to add from your Marine contacts, Chief Brold?"

"Other than the fact that deployment transports began less than two months before our departure. They've got the jump on us."

"Three months earlier wouldn't have mattered," said the XO. "Crax ships."

"Right," said the chief. "Better to deploy with full logistical support. I heard the Umbelgarri provided fast transports. Better speed than even Primus Crax."

The XO held up two fingers. That was all? Gudkov groaned. Haxon pursed his lips and shook his head.

"Anything to add, Specialist Haxon?" asked the XO.

"Just trying to get the big picture, sir." His gaze moved as if to focus on different regions of space. "The Crax would have to come through what remains of the Umbelgarri to get to us. We can't maneuver our units fast enough to support. Felgan loyalty to the Umbelgarri defines the term. But they're poor fighters. And the Crax have established a line of colonies and outposts between Felgan and Umbelgarri space. There's the Chicher." His voice trailed off.

Both the chief and the XO didn't have to say it. They wanted to be part of the defense forces moving against the Crax. But the *Kalavar* wasn't fit for combat by any stretch of the imagination, even with its additional patchwork armor plating.

"We don't know who's supporting the Crax," said the XO. "Stegmars, of course. The V'Gun would be a good bet. Others? Unknown. But the Crax Confederation," he spat, "Primus, Selgum and Coregar, is plenty enough."

"Back to the current situation," said the chief, "and what you're all itching your scalp over." He eyed the chronometer. "Negral doesn't believe all of the corporations are onboard for this war. At least to support the Umbelgarri. And it looks as if we're caught up in the inter-corporate and governmental squabble."

"Squabble is one way to put it," said the XO. "You three have volunteered for special duty. Identified because of your background, company loyalty, and especially because we believe you're not complicit in the recent sabotage and assassination." He leaned back a fraction. "I know there's friction between you, and the initial stages of our plan have played on the common knowledge of it. It has to end right here. Right now. Understood?"

Gudkov crossed his arms and nodded. Haxon elevated his right hand and nodded once. I followed suit. "Understood."

"First, the successful assassination," continued the XO. "Chief?"

With a tap the desktop screen angled up and pivoted. "You did two things right, Keesay. Still." The screen showed, with minimal distortion, a corridor approaching the first class passenger suites. A marine walked one step ahead of a well-dressed passenger, approaching the camera. The scene stopped.

"Keesay, you'll recognize the Senior Vice President of Recruiting for the Chiagerall Institute with Private Fleishman." With the distortion the ID helped, especially with Mr. Habbuk. Most executives his age have similar features based on common pre-selected genetic characteristics. "This is the only angle. Keesay, you ordered this sequence for priority isolation. Fortunately, we got as much as we did. Watch."

The scene continued with varying clarity. The strides of Mr. Habbuk and the marine shifted to the right. The marine's head turned as if to follow someone then faced forward. A fraction of a second later Mr. Habbuk looked over his shoulder and began to duck. Then the marine stepped and spun to interpose himself, MP pistol drawn to fire. The marine took an MP round in the neck. Aim disrupted, Private Fleishman fired off two shots before another round struck him in the face. He hadn't even moved his left hand to his damaged neck before a third round impacted his forehead. He instinctively fired off two unaimed rounds as he fell. Chief Brold stopped the recording.

"The marine call," said Commander Devans, "which keyed Keesay to save this sequence, we believe occurred just before the first wound. Now watch the senior VP."

Chief Brold started the sequence. Even as the marine fell, Mr. Habbuk dove to the right. A flash zipped past where he had stood. A crossfire. Mr. Habbuk went for the marine's pistol but never got to use it. He dodged several flashes and, based on movements, several MP rounds from the opposite direction before they finally nailed him with a laser blast in the back, followed by several MP rounds. An additional laser blast struck the downed marine, and two more rounds impacted Mr. Habbuk's prone body. Smoke emanated from the bloody corpses.

"What tipped you off, Keesay?" asked the XO. "Why did you relay to Specialist Club that the Senior VP required an escort?"

My eyes were wide. The meal with Specialist Tahgs felt weeks past.

"Actually, sir, Mr. Habbuk requested I escort him back to his quarters just after I was contacted by Specialist Muller to report to the colonist area."

"Any additional observations?" Chief Brold asked.

The screen remained frozen on the assassinated men. "Mr. Habbuk was insistent I escort him, but then said it would be fine and that I had others to watch. I told him to remain and I would send someone." I searched my memory. "During the boarding, Mr. Habbuk responded similarly. He turned toward the offender before any observable hostile act." Chief Brold nodded in agreement.

"You all noted," said the XO, "that someone, not picked up by the monitor, passed by Private Fleishman without raising an alarm. He didn't nod or acknowledge, so definitely not a marine. Probably not security. A passenger in the corridor should have raised suspicion. I believe a maintenance or engineering tech, or engineer. This assessment will tie in later."

"I saw the laser flash, light duty?" asked Haxon. "What other weapon was employed?"

"Small caliber MP," Chief Brold said. "Non-explosive rounds." He lowered the screen and tossed aside his toothpick. "Now for the primary targets." That statement raised four of our six eyebrows. Haxon remaining impassive. "Instructor Watts and her son."

My nose started bleeding again. "Not Lowell Owen?" I asked.

"Why would you say that?" asked the XO.

"It was my understanding that he was a corporate whistleblower." I dabbed my nose. "Although all that's happened seems pretty far to go to get him." I recalled Frost's inadequate reports and deleted sec-bot files. "He'd been roughed up pretty badly before. When I was in confinement. I filed an addendum report."

"No, Keesay," said the chief. "Colonist Owen was either an innocent bystander, or more likely Instructor Watts's white knight."

"Agreed," the XO said, rubbing his chin. "Up until now we haven't had much success in tracking the suspected infiltrator. Specialist Haxon, could you speak to that?"

"Sure," Haxon said, after a nod from Chief Brold. "The non-detection device. We tried to scan for alloys unique to Crax and V'Gun, hall by hall and, covertly, room to room without success. Senior Engineer McAllister programmed the security monitors to track civilian and personnel movements, and identified patterns and profiles. Also recorded sounds not matching visual. Scanned various spectrums, and on the outside chance, scanned for shadows. Maintenance Tech Gudkov designed and erected multiple covert spectrum irradiation sources to provide a possible signature. No success. The system attack destroyed the data files."

"From Keesay's report," Chief Brold said, holding up the note pad, "collected prior and follow-up interviews conducted by Specialist Club and

Muller, evidence collected from both assault scenes, and from Medical, this is what's been pieced together."

He plucked another toothpick from a miniature barrel. "Maintenance Tech Schultz is our man. That's why I wanted him to visit Medical." Gudkov's eyes widened as the chief explained. "Dr. Sevanto is scanning his bruised sternum right now. It'd help if we had a comparison, but Dr. Sevanto thinks he can locate any acidic suicide device couched behind the aorta. If he can, we'll know for sure." The chief gnawed his fresh toothpick. He had difficulty not grinding his teeth while uttering the last sentence.

"The blow to his chest was quite fortunate," added the XO. "It'll lessen suspicion. Even if Dr. Sevanto cannot confirm, we'll keep very close track of Tech Schultz."

"We don't know how fanatical he is," said the chief. "Nor do we know what could release the corrosive into his bloodstream. But he's our only lead to any other conspirators. Right now Specialist Club is surveying his quarters, workstation and then frequent stomping areas."

The chief held up his finger then, placed a hand to his ear. Over a minute passed. "Understood. Excellent work, Senior Engineer." He rubbed the back of his neck. "McAllister reports that the attack program was advanced artificial intelligence. We might have eventually gotten the upper hand on it, but the exploration shuttle software located the backdoor deactivation. However, while it was breaking the entry code, the artificial intelligence program laid virus mines throughout the system and then self-erased. One of those mines attacked the backup installation from the memory plates."

The XO interrupted, asking, "Did McAllister give you any idea how many more we might set off?"

"No. She's working up a profile on them. Apparently, she intends to use a derivative of Maintenance Tech Cox's Code Wars program."

"Benny?" asked Gudkov, a confused look on his face.

"You got it," replied the chief. "Apparently Benny modified it to overcome a virus mine set in the freezer system. McAllister said his program was able to temporarily limit the infiltrating intelligence program's access to the freezer systems."

"Well, of course," said Gudkov. "They're not a priority system."

"Actually, they were targeted," replied the XO. "What we now know is an A.I. program not only shut down the cooling system but initiated an emergency defrost sequence. According to Mer, launched from a mobile system, Tech Cox's program interrupted the defrost but couldn't restart the cooling. I'd speculate that the A.I. program set a mine in retreat, but one of Cox's routines overcame it."

"What's so important in deep freeze?" asked Gudkov.

"Guppies," said the chief. "And eighty percent of the stock was saved."

Gudkov asked, "Isn't the system Benjamin Cox cleared also tied into the one used by Medical to hold someone in cold sleep?"

"Bingo!" said the chief. "Leading to what we believe was the main target for the infiltrators. Instructor Lori Watts and her son."

Again, both Gudkov and I were surprised. Haxon managed to hold a straight face. This time I spoke up, "Why her?"

"Let's just say they are not accurately identified on the ship's roll," said the chief. "And that their continued health and safety may have a very large part to play in the war." He let that statement lodge itself. "I feared their identity might already have been compromised. Recall, the colonists suffered greatly upon revival from cold sleep. In the preparatory sequence, a defective drug was administered to the colonists. It was discovered late in the process and steps were taken to nullify the results. At that point Watts and her son were not believed to be the target. It could've been a screw up. It could've been an effort against whistleblower Owen. Or it could have been a corporate espionage effort to hinder Negral Corp. Such things are not unheard of."

"The incident," said the XO, "with your arrival on the Mavinrom Dock, Specialist Keesay, was a heads up." I noted he didn't state Representative Vorishnov. He continued ticking off on his fingers. "The abduction of Specialist Tahgs and the effort to access colonist files indicated that Watts and her son's cover wasn't completely compromised. The incident during boarding, the A-Tech explosive on Keesay's cart, and the suspected non-detection device, indicated there's a concentrated effort against them." His fists clenched. "We didn't single them out for protection because their identity would've been revealed without a doubt."

"And I had reports," said the chief, "that unusual activities had occurred on one of the decoy ships, where Negral planted information about Michael Watts. None of the measures taken was as extreme as what we experienced today. And those focused on abduction, not elimination. But the Crax invasion probably lit a fire under someone."

I said, "Could I ask someone *who*?"

The chief looked to the XO who shrugged and answered. "I believe a small minority in the government bureaucracy. Maybe a few military leaders. Several corporations. Capital Galactic Investment. Ask somebody else, you'll get a different answer."

"Some would list Negral Corp," suggested Specialist Haxon.

"Namely, CGIG," said the chief. "My mother taught me, when you point at somebody else, three fingers are pointing back at you."

"Speculation is interesting," said the XO. "But our main duty is to ensure the health and safety of Instructor Watts and her son until we reach our final destination, Tallavaster. We'll need to work up a security plan while we lay over at the Zeta Aquarius Dock."

"The ZQ Dock," said the chief. "We've got to get there. Let's go over details of the attempt on Watts and son. Then new duty assignments. Commander, did Dr. Sevanto verify his initial findings?"

"Yes. Instructor Watts had ingested Sigilligaste, a V'Gun drug which is essentially inert in the human body. Traces of it were located on a drinking glass in her assigned quarters. Undigested remains found in Watts's stomach. The latrine, where she'd vomited, contained amounts of Conwestrondian, another V'Gun drug. Some bound to the Sigilligaste. A lethal combination. Further examinations revealed small crystal like structures, almost identical to salt were found in the undigested food, digestive track, and vomit. The crystals were impregnated with digestive, time-released Conwestrondian, known to inhibit capillary constriction. Both drugs are colorless, odorless and very difficult to detect in food, blood and body tissues. The uncontrollable hemorrhaging in Colonist Owen set Dr. Sevanto and his staff on the trail. An antibody reaction in Watts tipped Dr. Sevanto off further."

Commander Devans stared upward to the right in thought before he continued. "Dr. Sevanto reported, if Conwestrondian is present, even as little as two milligrams, a quarter dose if given for medical purposes, and even a trace amount of Sigilligaste is present in the body, the results...well, Colonist Owen. The damage from the sonic blade may have been crippling but the internal hemorrhaging caused by the drug combination was fatal. Dr. Sevanto estimated that even with a fully functioning med lab and immediate knowledge of the lethal combination, survival would have been less than five percent."

"Okay," interrupted Gudkov. "Obvious questions. Why didn't the combination affect Instructor Watts? Why did it affect Owen and not the other colonists? Namely her son?"

"Any other questions before I am allowed to finish?"

I elevated my hand to get the XO's attention. He nodded. "Why didn't the assailant, presumably Tech Schultz, finish the job? And did Instructor Watts ID him?" Commander Devans didn't scowl at my question as he had Gudkov's, so I continued. "The non-detection device as evidenced by previous monitoring and by Private Fleishman and Mr. Habbuk would indicate that it's only effective against electronic surveillance, such as a security monitor or sec-bot."

"You want to take those, Chief?" asked the XO.

"Sure," he said. "First with Keesay's. Your sec-bot, Lefty, responded to the sounds of the conflict. His downloaded recordings indicate an intermittent scuffle, possibly a sound dampener associated with the non-detection device. Lefty arrived in the lavatory facilities, found Colonist Owen down and Instructor Watts huddled in the back of a stall. It transmitted a call for immediate assistance. The sec-bot registered no other individuals in the area but detected an anomaly in some of the scattered vomit and blood." The chief scanned some hand written notes. "I don't have it handy but the sec-bot recorded disturbances in the fluids on the floor, then scanned the ceiling for causation. It went into defense mode with both silent and siren alarm. It also fired two tranquilizer darts without success. The assailant then disabled the sec-bot with a powerful magnetic discharge. In defense mode the siren and silent alarm continued, but diminished in strength. We believe this is when the assailant fled the scene." He checked his notes again. "A colonist child, Vargus Idaduhut, responded, saw the scene and alerted his father."

The XO finished the answer. "Instructor Watts, at the time, was visually impaired due to the drugs ingested. She'll recover, and she did identify a tan-suited attacker. And as far as the other colonists, it appears the Sigilligaste was localized to the Watts's compartment. On the pitcher and one water cup. Apparently Michael Watts didn't drink from the pitcher that night or possibly the night before." He took a breath. "Colonist Owen apparently ingested the Conwestrondian like a number of other colonists. He picked up the Sigilligaste through his wounds from the instructor's vomit on the floor."

"And as the Watts family is under *special* protection," said the chief, "we can reasonably assume that they've been administered non-standard inoculations. One of them apparently foiled the lethal V'Gun drug cocktail."

I recalled the attempted assassination of Representative Vorishnov and my subsequent encounter with Field Director Karlton Simms and the resulting injection of an unspecified countermeasure drug to foil drug-assisted interrogations. But the chief's assumption about Instructor Watts and Skids fit.

Gudkov nudged me, pretty hard. "Keesay, your nose is drippin'," he whispered.

"Thanks." I grinned back, ignoring the pain as I dabbed and caught up on what the XO was saying.

"I believe the VP from the Chiagerall Institute was eliminated not necessarily because of his ability, but what he represents." He hesitated. "And his connection to the Watts family." The chief raised his eyebrows and his neck twitched, almost imperceptibly, but it did.

Specialist Haxon spoke up. "Not everyone feels what the Institute does is credible. But you saw how long their VP evaded a crossfire. Whoever took out that marine was a good shot. And Keesay reported his early response at the boarding incident."

"No sense debating that now," said the chief. "Not here. I've got duties to assign you, gentlemen." He looked to the newest member of the security team. "Haxon, rebuild the passenger and crew tracking system. Focus on Schultz. Find a pattern and a partner. And locate that non-detection unit."

The chief held up his finger and placed a hand to his ear. "Route it through my desk console and it'll be secure. Yes, agreed upon Marine encryption. Thanks, out." The chief looked up. "Dr. Sevanto's report on Schultz." He tapped his desk and waited for download and deciphering. He scanned. "Positive on the implanted device. Ninety percent. Says he noted other damage consistent with a scuffle. Minor contusion to the back of the skull. Also a wrist abrasion, knuckle scrape, and forearm bruise, the two former masked with some form of makeup. Schultz was freshly showered and clothed. Dr. Sevanto didn't question him other than about the contusion. He accepted Schultz's explanation. Conclusion, injuries consistent with minor scuffle, possibly one with Colonist Owens."

He looked up. "No need to examine his uniforms, make a count, etcetera. He's our man. Do DNA tests but let's not spook him. And that leads me to your assignment, Gudkov."

Gudkov sat up. "Yes, Chief."

"Maintenance and Auxiliary Security Specialist Anatol Gudkov, for failing to follow orders and involving yourself in an altercation with Specialist Keesay, your movements will officially be restricted. In addition, your primary assistant, Class 2 Maintenance Tech Heinrich Schultz, will be assigned to watch and observe you, in addition to assisting you." The chief smiled. "He'll be stuck to you like a burr on fur. And as such you'll be able to keep an eye on him. Restrict his, ahhh, shall I say, nefarious activities?"

"No problem, Chief," said Gudkov. "Wasn't his contract obtained from the Mori and Togo Frontier Mining Group? A subsidiary of Capital Galactic?"

"Yes, it was," said the chief. "You'll be taken off of program rebuilding and maintenance." That drew a frown. "Instead, as punishment you'll be assigned to cross check and rebuild the damaged cargo pallet manifest files. Other duties remain the same. Bot maintenance, et cetera."

"Inventory work?" growled Gudkov.

"Yes. And it should take you a while. We've taken the liberty of ensuring some of the hardcopy information has been misfiled and backup has been made inaccessible."

"And who'll assist Senior Engineer McAllister?"

"The captain feels that Maintenance Tech Cox is up to the task. His work is slow but solid."

"And," added the XO, "his code proved effective against the A.I. program."

"Didn't Tech Cox begin his career with Mori and Togo Mining?" asked Gudkov.

"That is true," said the chief. "But thirty-eight percent of the crew has some ties to the Capital Galactic Investment Group."

No need to suppress a smile. I figured my new duty would equally unpleasant.

"Keesay?"

"Yes, Chief," I replied, sitting up straight.

"Security Specialist Krakista Keesay, for your participation in the altercation with Tech Gudkov, you are reassigned to permanent stationing in the colonist area. You will pack up your cart with new quarters being those of Colonist Lowell Owen. From there you'll be able to keep a better eye on Instructor Watts and her son. With you there, and Schultz stuck to Gudkov, at least his access to the area will be limited."

"Understood, Chief."

"In addition," said the XO, "you will each receive ninety percent cut in pay for the remainder of this transport run, and will receive an additional reprimand in your career file."

Neither Gudkov nor I needed to voice our dissatisfaction.

"Gentlemen," said the XO. "The captain will amend the reprimand and reinstate all back pay, upon successful completion of the cruise."

The ramification of the situation began to run through my head. Depending on how it was worded, coupled with my previous conflicts with Pillar and McAllister, my career advancement could be truncated. I wouldn't be at liberty to explain the circumstances, not with the subterfuge needed to protect the two targeted and apparently significant colonists.

Someone in this meeting, I decided, must have strong ties to intelligence. Maybe Chief Brold. Probably Lt. Commander Devans. Calling the shots, and I was a bit player, a pawn to be sacrificed.

"Specialist Keesay," said the chief.

I was too busy getting angry to respond. Sure as shooting, my time aboard the *Kalavar* was limited. With McAllister and Gudkov around I'd go nowhere. My ability to get my contract picked up would be impossible. The Relic Army Ground Assault Support Force? No hope being recruited. Even if a war is on, who'd recruit me?

"Specialist Keesay," called Chief Brold.

I kept my voice level. "Yes, Chief."

"Report to Medical. Get someone there to look you over. Catch a few hours sleep before packing. Then report to the colonist area."

I wasn't looking forward to seeing Administrative Specialist Tahgs. "Chief, why the directive to Medical?"

He answered, "Your marbles were rattled a little harder than I thought." Gudkov chuckled and the chief shot him a glare before finishing. "You seem to be a little out of it."

"Really, Chief? Ever consider that I'm comparing my information with the gap-ridden set you've provided. Takes some concentration."

"Security, Keesay."

"Correct, you're concerned with my health so that I can safeguard two passengers whose protective custody has been compromised. Why not put them under twenty-four hour lockup with a dozen marines on guard?" I wiped my nose. It hurt. So what. "Instead, play some sort of shell game. Me and my career are expendable."

"Class 4 Security Specialist Keesay," said Commander Devans. "You lack the big picture. It's much larger than you think."

"Correct, sir. I'm only a C4 Sec-Spec. But good enough to place between Schultz and his pals, and Instructor—whoever and the youth masquerading as her son. I get that much of the picture."

The XO looked to the chief, then to Haxon, then back at me.

Before he spoke, I said, "Don't worry, sir, Chief. I will do my duty. They will be safe, or I'll be dead before they are." I looked at my watch and examined the chronometer. "Besides, I only need to do it for another four weeks until the ZQ Dock. I'll have to recalculate your deception from there to the Tallavaster Colonies. Correct?"

I held my wrist up to Gudkov. "Even relic equipment can provide data. How many seconds off is my watch? I'll tell you, thirty-two from what it should be. Should have only lost about twenty by now. If a C4 can figure it, surely someone else can." I slapped my head with my palm. "That's right. I need to visit Medical to be sure I can think straight."

The chief leaned back in his chair and locked his fingers behind his head. "If you don't want to go to Medical, Keesay, you could just say so."

CHAPTER 31

Interstellar tugs, vessels with the largest engine-to-mass ratio, play an important if rarely utilized role as primary responders in rescue and recovery. More commonly, tugs are employed to haul ships from orbital construction platforms to distant planets or docks. It's cheaper than on-site construction. Heavily armored and bristling with weapons for local defense, monitors are the most frequent hauls. Second, are strings of large pleasure yachts meant for intrasolar travel.

Capital Galactic Investment Group contracted for a series of Behemoth class transports with an internal bay capable of carrying vast amounts of cargo or several ships for interstellar transport. Seven were built before the Behemoth class construction was discontinued. Too few orders resulted in unjustifiably high per-unit construction cost.

Instructor Watts commented, "The Colonial Marines certainly have been ill tempered."

I tried to ignore her and focus on the relays the colonist children were running.

"The students miss the games with them. Especially Michael."

"Don't expect it to change any time soon," I said. "One of their number was killed. I can't imagine why that would alter their attitude and routine."

The race ended. Instructor Watts declared the winners and laid out the rules for the next competition. The colonist children began again, cheering on their teammates, except for Michael. This time, as he often did, he stood as if expecting to lose. I'd discussed the self-fulfilling prophecy with him in the past to no avail.

Instructor Watts pushed back my thoughts. "You haven't heard from the administration specialist in Medical?" she asked. "Has that placed you in an equally poor disposition?"

"Actually, I have. Once." I struggled to keep a sneer from my face. "She severed all communications. I'm a short-termer on the *Kalavar.* And not popular. Can't blame her."

"You're quite popular here. With the students. With the colonists, or most, despite your current bout of unhappiness." She rested a hand on my shoulder. "Father Cufter performed an exemplary service. I miss Lowell Owen, too."

A tip of my head signaled her to follow and avoid surveillance. "If that's what you believe. I'm confined here for reasons not of my own design, or directly of my own devices."

"And for that many of us are thankful. Even Stosh Meadows envisions you as a peer. Outwitted Senior Engineer McAllister. You were reprimanded for, as he says, 'Brawling with Champ Gudkov.' As such, he affords you respect instead of contempt."

"Fleeting. Soon as he decides he won't prosper. Give it another week." I shook my head. "You don't get it, but it's not your responsibility."

Trying to change the tone, Instructor Watts said, "It's my understanding the Chicher diplomat has learned to play dominoes, and proposes a tournament. Seven colonists have shown interest."

I shrugged, not really interested in dominos or much of anything beyond being effective in my assigned duty.

"Specialist Keesay, to remain bitter will benefit no one. Least of all yourself."

"Are you one of the seven colonists?"

"If you'll be the eighth, I'll be the ninth. I'm confident your participation will inspire more to compete."

"Why, to beat me?"

"Maybe. But we'll need more than just your one set. Maybe you can use your connections?"

"We'll see if I still have any. Think I'm still owed a pint of blowing bubbles." I couldn't help but return her smile.

I removed my riot helmet, winded. It doubled well for fencing gear. My durable uniform coveralls fit the bill for the rest. I walked back toward my quarters and pulled the curtain aside, allowing the Chicher diplomat to enter first. The rat-like alien, half my size, scampered past on his hind legs. I set the epee aside and poured two cups of water.

The Chicher removed his protective gear after setting aside his pair of triple-pronged hand blades and plucking off the four-edged tail weapon. He removed the sparring sheaths and scrutinized the razor-sharp blades. He chattered satisfaction before stowing them in an ornate wooden box. The metal of his tail blades reminded me of the alloy that jacketed my shotgun's barrel.

I removed the thin sheath and blunting device from the epee and hung the weapon on a peg before offering a glass of water to the diplomat. He signaled, "Hold." I did until the diplomat attached the circular translator to his leather harness and fitted the wired earpiece.

After chirping and chucking sounds, "Thank for ending thirst, Security Man," crackled from the Chicher's translating device. His mouth wasn't formed for drinking from a cup, yet through practice he'd mastered it.

"You're welcome, Diplomat. And thanks for lending me such a fine epee for fencing. Good exercise."

It took a while for the Chicher's device to translate and for him to interpret. I could've spoken more plainly, but he'd insisted I keep to standard speech patterns so that he might become more proficient.

"Good you do not use chop blade," he said. "Your point blade nimble."

"Yes. I agree. But I'm not used to combating one opponent's three weapons. And I am rusty. Not in practice."

"Like hibernation stiff, familiar movement journeys back."

I wondered at the Chicher diplomat's translation device. At their tech level, it was quite an accomplishment. Translating between the different human languages wasn't a problem for computers decades old. But humans think alike, or at least have a common point of reference. Human cultural differences affect language and thought, but are minor compared to aliens.

"Spirit Man said you, Security Man, ordered nest bound? First time task, make like under orb for you, Security Man?"

I scratched my head and hand signaled using the Official Galactic Sign Language, "Not understand." I'd gained some experience in it and simple one or two word concepts went smoothly enough.

The Chicher sign replied, "Satisfied?"

"Yes," I signaled, then pointed to my watch. "I'm back on duty in twenty minutes."

The Chicher spoke and his device translated. "Security Man task now. You watch. I return to temporary nest." He pointed to the epee. "Your hoard now. From my hoard."

"Thank you. We shall practice fencing again?"

"Yes. Not many orbs will cross the sky before we scrape metal." He attached the weapon case to his back and walked out on two feet, then dropped to all four and scampered past an approaching marine.

"You've built up a sweat, Keesay," Private DeLark said. "You're not romantic with that critter, are you?"

DeLark was one of the few marines who'd regained a sense of humor since Private Fleishman's death. "No more romantic than you are with that old couple's bulldogs." He laughed. I handed him the epee. "We were fencing."

"Really?" he said. "Even for a Relic this is an archaic weapon." He tested the blade for balance. "Tell you what. I cover for you an extra twenty minutes if you show me a little about this pointed stick some time."

"Anything to report?" I asked.

"All quiet. They should be getting up for breakfast in about thirty minutes."

"Good," I said. "Then I'll take you up on your offer. Thanks."

I was cleaning my duty revolver when a pair of shuffling feet stopped in front of my quarters. I pulled my backup from the ankle holster and set it on the blanket.

"Specialist Keesay," called a winded voice. "You in there?"

"I am," I said, and pulled back the curtain.

Mer stood there in his faded-black uniform holding a small crescent wrench. "Just making my rounds, checking. Haven't been this way in a long time."

"I try to make sure Maintenance keeps things in order around here."

"May I come in?"

"Your ship," I said, and stepped aside.

"True enough. Heard I missed a dominoes tournament."

"That is correct." I began to reassemble my single-action revolver. "Sorry, I didn't think to invite you."

He walked past my opened cart, sighed and took a seat near the head of the cot. "I miss the card games. Benny said you don't hear from Janice anymore."

"Correct." I shifted the contents of my cart and slid the cleaning kit inside. "I'm confined to this area."

"So I understand. What'cha still carrying all that water in your cart for?"

"Brought it on board. Probably will try to sell it when we get to the ZQ Dock. The chief cut my contract compensation." I slid my revolver into its holster and checked my equipment. "I'm not holding my breath for promises made. Perform my assigned duty. See what turns up."

"Would ya rest a minute?" Mer asked, patting the cot.

I locked my cart. "I'm back on duty in about three minutes."

"Been taken care of. Corporal Smith assigned Private DeLark to watch for a couple hours."

"Not quite fair to him."

"Life isn't fair. You've figured that out already?"

"Equitable then." Before I sat down I pointed to the pitcher. "Drink?"

"As long as it's on the *Kalavar*'s tab." He gave me a crooked grin. "I never told you how I came to own this ship, did I?"

I poured him a cup. "No, you didn't."

"We've got a few minutes." He took a sip and set the cup on the crate I used for a table and shelf.

"Are we going somewhere?"

"If we do, you can consider it part of your duty." He rubbed his hands together once then on his coveralls. "You know, I was married once, for thirty-one years. Saved all our money, Audrey and me, and took a once-in-a-lifetime cruise to Mars. The *Kalavar*'s maiden voyage. She was a luxury transport then."

He sat, silent. Then cursed. "Tragic accident. Negligence. The captain ignored routine maintenance." Mer looked off into space. "Took my Audrey. Took her from me." His gaze refocused on me. "Sued'em and won. Capital Galactic was just startin' out and having trouble. Paid me in stock, half a percent of the company. My lawyer advised against it. Said the company was bound to go belly up."

"I took my savings and gambled. I'd never owned part of anything big before. And if I could own enough, I could fire the corporate heads who allowed my Audrey to die. Stock rallied after five years. I kept working as a maintenance man, kept investing everything and wouldn't sell. Really took off during the Silicate War. Owned four percent of CGIG and made it on the board of directors. Got rid of those responsible for my Audrey."

He reached over and took another drink. "Pretty soon the fellas I knew left or were bought out, leaving a new, secretive crowd. I wasn't part of their circle. I'm not business smart, but knew they'd get me soon enough if I didn't leave. They were happy to see me go. Traded my stock for CGIG assets. Spent a lot of credits on lawyer fees," he huffed. "A major research and development lab, a couple of asteroid mining ships and rights to three lucrative asteroid fields, and loads of credits. I made them throw in the *Kalavar* for free. Don't like lawyers," he spat. "Especially the ruthless ones I hired. Do you?"

I sat, leaning forward, resting my forearms on my knees. "Can't say that I've found a likeable one yet. Haven't been looking long as you."

He licked his teeth and smiled. "Got together with a couple of my ousted buddies and formed Negral Corp. Capital Galactic really hates us." Mer's eyes became dead serious, matching his voice. "Never trust'em. Even less than lawyers." The old man placed his hands on his knees. "If you decide to end your contract with Negral, don't offer your services to Capital Galactic. If for no other reason than to avoid their lawyers."

"I'm not happy with Negral right now. But the chief hinted I should ride this through."

Mer leaned forward and tottered as he drew himself up. "Too much walkin' today." He rubbed his hands. "Why don't you come with me to a church service?" He saw the debate in my head. "Kra, won't any trouble come of it. Besides, Lori Watts and, what d'you call him? Skids? They're comin' too."

"Haven't been to one for a while, Mer. Thanks for setting it up." I pulled out my Bible and adjusted my com-set. I slid my backup revolver into place before locking my cart.

"It's been a rough run thus far. And not just for you," Mer said, elbowing me in the ribs as I drew the curtain aside. "Besides Security Specialist Nist, you're the only one who manages to get under Gudkov's skin. And he doesn't do it often enough."

I was going to ask Mer why Gudkov put up with Nist, but Instructor Watts and Michael stood waiting outside their room. Both were dressed in agricultural worker brown pants and collared shirts with brass buttons. It appeared my attendance at the missionary's service was preordained.

Mer and Instructor Watts walked ahead while Skids and I followed. Skids spent most of the time relaying the details of a fight between Little Elvis and Chopper. He described the parental punishment and said what the parents yelled at each other. Eventually he switched to asking about chess, and whether I played it, but I never got a chance to answer. He began describing a game he'd played against one of the other children. I gathered it was the sharp girl I'd nicknamed Athena.

"Beat by a girl, were you?" I asked, knowing the answer. "You need to take your time before moving. Concentrate."

"I do," he said. "I'm ready, so I move."

I recalled watching several of his games from afar. Skids moved without hesitation, but not randomly. He responded to his opponent, sometimes having eyed the piece he intended to move long before his adversary showed any sign of intent. "Don't let it bother you," I said. "I don't win all the time either. Even against girls." I knew his attitude about girls would change as he got older. But now, to him, girls were strange, annoying and weird.

His frown turned to a grin. "Really?"

"In some things."

A small group had gathered outside the meeting room. Benny stood next to Maintenance Tech Segreti. Next to Segreti stood the old couple with their bulldogs and Ensign Selvooh talking to them. I spotted the Chicher diplomat skittering from the opposite direction.

Michael asked, "Mom, can I go greet the Chicher diplomat?"

"Yes, you may," she replied. "Be brief. Don't annoy the diplomat."

Skids practiced the greeting hand signal before running forward. The two bulldogs also noticed the Chicher. A simple command from their master returned them to what their muscular bodies defined as sitting. Panting consumed their thoughts.

Someone came up behind and slapped my shoulder. "Specialist Keesay, heard you might be attending this small gathering."

"Corporal Smith," I said. "Didn't expect you. But I guess Colonial Marines are known to rise early. Unlike much of the crew."

The marine nodded to Instructor Watts. "What's the sacrifice of an hour sleep now and then, Keesay? Hope your singing doesn't set the canines to howling."

"Excuse me," said Instructor Watts as she slid toward her son.

Mer asked the marine, "Did ya request *Battle Hymn of the Republic* again?"

"Always do," Smith said. "My favorite." Corporal Smith crossed his arms and then put one finger to his chin. As a matter of fact, it was one of Winston Churchill's favorites. Had it played at his funeral about twenty years after World War II. You remember?"

"I studied history too, Marine."

"Sure, old man. Anything you say." Smith's grin was wide and teasing.

"If that's the case," Mer said, "I'll see to it it's sung at yer funeral. By your relatives and any other mutts I can round up." Mer slapped at the air, dismissing Smith and shuffling over to Benny.

"No black eyes or fat lips I see." Corporal Smith said with a wink.

"He'll give you one," I said. "Oh, me. Correct. Been quiet and boring."

Smith shook his head. "Such is a long transport through space. Right,

Ensign?"

Ensign Selvooh stepped over. "I should say. This run's been more eventful than any I've been on."

"And how many is that?" He looked up and down the young ensign.

"A little edgy, Corporal Smith?" I asked. Specialist Nist approached while studying a computer clip. "Something up?" I asked Smith.

"Enough to know," Selvooh replied, staring at Smith before he looked down. The Chicher diplomat joined us.

"Good orb rising," said the diplomat through his translator. "Warrior Small Group Leader, Captain's Hand, Security Man."

"Good morning to you, Chicher Diplomat," responded Ensign Selvooh.

"Diplomat," said Smith. "I heard you and Specialist Keesay were practicing swordplay."

"Hand blades never in this orb's combat. Strong for body work."

Smith crossed his arms, then slid a hand to his chin. "Except for the Coregar Crax. They prefer hand-to-hand combat. But their blades are more advanced. Molecular saws. Cut right through steel."

The diplomat thought a moment. Then signaled agreement.

"In other words," said Smith, elbowing me. "No bayonet charges."

"Not unless I can locate an Umbelgarri-forged blade." I pointed as the doors slid open. "Shall we, gentlemen?"

The room had three rows of eight padded, folding chairs. A red-carpeted aisle ran down the center. Candles burned on a table next to a crucifix. To the left sat a bowl with wafers and a polished gold cup. A podium holding a formidable leather-bound Bible stood to the right, while on the opposite side a projection hovered, listing the order of service.

Father Cufter greeted each as we entered. He didn't lead a traditional Catholic Mass when a mixed group attended. "Wonderful to see you again, Specialist Keesay." He placed a hand on my left shoulder and shook my right hand.

"It's good to see you again, Father." I led Michael to a front row seat. Corporal Smith slid next to me.

Michael asked, "Did you carve that cross?"

"The Crucifix? I did."

"Remember when you told me the angel named Michael fought Satan?" I nodded. "I can find it." I handed him my Bible. His mother hushed him as Father Cufter began the service.

"Emergency Code Red 14," crackled over my com-set. I observed to see who else had received. Corporal Smith looked at me. Ensign Selvooh stood while Larcher Nist whispered into Mer's ear and then followed suit.

"Sorry, Father," Mer said. "We have a situation." Benny and Tech Segreti followed the rest of us out.

"Chief Brold," I whispered over my com-set. "I'm in Meeting Room Three with Instructor Watts and her son. Where do you want them escorted before I report to combat station?"

It took a second for a response. "Bring them here to Security, for report."

Combat stations meant we must be near destination. I'd calculated another week before reaching Zeta Aquarius. Instructor Watts gave me a wide-eyed look. "I'm to escort you to Security. Come on, Skids." Only the old couple and their dogs remained seated. Even the Chicher had departed.

"Where'd everybody go?" the boy asked. "Want your Bible?"

"You carry it. Now follow." I adjusted my ocular and scanned the hallway before exiting. Two crew members, engineering techs, rushed past. "In places it'll be like someone kicked a beehive, so stick close until we get to Security." I got one of those feelings, realizing I should've ignored proper etiquette and brought my shotgun to church. Mr. Habbuk must've rubbed off.

"All passengers immediately return to and remain in your cabins," came the announcement over intercom, from the wall-mounted terminals, and over my com-set. "Information will follow." I scanned ahead with my ocular. There were a few passengers in the corridors, looking in wonderment but responding.

I pointed. "Let's use the access ladder." I set my ocular to scan the intersection ahead. One engineering tech heading away, trotted around a corner. We crossed, and I spotted Ms. Jazarine a short distance from us. I didn't bother to double-check my ocular before pushing Instructor Watts ahead and drawing my revolver. She dragged Michael with her. "Freeze," I yelled, aiming at the exotic dancer.

She'd already gone for her belt, ignoring my command. I fired on target. A wry smile crossed her face. Shield! My com-set squealed in my ear, then shut down. I fired again. *Blam!* My wrist dampener was dead, too. She clipped a black device back onto her belt and began running my way, drawing something else.

"Down, now!" I called to Watts who was pushing her son into the ladder tube. I thumbed back the hammer again and took cover around the corner. A laser blast singed the top of my right shoulder as the high-grade uniform deflected most of the energy. I fired back, not slowing her. I back pedaled and looked over my shoulder. Instructor Watts was in the access tube. Down the corridor I spotted the old male passenger with his two bulldogs. "Clear the hall," I yelled before trying my com-set with no response.

The old passenger ignored me and strode forward as Jazarine bounded around the corner. I rolled and fired before a laser blast burned past my right ear. The two dogs galloped our way. My expression must've tipped Jazarine as she craned her neck, still keeping the defensive screen between us. Off balance, she discharged her laser at the leading canine. The dog took a grazing hit, tumbled, but staggered to its feet. Smoldering and unsteadily the wounded dog tottered forward in the wake of its partner.

I pulled my bayonet with my left hand and charged, firing again. Jazarine snapped back around and fired, taking me in the stomach. I felt the burn, but my vest and coverall uniform absorbed most of it. The capacitor recharged her weapon faster than I'd expected. Still, I gathered myself, stood erect and smiled. She tapped at her belt and sprinted from view, back down the hall. I made it to the corner and fired off a shot, only to impact the trailing screen. The leading bulldog turned the corner as well.

"Call them off," I yelled at the approaching old man. "No sense getting them killed."

"Daisy, Brick, return!" he shouted. The lead dog, Brick, turned and trotted back, panting. Daisy, who'd just made the corner, pivoted and limped back to her master. It was amazing how fast the exotic dancer could run. She'd already disappeared around another corner.

"Thanks," I said. "Report to Medical. Tell them what happened and to treat your dog. Also, report the incident to that crewmember." I pointed to the approaching engineering tech. "Instruct him to contact Security." I holstered my revolver and dashed to the access tube wondering if Instructor Watts and Skids would make it to Security? Or might Tech Schultz, or another accomplice, be lying in wait?

CHAPTER 32

Corporate ship armament is limited to dual beam defensive lasers and close defense pulse lasers. It's an armament structure enforced by the government through threat of revoking all patents, licensures, permits, and asset seizure. Such actions are authorized and enforced by military personnel, even if the offending corporation developed, or is licensed to build and arm military vessels with the more powerful weapons and tracking systems. Civilian transports and freighters are permitted special armament upgrades for outer colony runs when necessary escort isn't available.

I sprinted to the nearest access terminal. "Security, this is Specialist Keesay."

Club's face appeared. "Acknowledged, Keesay. Situation reported. Specialist Haxon completed the escort. Report to Security. Out."

My stomach hurt. The exotic dancer's laser blast had burned an inch diameter hole through my duty vest, but the high grade coveralls, although singed, held. I was twenty yards from Security when my name was shouted.

"Specialist Keesay," called Colonist Carver Potts as he dragged my cart. "Private DeLark said to bring you your equipment. Hey, you've been in another fight." I looked at my shoulder and stomach and shrugged. Potts actually looked apologetic when he said, "Had to cut the chain. Sorry. Broke a wheel trying to disable the locking mechanism."

"Your efforts are appreciated. As are your talents." I pulled a key. "You're very lucky. This thing's booby-trapped." Potts let go of my cart and stepped away. I removed the padlock and unloaded my shotgun and a satchel filled with spare shotgun and revolver rounds. Then I dug for several stun and fragmentation grenades, removing them from an aluminum storage tube. "Just in case I run into the thug who messed up my uniform." His mouth transformed from one of awe to a nasty grin, matching mine. I went to the bottom for a particular box of shells and pulled the two popcorn nukes I'd disguised years back. I unbuttoned my vest pocket and inserted them, then buttoned. "Flare rounds," I lied.

"Ole Stosh said you just might be okay." He rubbed his jaw. "Maybe. Hey, you know what's going on?"

I loaded and checked my shotgun before grabbing my riot helmet, then locked my cart. "Negative, Laborer Potts. I'm just a C4. They tell me what to do and I do it." I tossed him several gum wraps. "Thanks. If you'd stow my cart over there between those pallets? Duty calls." I turned and trotted the rest of the way to Security. "I could learn to tolerate you, too, Potts," I called before rounding the corner.

I stood outside Security until Specialist Club admitted me. Instructor Watts sat, tapping at a console, with her son sitting beside her.

"Keesay," Club said, "go next door. You're late for the chief's meeting." She tapped and the door opened.

"Glad you decided to join us," said the chief. Around him sat Gudkov, Nist, Muller and Liu. "You missed the first meeting."

I set my equipment along the wall and almost fell as the *Kalavar* staggered in flight.

"That would be us decelerating with the assistance of a local moon," continued the chief. "Keesay, you neglected to factor in adjustments made to the cascading engine." He looked to the rest. "I'll be brief. From the first scrambled transmissions received while on condensed space approach, we believe a Crax scout force engaged a ZQ Dock patrol. Just before the Code Red 14, we think a closing enemy fleet was identified. Engineer McAllister knows her business."

He removed an abused toothpick. "The rest of our security team is dealing with the passengers while the marines patrol the ship. Captain's going to try to squeak through before the engagement. We'll have clearance due to our cargo." He held a hand to his ear. "Team, looks like the balloon is up. You all know your assignments. Dismissed. Keesay, you're assigned to monitor from Security. Club will brief you before you relieve her. Now go."

"Understood, Chief." I grabbed my equipment and marched back into the monitoring room. He turned and gave final orders to Specialist Liu.

"Keesay," said Club. "You're to remain here. Monitor. Keep communications up and running. Guard Watts and her son." She tapped a few keys. "The entrances to Security and to the chief's office have been set to register any weight variation. If someone with a non-detection device tries to get in, you'll know it."

"Understood," I said. "I'm not much on computer troubleshooting."

"Instructor Watts can assist." Club shook her head. "She'll report what you need to know." Club checked her laser pack and weapon. "She knows more than I do."

"All clear," announced Instructor Watts, and keyed the door.

"We'll get your dancer," Club said, tramping out.

I examined the monitors, then drew my revolver and reloaded. "Care to fill me in?"

"One moment," said Instructor Watts, turning to a flickering monitor console, stalling.

I checked my com-set. Dead, so I removed it.

"Can I see that?" asked Skids.

"You know something about this?"

"Tell him, Mom." Skids took the set and deftly removed the casing. He reached into a drawer and sorted through the tools.

"We are the target of a manhunt," she began. "Some in the government and several corporations would like to take us alive. But dead will suffice. Our cover as R-Tech colonists has obviously failed."

Skids returned my com-set. "That's old tech. A relay was shorted. It's fixed."

"Thank you, Skids." I replaced the set and scanned for reports. I stopped on the captain's relay frequency. "Since you both seem to be important." I set it to feed to one of the monitors.

Instructor Watts took it from there. She focused in on the tactical display.

"There's the ZQ Dock," I said. "Those are our ships." I checked the codes. "A monitor, two gunboats, and four police cutters." She further adjusted my display. "And two corvettes, one light cruiser and two destroyers."

"Where are we?" asked Michael.

"Not on the screen, thankfully." I pointed. "Over here."

Instructor Watts adjusted further. "Picking up enemy silhouettes," she said. "Large, some smaller. At least fourteen. We're tied into dock sensors but still can't identify them."

The captain's voice crackled over my com-set. I relayed it. "Progress report on the attachment of auxiliary rocket engines."

"Another thirty minutes," a steady voice replied.

"We're not going to make it," said the captain. "Navigator, download encoded reports 38-11-C and D to two emergency probes. Jettison and set to float for forty minutes. Don't want to give away our hiding spot between the debris field and this asteroid."

"Yes, Captain," said Navigator Pidsadaki.

"Chief Brold," called the captain. "Report."

"Captain, Dr. Sevanto believes he cannot remove the device from Tech Schultz."

"Acknowledged. Have Dr. Sevanto close Schultz up, keep him out for the duration and stash him somewhere. The exotic dancer?"

"Unable to locate her yet, sir. And we're unable to locate passenger Dabbit B'down. She's known to have associated with him. Recommend shooting on sight."

"Agreed. No chances. Too much at stake." She paused. "Chief, we're going to wait for our chance, then make a run for the con-gate. They might shoot us down, or they might disable and board. Any thoughts?"

"Affirmative. We've got the marines. We've got the cargo pallets containing the old-style assault rifles and some laser carbines. We can crash charge the power packs. Have the marines arm the passengers and colonists. Those that want to fight."

"Couldn't they do more harm than good shooting up the ship?"

"Depends on where we deploy them. I'll contact Keesay about the colonists and Ross about the other passengers."

"I believe Keesay is monitoring," said the captain.

"Correct, Captain," I said. "Chief, recommend a marine tap the diesel and agriculture instructors. They'll know the personnel and how to organize them."

"Right, Keesay. Even Potts, Meadows and Putin?"

"Affirmative, Chief. I don't believe they like aliens."

"Have the marines distribute CNS suppressor modules," said the chief.

"Good idea," the captain replied. "No need to tell what they are. If it comes to combat, we'll need them."

"Understood, Captain," said Chief Brold. "Out."

"Power systems down to minimum," ordered the captain. "Let's hide and hope the Crax aren't looking for too many surprises. Have weapon systems ready to go online. Have fighter and attack shuttle ready to launch."

"Crax vessels closing on the dock, sir," said the navigator. "Classic conical-wedge formation."

Instructor Watts updated the tactical monitor. "Exactly who are you?" I asked. "Not R-Tech." I reviewed the other monitors, waiting for an answer. "Well?"

"It might be better if you didn't know."

"Someone might torture it out of me?" I adjusted the view and saw DeLark lining up the colonist volunteers. An instructor handed each a standard R-Tech assault rifle. The chief must have had his recruitment plan already in motion. There were about sixty, most of the men and all the women. "It seems that Tech Stardz knew who you were. Ms. Jazarine knows. Who am I going to tell?"

Instructor Watts was silent, busy calling up more data. Organizing input.

"Mom?" I'd forgotten about Skids. But I wouldn't press him. It was his mother who had to speak up.

"You are very brave and dedicated to duty, Specialist Keesay. There's no reason for you to shoulder another burden. We won't remain on the *Kalavar* once we reach Tallavaster." She sighed. "But others will continue to pursue us."

She had a point. "I won't be on the *Kalavar* long after Tallavaster either. I'm only a C4 security specialist. But if they track you through me, it'll be a dead end, literally, for somebody."

"We'll all cross that star path if it comes," Instructor Watts said. "Look." Ship designs and known specifications appeared as she spoke. "The ones that look like two capital H's welded at the crossbar, those are Selgum Crax, lackeys of the Primus. Primus, they're in the spherical ships."

"I know," I said. "And the Coregar Crax don't have vessels other than troop transports and assault ships. Like our marines."

"My apologies," she said. "I forgot you've studied the Silicate War. The formation only has three Primus Crax. Heavy cruiser with two light escorts."

"That's probably more than the dock and defending ships can handle," I said. "There's one Selgum carrier, two battle cruisers, six heavy escorts or destroyers." I double-checked. "And two troop transports in back." She nodded.

"How can you tell?" asked Skids.

Instructor Watts looked to me. "The Coregar ships look like a disk," I said. "Not heavily armed, but well armored and designed for heavy atmospheric landings." I reviewed all of the monitors. DeLark was lecturing and affixing some device to the volunteers. It was white and extended from the base of their skull, down along their spine. Another marine thumb tapped a clamshell computer clip and ran a metallic baton up and down the length of the device. "Do you know what those are?"

"The CNS suppressor modules Captain Tilayvaux mentioned. What're they for?" She shrugged.

I reviewed the monitors again. "Maybe something to do with the Stegmar Mantis sounding?" I spotted Mer and Benny entering one of the hatches that led to the maintenance sleds between the hull and the armor plating.

"Who's that?" asked Michael. "Talking to the marines?"

I examined the monitor and magnified the picture. "That's Chief Brold. He's wearing servo-armor."

"Chief Brold and the captain must believe boarding is imminent," said Watts.

"Maybe," I said. "But the chief never likes to get caught unprepared. I hope he runs across Ms. Jazarine."

"Look," said Michael, pointing at a monitor. "They're getting closer."

They were. Our destroyers, flanked by the corvettes and cutters led the light cruiser into the battle. The dock's eighty fighters formed above the light cruiser while the gunboats accelerated away from the dock toward the con-gate.

"David and Goliath," I said.

"True, but David has been preparing to fight Goliath for some time," said Instructor Watts. "And look, a little assistance." She tapped the screen. Two vessels. A small one, the shape of a planarian flatworm sped away from a much larger vessel. The second resembled eight or nine mismatched crates half-hazardly welded together. The sleeker Umbelgarri frigate accelerated to engage the enemy formation from the ventral flank, while the slower Chicher battlewagon uncoupled its flotilla of midget frigates. The twin-boomed, oversized fighters circled their mother ship.

I was about to ask where the ally ships came from when a red light flashed on the main monitor. I looked up at the external camera. Someone had set off the mass detector, but the surveillance camera showed an empty corridor. "Damn, we have company."

"Oh no," gasped Watts. She tapped a few screens.

My call for assistance was overridden by the captain's priority call. "Security, engineering, locate and deactivate the sounding beacon. Communications, jam internally. Port section." Even in haste she articulated each word.

"We're on our own," I said, releasing the safety on my pump shotgun. "Look, someone's attaching some sort of charge to the door." *Ca-Chunk*. I handed the chambered shotgun to Instructor Watts. "Can you use this?" When she nodded, I drew my bayonet with my right hand. My left held my cocked duty revolver. I edged toward the door. "On three, open the door, then close it. They might be monitoring. Once I'm out there, call for help and hope it arrives in time." I looked to Skids, who sat wide-eyed and pale. "If necessary, escape through the chief's office. On three?"

"Be careful, Kra," cautioned Instructor Watts.

"Surprise is on my side." No sense worrying the kid so I winked. "See you in a few, Skids. One, two..." The *Kalavar* fired its engines. I leapt. "Three."

Perfect timing! And with a jig to the left I barreled into a gray-suited man as he placed a charge above the door. I drove him against the opposite wall. Ignoring what he dropped, I jammed my bayonet just under his ribs as he rebounded off the wall. Movement to my left signaled me to duck. A laser flash fizzled on the man's—Mr. B'down's—screen. Ms. Jazarine leapt toward the closing door. She wasn't fast enough.

I twisted behind the stunned and bleeding businessman, put my blade to his throat and dropped my revolver. The exotic dancer faced me. I reached to the front of B'down's belt and grabbed a rectangular device He started to resist. "Ahh Ahh," I warned, applying blade pressure to his throat. I slid my fingers along to detach the connected power pack. Before he came to his senses and sent an elbow or head strike into me, I jerked my blade across his throat and jumped away. "I did you a favor," I said, guessing my first wound would eventually have triggered acid.

Another flash fizzled in front of me. I smiled. The dying man gurgled as he tried to scream. I kicked my revolver to the right, keeping the screen facing Ms. Jazarine. "You're next," I said. She hadn't decided upon her next move. "What happens to your partner should be pretty upsetting."

I fumbled, clipping the screen generator to my belt. B'down's body began to fizzle and Ms. Jazarine stepped toward me. I raised my blade. "Wouldn't try it. Drop your laser and your screen."

Jazarine fired a blast at my face and the screen intercepted. Still, I flinched. "Damn!" She was already three strides into a sprint down the hall. I scooped up my revolver and looked back at the door.

"Go!" crackled Watts's voice over my com-set. I took off after the dancer.

Despite her enhanced figure, Jazarine was fast. I fired once before she turned a corner only to have my round impact on her screen. I slowed at the turn, and came around to find her still in full stride. She had a fifteen-yard lead. If I could keep her in sight, she'd eventually encounter another crewmember, maybe security or a marine.

She looked over her shoulder and must've drawn the same conclusion.

She spun, slid her laser into a pouch and drew her long slender knife. "Remember this?"

Before returning that same knife to her, I'd learned she coated it with a potent narcotic. I holstered my revolver and pulled my buckle blade. "Recall what happened to Engineer McAllister? Same stuff coats this," I lied. Recalling some of Corporal Smith's instruction, I crouched on the balls of my feet and approached. "Two blades to one. Drop it."

She came around with a kick. I ducked, came in, sliced with my bayonet and rolled away. Her blade slashed where I'd been standing. Although my blade had cut through her gray outfit, the garment had absorbed most of the stroke. Still, a line of blood formed along her hip. I said with a menacing smile, "My coveralls and body armor stopped your laser, and your blade's too weak."

Jazarine slashed again. I dropped my buckle blade and caught her wrist. She caught my right wrist as I thrust my bayonet upward. Before she could try anything else with her blade, I slammed my forehead into her chin. The tactic hurt my head, but I knocked her back. Unfortunately her slick gray outfit helped her to twist away.

"We seem to have a standoff," Jazarine said, wiping her bloody lip. "Ever consider joining me?" On cue the front of her already strained garment split to reveal even more cleavage. "You authorized my boarding. Your dispute with Engineer McAllister provided easy access to the computer system."

I circled, looking for an opening, and replied, "Recall our discussion of *Othello*?"

"Said if you discovered treachery similar to Iago's, you'd run him through with your bayonet. Wouldn't even waste a shotgun shell."

"Correct," I said. "There's a bigger game going on. Don't be a sacrificed pawn. Give up and tell us what you know." The floor shifted. The *Kalavar*'s gravity plates struggled to compensate.

She took a deep breath, forcing her outfit to spread open to the navel. Tears formed in her eyes. "I can't." If the fight continued, she'd fall out of her bodysuit. Her mistake. More opportunity for my blade.

"You've already tried to end me," I said. "I'd wager you had a part in the assassination of Mr. Habbuk and his marine escort." I shifted my blade. Her eyes followed. "Dr. Sevanto can freeze you and have the suicide device removed."

"This transport's heading into a trap."

"We're heading into combat now," I said. "Your option, or I'll end it here. Guaranteed."

"You won't survive," she said and sprung, fleeing to her right.

I tackled her, and slammed her against the grating when she tried to get up.

"Ahhieeahh," she screamed. I rolled her over, and jammed my blade under her chin, drawing a trickle of blood. I was wrong. Her uniform still retained her chest, but her knife had pierced both fabric and shoulder. She began to tremble.

I shifted and knelt beside her. With bayonet poised, I withdrew her blade. "Is it the narcotic?"

"They'll come for the boy," she sputtered. Pounding footsteps approached. She shoved me away and rolled against the wall, curling into a fetal position.

"Why?" I asked. She answered with a scream. Her clothing began to blister as the acid broke through. I staggered back into a cold embrace. I turned with blades ready but my arms were locked in iron grips. It was Chief Brold's servo-gauntlets.

"She said they're coming for the boy," I said. "Why?"

"No time to explain. We'll have to survive the firefight first. Get back to Security."

The acidic stench caused my eyes to water. "I have one of their screens."

"Give it to Watts. I've armed her. Now move, Keesay." He didn't wait to see if I followed his directive. He lumbered past the frothing pool that had only seconds before been an exotic dancer.

I slid her thin blade into my bayonet sheath, clutched my bayonet and jogged back to security.

Mr. B'down's odorous demise assailed my senses. Security's door opened, limiting the time I held my breath. Instructor Watts sat, working, with a laser carbine across her lap. Skids sat, wearing my riot helmet with visor lowered and holding my shotgun. He up looked from the monitors.

"Safety's on," he said. "What happened?"

I lifted my shotgun and checked the safety. "Very good." I affixed the bayonet before leaning it against the wall. "Both offenders eliminated." I moved next to Instructor Watts. "Do you know how to use this?"

She examined it. "A Crax defense screen. That's not a Crax power pack." She checked the readings. "Eighty-three percent power."

"It's yours. Report, if you would."

She tapped several screens. "Someone, possibly the two you dealt with, set off a radio beacon, announcing our presence. Engineering disabled it. The captain ordered full acceleration to the con-gate and is in consultation with Rear Admiral West. The dock and monitor have begun long range bombardment." She held up a finger and tapped the controls. Captain Tilayvaux's voice came on line.

"Navigator, angle toward the Chicher vessel. She'll run interference. Bay, launch fighter and attack shuttle. Form up with Chicher midget frigates." There was a pause. "Engineering, can you give me any more? We've got company on the way."

On cue Watts switched screens. Two Selgum Crax destroyers had peeled off from the attack formation to intercept. A half dozen fighters, two attack craft, and four breaching pods launched from a troop transport accompanied them. She queried the terminal. "They'll intercept us."

"The *Kalavar*'s armament is aft," I said. "We're meant to run from a fight, not into it." I retrieved my satchel and began to reload my revolver.

She shrugged, then stiffened. "A second Crax formation. Carrier accompanied by three destroyers. Opposite vector approach. Supporting an assault ship, almost certainly breach capable. The Umbelgarri have launched their eight fighters to box formation and are racing to intercept. Two police cutters have left the main defense formation to support."

"Provide more targets. Doesn't look promising." I pointed to the screen. "The two gunboats have altered course. They might slip in behind the two Crax destroyers."

I scanned the monitors. Specialist Tahgs approached Security carrying medical equipment and a shoulder pack. I keyed the entrance.

Tahgs avoided my gaze. "The captain's ordered inoculations," she said. "Ordered engineering to infuse the air circulation system with biological contaminants."

"Do you know what type?" I asked.

"These inoculations are for a UV resistant fifth generation tuberculosis and a strain of Chicher pox."

I cringed at the thought of the *Kalavar* carrying bio-weapons so virulent to humans. "I suppose both are lethal to Crax?"

Instructor Watts finished reading a screen. "The tuberculosis is, to Coregar Crax," she said. "The Chicher pox is known to infect Stegmar Mantis. Doesn't kill but inflicts blindness and crippling nerve degeneration."

I refrained from again asking Watts who she was. Specialist Tahgs prepared the shots. "We're short of med techs. I'm not very good at this."

"Practice on me," I said, and showed her my V-ID. "Anywhere in particular?"

"No time for V-ID's," said Tahgs. "Soft muscle tissue. If you've been vaccinated for Chicher pox, this will act as a booster. Dr. Sevanto doesn't think anybody is protected against the tuberculosis. This'll cause some local inflammation."

No sense being modest. I unbuttoned my coveralls, dropped them and leaned against a console. "Left side please." I still had my military style underwear.

Tahgs went right to work. Michael was second. He looked away, but flinched just before the needle touched. His mother went last. Tahgs returned the equipment to the case. "They're arming colonists and passengers." She still hadn't looked at me face to face.

"I know," I said. "Janice, this'll be like other scrapes I've been in. We'll get battered a bit, but we'll pull through."

"Genni says we can't win. We're outgunned. They've got more and better ships."

"Depends on whose opinion you value more," I said. "Mine or your roommate's." I fingered the laser burns marring my uniform. "I just bested two assassins armed with Crax equipment. Plus, there's an Umbelgarri on our side out there, so I wouldn't throw in the towel just yet."

She looked to Watts and Skids, then back at me. "Kra, I'm sorry."

I didn't know what to say. "Might request a weapon yourself." That didn't sound right. "We'll talk after this is over."

Janice gave me a quick hug. "Got more inoculations to give."

"I have duty to perform as well." I scanned the monitors after she hurried out. "Infecting the ship with some nasty microbes," I said to Watts.

"The Crax plan to exterminate us," she said, with no sign of doubt on her face.

"Guess we shouldn't pull any punches either."

"Mom!" called Michael. "They're opening fire!"

CHAPTER 33

Xenocartographers participate when translating the Chicher's written word. Although Chicher lettering resembles slashes, with similar design characteristics of human Chinese, the structure often refers to geographic regions of their home planet, in addition to symbolic references to pack structure and events in nature.

The dock and defending monitor continued to fire military-grade, long-range tri-beam lasers at the first enemy formation. As the range closed, targeting proximity improved until a grazing flash finally deflected off a Selgum Crax destroyer. Immediately the dock and vessels launched a wave of missiles.

"Should keep that destroyer busy," I said. "Either that or it'll have to turn its damaged section away from the missile tracking systems." The wedge of human ships also opened fire with their medium-range lasers.

"It'll keep advancing," said Instructor Watts. "They have highly effective point defense systems. But any damage before close engagement will improve tracking and targeting throughout the battle."

"How do you know so much?" I asked while scanning the security monitors and spotted several marines positioning armed passengers in the shuttle bay.

"My husband," she said. "A master of military tactics and knowledge. It's all he talks about. One can't help but pick up something."

I baited, "I know of no prominent tactician named Watts."

"Of course you don't." She returned to the combat-filled screens.

I looked at an adjacent monitor. The Chicher battlewagon's angle placed it between the *Kalavar* and the two approaching enemy destroyers. The *Kalavar*'s fighter and attack shuttle formed up with the midget frigates. I fidgeted with my com-set to find the fighter frequency. "Our pilots spent time learning Chicher tactics." I tapped several keys, connecting my com-set's output. "Here we go."

"Pack comrade pilots into shelter," translated a computer. "You duel the lizard with your shuttle's teeth."

"Roger that, Chicher flotilla. You get us there, we'll finish the job."

"You tell'em, Griffin," said Howler, above an echoing symphonic background. "We'll get'em."

The Chicher battlewagon opened up with eight ion cannons, all missing the approaching enemy destroyers. The midget frigates followed with a volley of balled electricity before the wedge shaped enemy fighters swooped in. The Crax fighters let loose with machine gun like turrets, sending streams of corrosive-filled pellets into the Chicher formation. The Chicher responded with reactive debris pods. The scatter of pods rocketed and burst in the line of fire, prematurely detonating some of the Crax rounds. Chicher short ranged fusion beams arced and slashed ineffectually while the corrosive hail pelted the midget frigates. One exploded and a second tumbled out of control while the nimble Crax fighters swung around for another pass.

"Mom, the light cruiser's firing its canister nuke," called Skids. I turned just in time to see the projectiles emerge from the internal rail gun.

"The *Black Riveter*," stated his mother. "Let's hope she has the range." Two of five thermonuclear canisters survived defensive fire and detonated in range. The blasts rocked an armored battle cruiser, causing one of its four aft engines to flare out. "Moderate damage."

"Missiles closing on that damaged destroyer," I said. "Look at all those point defense lasers." I watched as the destroyer and nearby ships obliterated the missile wave.

"Hold on," said Instructor Watts as both formations opened up with all weapons. "This'll decide it."

The Selgum Crax fired large and small corrosive canisters toward the charging wedge of human ships. Lasers and a new wave of missiles reached out toward the Crax.

"The Crax fighters are trying to flank our ships," I said.

"The dock's are engaging them," Watts replied. "They'll keep them off."

I said to her, "It'll be equivalent to old-style prop planes against jet fighters." She nodded, but I shook my head. "Won't last in a dogfight. Maybe they can hold them off, and take a few with them." I switched monitors. "Look, they're concentrating all laser fire on the damaged battle cruiser." The *Riveter* was on target as were most of its escorts.

"Oh no," whispered Watts. The three spherical Primus Crax ships opened up. Five emerald beams flashed out from each escort and nine from the heavy cruiser. The energy weapon reminded me of tracers, but the damage inflicted didn't. The Primus ships raked the length of the *Black Riveter*'s hull. "They're tearing right through the armor."

I watched, stunned. "Like BB's against aluminum foil. We can't stand up to that." The *Riveter* slowed and angled out of formation. "She's still firing!" One tri-beam turret tore into the damaged battle cruiser. Six more missiles sped from the light cruiser's racks even as internal explosions rocked her. A fiery disintegration followed. "No escape pods?"

"None," whispered Watts, double-checking the monitors.

I could barely watch as the caustic canisters closed. The corvettes and destroyers let loose with their point defense pulse lasers. "There're too many canisters," I said. Lasers blazing, the corvettes followed by the destroyers plowed into the caustic wave. One police cutter dove and evaded. The other took several hits and tumbled. Detonations riddled the destroyer and corvette hulls. A resulting debris cloud engulfed the ships.

I couldn't believe it. "They survived!" The destroyers and corvettes emerged from the cloud, launching missiles and focusing all laser turrets on the crippled battle cruiser. The dock and monitor added their long range fire.

"She's breaking up," announced Instructor Watts, as two of the battle cruiser's forward sections ruptured. Three missiles survived defensive fire and detonated their nuclear warheads against the dying battle cruiser's hull. "Scratch that one." She eyed my puzzlement. "Explosive armor. Reacts when caustic fluid impacts a ship. The outer plating is blown from the hull. It's an old armor trick."

"For all the good it'll do them," I said. The human escorts had swung broadside at point blank range to bring all turrets to bear. The Crax pulse lasers cut down every missile launched.

"Wise," said Watts. "They're targeting a troop transport."

"Too late." I said, leaning on the console. Streams of emerald energy bolts shattered the two destroyers and one corvette. "We're no match for the Primus." The surviving corvette executed a series of radical maneuvers to join the fleeing police cutter and fighters. The Crax cone formation ignored the evading ships and bored in on the dock and defending monitor.

"The dock can't hold up to that," I said. "Let alone us. They could take out the con-gate. Especially if it's energized, and it wouldn't be any use to us if it wasn't."

"They'll try to capture the dock intact," said Watts. "The con-gate as well. They'll want a base of operations."

I tuned into the *Kalavar*'s fighter frequency, but adjusted my com-set for command frequency priority. The Chicher battlewagon continued to scatter the area with ion cannon fire, with as much luck as the midget frigate fusion beams. "Their targeting and tracking just can't do it." I checked the console broadcast from my com-set. "Only two midget frigates left. One enemy fighter eliminated."

"Approaching optimum range," Howler's voice crackled through the outside interference. Just then the Chicher battlewagon scored a hit on the leading destroyer, followed by a second.

"Ion cannons," I said. "That should cause them some troubles." The Crax vessel slowed.

"Temporary," said Instructor Watts. "They'll be quick to reset affected systems."

The unaffected destroyer ignored the approaching enemy fighter flotilla and fired a canister barrage at the battlewagon.

"Viper one away. Viper two away!" yelled Howler. "From Umbelgarri with love."

"Let's get back to mother," said Griffin. "Chicher flotilla, evasive maneuver waterfall, on my mark."

"We gnaw nest raiders," replied the flotilla leader. "Return. Defend your nest." The Chicher demonstrated their intent by firing another volley of balled electricity at the stricken Crax. Several bolts found their mark, adding to the internal havoc.

"Acknowledged," said Graying Griffin and led the larger attack shuttle into a dive, away from the reforming enemy fighters. Three stayed on the midget frigates. Two broke off to chase the *Kalavar*'s combat shuttles, leaving a pair to bore in on the Chicher battlewagon.

The battlewagon continued to fire ion cannons and opened up with defensive fusion beams at the two Crax attack craft. "They made their run unscathed," I said. "Knocked out one ion cannon." The battlewagon launched debris pods in the path of the oncoming Crax canister barrage. The remaining pair of midget frigates raced behind Howler's two missiles toward the destroyer.

"She's recovering," said Watts. "Returning to course."

"Two bogies on our tail," called Bolt as he maneuvered his attack shuttle. "Gaining fast."

"Acknowledged," replied the fighter in the wing position. "We're full throttle."

"Run straight, preparing caltrops," said Howler, music still reverberating. "Keep running. Keep running. They're approaching optimum range. Release!" A trail of proximity-fused micro-explosives scattered in the attack shuttle's wake. From the wing position, Griffin's fighter followed suit.

"This had better work," said Bolt.

Flashes erupted around the Crax fighters as they blew through the barrier. The lead fighter slowed, but continued to close.

"Bank left," called Bolt. "Griffin, get on their six."

Howler opened up with the rear-mounted pulse laser. "Can't get a lock, going manual."

The Crax fighters bored in unfazed. Griffin's fighter was parallel to, and then slipped in behind the lead enemy fighter, risking all. The trailing Crax fighter was parallel to Griffin. The lead Crax began machine-gunning caustic pellets at Bolt and Howler as they strove to shake their pursuers.

"Can't get lock," called Griffin. "Second bogie is slipping behind me. Going to manual." Pulse laser fire from the fighter and the attack shuttle crisscrossed around the enemy fighter. It jinked side-to-side, foiling their efforts.

Static erupted from the communication signal. "We're hit," called Howler." Alarms sounded. "Aft turret out. Systems failing."

"Losing power," called Bolt. The shuttle shuddered. Another line of pellets impacted, eating through the skin and into the bowels of the craft.

"Eject! Eject!" cried Bolt, too late. The shuttle exploded.

"Yes," shouted Instructor Watts.

"What!" I said. "They just blew Howler and Bolt away!"

Watts looked over to my screen. "Oh, no," she said, catching the flaring embers that seconds before had been Bolt and Howler. "At least their sacrifice." She stopped and looked me in the eye. "Their missiles were Umbelgarri." She tapped the controls to replay the sequence. The missiles' installed defense screens absorbed the point defense lasers before they split into multiple warheads. "Eight of the ten warheads hit."

The switch back to real time showed the Crax destroyer's port side smashed inward. Both surviving midget frigates sped past, raking the crippled destroyer with fusion beams. Two Crax fighters raced in hot pursuit.

"Mom!" Skids pointed. The Chicher battlewagon rocked with explosions and began breaking apart. "They're still coming." He gulped and lost all color. As if to punctuate his fears, both the surviving midget frigate and Griffin's fighter exploded.

"Transport *Kalavar*, this is the destroyer escort *Samuel B. Roberts*," crackled over my com-set.

"This is the *Kalavar*," Captain Tilayvaux replied.

"Report situation, *Kalavar*."

"All Chicher vessels destroyed. Defensive fighters destroyed. Aft armament ready, limited to 70-degree arc laser, 135 degree target acquisition. There's a Crax destroyer, two attack shuttles, three breaching pods between *Kalavar* and the gate, and advancing. Our cascading engine won't recycle for another forty-eight minutes."

"Acknowledged. We're tracking them now. They've four fighters forming up with them." The destroyer escort captain paused. "Your priority cargo acknowledged. Come about, best speed. Form up with us and we'll punch you through." He paused again. "Gunboats *Thunder Child* and *Calling Thunder*, advance on the enemy flank. Use long-range fire if you can to end that crippled destroyer's fighting days."

"Acknowledged," returned both gunboat captains.

"Destroyer escort," I said to Watts. "She must've been pulled from mothballs and upgraded."

Michael removed my helmet. "Look there."

My eyes followed his to the monitor that showed, boxed by its fighters, the Umbelgarri frigate. Two trailing police cutters supported. "This engagement'll be decided as fast as the other?" They closed on the second, smaller Crax formation.

"It will," said Watts. "First, the wave of enemy fighters and attack craft will sweep through to disrupt the formation. Watch. The Umbelgarri won't miss."

On cue, golden, arcing energy beams, resembling the Chicher white fusion beams, emanated from the Umbelgarri frigate and fighters, striking out at the closing enemy.

"Advanced tracking systems," I responded. "Accurate and deadly." The frigate emerged pockmarked from the sweep, but unhindered. "I count six Umbelgarri fighters." I reexamined the display. "One cutter's falling back."

"Yes, Specialist," she said. "But see, two of the three squadrons are gone."

"Chopped to bits!" yelled Skids.

"They're circling back for another run," said Watts, resting a hand on Skids' shoulder. "They'll ignore the cutters."

The Umbelgarri fighters broke from their mother ship to intercept the returning fighters. "That's not standard tactics," I said. The frigate accelerated into the maw of the three Selgum Crax destroyers that supported the carrier and assault ship. "Think it can take them?"

All five Crax let loose with their canister weapons. "Maybe." Hope echoed through her voice.

"Really, Mom?" Skids' shoulders no longer slouched as he leaned toward the monitors. "Take'em out! Take'em!"

The Umbelgarri reached out with its main beam armament. The ghostly, golden-hued line slid downward, slicing into the assault ship. Smaller beams arced madly to obliterate the canisters as they approached. About one in three got through. The Crax laid in a continuous acidic avalanche.

"The assault ship's slipping behind that destroyer," I said. The Umbelgarri sliced into the intervening vessel, severing one of the sections at the elbow and, with an upward return stroke, tore into the main junction.

Watts adjusted the screens. "She's lost seventy percent of her defensive beams. They're getting through." The Umbelgarri sliced into the assault ship, clipping off a disk section before carving upward into the central hull.

"Two down!" cried Skids as internal explosions emanated from the assault ship. Then he frowned.

"She's losing power," said Watts as the Umbelgarri ship appeared to list. "She's not going to make it." Several escape pods popped from the hull, but instead of running, they rocketed toward the enemy formation. The Crax targeted them and destroyed two. The third detonated against a destroyer's port side.

"I think they picked that one up during the Silicate War." I said. "From us."

The Umbelgarri beam struck out again, targeting the damaged destroyer, but the weapon only scarred the hull. Flames erupted aft, near the sleek Umbelgarri ship's engines. Explosions followed.

I shook my head. "They're swinging wide to finish her off." Canister fire rained down on the faltering Umbelgarri ship. It reminded me of Ms. Jazarine's tortured demise.

The frigate lashed out, one final ineffectual blow, before breaking up. Eight Crax fighters and two attack craft formed up with the surviving carrier and two destroyers.

I slid into a seat and scanned the internal security monitors. Each marine had paired up with a sec-spec. Each duo had a score of armed civilians with them. I flipped from camera to camera.

"Are you okay, Specialist Keesay?" asked Instructor Watts. She rolled her chair close.

"Give me a minute." I said, and took several deep breaths.

"Michael, how about you?"

"I'm okay—I'm a little scared, Mom. They're coming."

I checked my equipment. Pulled Ms. Jazarine's slender blade and set it across the desk.

"Specialist Keesay?"

I looked at Instructor Watts. "I'd say call me Kra, but I don't know who you are." She pursed her lips. "The pilots," I said. "Griffin, Bolt, Howler. They were good guys. Really helped me out." I flexed my fingers. "Sorry, guess I just came off my adrenaline rush. Hope I got all the infiltrators."

"Me, too," she said, and switched off the room's internal monitors. "Dr. Maximar Drizdon." Her face had lost all expression.

"What?" I asked.

"Dr. Maximar Drizdon is my husband. His son, my son, is Maximar Jr."

"Maximar Drizdon?" I said. "The combat theoretician? Who masterminded the offensive against the Shards?" She nodded. "Anticipated a wormhole appearance and enabled a fleet to take the attack to them?" She nodded again. "I guess you would know something about fleet weapons and tactics."

"Yes." She smiled, and extended her hand. "Veronica Drizdon." I shook it. Skids, or Maximar Jr., stood next to me grinning ear to ear. "You kept the secret well," she said to her son.

"And you'll have to continue," I said to Maximar Jr. I scrutinized his mother. "I recall clips of you. Cosmetic surgery?"

"DNA manipulations too. At least for me."

"With war brewing, I can guess why some might be after you. Wonder how much Stardz, Schultz, Jazarine and B'down took to turn traitor on their own species."

"The Crax might not have paid them," she said. "But that's all I can say. You deserve that much, at least."

"Understood. Thanks. I'll continue to refer to you as Instructor Watts, and Skids. Not only for security reasons, but it's so ingrained."

"Lori will do, Kra." She flipped her hair back and rubbed her chin. "If I had to classify you, I'd say you're a hybrid. Rogue and good Samaritan."

"I think we know which genes are dominant," I said, reactivating the internal monitors.

My com-set crackled. "Transport *Kalavar*, this is the Zeta Aquarius Dock, Rear Admiral West." The voice was throaty and deep. "Con-gate set for condensation ratio 51.375K. Altering target. Will commence long range bombardment of blocking Crax vessel."

"Zeta Aquarius Dock," replied the captain. "Gate factor acknowledged. Negative on blocking vessel. Forming up with *Samuel B. Roberts*, *Thunder Child* and *Calling Thunder*."

"*Kalavar*, near zero probability of surviving enemy assault. We're set to self-destruct."

"Acknowledged. Situation understood. The longer you keep them occupied, the better our chances."

"Con-gate power setting for two ships, minimum two minute interval. Both will be at 22.833K. *Kalavar*, *Sammy Roberts*, good luck. We'll hold'em and take as many as we can." The admiral either forgot or chose not to close the channel. "Bays launch all attack shuttles and remaining fighters. Keep that carrier from crawling up our ass. Surviving cutters, flank them. *Stellar Inferno*, let's help the Primus bastards remember they were in a fight. Target escort on the heavy's port side. Lock will be inoperative, so go manual and shoot straight. All batteries open fire. Fire at will."

I turned away from the initial bombardment to watch Specialist Liu approach Security. She wore a sidearm on her hip and carried a satchel. I keyed the intercom. "Specialist Liu," I said. "Good day, how can I be of service?"

She gazed at the door for a second. "Busy day. I've brought breakfast."

"Now that you mention it, I am hungry." I checked Lori Watts and her son. They both nodded.

"The chief suggested chicken patties, your favorite."

"Very kind, Specialist Liu. I'll check with him."

"He thought you might." She spoke into her collar. "Chief, I'm at Security. Door remains locked."

"Keesay," came over my com-set. "Better eat up. May be a while."

"Understood, Chief." I double-checked the monitors and keyed open the door.

Skids whispered into his mother's ear. "Specialist Keesay," she said. "Michael needs to relieve himself."

Liu set the satchel on the desk. "Can you hold the fort?" I asked.

"No need," said Liu. She called up a screen and entered a code. "The chief's office has a back room." The connecting door to his office slid open.

"Really?"

"Long hours," said Liu.

"You keep them, too. Joint code," I said. "Makes sense."

"I'll take him," said Lori.

I asked Liu, "How go the preparations to repel boarding?"

"Actually, your colonists seem the most eager. How goes it out there? I heard not too well."

"Correct. We've got a Crax destroyer and some support between the con-gate and us. We've got a damaged destroyer escort, some fighters and a couple of gunboats to assist."

"They've got breaching pods?" asked Liu.

I nodded. "Captain's plan for a surprise run ended quick."

"The chief said you took out two infiltrators."

I opened up the satchel and set out the food and juice. "The exotic dancer and a business man. Both had Crax screens. Hope that's all because I was lucky."

"You always seem to manage, somehow," she said. "I caught part of it in engineering, but only your part of the conversation came through."

"Oh, Ms. Jazarine," I said. "Offered me a place in their conspiracy. I immediately accepted." Admin Specialist Liu's mouth dropped for just a second, until I broke into a smile and winked. I took a bite of the sandwich. "Actually, I slit Mr. B'down's throat. Ms. Jazarine fell on her own narcotic tainted blade. I'd have killed her just the same. Kept his blood on my bayonet and hers on that for analysis, should we make it through this."

"They've got Schultz rigged for cold sleep. Think there are any more?"

"No telling. No offense, that's why I checked with the chief." I nearly choked after recalling that I didn't challenge Tahgs.

"Just the same, if we get boarded," she said, "I'd like to be near you."

I looked over toward my shotgun. "Personally," I said, clearing my throat, "I'd like to be couched between Chief Brold with his servo-armor and one of the Colonial Marines."

"They're suited up in combat gear. Not powered like the chief's but they say it'll resist some of the Crax acid." She held a hand to her ear. "Got to get back to engineering."

"Engineering? Say hello to McAllister for me."

"She's too busy aft, working on the weapons systems. Chief Engineer Harkins is keeping ahead of Crax jamming." She swept across the wall with her hand. "Keeping your screens up." She turned to leave.

"If you do see McAllister, tell her I got roughed up pretty good. You'll make her day." Lori and Skids returned. I handed a key to Liu. "If you see a marine or the chief, give them this. In my old quarters under Benny's bunk I have two and a half cases of old-style grenades. A lot of shotgun shells, too. Hey, any chance of getting a spare CNS device?" I pointed to the back of my neck.

"Maybe. Distribution is under way. I'm awaiting myself."

I tapped at the console, closing the door behind Lori and Skids and let Specialist Liu depart. "Good luck and keep low." She waved into the security camera before hustling down the corridor.

"There's food on the desk," I said. "Chief Brold ordered my favorite."

"Chicken patty sandwich? I don't think I've ever seen you select one," said Lori.

I finished mine and drank some juice. "Got away from them after an incident with Senior Engineer McAllister. Got the notion I was too predictable for my own good." Then a flash caught my eye. "The gunboats got the crippled destroyer!"

"All hands secure," crackled Captain Tilayvaux. "Prepare for combat emergency maneuvers."

I said, "That's not what you expect to hear from a transport's captain."

"Aft engines, cut power," ordered the captain. "Port forward maneuvering thrusters, aft starboard thrusters, emergency burn on my mark. Three...two...one...now!"

The gravitation system struggled to maintain equilibrium as the transport began its spin. "She's bringing the aft weapons to bear," I said.

"Risky move," said Lori. "Exposes the main engines."

"But if we don't get past that destroyer, it won't matter."

"Computer control, adjust thruster's to halt spin to 180 degrees." Our bodies swayed the opposite direction.

Skids smiled, enjoying the sensation. I gripped his shoulder. "Too bad you're here. Probably more wild near the aft main engines, and cascading up front."

"Hold missiles," ordered the captain. "Aft batteries, open fire."

The *Kalavar*'s dual beams reached out and scored a near miss on the closing destroyer. The trailing gunboats fired long-range and went wide. The *Samuel B. Roberts*'s remaining dual beam succeeded with a grazing hit on a leading ventral elbow. "We're going to have to do better than that," said Lori.

"Fighters," called the *Roberts*'s captain. "Drop back, keep the breaching pods off the *Kalavar*."

"She's letting loose," I said, as the enemy destroyer opened up with a canister barrage. "What I wouldn't give for a canister nuke."

"Captain," called a weapons engineer, "the upgraded missiles are targeting in the tubes."

"Very good," said the captain. "Relay targeting information to laser batteries and to the gunboats and destroyer escort."

"Can't get through to the gunboats, Captain, jamming. *Roberts* received."

"It will do. Laser batteries, open fire. Fire at will."

"They're tearing into her," I said. The scarred elbow was now blackened with gaping holes.

"Captain," called Navigator Pidsadaki. "Incoming Crax fire. Recommend thruster burn to protect the engines."

"Was McAllister able to rig the missiles for transmit targeting after launch?"

"Negative, sir. Too complex."

"We need targeting to take down that destroyer." The captain sounded incredibly calm. "Navigator, give us a three second margin of error. We'll launch missiles, initiate spin. Calculate it."

The *Kalavar* opened fire again, scoring on the same section.

"McAllister," called the captain. "Affix coded transponder to one of the missiles. Relay vitals to *Roberts*."

"Acknowledged, Captain."

"*Roberts*," called the captain. "Will have to initiate spin in fourteen seconds to protect our engines. Will lose targeting. Have affixed transponder to advanced missiles. Have your missiles chase."

"Acknowledged, *Kalavar*. That'll get ours close. Will continue to fire.

Follow us through."

"Laser battery, let's make this last one count. One-hundred-ten percent power."

"Acknowledged, Captain. Emergency overload."

The *Roberts*'s point defense weapons began firing on the closing canisters. Denude of her reactive armor, she began to take hits.

"Dual beam lasers hit on ventral elbow. Pulse lasers opening up," called the weapons engineer. "Aft missiles firing,"

"Initiating burn," said the navigator. "All sections verify ready for impact, secured for hull breach."

"We'll see if Mer's armor project pays dividends," said the captain.

We hung on as the *Kalavar* spun 180 degrees. A patter of dull thuds sounded through the hull. "That's the caustic canisters," said Lori, holding her son close.

"I've seen the outer armor plating. It's ugly and formidable." I said a quick prayer.

One exterior camera still functioned. I focused it and forwarded the view to the navigator's screen.

"Captain," he said, "hull remains intact. Exterior armor port side sustained eighteen hits. Fourteen burn-throughs." He paused. "Primary antigravity array damaged. Secondary antigravity network still intact."

"Acknowledged. Initiate main engines, flank speed. Swing by the *Roberts*. Shuttle bay prepare to receive escape pods."

The *Samuel Roberts* was dead in space, slowly tumbling with its forward momentum. "Looks like buckshot through a steel can."

"Three of her missiles are trailing ours," said Watts. "Four escape pods vectoring our way. Crax destroyer is opening up again, trying to disrupt escape pod retrieval."

"She'll do more than that," I replied. "If those missiles don't hit, we're dead. They'll be ready for any advanced equipment surprises like Howler's missiles."

"Navigator," said the captain, "reduce engines to one quarter. Protect the cascading atomic engine compartment. Present starboard side.

"Initiating maneuver, Captain. Barrage strength down sixty percent. Canisters angling toward us. Point defense lasers opening fire."

"I suspect, Lieutenant, she's saving some for the incoming missiles. Lost some of her point defense lasers. Won't be fooled like her sister."

"Long-range fire from the gunboats ineffective," replied the navigator as the shots went wide. "Missiles initiating terminal dive."

"There they go," I said. The Crax destroyer let loose with everything. A canister destroyed one advanced missile before it split into multiple warheads. The second split, but all were taken out. Then two large flashes. "*Roberts*'s missiles got through! She's buckling along the horizontal crossbar," I said, just before the Crax ship split in two.

"Prepare for impact," called the navigator. A second series of dull thuds sounded.

I sent a message to the navigator.

"Hull integrity remains intact," he reported to the captain. "Both external starboard monitors damaged or destroyed." A second later he added, "Tracked repair bots report twelve impacts, nine exterior armor breaches."

"Return to course," ordered the captain. "Flank speed. Now all we have are those shuttles, fighters and breeching pods. Shuttle Bay, how many escape pods from the *Roberts*?"

"Two, with nineteen crewmen total."

"Good. Those that are fit, have them report to Chief Brold. Get the others to Medical." She switched frequencies. "Fighters, recommend Finger Four Formation. Put some maneuvering distance between us. Keep them off as best you can."

"Acknowledged, *Kalavar*. Out."

"Kra," said Watts. "One of the Primus escorts broke off. Toward us." She finished calculating. "She'll get in range before we reach the gate. If only we had the auxiliary rockets."

"The gunboats won't even slow her down," I agreed. "Look, dock's attack shuttles damaged the carrier. She's disengaging!"

"I count nine attack shuttles and one fighter still in pursuit."

"May as well," I said. "I don't think there'll be a dock to return to. The Crax are in range." The dock and monitor continued to fire all batteries. They'd scored several hits on the Primus escort. Superficial damage. "Pray the lasers penetrate when they close. The Crax troop transports are staying out of range."

"The Crax are firing canister weapons," said Watts. "Difficult to say who they're targeted on. Wait, they're firing again. Two waves."

"They're learning," I said. "Take out the reactive armor on the first wave and penetrate with the second." The Primus heavy cruiser and escort opened up. Emerald flashes scattered across the dock. "They're targeting weapon systems." Flashes followed by explosions reverberated across the dock. Only one dock laser battery answered when the monitor returned fire. Again, they scored several hits. "She's too heavily armored. They'll never penetrate the Primus armor."

"Not before they're destroyed." A forty missile wave rocketed from the ZQ Dock and the *Stellar Inferno*. "The dock's rotation is bringing more batteries to bear. This time she fired on a Selgum Crax destroyer. "The monitor's combining fire." The first wave of corrosive canisters impacted the *Stellar Inferno*'s hull. The reactive armor combined with defensive fire minimized penetration. Laser batteries emerged from the cloud around the monitor, tearing into the targeted destroyer.

"The Primus ships have taken out more dock lasers," said Watts. "Pinpoint accuracy. The one chasing us will get our engines before we make the gate."

The second wave of canisters raced into the cloud, resulting in explosions. The *Stellar Inferno* and Crax destroyer perished simultaneously. "They'll take out the remaining batteries," said Watts. "Then target the pulse defense lasers. See, the breaching pods are already launching from the troop transports."

"Sitting duck," I agreed. I scanned the internal monitors. The chief was speaking to the group of *Roberts* survivors. "You okay, Skids?" He was sitting in corner a little pale. "You going to get sick?"

He shook his head. His mother knelt next to him. "It'll be okay. Everyone on the *Kalavar* is armed. If they board, we have marines." Skids remained unconvinced. I couldn't blame him.

"You stick with me, Skids," I said. "I'm a survivor. So's your mom. So are you. If it comes down to it, do what I do. Do what I say, when I say." I patted his shoulder. "I've been in tougher scrapes." He looked up with hopeful eyes. "Really," I told him. "Ever hear of the Colonization Riots? I was there. When we get through this I'll tell you about it."

"You might have been a little young, Max...Michael," his mother said.

"Then you'll get a history lesson."

"I like it when you teach stuff, Specialist Keesay."

"Okay then. Remember, do what I say, when I say." He nodded. "Now, I'm assigned to monitor the situation and keep the chief and captain up to date. Computers and R-Tech, I need your mother's assistance."

"Mom says you're better at tech manipulation than you think."

"Maybe, Skids. Now hang in there. Lori." I pointed to the approaching Primus escort. "She's swinging around behind. Trading closing distance for a straight shot."

Lori Watts recalculated. "She's delaying intercept by four minutes. We'll have a chance to get through the gate first."

I shook my head. "No, the Primus are too smart. Got something up their sleeve, or should I say, scales." Some of the screens began to lose clarity. "Jamming. What's that coming out of the Primus ships? Looks like breaching pods."

"That's not good," said Watts. "They'll be carrying elite forces. Coregar Crax."

"Gar-Crax in battle armor." I tried to disguise my sinking feeling. The screens continued to distort. Watts worked to retain the relay, but shook her head.

I tapped the console. "Captain, this is Security. Transmissions from the Zeta Aquarius Dock have been jammed. Switching exclusively to *Kalavar* feeds."

"Acknowledged," said the captain.

I asked Lori Watts, "When were you granted access to security systems?"

"After the attack on the systems, as a precautionary measure."

"Your access is broader than mine?" She nodded. I shrugged.

"Captain," reported Navigator Pidsadaki. "Our fighters have engaged the enemy fighters. They're outmatched. Totally defensive, sir. Enemy attack shuttles slipping past. Breaching pods following."

"Maintenance," called the captain. "Are those maintenance-bots ready?"

"Two are, Captain." I recognized Gudkov's voice. "Chief Brold ordered me to get them to the tracks. At the hatch now. Estimate three minutes 'till operational."

"Acknowledged. Navigator, how long until we reach the gate?"

"Eight minutes, fourteen seconds. Sir, the Primus escort is getting behind us."

Cut power to starboard engine. Adjust aft thrusters to port. Increase their angle."

"That'll increase approach time by," he did the calculations, "one minute, eighteen seconds. Sir, Primus appears to be altering angle of approach. She's opening fire."

I waited for impact. When none came I examined the screens. "Navigator, screen feed four."

"Sir, they targeted the gate." He paused. "Getting unstable readings."

"Damn! All engines on line. Give me 105%. Navigator, come about. Keep our tail away from her as long as we can."

"She'll close. Enemy attack shuttles coming about, looks like they're going to target engines."

"*Calling Thunder*, *Thunder Child*," called the captain. "Gate inoperable. Primus escort closing. Three breaching pods, on approach supported by two attack shuttles and three fighters. Our fighters eliminated. Appear to be targeting our engines. Twenty-eight minutes until our cascading atomic engine recycles."

"*Kalavar*, two minutes till intercept. Unable to target lock enemy units."

"Engage Primus escort. Keep her off our tail."

"Acknowledged," called one of the captains. "*Thunder Child*, come around behind. I-formation. Forward batteries, manual targeting. Fire on the Primus escort. Fire at will."

"Sir, pulse lasers opening fire." The navigator's voice went monotone. "Verified, pursuing Primus escort has launched two breaching pods."

"Give me aft view. Aft batteries cease fire. Port main engine, cut thrust to one-quarter."

"Thrust cut to one-quarter."

"Initiate fuel dump, portside auxiliary thrust rocket. Jettison portside auxiliary rocket."

"Sir?"

"Do it now. Emergency release. Ordered sequence."

"Fuel dump initiated," stated the navigator. "Emergency release." The fuel-filled rocket tumbled away.

"Good. Main engines failed to ignite it. Aft batteries, target auxiliary rocket. Fire on my order."

I switched to the back view. "They're swinging wide of the thrust rocket," I said.

"But what would happen if those attack shuttles came near the vapor trail?" asked Watts. "Their corrosive canisters won't ignite it."

"Aft batteries fire!" The explosion rocked the *Kalavar.*

"Got one of them, sir. The second is limping away. Light damage to portside engine. Loss of ten percent thrust."

"Good trade," said the captain. "Bring her down to sixty percent power, then have her flame out."

"Relaying the order, Captain."

"Have all shuttles capable of condensed space travel energize and prepare cascading engines. Even the exploration shuttle in the cargo bay. We'll fail to mission accomplish without taking a few more risks."

"Sir, enemy fighters strafing forward pulse laser turret. Turret destroyed. Breaching pods on approach."

"Navigator, random thruster fire. Keep her bouncing. Let's not make it easy. Chief Brold, Corporal Smith, prepare to repel boarders."

CHAPTER 34

Aliens consider humans an aggressive, militant species. Most aliens consider the Colonial Marines, one-on-one, among the most dangerous of combatants. The only species more greatly feared, not only for its advanced technology, but also for size, strength and sheer ferocity, is the Coregar or Gar-Crax.

A most unusual sight, Specialist Club sprinting. Her stocky frame carried her and her equipment with ease. Before entering Security she examined the door, and plucked something from the frame.

"Move over, Keesay. Company's knocking." She slid into the rolling chair and took command of the consoles. "Here," she tossed.

I caught two items. The first, a miniature computer clip. The second, a thumb-sized, clay-like substance. It wasn't C4 or a familiar explosive.

"Insert the clip electrodes," she said. "Push in the three side buttons simultaneously. Standard timing, 4.5 seconds and you'll have a nice blast." She re-sequenced the monitor displays. "Chief, ready to go," she said into her collar. "Keesay, your job is to make sure anyone who approaches Security who ain't human doesn't get in."

She reached into a thigh pocket. "Before you post yourself outside," she said, tossing a slim box to Watts, "a CNS modulator." She followed with a small baton. "This will attune it to his nervous system. Just follow the instructions."

Lori Watts went right to work. The oblong, leaf-shaped device felt smooth to the skin. Watts slid the CNS modulator inside my uniform collar, and affixed it just below the neck. Its cool touch extended halfway down my spine. "It'll hurt when it gets peeled off," Lori said.

"Good to know," I said, watching Club at the screens.

Club pointed. "You, Michael Watts. Sit and monitor those two screens. Let me know immediately, yell, in fact, if you see any non-human." Michael hopped to it.

"Instructor Watts, as soon as you're finished, assist me. Chief Brold says you're familiar with the system." She might've been skeptical, but the chief's word squelched question.

"Okay, Keesay," said Watts. "If you notice a sharp pain along your spine, described as being similar to burning needles, remove the device immediately."

"How?"

She took my right hand and directed it over my shoulder. "Tug here. Pinch for three seconds and it will release. Painful, like I said."

"Understood. I've experienced Stegmar Mantis sounding. Anything that'll help." I carefully fitted my riot helmet before dropping the visor and testing my com-set. I grabbed my satchel of ammo and my shotgun. "Specialist Club. I'm going to retrieve a riot shield and equipment from my cart down the hall."

She nodded. "I saw it. You'll need the stuff. Thirty seconds."

"Acknowledged." I ran, and retrieved my collapsed shield, slid it over my left shoulder, slid a few more shells in my pockets, and grabbed my plasticized breast, arm and leg armor. Probably useless against Crax caustic rounds, but maybe not against the Stegmar Mantis weaponry.

"Keesay," called Club. "All clear. They haven't boarded yet. Suit up."

I needed access to my coverall pockets, so I unbuttoned and strapped the body plates under my vest and uniform. It was a snug fit. Never can have too much, I thought, if it doesn't hinder mobility. I strapped on the shin, calf and thigh shields. *Thunk*! Something stuck the hull. I strapped on the right forearm plating and set the rest aside. I adjusted my com-set to prioritize, Command primary and Security secondary frequency.

"...losing command contr...bot attached." It sounded like Gudkov. "Other...imity. Det...cutti...arm... Losi...deto..." Two blasts reverberated near the hull.

The door opened behind me. "They're jamming all frequencies. Our system upgrade was supposed to handle it." Club worked frantically. "Cameras are still up. Mer insisted on running lines. No audio. No send and receive."

"The marines' equipment should be." I switched to their frequency exclusively. "I'm receiving Corporal Smith."

"In here, Keesay." I ran to Club and pulled my headset. She took it. "Club, Alpha Alpha Mars, breaching pod aft destroyed. Ventral pod knocked away, damaged but maneuvering to re-attach. Portside forward pod attached, just aft of engineering." She examined her monitors. "Squad 2, 3, 8 to forward engineering. Squad 1, 5, 9 to shuttle bay."

I unclipped my com-set and attached it to Club as she continued to survey the situation. Watts assisted. Fighting broke out near engineering. DeLark led two dozen colonists against a wave of Stegmar Mantis. The 30-inch high insectoid aliens advanced at a heavy cost.

Then a large reptilian biped leapt through the hull breach. It was mottled green and resembled a prehistoric predator, except it carried a halberd with nasty hooked blades. A second and third followed. "Gar-Crax trio with shields," called Club, "accompanying Stegmar boarders near forward engineering." The Gar-Crax, like the Stegmar, carried equipment on belts, harnesses, and bandoleers. The Crax leveled their halberds and sprayed the defenders. The assault weapons' return fire failed to penetrate the shields. The defenders fell screaming beneath the caustic pellet barrage.

"Squad 4 and 6 fall back." Club tapped and a bulkhead dropped, providing temporary respite. "Smith, get heavy-duty lasers to forward engineering."

The Crax halberds sliced through the door. "Estimate seventy Stegmar, ten Bulldog Beetles, supported by three Gar-Crax." *Thunk*! "Pod reattach aft of shuttle bay."

"Specialist Club," said Watts. "Two Primus-launched pods on approach. Gunboats moving to intercept Primus escort. Several flotillas of pods approaching dock."

"Acknowledged." She dropped another door to shield DeLark and his half dozen survivors. "Stegmar scattering into groups of five." The ship lurched. "Captain's making evasive maneuvers."

"She just fired rear batteries. Two missiles," called Watts. "Gunboats closing on Primus frigate, opening fire." The *Kalavar* shuddered. "Primus firing on us. I think the main battery is out. Primary engine failing."

Michael was huddled in the corner. "Skids!" I ordered. "Remember what I said?" He nodded. "Specialist Club directed you to watch those two monitors. Perform your duty."

He blushed and pulled himself to his feet. "Sorry."

Chief Brold led a counter assault near engineering. Hefting a large shielding steel hatch and carrying a long pole, he charged ahead. Behind him, two marines fired heavy laser carbines wherever they found an opening.

"The chief's got his Umbelgarri stabbing pike," said Club. "Goes with the armor."

"Looks like a medieval knight," said Watts.

"More like a Crax nightmare," I said, before another monitor picked up a sprinting man in gray-green coveralls. "Here comes Haxon." He pulled up outside Security, almost losing his Marine helmet. "All clear."

Club keyed the door open while reporting, "All weapons out. Engines out. Forward momentum and thrusters only. Two more pods on approach. Primus escort light damage. *Calling Thunder* destroyed. *Thunder Child* pressing attack. Shuttle bay under attack. Advance on forward engineering repulsed. Stegmar Mantis raiding parties on forward decks 3, 5 and 11."

"Keesay," said Haxon, catching his breath. "We're to get those two to the shuttle bay. Reinforcements have been sent to hold the bay. We've two shuttles manned and ready for launch."

"What? With that Primus escort out there?"

"Main engine's dead, even if we repel this wave. Captain's orders. Two yachts for decoys and something else planned."

"Understood." I checked my shotgun and gear.

Haxon produced three disposable injection packets. "To neutralize Stegmar Mantis toxins." He injected me first, Lori Watts second. He carefully administered Michael a half dose. "There. Chief said not to put our eggs in one basket. You take one. I'll escort the other."

"Did you catch that, Club?" I asked.

She held up a finger. "Thrusters, ten percent burn. Not fast enough for them to target, but get the nose lined up with the frigate." She spun. "I got it, Keesay. Orders confirmed. If you get cut off or the shuttle bay falls, Plan B, go for the cargo bay. McAllister and Gudkov are prepping the bay for emergency decompression. The exploration shuttle has a cascading engine cycling."

My eyes locked with Lori's. She embraced her son tighter. "Skids, you're with me."

She unclipped the Crax screen.

"No." I shoved it back. "You can utilize it best." I unfolded my riot shield. "He'll carry this."

"You sure?" asked Haxon.

I removed Haxon's helmet and adjusted the straps. "You're with intelligence."

"What?" asked Haxon. He donned his helmet and looked away. "Specialist, time to move."

"Right." I eyed Watts and slipped on my helmet. "Same R-Tech rigging. What sec-spec wouldn't know how to adjust it? You'll need the screen." I'd gotten used to checking with my com-set's ocular but Club needed it to relay information. "How's it look, Club?"

"They're shooting out cameras wherever they spot them. Bugs are crawling everywhere. Mainly in twos and threes."

"Keesay, you go portside route," said Haxon. "We'll go aft."

"Understood." I tugged Skids away from his mother. "Michael! Time to move."

"Kra's right." She grabbed her laser carbine and checked her shield. "I love you, Little Max."

I pulled my stun baton, handed it to him with the shield. "I'll need both hands for my shotgun. Be careful, that tip will send a charge through anything you touch, including me or yourself." I showed him how to telescope the baton in and out. "Arm it only when you intend to use it." I adjusted the shield straps. "Grip it here. Cradle behind it like this. Understood?" He didn't respond. "Understood?"

"I want to go with Mom!" Tears welled in his eyes. His mother was little better off.

I eyed Haxon, then put my hand on Michael's shoulder. "Duty, remember? Do what I do. Do what I say, when I say. Now form up!" He stood straight. "We'll make it," I said to Lori. "Be sure you do."

"Get a move on!" ordered Club.

"Always the charmer." I winked and shot a glance to her heavy duty laser. "Happy hunting."

"Thanks, Relic." She winked back. "All clear." The door slid open. "Now, MOVE OUT!"

The shouted order jarred Watts and her son into action. Lori and Haxon went right. I stepped out and pulled Skids left. "Trot."

We made it to the first intersection. He dropped my shield and stopped. I swung back and pushed him from behind through the intersection. Kicked the shield to him. "Skids, I have my orders. I'll drag, or carry you."

In the distance I heard an eerie sound. It wasn't as bad as the simulation. "Those are Stegmar Mantis." It got Skids' attention. He picked up the shield and clutched the baton. "Skids, I'm scared, too. If we weren't, we'd be foolish. This way. Ignore the sound. Stay right behind me and keep your eyes open."

"Understood, Specialist," he said through gritted teeth.

We made it to an access ladder. I listened. Stegmar predatory sounding, but distant. Shotgun ready, I looked up and down. "Let's go." He nodded. I descended first. Skids followed. Two decks down the sounding grew. "I stuck my head out. "Quick," I whispered. The volume increased from below. Small arms fire blended with yells and screams.

I increased the pace, checking occasionally over my shoulder. We came to an intersection and found a passenger, partially dismembered. "Don't look, Skids." Fallen next to him was the old dog trainer, still clutching his assault rifle. Body swollen with venom. I felt for a pulse. None.

"Specialist, look," Skids said. A lacerated bulldog whimpered twenty feet away. A foreleg dangled as it hobbled toward its fallen master. Green blood was splattered across the canine's face and jaws. Three large welts lined its back.

The dog ignored us in its trek. I led Skids wide around. "Beetle toxin. It wants to die with its master, in peace." I urged Skids along, trotting past two fallen Stegmar. One bullet ridden, the other mauled. "Old man and his dog cleared the way."

We made it to the next access ladder. Hearing nothing, I looked down just as a Stegmar leapt onto the ladder two decks below. *Blam*! No way I missed. I pumped a fresh round into the chamber and I grabbed Skids. "Come on." A sounding stirred from behind. We turned at an intersection before they emerged from the tube. The sounding tore at Skid's nerves but my modulator held it at bay. I tossed Skids over my shoulder and ran to an elevator around the next turn. I flopped him down, stood ready, and tapped the call button.

A five-second eternity passed before the elevator arrived, empty. "This won't lead to the shuttle bay, but to an observation balcony. There's an access ladder down. Can you climb?"

The elevator door blocked the sounding. Skids nodded.

"You're a tough kid."

He looked down. "I wet my pants."

"Marines have been known to do that."

"Really?"

"Seen it in simulations," I lied.

"Did you?"

"Naww, I'm a Relic, remember?" He smiled. "Get ready!" I said.

The door slid open. I knelt, peeked out. "Set the elevator for four-minute delay service. I don't hear them so they're not climbing down." I checked again. "Come on, the balcony."

A cacophony of sounding, cracking MP fire, and bursts of automatic gunfire increased as we approached the bay opening. I spotted the bodies of two passengers. One lay prone, acid having eaten through his abdomen. The other, doubled-over the railing, was covered with needles from Stegmar guns.

I crept forward to survey, using the corpse on the railing for cover. Smith and Muller were in a firefight with two dozen Stegmar and a Gar-Crax. Less than twenty yards away three passengers inexpertly covered their flank. Haxon and Watts were pinned down behind some crates about thirty yards from the shuttle. Shattered human and alien bodies littered the bay.

Thunk! A pod. Its impact sounded close.

I looked again. An energy beam emerged, slowly cutting an arc through the shuttle bay floor. Two of the covering passengers were down with one falling back. I pulled two fragmentation grenades. "Smith, Muller, DOWN!" I hurled the old-style grenades in the path of the Stegmar swarm now hurdling toward Smith. Before they exploded, I threw a stun grenade to suppress the group pinning Haxon and Watts.

The sounding faltered for a second, but a hail of needles and acid rounds convinced me the bay ladder down was a bad idea. "We'll go Plan B," I shouted into the bay.

I dragged Skids from the balcony. "Skids, I just cleared the way for your mom. Corporal Smith's down there." I tugged at his shoulder. "He'll get her out. We'll go for the exploration shuttle." I keyed the balcony's door closed, and the sounding lost most of its grip on the boy.

"My mom?" He refocused his thoughts. "Why?"

I didn't want to mention that in about 30 seconds there'd be a new boarding party climbing into the bay. Elite forces, as Lori Watts suggested. We picked up the pace and passed the elevator. I didn't dare risk one again. I raced to recall the ship diagrams. Maintenance accesses had lines running. Some would be grated and some covered, but they ran along decks, not from deck to deck.

Then I remembered the leaking pipes installed in the colonist area. Mer brought me along to examine the repairs. They ran along a main vertical conduit and passed through the gravity plate. "I have an idea. Quick now."

A blast nudged the *Kalavar*. "What was that?" A larger one rocked the ship.

"Don't know, Skids. Maybe the *Thunder Child* got lucky." We made it to the center of the ship. "Unlike the tube ladders, this has limited access." I keyed and spoke my password. "Hope the system's still up."

"Did you almost forget your access code?"

Thud. I did my best to ignore the fact that another breaching pod just attached. "No, incorporated a required pause for impatient I-Techs like you," I teased. Despite the situation, Skids cracked a smile.

The thick titanium alloy access, disguised as any normal door, slid open. I peered in, shotgun ready. The standard three-meter-diameter tube housed hundreds of wires, pipes, and lines, among other things. What remained was a one-meter diameter area with varying degrees of lateral access. "They haven't made it to this yet. If they do, they could sever a main artery of the *Kalavar.*" A platform descended. "Hop on, strap in." I keyed the door closed. "Lift, elevate two meters per second." I didn't recall the deck number the water pipes split off, but I knew Mer had marked them with yellow duct tape.

I pulled my pen flashlight. "See, we follow the line with the yellow tape." I handed him the flashlight before we reached the orange line. "Hold on." The platform pivoted 180 degrees as we passed through the gravity plate. We continued up while I settled my stomach.

Skids slid the stun baton into a pocket. "Where to?"

"Colonist area. Those are the water lines to the lavatory." Then, I thought better. "No, the wires running to the recessed surveillance equipment." But I hadn't inspected that and didn't know for sure which cable bundle they were. "Damn, stick to the water line."

"There, they go in," Skids said, pointing.

"Good work. Lift, slow ascent to one half meter per second…stop ascent." I collapsed Skid's shield and unhooked him. "Crawl quickly but quiet. Follow the lines."

He slipped the penlight between his teeth and took off like a tunnel rat. Toting my shotgun and equipment proved more difficult. I sheathed my bayonet and still twice I hooked my satchel or sling before catching up with Skids.

"The sounding noise," he moaned.

I listened. That and automatic gunfire. "Can't be helped. This way." I led him to a section of temporary ceiling paneling. "Light off." I pried up a panel with my bayonet to find we were above one of the colonist's quarters. Nearby, the sounds of desperate fighting raged.

Skids gritted his teeth. I pulled my bandana and cut small strips and wadded them up. "If we get separated," I whispered, "make it to the exploration shuttle in the cargo bay. You know where the bay door is?"

Skids shook, but was coherent. "Yes, Specialist."

"Know where the access hatch is?"

Nervous sweat dripped down his face. "Nne--near the diesel engine work station."

"Correct. You've been brave. Stuff these in your ears. It'll help some." I removed the panel, crawled over and then dropped. I signaled for my shotgun. Then Skids followed.

"This is Vargus's room," he said.

"We're near the dining area." A spray of bullets ripped through the temporary walling. I yanked Skids to the ground. I signaled for him to stay and crawled to the half-drawn curtain. Toward the dining area, about 25 yards away, stood three Gar-Crax, each with a Bulldog Beetle clinging to its shoulder. They were shielding ten Stegmar Mantis forming up for a charge.

The sounding intensified until it rattled my bones. I looked back to give Michael instructions, but he was curled into a ball, paralyzed. Before the aliens could move, I pulled my last stun grenade and sent it skidding across the floor. Then I stood and emptied my shotgun into the surprised bundle of aliens.

Crewmen from the other direction opened up, catching the aliens in a deadly crossfire. The sounding ceased. I turned to get Skids when heavy footsteps, metal on metal, caught my attention. Two huge Gar-Crax, suited in metallic armor, approached. Like an armadillo's overlapping bands, the armor covered them from snout to tail, and each hefted an ornate halberd similar to its unarmored brethren.

I didn't have to see the elite soldiers' grins as they strode closer. "Holy crap!" Shotgun empty, I drew my revolver, wanting to shoot myself for not loading AP rounds. "Skids, don't come out!" The Crax duo increased their pace. I backpedaled faster, and fired once, generally for the crystal eye slits. The headpiece jerked slightly at the impact, but the round ricocheted off without leaving a mark.

I knew Gar-Crax were faster than any human, even one running for his life. Maybe the armor would slow them down. I broke into a sprint, holding onto my firearms, who knows why. Maybe training—maybe stupidity.

I made it to the last set of quarters and hurdled the pile of fallen aliens, fully expecting to be bisected in mid-leap. As I landed, a temporary wall crashed into the pursuing Gar-Crax, knocking one flat while the other staggered through the opposite wall.

Chief Brold hauled himself up and drove his pike through the walling, through the armor, and into the chest of a fallen Gar-Crax. Its snarl curled to a screech when the chief energized the pike's tip.

Chief Brold didn't have time to gloat. The second Gar-Crax recovered and swung its halberd at the servo-armored human. The chief ducked and the alien's molecular blade struck his pike. Somehow the chief retained his grip.

Unfazed, Chief Brold lowered his shoulder and drove into his eight-foot opponent, hauling the pike behind his churning feet. I took the opportunity to load lead slug rounds into my shotgun. They wouldn't penetrate but might jar the alien a bit, if I got a clean shot.

The chief came around with a right fist to the head, toppling his opponent. The Crax got its left foot under the chief, kicked and sent him flying into the meal benches twenty yards away.

Blam! *Blam*! I sent two rounds slamming into the Crax before it got up. That got its attention. Swell. "How 'bout another." *Blam*! That one deflected off the faceplate.

"Keesay!" shouted the chief. "Get the hell out of here!"

"You look a little overmatched, Chief!" I circled to my right. The Crax would have to turn his back on the chief to face me. It leveled its halberd. Knowing what that meant, I dove and rolled. Three caustic pellets whizzed past, inches off target.

It turned back to face the charging human. The chief knocked aside the halberd and slammed his pike's shaft into the Crax's midsection, driving it back a step. The Crax swung its weapon, slashing just over the crouching human. Chief Brold responded by plunging the point of his pike through the armored abdomen, driving the elite soldier back.

The chief activated the tip, sending energy through the impaled alien, but not before it brought the halberd down, shearing through the chief's leg and into the floor. I slid two buckshot rounds into my shotgun and scanned for more aliens. I spotted *Kalavar* crewmen climbing from behind a barricade.

"Chief's down," I yelled. When I got to him, the chief had thrown the alien aside. It lay stiff, with armor locked in place. I knelt next to the chief. His leg had been severed at mid-calf, down at a sixty degree angle.

Blood gushed out. "Lie back, Chief." I examined the leg armor for the release catches. With it in place I couldn't apply pressure or other first aid.

"Report. Where's the boy?"

"Right there, Chief." Michael crept forward. "See, now lie back." The pool of blood spread. Chief Brold was going into shock. With two quick snaps, the armor fell back. Carver Potts shoved a cord into my hand. "Anybody have a first aid kit?" I asked.

Potts shouted, "Tahgs, hustle up!"

"Colonist Potts," I said. "Post guard. Still aliens about."

He checked his assault rifle. Changed clips. "Sure thing, Specialist. Knew that was you blasting away. Glad I never really tangled with ya."

I looped the cord and tightened it over the leg stump.

Tahgs slid next to me. "Kra, not too tight. Hold the leg up." She pulled a packet of synthetic skin. "Mer, open this."

The old man peeled it open. Tahgs sprayed an antiseptic followed by a blood vessel constrictor. "Quick, Mer. Place it over the wound."

When the synth-skin attached to the wound, blood proteins activated the bonding seal. Tahgs moved around and checked Chief Brold's pulse. She reached in and pulled an emergency injection syringe and administered pain meds.

"He'll make it," Mer said.

"Kra," said Janice. "Potts claimed you're a brave SOB. I'll have to admit, crude but true."

"Did you miss the running part? Chief did all the work."

She looked around. "And who shot those Crax and Stegmars?"

I looked to Mer who was holding a marine-issue hand radio to his ear. "I've got to get to the exploration shuttle," I said. "Captain's orders."

He looked determined. "Club says we can expect company. Two decks below moving up. She'll try to send help. And good news, four pods on approached, turned back."

I searched my pockets, and switched loads in my revolver. "AP rounds," I said to anybody who was listening, "for what they're worth."

"A couple of Crax with shields got past us," said Mer. "Some Stegmars, too. Might've been heading for the cargo bay. There's a squad of colonists up there."

"Any marines?"

Mer shook his head. "Them and the shuttle crew. Might have been some gunfire, but hard to tell."

"Engineer McAllister and Tech Gudkov, too," said Tahgs. "Just before they hit us."

"Skids, my shotgun. We'll get by them."

"Lefty got two of them," Skids said, pointing. My sec-bot had deployed its stun net over two Stegmars before becoming an acid-pitted husk.

Mer ordered, "Colonist Potts, go with Keesay."

"No," I said. "You're expecting company, remember? I'll need you to hold them while I figure a way around the Crax."

"Raccoon," said the chief, propped up on an elbow. "Damn foolish of you. I'd been stalking them since they boarded. Chicher's been shadowing them, too."

"Glad to flush them for you, Chief." I finished loading my shotgun and said to Potts, "Help me haul the chief to the barricade."

Mer, Tahgs and Skids followed. "Get my leg," ordered the chief. "Maybe Sevanto can sew it back on."

Mer retrieved it, shaking his head. He wrapped it in a sack and set it in a dish tub.

"Thanks," said the chief, and pulled his laser pistol.

Mer followed by slamming a fresh clip into an old-style .45 semi-automatic pistol, and holstered it before grabbing an assault rifle. "You ain't the only one with Relic weapons, Kra." He grinned. "We'll hold'em." Potts affixed a fresh laser module under the barrel of Mer's rifle. Mer spoke into his hand radio. "Club, Keesay escorting package to expo."

Tahgs looked up from two wounded colonists. "Kra," she said stoically, "be careful." The frightened, desperate expression betrayed what her voice hid.

"Will do." I winked. I took her right hand. "We'll have dinner again sometime. Promise." I wanted to ask about Benny, but didn't. Before she responded I nudged Skids forward. "Unfold that riot shield."

The chief issued orders as we trotted away. "Mer, colonist, over there. Tahgs, you know how to use that laser carbine?"

Skids looked back. "I won't lie to you," I said to him. "But if they don't make it, they'll take a lot of Stegmars and Crax with them." I urged him on.

"If we don't make it, their bravery will be wasted."

We slipped past more colonist quarters and the rec area, all the time circling upward toward the cargo bay. "My ears are ringing a bit," I whispered. "You hear anything, let me know."

We crept through the diesel farm equipment, avoiding several dead Stegmar and colonist bodies, and one engineer identifiable only by a few tatters of dull orange fabric. "Listen, Skids." He'd already stopped. A voice or two echoed. "I think it's coming from the cargo bay door." Skids nodded in agreement.

We crawled around several carts, a large tractor, and a combine.

"Go warp-screw yourself!"

"That's Maintenance Tech Gudkov," I whispered.

"Information or the female ends, human," ordered a synthetic voice. It accented the command with a gurgling hiss.

I crawled forward. Backed against the main door stood Gudkov, facing three Gar-Crax. Behind him stood McAllister. One Crax was an elite in armor. The others appeared to have defense screen generators on their belts. Posted were two Stegmar Mantis. One Gar-Crax faced the access terminal, manipulating a boxlike device.

"Skids," I whispered. "Sneak over to the right, past the diesel engines."

"Access door?" he asked.

"Correct. I'll distract the Crax. You sneak in, get to the shuttle and go."

"That armored Crax. He'll kill you."

"Keep your voice down. I've no intention of letting him catch me." Skids was smart enough to know the odds. I reached into my breast pocket. "Know what these are?"

"Shotgun shells."

I shook my head. "Popcorn nukes." His eyes widened. Distant gunfire erupted. "That's the chief and Mer. Now go." I collapsed his shield. "Fast as you can. Be silent." He crawled back behind the carts and began a circular approach.

"Time gone," said the elite Crax, and knocked Gudkov aside with a backhand.

I took aim at the Crax with the computer, hoping his screen was drained or facing forward. *Blam*! It went down with a hole in the base of its skull. I fired twice more, the first round of buckshot whizzed into the Stegmars, knocking one down and injuring the other. The follow up slug struck the injured Stegmar in the lower thorax, knocking it back. It kicked and spun, but never got up.

To my right, Skids was slinking, making for the door. I ducked as caustic pellets raked the intervening tractor. I slung my shotgun and drew my revolver. I climbed and took aim at the advancing elite soldier. *Crack—Dthzthing*! The AP round struck the helmet, didn't penetrate, but left a mark. I stood my ground and fired again, hitting its chest without slowing it.

The elite Crax leapt on top of the tractor. I jumped down and faked to my right, before diving under the tractor. The Crax went for the fake giving me the chance to roll under. I didn't have time to fire before the elite spun and sent caustic fire my way. Tires and metal sizzled.

I made for a cart, the Crax pounding in pursuit. I felt a round impact my helmet and I flipped it off before acid reached my flesh. I slid under the cart wildly returning fire.

I saw the Crax's feet leave the ground, and I scrambled to reverse my momentum. *Thunk,* in the wagon. *Clump*, the Crax hit the floor. I scampered back under, and holstered my revolver. My only hope was to get the eye slits. I unslung my shotgun. Diving and rolling with bayonet fixed had been reckless, but I was happy to have it now—sort of.

The elite soldier took my action as intent to engage in armed combat. His A-Tech blades against my bayoneted shotgun. I had no intention of honor and let loose. The steel buckshot rattled harmlessly off its elongated faceplate.

I backed away. A flick of its halberd clipped away the tip of my bayonet. I fired again with no results. The elite Crax charged, swinging its blades down. I braced my shotgun above my head. The blow drove me to my knees, but the barrel's perforated sheathing held. Like the chief's pike, the Umbelgarri alloy withstood the molecular saw.

Surprised, the Crax pressed down. I gritted, resisted. His bulk and armor-enhanced strength tore at my shoulders, compressed my entire body. Something landed on the armored soldier's back.

It was the Chicher diplomat. In a flash he whipped his tail blade around and drove it into a vulnerable spot. The rat-like alien left the quad-blades imbedded in the Crax's armpit and vaulted off the elite soldier's back before it could react and grab him. From on top of a tractor cab the Chicher spit on its remaining hand blades in defiance.

The soldier grasped at the quad-blade. I rolled away and fired upward before it succeeded. The Crax snarled and turned on me.

I scuttled back, seeing a thin stream of red running down from under its arm. "We hurt it," I yelled. "It's bleeding."

The Chicher clucked and chattered something, drawing the injured Crax's attention. The soldier turned, stumbled, then lunged at the taunting Chicher, but didn't quite make the top of the tractor hood. Still, it deliberately swung its halberd, slicing through the cab, sending the Chicher scurrying over the side.

I slid a flare round into my shotgun and aimed for the faceplate when it turned. Blam! The yellow flare ignited, blinding the soldier. It dropped its halberd and fell to the ground. A gauntlet clumsily knocked the ignited chemical paste aside. I sidestepped, drew my revolver, and took aim. The AP round penetrated the crystal eye slit. The body slumped before the armor locked in place.

I sighed before turning toward the bay door. A Gar-Crax was still up, engaged in hand-to-hand with Gudkov. I holstered my revolver, not chancing an AP round into the bay door. Instead, I slid two slug rounds into my shotgun.

The Crax's jaw hung at an odd angle, but Gudkov looked worse off. Blood poured from a head wound, his blood-soaked uniform was rent from shoulder to hip, and his right arm hung, dangling. McAllister lay dazed behind him.

I fired from the hip just as the Crax leapt and spun, slamming its tail into the battered human. My slug took the Crax in the thigh as it landed, causing it to stagger and fall. My second shot clipped it in the tail.

The Crax climbed erect with a snarl. Its screen intercepted my next shot. It hobbled forward to retrieve its halberd. I searched for cover as it took aim.

From behind, a red-haired dervish leapt onto the Crax's back, grasped its broken jaw and yanked. The Crax snarled and screeched. Instinctively it spun, grasping for its attacker. I fired another lead slug into its ribs. The Crax's wounded leg collapsed and it crashed to the floor. McAllister rolled away while I charged and fired again, and again. *Click*. I drove what remained of my bayonet into the alien's neck and twisted before it could rise. Blood sprayed. It grabbed the shotgun muzzle, then fell limp.

I loaded more shells and searched for enemies. "Skids," I yelled. Maybe he hadn't made it into the bay yet.

"No!" cried McAllister. "Keesay, help me." Covered in blood, one eye swollen shut, she looked up. "He's dying!" Frantically she applied pressure to his chest and abdomen. Blood welled over her fingers.

I jumped and leveled my shotgun at two approaching forms. I nodded to the Chicher and said to Skids, "Post. Yell if you see anything." I knelt across from McAllister. "Do you have a first aid kit?"

"No," she sobbed. "Help him."

I surveyed Gudkov's injures. "Right shoulder dislocated," I mumbled. "And forearm broken." I looked further. "Lacerations, a bite to the scalp. No cranial penetration." I recalled the tail blow. "Ribs broken, possible punctured lung." I lifted McAllister's hands. "Deep abdominal wounds."

"Shut up and help him!"

Somehow Gudkov had retained consciousness. "Never liked. You rugged damn Relic." He knew he didn't have long and locked eyes with McAllister. "Nova, go with Keesay."

She cradled his head. "No! Don't leave me."

"Can't help it." He looked back to me. "Keesay?"

"I'll protect her."

Fading, he searched with his good hand for McAllister's. "Relic, say something. A prayer for me, for us."

I was at a loss. McAllister hovered close, listening to Gudkov's faltering words. "I love you, too." She looked to me. "He's dying," she cried.

I placed my hand on his head, and recited as best I could from memory, a verse from my grandfather's funeral. "For everything there is a season, and a time for every purpose under heaven. A time to be born. A time to die."

McAllister sniffled, eyes locked with her companion. Until that moment I hadn't even considered Gudkov as her love.

"A time to plant," I continued, "and a time to pluck that which has been planted. A time to kill, and a time to heal. A time to break down, and a time to build up. A time to weep, and a time to laugh. A time to mourn, and a time to dance. A time to embrace, and a time to refrain."

McAllister was calming. Gudkov was struggling to hang on, somehow smiling.

"A time to get and a time to lose. A time to rend, and a time to sew. A time to be silent, and a time to speak." I took a breath. "A time to love, and a time to hate. A time of war, and a time for peace." I slowed. "Anatol Gudkov. It's now your time for peace."

His hand clenched McAllister's. Then his eyes rolled up and closed. She pulled him to her. "No!"

Her cry haunted me, same as years before. I got up and looked around. Skids had watched Gudkov die while the Chicher stood guard. The alien signed, "Move."

I signed, "Agreement," and pulled McAllister away from Gudkov. "We've got to go. More Crax and Stegmar on the way."

"So?" she asked.

Empathy would get me nowhere. I spun her around, clenched the front of her shirt and pulled her close. "I just made a promise to a dying man. I intend to keep it." I let her go. "You might consider survival. It's what *he* wanted. Otherwise his sacrifice means nothing."

She gazed down. "Now," I said. "Get us into that bay!" I tugged a platinum ring from Gudkov's finger and slapped it into her hand. "Put this in your pocket and get moving."

Skids ran up and yanked on my vest. "The system says the bay's depressurized."

"Damn! McAllister."

A glimmer of a smile crossed her lips. "Inverted the reading. Let's go."

I signaled to the Chicher to follow. As McAllister entered her code, gunfire and flashes emanated from beyond the agricultural equipment.

McAllister halted the door's elevation at thirty inches. "Get under. It'll drop and lock in fifteen seconds. Depressurization will begin thirty seconds after that."

I followed Skids, McAllister, and the Chicher. The exploration shuttle rested in the center of the cargo bay, surrounded by secured crates and equipment. It looked like a modernized ground assault shuttle on steroids. McAllister turned and stared at Gudkov, solidifying the scene in her mind until the door dropped. I waited with her, and urged Skids toward the shuttle.

McAllister clamped the ring between her hands, raised it to her forehead, and whispered. Then she snapped, "I'm fine. Get going."

"You know anything about shuttles?" I asked as we ran. "Spotted some of the crew dead back there."

Her battered, reddened face betrayed more than her words. "What do you think?"

"I was hoping so."

A shuttle crewman ushered us up the ramp. Except for her midnight skin, she could've been Club's twin, angry expression and all. "Inside," she said. "Either of you know anything about shuttles?" She recognized McAllister. "Okay, you do."

"I know something about pulse lasers," I said.

Club's twin slapped the wall panel. The ramp retracted and the door slammed shut. She grabbed my shotgun and thumbed, "Aft, ventral." She looked to McAllister. "We're short-handed. Man the cascading engine. You, kid, get yourself and your furry friend strapped in."

"Hang in there, Skids," I said. "We're just a little behind your mother."

The exploration shuttle was huge compared to standard shuttles. I climbed around a land survey vehicle to find the ventral turret just forward of the engine compartment. I lowered myself into the control seat and slipped on the auxiliary com-gear before surveying the controls. The engines began to hum. I doubted the computer targeting system would lock on, so after activating the system I keyed manual control. It queried twice before enabling manual control of the dual pulse lasers.

"Ventral turret, status," called the pilot.

"System powered. Manual control selected." I continued to study the system. It was more advanced than the simulator's.

"Cascading controls, status."

"All systems cycled," replied McAllister. "Antigravity field standing by. Can initiate condensed space with twenty-eight second lag. Condensing factor of 65.250K."

"Guerrero, status."

"Thrust engines check out," replied a female crewmember. "Ready to initiate full burn."

"Shiffrah, status."

"Dorsal turret powered and ready," replied Club's twin.

"Outstanding," said the pilot. "Eighteen seconds until full bay depressurization."

"Pilot," I called. "Disposition of nearby Crax vessels?"

"Ventral turret, two Crax attack shuttles in vicinity. Several fighters in support."

"The Primus escort?"

"Destroyed," said the pilot. "Ten seconds to full depressurization."

Crax escort, destroyed? I rechecked turret systems.

"*Kalavar*," called the pilot. "Cargo bay hatch open, thrusters at one-third." The floor fell away. "Clear. Full acceleration, now!"

Without the gravity plate energized, I braced for the inertia change.

We accelerated across the top of the *Kalavar* and came about. The *Kalavar*'s portside engine ignited as we sped away. "She's damaged but going to make a run for it," said the pilot. "Take some of the heat off us. Look sharp! We've got to build up speed before engaging the cascading engine."

"Two bogies six o'clock high," called the dorsal gunner.

I spun my turret, seeing none. The shuttle rocked as the pilot took evasive action. Several taps ran across the hull. Muffled explosions responded. Reactive armor? "Be ready, ventral turret."

The two fighters shot past. I adjusted and fired, going wide left. "They're coming about, paring up with another two."

The pilot fired thrusters randomly causing the shuttle to jink as it fled. "Maximum thrust," he called.

This exploration shuttle was fast. The Crax fighters were gaining, but slowly. I fired several long-range bursts, gauging the deflection angle. Then I poured it on. Bursts from the dorsal turret reached out as well. I came within twenty yards of one when we climbed to evade.

"Scratch one," called the dorsal gunner. She still had the arc to fire.

I searched for targets without success. The shuttle spun and dove. I snap-fired several bursts as five fighters came into view.

"Two bogies on dogleg approach," called the pilot. "Four o'clock low. Get them, Ventral."

"On it," I said, spinning the turret. Just like skeet shooting I told myself, then opened up. The lead attack shuttle crossed my line of fire, taking two hits. It continued to bore in with its wingman. I fired again going wide left.

"Can't keep the fighters off," called the dorsal gunner.

"Attack shuttles getting through," I said, trying to keep calm and focused.

The pilot responded with a series of radical spins and maneuvers. Twice I snap fired when I spotted the enemy. Several thuds sounded forward.

"We've taken hits in the nose," called McAllister. "Engine stabilizing. Recalibrating."

"Prepare for condensed space. Emergency initiation." The pilot leveled out. "Let's hope we're pointing in the right direction. Now, Engineer." A distinctive hum ran through the ship. "Gunners keep them off of us. Twenty seven seconds."

I searched for targets. The five fighters formed into a wedge and gave chase. Again, I test-fired to estimate angle of deflection. The dorsal turret had already opened up.

"Get on them, Ventral Turret," called the dorsal gunner. She connected with a wingman. It slowed and spun out. "Come on, Ventral."

I took my time, estimated, and then fired a burst. Too far ahead. I adjusted and laid another stream. One crossed into it, taking a blast to its engine and fell out of line.

"Ten seconds," announced the pilot.

The fighters opened up. We fired back. I clipped another while the dorsal gunner hammered the lead fighter. "Where are the attack shuttles?" I asked.

"Don't know, don't care," called the dorsal gunner. "Keep on the fighters."

I sent another string of fire and missed low.

"Attack shuttles broke off," said the pilot.

Several more thuds rattled the hull. "Damage to port engine," called Guerrero from the engineer compartment. "Seventy percent loss in power."

"Adjusting," said the pilot. "Six seconds. Anti-gravity field activated."

A fighter exploded. The dorsal gunner cheered, "Take that, you sel-scum Crax!"

I fired again, low and to the left, then felt the wave of disconnect pass through me.

"Condensed space travel," called the pilot. "Crax out of range. Now, let's see where we're headed."

CHAPTER 35

Most humans consider the Shiggs, fibrous scarecrow-like aliens, as different from humans as are the silicon-based Shards and Flakes. It's an inaccurate belief, as the Shiggs' biological makeup is carbon-based. When it is argued how physically different they are, a xenobiologist only needs to point to the depths of Earth's oceans. Compared to some of the most bizarre native ocean organisms, the Shiggs may look like mankind's distant cousin. In the scale of differentiation, compared to a Shard, giant tubeworms are humanity's fraternal twin.

Three hours after our escape from the Zeta Aquarius Dock Pilot, Calvo Odthe called a meeting. We crowded into the conference room on the upper deck, behind the pilot's cockpit. Besides meetings, it doubled as a dining and rec area.

Pilot Odthe looked rugged with a rough weather-beaten complexion. His graying hairline had receded, exposing more of his already bulging forehead. He closed his eyes and brought his hands together, pressing the tips of each finger and thumb against its opposite. "Engineer McAllister, report on the cascading atomic engine." The wispy character of his thin mustache and beard did little to camouflage the hard lines as he spoke.

"I've been able to stabilize the system. We are at 50.135K and will be able to maintain for a maximum of 119 days." I noted her left hand resting on her lap, balled into a fist. "However, the containment housing has been damaged. As long as the anti-gravity field remains intact, we'll be fine. But the engine cannot be recycled."

"Could the damage be mended?" asked the pilot.

McAllister forced air through her teeth as she thought. "No," she said, shaking her head.

Guerrero, wearing sky-blue coveralls with a communications insignia, interjected, "This is a long-range exploration shuttle with extensive fabrication and repair facilities."

McAllister glared at the wavy-haired brunette. "I am quite aware of the standard exploration shuttle model 3X-19's design specifications, engines, systems." McAllister's eyes narrowed. "And in the case of the *Bloodhound III*, classified systems and parameters of its upgrade equipment." The stress on 'upgrade' hung in the air.

"Engineer McAllister," said Pilot Odthe in a level, but menacing voice. "I realize you are a brilliant engineer. Your skills and knowledge clearly surpass all onboard my shuttle." He leaned close. "Note, I said *my* shuttle. I am the pilot. Let me refresh your memory on exploration shuttle command authority. There's the pilot, me. Sometimes I consult God in command decisions, but often He and I are too busy. I'm always right anyway."

He leaned back. Behind her swollen eye, McAllister appeared unimpressed. "Engineer McAllister, what happens when someone's face gets too close to an active cascading atomic engine?" He didn't await a response. "You know, their nose extends beyond the anti-gravity barrier?" He paused. "Kind of like crossing a black hole's event horizon. I would imagine it to be agonizing, for what would seem an extended period." He very gingerly pointed. "Monitor your conduct or I will give you a personal tour as to the internal workings of my cascading engine."

There was a long moment of silence while McAllister and Odthe glared at one another. The Chicher diplomat twitched nervously upon receiving the completed translation.

"Now, Engineer McAllister," Pilot Odthe said. "Would you please explain to Communication Specialist Tia Guerrero, who has served under me for fourteen years, why her assertion lacks merit?"

McAllister looked at the table, red-faced and silent, weighing her options. I could figure them for her. Odthe had the loyalty of Guerrero and Shiffrah, and the command authority of an exploration shuttle pilot. He correctly assessed that I wouldn't back her. The Chicher was out of his element, and Skids was only a kid.

"My apologies," said McAllister.

"It's alright," said Guerrero. "We just came through a difficult crisis. We all lost fellow crewmen and companions."

McAllister nodded and stared at the pilot. "With the proper equipment and materials, a patch can be made over a structurally weakened containment housing. However, the risk of containment breach due to nineteen damage-related variables is increased a minimum of five-hundred fifty-seven point six percent."

McAllister looked back to Specialist Guerrero and then around to the rest of us. "The molecular effect of Crax corrosive weapons on the housing makes the patch, using standard methods and materials, unstable. Without proper facilities to study the particular corrosive introduced to the containment housing, which could take months if not years, my confidence of any patching effort would be near zero."

I think she avoided what I believe to be fact, that Phib tech was probably integrated into the cascading engine. I'd never read of an exploration shuttle housing one with such a high condensation factor.

"Thank you for that assessment, Engineer McAllister," said Odthe. "So for the time being, wherever we happen to drop out of condensed space, we find assistance, or plan on raising grandkids." He tapped at the table, bringing up star charts and allowed us a moment for orientation.

He extended a line from the shuttle's location, indicating the direction of travel. Then he highlighted Tallavaster. "As you can see, our running battle with the Crax knocked us off course." He extended the line of travel into a narrow cone, and then truncated it. "Not only did they damage our cascading engine, lessening the condensation factor and eliminating the possibility for re-initiating condensed travel, but they damaged our port thrust engine, further limiting our range."

I voiced the obvious question. "Are there any colonies within the parameters of travel?"

"Dr. Shiffrah?" asked Odthe, again with eyes closed and finger tips pressed together.

"First, our food and recycling capacity is diminished due to improper stowage of necessary supplies. That being said, even if we decide to stop, jettison a message rocket, and put half our number in cold sleep." She paused, shaking her head. "With the Crax invasion it would be very risky."

"Yes," the pilot said. "Discussed and rejected."

The xenobiologist continued. "Standard charts do not show any habitation within our parameter of travel. Colonies, docks, or mining operations." She tapped the screen and entered an elaborate code. She looked up to the pilot who then followed suit. Immediately four red dots appeared on the screen. One was within the cone. "We have one option."

I gestured, holding my hand up in front of me. "Don't feel obligated to respond. Your specialty is interstellar espionage?"

Pilot Odthe kept a strong poker face. "And what would lead you to that conclusion, Specialist?"

"Experience," I said. "Past experience."

"Oh," he said. "Dr. Shiffrah, would you continue?"

Skids asked, "Is this a spy ship?" His speaking up surprised everyone except me.

"Skids, that's a question the pilot will neither confirm nor deny."

That didn't satisfy him. "Specialist Keesay isn't afraid of you. Colonist Potts is the meanest man I know." Nodding his head, Skids' eyes widened. "And he said he was glad he never messed with him. Said Specialist Keesay was a brave SOB."

I put my hand on Skid's shoulder. "It's okay. Regulations won't permit him to."

But Skids was on a roll. "He did tangle with him once. Specialist Keesay broke his jaw. Colonist Potts was hit so hard he couldn't even remember. And he killed a bunch of aliens, too. More than you, I bet."

"Young man," interrupted Pilot Odthe. "I am well aware of Specialist Keesay's exploits. I will be happy to discuss the issue at length some other time."

I squeezed Skid's shoulder. "Pilot Odthe has the floor."

Odthe nodded to Specialist Club's twin. "As you can see," Dr. Shiffrah continued, "I have identified one destination within range."

"Please report," said Odthe.

"The planet has been stricken from most charts. Listed is a corporate research facility." She called up a file. "It's a level-one quarantine planet. Details are few. Habitable oxygen and nitrogen atmosphere. Water present."

"What corporation?" asked Pilot Odthe.

"Primary research funding is through the Capital Galactic Investment Group."

"Any other available data?" he asked. Dr. Shiffrah shook her head. He frowned. "Reason for quarantine could be critical."

"If we reach the planet," said Specialist Guerrero, "they could at least provide supplies. Send a message rocket."

The Chicher diplomat, who'd been following via delayed translation, interjected, "My pack temporary nested in that orb's gravity." All eyes shifted as he continued. "Abandoned far migration when human pack marked territory."

"Do you have information on this planet?" asked Pilot Odthe.

"My pack has scratched knowledge. Other pack member's task. Story of planet, its packs breed no more. Water giants, scratch knowledge longer tell my pack war of unseen death and decay end packs. Leave nests empty. Crumbled."

Dr. Shiffrah asked, "The Umbelgarri say germ warfare killed all inhabitants?"

The diplomat signed, "Yes, unsure."

"How long ago?"

"Orb not rise on my pack. Not on any pack."

"Before the Chicher," said Dr. Shiffrah. She looked to us. "The Chicher don't account for time before their race came into being. So we can figure at least 45,000 years."

"How long have the Phibs been around?" I asked.

"One of their many secretive points," Dr. Shiffrah said. "We estimate Umbelgarri civilization to be at least 90,000 years old. Possibly more." She rubbed her chin in thought. "Studies, which factored in long life span, peculiarities in reproduction and development, known rate of interstellar expansion compared to the known extent of expansion, bits of information on technological advancements and the time in between, the Umbelgarri may have been in space as much as 60,000 years ago, or as little as 18,000 years ago."

"But they knew of this planet," said Odthe. "Indicated its inhabitants were destroyed by warfare. High probability it was biological, but possibly chemical, or even radioactive fallout."

"The planet is under level-one quarantine," said Guerrero. "Possibly due to residual microbial contamination. However, if there was a civilization there, and Capital Galactic was the first to locate it, mightn't they jump at any chance to keep competitors at arm's length?"

"I wouldn't put it past CGIG," said the pilot. "Level-one restricts any unauthorized vessel from establishing orbit." He stroked his wispy mustache twice before looking across the table. "Chicher Diplomat, did your pack members take any precautions or suffer any illness?"

"Pack stronger than many unseen deaths. Stronger than anywhere human pack marked territory."

"I take that as a no," said the pilot. "Human immune systems are as effective as the Chicher. Correct, Dr. Shiffrah?" She nodded. "So my guess would be that they're engaged in biological warfare research. If we establish orbit, the invasion may be news to them. It may also be our ticket for assistance. Knowing CGIG scientists, a reasonable chance it won't be." He rubbed his hands together and resumed his favored finger-to-finger position. "I will double-check my calculations and initiate course alteration to the quarantined planet. Next?"

"You'd already determined our destination," said McAllister. "Why didn't you simply inform us?"

"To ensure it was indeed our only viable option."

"By sitting here," added Guerrero, "Pilot Odthe considers you a member of his crew. And by doing so, we've combined our knowledge about the objective."

I knew McAllister was hardly flattered, so I changed the topic. "Is our ultimate destination Tallavaster? Did any of the other shuttles escape?"

Guerrero said, "Our monitoring of the situation indicated that one shuttle escaped. One damaged yacht crash-landed on the ZQ Dock." She looked to Pilot Odthe.

"Last tactical report from the *Kalavar* estimated seventy percent casualties among marines, crew, and passengers. With an estimated two dozen Stegmar and maybe half that number of Crax still onboard, victory is unlikely but not impossible. According to communications intercepts, thanks to Specialist Guerrero, we know that except for the elite troops from the escort, the boarding troops were reserves."

"They didn't expect large or organized resistance," said Guerrero. "And I was able to send a false recall order to a flotilla of reinforcement pods."

"Even if they do prevail," said Dr. Shiffrah, "with any luck they'll intermingle and infect their associates with the pox and pneumonia."

"A tuberculosis was to be released," said McAllister. I nodded in agreement.

"Misinformation," said the xenobiologist. "If any crew or passengers from the *Kalavar*, except Dr. Sevanto and the captain, were questioned, the Crax would obtain inaccurate information. TB and the strain of pneumonia have similar initial symptoms in Crax, but it's estimated to have a ninety percent mortality rate. Very contagious, and unlikely they'd find an immediate cure." She thought a moment. "And the Stegmar are immune, but would be carriers."

"Now, tell them the really interesting news," said Pilot Odthe.

"Humans are unable to resist the microbe as well, and there is no cure once it takes hold." She held up her hand and continued. "However, the Chicher immune system is able to produce effective antibodies. What you received, in part, was a dose of antibodies which should enable the human immune system to get the upper hand and eliminate it." She checked the shuttle's chronometer. "We'll know in about five hours. Specialist Keesay, Colonist Watts, and Specialist Guerrero, if you pass the test you'll be prepped for cold sleep."

"And if not?" asked McAllister.

"We get some more antibodies from our Chicher crewmate and hope the second dose does the trick."

"I don't want to go into cold sleep," cried Skids. His face was white, as if he was experiencing a Stegmar sounding.

"I've heard recovery isn't as bad the second time," I said. "Plus, exploration shuttles are equipped with better chemicals. Correct, Doctor?"

"Right on both counts. You might even be hungry this time when you awaken."

Skids took several deep breaths. "I'm hungry now."

"I think that last statement applies to everyone," Pilot Odthe said. "Meeting adjourned." I stood. "Specialist Keesay, come forward with me a moment if you would."

Specialist Guerrero walked around to the boy. "Skids?"

"That's my nickname. Specialist Keesay gave it to me."

"Why don't we find something to eat?" Specialist Guerrero was a head taller than Skid's mother, and her hair, even though it wasn't straight and considerably longer, was the same color. They might pass as first cousins. I looked closer. Guerrero bore traces of Pilot Odthe's weather-beaten features.

"Can the Chicher diplomat eat with us, too?" Skids asked. "He chews fast, and he's a good umpire."

After their exit to the galley, I followed the pilot. I climbed into the co-pilot's seat. Odthe began entering information into the flight control system. "What do you know about the boy?"

"That his safety and security is vital," I said.

"Know why?"

"I have been able to piece it together."

"He's not an R-Tech colonist. Who is he?"

"I think you would classify that information as need to know," I said. "And someone from intelligence has pumped me full of drugs to resist interrogation." If something happened to me, I suspected McAllister knew. I doubted Pilot Odthe would ask her.

His eyebrows rose as he chewed on my statement. "His survivability, having been in cold sleep once, is virtually 100%. He'd be more likely to get killed moving about on board." He continued to enter information. "Considering your assigned responsibility, is there any problem with your cold sleep?"

"Other than the fact that McAllister despises me a shade more than you? No." I looked over the controls. They were similar to the Graying Griffin's antiquated fighter. I thought about him and Benny, Janice, Smith, the chief, and Mer.

"You all right, Keesay?"

I responded an unconvincing, "Yeah." He didn't say anything. "Just thinking about some friends I lost. Maybe all of them."

He shook his head. "War. We lost Spinazze and Jutte." He stopped entering data. "Didn't mix much among the *Kalavar* crew. Stuck to ourselves. Did work with Corporal Smith a bit. Said you're a real lightning rod for trouble. Too hard-headed to take advice, but a real survivor. Chief Brold remarked as to your tenacity."

"I'll miss them," I said.

"That boy thinks pretty highly of you."

"Seems so. Do you think the ZQ Dock will hold?"

"What do I know? I'm only a pilot." He winked and tapped in more data. "Two-hundred Colonial Marines stationed there, twelve-hundred on layover. Eighty security, five-hundred station personnel, maybe four-hundred civilians willing to fight. They were holding their own when we made our escape." He ran his left hand through his thinning hair. "If they fought as well as the *Kalavar* crew, and the Crax want the station intact, it may come down to who gets there first. Our reinforcements or more landing troops."

"Do you think the *Kalavar* will make it?"

"Captain Tilayvaux managed to keep one thrust engine intact. Her cascading engine was nearly cycled." He paused. "We downloaded all of the combat information and communications. You did more than your fair share."

"Do you think the *Kalavar* will be captured?"

"After we sanitize the information, we'll jettison a message rocket. Let Earth know what happened. Many'll be in line for medals, especially the *Thunder Child*."

"Exactly what happened?"

"Managed to ram the Primus escort after your captain rigged a message rocket's cascading engine. Distracted them by detonating an aux thrust rocket. Crippled it." He smacked his fist into his palm. "*Thunder Child* finished her." Odthe made a final data entry. "Let's just say I feel for the med team that'll have to board and decontaminate that battered old transport."

I learned several things over the next five days. Injections in preparation for cold sleep keeps one on the constant edge of vomiting. Skids did an exceptional job of hiding his technical knowledge while aboard the *Kalavar*. And if McAllister managed to make sure I didn't wake up from cold sleep, she'd be doing me a favor.

"Keesay," said McAllister, "you need to plan more than four moves ahead. Check."

"Thanks for the tip." I advanced a pawn and blocked.

"Let me amend my last statement. Three moves ahead. Check."

"Ever consider applying to the Fleet Academy?"

"Not a bad move, Keesay, but thanks for the bishop. Even you must realize I'm poor officer material."

"No, a think tank. Tactics and logistics. Life should be rougher without that knight."

"It would be if I weren't going to win. I work better alone. Check."

Three moves later I tipped my king. "You excel at games of strategy. Ever play euchre?"

"Thanks for the compliment. And thanks for helping me and Anatol." Her voice fell to a whisper. "And for what you did at the end."

I wasn't sure of her angle, if there was one. "You're welcome."

She gave me an icy stare. "I'll still never forgive you for killing Steffon."

Maybe McAllister wanted me to pick a fight. Like point out her fiancé had pulled a sonic blade. They were members of a riotous mob. "Every action we take has consequences."

She cleared the screen. "At least you don't attribute your poor play to the cold sleep meds. Euchre, you say? Isn't that a game of chance?"

"Some. And skill. And getting to know your partner."

"Think there's a lesson in there for me?" She sat back and began to unbraid her hair. "I suspect you excel in that game. Skill, luck, depending on others."

"Nothing wrong with partnering to achieve a goal."

"I'll study it while you're in cold sleep. You partner with me against Odthe and whoever he picks?"

"I'm not getting into your feud. I like him better than I like you."

"You like that creepy rat, too. Can you believe Shiffrah laid down with it?"

"Next to it," I said. "Empathy. While you're in the E's, look it up. His species depends on close pack ties. See any other Chicher?" I mock scanned the compartment. "I don't. Physical contact eases a Chicher's hibernation."

"I know. Supposedly it'll steady the brain waves." McAllister raised her hands using two fingers to emphasize quotation marks. "Fewer nightmares." She undid another braid. "Xenobiologists are weird."

"Ever heard of the phrase, 'Pot calling the kettle black?'"

"No."

"A binary sort calling a shaker sort routine, slow?"

"On the intergalactic weirdness continuum, where would you fall, Keesay?"

"Depends on who you ask. And I wouldn't ask you."

"At least you've only got another seven hours of consciousness."

"You could always clean and maintain my equipment."

"No thanks. Odthe'll do that." She gestured. "I'll ask him to repatch those laser burns."

I examined my handiwork. Sewing isn't my forte.

"The *Bloodhound III* has extensive files," continued McAllister. "Odthe has made two runs beyond the outer colonies. Has some files on Shigg tech. Even a few programs."

"That should keep you busy for, say, eight hours?"

"Depends," she said. "Odthe's limited my access to the system."

"Can you blame him?" She glared at me. "Seriously," I said. "Look at what his shuttle's built for. Even I can see it. How much do you think is classified?"

"Another game?" she asked.

"What, last one went all of twenty-six moves? Ever play draughts?"

"Nope, never heard of it. Involve luck?"

"Only in determining who goes first." I searched the files for the program.

"Oh, Checkers. Haven't played that since," she paused, "I was younger than Skids. You can go first."

"Thanks," I said. "Skids has done pretty well. Saw a lot of carnage."

"Seems to have locked onto Guerrero. Likes her almost as much as you. Even so, I don't think he'll need to see a psychologist."

"Tough being popular," I said.

"I wouldn't know."

"Who'd've figured?"

I sat huddled with Skids and Specialist Guerrero. Misery loves company. "Told you, Specialist Keesay," Skids said. "Waking up's terrible."

I pulled him close. "I've been thumped by one marine in my life. This is close." I smiled at the communication specialist. "We should be more like Guerrero."

"Been through it many times," she said. "They say it's best to sleep through the recovery." She forced a smile. "Difficult to do after nearly three months of induced slumber."

Dr. Shiffrah examined each of us again. "Another four or five hours," she said, "and this will be an unpleasant memory."

Pilot Odthe stuck his head around the corner. "Thirty-four hours until we drop out of condensed space travel."

Twelve hours later and after a nap, the nausea was only a vivid unpleasant memory. I still had a metallic taste in my mouth, reminiscent of poor quality water reclamation systems.

"You still look unhappy, Keesay," said Pilot Odthe. "Shiffrah said you checked out."

I licked my teeth. "Aftertaste of the recovery drugs. And those tubes."

"I have something that might get your mind off your troubles." He held out a folded cloth and withdrew an exquisite blade. "Bayonets and shotguns go way back. Maybe during the U.S. Civil War, but definitely WW I. Should replace the one that Crax warrior chopped off."

"Sawback blade," I said, noting how light it was while admiring the workmanship.

"Well, true. Exact design replication of yours, except for the top, saw blade edge." He tapped at a monitor screen. "Checked your scabbard. Used *Kalavar* surveillance recordings to ensure the exact length." He adjusted. "See, right here is where the Crax took off the tip."

I watched the scene play through, amazed that I'd survived.

"Best thing, Keesay. This one's made of the same stock as your shotgun's sheath. Damn lucky you had that. Could be someday someone else will remark the same about your new blade."

"Sawbacks are pretty cruel. Early 1900's in the trenches. If you were found with one."

"Things would go rough," nodded Odthe. "I figure the Crax've got it in for us one way or another. So, a captured human toting a little nastier-than-average blade? Won't make his lot any worse."

"Thank you," I said. "Working with Phib alloys. Expensive, and time consuming."

"You're welcome. We have excellent facilities for small projects. And long voyages encourages one to find projects." He shut down the terminal. "There was novelty in researching equipment for a space-faring relic."

"This engraving, like scratches. Is that Chicher?"

"*Nemo me impune lacessit,*" Odthe said. "Ancient Latin for, no one injures me with impunity?" He saw the anger and suspicion on my face. "Chief Brold mentioned it. Your motto."

I recalled that conversation. "If you inserted 'pack' for 'me,' it would sound Chicher." Interesting, I thought. Chicher mores inscribed upon forged Umbelgarri tech, wielded by a human.

Pilot Odthe interrupted my moment of introspection. "You know anything of euchre?"

"Sure," I replied. "Why?"

"After McAllister and I stalemated eleven times at chess, she suggested a game when you came out of cold sleep." He smiled. "You want to partner with her?"

"I don't have my deck. If she's had access to your system, partnering with her may be the only way to win."

"You're assuming she's a better programmer than I am."

"I'll team with the Chicher. You get McAllister."

The Chicher diplomat had a knack for card playing and must've considered me part of his pack. We anticipated each other and managed to keep the upper hand on Odthe and McAllister until Specialist Guerrero climbed up the ladder and interrupted.

"Pilot Odthe, we've picked up some unusual communications."

"What is it, Guerrero?"

"You'll want to check this out yourself."

"We're all a team. Send it through up here."

We cleared the table while Guerrero returned to her duty station. "At this distance, nine hours twenty-one minutes out," said McAllister. "The communications must be almost three months old if the planet is point of origin." Pilot Odthe nodded in agreement.

McAllister pushed away from the table. "No need to assist her," said Odthe. "She's highly skilled and experienced in this area."

"Does our team eavesdrop often?" I asked.

"If they don't want someone to listen, they should encrypt their information more carefully."

"Or at least minimize signal strength," I said as Dr. Shiffrah led Skids into the room. She handed me a com-set similar to the one I left in Specialist Club's possession. No ocular.

Pilot Odthe examined signal characteristics. McAllister followed suit. Her eyes widened. "Very sensitive equipment. Keesay, this is a controlled signal. The *Kalavar* would never have picked this up."

Pilot Odthe spoke into his collar, "Assessment?"

"Not civilian encryption," said Guerrero over ship's communication. "Possibly military. Alien."

"Crax," said McAllister.

"Can you break the encryption?" asked Pilot Odthe.

"Working on it," said Guerrero. "An unusual variant. Maybe as the signal strength increases. If the communication continues."

"And we can reduce distortion," added McAllister.

"Belief," said the Chicher over his refurbished translator. "Worker Crax tools. Not Crax pack member voice."

CHAPTER 36

Three decades before the Silicate War, Earth's civilization underwent a crisis. When an apparent technological plateau had been reached, trailing nations and their associated corporations strove to close the gap. Several countries that enjoyed the technological, and thus the economic, advantage actively worked to undermine the advancement of others.

One impoverished nation developed low yield radioactive, high burst electromagnetic pulse nuclear weapons and secretly sold all it could produce. The economic and espionage struggle erupted into one centered around sabotage detonations of EM pulse weapons which leveled many things, including communications networks and robotic manufacturing. Mankind learned a number of lessons from the EM Pulse War.

"Upon establishing our course, we knew we were on a one way trip," said Pilot Odthe to the assembled *Bloodhound III* team. "And we don't know what to expect upon arrival at the quarantined planet. At the very least, the researchers will be unhappy to see us. Being the bearer of bad news won't necessarily motivate them to provide assistance for our departure. At the worst, the Crax have captured the planet and we are heading straight into..." He looked at Skids. "Well, you fill in the blank."

He ran a hand through his thinning hair. "Guerrero and McAllister haven't been able to break the encryption. They estimate sixty to seventy hours outside of condensed space travel before making any headway. If it can be broken."

He tapped the tabletop screen. "Damage to the port thrust engine has been repaired, but remains unstable." He powered off the terminal. "Reinitiating space condensation on our own isn't a viable option." He looked toward Skids, who averted his eyes first to me, and then to the floor. "And a priority is the continued safety and security of Colonist Michael Skids Watts."

Pilot Odthe took a deep breath, closed his eyes and pressed his fingertips together. "I've decided that we will cease condensed space travel as close to the inner orbiting moon as possible. From there we will assess the situation. Give Guerrero and McAllister a chance to complete their task."

Odthe took everyone's approval for granted. "What happens from there will be played by ear. Twenty minutes. All systems checked. All equipment secured. Everybody knows their job." He opened his eyes. "Report to your stations in ten minutes."

Skids followed me back to the ventral turret. His assigned duty was to assist in the nearby engineering compartment, monitor systems, report, and take action if directed.

After watching me run a systems check, Skids pulled his laser derringer.

The pilot had armed him with the BB gun of lasers. "I don't think Pilot Odthe likes me."

"Why not?" I asked. "He gave you that sidearm. Showed you some Code War programming tricks. Remember, even McAllister thought they were pretty slick."

He slid the laser back into its holster. "I don't know. I don't think he does."

"Skids, there are all kinds of people. Some like you and show it, while others don't. Same way for those who dislike you."

"What kind do you think Pilot Odthe is?"

I adjusted my seat. "He's the kind who doesn't like a mystery. And that's what you are to him."

"Mom told me not to tell anyone. I can't believe she told you." He looked forward. "She wouldn't have told him."

"Maybe not," I said. "Specialist Guerrero likes you."

"Yeah, she's pretty fun. I told her she should have kids."

That caught my attention. "What'd she say?"

"Travels too much. She even showed Engineer McAllister some stuff!"

"That I'd like to have seen."

"I think Engineer McAllister's mother must have traveled a lot."

"You might be right."

"Here she comes now," Skids whispered, as Guerrero stepped through a hatch.

"Why don't you go say good luck to the diplomat?" I checked my watch. "You've got four minutes, thirty eight seconds."

"Okay!" he said, scampering off like a Chicher.

I asked Guerrero, "Any luck with the signals?"

"They're Crax. With the software and equipment we have onboard, it'd have to be A-Tech."

"Could be the Phibs?"

"No. The Umbelgarri utilize more subtlety in their technique. The Crax simply put up a wall to break through." She turned back around. "More complicated than that, but I don't have the time and I'm not sure you have the intellect."

"Appreciate the vote of confidence," I said. "Just remember, this dullard is manning the guns keeping any Crax, real or imagined, from shooting you up, along with our engines."

She shook her head with a smile and slapped the controls switch, shutting the door to engineering.

I relaxed, and looked over my stowed equipment. Not much to speak of. A couple of firearms, some ammunition. Everything else was lost aboard the *Kalavar*.

"Keesay, you set?" Shiffrah called from the dorsal turret over the com-system.

"Right. Now which screen do I tap to turn it on?"

"Want me to drill a hole in your turret so you can fire that shotgun through instead?"

"Clear it with the pilot first." When she didn't laugh, I said, "I'm ready. Won't fire up the guns or targeting system until I get the okay."

"Good, because Pilot Odthe rigged the ventral turret to jettison on his or *my* command."

"Oh, I shouldn't have wedged the capsule door open?"

"Just keep your eyes open," Pilot Odthe said. "Ten minutes until cessation of condensation."

The pull of gravity decreased as the capacitors in the gravity plate lost energy. Minor as the gravitational fluctuation might be, Pilot Odthe felt it might be detected. The plate would be used to assist in slowing the shuttle, and then shut down. The wash of constant disconnect and anticipation disappeared. From my encased turret view, nothing changed.

"Trouble," called Pilot Odthe. "They've got a base on the moon and at least one orbiting satellite. They'll pick us up before long. Guerrero, cascading engine status?"

"Completing shut down."

"I'm collecting transmissions. Routing them to engineering until you get up here. McAllister, evaluate until Guerrero can take over."

"Acknowledged, Pilot."

"Too late," called the pilot. "Picking up tracking signals. Monitor that port engine. Let's make nice and head toward planet. Two-thirds thrust."

"Unidentified vessel, we are tracking you on approach to the planet Selandune. Please identify yourself." The voice was male, and human.

"Tracking Station," said Odthe. "This is the exploration vessel *Bloodhound III*. Negral Corporation. We have suffered systems damage and request assistance."

"Selandune is a level-one quarantine planet. Do not approach."

"Acknowledged, Tracking Station. Our outdated navigational system records did not indicate this. Our cascading atomic engine needs repair. Or we need a tow."

There was a moment of silence, probably while the tracking station sent the contact up his chain of command.

Guerrero said, "Intercepting a transmission from the lunar base."

"Reducing thrust to thirty percent," Odthe said. "Give them less to complain about. Engaging sensors. Look sharp, team."

We continued our glide toward Selandune. "Transmission from planet," said Guerrero. "Can't decipher."

"McAllister?" asked Odthe.

"Similar pattern. Apparent decrease in transmissions since our arrival."

"Shuttle *Bloodhound III*, what is your point of origin?"

"Zeta Aquarius Dock," said Pilot Odthe. He switched channels.

"Guerrero, I've got a bad feeling. Download file three-three-six dash B to message rocket. Include communications with Tracking Station and all ship readings. Prep rocket for launch."

"Be advised," said the tracking station, "friendly fighters en route to escort you to proper orbit around outer moon."

"Acknowledged, Tracking Station." He paused. "Folks fire up tracking systems."

"*Bloodhound III*, cease acceleration toward Selandune. Come about and await escort."

"Here's where it gets interesting," said Odthe. "Negative, Tracking Station. Will continue on course for escort intercept."

"Selandune is a level-one quarantine planet. Approach is restricted."

"They're hiding something," Odthe decided out loud. "Maybe legitimate, maybe not." He paused. "Tracking Station, our port thrust engine has received damage. Minimal maneuvering recommended by onboard engineer. Will continue approach under reduced thrust."

"Negative, *Bloodhound*. Approach route denied. Come about."

"Pilot Odthe," said Guerrero, "picking up analog low-band traffic. I think the lunar station just went to combat stations."

"Two fighters on approach," called Shiffrah. "One standard colonial defense, one Crax!"

"Okay, team. Things are going to get tight. No hitches, full scan. Focus planet surface. Find any bases. Locate and identify satellites. Download information to the light land transport vehicle." He paused. "Correction, download information to the LLTV from Mavinrom docking till now."

"Exploration shuttle *Bloodhound III*, cease approach to level-one quarantine planet."

"Tracking Station, have identified one fighter on approach. My communications officer cannot give a positive ID on number two. She says the second fighter is not of human manufacture."

"Irrelevant, shuttle *Bloodhound*."

"Transmission from planet," said Guerrero.

"Shuttle *Bloodhound*, fighters have been authorized to disable your engines if you fail to cease approach and come about."

"Tracking Station," called Odthe. "Is that a Crax fighter?"

"Irrelevant, shuttle *Bloodhound*. You have ten seconds to comply."

"It is relevant. Reports indicate that the Crax are at war with our ally, the Umbelgarri. I can transmit the information to verify." He paused. "Turrets, stand ready."

"Keesay," called Shiffrah, "you target ours, I'll take the Crax."

"Understood."

"Negative, *Bloodhound III*. Will verify claim upon boarding. Five seconds."

"Tracking Station," called Odthe. "The Crax have launched an invasion of human space in violation of Interstellar Treaty."

"We will verify claim upon boarding."

"Nobody is boarding my shuttle." He cut the channel. "Take them out."

The Crax had already begun to maneuver. My target was slow. Tracking had him locked and, even at maximum range, four blasts connected.

"We're at maximum thrust, pilot," called McAllister. "All systems stable."

"Hang on, team. Take out that Crax."

Odthe took the ship into a twisting roll. Tracking wasn't able to keep up and lock on the Crax. I snap fired as it passed my turret.

"Good hit, Keesay," shouted Shiffrah.

Pilot Odthe continued to corkscrew and I caught a glimpse of the fighter. My snapshot went wide. "Pilot, cannot lock with your maneuvering."

"Hold on, Keesay. We've got two lunar-launched missiles incoming. Deploying caltrops." A shockwave pushed the shuttle. "Okay, fighter in retreat. Finish him!"

We pursued. "Can only get proximity lock," I called, opening fire.

"Go with it, Keesay," called Shiffrah, following suit. Two, then three of her blasts found their mark. Then both of our arcs centered on target.

"Good work, team. Prepare to jettison message rocket. Estimate to condensation?"

Guerrero answered, "Message rocket condensation, eight minutes."

"Team," Pilot Odthe said, "nowhere to go in space. Will attempt landing on planet and evade. Guerrero, download including these words, complete?"

"Affirmative."

"Jettison rocket."

"Jettisoned."

"Let's play with their head," said Odthe. "Maybe some will recognize the truth. Prepare transmission. Eliminate all reference to the *Kalavar* from combat data around Zeta Aquarius Dock. Every frequency available. Transmit to planet and lunar tracking station."

"Will do," said Guerrero. "Estimate twenty seconds. Have information on satellites and ground stations."

"Report," said Odthe.

"Two major land masses," said Guerrero. "Transmissions originated near ocean along northern coastline. Information on screen."

I didn't have time to look. More fighters would be on approach at any time.

"Nine satellites identified," said Guerrero. "On screen."

"Shiffrah," called Odthe. "Target two kill-rockets on each. That will leave six for any surprises."

"Acknowledged. Targeting. Automatic launch when in range."

"Have located a tropical storm system," said Odthe. "That will be our landing zone."

"If we make it," said the dorsal turret. "Tracking sixteen fighters on approach. All standard colonial defense models."

"Okay, team. Guerrero, ID their frequency. I'll transmit a message to them, then jam their communications. We'll blow through and make a run for the planet."

"Frequency identified and locked in. Jamming pod standing by."

"Approaching fighter squadron," Odthe announced. "Crax vessels have encroached on human space. We escaped Zeta Aquarius. It was under attack by a large Crax fleet. Cooperation with the enemy is treason. Break off and stand down."

"Jamming pod active," said Guerrero.

"In maximum range for our weapons," said Shiffrah. "None have broken formation."

I said, "They've sent up their loyalists."

"Approaching their maximum range," Shiffrah warned.

"Burn'em," Pilot Odthe ordered.

"Keesay, you start from the left. I'll start from the right."

She opened fire before I replied, "Understood."

I'd critically damaged one and destroyed a second when they opened fire with pulse lasers and 20 mm cannon fire. I damaged one more and Shiffrah finished her fourth when the turret warning light flashed. My seat ejected into the main shuttle and a safety door slammed shut.

"Ventral turret destroyed," I called, catching my breath.

"Jamming pod inoperative," called Guerrero. "Hull breach in forward engineering."

"We've blown through," said Pilot Odthe.

"Good armor for an espio—I mean exploration shuttle," I commented.

"They're turning to pursue," said Guerrero.

"They've had their noses bloodied," said Pilot Odthe. "Dorsal gunner, keep them off. Once we're in the atmosphere we can lose them."

"Should be easy enough," Shiffrah said. "My guns have better range." She was correct. None of the surviving eight showed interest in charging up our six.

The shuttle's continued acceleration provided enough gravity to permit easy movement forward. I joined the Chicher at the meeting table. We signed, "Greetings," before I strapped into a chair and accessed the system. He continued to collect data on transmissions.

"Pilot, look at this," said Guerrero.

"That's a Behemoth class transport," he replied. "Wonder what it's doing here?"

"Take a look at what's unloading and guess," said the communications specialist.

"Somebody's in this deep," Odthe said. "Download this recording. For this I'll risk our last message rocket."

"What's so interesting?" asked McAllister.

"Our friends at CGIG are transporting Crax frigates," Odthe said. "ETA to atmosphere, two minutes."

"Intruding shuttle, this is Research Command." The voice could have been synthetically generated. "You are in violation of corporate and governmental law. This is a level-one quarantine planet. We have the authority to destroy you if you continue approach and establish orbit."

"Research Command," replied our team leader. "You have already fired on us, and failed in your objective. If you have any yellow neckties down there, you might query them. What might the penalty be for rendering assistance and harboring the enemy of Earth and her colonies?"

"Negative, invading shuttle. You opened fire first."

"Simply enforcing the law. Check with your legal team. Shuttle out."

"Crax frigate clear of the transport," warned Guerrero.

"McAllister," called Odthe. "Estimation on how long it'll take that Crax frigate to cold start her engines?"

"During the Silicate War, standard Crax frigates required an estimated twenty-four minutes. Their design may have improved."

"They may have been prepping since our arrival," I added.

"Shiffrah," called Odthe. "Prepare to engage fighters. I'm coming about."

"What?" questioned McAllister.

"Calculated risk. More fighters we eliminate, the fewer available to search for us planetside. Now monitor those engines."

I held on as the *Bloodhound* turned. "Jettison message rocket."

"Rocket jettisoned," said Guerrero.

"Keep on them," said Odthe.

I watched on monitor as Shiffrah took out two, then three. Another limped away.

"Coming about," said Odthe. "That Crax'll fire her engines any moment."

"Five fighters remain intact," Shiffrah said. "Three of those damaged."

Guerrero warned, "Crax frigate firing up engines."

"Not fast enough, team. We'll make it. Find a nice ocean to hide under."

"Fighters intercepted and destroyed second message rocket."

"That's okay, Guerrero. Our first is long gone."

"Kill rockets launching."

"More good news," said Odthe. "That should yank a warp cord in their shorts. Wager they don't have replacements."

"Crax moving to intercept," said Guerrero.

"We have the planet on our side. Brace for atmospheric entry."

The *Bloodhound* rocked. "Hull temperature rising," said Guerrero. "Increased friction due to hull damage." Shuttle vibrations increased.

"Have to go in fast or that Crax will get a shot at us."

"Forward hull temperature increasing beyond safety parameter."

"Firing braking thrusters," called Odthe. "Hang on."

I jerked forward, not realizing how much difference an energized gravity plate made.

"Heading into a tropical storm," Pilot Odthe said. "We'd better set her down for inspection before submerging."

"Warning lights on port engine," called McAllister. "Recommend shutdown."

"Acknowledged. Shutting down. Continue to monitor."

We survived a rough ride to the surface and landed with a *thump*. Pilot Odthe climbed from the cockpit. "Keesay, with me."

I followed him to the exit ramp. "Wicked storm out there," I said.

"Here." He handed me a nylon line. "Secure yourself with this." As soon as I did, he opened the hatch and signaled to follow him out.

The wind whipped rain into my face. "What are we looking for?" I yelled.

"Hull damage." Odthe struggled to read his portable scanner through the downpour.

I staggered around the front with him. "Not good." He pointed. Several 8-inch diameter holes marred the lower shuttle nose. He adjusted his scanning device. "Lift me up." I locked my hands' fingers, forming a step. Pilot Odthe stepped up and kept his balance despite the battering gale. "Damn, radiation," he yelled before hopping down and tugging my line. "Let's get inside." We did.

I leaned back to avoid dripping on the table. Pilot Odthe didn't. His shuttle.

"Team, we have a serious problem." He didn't close his eyes, but instead met each face. "The cascading engine containment has a hairline fracture. It's leaking radiation. While the amount isn't lethal outside the shuttle for short periods, it's a beacon announcing our location." He leaned back. "The Crax frigate should be able to locate us within hours."

"That's if they know what to look for," said McAllister.

"Their surviving fighters will have recorded damage to our nose," Shiffrah said.

"It is unlikely they'll approach until this storm abates," said Pilot Odthe. "Dr. Shiffrah, any additional precautions we should take?"

"Atmospheric readings indicate habitable. At this latitude, moderate temperature and an abundance of plant life, similar to Earth. As far as the potential latent bio-weapon? Our chances are better down here than up there."

"Does anybody have anything else to add?"

The Chicher diplomat stood. "Not burrow from hawk. Raid enemy pack. Snatch ship."

Pilot Odthe nodded. "Thank you. The suggestion has merit. Anybody else?" No one spoke up. "Team, how are we doing on their codes?"

"Not enough time to tell," said McAllister. Guerrero nodded and the

Chicher signaled, "Agreement."

"Final input?" No one made any additional suggestions. "Okay. Give me five minutes."

We all departed the meeting area. Skids followed me down to the lower deck. "What's all that rain like outside?"

"Kind of like being sprayed with a fire hose. Hard to see. So windy, hard to stand."

"I've never been in a storm like that." His eyes widened in anticipation. "Think we'll get to go out in it?"

"I hope not, Skids. My coveralls are moisture repellant, but some got in. It's uncomfortable." He frowned. "What do you say we go to the dorsal turret and watch the storm?"

"There's only room for one, Specialist."

"I've seen enough of the storm," I said, leading him aft. He sat on my shoulders while looking out and started asking questions about rain, clouds, and wind until Pilot Odthe called us back.

"Team, we're going to split up." He didn't wait for comments. "The LLTV is designed for four, but five, with a smaller passenger could get by." He pointed. "Skids, you'll go along with Guerrero, McAllister, Keesay and Shiffrah. The Chicher and I will remain with the *Bloodhound III*."

"What is the plan?" asked Dr. Shiffrah.

Pilot Odthe closed his eyes and pressed fingers. "You five will work your way towards the research station. Break their codes along the way. Learn what you can. Guerrero should be able to handle that. If anything breaks or Guerrero needs assistance, McAllister. Shiffrah, your expertise will be needed should there be an issue with microbes. Namely, any residual strains from biological warfare. Keesay, you seem to be able to handle yourself in a fight, and there's a good chance your skills will be needed." He opened his eyes and stared at Skids. "Young man, I've no idea as to your identity. But you're knowledgeable and brave. They'll need your assistance."

He allowed time for the Chicher's translator to catch up. "Diplomat, you and I will stick with the *Bloodhound*. Move around. Keep them off balance. You'll assist with the decryption efforts here and man the dorsal turret if needed." He leaned back. "We don't want to know anything of your plans other than what I've outlined."

"In case you're captured?" Guerrero asked. By the expression on her face she already knew the answer.

"Affirmative. I suggest you get packing while I instruct the Chicher in turret gunnery."

Two hours later we'd selected and stowed gear in and on the LLTV. The storm was letting up. We'd decided to travel along the ocean, using it and terrain for cover. The LLTV could submerge. It couldn't supply oxygen for long, but had snorkeling ability. About 1400 miles to the research station.

Pilot Odthe called one last meeting. "Team, storm's abated. Time to move. Keesay, I'm putting you in charge of the LLTV team. You think fast on your feet and that's the most important quality in a leader. Dr. Shiffrah, you're second. Any questions?"

I saw McAllister holding back. Too bad.

Pilot Odthe offered his hand. "Specialist, good luck."

"Same to you, Pilot." We shook hands even though we both knew his fate was to be hunted, ending in death. Capture might be part of the equation, leading to the same result by way of interrogation and torture.

"Better get your team moving. I'll need to consult with Dr. Shiffrah a moment." He'd already said his goodbye with Guerrero.

I looked around and slung my shotgun. "Engineer McAllister, assist Guerrero deploying the LLTV. She's driving. Skids, you double-check to make sure everything is locked down." I strode down the ramp before McAllister could complain. The Chicher followed.

We stood in the stiff breeze off the ocean that brought in the salty air. It also carried the remaining clouds inland, away from the gritty beach that ran into the rough surf fifty yards away. "Security Man, different trails. Still surrogate pack member."

"Agreed. We will fence and play dominoes again."

"No. Pilot Leader and I will nest and run until cornered."

I offered my hand. "Chicher Diplomat, you never know. Us R-Techs are tough to kill." I craned my neck to view the front of the exploration shuttle. "Let's get moving," I yelled. "Radiation won't do us any good."

Two shadows shot from the cliffs and sped out over the ocean.

"Fighter's, two!" I shouted. "Get that LLTV clear." Into my com-set I called, "Pilot, we've got fighters."

The *Bloodhound*'s dorsal turret spun to life. The shuttle ramp retracted and the hatch slammed shut. The LLTV deployment platform elevated. I was three steps behind the Chicher, dashing for a rock outcropping.

The pair of fighters, one Crax the other human turned and accelerated in on the deck. I pulled my revolver and ejected the hollow point rounds and loaded armor piercing. The thudding roar of pulse laser and cannon fire mixed with the sizzling impact of corrosive pellets.

The *Bloodhound*'s engines sputtered. The Crax was on target and its corrosive chewed into the shuttle's rear. Pulse lasers tore at the beach, raked into the nose, and erupted up the cliff face.

"Engineering's gone!" I said. Rocks and debris rained down on the shuttle. I pointed to the north. "Dorsal turret, on your six, circling toward three for another pass."

"Thanks, Keesay," called Shiffrah and rotated her turret to engage. "System's down. I'm manual." She engaged at long range.

Pilot Odthe dropped from the emergency hatch, toting a heavy-duty laser and tripod. A power cable trailed behind. "Keesay, get your team out of here!"

"Guerrero, go north," I said. "Will follow on foot."

"Negative," called McAllister. "Preparing to engage."

"Your pulse laser won't punch through," I said.

"We've got tracking," said McAllister. "Enough hits will."

"You don't have the energy reserves. Even I know that!"

"*Bloodhound* is jamming, Keesay. If we don't take them out now, they'll be all over us."

"Agreed," I said. The Chicher's chatter transformed to a shrill clicking. "I agree with that, too." They were coming about again. I rested my arm on a rock, estimated lead and waited.

Lasers and caustic pellets crossed long before I could take my shot. Shiffrah focused on the Crax. Odthe and McAllister fired on the colony fighter. I prepared to combine my feeble firepower with theirs.

The colony-grade fighter broke apart on approach. The Crax fighter absorbed one hit from Shiffrah before popping up to release a rocket from its belly. "Incoming," I yelled, and pulled the Chicher down with me. The concussion hammered us against the sand. I struggled to breathe in. Finally, breath came. I said to the recovering Chicher. "Crax don't bomb with explosives."

The rocket had penetrated the *Bloodhound*'s hull before exploding. What was left resembled a blackened canister, jaggedly split across the center. I leapt from the rocky concealment and ran to Pilot Odthe. He'd been thrown twenty feet. I didn't bother checking his broken body for a pulse.

The Chicher had already reset the tripod and was struggling to lift the heavy laser despite the severed power cable. I hefted it in place and checked the power reserve. I held up two fingers and said, "Two blasts."

He signaled, "Understood," and swung the weapon away from the smoking wreck and into the ocean breeze.

I adjusted my headset and called, "McAllister, report."

"Thought you were dead, Keesay. We'll swing back for you. Only enough power for a few weak bursts."

I reached into my breast pocket. "Swing back this way. Provide a moving target. Fire if you want, but don't pick us up."

"What?"

"I've got an idea."

"This ought to be good."

"It will be," I said. "Shut down and secure all vulnerable electronics equipment you can."

"Why?"

"Just do it, now. Here he comes." I deactivated my com-set and set it on secure mode.

I loaded one of my disguised shells, estimated the wind, stepped twenty paces from the Chicher, and held my shotgun at a thirty degree angle. The Crax swung around and again raced in on the deck. I pulled the trigger before anyone else opened fire. The shell's rocket assist knocked me back.

Pellets raced toward the LLTV. The vehicle spun around, throwing sand as it evaded. The Chicher opened up just before McAllister did. All missed. Any time, I prayed.

A concussion of water erupted one hundred yards ahead of the Crax. The fighter slammed into the water wall. It broke through, skipped on the surface, flipped, and cartwheeled into the surf.

The Chicher chattered, clicked and pointed at an ejection capsule rocketing above the waves, moving away. The Chicher pulled the heavy laser's trigger. Nothing. I switched on my com-set. "McAllister! Take out that capsule."

"We're out of power. What'd you do?"

"Dump energy into it and take it out, NOW!"

Seconds later blasts streaked from the LLTV's roof turret. Three found their mark, bringing down the defense shield. The fourth sent it burning into the ocean.

I climbed to the top of the rock pile and watched the Crax capsule sink. Nothing surfaced. "Over there," I yelled. Off to the right a smaller capsule bobbed along the surface. "McAllister, can you get a fix on that?"

"On what?"

"Two o'clock straight out, four-hundred yards."

"Got it. There's movement inside."

"Colony fighter pilot," I said. "Ocean's bringing him in. Jam his transmissions."

"Have been since the engagement started," said Guerrero.

"Odthe and Shiffrah are dead," I said.

"I know," she replied.

I stood on shore and watched the capsule approach. I held my shotgun ready. It bottomed out and tumbled with the next wave. "Out now," I shouted.

The hatch blew and the pilot dove out, under the surf. "She's armed," I yelled and dropped to the sand.

She came up behind the capsule. The crack of MP fire echoed above the surf. I returned the favor. "*Blam*! *Ca-Chunk, Blam*! A wave swept into the pilot and the capsule. I couldn't see her so I moved right.

Skids ran up with his laser derringer.

"Get back!" I yelled before spotting the pilot surfacing. I changed orders. "Get down!"

Crack! *Crack*! *Crack*! Sand divots popped in front of me. I rolled. The pilot switched targets and exchanged fire with Skids, who'd mimicked my prone position.

Skids rolled right, just before several rounds struck his former position. Rolled left to avoid a second volley. It reminded me of Mr. Habbuk. That pilot was a marksman.

I took aim. *Blam*! A slug slammed into her ribs, knocking her back into the waves.

Guerrero dashed forward, grabbed Skids by the collar and pulled him toward the LLTV. McAllister stalked forward with two laser carbines. She saturated the water around the pilot with fire. "Keesay, may not want to kill you," she screamed over the surf, "but I have no problems with it." She sent a few more blasts. "Hands up now or no quarter!"

We both eyed the water. McAllister said, "I thought you were blood thirsty."

"You've been misinformed," I said. "Besides, I just nailed her. See, there she is."

The pilot had raised her left hand. Her right cradled her ribs. She'd shed her equipment belt and weapon. I fixed my bayonet and escorted the injured pilot to shore.

McAllister accompanied us. "You've been itching to do that," she said.

"Do what?" I asked. "Keep moving."

"Use your fancy new bayonet."

"PhD in R-Tech psychology?" I chided, before motioning with my bayonet. "That's it, past the man you killed."

"Man I killed?" said the pilot. She turned and whipped her dripping bangs aside. "How many of my squadron did you kill?"

"Remorse from us? For killing a pack of traitors?" Proper gesturing with my shotgun halted her reply. "Over there."

McAllister said, "See why you don't have any friends."

"Stop," I ordered the pilot. "Off with your coveralls." To McAllister, I said, "Jealousy rears its ugly head."

"Just looking in the mirror, Keesay."

"Pilot, I suggest you comply. My slug may not penetrate your flight coveralls, but it'll split your skull. Boots, too." I took a step back. "McAllister, I've got friends."

"The rat and kid don't count."

The pilot disrobed and stood in soaked undershirt and shorts. "Socks, too. McAllister, you get to make a new friend. Search her."

"Bashful?" asked McAllister with a wicked smile.

"Polite. Besides, who knows what tech stuff I might miss. They've sided with the Crax, remember?" That motivated McAllister.

Despite the fact that the pilot was a half foot taller and fifty muscled pounds heavier, McAllister was anything but gentle. After working her way down, she reached up and snatched a handful of the pilot's pageboy-cut hair, and yanked. "See this ring?" She held it in the pilot's face. "Your Crax buddies killed my only friend. Only reason I tolerate that Relic is because he's good at killing Crax." She spat in the pilot's face. "And traitors."

The pilot's lip curled, but she gritted her teeth and remained silent.

"I know," I said. "Thinking your pals will rescue you. And if not that, avenge you?" I looked over toward Guerrero who was rummaging through the washed up capsule. "Don't count on it."

"Got a name?" McAllister asked. No reply. "Give me a name or I'll let Keesay name you. And he's not too bright."

"Bright enough to bring down that Crax fighter," I said.

"How'd you do that?" asked McAllister, again pointing her carbine at the pilot.

"Popcorn nuke."

"Popcorn nuke? Where'd you get that?"

I didn't want to tell her the truth, during the Colonization Riots. "Skids," I yelled. "Get some clothes for...What's your name?" No answer. "Loser. Pilot Loser. Sit down, Pilot Loser."

She refused.

I walked behind her and swung my gun's barrel at her calves. I caught them tensing at the last second, pulled the swipe and leapt back. Pilot Loser spun and landed. Her leg's reach was inches short.

I took another step back and leveled my shotgun. "Forget the clothes," I yelled. "McAllister, keep your eye on our Pilot Loser."

"Where'd you get those?"

"What competent security specialist would be without handcuffs?"

"Now I see how you keep your friends around," said McAllister.

"I'm done playing now, Loser. On the ground. Face down and spread them or this spot'll be your grave."

"Keesay's a lot of things, but squeamish about killing isn't one of them."

The pilot complied and I handcuffed her. "Commerce raiders," she spat.

"Incorrect," I said, and reached into my pocket and unspooled a small cord. I tied each ankle with about ten inches of play between them before pulling her up.

"Why do you carry that?" asked McAllister.

"So my friends can't get away."

"They must've known you had it." McAllister grinned broadly. "Is that how you convinced Captain Tilayvaux and Chief Brold to let you carry popcorn nukes?" Before I could berate McAllister for divulging information she held up her hand. "Hey, I think Pilot Loser knew the captain."

I picked up her flight coveralls and located a Firewings patch. "Pilot Loser flew in the Red Phoenix Wing. Didn't Captain Tilayvaux?"

Pilot Loser spat. "Tilayvaux'd never captain a commerce raider."

I tossed her dripping coveralls over my shoulder. "First correct thing you said since we met. Captain Tilayvaux went down with our ship, a civil transport." I pointed to my *Kalavar* patch.

"You're lying."

"I haven't got time for this. We've got dead to bury, and clear the area before the radiation gets us. Watch her," I said, and prepared myself for the carnage.

It was dirty work. I climbed into the *Bloodhound*'s smoldering husk and wrapped what I could find of Dr. Shiffrah in a duffel bag. "Not much survived forward," I said, coughing. "Better make this quick or Pilot Loser's Crax buddies will finish the job."

Skids scanned the sky.

At McAllister's insistence, Pilot Loser dug the holes in the sand.

"Shallow will do," I said.

Our prisoner asked, "Should I dig a third?"

"Depends on how you act," I replied.

Upset at the death of her comrades, Guerrero glared at me.

"Pilot Odthe put me in charge. It'll be cramped, but I've no intention of killing Pilot Loser in cold blood. Not yet."

"It's what she deserves," said Guerrero.

"What we deserve and what we get have little in common." I set the remains of Dr. Shiffrah in one hole. "McAllister."

She handed her carbine to Guerrero. Together we placed Pilot Odthe in the other. The Chicher clucked and chattered, and took the shovel from Pilot Loser. He dug a channel between the two graves.

I signaled, "Good," before reattaching the cord and cuffs to Pilot Loser. "Wind getting cold?" I asked her. "At least you can feel it." Skids and Guerrero cried as I shoveled and buried our fallen team members.

McAllister scowled, holding back. "Say something, Keesay. You're good at it."

"Please," said Guerrero, holding Skids close.

"Was either religious?"

"Pilot Odthe more than Shiffrah," said Guerrero.

My prayer for Pilot Calvo Odthe and Dr. Nikoya Shiffrah was another partially memorized verse from my youth. "The Lord is my light and my salvation, whom shall I fear? The Lord is the strength of my life, of whom should I be afraid? When the wicked, even my enemies and foes, came upon me to eat up my flesh, they stumbled and fell."

I watched Guerrero's solemn reaction, and continued. "Though a host should encamp against me, my heart shall not fear. Though war should rise against me, in this will I be confident. One thing have I desired of the Lord, that will I seek after, that I may dwell in the house of the Lord all the days of my life, to behold the beauty of the Lord."

My stomached knotted and I hesitated, knowing I'd forgotten some. "And now shall mine head be lifted up above mine enemies round about me. Therefore will I offer in his tabernacle sacrifices of joy. I will sing praises unto the Lord."

Anger rose in me and I glared at our prisoner, accomplice in the death of Pilot Odthe and Dr. Shiffrah. "Teach me thy way, O Lord, and lead me in a plain path, because of mine enemies. Deliver me not over unto the will of mine enemies. For false witnesses are risen up against me, and such as breathe out cruelty. Wait on the Lord: be of good courage, and he shall strengthen thine heart. Wait, I say, on the Lord."

I took a breath, and gazed into the breeze and surf. Then at Skids dragging his sleeve across his nose. And to Guerrero who stifled sobs while standing behind him. McAllister was red, maybe in sadness, but probably seething anger. "Calvo Odthe and Nikoya Shiffrah, the Lord is waiting. Be with Him. We will miss you."

"We will avenge you," McAllister promised.

Recalling Mer and Corporal Smith, and all aboard the *Kalavar*, I sang all four stanzas of *Battle Hymn of the Republic* as I set a pile of stones over the graves. Skids accompanied through sniffles, and all but our prisoner joined in the chorus.

I was struggling to hold back my tears. "I sang that for all our friends, and fallen crewmen. Including the *Kalavar*. Even your associate, Captain Tilayvaux." I collapsed the shovel and shoved it into Pilot Loser's cuffed hands, daring her to say something. "I'm sure she'd be proud of what you've become. Let's get the hell out of here." I slung my shotgun and checked my equipment. "Let's move. McAllister, you're finished?"

"The internal reactor and the cascading engine are rigged." She tapped a clamshell clip. "Twenty minutes from now."

"Good. Guerrero, you're driving." I checked the trailer. Hitched and sealed. I was the last to pile in. Guerrero drove with McAllister and Skids next to her. To their back, facing rear were seats for myself and Pilot Loser, followed by tied down gear and supplies. The Chicher had formed a small area between some cases.

I showed Pilot Loser my bayonet before resting the sawback edge on top of her shorts and drawing back. The teeth snagged, dug in and sliced. "Remember, if I use this, you killed our only doctor." I strapped her in.

"Ready, Keesay?" asked Guerrero.

I strapped in and checked my watch. "Seventeen minutes. Best speed."

"We've been recharging the batteries," said McAllister. "Need them to remain submerged. Estimate we'll burn all metallic hydrogen fuel in three days. Will have to use ocean water to refuel, along with solar."

"Understood." I was surprised McAllister hadn't balked at my assertion of command. But then I hadn't asked her to do anything difficult. "How fast are we clearing the area?"

"Seventy-six kilometers per hour," said Guerrero. "Sand's not the best medium. Especially this close so the surf will erase our tracks."

"We'll be clear," said McAllister.

"I hope so," I said, and actually did for another fourteen minutes.

"Picking up communication signals," said McAllister. "Overhead search."

"Let's see how stealthy this vehicle is."

"Don't want to be near the ocean after detonation," McAllister warned.

"Up the rocks, find some shelter. Not too close to the cliff edge. It's almost show time." She craned her neck. "Your friends'll love it." She grinned wickedly. "I could delay and let them land."

Thruster rockets fired as the antigravity sled kicked in.

"Negative," I said. "They may already be there. Plus, they might pick up the signal."

"Unlikely, Keesay, but, ten seconds." She raised the window shielding.

A little over twelve seconds later the ground rumbled, the sky roared, and the LLTV rocked while light debris bounced off its roof. Our prisoner didn't react.

"That should hinder their search efforts," said McAllister.

I said, "Let's put a few more miles behind us while they're occupied, then shelter."

CHAPTER 37

Convergent evolution appears to be rampant across the galaxy. Organisms living in similar habitats resemble each other in outward appearance, but have different evolutionary origins. An example from Earth's history would be the Thylacine, or Tasmanian Wolf. Being a marsupial, it was not a wolf in any true sense. It adapted to a similar environment and way of life as placental wolves. The Chicher nose-tracking beast, which could be mistaken for a striped wolf with large jaws, is another example.

I sat back, leaning against one of the LLTV's tires. "Maybe I should try cooking one of those giant slugs."

"Nuh unh," said Skids. "Yuck."

"These cal-packs can't be much better." I tore open the finger-sized packet and squeezed the nutrient paste into my mouth. "Vanilla," I said, after swallowing. I crumbled the packet and chewed it. "Graham cracker. At least we have variety."

Skids said, "I got grape and buttered cheese bread."

"So far it's the slugs, or some of the eel worms trapped in the tidal pools."

"Would you cook them?" asked Skids.

"Might even show you how to build a fire using friction."

"Would it be safe?"

"From the fighters?" I asked. "Or the toxic smoke Guerrero insists would come from the wood?" I stood up. Skids followed suit. "Probably have to stick to solar pan frying."

"I don't want to try any of it," Skids said.

"If we're here a while, we'll have to. Maybe we can get McAllister to try it first."

"I don't think so."

"We'll pick up a few tonight when they come out," I said. "Maybe slice them up. Dry them into jerky."

From atop the vehicle the Chicher chattered, pointed and signaled, "Return."

"McAllister and Guerrero are coming back," I said.

"When are they going to fix the Chicher's translator?"

"McAllister said my popcorn nuke did a number on it. But that's not the problem. Reprogramming it is." I chuckled. "Never thought I'd hear her say that."

"She was cussing about it last night," said Skids.

"I know. Something about reduplication." Skids looked at me. "Like for the word 'fighters,' the Chicher say 'fighterfighter' for plural." Skids nodded.

"It gets worse. That's for non-living things. For living, they have singular, dual, trinal, and plural nouns."

"That'd be easy for translating to us," said Skids. "But our words to him wouldn't work."

"That's only one of the problems. McAllister solved it, I think." I watched the Chicher scamper off the LLTV. "Gives her a hobby."

Skids followed the Chicher into the woods. I walked next to the tree where I'd cuffed the prisoner. "McAllister will be back in a minute. She'll escort you to the stream."

"I don't trust McAllister," said the pilot, stiff from sitting with her arms around a tree. "You shouldn't either. Let Guerrero take me."

"I doubt if Guerrero would hesitate to shoot you. But I *know* McAllister won't. I prefer it that way."

She climbed to her feet. "You take me, then."

"Your buddies are still out there searching. You haven't provided any information. No favors for you, Pilot Loser." I pointed my shotgun at her and tossed the key. "I won't lie. You're proving to be excess baggage. Securing you is my responsibility and I'm tiring of it, real fast."

"Thank you for returning my flight suit."

"McAllister checked it out. It's getting colder. May give you your boots back. Your feet are toughening up anyway."

"What do you think I'd do if I got away?"

"Same thing I'd do. Disable the vehicle, put distance between us, then signal my buddies." I looked her up and down. "Your training, you'd probably do a better job."

"Escort me. You won't regret it."

"McAllister," I called. "Give me your carbine. I'll monitor Pilot Loser this morning."

McAllister smiled and handed me the laser carbine. "Been that long, Keesay?"

"I'm not about to propose." That raised an eyebrow. I tossed her my shotgun. "Can you figure the mechanical workings, Genius?"

"Is this the safety or the trigger?"

"Ask the Chicher," I said. "Oh, that's right you're stumped on that project. Come on, Loser." I pointed with the carbine. "This'll burn through your coveralls." She led the way toward the stream. "Unlike McAllister, I can figure out her weapon."

Both Pilot Loser and I avoided brushing against certain branches as she led the way through a break in the thicket. The more red-tinting in the predominately green leaves, the more irritating the resulting rash.

"The ones with the orange stripes are best," she said.

"What?" I asked, watching for any false moves.

"Slugs. The ones over ten centimeters. The green florescent ones are okay."

"Speaking from experience?"

"Yes. As far as I know, of the eel-worms, only the yellow are edible." She stopped at the stream where it elbowed with some depth. "There used to be vertebrate life on this planet." She removed her coveralls.

"Cuff your ankle to that sapling," I said. "I'll give you one minute. Keep talking. If you shut up, no questions. You'll be dead. Now toss me the key."

"Do you trust anybody?"

"Depends on what I'm counting on them for."

"That boy, Skids. He thinks a lot of you."

"So I've been told. Most recently by someone you killed."

"Back to that?" she asked.

"What else is there? It's the essence of our relationship."

"What about my friends you killed?"

"That Crax," I said. "What about it?"

"Don't play dumb. You're anything but that."

"Is this conversation going somewhere?"

"You said to talk."

"Sing then." I checked my watch. "Thirty seconds."

"I'd rather talk. Skids told me about what happened on the *Kalavar*. Said you killed at least twenty Stegmar, four Gar-Crax. Helped your security chief kill two elite Crax, and teamed with the Chicher to get another."

"So?"

"He also said you get beat up sometimes, but never quit." She paused before saying, "I'm finished."

I stepped toward her, keeping eight feet between us. "Show me your hands." I tossed the key. "Leave the cuffs there. Enter the water if you like. Keep your back to me. I don't want you to see where I am."

She began to remove her undergarments. "You mean you don't want to see me."

"Either way," I said. "Two minutes."

She waded out. "It's cold."

"By the way, my duty revolver will find you if you dive."

"Guerrero, she's a follower. The Chicher considers you a pack member." She splashed in the waist-deep water. "McAllister. Don't know why she follows you. Clearly thinks she's superior."

"She is, in most ways."

Pilot Loser sat in the steam and continued to wash. "Then why does she follow you, an R-Tech?"

"We go way back. It's complicated." I thought a second. "A tolerate-hate relationship."

"What do you mean?"

"We'll tolerate each other until…" I shook my head. "Forget it, Pilot Loser. Time's up."

She turned and stood, hands on hips. "I've still got a minute."

I stared her in the eye. "I changed my mind. This hasn't been worth my while."

"Is this all an act?"

I leveled the carbine at her chest. "No. Out now, Loser, or plan on feeding the eels."

"Boyd," she said, climbing out. "My name is Jackie Boyd."

"Doesn't matter to me, Pilot Loser." She was attractive, but I hated her. The faces of Smith, Brold, Mer, Benny and Tahgs stirred me. My eye caught the tattoo high on her right breast. Three red obtuse triangles, each connected at the base forming an equilateral triangle. A Silicate War Ace, three times over. Fifteen kills.

She knew I recognized the design. "It should, if you want me to work with you."

I stood ready as she began to dress. "You guessed right. If Guerrero can't figure out the serum mix by tonight, I'll bury you tomorrow morning."

She stopped pulling on her undergarment top. "Pretty damn cold."

"It's war," I said, waiting for her to continue dressing. "You're on the other side."

"You've killed, but you're not a killer."

"No, you're right. I'm not a killer. It'll haunt me. I'll do it because it has to be done."

She finished dressing. "McAllister'd do it."

"She would. But I'd do it right. Now cuff yourself."

She straightened. "Convince me we're at war. War with the Crax and I'll join you."

"Why would we trust someone who'd switch sides?"

"Because until we met, I didn't know there were sides."

I stared out the window of the LLTV while Guerrero spoke. Outside, the Chicher held a carbine on the pilot, despite the fact that she was cuffed to a tree. Not trusting.

Sitting next to me, Guerrero said, "Pilot Boyd has indicated the broad spectrum anti-viral medication Dr. Shiffrah provided should protect us."

Across from Guerrero, McAllister said, "How kind. I think that Keesay here softened up after spending a little intimate time with Pilot Loser."

"Would you like to clarify that statement?" I asked.

"How else could you have identified the triple-ace tattoo if she didn't give you an eyeful?"

I sat back, shaking my head. "And you believe that encouraged Pilot Loser to cooperate?"

"You authorized that exotic dancer to board the *Kalavar*. Look how that turned out."

"She's dead."

"Right, Keesay. You killed her just a little too late."

I couldn't argue that. She'd had a part in the death of Mr. Habbuk and the marine. Maybe in Lowell Owen's. She could've triggered the beacon that alerted the Crax fleet to the *Kalavar*'s presence. How many died because of that?

"Security failed aboard the *Kalavar* before Keesay arrived," said Guerrero. "Blaming him for that isn't relevant to our situation now."

"Why isn't it?" asked McAllister. "His track record in this area is poor."

"And what's your expertise?" I asked McAllister.

"Let's keep our voices down," said Guerrero. "Let's look at the facts. We're stranded here and hunted. I believe we could evade indefinitely, but they could always get lucky, especially if the Crax focus on the effort. Agreed?"

McAllister and I nodded.

"Second, even if our message rocket is received, with the war, what are the chances that an effort would be mounted to recover us?"

"With Skids," I said, "better than you might think. But it could be a year. Two years. If we're losing, maybe more or never."

"And Pilot Loser has kindly offered her assistance to get into the research facilities and help us escape this planet," said McAllister. "What convinced her to turn on her company and comrades?"

"Her observation of us," I said. "Plus the *Kalavar*'s combat recordings. She flew with Captain Tilayvaux, and trusts her."

"I could've easily created a fictitious recording," McAllister said. "Guerrero as well. Maybe even Skids."

I watched Skids pitching rocks at a stump. "Consider that Pilot Loser has been observing us since her capture. I think Skids is why she believes us."

"You realize," said McAllister, "that if she is to help us get into the base, we'll have to return her hand and ear chips. Increases her ability to betray us."

"Brilliant deduction, McAllister." I shook my head. "That's the whole point. Weighing the odds of her betraying us compared to the assistance she could render."

"She's our best chance to escape," Guerrero said. "She knows the research station. Knows its security. She's a pilot. She may be able to recruit assistance."

"If we get into the station," I said, "I intend to damage or destroy it." Guerrero's eyes widened. McAllister tilted her head. "Look. Whatever Capital Galactic is doing here can't be good for the rest of humanity. I wager they're researching bio-weapons."

McAllister shook her head. "More likely they're working with the Crax to unlock some lost technology."

"Either way," I said, "it'll benefit the Crax."

McAllister nodded. "You'd risk the kid?"

"I figure that we'd need some sort of distraction. What greater distraction than sabotaging their project?"

Guerrero gazed out the window. "Pilot Boyd probably has more information on the research goals. She'd be necessary for Keesay's plan."

"It could result in the death of some of her comrades," warned McAllister. "How many moves ahead are you thinking?"

"This isn't chess," I said. "If you move your knight to capture a pawn, it takes the pawn out every time. Real life isn't that neat and tidy. Pawns fights back. Even if it doesn't win, it could injure the knight."

"You consider us a knight and the Crax and CGIG scientists, engineers, and security forces pawns?"

"You missed the point. There isn't a black and white answer." I thought back. "Euchre. We don't have both bowers and the trump ace. We have to count on our partner for a trick or two."

"And Pilot Loser is our partner."

"Correct. And I suspect that our opponents have strong hands. Do we let them call trump?"

"So," said McAllister. "You say trust her."

"No. That's the problem. I don't know whether to trust her or go it on our own."

"You'd kill her?" asked Guerrero.

McAllister answered, "Until Pilot Loser opened her mouth, he was going to do it tomorrow morning."

CHAPTER 38

Seven basic characteristics classify life: composed of cells, requires energy, reproduces, displays heredity, responds to environment, maintains homeostasis, and evolves and adapts. Until the Silicate War all seven applied. Like many of man's previous assumptions of the universe and its workings, exploration, discovery, and experience changed long-held views. An example might be a subgroup of a species sacrificing the rest of its kind for power and profit. A contrary view would consider such an action to ensure survival, rather than the utter annihilation.

Being crowded in the LLTV for long periods didn't help anyone's mood, but the travel northward, and frigid weather, made it necessary. "McAllister," I asked, "progress report on your infiltration program."

"Nearing completion. They've utilized Crax elements in the security programming." She didn't complete the sentence. Instead she continued tapping at the mounted console.

Skids rode crowded in back with Pilot Boyd and me while Guerrero handled the submerged LLTV. The Chicher always managed to locate a perch somewhere.

"Well," I said, "it would've been much harder if Boyd hadn't provided insight into the equipment salvaged from her fighter." McAllister ignored me and continued to work. I leaned toward Pilot Boyd. "How much longer?"

Boyd looked up from her sewing, through the windshield and into the blue-green water. "Less than a week. The snorkel device really makes a difference." She went back to binding the white fabric to the sleeve of a survival jacket.

"When the surface isn't too rough," reminded Guerrero. "That's less and less often."

I held out a long strip of dried slug. "Anyone?"

There were no takers except the Chicher. "I will nibble with you, Security Man."

I tore the eight-inch strip in half. The diplomat relished the treat. I chewed and suffered its salty, bitter taste. "If you're going to eat this stuff," I said to no one in particular, "may as well make a meal of it and get it over with. One bite or ten, aftertaste lasts for hours." I pulled another strip and choked it down.

Skids said, "We still have cal-packs."

I swallowed. "For now. Better to save them."

Skids sat up straight. "But we're going to escape with Pilot Boyd's help."

I stared at Boyd and answered, "Nothing is guaranteed."

I didn't sleep well the last night in the LLTV, but weeks of boredom compensated. "So the plan remains. You, the Chicher and I will tramp ahead and shelter. You'll return to pick up McAllister, Guerrero and Skids."

"Correct," said Boyd. "I'm the only one with arctic survival training. You and the Chicher have some outdoor experience."

"Then the Chicher and I forge ahead." I pointed to a map. "To this ridge and establish a second shelter and wait."

Boyd nodded. "With you two R-Techs, restricting electronics or other detectable equipment shouldn't be a problem."

"Do you want to demonstrate this magnetic locator again?" I asked, smiling.

"No. Nine times should suffice. Just make sure you don't break it or we'll never locate the second shelter."

"Understood," I said. "We'll be within two kilometers of the station's outer perimeter."

"I'll secure the LLTV," said Guerrero. "It should remain hidden if we need to retreat."

"We'll set it to self-destruct after twenty days, or if tampered with," added McAllister. "Everyone but Pilot Boyd will have the code."

"Fair enough," Boyd said. "Let's get under way." She set the example by donning her white-covered coat.

"Layers," I told Skids. "I've got thermals under my uniform and two sets of socks. Keep your head covered. That's where you'll lose heat."

"Is that why you've started a beard?"

I rubbed the quarter inch stubble. "It couldn't hurt. You follow instructions and stay tough." I offered my hand.

"You too, Specialist Keesay," he said, shaking it vigorously.

The LLTV surfaced and used its antigravity sled to land on an ice shelf. We climbed out before we started to sweat.

"Skids," I said, "you make sure McAllister has that program finished."

McAllister flung our equipment out onto the snow-covered ice and cycled the hatch. Boyd, the Chicher and I went right to work, each loading and tying down our sleds. They were nothing more than logs split into rough planks, secured to carved wooden runners. Then we secured a rope between us.

Boyd checked her compass, then yelled from beneath her white scarf, "Let's get moving." She led with the Chicher second, pulling the lightest load. I tied a white scarf over my floppy brimmed hat and brought up the rear.

We tramped on through the glaring snow, cold, and wind. I couldn't tell at first if it was snowing or just blowing. Once we moved away from the coast the wind died down. The polarized goggles reduced the glare. The Chicher struggled more than me, and far more than Boyd.

Pilot Boyd stopped. "Three minute rest." She handed us a broth-filled thermos. "Keesay, how are you doing?"

"Cold, but okay. My feet are starting to get numb."

"Stomp," she suggested. She signaled to the Chicher.

He signaled back, "Big cold."

Boyd adjusted his garments and wrappings before working on his boots, which had been converted from thermal mittens. "He loses a lot of warmth through his stomach traveling on all fours."

I brushed off the sleds. "Should I pull him?"

"No," she said. "If he clutches, can you carry him over your shoulder?"

"Be like a fur muffler?" I said. "I should be able to."

"Okay," said Boyd. "I'll pull his sled."

After the Chicher finished his steaming drink, I signaled to him, "Carry you."

He signaled, "No."

I signaled again, stepped forward, and hoisted him across my shoulders. He chattered for a few seconds. I shifted his manageable fifty pounds. He clung like adhesive, making my job easier. Having his tail bound in his garments flustered his efforts to hang on.

"Here," Boyd said, tossing a bleached white blanket over my shoulders and tucking it around the Chicher. "If his shivering increases let me know."

I labored to knot my line to Pilot Boyd. "Understood."

Hours passed. I stumbled several times as my feet continued to numb. Finally, Boyd called a halt. "We'll shelter here. How is the Chicher?"

"Alive," I said. "How about you?"

"Good, considering how ill prepared and poorly clothed I am. You?"

"Just this side of sitting in a cycled space lock."

"Can you dig?"

I nodded before setting the Chicher on a sled and covering him. I stretched my shoulders and knocked ice from my beard.

Boyd handed me a folding shovel. "I'll tunnel. You move the snow out and around on top. Pay attention."

"I will. I recall your instructions. Start low, tunnel upward. Hollow out. Only big enough to shelter."

Boyd worked fast and hard. I took over, and then we alternated. It was getting dark when we completed the task. The last thing she did was drill a ventilation shaft. We climbed in, dragging some of our equipment behind us.

Boyd activated a chemical glow light while I set the Chicher on a tarp-covered sled. "Keep off the ice and snow," I said, then signaled as best I could.

"The key is to conserve heat." Boyd nodded, placing a cloth over the entrance. "Not airtight." She lit an oil candle. "Now let's eat."

The Chicher stirred as the enclosure warmed up. I commented, "Even this green slug tastes good."

Boyd laughed. "I wouldn't go that far." She signaled the Chicher, "How you?"

"Bad, cold, better."

Boyd checked a thermometer. "Negative sixteen degrees outside and falling. Already up to negative four in here."

I did some mental conversion from Celsius to Fahrenheit. About four or five degrees outside and almost twenty-five in here. "How cold will it get out there?"

She shrugged. "Maybe negative thirty." She knocked bits of ice and snow from the sacks and produced a handful of cal-packs. "The wind makes it feel colder."

"Wind chill," I agreed. "I read that at minus fifty degrees Fahrenheit, your spit will freeze when it hits the ground."

She thought a moment. "You R-Techs. Negative forty-six Celsius." She checked on the Chicher who was beginning to move around. "Should reach, forty-five or fifty degrees Fahrenheit in here."

"Good. I'm tired. Is leaving our two sleds outside wise?"

"Remember your rash and blisters from carving the runners?" She watched me nod.

"The hardest wood I could find was also toxic." I pointed. "Except to him."

"We'll chip them loose if needed. Let's get things situated and prepared for morning. Then sleep." We worked while the Chicher ate and drank.

Boyd asked, "Will you be able to make it with him?"

I removed my boots and one layer of socks. "I can." I stretched and rubbed my feet.

"Will you abandon him?"

"Won't have to. Even, if I have to carry a corpse." The Chicher recognized we were discussing him.

"We're depending on you," Boyd said. "You don't make it, your friends, including the boy, will die."

"I'll make it. I do what has to be done. Just make sure you do." I looked from the Chicher to the pilot. "We're counting on you not to betray us. If you do, I and all my friends, including the boy, will die," I lied, knowing they'd spare Skids if they discovered his identity.

She stared hard. "Point taken."

We finished preparing the sleeping shelf in silence and piled together to conserve heat.

Morning arrived. We ate in silence before packing. Some equipment was wrapped and stored for Boyd's return trip with McAllister, Guerrero and Skids. Boyd hauled a small amount for her trek back while the Chicher diplomat and I prepared to drag the rest to the forward site.

"Good luck, Keesay," Boyd said. "If all goes well, we'll see you in three days. Maybe less."

"Keep your earmuffs tight," I warned, "or your head will explode from McAllister's bellyaching."

"Good advice. She doesn't deal with adversity well when elements are beyond her control. Add that to her dislike of cold." Pilot Boyd slid on her polarized goggles before signing to the Chicher, "Farewell. Meet again."

"Soon," he signed back, then chattered something my direction.

"I agree," I said, knotting his rope to me. "Keep up." I didn't look back. Instead, I checked my compass as I would every fifteen minutes, and hiked on.

Only once during the arduous trek did we spot a shuttle. We lay prone for ten minutes while it passed overhead. By lunch the Chicher was slowing. After lunch he caught his wind for another hour. Soon after that, despite his protests, I attached his sled to mine and carried him as before. I spotted the ridgeline not long after that, but it seemed an eternity before we reached it.

I selected a spot. The Chicher, chilled but well-rested, began the excavation. I climbed the ridge and spied part of the research station and signaled success to the Chicher. We finished the shelter minutes after nightfall.

That evening, the following day and evening crawled by. We dared not activate the Chicher's translator, and I hadn't brought any entertainment games. Learning Intergalactic Sign Language without verbal explanation or reinforcement is difficult. Tic-Tac-Toe using sliced bits of yellow eel-worm and orange slug on a grid scratched into the ice only goes so far, although the diplomat taught me the Chicher version where one wins by forcing the opponent to get three in a row.

Midmorning of the third day we dug, increasing the size of the enclosure to house six. I set the magnetic locator in the early afternoon and we waited. The signal's housing limited location to a 165-degree ground-level arc. Even that small traceable signal felt like a searchlight beaming skyward from the snow-packed tundra.

I used the excuse of cleaning my weapons to hide my discomfort. The Chicher tended to my .38 caliber backup. Boyd and company would be hauling the lasers and MP pistols in a shielded case to minimize detection. My remaining popcorn nuke was with them as well. It was an EM Pulse War vintage weapon that'd been designed for stealth. Carrying it in or out of the shielded case McAllister carried made little difference. It was paranoia not bringing it myself, but one mistake or unlucky break and we'd be discovered.

I increased the detection arc to 180-degrees two hours before nightfall. To pass the time, the Chicher and I exchanged simple words such as, 'no', 'yes', 'stop', 'go', and 'help'. We learned to utter close approximations. Human anatomy proved to be more adaptable and counter balanced the diplomat's experience. We both jumped at the ice crunching outside our shelter.

"That bayonet had better be pointed elsewhere," McAllister puffed through muffling garments.

I gave her a hand and pulled to assist. Skids was next. He looked near frozen. Guerrero followed, and Boyd squeezed in last. I crawled to Skids and the Chicher followed with a cup of broth warmed over the lamp. The boy was huddled tight, shivering. "How long has he been like this?"

"Two hours," Boyd said. "Get his coat off. Boots, pants. Keesay, you and the Chicher under the covers with him. Pack close."

I did immediately, holding him and whispering all would be fine. He whimpered and shivered. The Chicher set into a clucking purr. I told Skids several Aesop's Fables, and fifteen minutes later he stopped shaking and sipped some broth. A half hour later he fell asleep.

"Will he be ready tomorrow?" I asked.

"Should be," Boyd said. "His toes don't appear frostbitten. His nose, maybe a little."

"Everybody else?" I asked. "We have enough food for three more days."

"We're fine," said McAllister. "We had it easier than you, except for the last two hours. Cold front set in. Wind picked up."

We huddled and made final plans that night.

McAllister risked checking her equipment. "First trick will be getting past the perimeter sensors. With the information Boyd provided, I should be able to dampen an area, undetected, while we pass through. If the wind keeps whipping the snow about, the motion detectors will be easier to bypass. But this'll go nowhere if you can't get us inside."

"I can," Boyd responded. "I doubt they removed my access code. They hadn't after a pilot's death a while back in a training exercise."

"Sloppy," said McAllister.

"True, but all resources are going toward isolating what destroyed the planet's civilization and discovering its lost technology."

I said, "With our arrival, maybe they've wisened up."

"Won't know until we try," Boyd said. "The hangar section is two point three kilometers over the ridge. Once we enter, we'll split up. I estimate it'll take me about fifteen minutes to get Guerrero and Skids to the warehouse area adjacent to the fighter and shuttle launch. Then I'll contact some of my squadron and effect our escape."

"Understood," I said. "That should take another twenty minutes, assuming your pals believe you, and care to assist us."

"We've been over this. We'll need assistance. Most of the pilots you shot up ejected and survived, so it should be more bruised egos than vengeance. And we'd just received a new shipment of fighters."

"Do you really think your pals will be able to commandeer the tug for their escape?"

"If it's still in orbit," reminded Guerrero. "It'll be manned by a CGIG crew."

"Once the pilots know the truth, they won't want to stay here. Tug crews are small, and they won't be expecting it." Boyd scratched on the ice floor. "In the hangar, there're two shuttles capable of condensed space. Not fast but capable. We'll take one. Anybody else who has an itching to depart can take the other."

I grinned and winked to McAllister. "Like the depressed scientists, once our friendly engineer trashes their system and files, and I do whatever I can to increase the mayhem."

"You sure you can do it?" asked Guerrero.

McAllister turned a little red, but controlled her temper. "Even incorporated some of Odthe's programming obtained from the Shiggs. That should provide some additional assistance, along with Boyd's access codes."

"Assuming the codes are still active," I said. "If not, we play it by ear."

"They'll still have the backup files on the orbiting platform," warned Guerrero.

"Our escape will be bad enough," I said. "Any damage we do down here will be icing on the cake. Even if we could fire on the platform, they'd be on us that much sooner."

"We have to be on the move two hours before dawn," Boyd said. "Let's pack and sleep."

No one argued. No one mentioned the elephant in the igloo: The question of Pilot Boyd's loyalty.

We stumbled into a perimeter relay just before sunrise. McAllister's techno-wizardry slid us past the first hurdle. The frigid weather held, and the wind worked in gusts. We utilized it to penetrate the perimeter, figuring the blowing snow would degrade motion sensor and the camera effectiveness. McAllister had torn equipment from the LLTV and reconfigured it to generate a short-range deflector. It worked like a glass shield to foil infrared detection. It was my job to pull along the chemical fuel cell that powered the device. Once activated, we had fifteen minutes of power.

"Five minutes left and three hundred meters," I estimated as we crouched behind a drift. I looked over the top. The dome was shut. "No launches imminent. Nothing moving outside." I slid back down. "I'll go first. Boyd, you help push the sled over this drift. Everyone close in line after me, and hope McAllister calibrated the motion dampeners properly."

"Let's hope you don't slip," said McAllister. "And dump my deflector."

"Both are equal in probability," I said. "Right, Skids?"

He snickered. McAllister grumbled. Boyd and I climbed ahead.

After a minute of steady progress, we dashed to where the dome connected to an above ground maintenance garage with one large elevating door overshadowing a smaller access door. We stood next to the access door and caught our breath before removing our winter gear. Boyd raised the automated access panel's protective cover. She ran her hand over it and spoke a password before typing in a twelve digit code. A buzz and click sounded above the whipping wind.

"Hope nobody's home," Boyd said, and led the way in. I followed with fixed bayonet. It took a second for my eyes to adjust to the dimmer overhead fluorescent lighting.

A deep, masculine voice said, "Who the? Pilot Boyd? Hey!" It came from a bearded man wearing maintenance overalls that covered his bulging stomach. His right hand clutched a large crowbar.

I lunched forward, but Boyd grabbed my shoulder. "Wait," she said. "Kalger, where are Weitz and Bruhmhaur?"

The man stood for a second, deciding whether to answer, fight, or run. He squared up, eliminating retreat. He looked past me. "Who's yer friends?"

The other four were in. I pointed to a camera. "Bad place to stand."

"Not now, Kalger," Boyd said. "Trust me."

Kalger shifted weight from foot to foot. "You, okay." He lowered his bar and lumbered to a console.

I followed, and leveled my shotgun. "Nothing fancy."

"Would ya care I don't shut down the monitors for temporary maintenance?"

I warned, "Just so you know where things stand."

"Keesay," Boyd said. "Relax. Do it, Kalger."

McAllister moved to observe as the big man tapped away. He smiled down at her. "You wouldn't be from that hostile shuttle that was shot down, would ya, sister?" He finished his task and eyed us again. "Usin' a Chicher for a sled dog. Now that's creative." He wiped his hands on a shop rag. "What was yer first question, Pilot Boyd?"

"Weitz and Bruhmhaur?"

"Oh, breakfast. We heard you was dead. Explain that one." He checked a wall chronometer. "Quick-like. The maintenance routine will complete in about six minutes, about two ahead of my breakfast. Weitz knows better than to be late."

"We can trust him," assured Boyd. She explained to Kalger what she'd learned from us about the Crax invasion.

After she finished he scratched his neck and beard. "This could affect my pension." He looked at me. "You know how certain corporations are. Lookin' out for C3 maintenance techs in our old age, eh, Keesay?"

I figured his contract compensation was marginally better than mine. "Nothing is secure," I agreed.

"Not the trusting sort, is he?"

"No," I said. "But you know the score. Stegmars don't draw pensions. If the Crax have their way, few surviving C3 maintenance techs will either."

"Hey, I'm convinced. Boyd's word here is good as asteroid gold." He eyed the chronometer. "This way."

We followed until Kalger stopped and keyed a panel. He opened two transport crates along the wall and stepped inside one. Pulling a power drill from his belt, he locked a bit and went to work. "Should be enough room and air for three to hide in this one, till Boyd sets things up." He moved to the next.

"No," Boyd said. "That's all we'll need. Diplomat, Guerrero, Skids, in there." They hesitated until I nodded.

With the fur on his neck standing erect and his ears back, the Chicher said through his translator, "Not nest in box."

"What about the Chicher?" asked Guerrero.

"Shelter in false tunnel," the Chicher said. He pulled his small MP pistol and backed into one of the stacked conduits that ran parallel to the wall.

"Good enough for me," McAllister said, and strode over to the transport crate console. She tapped away before holding her finger over the pad. "Guerrero, say something."

Nodding with approval, Guerrero stepped forward. "Open crate."

"No sense getting locked in," McAllister said, stepping back. "Give us forty minutes."

"Stay here, Skids," I said. "I'll be back for you. Until then, stick with Guerrero and the diplomat. Understood?"

"Understood, Specialist," he said in a weak voice before checking his laser pistol's cross-draw holstering. Guerrero pulled him close.

"What're the rest of you doin'?" asked Kalger, as he ushered Skids and Guerrero into the crate.

"Classified," I said while he closed it.

"Sure." Kalger lumbered back to his workbench. He was puzzled but dropped it. "I'll distract my boys while you slide out. Then, I'm packing." He regarded our expressions. "What? You think I'm stayin' here?"

"Of course not," Boyd said. "Pack light. Be discreet. Nobody else."

He directed us to a recessed area. "You know how many friends I got."

"Do the cooks count?" Boyd asked. His belly shook as he laughed.

"Kalger," I said. "Internal security. Monitoring. How tight is it?"

He shook his head. "Scientists run the place. Except in their labs, they don't want to put up with hassles and delays. Not on an uninhabited quarantine planet."

I tore his CGIG patch from his shoulder. "Mind if I borrow this?" I dumped a tool case and handed it to McAllister. "Here, put your laser carbine in this. I'll carry it." I grabbed a tube of adhesive and replaced my Negral patch with the Capital Galactic one. Wear a logo bearing 'CGIG' across a glittering Milky Way background agitated me.

Boyd asked, "How many Crax on the ground?"

"Three dozen," said Kalger. "Mostly Selgum. There's two Gar-Crax, but they mightn't be planetside."

"Know what's orbiting?"

He shrugged. "Sorry, Pilot." He checked the chronometer. "I'll swing by the cafeteria and make a quick meal. Otherwise might raise suspicion. I'll be back here and deal with my boss and Weitz. Retrieve your friends." He started to leave, then turned back. "Hey, any code word so I don't mix up anybody?"

"Relics rule," I said. "Nobody should say that by accident."

"Bayonet?" asked McAllister.

I sheathed it and we hid until two maintenance men entered. Kalger led them to the far end of the maintenance area. Boyd, McAllister and I slipped out.

"Interesting friend," I said, winking. "But then again, look at me."

"Forty minutes," Boyd replied. We walked together down uniformly cream-colored hallways for about fifty yards before she split off. Every hall looked the same except for the bold black numbering system painted on conduits, doors and intersection floors.

McAllister walked a half pace in front of me. "Remember, I do the talking."

"Understood," I said, knowing she could talk us past better than I could. We ignored several maintenance techs, a white-coated scientist, and an engineering tech. The latter turned and stared at us as we passed, but said nothing. We came to the area Pilot Boyd had described.

"Next hallway, center door," whispered McAllister. "Let's keep it quiet."

"Understood, Engineer," I said, following McAllister into the system maintenance room.

Inside stood an engineering tech with his back to us. McAllister walked up to him and placed a hand on his shoulder. "Excuse me, Engineering Tech. I need to utilize that work station."

The tech turned. He didn't recognize McAllister, but did observe her dull orange engineer coveralls. "Engineer, there are several other stations. I'm engaged in a project."

McAllister turned to me. "Specialist, please explain it to him."

I stepped to the side, out of view of the security monitors, and beckoned him toward me. "I know it's a hassle. This should only take a second."

"I haven't seen you before," said the tech. He approached anyway, eyeing my slung shotgun.

I rested my left arm on his shoulder. "Just transferred." I looked him in the eye. With an uppercut I slammed my brass knuckles into his chin. I caught the dazed tech, held him against the wall and gave him a left to the stomach. When he doubled over, I held his head and drove my knee into his nose. "Quiet enough?" McAllister was already at work and didn't respond.

I stood beside the door. Three minutes passed. "Progress?" I asked.

"This fellow has better access than Boyd. I just finished his project. Won't raise any flags that way."

Time dragged while my heart raced. Waiting was hard.

"Thirty more seconds," McAllister said, before the door slid open.

Two people dressed as Capital Galactic engineers entered. The first missed me and focused on McAllister at the console. The second had scales the color of green bananas beginning to ripen. The bulbous forehead identified it as a Selgum Crax.

I caught the Crax's eyes. They widened, and its dangling chin flap retracted. The door slid closed and a round from my revolver dropped the alien before it could hiss.

The engineer heard the dampened sound of my revolver and the alien hitting the floor. Instead of addressing McAllister, who hadn't bothered to acknowledge his presence, he turned and asked, "What is this?"

I thumbed back the hammer and took careful aim. "Unless you desire a hole in your cranium as well, I suggest you shut up and place your hands in the air."

He complied after seeing the bloody pool at my feet.

"Kneel." I moved behind him and pulled an anesthetizing patch from my pocket. I slapped it on his neck. He reached for it, so I slammed my revolver butt against his skull.

"Finished," said McAllister. She looked at the bodies. "Only one dead?"

"I noted your confidence in me. Security's sure to have picked this up."

"Sort of," she said. "I scrambled the content and the origin. They may have seen you waste the Crax, but monitors will have shown it happening in the corridor outside Security, and the system tag should indicate the waste incineration complex."

I pictured a surgery occurring on a dining table. "Anything else I should know?"

"The system should be slowing, especially if the writers aren't familiar with Shigg code. I wasn't." I stepped over the dead alien on the way out. McAllister stepped on it. "Access 3344 A, B, C, lock," she said grinning. "Keyed access commands to our voice patterns."

She led me to the left, down the main corridor. "McAllister, why didn't you tell me this before?"

"You're R-Tech," she said. "And I wasn't one-hundred percent certain it would work."

Some personnel moved along the corridors unaware. Others proceeded with concern and purpose. I leaned toward McAllister. "This is where we'll find out if Boyd—does everyone else know about the access commands?"

"Is anyone else R-Tech?" She picked up the pace, mimicking those with striding urgency. "I think we'd be dead if we were betrayed. Keep up."

Next stop was an administrative supply office. McAllister walked in and announced, "System troubles."

A sky-blue dressed S2 information specialist stood next to his console. "Yes, Engineer." He started to say more but spotted me. He raised his eyebrows at McAllister. "Who are you?"

"Doors lock," said McAllister.

I leveled my shotgun. "Hands up. Away from the consoles. Anybody speaks out of turn will regret it." All four info specialists complied. "Okay. Line up against that wall. Hands straight up."

They filed toward the wall. "I don't know—," began the supervisor.

I slammed the butt of my shotgun into his kidneys. The others observed their supervisor grimacing on the floor. I reached into a pocket and tossed four patches to one on the left. He looked the meekest. "Apply one of these knockout patches to your boss's neck." He hesitated. "The other options are for me to beat you all to unconsciousness, or kill you."

The meek C3 complied. Then he applied patches as directed to his other associates and himself.

"You're most efficient," McAllister said. "I only heard one in pain."

"How goes it?" I asked. "And what are you doing?"

McAllister didn't look up from the screen and her oversized computer clip. "Their system is running at 4.88 percent normal speed. I've just launched an attack on communications." She shifted from clip to console and back. "Their systems engineer is competent. Problem for them is, most defense and firewalls are focused on securing their research information." She disconnected her clip.

I picked up the case with her carbine and spare equipment. "Next stop, reactor control?"

She nodded. "I've avoided the internal transport system as much as possible. Main access door, open, then close and lock after three seconds."

We hurried to a busy shuttle access and waited. The arriving shuttle looked like an oversized golf cart with facing seats. And like virtually every other piece of equipment, it was cream colored. Its eight seats filled immediately. The next was only half full with us sitting across from a scientist and a C2 maintenance tech.

"Reactor control," said McAllister, causing the shuttle to accelerate down the tubular route.

"Must have fixed that glitch," said the C2.

"Must have." McAllister grinned. "Specialist?"

I drew my revolver. "Hands up."

McAllister giggled. "Hand over all your credits."

Puzzlement stretched across both faces.

I didn't bat an eye. "You," I said to the C2. "Slowly extend your right hand." When he did, I slapped a patch on it.

He sat stunned. Within three seconds he slumped.

I thumbed the hammer of my revolver. "Care to tell me anything about your research?"

"I, ahh," the scientist muttered. "It's classified."

"And probably over my head. Correct?"

Hesitant, he nodded, staring wide-eyed down at the C2.

"I'm out of patches," I said. "Shuttle stop." As it slowed I asked, "Do you have any, Engineer?" When the scientist's eyes darted to McAllister, I caught him in the chin with my brass knuckles. I removed both men's collar communications and then dumped them in a maintenance alcove. I checked my watch. "Time's running out."

McAllister studied her clip as we sped on. "System speed is up to 12.41 percent. They should defeat the communication attack in twelve minutes. Security system remains scrambled. Shigg code is *very* effective."

"I really am out of patches." I replaced the used round from my revolver. "This next one we'll have to be a little more aggressive."

"Violence is your style, Keesay. Remind me to tell you what I'd planned to do to your files on the *Kalavar*."

"You say that after noting my violent tendencies?"

"Keesay, you may be able to intimidate others. Not me." She wasn't lying.

I shrugged. "I can see why you and Gudkov worked so well together. I'll never match him. But I can sure try."

Her face grew dark. "I'll never like you, Relic."

I hid my surprise. "McAllister, the feeling's mutual. But together we get the job done." The shuttle slowed. "What else is there?"

She set the opened case beside her, hand inside on the laser carbine. Two sec-specs stood posted outside. "Keesay, you take the one on the left."

"Understood." I climbed out, drew and fired my duty revolver. I missed his face by six inches to the right.

McAllister took hers with two blasts. Mine returned MP fire before I hit him in the chest, knocking him back. McAllister finished him. "Losing your touch, Keesay?" She stepped past the dead men. "Shuttle, remain for eighteen minutes."

"Didn't have time to aim," I said. "That's why I carry this." I affixed my bayonet and said, "Main access to reactor control, open."

There were only two security inside the main access. We surprised them along with the other personnel. In the end we killed or incapacitated the security along with nine engineers and maintenance techs. Three managed to escape into the reactor area despite McAllister's lockdown command.

"They'll be able to call for assistance in eight minutes," McAllister warned.

"We'd better be gone by then."

"Maybe," said McAllister, working again. "System's up to 25.74 percent. They'll regain security monitoring in eighteen minutes."

"I'm going to see what damage I can do," I said. "Which door do you suggest?"

Without looking she leaned to reach another console, and tapped. "That door. Straight ahead." She hesitated. "You're not planning to use that popcorn nuke?"

"No suicide today." I pulled out B'down's timed explosive I'd been carrying since killing him. "And I have this and AP rounds." I began to eject jacketed rounds and load AP. "We'll never make it to the alien underground facilities. But I may be able to make it harder to access them in the future."

"Hey, Keesay," McAllister said with a grin. "They're in the middle of loading radioactive fuel. That door instead. Look for a large tracked forklift-bot carrying something with a 'Danger Radioactive' sign on it."

"I'll be back in five minutes," I said before stepping over several bodies. I should've felt guilt, but picturing my dead friends aboard the *Kalavar* trumped any sympathy.

"Don't get too close," said McAllister, "or hang out too long and get a lethal dose."

"Didn't know you cared."

"About you, no. About your ability to help shoot our way to the escape shuttle. Yes."

"Close enough." I held my shotgun ready. "Door, unlock and open for two seconds, then close and lock." I entered a corridor and headed for the stairwell up. Movement caught my eye. I filled a fleeing maintenance tech's back with buckshot.

He was still conscious. I stood over him. "The Crax have invaded and you guys are assisting them," I said before kicking him in the face.

I climbed three flights, then ran down another corridor. *Crack*! *Crack*! MP fire from ahead. One shot impacted my chest. My high-grade coveralls and plasticized breastplate beneath absorbed the hit. I scattered two buckshot rounds down the hall before I spotted the enemy fire source. *Crack*! *Crack*! An armored door with a slot. Another hit in the chest staggered my step.

I dove. "Armored access door to reactor area, open." When it ratcheted up I sent buckshot into the guard's legs and followed with a killing shot after she fell.

I reloaded my shotgun and climbed to my feet. Two sec-bots stationed themselves at the entrance to a cavernous reactor area, next to the fallen security woman. I threw my shotgun at the right-hand one when it prepared to deploy its stun net. The other grazed my cheek with an MP round.

My shotgun entangled the stun net and clanged off the sec-bot. I dove and rolled so that the right-hand bot obstructed its partner's line of fire. An MP round ricocheted into my right leg. I aimed my revolver and sent an AP round through the firing sec-bot. I took out the second when it maneuvered to fire on me.

I wiped my bleeding cheek and held my bandana against it. My leg hurt and would be bruised. I pried open the access panels of both sec-bots with my bayonet and scrambled a few circuits before checking my watch. Almost out of time. I spotted several retreating engineers and the abandoned industrial forklift-bot. The blazing-red radioactive symbol marked a two ton canister resting on the floor in front of it.

I ran forward and set the explosive for triple delay setting, 13.5 seconds, and slapped it onto the industrial-bot's hydrogen fuel tank. My bruised leg didn't slow me much as I ran back toward the door. "Armored access door to reactor area, lower in five seconds." I cocked my revolver, and sent four AP rounds at the canister. Two deflected off. Two penetrated. When the door ratcheted down, I ran.

The lights dimmed after the muffled explosion. I ignored my throbbing leg while sprinting back to McAllister.

She was standing against the wall. "About time. Three security out there."

"How are they deployed?" I pulled a bandage from my belt pouched and slapped it on my cheek. "How're they armed?"

"MP carbines," she said. "They're outside trying to override my lockout."

"I used my explosive. Can you cut the lighting in here?"

"That'll be easy. I just scrammed their online reactor." She tapped at a console. "They're on backup generators and battery reserve. With any luck, it'll go critical after they restart it. Want their lights out, too?"

"No. We want to see them."

"What if they have infrared?"

"They're cheap here," I said. "Minimal equipment."

McAllister grinned as our lights faded. "Theirs are strobing."

"Okay, you call it. I'll take the center and right. You get left."

"Counting down," she said. "Three, two, one, entrance access door, open."

We achieved complete surprise. Their uniforms couldn't withstand buckshot, let alone laser blasts.

"They've locked out the shuttle," McAllister said. "Not good." She pulled her computer clip and attached it.

"We'll never make it on foot," I said, looking down the strobing transport corridor. "Not on time." I dragged the one surviving sec-specs to the cart and threatened her. "Get it running or join your friends."

The C3 sec-spec was bleeding from her abdomen and shoulder. "Warp-screw you," she spat.

"One brave one in the lot," I said, trying to ignore the pulsing lights.

McAllister smiled. "No need. Get in."

The C3 slumped. I pulled her up by the hair. "Crax are busy killing marines and civilians. Here you are defending them." I took her MP pistol and threw her down. "Hope you can live with your treachery." My brass knuckles broke her jaw. "Six minutes." We sped away.

"That blood'll give us away," said McAllister, glaring at my cheek. "As if your R-Tech cap and button uniform wasn't bad enough."

I removed the patch from my face while dabbing a fresh one over the blood stain on my shoulder. "Still bleeding?"

"Barely," said McAllister. "Enough to show."

"Here." I handed her a tube of skin-seal.

She applied it. "Where'd you get this?"

"From the LLTV first aid kit. How'd you get this running?"

"Same program that enabled our system voice command. It should self-erase in about forty minutes. We should be on our way before then." She handed back the skin-seal. "Should hold."

"We'd better be." We sped out of the strobing shuttle corridor section. "They're getting organized. And if your reactor trick works..."

"Looks like we may have company," McAllister said after examining the onboard monitor. "Shuttle, slow to thirty percent."

I checked the screen. "Two security. Damn, it could get rough. Maybe not." Most of the security team's response demonstrated training equal to Kent O'Vorley's. "Should we risk contacting Guerrero?"

McAllister spoke into her collar. "Party Four, are you in position?"

"Affirmative, Party Five," replied Guerrero without delay over McAllister's implant and my com-set. "With our new found friend."

"Associate One?" McAllister asked.

"No word," Guerrero replied. "Things are happening around us."

"Acknowledged. Out." McAllister examined the shuttle's chronometer. "Three minutes, fifty seconds." She replaced the power pack in the butt of her laser carbine. "Shuttle, one-hundred percent."

Ca-chunk! McAllister watched as I pumped a shell into the chamber. "We won't be able to talk our way past those two security." She nodded. "I'll run interference. You watch our back. If we run into any sec-bots, you hammer them with your laser." I handed her the lifted MP pistol. "Here's a backup."

The shuttle slowed. "You get the one approaching," I said. "I'll take the other."

Before the shuttle stopped I raised my shotgun and fired twice. The buckshot took out the unprepared man. McAllister knocked hers down with her second blast. We leapt from the shuttle and made it into the corridor. Station personnel scrambled to get out of our way. I was able to load two shells.

Crack-Crack! *Crack-Crack-Crack*! Two sec-specs had taken cover near the maintenance room we had to get past to reach the hangar. "Keep behind me." I ran forward and exchanged fire. One fell. The other hit me with two rounds. A sharp pain knocked me off stride. I stumbled and unloaded on him before he could do any more.

McAllister caught me under the shoulder. "Keesay, how bad?"

"Took rounds in the thigh. Didn't penetrate." I hobbled forward, then continued in a galloping run toward the last cross-hall. Ahead, two more security blundered into view.

McAllister burned them before they recognized their peril. "I'll take lead."

"No." I loaded a shell as I galloped. "Take out that camera. Watch our back." She did, and we made it to the hangar area. Shouts, screams and the cracking of MP fire echoed from within the shattered entryway. Arctic air rushed past us.

Inside we encountered a melee between pilots, ground crews, maintenance and engineering techs. At least fifty fought across the entire hangar.

"Which shuttle?" I asked.

"We're on the far right," came over my com-set. "Hurry!"

A fighter hovered before accelerating through the gaping hangar doorway.

"Let's just run for it," I said.

McAllister was wide-eyed. "Go!" she yelled, tearing past. "Crax behind us!"

I didn't bother to look. I simply tried to keep pace.

The fighting raged with fists, stun batons, makeshift clubs. It was impossible to tell who was on Boyd's side. McAllister was almost there, with me ten yards behind. The shuttle ramp was extending when I got blindsided. I went down hard with a brawny engineering tech on me, grappling for my shotgun.

He'd succeeded in tearing it from my grip before rolling away, bellowing. He'd dropped my shotgun and came to one knee, struggling with a brown-furred mass gnawing into the base of his neck. Somehow, the tech had snagged the Chicher's tail, holding the deadly tail blades at bay.

I grabbed my shotgun and rammed my bayonet into the engineering tech's chest, but not before he'd slammed the Chicher to the floor. I grabbed the stunned diplomat by his harness and ran for the shuttle. McAllister and Kalger stood atop the ramp. Instead of urging me forward, they sent a rain of laser fire over my head. I didn't have to guess why. A line of caustic bubbling burned alongside my path up the ramp.

Kalger yelled, "He's in!"

We all staggered and fell to the floor as Guerrero lifted off. McAllister managed to close the hatch before anyone tumbled out.

I rolled over to see the Chicher writhing in agony. "Pain meds!" I shouted. "First aid kit!" Kalger crawled on all fours to comply.

"McAllister, get over here," I said. Along the Chicher's ribcage a fist-sized hole frothed. I recognized the caustic stench. "Hurry."

The diplomat stared at me, eye-to-eye, and chattered something. I couldn't hear, so I leaned closer.

The Chicher chattered a short pattern, three times. It was strained. His smashed translator dangled from its harness. He beckoned me closer. I leaned in and his jaws shot forward. His teeth pierced my neck, but his jaws didn't close. He fell back before I could respond.

I sat up. Kalger shoved something in my lap. The diplomat's ears and face were drawn back in agony as he squealed. I took his hands. "Hang in there, Diplomat. Pain meds, man!" His tail curled around my leg.

Kalger took back the meds and injected two emergency doses.

"That should help, Diplomat," I said. I spoke in Chicher, "Help, yes."

The diplomat chattered the same short phrase as before, three times before clenching his teeth. His tail tightened, as did his handgrip. Then he fell limp.

"Acid got his innards," said Kalger.

"Brilliant observation," I snarled, causing Kalger to back away. McAllister was nowhere to be found. But Skids sat strapped to a nearby seat, taking the horrid scene in. I took a breath. "I'm sorry, Skids."

"Better stow yer gear and get seated," warned Kalger. "I'll show you where you can lay yer friend."

I lifted the diplomat by the harness, mindful of the acid.

Kalger grabbed my shotgun. "Darn brave alien," he said. "Interestin' death ritual."

CHAPTER 39

The use of modular docks established a more rapid system of expansion across the galaxy. A series of specially designed ships travels to a destination. Upon arrival, each ship's aft thrust engine section and forward cascading engine compartment detach from the vessel's central hull section. Engineers and construction-bots weld center sections together, forming a functioning dock. The forward and aft engine sections then unite for a return trip.

The modular docks require higher degrees of maintenance and the return trips are difficult on crews as ship facilities are limited. The price endured for the ability to swiftly establish distant footholds.

The gravity plate's strength fluctuated between 80 and 110 percent during the rough ride out of the atmosphere.

I asked Kalger, "Grav control's shot. How old is this shuttle?"

He held his stomach. "Shoulda known better than to eat before boarding this ol' boat." He burped. "Was refurbished before her trip out three years ago."

I said to Skids, "Stay here," and went forward, entering a cabin lined with cold sleep tubes.

A med tech with a curly mop of hair and straight, manicured beard, smiled. "Specialist," he nodded.

"Thanks for all the help." I brushed past him.

"Heard you were a real Crax killer," said the med tech. He shook his head. "Saw more running than killing."

I turned. "In a minute you're gonna be doing more bleeding than grinning."

"Whoa there, fellas," called Kalger, lumbering into the tight area. He put his hand on the med tech's shoulder. "Stenny, you don't wanna mess with this fella. And you, Specialist, probably don't wanna piss off Tech Stenny here."

I checked my temper and strode out. I heard Kalger telling him about my buddy, the dead Chicher. I climbed the access ladder and continued forward into the cockpit where Guerrero sat at the controls.

"Keesay, got an open seat," she said. "How's the diplomat?"

I plopped into the co-pilot seat. "Dead," I said. "Situation?"

"Sorry." She didn't look up from the controls. "McAllister is down with the cascading engine. Engineering Tech Popova is in the rear getting the most she can out of the thrust engine."

"One engine?"

She nodded. "And it's an old one. We're tailing Boyd and four of her squadron. Two yachts launched ahead of them. I think they destroyed the second shuttle on the ground." She glanced my way. "Heard the Crax are scrambling fighters. Five station fighters are forming up with them." She checked the controls. "We may be joining the diplomat very soon."

"Those fighters on the ground looked like military trainers."

"Tech Kalger informed me of that. At least they have weapons."

McAllister announced over the intercom, "Eighteen minutes till the cascading engine will be cycled."

"Acknowledged," said Guerrero. "Following escort. Twelve minutes until we're aligned for Tallavaster."

"Rogue One to Rebel One." It was Boyd. "Tug destroyed yachts on approach. Two friendlies on your six. We'll get you through."

"Acknowledged, Rogue One," said Guerrero before turning to me. "We couldn't do anything about it if they were hostile."

I scrutinized the display. The orbital platform came into view over the horizon. "Tug accelerating. Moving away. Five hostiles, possibly nine, if those four shadows are Crax. On intercept course." I cautiously manipulated the display.

Guerrero reached over and tapped. "Here. This rotates the tactical display."

"Thanks," I said. "Two closing on our tail. Four bogies exiting the atmosphere in pursuit." I watched. "Friendlies turning to engage."

"Tech Popova," called Guerrero. "Any more?"

"Negative," she replied. "Maximum thrust, plus three percent."

"One Behemoth class transport in orbit," I said. "No Crax vessels."

"Rogue One to Rebel One," said Boyd. "Good luck. Rogue Two with me. Rogue Three, Four and Five, cover Rebel One."

"Two friendlies are splitting off," I said. "Vectoring toward the Behemoth." I worked the display. "Three shadows appear to be leaving enemy formation."

"Going to protect any Crax ships they might be harboring," said Guerrero.

"Correct," I said, adding the understatement, "but one Crax and five trainers might be too much for our escort to handle." I watched the display. "Looks like a real dogfight behind us." Fighters disappeared from the screen. "Three fighters left. Two are friendlies. What happened on the ground, Guerrero?"

She continued to monitor, but answered. "Apparently Boyd made contact with some loyal ground crews. They loaded and fueled the fighters, yachts and shuttles. Word must have gotten out and a group of maintenance and engineering techs arrived, at first to inquire. Then fighting broke out. I think communications were down because only a few more reinforced the bad guys."

"It'll go hard for those left behind," I said. "Gar-Crax were on our tail into the bay. Fists and clubs won't do it."

"I think that many were looking for a chance," said Guerrero. "Kalger said they're pretty isolated here. Information is controlled."

"I could do without that med tech," I said. "A real Thud."

Guerrero smiled at my R-Tech putdown. "That's another story. Look! Boyd and her wingman are making a run on the Behemoth." She manipulated the controls and intercepted a visual relay from the orbital platform.

"They'll only get one pass," I said. "Those chasing Crax are just out of range." Boyd and her wingman split. One angled toward the aft section, the other the forward ventral.

"Trainers," I said. "Only armed with a rotary cannon and a single pulse laser." Both friendlies opened fire just before the Crax. "They're not pulling up!"

"They can't," said Guerrero, "they're hit and out of control."

Fiery explosions erupted against the Behemoth's hull. "For I am already on the point of being sacrificed," I mumbled. "The time of my departure has come. I've fought the good fight. I've finished the race. I've kept the faith."

"What?" asked Guerrero.

"Second Timothy," I said. My mother said one day I'd be glad I memorized verses. I'm getting tired of praying for the dead." I adjusted the display. "Boyd, she turned out to be okay."

"You were right about her," sighed Guerrero, before pointing out, "secondary explosions in the aft section. She's beginning to roll."

I sat up. "One must've rammed internal docking control." We watched the enormous transport's engines flame out. A maneuvering thruster flared to life only to ignite leaking fuel.

"She's tumbling toward the planet," I said before several escape pods rocketed from the Behemoth. "Fewer crew. That won't help."

"The tug will have a tough time saving her and any cargo." Guerrero's attention diverted. "They've got their troubles. We've got ours."

I re-evaluated the display. "Three friendlies angling in. Three peeling off to intercept. Doesn't look good. Time until intercept?"

Guerrero altered our course. "Now five minutes till alignment. Seven until cascading is cycled."

"Crax accelerating," I said. "Guess this was a bad idea. Wait!" I checked the screen. "A bogie just slid in behind the Crax and opened up." A second followed suit. "They've crippled her!"

"Rebel One," called an unfamiliar voice. "Way is clear. Going to help our friends." The two fighters peeled away from the damaged Crax.

"We can outrun him now," replied Guerrero. "Many thanks. We won't forget."

"What's that, Guerrero?"

"Spike in planetside radioactive readings," she said.

"McAllister," I called. "You must've convinced a reactor to go critical."

"Why, Specialist Keesay," she replied, "you sound surprised."

Med Tech Stenny shook his head. "I can't believe how many pilots and ground crew turned on Capital Galactic."

"How many were former military?" Guerrero asked.

"They'd just shipped half of their competent security," said Stenny. "Engineers, too." He looked to Popova, a young Engineering Tech. "Remember that new sec-spec? Toaver, what an asshole."

I held my tongue. Stenny was a rude bastard himself.

"Nasty," she agreed. "Aggressive." She swiped a patch of dusty curls from her face. "I bet he was the one who sexually assaulted Tech Crayonit."

McAllister hissed, signaling she'd had enough. "I'm sure Keesay bayoneted him. We can check the blood on his blade later." She looked to me before stepping forward. "So, Medical Technician Stenny, how competent are you with the cold sleep equipment?"

"Who put you in command?"

"I did," I said. "Answer her question."

"Do it, Stenny," Kalger warned. "You don't wanna mess with this R-Tech."

"I'm trained on the equipment. I've been through seven simulations in administering proper prep dosages for cold sleep." He glared at me. "Although I could always screw up, by accident."

"Keesay dies, you die," McAllister said, presenting her menacing smile. "And, I've already programmed the system. Anything happens to me, this old interstellar shuttle will die too. Guess who goes with it?"

"Believe her," Kalger said. "You saw what her code did to the station. Can you match that?"

"Why'd Boyd tap you?" asked McAllister.

Stenny replied, "Think about it. Everyone in science and medical is hard core Capital Galactic. I'm the only one with skills who'd be willing to warp-screw them without question."

"I can see why you weren't popular," I said, trying not to sneer. "Neither am I. McAllister has more reason to hate my guts than you could ever dream up. She's learned to live with it. We do our task." I looked around. "We don't have enough stores and recycling capacity for all of us. Only three can stay awake. You'll prep Skids, myself, Popova, and Kalger, and see that we successfully enter cold sleep."

Tech Stenny crossed his arms and stared at the ceiling.

"Now yer pissin' me off," Kalger said. "Grow up, boy. These ain't just a group of refugees. Get with the program. The Crax are tryin' to make us extinct."

"McAllister," I said, "you're a genius. If Stenny can figure the equipment, so can you. We won't risk Skids. You and Guerrero will stay awake with him." I drew my revolver and thumbed back the hammer. "You, Tech Stenny, come on back with me. No reason for the others to watch."

Stenny's jaw dropped. He looked to Kalger for support.

Kalger held up his hands. "I warned ya. Can't say I blame'em."

Tech Popova jumped between Stenny and me. "You can't." She was shaking. Her brown eyes wide. "He'll do it. Won't you, Stenny?"

"I'll do it," agreed Stenny. "Yes. No problem."

"There is a problem," I said. "I don't trust you. I trust McAllister to try harder."

"Ludmilla," said Kalger, taking Popova's arm. "Stenny messed with the wrong crowd."

"Bide," McAllister said to me. "Tech Stenny will teach me everything he knows. I'm always interested in acquiring new skills." Stenny sighed. "Don't relax just yet. After you instruct me, I'll apply my new knowledge." Her grin transformed from menacing to sinister. "On you first. If things go well, you'll live." She looked around. "Fair enough?"

Stenny sat forward. "Yes! That's fair." He gulped afterward.

One week later, Stenny, Kalger and Popova were in cold sleep. I was on the platform, ready to be knocked out before the tube insertion. "Think she can go four for four, Skids?"

McAllister's impish smile preceded her question. "What makes you think I went three for three?"

Skids shot a worried look at the red-headed engineer.

McAllister laughed. "Keesay didn't teach you how to identify a joke?"

"He never jokes when he talks about you, Engineer."

"Only when you're not around, right, Keesay?"

"Skids, do me a favor. Beat her at chess, would you?"

"Sure thing," he said. Then he met McAllister's gaze. "I'll try."

"Make sure she maintains my equipment."

"We'll clean your guns." She pulled a needle and calibrated the dosage. "Remember, we won't risk bringing you out until we land on Tallavaster. So, my face won't be the first thing you see."

"Six months from now. Until then." I nodded to Guerrero. "You're in charge. Keep an eye on them." I winked at her. "I know. You're welcome."

I woke up retching with nothing to spit up. Every nerve ending ached.

"It doesn't get any better, Specialist Keesay. Does it?"

I knew that voice. "Skids?" I rolled over. A nurse helped me sit up. "Careful," I said, every orifice throbbing.

"Specialist Keesay," said Skids, "you'll never believe it. Both sides almost shot us down. But Guerrero got us through!"

I squinted. McAllister and Guerrero stood nearby. I heard Stenny across the hall, moaning. I forced mirth through my dry vocal cords. "Glad you made it, Tech Stenny. If for no other reason than to know how terrible you feel."

"My eighth time," Kalger chimed in from nearby. "It never gets better. You okay, Ludmilla?"

She groaned in response.

I took a second to get my bearings.

"Guess who's here, Specialist!" said Skids. "Guess!"

"Michael, I'm sure he isn't up to guessing."

I rubbed my eyes and refocused. "Sorry, Instructor Watts. I thought you were Guerrero. You made it!" I felt dizzy. The nurse laid me back down.

"We must go, Kra," Lori Watts said. "Michael and I." She leaned over the table and hugged me. "I can't thank you enough." She kissed my cheek and whispered, "I'll never be able to repay you."

I looked her in the eye. "I had some help. And Skids mostly took care of himself."

"Not if you hear him tell it."

"He's a fine young man," I said.

Skids frowned. "I didn't beat Engineer McAllister."

"He did stalemate me once," McAllister said with hands on her hips and sporting a new French-braid hairdo.

Skids shrugged his shoulders. "Engineer McAllister wasn't paying attention."

Watts leaned close and whispered again. "My husband hand-picked you to save our son. He knew you would. And my husband would say you preserved a chance for *our* future."

The stress on 'our' caught my attention.

She stared deep into my eyes. "My husband knows about such things. But I know what I know." She held her son close. "Thank you."

I fought back the nausea. "You're welcome."

"We have to go," Watts said. She held up the bust I'd carved of her son. It seemed like ages ago. "We won't forget."

Its presence went right over my head. I extended my hand, and struggled to hold it steady. "Skids, you're okay. Don't let anyone say otherwise." I managed a smile and wink.

Skids shook my hand through tears. "You're great."

"Take care of your mother."

"Take care of yourself," Lori Watts said.

My mind raced as I replayed what Watts said. I was too ill to concentrate so I curled up and tried to sleep.

Two days later a marine major and someone dressed in a gray quasi-military uniform debriefed me. Had to be Intelligence.

"Any questions, Security Specialist Keesay?"

"Yes, Major Voisard. Several." He sat silently. "What happened to the

Kalavar?"

"I do not know."

"How did Instructor Watts get hold of a bust I carved?"

"I cannot verify that she had such an item. If she did, it may have been a replica."

"Where are they?" Both men sat silent. "Are they still planetside?"

"They looked at each other. The intel man spoke. "We cannot verify if they have yet to depart."

I didn't trust a word he'd uttered. "But the blockade around Tallavaster?"

"Has gaps," said the major. "Anything else?"

"What became of the Chicher diplomat's body?"

The intel man spoke up. "Turned over to the Chicher enclave. Different pack." He shrugged. "They're cut off too. Best we could do."

"Understood," I said. "My equipment, sir?"

The major called into his collar, "Private, the security specialist's equipment." A marine entered carrying my uniform, firearms, belt, everything.

"You've been drafted," the major said. "We took the liberty of dying your security uniform to Marine camouflage. It's higher quality that we could issue."

After what I'd survived I knew that was an understatement. "Thank you," I said to the major, and thought back to Field Director Simms. I examined my uniform. The brown, gray, green design appeared of moderate quality. I stood and saluted.

"No need to salute, Keesay," Major Voisard said. "Untrained conscripts outnumber trained military. Just follow orders." They stood. "Dress in here. Your squad leader is waiting outside."

"Understood, sir." I watched them leave, then dressed. I slipped the breastplate on under my coveralls and buttoned my armored vest over it all. I checked my equipment before stowing the hospital coveralls and canvas slippers in my satchel. Then I exited.

"Security Specialist Keesay," called a deep, booming voice. "Fancy meeting you in this part of the galaxy."

I did a double take. Then grew angry and sick. "Private." I looked closer. "Corporal Ringsar?"

"Pillar," he said. "A medical treatment center seems appropriate. Glad you're part of my squad." He recognized my disbelief. "Heard your name and urged my captain to request you."

"Why is that?"

He signaled me to follow him down a tan-painted cinderblock hall. "Things are tough out there. Going to get worse. Crazy or stubborn, doesn't matter. Told my captain you wouldn't break and run under fire." He puffed out his chest. "Prove me wrong and we'll finish that fight." He led me down some stairs. Each metal step reverberated with our booted steps.

"You're right," I said, stepping aside for a woman before exiting out the glass doors. Her stomach bulged under a loose blouse. My voice trailed off as I watched the woman. "I know how to fight."

Pillar laughed. "Too much time in space, Keesay. No birthing up there. Kind of reminds you what we're fighting for."

I spotted a black and yellow fallout shelter sign near the hospital entrance. "Correct." I squinted in the warm sunlight. It was shining down between the rows of cut stone and concrete buildings.

"Crying infants," said Pillar, "reminds me of some wimps in the trench line." Pillar snapped his head for me to follow him to the right. "Scuttlebutt is, Keesay, you're some kind of Crax-killing specialist. I'll have to hear about it."

"Who told you?" I asked, watching a mixture of diesel and humming, hydrogen-burning vehicles speed by.

"Some firebrand engineer. That's how I heard you were planetside. She wanted to know if I was the same marine that thumped you on the Mavinrom Dock."

"Figures." I looked up and down the street. The rows of buildings were of uniform block design, eight to ten stories tall. All unmarked. "Anywhere to eat? I've been in cold sleep. Just getting my appetite back."

He laughed. "Already trying to avoid field rations. Our rations really are field rations." He jerked his head, still chuckling. "This way. Hey, guess who'll be sharing your fox hole?"

I wasn't sure I wanted to know the answer. "His name better not be Stenny."

We'd hitched a ride to our forward position. The diesel tractor pulling the wagon rolled past fields of buckwheat, sorghum, and clover. Goat herds devoured the latter. Pillar did most of the talking, about his prowess on the battlefield and in the bedroom. I decided to interrupt him.

"Buckwheat," I said. "Good for honeybees."

"Huh? Bees? Negral's got beehives everywhere. Need them for the crops."

"I know. My uncle kept bees. Made a decent living off the honey."

"Hard to believe," Pillar said. "A couple years ago this planet was basically all rock and water. A few primitive lichens and algae. I heard the Phibs sold Negral some alien engineered bacterial strains. Metabolized rock, gave off organic wastes." He lifted his helmet and scratched his head. "I don't pretend to understand it. The initial bacteria had genes that limited the number of times it and its offspring could divide. Them Phibs have it down to a science."

"They should," I said. "A xenobiologist told me the Phibs have been in space as long as 60,000 years."

"There're some on the planet."

I was skeptical. "Have you seen any?"

"No. But I've seen a couple of the big crabs that serve them."

"Bahklack? Umbelgarri thralls?"

He nodded. "If they're around, and they're helping Negral establish Tallavaster, makes sense there're some here." He leaned close, so the farmer had no chance of hearing over the tractor's dieseling purr. "Hidden in the city are some Phib defenses. The Bahklacks maintain them."

"How big is New Birmingham?"

"Housing for forty thousand," he said. "Only about twenty-five thousand colonists though. Twice as big as Volsar and Sola Two."

"How many residents are in the field?"

"What, farming or defending?" He shrugged. "Defending, maybe fourteen thousand conscripts. A reinforced regiment of colonial marines." He looked up. "Getting close. We'll hold out longer than Volsar and Sola Two."

I looked ahead. Several tents and a series of trenches broke the otherwise flat terrain supporting endless fields. "How'd you get here?"

"Intel predicts we've got long hours of static defense ahead. I'll let your foxhole buddy tell you."

We hopped off the wagon and waved. The farmer waved back and continued past the defensive position.

"This way, Keesay." Pillar led me away from the sandbags and tents, down a stone stairway, into a large trench, and finally to an underground outpost. I saw hints of fortified concrete construction, but most of the ground was a layer of dirt on solid layers of gray rock. A young captain and middle-aged NCO stood near a table. Pillar saluted. I stood at attention.

The captain returned Pillar's salute. He looked to me.

"Sir," I said. "C4 Security Specialist Krakista Keesay, reporting." He was silent. "A major directed me not to salute officers."

Sergeant Trahk stepped forward and scrutinized me. "Salute or not. Follow orders without question and fight. That's your duty."

"Understood, Sergeant."

He removed my com-set. "Nice equipment, Keesay." He adjusted the settings. "This'll be hard to trace. Our platoon's name and call signal is White Mule." He continued to manipulate the settings. "Command is Channel A. Our frequency is Channel B. Rock Mole platoon to our left is Channel C. Copper Mink platoon is to our right. Channel D." He handed it back. "Alternate frequencies are A1, A2 and so on."

"Understood."

"Areas in the trench line marked in red paint, don't say anything important. Troop movements, dispositions. Got it?"

Those would be areas vulnerable to enemy eavesdropping. "Understood."

"How are you armed, Keesay?"

"Twelve gauge shotgun, .357 Magnum and .38 caliber revolver."

"Can you handle anything more advanced?"

"Yes, Sergeant. I am competent with MP pistols and carbines, and trained in light and medium-duty laser carbines. I also have a CNS modulator to nullify the Stegmar sounding."

The captain nodded and spoke up. "Corporal Ringsar informs us that you'll stand and fight. What combat experience have you?"

"Our transport was caught in a firefight on approach to the Zeta Aquarius Dock. We were boarded."

"You were successful in repelling boarders?"

"Unknown, sir. I was ordered to escort an important civilian to an escape shuttle."

"So," sighed Captain Ermot, "you haven't seen combat."

"Incorrect, sir." May as well toot my horn. "I wasn't counting, but estimate killed or incapacitated a dozen Stegmar. I killed or assisted in killing three elite Gar-Crax and four Gar-Crax while defending the transport and the civilian." He and Sergeant Trahk exchanged glances. "However, I was led to believe that the majority of the boarders were reserve troops."

"What was the transport?" asked the captain. "And who was the civilian?"

Pillar knew I'd departed on the *Kalavar*, so I was willing to provide that much. "Civil transport *Kalavar*. I was not given the civilian's name."

"You were part of Security on the transport?"

"Correct, Captain. That is all I can say."

He frowned and glared.

"If you want to know more," I said, "Major Voisard will have to authorize it."

All three pairs of eyes rose at my statement. "That will be all," Captain Ermot said. "Corporal, issue Keesay a medium duty laser carbine. We've enough recruits with old-style assault rifles. Show him the map, and give him the tour."

Ringsar saluted. "Yes, sir."

Pillar handed me a medium-duty laser carbine. "The captain wants everyone to have some ranged firepower." He handed me a helmet, backpack, bedroll and canteen before leaving the storage bunker. "Okay, Keesay. Point the direction of the three pillboxes."

Despite standing in a seven-foot trench, I pointed three different directions.

"And HQ? Good. Our tank-bot? Good, Keesay. Even I had to think on that one." He smiled and put his hands on his hips. "And your assigned position?"

"That way," I said, pointing south. "It's the only place we haven't toured. And I haven't spotted a known face yet."

"Right, Keesay. Let's go."

We trudged, retracing some of our steps. The trench walls showed signs of mechanical digging and high-energy laser slicing, without a doubt A-Tech, Umbelgarri. A foot or so of compact soil lined the rims. What had eroded, formed a muddy trench floor. Carved or emplaced stone along the trench floor provided steps for firing positions along the wall. Scattered aluminum ladders provided easier exit and entrance to the trench line.

"White Mule defends a one-kilometer front," said Pillar. "You're on the end of the line. Next to you will be the Rock Mole platoon. Weak outfit."

"Thanks," I said. "We're stretched thin as it is."

"You know the fallback position and rally points?"

"I do," I said, and named them off.

We made it to the end of our assigned trench line. Pillar bellowed, "O'Vorley! Front and center."

The muddy face of Security Specialist Kent O'Vorley emerged from a tunnel. He looked as surprised as me.

"I'll leave you two little girls to get reacquainted," said Pillar. He turned. "Moorsheen, you're on duty."

"Kra!" called the young sec-spec. He removed his helmet and gave a mile-wide grin.

I extended my hand. "Security Specialist Kent O'Vorley." We shook, then patted each other on the shoulder. Kent looked youthful but tired, except his eyes. They were dark and held understanding beyond his years. Nothing like our first meeting back on the Mavinrom Dock. I wondered if my eyes mirrored his, or worse.

Kent couldn't stop grinning. "Pillar warned he had a new recruit lined up. The last was Moorsheen, a marketing and sales analyst. Let's go inside."

He led me through a three-by-three foot opening made of rock and cinder blocks. After the small entryway, we took a narrow set of steps down about eight feet. A small room had been carved out of the rock. The hanging chemical lantern cast shadows, emphasizing the hewn walls.

"Sturdy construction," I said, before sitting down.

"Excavation." O'Vorley sat down next to me and rested his back against the stone wall. "Thirty centimeters of soil, then rock. All this was carved and tunneled several months before the invasion. Or so I'm told."

"How'd you get here? Mavinrom is a long way off."

"We were hit by a Crax fleet. They destroyed half the station, but we drove them off. Mavinrom was a staging area. A battle group was preparing for departure when the attack came."

"You don't speak of it as a victory."

"A Primus heavy cruiser led the attack. Took out two battleships, one battle cruiser and a heavy carrier. We held our own against the Selgum Crax. I think some new ship armor. But by the time the Primus was destroyed only a monitor and several escorts survived."

"And the Crax? What about them?"

"They recalled the boarding troops on the dock. Many of their ships were damaged, almost half escaped." He stared off into space a moment, reliving fragments. "Most of the surviving dock personnel were offloaded before the second attack came. They finished the job. Destroyed the dock. Wiped out the mining operation."

"And they shipped you here?"

He nodded. "A fast transport. I heard it was destroyed in orbit when the Crax attacked Tallavaster." O'Vorley paused. I knew he was recalling lost faces. "Pillar and a few other marines, and nineteen station personnel came here with me." He glanced up through the rock to the sky. "One pilot told me they're pretty thick up there now. How'd you get through?"

I shrugged. "I was in cold sleep. Probably because we'd commandeered a CGIG long-transport shuttle. They're working with the Crax." His eyes widened. "That's the truth."

I told him of the combat aboard the *Kalavar*, and the escape to and from the Capital Galactic quarantined planet. I paused. "Don't think the CGIG corporate heads ever read Machiavelli."

"Name's familiar," said Kent.

"Ancient author of politics and strategy. One of his suggestions mentioned when dining with the devil, bring a long spoon."

"You think Capital Galactic cut a deal with the devil?"

"The Crax are close enough."

"Kra," O'Vorley said. "Thanks. I never understood why you looked out for me on the Mavinrom Dock." His voice trembled in a hoarse whisper. "It was a nightmare. The Stegmars tore us limb from limb. The Crax had shields." His back stiffened. "The marines took it to them. You got one to train me. Or I'd never have survived."

"I try to do what I think is right. This time it worked out. You don't know how glad I am." Now I struggled. "Some of the decisions I've made cost lives."

"We're in a war," Kent said, his eyes filled with empathy. "We can only do our best to survive and win it."

"Easy to say," I said, pushing faces of the dead back into hidden corners in my mind.

"We'll get our chance soon, I think," Kent said. "They took the two other colonization cities. I've spoken to a few refugees. The Crax used a kind of neutron explosive. Like a tactical nuke, but high radiation, short duration. Kills defenders, but leaves buildings intact."

"Is that why we're entrenched eight miles outside the city?"

"Could be. General Yakumi planned some radical tactics. Trenches. Mixing R-Tech arms and I-Tech. I saw old-style, towed artillery and what I think was fission artillery shells just behind the Mink position."

"Chances of survival are pretty grim?"

"Maybe not." He led me back to the entrance. "Crab aliens supervised the digging of the trench network, or so Pillar said." O'Vorley lifted a fitted section of rock. He pointed, and I looked at a dull metal rod imbedded there. "Some kind of shield tech, like the Crax." He replaced the floor slab. "Captain calls them static defense screens. A-Tech, but crude he said. Don't try to cross an activated one. They surround the artillery and pillboxes. Most bunkers like ours have one."

"So when the nukes fly, we hide in here and pray we don't get buried."

"That's the plan. When they send the ground troops, we rise and resist."

"I showed him my CNS modulator."

"Got mine last week. We're not supposed to talk about them."

"They work," I said. "You've heard the sounding?"

O'Vorley nodded slowly. "On the Mavinrom Dock. I could hardly think, let alone aim and shoot."

"This'll even the odds."

Someone tramped down the bunker steps. "Colonist Carver Potts?" I said. "You made it!"

"Refugee," he corrected. "That red-headed engineer recognized me. Said you were in town."

"What happened to the *Kalavar*? Who else made it?"

His face twisted and he bit his lip. "To you, this'll sound kind of funny. It's classified?" He looked to O'Vorley. "Brought supper." He hefted a sack and chuckled. "Field rations again."

O'Vorley groaned and stood. "Don't you ever get tired of that joke? I'll let you two eat and catch up." He turned to me. "Don't want to leave Moorsheen on watch alone. Still trying to train him. We can finish later." Carver Potts sat down and handed Kent a set of binoculars as he went by.

"Specialist Keesay, you're a tough one," said Potts while pulling several pouches and a long loaf of bread from the sack. "We'll see how tough you are after a few weeks of this."

He set to work. "Hand me those plates." He tore the bread in half and set one portion aside. Then he mixed a pouch of golden liquid with a dried powder, making a paste. He poured a dark syrup in it. "May I borrow your blade?"

I handed it to him.

He whistled. "Where do you get your equipment?"

I shrugged. "Here and there in my travels."

He sliced the bread in halves and applied the pasty mixture. "It's okay the first dozen times. It's filling." He offered my quarter portion.

I tasted a wheat bread with wheat paste, a hint of apples and an unusual, not sugary syrup. "Kind of sweet."

"Syrup comes from the sorghum. What the goats don't eat. That's one of the other staples. Goat meat, goat milk, goat cheese, and sometimes honey." He began to eat, speaking between bites. "We've cal-packs in the bunker, but may need them if we get isolated."

I ate fast, and waited until Potts finished his meal. I handed him a canteen. "What happened to the *Kalavar*? Her crew?"

"Don't know much. I think some of the security recordings survived. Of course, they didn't share any with me, but I'll tell you what I can." He sat back. "After you left with the kid, we got in a firefight with some Crax and Stegmars. They got Mer. Winged the chief, but Club's reinforcements took them from behind, like you did." He held up a hand, then patted his slung firearm. "Unlike you, it took six with assault rifles."

"They killed Mer?"

"Yeah. They did. Then we got into condensed space with a bunch of them still on board. We got them all, but they got most of us." His eyes became distant. "Club went down in a firefight. DeLark finished the Gar that got her."

Potts's feet shifted, alternating. I don't think he was aware as he continued. "Had to climb over the Stegmar corpses to reach her body. The XO lured one Gar onto a tarp that he'd pissed on. Burnt out a section of the electrical system when he discharged a cable into it. Got caught in the backlash. Died of the burns, later." He nodded with strong affirmation. "But he drained that Crax's shield."

Potts began to rub his hands together. "Played cat and mouse for about ten hours. They getting us, we getting them. But without the Gar-Crax the Stegmars were pretty easy."

"Who survived? Tahgs, Benny? Who?"

"Yeah, Specialist Tahgs made it. Like I said, the chief, the captain, me, DeLark, some colonist kids. You called them Athena, Little Elvis, Chopper. A doctor, two maintenance techs, a med tech, an engineer, and a weapons tech from the *Roberts*. Sorry, I don't remember their names. I'm the only colonist that took up arms, and survived.

"Oh, and seven first-class passengers," he spat. "Hid and didn't fight." He rubbed his chin. "You know that priest? Lured a gang of Stegmars from those three kids. We never found him."

We sat until I broke the silence. "What about the *Kalavar*? Where is she?"

"I'm not sure," he said. "Hell of a busy trip here. Even the first-classers pitched in. Something about *Kalavar*'s structural integrity and call for decontamination." He scratched his head. "I helped a little with the grunt work, unloading pallets. While I was doing that, I think they pulled the engines and the weapons."

"I'd heard they spread a nasty microbe or two through the ventilation system," I said. "Sounds like they salvaged what they could."

"I think they cast her off into space. Maybe for retrieval, later. Told me to be quiet about the *Kalavar*. Anyone asked, I'm a refugee. That was just before the Crax came. And good thing we had time to unload." He thumbed his rifle. "Had twenty thousand of these on board. Bunch of the neck modules that quiet the Stegmars." He shook his head. "A bunch of other stuff. Even frozen little fish. There was another Negral transport in orbit unloading too. Weird name. Something *Boxcar*."

"The *Peripatetic Boxcar*?"

"That's it. Mer owned it too?" He took a swig from his canteen. "You were buddies with Mer. That's how you knew?"

"No. My cousin Oliver's a turret gunner on her. Travels to the outer colonies. I think he knew Mer better, and got me a contract with Negral."

"Heard it came from Umbelgarri territory. But I'm not so sure." He saw my apprehension. "Unloaded its cargo. Loaded food stores and days gone before the Crax attacked."

"I'm glad you made it," I said.

"Well thanks, Specialist. Never thought you liked me much." He rubbed his stubbled jaw.

"I didn't. But you proved yourself on the *Kalavar*."

"I won't claim to be the straightest man alive. But anyone who doesn't step forward now." He stretched. "I've got another few hours of watch. Keep looking for relief. They say help's on the way."

"Don't they always say that?"

"You're a true optimist, Specialist." He rubbed his eyes. "Maybe you're right. But with all this cargo they dropped. If you listen to the right people."

"You the only *Kalavar* refugee planetside?"

"Well, I saw McAllister. She was programming our tank-bot. That purple-eyed Tahgs is somewhere in town. The colonist children, and DeLark. He's with the Iron Turtle platoon." He rubbed his chin and scratched his neck. "Heard Captain Tilayvaux signed on as XO with a damaged escort carrier. Your chief got a robotic leg. I think he and the rest of the *Kalavar* crew went with the captain. Come to think of it, maybe that's where they transferred the weapon systems and engines."

He inched toward the steps. "Glad you'll be in the trenches next to me."

"I'm just glad to be alive."

"Me, too," said Potts. "O'Vorley's okay, but next to Pillar, I think I'd rather have you at my back."

"You've made it this far. You can't be a slouch."

"Well, while I watch, you pray for reinforcements."

I tried, but didn't sleep well. Too many faces. I did pray. I prayed for lost friends and comrades, surviving friends and comrades. I prayed for the traitors. That was hard. But couldn't bring myself to pray for the Crax. I finally dozed off, holding my neck, the diplomat's death chatter rattling in my thoughts.

CHAPTER 40

The introduction of organisms on planets and moons identified for colonization is tightly regulated with infractions severely punished. Years of study and experimentation have resulted in establishment protocol. Ecosystems, inhabited by indigenous organisms complicate controlled efforts.

Ignoring microbes, human explorers have never succeeded in 100% control of species imported, be they plant or animal. Xenobiologists believe no alien colonization effort will ever escape contamination over an extended period.

Splat! My hand stung as I pulled it away from the bunker's rock wall.

"Got another one?" asked Potts.

I flicked away the smashed brown insect. "German cockroaches you say?"

"Yep. They've got little dark racing stripes on their heads." He looked around the bunker. "One of the unintended six-leggers on Tallavaster."

"Not counting the Stegmar." I checked my watch before sliding my helmet on. "My watch."

"Sure are punctual," said Potts.

"It's only been two days and I can hardly take Moorsheen in small doses. O'Vorley's been here longer." I rechecked my gear. "Seems hopeless. Like O'Vorley said, Moorsheen won't even try to learn."

"Yeah. Now the little bugger'll be in here with me."

"Correct. But you sleep like a rock so it doesn't matter how much he whines and complains." I waved and made my way out. I found Moorsheen huddled in the darkness. "You're relieved."

He jumped. "I was listening."

"Sure," I said. "Hush your voice. Give me the binoculars."

"Okay. My shift's over?" The marketing 'expert' looked around. "Good. It's cold out here tonight."

I watched my misting breath in the starlight. "I've endured worse."

He knew better than to challenge me on that. "Why do you carry your shotgun and the laser carbine?" asked the marketing analyst. "Kind of heavy and awkward."

"I've been caught with too little firepower too many times. This time I know bad guys will be coming."

"I wouldn't bother. They'll bomb us to oblivion first."

"Maybe. If they don't, I'll be ready. If they do..." I shrugged. "You should clean your rifle." A suggestion he was sure to ignore.

"O'Vorley just left for the Rock Mole boundary. Good night," he said before trudging away.

I extended the binoculars so that they periscoped over the top of the trench. I didn't bother looking before I pulled them down and moved a dozen yards to the left. Then I scanned. Nothing, even with the light intensifiers. Slogging footsteps approached. I drew my revolver.

"Six chambers," whispered O'Vorley.

"Falling rocks," I replied before Kent's silhouette approached. I rubbed my hands together. "Snuck up on Moorsheen again. I'm becoming convinced he's worse than useless."

"Tell me I wasn't that bad," said O'Vorley.

"I'm not saying either of us is that good. But at least we try."

O'Vorley sighed. "Not like those Groundhogs out there."

"They must be good," I said. "Haven't seen one since I've been here."

"Doubt if you will, unless one is relieved. They hide out there for ten days at a time. No electronics. Just an optical scope and a .50 caliber sniper rifle."

"And their job is to pick off the enemy when they attack? Doesn't sound like retirement benefits in their future."

"Individuals, or their combat-bots," O'Vorley said. "Whatever they think their AP rounds can take out." We moved and surveyed. "Think we'll make retirement age?"

"So they'll die first," I said. "We'll be second."

"Unless they succeed in bombing the city. Then they'll be second and we'll be third."

"Or the lucky last."

"You're so cheery tonight, Keesay. Think it might rain some more?"

"You want me to get Moorsheen back out here?"

"Keesay!" boomed Pillar's voice. "You've got company." His hulking form sauntered down the steps. Only he could accomplish that hunched over.

I was up and buckling on my equipment belt. "Corporal?"

"He's decent, ladies," Pillar called over his shoulder. "Might try a mint, Keesay."

A small figure slid past him, then a second, taller one. I was tired and the light filtering down made it difficult. They were in civilian camouflage uniforms. One with a dull orange armband and the other with a dark blue.

"Specialist Keesay," said McAllister. "Living in a cave. Right at home."

"Unless you're planning on moving in," I said. "Tahgs?" I didn't recognize her at first. She'd cut her hair short. McAllister carried a satchel with computer equipment plus a laser carbine. Tahgs had a satchel and an MP sidearm.

Tahgs stepped forward. "Remember you promised me dinner some time?"

"Keesay," Pillar said, shaking his head. "How do you attract them?"

"Charm," voiced a bedroll. "Something they apparently don't teach Colonial Marines."

"You get up too, O'Vorley," Pillar said. "Engineer McAllister is here to check our equipment and update our tank-bot. You'll assist her."

"What about Potts or Moorsheen?"

"Farmer Potts? Salesman Moorsheen? The engineer would appreciate real assistance."

O'Vorley managed to slip into his coveralls under his blankets. He tugged on his boots and grabbed a canteen.

"You're young," Pillar said. "Keesay might want some privacy."

O'Vorley grabbed his helmet and carbine. "Sorry, Keesay."

McAllister said to O'Vorley, "I'll catch up with you in a minute."

"If you need any assistance, Keesay," leered Pillar.

I glared up at the marine. "Get lost, Corporal."

"Come on," said O'Vorley. "Remember what happened last time you messed with Keesay?"

Pillar turned. "Sure do. Laid you flat and sent him to the infirmary."

"How's that knee?" asked O'Vorley as he led the marine out. "Didn't you spend more time there than Keesay?"

"You want a transfer to Rock Mole?"

"Keesay," said McAllister. "Who in the galaxy haven't you gotten in a fight with?"

"How many have you had a civil conversation with?"

"You owe me, Keesay." She rested a hand on Tahgs' shoulder. "He's all yours. Half hour," she said before grumbling up the steps.

I ran a comb through my hair. "Sorry. I look like crap. This place is a mess."

"No, Keesay. This is a bunker. You look like a soldier in the field."

I activated another light and tied up bedrolls. "I really don't have much to offer for dinner but bread, cal-packs, and water."

"That's okay, Keesay," she said. "One thing this planet has is food. I think I've found most of it. Can't you tell?"

Her face did look fuller, but I'd attributed it to the haircut. Maybe her hips. "No."

She unshouldered a satchel. "Just as well it's dark in here. Anyway, I brought the meal."

I cleared the salvaged half pallet. "Our table."

She grabbed a crate. "Chair?" We sat. She began to pull food from her satchel.

"Potts told me you made it," I said. "How have you been?"

She averted her eyes. "The meds help. Let's not talk about it."

I changed topics. "What'd you bring?"

"Goat," she said. "Pretty basic this time."

"Overpaid last time, but it was worth it for your company. Then and now."

"McAllister said she fixed your account, whatever that means? Hope it's good."

I shrugged. "McAllister and I've been through a lot together. I wouldn't say we've bonded. But until the Crax are driven off, we have a common enemy."

"She said you saved her and almost saved Gudkov."

"You see her much?"

"A little. Her apartment is in the same building. It's almost like a ghost town. They spread out everybody who's left."

I nodded. "What assignment has Negral given you?" I began to arrange the food.

"Emergency med-unit records. Saw your name. McAllister mentioned she had an idea where you were posted. I asked if she could take me if she visited your platoon." Tahgs looked down and noticed everything was set. "Sorry."

"You brought it. Least I could do is help serve it."

"And eat it," she said. "I was surprised when McAllister agreed, even pulled some strings to get me out here."

"She's not as self-centered as she once was. What's in the bottle?"

"Some type of whiskey."

"One cup." I held up the chipped ceramic mug. "We'll have to share."

"No thanks." Tahgs pulled out a plastic pillbox. I handed her my canteen. "Can't mix this and alcohol." She swallowed. "My dosage is down to one quarter."

I pulled my bayonet and sliced the bread and made goat chop sandwiches. "They do make good bread."

"I saw Colonist Potts. Did he tell you what happened on the *Kalavar*?"

"Yes, Janice, he did."

She bit her lip. "It was horrible."

I slid over and put my arm around her. "Sure you don't want to talk about it?"

"It was terrible, Kra. They killed Benny, then Mer. The bodies. Even after we jettisoned them, the smell of blood." Her face twisted. "Rotting decay." She started to heave, but held it down.

I took her hands. "It's okay."

"No, it's not. Look at you. You saved us." Shaking while tears welled, she stared into my eyes. "I saw those Crax warriors. They came at you and you knew what to do. You didn't flinch." She looked away. "Nobody confirmed it to me, until McAllister, that Chief Brold ordered you to escort some cargo off the *Kalavar*. She said you and her did some bloody work. Wouldn't tell more." Janice clenched her fists. "Death all around and you moved on. I can't."

"I haven't moved on. I've tread water. Kept just ahead of it." I debated what route to take before gently squeezing her hands. "Besides the fact that I'm an R-Tech, and have such a radiant personality, ever wonder why McAllister took to me so well?"

"There's another reason? I thought she disliked you just a little more than everybody else. Because she couldn't intimidate you."

"Let me tell you a few things." She turned her head and waited for me to continue. I almost didn't start. "Janice, between you and me only. Some is classified, and I'll deny ever saying it. Understood?"

She nodded, curiosity rising.

"No sense wasting good food with good company," I said. "Let's eat while we talk."

I told her about the Colonization Riots and how I killed McAllister's fiancé. I told her about the shootout on the Mavinrom Dock. How a woman died because of me, and how I survived by crushing another man's skull. She, of course, knew about the time she was abducted by rogue security on the dock, but I mentioned it. I described how Mr. Habbuk and his marine escort died. I told her about how I slit Mr. B'down's throat, and how Ms. Jazarine died screaming. About Gudkov's death, those I killed on the quarantine planet, and the all friends I lost, especially the Chicher diplomat.

"How do you go on?" she asked. "How do you manage?"

"Faith. Prayer. It helps. Friends. But the memories haunt me, usually nightmares." I hadn't noticed my grip on her hands had tightened. "Morning always comes. Learn from the past. Work toward the future."

"Kra, I think I know where your cart might be. A warehouse in the ninth district. I think Chief Brold put your Bible in it before locking it."

"Really? My equipment?"

"I'm sorry, I meant to tell you right away."

"No," I said. "That's' okay." I reached into a pocket. "Here's the key. It's rigged otherwise." I smiled. "I think the chief had Club make duplicates."

"I know. Chief Brold said. He was laughing when he packed everything. He missed you. I know I did."

"I missed you, too." We held each other for a moment. "My equipment. The Bible's yours. Read some of it. Ecclesiastes, third chapter. It's good. Helped me in some tight situations."

"I can't take your equipment. The chief said some of it's pretty valuable. Wood on this planet is like—"

I cut her off. "Like a good friend. Being able to unload. To talk to you, and you listening. I've never told anyone like that."

"Thank you for confiding," she said. "I'm so happy. I thought you might not want to see me after." She stammered. "Well, when I..."

"How could I blame you? War changes things. Doesn't it?" Her hair bounced as she nodded. "Janice, tell you what. You harbor my equipment, and I'll carve you something."

"I've seen your work. How about a bust of yourself?"

"How about one of us?"

"Would you?"

A shadow darkened in the entrance. "You've got ten seconds to get decent," bellowed Pillar.

That let the air out of us. She slid the remaining food back into the satchel. "Keep it."

I helped Janice to her feet but tugged her down before her head hit the rock ceiling. She grimaced, and then grinned.

"Even I have to duck in here." I grinned back. "Thanks. A better lunch than I ever expected," I said before yelling. "Corporal, ever hear of military discipline? The Crax can hear you from high orbit."

"They're not coming today." He swaggered down and looked around. "I'm disappointed in you, Keesay."

I stared at Janice and kissed her on the cheek. "I'm not disappointed. I'm glad you came."

She hugged me and placed a quick kiss on my lips. "I'll try to visit again."

Pillar said, "You'd better because Keesay ain't due for leave."

"I still have my brass knuckles, Corporal."

He shook his head. "Don't know how you hooked a keeper."

I escorted Janice past the grinning marine. "She doesn't have any sisters on Tallavaster." McAllister leaned against a trench wall, talking to O'Vorley. "Thanks, McAllister."

She shrugged. "My good deed for the year."

Squeezing Janice's hand one last time, I said, "McAllister, don't let Tahgs hang around you too much."

After the two women passed the first bend in the trench line, O'Vorley spoke up. "Corporal Ringsar, got about ten minutes? You, too, Keesay."

We followed him into the bunker. "McAllister conveyed some information I thought you should know. She'd probably have told you, Corporal, but she had more work to do. Engineer McAllister altered the programming in our communications equipment as well as the tank. The Copper Mink's and the Rock Mole's equipment, too. The captain is meeting with Colonel Rakeshaw, so I was the next best thing."

We pulled up crates and listened.

"Volsar City's been destroyed. A hundred-megaton ground burst."

"That should put a crimp in the lizard's plans," Ringsar said. "A last-ditch gift from the resistance fighters. Reports said the lizards were staging a lot of troops and equipment there."

"They've broken the plague in Sola Two," O'Vorley said, looking at me. "About a day after Keesay's shuttle landed, intel uncovered a cell of collaborators. They sent medical information on the virus to the Crax. Any or all of our codes could be compromised. The Crax have been alerted to the inoculations against chemical weapons."

Ringsar ground his teeth. It took me longer to piece it together. "So they'll be protected?"

O'Vorley nodded. "Engineer McAllister says the glass and plastics plants just started producing, phosgene?"

I recalled the name from my study of WW I, but Corporal Ringsar spoke up. "That's an old one the Reptiles might not expect. Smells like mowed hay. Perfect for the fields." He rolled his eyes in thought. "Gets in the lungs, contacts moisture and produces hydrochloric acid and carbon monoxide. Not an immediate effect."

"That," said O'Vorley, "and if they get the chance." He stumbled over the name. "Dichlorethylsulphide."

Ringsar nodded. "Mustard gas. Blistering agent."

"Doesn't it accumulate in low areas, like trenches?" I asked. "We don't have any protections."

"There's an iodine-based solution for the mustard gas," said Ringsar. "If they have it. And a proper air filtration system will work against the phosgene."

"May explain a mentioned equipment delivery," O'Vorley said. "Anyhow, Engineer McAllister said they intend to launch on distant troop formations through artillery and missiles. Said the delayed onset would make it useless once they close."

"Unlike the specialized nerve agents we'd planned," said Corporal Ringsar. "Does the enemy know their informants have been compromised?"

O'Vorley nodded.

Ringsar frowned and shook his head. "I was wrong, Keesay. They'll be coming soon, maybe today." He stood. "I'll pass the word. Make sure you've got your shit together."

The night was cold and still. A beam of golden light flashed in the cloudless sky. Then three more. There, for an instant, arcing only a few degrees.

O'Vorley asked, "What was that?"

"Umbelgarri energy beams," I said. "Seen their likes around Zeta Aquarius."

The rumble of artillery began. Friendly, low flying missiles, streaked overhead. Distant sirens wailed.

"It's starting." O'Vorley took a steadying breath. "Nothing on my receiver."

"Wait," I said, adjusting my settings. "Crax are launching ballistic missiles. Some from orbit. Take cover." I switched to Channel B. "White Mule Command, Keesay reporting. Enemy jamming affecting some equipment."

"Acknowledged," replied Corporal Ringsar. "Command is getting through. They're launching nukes. Hold." Three seconds later he ordered, "Send a runner, Potts, to Rock Mole. Inform them to button up in their bunkers. Defense screens will be activated in two minutes. Yours will be kept off-line until he returns."

"Potts," I called. "Run to Rock Mole and order them to bunker. Nukes incoming. Then get back here yesterday!"

"Don't have to tell me twice," he said, already in a hunched sprint.

I watched the staccato Umbelgarri beams. A second wave of missiles raced not twenty feet overhead.

"Shouldn't we get under cover?" said O'Vorley. "Something's bound to get through."

"I feel guilty sheltering after sending Potts. Besides, our screen won't be up until I call."

"Orders," he said, taking my arm. "Better to be alive with a little guilt. Cover from above and some protection from radiation even without the Phib screen."

"Easy for you to say," I said, following his lead. I picked up the rock wedge that protected the screen device.

Moorsheen lay huddled in his bedroll. We waited. Potts scrambled in on all fours, gasping for air. "Mission accomplished."

"Command, this is Keesay. Activate our screen."

We sat in darkness. After a half hour the artillery's rumbling stopped. Two hours later we counted two deafening detonations.

Shortly after that, Captain Ermot called over the com-set. "Two enhanced radiation warheads detonated over New Birmingham. Five-megaton warheads. Our allies took out the big ones."

Potts listened over his hand radio. "What does that mean?"

"Neutron bombs," I said. "Minimal blast, excessive short-term radiation. Kills people but leaves buildings and equipment intact."

"How do you know that?" asked Moorsheen. "You haven't had military training."

"No, but I've spent time on an exploration shuttle with engineers and scientists familiar with war and the Crax. Pillar mentioned them. Plus, I used to read a lot."

Potts jammed his heel into Moorsheen, still huddled in his blankets. "If Keesay says they're firing flaming goat crap at us, believe him!"

Twenty-eight hours, or a little less than a day on Tallavaster, passed in silence. Boredom mixed with anticipation and sweat. The first few hours were filled with speculation, Moorsheen's whining concerns, and Potts's muttered threats. We took turns catnapping and whispering.

"Wish I had my deck of cards," I said to O'Vorley. "Tic-Tac-Toe, even Chicher-style doesn't last."

"Too dark right now," replied O'Vorley. "You notice Pillar's change?"

"What do you mean?"

"Well, maybe it's because we're soldiering under him. He's not as mean. When I found out he was leading my squad, I figured I'd get a daily thumping. We all would."

I shifted my seating position from a cross-legged to a crouch. "He's a Colonial Marine, trained for combat and killing. Without a war or an enemy, he'd settle on any target." I stretched my legs. "Now that he has one." I recalled the pregnant woman. "And a cause to fight for."

My com-set crackled to life. "Enemy forces are on the move," called Captain Ermot. "Shutting down bunker defense screens."

Everyone heard it. O'Vorley and Moorsheen over their implanted chips, and Potts over the hand radio next to his dried alfalfa-stuffed sack pillow. Potts reached under his bedroll and pulled a machete from its sheath.

"Where'd you get that?" I asked.

"A farmer gave it to me."

"Gave it to you?"

"He owed me."

Potts's antisocial tendencies were re-emerging, but I'd worry about that later. "Useful if they make it to the trenches."

"Yep." O'Vorley smiled, checking his gear. He slipped a chisel-tipped rock hammer into his belt.

"What about me?" whined Moorsheen. He grasped his assault rifle. "Nobody told me."

O'Vorley checked his MP rifle and snapped its scope in place. "Have I ever forgotten about you?"

We all continued to prepare our gear. I took a drink and handed the canteen to Potts.

"Yes, you have," Moorsheen complained. "More than once. This is life and death."

O'Vorley hefted the two-kilo hammer used for chiseling shelves in the wall. "I told you about this two weeks ago. Remember? This'll crack Stegmar exoskeletons and Crax skulls."

"Oh, right," Moorsheen said. "Thanks." Then he turned pale. "If they make it to the trenches—"

"We'd better hold them," I said. "They aren't likely to take us prisoner." What I didn't tell him was that if they made the trenches, we'd better get reinforced, quick. I stood and performed a double-check of my revolver, shotgun and laser carbine. I strapped on my helmet. "Everybody out. Positions and keep low."

CHAPTER 41

Nine dots, in three rows of three, represent the foundation of the Umbelgarri written language. The pattern of colored dots translates to sound. Any gray lines connecting one or more of the dots adds deeper meaning.

Oral communication between the Umbelgarri takes place through vibrant body colors and patterns emphasized by variations of low frequency sound similar to that of pachyderms, or elephants. The dots represent the color patterns, the lines the sound pattern.

The rumble of artillery fired from secured emplacements was infrequent but welcome. A soldier's surprised scream followed by silence was not. The prolonged screams were sure to haunt me. Dawn approached, and traces of whatever the enemy was firing zipped overhead. I could guess.

"Corrosive canisters," I called to O'Vorley on my left, who was surveying with periscope binoculars. "Countering our high explosive artillery."

"Maybe chemical laced," he replied. "Wind's in our favor." He pulled down his binoculars. "Damn, here they come."

I chanced a peek with my old-style 12x binoculars through the heavy rocks I'd piled along the lip of our trench. The enemy was two miles away, advancing across the flat cropland. A distant, eerie call sent chills down my spine. "Correct," I said. "Mechanized units closing. Stegmar must be closer."

"White Mule," called Captain Ermot over my com-set. "Activate CNS modulators. Self-administer one dose of Stegmar weapon anti-toxin."

I'd already performed the first action. To my right Moorsheen fumbled trying to carry out the directive. "Moorsheen," I called. "Relax. CNS first, then the anti-toxin."

He turned, wide-eyed and reached behind his neck. "Right. Thanks."

I gave him a thumbs-up and edged closer to support our weak link. Black dots appeared in the distant sky. Hundreds. As they closed, I spotted movement on the ground, passing over the groundhog positions. Knowing the answer I called to O'Vorley, "What do you see?"

"Fighter and attack shuttles, troop carriers and tank-bots," he said. "Oh, damn!"

I saw it, too. A curtain of advancing impacts. The crops disappeared. The ground sizzled. Everyone ducked into alcoves and under trench ledges. "Trying to take out our minefield," I yelled to no one in particular.

Five yards to the right the trench lip cracked and sizzled. Hundreds of acidic droplets splattered. I dug my shoulder deeper into the rock hollow and observed three inch-wide holes fizz near my boots. Continued impacts permeated the trench line with an acidic stench that mingled with screams. I said a quick prayer.

A flash followed by an explosion reverberated through the rock. It had to be a tactical nuke. Friendly.

Minutes later I opened my eyes. Friendly artillery impacted closer. Smoke trails crisscrossed the sky as our side's surface-to-air missiles raced toward targets. "SAMs, take them out," I urged. Nobody could possibly hear.

I ventured a look. A vanguard of enemy dome-shaped tanks advanced across the crater-filled fields. Smaller wedged-shaped combat vehicles raced along in support. My com-set sizzled and crackled. I shut it down before the crisscrossing electronic warfare destroyed it. Mine detonations mingled with the artillery, hammering the enemy.

I ventured a second peek. The artillery found random success, but the minefields were taking a toll. Enemy defense screens angled forward or above, not beneath. Some smaller combat vehicles simply stopped. One even turned and fired on its leader.

"McAllister," I whispered into the increasing rumble, screeches, and explosions. Several more enemy units went rogue. "That should upset them."

Overhead, more SAMs sped, most almost vertical. The enemy was above. Out of the corner of my eye I caught movement. An enemy attack craft had lined up to strafe our trench.

"Cover," I yelled, and hip shot a laser blast before tucking into my alcove.

O'Vorley saw my fire, looked at me and followed suit. A squeal of pain, then silence, reported Moorsheen hadn't.

I ventured another peek. Less than a mile. From behind our lines an odd combination of old-style helicopters and prop attack planes raced forward, firing air-to-ground missiles while I-Tech jets engaged enemy shuttles. The effort momentarily stymied the advance, until the enemy blotted the old-style aircraft from the sky. Only two helos retreated.

A wave of friendly tank-bots mixed with manned tanks rumbled over the trenches. Dirt and crumbling rock threatened to give way but held as the tanks spanned our trench. Too heavily armored for efficient use of anti-grav sleds, the theory was that what they lacked in mobility they could make up for in staying power.

I snuck my laser carbine between a pair of rocks, aimed and fired on what I guessed to be a smaller troop carrier. I pulled back before someone returned the favor. My primary firing position fizzed and sizzled. Lasers offered more killing power, but also gave away a position as surely as any tracer round. "Think I'll wait," I muttered.

Friendly troop carriers rumbled overhead, some on anti-grav sleds. A follow-on-formation of Colonial Marines in servo-armor leapt across the trench. Two fell back between O'Vorley and me.

O'Vorley checked the bodies. "Casualties," he called. "Should we advance?"

"No," I shouted back. "Hold the line was our order." I peered through my rock wall's gaps. Strafing attack craft and enemy armor hammered our tanks. About half the time they took it, shed explosive armor, maneuvered and returned fire. A second wave of friendly aircraft engaged. The pilots were skilled and brave, and outgunned. The Crax obliterated them in short order, same as the first wave.

We gave the marines support fire. O'Vorley shifted to within five yards. "They're outnumbered. The Stegmar are tough to see in the crops."

I scanned the carnage. "What's left of them." Twenty miles away the mushroom cloud from the friendly nuke climbed skyward. Maybe it took out the reserves or command and control. Five more SAMs rocketed into the sky. Two explosions.

"The marines are getting torn up," O'Vorley shouted over the din. "They'll fall back."

I watched and fired as the surviving marines engaged the closing enemy with small arms fire and larger anti-armor rockets.

"Here they come," I said.

A damaged tank and a scattered platoon maneuvered over our trench. I scanned for pursuing targets and spotted a trio of Gar-Crax. I poured a series of blasts into the leader. O'Vorley added his MP rifle. The Crax ignored us and continued to keep six marines pinned thirty yards to our front. Two Stegmar squads leapt forward in a pincher move.

"Not enough firepower," shouted O'Vorley. He switched to the Stegmars.

I followed his lead. A rain of needles tore at the ground and rocks near our position. "That got their attention," I said more to myself than anyone else.

I was caught by surprise when a squad of women marines dropped next to us. The delivering armored personnel carrier swung left, lending cover fire with its auto cannon.

A husky, freckled marine yelled, "Keep firing!" She slid her heavy-duty laser rifle over the trench lip while her partner inserted the line into the crate-sized power pack. Three marine teams opened up.

I took out two more Stegmars while the female marines cleared the fire zone of Crax. A second retreating tank rumbled overhead, followed by a supporting troop carrier. Three marines dropped into the trench. "Thanks," said a narrow-eyed, black marine.

I thumbed over my shoulder. "Thank them, Private Zalton."

The freckled marine shouted, "Move now!" and pointed my direction. Everyone ducked and ran. Seconds later my home of the last few weeks erupted into a frothing crater. Before the air cleared we shifted partway back.

"They're regrouping," said the freckled sergeant. Her nametag read, Sayrah.

"How are we doing, Sergeant?" I asked.

"We're getting our ass kicked, soldier. This is a secondary effort. They've broken through north. All reserve assets are closing the breach."

I replaced a drained power pack and handed my laser carbine to a marine armed only with an MP pistol.

"Thanks, soldier," he said. "Acid bolt got my rifle."

I tossed him two remaining power packs. I unslung my shotgun and fixed the bayonet. *Ca-chunk*. "I prefer this anyway."

"You'll need it," said Sergeant Sayrah. She shouted up and down the line. "We've got to hold!" She looked at my nametag. "Keesay, they'll be sending bulldogs. Take them down. Leave the rest to us."

"Understood, Sergeant."

Private Zalton peered ahead with his narrow eyes. "They're almost regrouped. Only cover they got are those two acid-killed tanks."

"Let's hit'em before they're ready," Sergeant Sayrah shouted. "Pick your targets and fire at will."

In less than a minute we cut down dozens. Return fire burned huge gouges into our defensive position. I spotted only Zalton, Sayrah, and O'Vorley standing. Experience had numbed my nose to acid-burned bodies. O'Vorley had some experience but still struggled with the rising stench.

Sergeant Sayrah growled out, "Marine communications failing."

I turned on my com-set. Selected Command on Channel A. It crackled. "Command, this is White Mule Position. Do you read?" I tried again. "Nothing," I said to Sayrah.

"We'd better do something." She took a second and reset my com-set. "Try that one. Artillery. Call down fire on White Mule grid sixteen."

"Artillery control," I called, "this is White Mule, star-crimp-two-laugh. We're under heavy assault. Request fire on White Mule grid sixteen. Repeat, WM grid one six." I waited a second. "Do you read, over?"

A distorted response crackled over my set. "Gun...ments...d...hold...ing your...to..."

I repeated what I heard to Sergeant Sayrah. Listened for more, then shut it down.

Before she answered, Private Zalton barked a string of oaths, then finished. "They've got a company of armored reserve and we're out of anti-armor rockets."

"Lasers are down to eighteen percent," reported O'Vorley, leaning over the first power pack. He examined the second. "And twenty percent." He dragged a third power pack from under some fallen rock. "Four percent."

"Plenty of small arms and lasers," Sergeant Sayrah said. "Not enough anti-tank, tactical nukes or even grenades and mortars."

"Crax intercepted some transports," agreed Zalton, still peering with his standard Marine-issue binoculars.

"I wouldn't doubt if CGIG informed them of routes and destinations," I said.

Sayrah scowled. "I heard something about that. You one of those that ran the blockade?"

"Technically. I was in cold sleep." I reached into my breast pocket. "But I managed to import a popcorn nuke."

"Relic conscript with a nuke." Sayrah adjusted her helmet. "Ever heard of that, Zalton?"

"No," he said. "But he'd better get ready to use it. They've formed up. And with the pillboxes wiped out."

Two more female marines, followed by Potts, climbed over a collapsed section of the trench line. The lead marine reported to Sergeant Sayrah, "This is all that's left. Mink section is nothing more than a crater."

"Acid's still percolating," Potts added. He set a heavy laser power pack down.

The private held up Potts's hand radio. "We've been ordered to hold. Reinforcements are on the way."

"Damn," Sayrah cursed. "Well, without transportation we'd never make it anyway."

"Damn nothing." Zalton sent a laser blast. "Get on the line here before they overrun us."

Sergeant Sayrah glanced at my tag again. "Keesay, you know what to do?"

"When they get to three-hundred fifty yards," I said, "I'll do what I can."

"Let's hold, Marines," she urged. They were already firing.

I handed Potts a salvaged laser carbine. "Just aim and pull the trigger."

"What're you going to do?" he asked while looking over the weapon.

Zalton called, "Shotgunner. Two o'clock low."

I popped up and sent four loads of buckshot into a swarm of bulldog beetles. Three of the five went down. O'Vorley picked off the other two.

"Ouch!" O'Vorley plucked a needle from his face. His right eye and cheek went slack. He administered another anti-toxin injection.

I spied over the edge. "Stay down." A trio of medium tank-bots was less than 400 yards out. I thumbed in the popcorn nuke and pumped it into the chamber. "Nuke away!"

The ground rumbled with the explosive blast. Before it stopped we were following Sayrah to the Rock Mole position. I stepped over what had once been Moorsheen.

Potts grabbed his assault rifle. "Undamaged," he said. "O'Vorley, see if there's any ammo. My hands are full." O'Vorley did as Potts lugged the last power pack.

Our previous position erupted in acidic fumes.

"They're in the line," called Zalton. He laid down a line of laser fire, slicing through a dozen Stegmars.

"Push on," ordered Sayrah. "Get to the tee. We have to fall back."

I popped up to peek over the edge. "Move! Move!" I fired three shots into an enemy wave, forty yards and closing. "Stegmar!"

No more encouragement was needed. We charged ahead, over the rubble and corpse-filled trench. Zalton went down. Sergeant Sayrah drained the last of the power pack and threw the heavy laser aside. O'Vorley, Potts, and I laid into the wave of Stegmar. The two marines near Potts died while downing a Crax trio.

They came on. Thirty yards. Twenty yards. I reloaded. O'Vorley turned and fired on Stegmar in the trench line to our rear.

I emptied my shotgun and Potts did his assault rifle as the insectoid enemy leapt over the edge. Everything was a blur. Stab, slice with my bayonet. Block with stock, smash with shotgun butt.

Potts's machete flashed. He beheaded one Stegmar and whacked two arms from another before three came down on him. He bellowed, hacked and punched. I smashed one on his back before it could tear into him with claws and hooked knives.

That was all I could do. Instinct called. I swung my barrel overhead and clipped one in mid-flight with my A-Tech bayonet, shearing through its abdomen. I stomped what was left of the tenacious mantis warrior, only to have three close and fire needles. Most deflected off my helmet or didn't penetrate my combat gear, but two pierced the flesh of my left hand.

I had trouble holding my shotgun so I dropped it and drew my revolver. Another needle nicked my chin as the first AP round burst through a chitinous head. I thumbed back for the second when a grayish beam, maybe gold, sliced the remaining two in half. Several more beams arced.

"Phibs on the ground," I shouted. My jaw was numb but workable. I turned and kicked a Stegmar Mantis struggling with Potts. It landed four feet away. I aimed and killed it.

Potts staggered to his feet, then fell back. Blood flowed from his neck, face and chest.

"Hold on," I said, administering anti-toxin to my numb left hand and chin.

"Kra!" O'Vorley shouted. "You've got to see this!"

I ignored him and focused on Potts. I tugged open the first aid kit on his belt. "Let me see." I pried Potts's hand from his neck. Blood pumped from a deep jagged tear. I slapped a bandage on it and applied pressure.

Potts gazed up at me, struggling to speak. Nothing came out except a trickle of blood. His eyes bulged in terror. He clasped his hands over mine.

"I'm right here, Potts," I assured him. "The Phibs are on the move. Hold on." I knew the wound was mortal, unless a medivac arrived within minutes. Maybe not that long.

A pair of hands injected pain meds. Sergeant Sayrah's eyes met mine. She knew it, too. "You fight like a Marine," she told Potts, wiping blood-matted hair from his forehead.

His eyes met mine again. More relaxed. The throbbing weakened.

"Would it be okay if I said a prayer?"

One crimson-stained hand slid up my arm and he nodded ever so slightly. His frightened eyes never left mine. I recited the 27th Psalm as best I could remember. It seemed appropriate. By the second verse Potts managed a grimaced smile. By the end of the sixth he was gone.

Sergeant Sayrah pulled my hand from Carver Potts's neck. "Fine words, Keesay. You a preacher?"

"No. Practice," I said. "Too much damn practice." I pulled and pocketed Potts's CNS modulator. No sense leaving intelligence assets. "Like they won't recover any."

"War's like that," Sayrah said. "A better death than acid or toxin." She thumbed over her shoulder. Zalton was propped up, struggling to salvage an MP carbine. "Private Lazarus," she winked. "Additional anti-toxin kicked in." She whispered. "May be permanent nerve damage, but he'll live."

"Uh-oh," said O'Vorley.

Maybe not, I thought, and stood to see what Kent was looking at. Sayrah did the same while helping Zalton to his feet.

A sleek, oblong war-machine maneuvered a half mile away. Enemy attack craft and fighters dove on it. Hostile artillery and armor fired on it. In response a beam emanated from the Phib tank. First flashing above, then behind. Where it touched, a fighter fell, or an enemy tank took damage, unless its shield was down. Those exploded.

The remnant of a smashed marine tank company fired on the enemy's right flank. The Crax all but ignored them and concentrated fire on the Umbelgarri battle tank.

"Nine smaller combat bots were defending it," said O'Vorley. "Some of the acid's getting through. Only four now."

"If they've got enough firepower to stop that Phib tank," Sergeant Sayrah said, "they were just toying with us."

"Lured them out," agreed Private Zalton. "Look, they're retreating."

The Umbelgarri had inflicted damage in minutes that equaled what our armor had managed since the attack began. "If they call that a victory," I said, loading my revolver. "They're getting slaughtered."

"So will we if we don't get out of here," said Sergeant Sayrah. "Everybody out." She hefted Zalton, then held her hand as a step for me. "You're next."

Crack Crack! MP fire. I made it out of the trench just in time to see Zalton die. An elite Gar-Crax warrior stepped over the bisected Marine.

"Gar warrior," I yelled, diving and rolling. It followed. "Get clear. I'll hold it." I didn't dare take my eyes from the towering, armored alien. I spit on my bayonet and held my shotgun in challenge.

It charged and swung its halberd. I retreated and deflected its strike. It seemed surprised. I sent buckshot into its face armor and charged. It blocked my thrust and slammed me in the side with the haft of its weapon.

Laser and MP fire bounced off its armor. It turned hissing and snarling.

"Get out of here," I shouted. "I can take it."

"Like hell," Sayrah yelled. She fired laser blasts into its face, blinding it. It raked a stream of caustic pellets just over her and O'Vorley's head.

I searched for a weakness and spotted where the armored bands met at the base of the tail and the leg. I stalked forward and drove my blade in.

It snarled and spun counterclockwise, flinging me to the ground. I held onto my gun and scrambled to my feet. My sawback blade was covered in blood and gore. I'd pissed it off and readied for its charge. A rip of cannon fire tore up the ground between us, and then slammed into the elite warrior. I ducked and fled the explosions. The auto cannon didn't penetrate, but pounded the alien back. A round caught its halberd, knocking it away.

O'Vorley and Sayrah were already boarding the troop carrier. I circled wide and leapt up the ramp. "Go!" shouted Sayrah. The APC tore away before the ramp cycled shut.

"Look," said O'Vorley. Fifty yards from the trench line the pitted Umbelgarri battle tank stalled. Five giant armor-clad crabs, Bahklacks, emerged, surrounding a twelve-foot, low-slung quadruped. At first I thought it was an alligator. But then I noted the more rounded features and scintillating flesh. Harnessed to its back was a large tube. Like an intense floodlight, it rotated and flashed, slicing out at the closing enemy. The Bahklacks supported the foot-retreat with laser blasts.

"We can't abandon them," I called forward. I grabbed Sayrah's sleeve. "We can't."

"They gave the order," said the gunner. "We're to defend the city."

"No," I said, peering out one of the ports. Several Bahklacks fell, their defense screens overwhelmed by acid. "They won't even make it to the trench line."

"Their choice," Sayrah said. "Just like you intended to stand against that elite while we retreated."

"But I had a chance." She cocked her head in doubt. "I wounded it," I said.

"You cut it." She held up a hand. "No minor feat. But until then it didn't think you could harm it."

I detached, wiped, and sheathed my bayonet. "Why didn't you run?"

She pointed to her stripes. "Sergeant." Then she pointed to me. "Conscript. I'm your superior." She sat back. "Who do you think is the senior partner in our alliance?"

O'Vorley pointed at me. "I prefer you alive, and that Crax knocked senseless in a trench." He shouted forward, "Thanks for the pick up!"

"How long will we last?" I asked.

"Until reinforcements arrive," said Sayrah.

"Oh shit," screamed the gunner. "Attack craft!" The auto-cannon spit rounds skyward. The APC swerved.

I held on with one hand and threw MP reloads to O'Vorley. "More explosive rounds!"

"Good idea," said Sayrah, discovering a cache of medium-duty power packs. "Damn lucky, Keesay," she chuckled, and tossed me a bandoleer of shotgun shells.

Concussions echoed through the APC. "Reactive armor," shouted Sayrah.

O'Vorley and I belted in and held our hands over our ears.

"Reload!" shouted the turret gunner.

Sergeant Sayrah yanked a box and slammed home a replacement. "Loaded!"

The gunner fired several more rounds before the APC banked sharply. First the driver, then the gunner screamed. The familiar acidic stench of dissolving metal and flesh filled the troop compartment. The APC straightened and rolled to a halt.

Sayrah manually lowered the ramp. "Keesay, O'Vorley, out!"

We grabbed our gear and ran. He went right. I went left and hit the dirt near a clump of buckwheat.

Sergeant Sayrah bolted past, and shouted, "Coming around for another pass!" She knelt and opened fire.

I drew my revolver and added several AP rounds, and O'Vorley cracked away with MP fire. Several of Sayrah's blasts were on target. I think one of my rounds hit. It was hard to gauge what volume of O'Vorley's struck.

At the last minute we dove for cover. It strafed and missed. The tail gunner sent a wild stream that came closer.

"She's smoking," said O'Vorley.

"And coming around again," I said. "Any ideas?"

Sayrah pointed. "Cover." She ran toward a decimated artillery battalion.

"That's why she's a sergeant," said O'Vorley, pounding on her heels.

I pushed to keep up. "And I'm a relic conscript."

"Spread out," ordered Sayrah.

I dove behind a half-dissolved 6-inch towed howitzer.

A dozen assorted firearms added to our effort. The Crax attack craft pulled out before completing its pass. A ragged cheer rose from the destroyed gun emplacements and surrounding foxholes.

"Form up," barked Sergeant Sayrah. She stood. "Form up and form up NOW!"

Fourteen conscripts emerged. All scanned warily behind and to the sky. An elderly conscript limped forward. "There's two shell-shocked ones won't move for anything," he said.

I clicked on my com-set and searched frequencies. "Jamming is weak," I said.

"See what you can hear while I round this rabble up. O'Vorley, check those trucks. We can't stay here long."

It was a sorry lot. No question why they weren't defending the trench line. Old men and others obviously not up to combat.

I picked up communication bits and fragments and tried to piece them together. Sayrah huddled the group between a half-dissolved emplacement and a burned-out ammo wagon. I approached and waited for her attention. She interrupted her organizational questioning. “Report, Keesay.”

“The north line collapsed. Ground assault shuttles are dropping Crax and Stegmar in the city. I heard the Stickley Café mentioned as a rally point. Ate there once before my assignment.”

“I know it,” said Sayrah. “It’s near the west end of the city. Good tea. Decent service.” She turned to the conscripts. “You heard that? That’s where we’re going. They’re fighting in the city. We’ve got to hold it.”

“Why?” asked a teenager. “We can fight just as well from here.”

Sergeant Sayrah’s freckles disappeared in red. “Because,” she said with forced calm, “a reinforced mechanized regiment is on our ass. And they want the city intact. They’ll be willing to waste more than a few Stegmar and an occasional Crax in taking it. But it’ll take time.”

“Time for our reinforcements,” I added.

They all looked less than convinced. Pursed lips, shaking heads and sighs. Marine Sergeant Sayrah trembled on the verge of violence.

I stepped closer. “Besides, that attack craft got away. They carry comsets. Think he’ll forget to tell that closing regiment?” I pointed at the rising dust column. “Stay here if you want. I’m following the sergeant.”

O’Vorley ran up to Sayrah. “Sergeant, there’s a truck and an ATV with a small wagon full of rations. Looks like they’ll run. Everything else is wrecked.”

Sayrah scanned the area. “Good. A little luck. Any heavy weapons around here?”

“None of the artillery works,” said the teen.

The elderly man shook his head. “There’s a couple of heavy-duty lasers. None of us know how to use ’em. All we got are these.” He held up an MP carbine. Most had carbines with a few MP rifles and pistols.

“Where?” Sayrah followed the limping man to a bunkered ammo dump. “Keesay, O’Vorley, bring the vehicles here.”

O’Vorley looked at the two-and-a-half ton transport truck.

“I’ll take it.” Luckily I’d observed a colonist session on driving aboard the *Kalavar*. One of the instructors let me put theory into practice in repayment for keeping an eye on Carver Potts. Thinking of Potts caused me to stall it once. After that I shifted gears smoothly. I followed O’Vorley on the six-wheeled ATV with wagon in tow. It was a smaller version of the one that delivered our daily rations.

“O’Vorley, Keesay,” ordered Sayrah, “load one of these heavy lasers onto that wagon. The other on the truck.”

Several of the conscripts helped load crates filled with small arms and ammunition. Two others refueled the truck from a ten-liter canister. The diesel fuel fumes again reminded me of the *Kalavar*.

I shook it off and followed Sayrah into the bunker. "The armored column is moving slow but closing," I said. The bunker was half empty but still held rows of artillery shells and crates of weapons.

She went to work. "Just setting a little surprise." Sayrah connected a wire to a laser pistol, wedged and aimed at a stack of diesel fuel cans and broken artillery shells. She picked up a can of diesel. At the top of the steps she tipped the can, allowing fuel to spill onto the soil. "Cover the smell below."

I nodded in approval and looked over my shoulder.

"Keesay," said Sayrah. "You're competent under fire. In the wagon. Man the laser. O'Vorley, on the ATV." She climbed behind the truck's wheel and yelled out the window. "Old man, up here next to me. Anybody else who's coming, in the back now." She put it in gear. Everyone boarded. "O'Vorley, go on ahead. If any Crax are ahead of us, you be the rabbit they'll chase. We'll rumble on behind."

"Sure thing, Sergeant."

I tossed a couple of the wagon's food sacks into the window and then to some of the hands calling over the truck's railing. I handed O'Vorley an abandoned canteen. He took several swallows. I took two gulps and tossed the half-empty canteen to Sergeant Sayrah. "Let's go." I looked back. "They're closer to us than we are to the city."

"Where to?" he asked.

I scanned the pillars of smoke rising from the distant city. "Know where the hospital is? It's near the café. Let's try for it until something better comes along."

Kent gave a lopsided grin. Most of the paralyzing toxin had been neutralized. "Hang on, Kra. And look sharp." He gunned it.

We'd raced for almost two miles through the fields, leading Sergeant Sayrah's truck and pulling away from the mechanized Crax regiment. O'Vorley managed to avoid most of the ruts and ditches, making my wagon ride tolerable. He slowed as we passed by a dozen dead, bloated goats scattered among the dying vegetation. I knew the soil was dead as well. I signaled for O'Vorley to move on. I didn't want to picture two days hence when fallen soldiers would similarly litter the countryside.

"From what I'm getting over the com-set," I yelled to O'Vorley, "they've advanced through the north side. Scattered troop drops throughout. Street-to-street fighting."

"Better chance there than out here in the open," replied O'Vorley.

I scanned the sky again. "Oh, crap! Ground assault shuttle three o'clock." I swung the heavy laser around and waited for it to come into range. "Any cover?"

"Their sensors can read through concrete. If they take an interest in us." He hesitated while negotiating a steep bank. "You'll have to take them down."

"Understood," I said, trying to keep the tripod in place. The food packed around helped. "Slow down. Here they come." I lined up, giving much less lead than I would with my shotgun or revolver. I depressed the trigger. Right on target. "It's got a shield up!"

O'Vorley accelerated. I sent several more blasts. The rough terrain made all go wild.

"We'll head for the quarry," said O'Vorley.

I'd seen a gravel pit on the way out to the trench line. "Good idea. Cover." I watched the shuttle approach. "They're trying to decide on us or the truck."

"The more they hesitate, the closer we get."

"I'd hate to see Sergeant Sayrah have to face them with that crew." I aimed and fired, on target. The shuttle vectored toward us. "Made up their mind."

"What's the plan?" asked O'Vorley.

"Plan? Gravel pit's your idea."

"Figured we'd stand a better chance in the rock piles and equipment. Against ground troops, too."

"Sounds good," I said. "If we can get there. We'll split up so we can get shots from behind." I fired again and missed.

"Avoid the shields," said O'Vorley, looking over his shoulder. "They're getting close."

The ventral turret spun to life. "Turret active!"

O'Vorley slowed and turned sharply toward the shuttle. "Take a shot when she flies over."

I struggled to keep the wagon from tipping and the laser from going over the side. "Sounds good."

A stream of caustic pellets raked the ground ahead. O'Vorley cut left, too sharp. The wagon tumbled. I rolled away as it unhitched. Several pellets stuck its bottom and ate through.

I staggered to my feet. O'Vorley pulled around. "Get on!"

I eyed the quarry a few hundred yards away. "No. Split up. Without the laser they can close and nail us. With me on it'd be too slow," I lied. I didn't wait for his answer. Shotgun in hand I broke into a sprint.

The returning GAS didn't give time for debate. "Keep low, Kra!" He gunned the throttle.

I waved but didn't turn. I concentrated on hurdling a ditch. A second ditch thirty yards beyond angled toward the road leading into the quarry. It'd offer some cover.

The sound of the ATV faded. I looked over my shoulder just in time to see the GAS make a touch landing, dropping a squad of Stegmar and one Gar-Crax. The shuttle then flew off after O'Vorley.

I had a 120 yard lead when they touched down and added thirty before they organized for pursuit. I gave up on the ditch and headed straight for the gravel pit road. If they got a lucky shot, oh well.

A few pellets flew past as I huffed through the quarry's chain link entry. No one had bothered to close it. The Stegmar sounding intensified. With the CNS modulator it wasn't a problem, but it told me they were closing. Stegmar can't run as fast as a human but they can fly for short spurts, and Gar-Crax can reach thirty miles per hour.

I made it around a rough boulder marking the edge of the descending road. It sizzled with impacts. I popped over the top and returned fire. I caught the ten Stegmar and Crax leader at forty yards, charging in the open. I dropped three Stegmar and injured one. I didn't bother with the leader. Two Stegmar returned covering fire while the rest made for the ditch. I wounded two more with buckshot. The leader kept coming so I fled left, descending the dusty road along the quarry's west wall.

What I wouldn't give for a grenade, I thought. I slid behind the fourth edge-lining bolder just before the Crax leader made it to the first. Unless he was both blind and stupid, the settling dust would indicate my location. But he'd abandoned his support. Unwise, just like armor outpacing supporting infantry. But what if they were spreading along the ledge?

I peered over the edge at a sixty-foot drop. A shallow pool of water ran along the rough wall. I slung my shotgun and slid over the edge. Not enough time to descend, so I located handholds and perches while maneuvering to my right, toward the distant fifth boulder. I made it under a six-inch overhang before drawing my revolver left-handed. I thumbed the hammer and waited. It was a fifty-fifty chance. If the Crax came around the boulder and looked, I was betting he'd look around to the right first. I might get one shot inside his shield.

Thirty seconds passed. I'd caught my breath but my right hand began cramping. Then the fourth rock sizzled. Heavy treads approached the edge followed by a clucking hiss. The big reptile's halberd-rifle emerged over the ledge first. The Crax leaned and searched right. I risked a quarter-second aim.

The AP round struck the Crax in the jaw and burst through its skull. The Gar-Crax tumbled into the pond below.

I holstered my revolver and risked a wild descent. Twice, I almost fell before hang dropping eight feet. The Stegmars reached the ledge but their angle was poor. One attempted a scaling descent. Another flew out and around. I nailed the one in flight and popped away from the wall to waste the second. Then, I waded through the thigh-deep water to the dead Crax. I searched his body. Anything electronic I smashed, thinking something might be a locator. Grabbing its halberd, I moved away and depressed the trigger. Nothing. No safeties. Must've been protected from unauthorized use, so I tossed it on the floating corpse before shooting an AP round into the magazine. That did it. I ran from the water when the torso erupted in froth.

I looked over my shoulder. Near the entrance two Stegmar pointed. One held up a small box to its mandibles. A radio. They backed away when I turned to fire. "Damn," I said. "Reinforcements."

I made my way past several huge gravel mounds and the conveyers that had piled them. I climbed onto a large dump truck to survey the quarry. There was only one exit with two Stegmars posted there, watching my movements. How long before reinforcements? The armored regiment couldn't be far behind. Trapped. I wondered if O'Vorley or Sergeant Sayrah would make it to the city.

I'd read that Stegmar eyesight was better close than far, picking up only distant movement at best. I estimated my distance as 300 yards before raising my shotgun as if to fire. They took cover. I maneuvered around more equipment, stepped in view and repeated the threat. They retreated after hesitation. Was it sight, or disbelief that I'd fire? I guessed a little of both.

If I was fast enough, I could reach the east wall and attempt to climb. I picked my way, going under equipment, staying in shadows and between gravel piles and debris.

In the base of a refuse pile I spotted a frosty plastic box. I'd seen similar aboard the *Kalavar*, holding some of Mer's frozen fish. The scanable ID marking was missing. I looked around and spotted an area surrounded by a tall, rusted, chain link fence. Razor wire lined the top. Scattered beyond rested broken-down equipment. It reminded me of the junkyard near my uncle's farm. The fence was chained with an impressive padlock. Nothing else I'd seen was locked. Why this?

Further inspection revealed holes in the fence and the rock beyond. This wasn't the only place Crax caustic bombardment had gone astray. I crawled through instead of risking the razor wire, and also revealing my position.

The distant rumble of war accented by nearer tank and artillery fire kept me alert. I wove my way to the back where the most stripped and useless equipment rested. Behind a damaged bulldozer blade was a large cast iron door. Weather had taken its toll. A battered sign whose red paint had faded to pink hung by a single bolt. It read, 'Danger, Demolition Equipment.'

A bolt of Crax acid had dissolved the base of the iron door. An oval hole two-feet high and nearly as wide invited inspection. A few gravel tosses convinced me the acid residue was inert.

I peered into darkness. My penlight didn't reveal much more. It offered possible concealment, so I shoved my shotgun ahead and climbed through. Inside I found a few scattered crates, and some sort of glassy wires running into holes along the walls, and one into each crate. The wires gathered together in a bundle. I followed them down a thirty-foot corridor to a wide set of stairs. No lighting was apparent.

I returned to the door, climbed out and looked around. I found a flat tire still on its rim and hauled it back. After climbing back inside I maneuvered the tire in front of the hole. Then, I reexamined the stone stairway. Before my boot touched the first step a pulse of energy coursed through my body. Blackness followed.

CHAPTER 42

The number of extinct alien cultures far outnumbers those currently known to exist. Those that never reached the stars most frequently perished because of natural disasters, followed by disease, and then war. Clues of cultural decadence are rare but not unheard of during the waning period of a sentient race's existence.

For those far more rare species that reach the stars, a natural disaster may be a catalyst, but rarely the ultimate cause of its demise. Except for two documented instances where disease drove a space-faring race to extinction, all others were directly related to war. Sometimes an invading race is the cause. Sometimes an aggressive or unwise race incurred the wrath of a more powerful foe. Sometimes internal strife and resulting conflict brought a race to its end. Internal strife and an external aggressor are common denominators in almost three-fifths of known lost space-faring cultures.

I awoke, but didn't open my eyes. I was on my back, level. A band constricted my chest. As I exhaled, my breath sifted through cloth or a mask. I listened and heard breathing mingled with tapping. Breathing regular, tapping, no pattern. It struck me as familiar. A clicking of sticks on stone approached.

"Keesay, it knows you're awake."

I flexed and discovered I was strapped across not only my chest, but arms, wrists, thighs, and ankles. "McAllister?" My voice was muffled. I craned my neck to see. "What are you doing here? Where's here?" I caught sight of eyes on stalks examining me.

"Probably hasn't seen a living relic up close before," McAllister said. Her mismatched green and blue eyes sparkled above a white surgical-type mask.

"Is there a reason I'm tied down?" I scanned the small room. Beyond my feet, a wall of computers hummed with activity. To my right, gray stone. To my left, a wall with large wire-reinforced windows showing a stone corridor. "We're all on the same side." A hinged metal door stood ajar.

"I vouched for you, but here I'm only an apprentice engineer."

The Bahklack sidestepped around the table before clicking its way over to a control panel.

"Where's here?" I watched the crab-alien manipulate controls. The displays pulsated a rainbow of colors.

"Can't tell you."

"Can't or won't?"

"I won't because I'm not in a position to do so." She shifted positions on the tall stool. "A higher authority will have to sanction it."

"Being a junior engineer doesn't upset you?"

"Not under these circumstances."

"What?" I asked. "That New Birmingham is under assault?"

"Give me more credit than that."

"The Phibs recruited you? They take their pick from the brightest. Intelligence, you fit."

"They prefer the term Umbelgarri."

I looked around, realizing they'd be monitoring. "Umbelgarri then. I'm on their side."

"This place is pretty important to them," McAllister explained. "They're pretty secretive."

"I know, but strapped down hampers my ability to kill their enemy. Our enemy. Last I knew, the Crax were routing us."

"I think that's the only thing keeping you alive. How'd you know that Gar-Crax would look right first?"

"What? You saw that?"

She nodded.

"A guess. Figured it was inexperienced because it left its Stegmar support. It was working on impulse. My first impulse would've been to look right."

"I told them about your efforts aboard the *Kalavar* and on the quarantine planet."

"Can't do much more to convince them," I said. "If I found this place, they'll find it."

"I think that's what has them worried. Collapsing the entrance now would attract undue attention."

"Let me go and I'll leave. Not a word."

"What if you're captured? Unlikely, but possible."

"I can be pretty tight lipped when I want to be. Besides, an intel guy on Mavinrom shot me up with something to prevent me from being chemically forced to reveal information."

McAllister stood. "Really? Why?"

"Classified," I said. "What if this is an elaborate hologram?"

The Bahklack turned. A rectangular patch on its large claw flowed patterned colors. A speaker in the ceiling voiced the translation. "Tell us."

"No. It's classified."

"We require the information. Proof or we will terminate you."

I tried to move my hands. No luck. Damned if I do and damned if I don't. "Do what you have to."

"In my expert opinion," warned McAllister, "I'd say they're serious."

"The least they could do is drop me on a nest of Crax. At least I'd go out fighting."

"This isn't a hologram, Keesay. It's not that they don't think like us, but they won't hesitate to end your life." She stood. "Actually, they might think more like you. You don't seem to hesitate before killing."

"In the line of duty, no," I said. "Do you know if O'Vorley got away from the ground assault shuttle?"

"O'Vorley?"

"Young guy. You saw him in our bunker."

"Shouldn't you be worried about your own life?"

"Out of my hands. I doubt I'll manage to escape. O'Vorley?"

" I don't know. The Umbelgarri have been monitoring communications. Seems there's one Gar-Crax, equivalent to a colonel, who the Umbelgarri think is hunting for you."

I thought a second and smiled. "Probably the elite Crax I stabbed in the rump."

"He's on his way to your last sighting. Human with an advanced speargun that expels lead balls."

"Translated from Crax to Umbelgarri, and into English. Still coherent. What about Tahgs? Is she okay?"

"Last I saw her," said McAllister, "she was assigned to a mobile medical squad. Coordinating communications." McAllister looked away.

"What is it?"

"I don't know, Keesay." McAllister's gaze hardened. Then she shrugged her shoulders. "When Tahgs heard you were planetside, she suddenly believed we'd repel the invaders. She had more questions about you than I could ever answer. I said you're an accomplished killer with tenacious sense of duty, and would make an ideal soldier. I explained that our survival rested on reinforcements, not an R-Tech security specialist."

McAllister shook her head. "Tahgs was sure you'd be there if things got desperate. You know, her knight in shining armor."

I knew why Tahgs felt that way. More than once I'd saved her. But my feelings for Janice were none of McAllister's business. "Accomplished killer?" I asked.

"The truth, Keesay. You're effective. Nothing more."

The fate of O'Vorley and Tahgs was out of my hands. "Are there any guppies down here?"

"What? Aren't you worried about the Crax warrior?"

"No. Our allies are going to do his job for him. I saw something in a debris pile."

"Maybe. You're not all there anymore, are you, Keesay?"

"And you're one to judge?" There was momentary silence. The crab-alien moved busily around the room. "The Colonization Riots," I said. "I'm truly sorry about killing your fiancé."

McAllister's face darkened. "They know about that," she said. "Don't try to bring me down with you."

"I didn't mean it that way," I said. "Really. Just trying to clear the slate." I closed my eyes. "Honestly, I can't think of a way out of this situation." That was the truth. I wouldn't kill any of humanity's most important ally to save myself. One of them meant more to humanity's survival than one of me.

I opened my eyes to see McAllister's raised skeptical eyebrow.

I closed my eyes. "Even if I *somehow* got out of this bed, I'd have to best you and at least this Bahklack, barehanded? And if I did, where would I go? Unarmed out into the quarry, if I could find it before I tripped some A-Tech security measures, or was brought down with one of their golden energy beams?"

I took a deep breath and opened my eyes. McAllister was standing next to me. "I see you got a chain for Gudkov's ring. Do me one favor."

"What would that be, Keesay?"

Request your superior to give me two minutes notice before they follow through."

"This doesn't sound like you, Keesay. Giving up."

I shrugged as much as my restraints allowed. "Believe me, my mind is working. At least you spoke up for me."

She rubbed the platinum ring. "Two minutes. I'll do that." She paused. "Would you want me to pray for you? The same words you said for Anatol?"

"No. That'd be really out of character for you." I peered into her mismatched eyes and re-evaluated. "It would be comforting. For me. Maybe for you, too."

"You'd do it for me," she said. "Yeah, I'll make the request."

"I should've taken your advice. Learn to think more than three moves ahead. Good luck in your new assignment."

I stared a moment at the silent Bahklack. "I am thirsty." I tried to move and get more comfortable despite the restraints before closing my eyes. "Who'd have figured," I mumbled. "Put to death like a common criminal for trespassing." I heard McAllister slip out.

I was exhausted from combat, but I didn't expect to doze off. My first thought upon being startled awake was that they'd drugged me. Someone tugged at my straps.

"They're going to let you go," McAllister announced as she moved from my chest to my arms. "Some luck you have."

"How long have I been asleep?"

"I don't know. I left you a half hour ago."

"Did you talk them into it?"

"No," she said. "All I did on your behalf was to relay the requested two-minute notice. We've got to hurry." She watched me stand and stretch.

"I smell pretty bad, don't I?"

"I was thinking you could use a shower, Keesay. Our masks don't filter that out." She turned toward the door. "This way. Don't touch anything."

I grabbed her shoulder, figuring she meant touching equipment. "What's the deal?"

"Deal? No deal really. I'll explain along the way."

I followed her into the corridor. She went left. The ceiling was irregular in height and texture. Cement had been poured to level the floor. It was damp, and small water channels ran along the walls.

"Wet in here," I said. "Necessary for the Umbelgarri?"

"Comfortable," she said. "We're in a cavern complex. I'm leading you to the quarry. You'll get your guns and equipment there."

"And?" I slowed.

"Go out and fight the Crax."

"Go out and get killed."

She stopped before crossing a carved, stone-block bridge spanning a shallow pool. "More than likely. That elite soldier just landed outside the quarry. It's looking for you."

"Yes, it'll kill me, but that won't solve the problem. They'll still find this place."

"I'll explain more as we near the exit."

"I don't get my equipment until you tell me the plan? They assess. In case I want to back out."

"After Capital Galactic's, ahh, shall we say treachery, they're less open to simply taking a human's word."

Movement in the pool caught my attention. I climbed on the bridge and peered into the shallow water. An algae film covered parts. Small fish, guppies, poked at it. Larger forms, mudpuppies, moved along the bottom. "Are those Mer's fish?"

McAllister said, "Better keep moving, Keesay."

"Understood." One of the mudpuppies snapped at a guppy. "Are those immature Umbelgarri?"

"No," said McAllister. "They're not native to Tallavaster. I think the Umbelgarri imported them. Food for the Bahklack."

"Makes sense," I said. "Grow local food to their tastes. Don't care much for goat or buckwheat?"

"No, they don't." She sighed and gestured with her hand. "Faster would be better."

We were pretty deep down, maybe a half mile. We crossed several branching areas and one more pond. Lighting became less frequent as we ascended.

Just before we came to a heavy door McAllister faced me. "Here's the plan. You're to wait in or near the spare parts yard until the elite Crax locates you. Lure him in and the Umbelgarri will detonate the explosives. Get out if you can manage it. Nevertheless, it'll appear to be your handiwork while sealing the cavern entrance."

"That Crax took at least ten rounds of auto cannon fire. Point-blank range. Even an explosion that kills me outright won't get him. And too much will be suspicious." Then it hit me. I stared at McAllister. "Got to admit it, I'm thinking more than two moves ahead."

"No," said McAllister. "That's not it."

"It's okay, McAllister. I can show my face, and then fall on my sword.

Make it look otherwise. I know what this place is. How important it is to the Umbelgarri."

"No, no," McAllister said, grabbing my shoulders. "You're right. Any explosion big enough to kill the Crax would draw undue attention." She led me to my equipment, stacked and cleaned.

I buckled on my belt. I examined my equipment and began to load my shotgun.

"Here," said McAllister, holding out a .357 round. "This is what they expect you to use on the Crax. You've already proven to have advanced equipment, so this shouldn't raise too much of a lizard brow."

I forced a smile at her humor. "One shot?"

"That's right. With your archaic equipment, that's all the time you should have anyway."

"I can live with that," I said, taking the bullet. "Umbelgarri alloy?"

"It'll penetrate."

"Is this Crax hunting alone?" I loaded the Umbelgarri round and spun it into position.

"No, he'll have company. Witnesses?"

"Until I waste him. Then—"

"Then you use these." She shoved two micro explosives into my hand. "Similar to what you used on the quarantine planet. Set for three seconds. Anything except the armored Crax will be taken out in a fifteen-foot radius." She hesitated in thought. "Correction. Will weaken, but won't take down a Crax shield. Not if it's above thirty percent charged."

I looked the micro explosives over. "Good to know." I tested the cover that prevented accidental activation. "I'll push the red button and toss it over their heads. Looks like your handiwork."

"Might give you a chance."

"Appreciated. Any wire cutters for the fence?"

"I understand it's taken care of."

"What's the situation, if I make it to New Birmingham?"

"Fighting is still going on," said McAllister. "They control eighty percent of the city."

I offered her my hand. She took it. "Learn all you can from the Phi—Umbelgarri." Her shake was limp. "Ask the Bahklack to demonstrate a proper handshake. With its claws it ought to be firm."

"You're a jerk, Keesay."

"I'm going out there, calling trump on a queen and ten." I patted my belt pouch where I'd stowed the two detonators. "Thanks for the off-suit ace."

"Saying thanks an awful lot," accused McAllister.

"You're right, I'm stalling." I handed her my sterile mask and then lifted my leg and pulled my backup .38. "If you see Tahgs again, give her this relic. If you can't find her, keep it yourself." I held up a hand. "Or sell it. I'm going to have to be fast on my feet." I grabbed my shotgun. "No more stalling." I jogged up the stairs.

My penlight helped me find the door and avoid tripping over the wires. Several new ones ran under the door. I avoided them, crawled out the hole and replaced the tire. I crawled toward the fence. To the right of two poles, a three-by-three foot section had been weakened. I tested. A little pressure and the metal fractured. The chemically-induced fault was barely noticeable.

Movement caught my eye. I crawled back behind a broken axle that supported a heap of twisted sheet metal. It was the elite Crax, and a partner! So much for Umbelgarri intel. Behind trailed a dozen Stegmar and a Gar-Crax leader.

They'd searched most of the quarry and made it to this side. The sun would set in an hour. Their armor surely had advanced optics and night vision. No sense giving them a greater advantage. Sliding the action, readying a slug round, attracted their attention. I took aim and fired.

The first slug hit a Stegmar square in the chest. Not bad for a hundred-twenty yard shot. The Mantis soldiers hit the dirt before I could get a clean second shot. My third nailed one on the ground. They returned fire. Needles clinked off the scrap metal and rusted equipment.

One of the elites swung his arm and the firing stopped. Both elites advanced. One stalked with a limp.

May as well make this look good. I fired another slug into the limping one. "Back for more?" I shouted. "Come on in here and get me. If you dare!"

The limping one raised its halberd and continued its approach. The other remained forty yards back. That'd be a tough shot. "I see you have a translator. Is your partner afraid of getting too near combat?" I fixed my bayonet and backed farther into the yard. The second didn't move. "Thought so. Why don't you just stay there. Won't see anything, but you'll be far enough to run away when things get violent."

The second elite strode forward, halving the distance while the first sliced through the fence with its halberd. It knew right where I was. I moved around a huge fractured backhoe shovel. His gurgling hiss had to be laughter.

"He who laughs last doesn't get the joke," I said, hoping to confuse it.

It only motivated the elite as its gurgle evolved to a growling hiss. It bounded forward and landed opposite the shovel, swinging its weapon menacingly. It brought the blade across the steel shovel and sliced a sliver off before lopping off a corner with a controlled backstroke.

The elite moved right, I followed suit. It stopped. I stopped. I guessed what was next. As soon as the elite leapt I fired a slug into its leg and dashed for the fence. I must have connected, and knocked it off balance because I didn't get cut in two. I tossed one of the detonators a few yards ahead of me. I ran straight over it toward the other elite Crax.

The micro explosive's concussion knocked me forward. I kept my feet and barreled through the weakened fence. The waiting Crax watched as I rolled to a prone position with my revolver cocked. The observing elite's split-second indecision gave me the time I needed to aim for a headshot.

The elite outside hadn't collapsed when the ground reverberated. Gravel and bits of metal flew up and rained down. Nothing large hit me while I struggled to regain my wind.

I spotted the other elite soldier picking itself up off the ground twenty feet away. I reached into my pocket and slid a flare round and pumped my shotgun. Not in time. The elite Crax was finished fooling around. It took aim. I rolled onto one knee and fired.

Two caustic rounds took me in the chest. They immediately ate through my outer uniform and worked on the lower half of my breastplate. I'd never get it off in time.

The elite wiped the flaring mass from its faceplate. I charged, feeling the burning going through my vest armor, attacking my skin. The pain almost doubled me over. I thrust, but my momentum and strength faltered. My bayonet only scarred the armor across its chest.

With one hand it slammed me aside. I screamed. Each breath brought in the odor of dissolving flesh. I struggled to regain composure. My layers of armor must have dissipated the acid. I realized I was going to die. Just not yet.

The Crax stared down, laughing. I couldn't even muster spit. Fiery, sizzling pain emanated from my core, reaching for my extremities. The acid was in my blood. I looked up again to see the Crax ignoring me, waving its gauntleted arm, giving orders.

I struggled to reach my belt, found McAllister's second micro explosive. My hand shook as I flipped the cover. I pressed the red button, and then placed the device between the Gar-Crax's armored toes.

"*Nemo me impune lacessit*," I said, struggling to roll away. The second time my stomach touched I screamed again. I was sure the elite was laughing. Why I rolled away? I'm not sure. Did an explosion follow? I don't remember.

I floated to consciousness. Pain meds coursed through my veins. I was alive? Nearby, small cooling fans and the hum of lights. My head and neck hurt with a dull burning ache, but nothing else did. Maybe the pain meds made it tolerable. Bright light penetrated my eyelids.

I replayed my actions up until the micro explosive's detonation. There must've been one. Now, I was lying horizontal, indoors, receiving medical care.

I tried to move and couldn't. My arms weren't strapped. I just couldn't move them. Same with my legs. There was a new sound, footsteps approaching.

"Security Specialist Keesay," said a nasal voice. "Right on time."

No sense feigning unconsciousness. Monitoring equipment reported otherwise. I opened my eyes and tilted my head. My vision was blurry. Even my eyeballs ached. They responded slowly to the light. It even hurt to shut my eyelids.

"I was assured your vision, hearing, and voice are intact."

"Water," I asked in a raspy voice.

"Not a good idea at the moment," said the nasal voice. "Maybe later."

I opened my eyes again and licked my dry, cracked lips. "Sponge my lips."

"A moment on that." A shadowy form moved from sight. His deliberate speech emphasized the nasal tone. "May the patient have moisture applied to his lips and tongue?" There was a pause. "Negative, not a drink to reach his digestive track. Moisture so he can speak." More pausing. "No, it is not vital, but it would be convenient." Pausing. "Understood. Thank you." The man left the room.

I opened my eyes again and tried to focus. It was easier this time though no less painful. The overhead lights told me I was in an operating room. I could only move my head left and right and lift it. I couldn't arch my neck to see anything else. Each muscle contraction burned.

No hum of engines. Not on a ship, not in condensed space. The walls and ceiling were white, painted concrete. Metal conduit ran wires to a bank of computers along the left wall. They appeared idle. I was still planetside.

A white curtain was stretched five inches below my chin. It extended several feet beyond my bed. I tried to move my fingers to determine bed or table. No movement, no sensation. I wondered if the explosion broke my back.

The man returned. I guessed he was average height for an I-Tech, with a round face and slicked-back, blonde hair. He wore a business suit and sported a yellow tie, only about a third of which was covered with black rectangles.

"Why the frown?" said the lawyer. "I've brought you some water." He dipped a stick topped by a small yellow sponge into a cup. He then gently applied it to my lips and tongue. As he leaned over I saw a CGIG tie tack. I considered spitting, but figured to save my strength and determine his intentions.

He repeated the procedure twice. "Is that better?" he asked. "Can you talk?"

The water was cool and eased some of the pain in my throat. "Depends on what you want me to say." The effort to speak burned just as it did when I moved my neck. But it wasn't as intense.

"I'm Mr. Heartwell. I'm here to interview you. I was told you'd be a tough case, Specialist Keesay. This can go fast and easy, or long and difficult. We'll get the information we desire."

"Ask," I said. "You appear to be in a hurry."

"Why would you say that, Specialist?"

"Most lawyers don't question people in an operating room."

"Observant," he said. "There are few rooms available. Overflow of patients. You're third on my list of interviews today and you just happened to be available."

"Is that why you were waiting on me?"

"Trust me on this. Your surgeons are extremely knowledgeable. I knew of your availability within a thirty-second time frame *and* I happened to finish my second interview early."

He pulled up a stool. "Actually, you are quite fortunate the Capital Galactic Investment Group has taken an interest. The Crax are very interested in taking possession of you, especially a particular crippled Crax. If you're cooperative, he may no longer be planetside when you become available."

He watched my eyes, my facial expression. I tried to keep a straight face, but the pain meds and headache made it difficult.

"Yes, we are aware of your activities on Selandune. Rest assured, the little rebellion you precipitated was put down." He leaned closer. "You're quite an irritant, but one we are willing to work with."

"Work with you?"

"Yes, you owe CGIG a great debt, but you could repay it." His voice became cheery. "I'm your representative, Mr. Jerden Heartwell."

Good lawyer name, I thought, before asking, "What debt?"

"The damage to the research facilities on Selandune. Compensation to the company for loss of property and personnel."

"Compensation for a corporation aiding and abetting the enemy?"

"Depends on who you deem the enemy."

"Isn't that obvious," I said, ignoring my throat's burning. "I don't switch sides."

"Even if yours is destined to lose?"

"I'm not a traitor to the human race. We won't lose."

"I'm no soldier or military expert." Mr. Heartwell chuckled. "But I've not heard of one victory for your side."

"This isn't the best we have," I said. "Nine out of ten are untrained conscripts."

"Like you?" He stood and paced a little, before looking behind the curtain. "The Crax sent second-line combat units with obsolete equipment. The first-line troops and equipment smashed through the Felgans and are overrunning Umbelgarri space." He nodded approval. "Although I do believe the Crax underestimated human combat abilities." Mr. Heartwell returned to the stool. "I've heard a little of your prowess as a killer. Took out several Gar-Crax on the *Kalavar*." He folded his arms, then placed a finger on his cheek. "And you kill humans, too. On the Mavinrom Space Dock?"

"Two of our crew had been abducted. My duty called for it." He seemed pretty talkative for an interrogator. "Probably your operatives."

"Saved a certain Representative Vorishnov?"

I feigned ignorance. "Who?"

"Nice try, Specialist Keesay. Look, I want two things from you. One, verification of the location of Maximar Drizdon Jr. Two, you to sign on with Capital Galactic."

"One," I said. "Even if I knew any information, giving it to you would simply sign my death warrant that much sooner. Two, don't patronize me. Capital Galactic has little use for a 4th class security specialist. I'm not a Chip. Are you?"

Mr. Heartwell shook his head. "I believe that you have valuable information. And you would have continued use to Capital Galactic. You have connections with the Chicher, or at least one of their packs."

"Wrong again," I said, coughing. "Both counts."

"Those marks on your neck say otherwise. You'd be an exceptional inside man. And the compensation is excellent."

"Not when I'm executed as a traitor."

His face remained passive, all except his eyes. They sparkled. "I'm not sorry you've refused to work with us. I spoke against offering you that option. But as to the information issue, we'll keep you alive as long as it takes." He walked around my head to the other side of the table. "If we have to resort to drugs, I guarantee it will be a long and painful end. Let me stress, *long*."

"Mr. Heartwell, I've never liked lawyers. Never trusted them. You only reinforce my opinion. But to save you time, your drugs won't work, and I won't talk."

"A common assertion." He laughed again. "We own the patents to the resistance drugs Negral dispenses. Besides, any secrets Negral has will be ours."

He sat again, very pleased with himself. "The war has eliminated many of your corporate sponsor's assets. Capital Galactic Investment is responsible and efficient. A hostile takeover in the works last I heard. Already completed by now I should imagine."

I grinned. "Be my guest."

Heartwell's smile turned sinister as he reached for the partitioning curtain. "Let me introduce your surgeons." He pulled the curtain aside.

If I could've jumped, I'd have been on the ceiling. Across my chest and groin stalked two hideous creatures. Half spider, half squid, with a dozen eyes. I tried to swat them away but my arms wouldn't move.

"I thought you'd be impressed," Mr. Heartwell said. "A bit gruesome, but unsurpassed surgeons."

I got a hold of myself. "Not what I expected." Each creature was the size of a Chihuahua with their downy brown squid part perched upon a tarantula torso. They had two long, wispy tentacle arms and six shorter. "At least they have the decency to wear sterile leggings."

The two creatures turned their sparkling red and white eyes back to their work. Tubes, needles, and syringes moved rapidly along festering sections of my abdomen. Some tubes and sensors ran into my chest.

The lawyer nodded his approval. "Impressive. You didn't even scream." He walked around, observing the aliens' work. "Sterile measures are for their benefit, not yours. V'Gun are medical geniuses. They're your lifeline, Specialist Keesay. Obviously, their size limits their combat ability. But all allies can contribute."

"Explains why the Stegmar were able to conquer them," I said.

"And the Crax subjugated the Stegmar." Heartwell clasped his hands together. "The V'Gun were a bonus."

"Do you intend to be a bonus?" I asked. "I doubt the Crax will have much use for human lawyers."

He cocked his head while gazing down at me. "So, you admit the Umbelgarri-Chicher-Human alliance is doomed to failure."

"No, just pointing out a flaw in your logic. Ever play chess?"

Dimming lights interrupted Mr. Heartwell's reply. Commotion in the halls followed. One of the V'Gun climbed over to a miniature computer console. After a moment Mr. Heartwell moved to read a large screen. Its angle was just beyond my view. For just a second he lost his poker face.

Mr. Heartwell said, "Administer the interrogation drug regimen."

One of the aliens climbed onto a tray and returned with a syringe. It climbed to my neck.

"I recommend you hold still," Mr. Heartwell warned. "Those long tentacles carry a painful venom."

I turned my head to expose a good vein. "My standard nightmares are worse."

The prick was fast, and an icy burning sensation followed. The V'Gun scrambled back to its partner where they monitored their equipment.

"Since you force me to resort to chemically-induced cooperation, I will inform your Crax handler that your nightmares are worse than anything he can dream up." My smile surprised him. He shook his head. "You are a fool, Specialist."

"Really, Chip?" The pain in my throat seemed more manageable. "I think your allies crave your attention."

Mr. Heartwell read the screen. "What? Are you sure?" He read the reply. "Is he stabilized? Good. Close him up." He read further. "Prepare him for interrogation. We may have time. After that you may do as you please with the Bahklack." He raised one eyebrow to me. "I have arrangements to make." He turned and left.

I closed my eyes while the two V'Gun surgeons worked. It was better than watching. I dozed off and awoke to my bed moving. Both V'Gun surgeons stood perched next to their equipment, tentacles controlling my bed's movement.

Passing on my right, taking up my former position was a wider table, or plexiglas box. It was six-by-six feet, and about two feet deep. Inside, partially submerged in some sort of blue-tinted gel, rested a Bahklack. Additional restraints held the crab-alien's claws and body immobile. It didn't appear necessary. Several holes and surrounding foam on its exoskeleton told of damage from Crax corrosive pellets. Its limp eyestalks swayed as the holding tank rolled into position.

The V'Gun surgeons discarded their old leg sheathes and stepped into sterile ones. They leapt onto the Phib thrall and began attaching monitoring equipment. It would've been difficult to watch, but the V'Gun had directed my bed parallel to the wall. I decided that my central nervous system had been deadened. If not, the torture Mr. Heartwell envisioned would be limited.

While the V'Gun leapt to retrieve more monitor wires, I spotted an eyestalk follow the move. A strap, bound to the large claw, tightened. Questions raced through my head. Had it been playing possum? Could it escape? Is that its intention? What could I do? If the V'Gun attached all the monitors and activated them, the ruse would be over.

I couldn't move but I could yell. That might work. Could I force myself to vomit? That'd get their attention. I could hardly swallow. All sensation below my neck remained dead.

"Hey," I said. "You V'Gun, I think something is wrong." I coughed. "I'm having trouble breathing." I coughed and groaned.

The V'Gun halted their activity and stared in my direction. A snap and suction popping sound alerted the two spidery aliens, but not before the Bahklack's small claw snatched one of the V'Gun and crushed it. The second leapt straight up, and clasped the lights. Its sterile leg sheaths hindered its grip and it fell onto the Bahklack. The gore-covered claw clamped onto the second squid-spider alien.

The V'Gun struggled. Tentacles lashed at the claw. A crisp crack followed by a grating crunch pronounced the second V'Gun's death.

I watched helplessly while the Umbelgarri thrall struggled to free itself. First it managed to fray and finally snap the strap restraining its large primary claw. Then the Bahklack pulled and freed its primary claw from the gel's grip. After that both claws went to work slicing at the restraining gel. Progress was slow. Finally the thrall worked to lift itself.

"Push out the sides," I said. "Break the gel's retaining walls."

The alien paused, then braced claws on opposite sides and pushed. The sides bowed. Then the right, forced by the larger claw, cracked. The alien clamped onto and tugged at the broken side until it pulled one half into the air. The retaining gel sagged over the edge. The Bahklack used the snapped edge like a knife and sliced deeper into the gel around its body. After shifting the plexiglas sheet to its smaller claw, it was only another thirty seconds before the crab pulled free.

"Good luck," I said. "Take a few out for me."

But it didn't leave. Instead it walked over to the computer equipment and tapped away with its smaller manipulating claws. Its eyestalks scanned the door, and occasionally my direction. Then it clicked over to me.

I watched, unable to do much else. It stopped inches from my bed and its black, bottomless eyes peered into mine. I stared back into them. Slowly it interposed its huge claw. A patch on the claw began pulsing with colors. Two stalks peered over the top. I looked at them a second, but then stared back into the mosaic swirl. It was trying to tell me something.

I don't know how long I stared. The dominant colors were flashing reds, blacks, and browns. The display mesmerized me. I couldn't discern any message. The colors continued to flow and flash but now with yellow and black at the center. That annoyed me. What was the alien trying to say?

"Get on with it!" I snapped, surprised by the harshness of my voice. I tried to calm myself before continuing. "That lawyer will be back any time." My teeth ground as I thought about the lawyer.

A yellow triangle formed in the center of the flashing and swirling colors. Specks of black bubbled within it. The triangle elongated into a diamond, then a narrow pyramid, with a second smaller forming on one end.

Furious, I bit back curses. "Get moving. Kill those Crax and lawyers," I hissed through my teeth. "Get revenge. They're traitors." I seethed. I'd have bit the claw if it were closer. My head throbbed, pounded. It was external. I was slamming my head up and down. I didn't care.

The Bahklack's smaller claw held my head down. The colors abruptly stopped.

I was exhausted. "I'll bide my time," I panted. "They'll pay."

Someone entered the room. I couldn't see but I heard Heartwell yell, "Guards!"

The Bahklack charged the door. On the way he toppled computer consoles. Then he wedged his claws into the sliding door and pried it open. Yells erupted as he ran out. Screams and MP fire cracked.

Fifteen seconds later Mr. Heartwell entered. He looked down at the crushed V'Gun, and stepped over them toward me. "Your ally is dead."

I started at his tie. I wanted to strangle him with it. "So are you," I snarled.

"Get him to surgery," the lawyer called over his shoulder. "And get two more V'Gun surgeons."

A security supervisor, an S2 wearing a CGIG logo, came around and maneuvered my bed out of the room. The lawyer followed. We passed a concrete wall. Among the posted signs was an arrow inscribed with the word, Maternity. The hospital. I forced myself to concentrate, not on Heartwell, but my surroundings. But every word he spoke shattered my concentration.

"We can't count on the Crax to hold off the fleet long enough," the lawyer said into his collar. "Besides, once they find what they're looking for, they might pull out. The V'Gun said they could black out selected parts of Specialist Keesay's memory. Be sure the new surgeons know what we want."

We stopped at an elevator. "Reinforcements made it," I said. "You and your company are warp-screwed."

The S2 pushed me into the elevator. Two security stepped out, leading several battered prisoners. "Tahgs?" I said. One purple eye was swollen shut. Her face was bloody and bruised, and wet with tears.

Before she could say anything a trailing sec-spec yanked her by the hair and shoved her forward. "Get moving, bitch."

"Bastard!" I yelled. "Your time'll come."

The S2 pushing the bed backhanded me across the face. "Shut up!"

We entered the elevator. "Don't worry, Supervisor Royer," said the lawyer. "Specialist Keesay will get his. Most assuredly." He handed the security supervisor a memory chip. "See that this gets downloaded. It's encoded to override any attempt to erase, should it come to that."

"Understood," said the supervisor. "I'll load it into the main and backup system."

"See to it," said the lawyer, "and that it is placed on several clips as well. Should the Umbelgarri and Marines break through, we don't want any *incriminating* information on Specialist Keesay here to become lost."

Lawyer Heartwell looked down. "Don't worry, Specialist. The files will be damaged, but they'll survive, even if you don't." The elevator door opened. "I'll take it from here." The S2 strode out.

"You think you've got it all figured out," I said. "I wouldn't count on it. I'll make sure you and every lawyer and board member of Capital Galactic pays." I flashed back to Mer. "It's been done before."

"You'll get your chance," Heartwell said. "But of course you'll be hampered by the fact that you won't recall a thing. If Tallavaster falls, we'll get you back. Capital Galactic is, after all, a very influential company supporting the government and military. We'll get the information we're after."

"I know a thing or two about Crax wounds," I said. "I won't last that long. I felt the corrosive in my blood."

"As I told you, the V'Gun are medical geniuses. They were instructed to stabilize you. There's a buffer in your system, and your organs have been repaired. We'll keep you alive as long as we want. No longer than we need to."

We passed by two security posted outside an operating room. "It is fortunate that you already have the cold sleep chemicals in your system. You'll survive at least that." He stopped the table. "And now, I have to see that the few prisoners we intend to take are prepared."

He turned to leave, but hesitated. "Oh, yes. Your friend, Tahgs. I worked with her. Charming girl. Didn't have the inhibiting serum you did, so I only had to torture half the information out of her."

"You," I said. "You'll rot in hell."

"She dislikes lawyers too. Can't imagine why. I'll be sure to ask when I see her again." His sinister smile returned. "That and a few new questions."

He wheeled me under the lights. Two V'Gun and one Selgum Crax stood over me. I tried to move my hands. No success. I shook my head and bit as the V'Gun tried to stick a needle in my neck. The Selgum Crax held me. I felt the sting. Everything went fuzzy, then black.

CHAPTER 43

Light shined through my eyelids. The familiar sound of cooling fans mixed with the hum of computers. I braced for cold sleep nausea and pain from my wounds. I felt neither.

Good pain meds? A tightness and tingling danced within my abdomen. I didn't have time to debate. Monitors would reveal conscious brain activity. My right index finger scraped against cloth and I could wiggle my toes. No oxygen tube. I listened. Breathing and footsteps coming toward me.

Loose restraints bound my arms above the elbow and across my chest. No time like the present to test their strength. They'd botched the memory erase, or had they? Only one way to find out. I relaxed and counted to three.

I opened my eyes and jerked my arms, pulling with everything I had! The restraints loosened. A lady doctor jumped back. I tried again, gaining more slack. I was in a rock-walled lab, still on Tallavaster?

"Specialist Keesay," the short, gray haired doctor said in a soothing voice. She smiled, held out her hands and stepped closer. "Relax. You're safe, it—"

Her mistake for getting too close. After my third try I broke free, grabbed a handful of white lab coat and yanked her toward me. "You're going to help me get out of here."

"Okay, Specialist Keesay," she said, a hint of panic in her voice. "Anything you want from me, I'll do."

The room was small with two banks of overhead fluorescent lights and tons of advanced equipment lining the walls. One door.

"Don't move," I said before relaxing my grip. "You do and I'll get out of here without your help." I reached down, detached the slack chest strap and sat up, keeping my eye on the doctor. Something was wrong. I could sit up.

The doctor spotted my surprise. "Kra, you've already been rescued. You're safe."

A young Colonial Marine, followed by a tall woman, rushed into the room.

"Stop," ordered the doctor without turning. "Specialist Keesay is having difficulty orienting. It is to be expected."

I clamped onto the doctor's wrist. "No tricks," I warned. "V'Gun's mistake for fixing me up too soon. Stand between me and that, marine." I stared at the doctor. I knew her. "Dr. Goldsen?" Both eyes worked, no blurring.

"That's right. I am Dr. Goldsen." She turned slowly. "Special Agent Vingee. We are on Io. Remember?"

Their faces were familiar—from the past, a trial. "The Cranaltar." I fell back to the bed. My stomach burned and ached. I couldn't see any blood seeping through the white gown. Where? What happened?"

"You mean what's happening," Agent Vingee said, moving up next to Dr. Goldsen.

Looking up, Dr. Goldsen said to Agent Vingee, "Not now. I should have kept him sedated longer."

"What do you mean?" I asked. "Longer? How long has it been?"

"Been?" Agent Vingee said. "You were hooked to the Cranaltar for weeks, and then under the medical care and recovery of the Umbelgarri for over a month."

Dr. Goldsen looked at me over the rims of her glasses. "Now be still while I see if you have injured any regenerated organs. Private Mulldoag and Agent Vingee, if you will step out a moment."

"Wait," I said. "This could be a trick. Before I submit to anything, I want out of this room. I want another bed."

"Why?" asked Dr. Goldsen with an annoyed look on her face.

"I had Crax acid in my blood. The V'Gun or Primus Crax would have the knowledge to cure that." I eyed Dr. Goldsen. "The Cranaltar destroys the brain. This could all be a drug-induced hallucination, maybe combined with a holo-cast."

Dr. Goldsen's stood with a furrowed brow. "If you insist. I do not know how that will convince you."

"No," said Agent Vingee. "It fits. I watched most of the Cranaltar's, *Documentary*."

"Documentary?" I asked.

"That's what your recorded experience is referred to," explained Agent Vingee. "Its official run for the trial is nearing completion. But I've been privileged to preview the ending. Would you like to see?"

"You are not going anywhere," Dr. Goldsen said. "Not until I examine you. You could have damaged the new tendons or caused internal bleeding."

"I'll risk it," I said. "Once I'm convinced I'm on Io."

The doctor crossed her arms over her chest. "The Umbelgarri were gracious enough to heal you once. This is foolishness."

I looked around, spotting one obvious surveillance camera above a cupboard. "If what you say is true, the Umbelgarri will appreciate my caution."

Agent Vingee nodded. Dr. Goldsen frowned.

The door slid open and everyone turned to watch a Bahklack enter. Dr. Goldsen stepped aside as the thrall clattered to my bedside. It raised its claw, presenting the color-shifting area. I watched the colors pulsate. And comprehend it!

"Human resistance fighter," it began. The colors continued to shift but, without the associated sound, the communication was bereft of emphasis and emotion. "You are witnessing reality. Your unrelenting hostility toward our mutual foe, your loyalty to your race, and your willingness to safeguard the

Masters' breeding ponds without question gave reason for extraordinary action on your behalf. As assigned, I have assisted in the assemblage, organization and restoration of your higher brain function. It was successful. I was instructed to infuse the ability for you to comprehend the Masters' visual and graphic communication. I provided technical assistance to your physician and her subordinates in detoxifying your body fluids and tissues and in cultivating the regeneration of damaged organs."

The Bahklack paused. It took a second to place proper emphasis on the string of merging visual images. "Understood," I said and signed.

Dr. Goldsen placed a hand on Vingee's arm, telling her not to interrupt.

The colors shifted again. "The images of your locating the breeding pond have been omitted from the record. Do not reveal this. Those that are authorized to know, do know. A suitable sequence was inserted."

Understood," I said and signed.

"The deep message of hostility and resistance to the yellow-tie worker classification administered by my kin has been eliminated. You retain your innate dislike of the yellow-tie classification. You must now follow your physician's guidance. This revelation session has delayed my assigned tasks. I must go."

"Thank you," I said and signed.

It held up its claw as it moved toward the door. "Your actions indebted the Masters."

"Well?" asked Dr. Goldsen.

"Well," I said, lying back down. "I don't like the fact that my thoughts and actions have been accessed, then manipulated and reloaded. How will I know what I think are really my own thoughts? Especially the infusion of Umbelgarri language."

Agent Vingee and Private Mulldoag eyed each other before following the alien thrall out.

Dr. Goldsen frowned. "I monitored the process. It was primarily an Umbelgarri program and procedure. The language bridge was necessary to ensure proper connections to recover your memory and thought processes."

"So, I think like an Umbelgarri? How they want me to?"

"No," said Dr. Goldsen. "Agent Vingee deems your action upon awakening as consistent with previous behavior."

"I don't like the way the Bahklack referred to the Phibs as its master."

"I think you just answered your own question," Dr. Goldsen with a knowing nod. "If your thought processes were altered, would you refer to them as Phibs?" She finished hooking up the equipment and stepped over to the computers to run the tests. "Would you accept their dominance over the Bahklack?"

I looked down. Round fleshy scars covered my stomach and side. My leg had numerous white linear scars.

"They'll fade," she said. "But never disappear. The leg wound occurred, I understand, from shrapnel due to an explosion of your own making." She examined the results. "And your eye was damaged by the haste of the V'Gun in severing part of your conscious memory. It was surgical in nature and easier to mend." She returned and removed the attachments. "And I personally saw to repairing your damaged hearing. Firing archaic weapons in confined areas is not wise."

"I suspect explosions not of my own design and front line combat contributed."

"Nevertheless, I hope that you will be more careful in the future."

"Do I check out?"

She pulled an old-style stethoscope from her lab coat pocket and listened to my heart and breathing. "Mr. Keesay, in ten days, you should be fit for duty." She spoke into her collar. "Special Agent Vingee, Specialist Keesay checks out."

The door slid open. Agent Vingee handed me a pair of gray-green security coveralls, along with socks, boots, undershirt and an unusual synthetic I-Tech pair of briefs. "Get dressed, quickly."

"You might assist him with the socks and boots," said Dr. Goldsen. "The monitors indicated you are experiencing pain despite the medication."

They politely turned their backs. Agent Vingee talked while I dressed.

"They're almost to the part in the Documentary where the Bahklack breaks free and kills the two V'Guns. After it ends, things should get interesting."

I buttoned the coveralls. "Thanks for the R-Tech touch. If I recall, much of my, uh, Documentary was interesting. At least to me. Help with the boots?"

"You're one lucky security specialist," Vingee said while sliding on my socks and then my boots. She finished with a double knot.

"I can't argue with that," I said. "The *Kalavar*, the quarantine planet, combat on Tallavaster. It seems somehow, distant. The trial, the destruction of the *Iron Armadillo*, you and Dr. Goldsen. More like a dream."

Agent Vingee helped me up. Steadied me. I was stiff, sore, and weak.

"All those people dead," I said. "They were real. They were my friends. Are any of them alive? What happened on Tallavaster?"

"No over exertion," interrupted Dr. Goldsen as Agent Vingee assisted me into the gray stone corridor, followed by my Marine escort.

I waved before switching to a salute. "Understood, Doctor."

"You'll be briefed," Vingee said. "Soon."

I stopped, hands going to my belt and pockets.

Vingee asked, "What's wrong?"

All my pockets were empty. No belt, no holster or equipment.

"Feeling somewhat naked, Specialist?" She pulled out a small firearm and handed it to me. It was an old .22 semiautomatic. Blued steel, rosewood grips.

"This is Inspector," I started before correcting, "Deputy Director Simms's." I checked the clip, safety, and slid it into its holster before pocketing it.

She urged me forward. "Promise not to shoot anybody."

"Not without cause. I've enough on my conscience."

We took a secluded route too narrow for cart access. I had to rest, which annoyed Agent Vingee, but not the marine. He looked green. "Seen any combat, Private Mulldoag?"

"None yet, Specialist. I've applied for transfer of duty twice."

I stood with his assistance. "You'll get your chance."

"Scuttle-butt has it, Specialist, that you've killed your share of Crax."

Vingee frowned. "Can't confirm that," I said. "But you appear to have good ears."

We made it to an elevator. Private Mulldoag stepped in first. We went down. He was the first out, checked the corridor, and signaled all clear.

After we exited, Private Mulldoag re-entered the elevator. I nodded to him before Agent Vingee steered me toward a set of doors guarded by two armed and armored marines.

They watched as Agent Vingee scanned her hand chip and eye. I scanned my eye and fingerprint. I needed to rest again, but pressed on.

"Does Falshire Hawks know I survived? I'd like to see his face."

"No," said Vingee. "You won't get to see him. A week after the Documentary began he departed. Since then a trio of subordinates and support staff have been in attendance."

I tried to hide my disappointment. "Anybody I'd know?"

"I doubt it. You need to rest."

There were no chairs in the corridor, so I leaned on her for a minute.

Agent Vingee said, "Deputy Director Simms might be alive."

"What? How do you know?"

"Intelligence doesn't know for sure. We believe that the Crax and their CGIG allies are holding prisoners. If he survived he'd be an important captive."

"What about Janice Tahgs?"

"I don't know, Specialist. Maybe. Tallavaster was retaken. Administrative Specialist Tahgs is listed among the missing." Her tone didn't inspire confidence.

"Let's go," I said. "Guess your security clearance has improved."

She grinned.

"At least someone benefited hanging around me."

"A lot of people benefited."

"It's going to take some getting used to," I said through pursed lips.

"What is?"

"The fact that my life, my thoughts and actions have been downloaded and viewed."

Agent Vingee slowed our pace. "I see what you mean. But I think very few people will ever see the Documentary."

"Besides those viewing the first run. Consider military planners, analysts, and their staff. Corporate lawyers. Researchers on the Cranaltar IV Project, and probably a dozen other groups I haven't considered."

She nodded. "True, but still pretty small in the big scheme of things."

"Didn't I request it to be a part of the public record?"

"I believe so. But I doubt that will ever happen."

"Not until I'm long dead. I hope."

I wanted to sit down and sort things out. What had happened—really happened. All of the people returned to me through advanced technology. Through the Cranaltar. But the Documentary, my Documentary, was coming to an end and I didn't want to miss that. Not for anything.

Agent Vingee led me to another door guarded by a marine. He nodded to Vingee and then to me, and stepped aside.

Beyond was a small room with a row of padded, flip-down chairs reminiscent of old-style movie theaters. They faced a window, beyond which action on a circular screen played. A trio of angled monitors sat above the window with the same, visually modified scene. Muted sound accompanied. I recognized what was happening. The screen showed the freed Bahklack making its way out the door. It was like I'd carried a recording camera mounted on a helmet. Every movement captured. Every sound. Even thoughts.

Vingee steadied me. She helped me to a chair. I was so caught up in the action I didn't notice the man three seats down.

"Greetings, Specialist Keesay," he said.

It was my nurse from pretrial. He'd helped me escape the *Pars Griffin*. "Greetings, Caylar?"

He slid down next to me and offered his hand. "Special Agent Caylar Guymin."

I shook his hand. His grip was firm but gentle, considerate of my weakened state. "Sorry," I said. "Caylar was all I could recall."

"No problem," he said. "Caylar is fine."

"Call me Kra."

Vingee sat down next to me. The seats were a little high off the ground for me, a little shallow for her.

Onscreen I watched Mr. Heartwell speaking to me. "I really hate that guy."

"Understandable," Caylar said, his attention returning to the screens.

I leaned close to Vingee. "Did he and Mr. Loams ever locate Diplomat Silvre?"

"Her body," said Caylar, "among the *Iron Armadillo*'s debris."

"I'm sorry to hear that." It reminded me of how many had died. I thought of the colonies on Tallavaster. The Zeta Aquarius Dock, and all the ships. The men and women who manned them. The colonist children.

"Thank you." Caylar's attention was no longer on the screens. "What do you think?"

"Of that?" I asked, refocusing on the present. "Really weird. The sound of my thoughts matches exactly how I hear it in my head. Like I'm really talking to myself, but from outside in."

"If you look," Agent Vingee said, pointing, "you can see some of the Capital Galactic personnel watching."

I got up and walked over to the window. We were at the four o'clock position. Eight viewers in two rows sat in near darkness, except for the faint glow of dimmed computer screens set into the desks. They reminded me of Chief Brold's desk.

The viewing screen didn't project light into the area.

Vingee stood next to me. "There's a fleet captain, Colonial Marine colonel, two intel agents, a lawyer from the Criminal Justice Investigatory Squad and two Capital Galactic reps, and a diplomat to the Umbelgarri. Several rooms like ours have a Chicher diplomat, researchers, and legal teams from selected agencies, and former Negral Corp reps, watching."

I was going to ask her about the 'limited number of spectators' when a ratcheting sound reverberated in my head. I looked from Vingee to Caylar.

The next thing I knew I was seated with Vingee holding my hand and Caylar kneeling in front of me.

"Specialist Keesay, Kra," Caylar said. "Are you okay?"

It took me a second to snap out of it. "I think so. What happened?" I felt a warm sensation in my shorts. I looked down. Now I knew what the synthetic underwear was for. "I blacked out, didn't I?"

Caylar nodded.

"How long?"

Agent Vingee replied, "About a minute and twenty seconds."

"You knew this was going to happen."

Neither spoke at first. I waited. Dr. Goldsen, trailed by an assistant lugging portable diagnostics, strode into the room.

"You knew this was going to happen!"

Dr. Goldsen ignored my question and flashed lights into my eyes. The assistant stuck several relays to my scalp and neck and began a scan.

"Right?" I asked.

"We suspected it might," said Dr. Goldsen. "You had similar episodes while you were unconscious. How long did this one last?"

I pushed away Vingee's hand. "Episodes?"

"Eighty-one seconds," Vingee said, watching me carefully.

"Wait," I said, trying to get up.

Caylar pushed me back into the seat. "Take it easy and let them treat you."

I relaxed and let them work. I gathered my thoughts and realized how little I knew about my situation. I wasn't happy. "It's better than being brain dead," I admitted.

Agent Vingee held my hand while Dr. Goldsen monitored and analyzed the results.

"Did you notice anything before the episode?" asked Dr. Goldsen.

"Episode," I said. "Exactly what is an episode?"

"A seizure," she said. "They have been decreasing in frequency and length. They may disappear altogether, or may be medicated. Did you notice anything?"

"Yes, I did. A clicking or ratcheting sound just before. Next thing I knew I was seated, in wet drawers." I looked at the concerned faces around me. "Oh, and thanks for the absorbent pants."

"Good to see you are taking this well," said Dr. Goldsen.

"I haven't the energy to do otherwise. Besides, the Cranaltar should've scrambled my brain. All things considered, I've faced worse."

"I believe you have," said Dr. Goldsen, continuing her work.

I smiled. "Anyone supply the CGIG lawyers with absorbent undergarments?" That got a round of chuckles.

I waited while Dr. Goldsen and the med tech completed their monitoring. I was tired, but not enough to sleep. I spotted movement in the viewing room. "What's going on out there?"

"The Documentary has ended," said Caylar. "They're debating it right now."

"Pipe it in," I said.

Caylar looked to Dr. Goldsen, who nodded.

"The defendant's version is unreliable," said a Capital Galactic lawyer. "If he wasn't already criminally insane, which would alter his perceptions and interpretations, the manipulations and incorrect transcriptions made by the *experimental* Cranaltar IV certainly have altered our viewed version of the defendant's perceived *version* of events." He scanned notes from his clip. "We have not had time to analyze the defendant's distorted perception instigated by the Bahklack's hypnotic suggestion."

An intel man stood. "Thus far, information presented with respect to events on the Mavinrom Dock is accurate. Ships to investigate concerns about the quarantine planet and Tallavaster are en route."

"Already there," whispered Agent Vingee into my ear. "No sense letting CGIG know that."

"Really?"

Agent Vingee looked around. Neither Dr. Goldsen nor her assistant were within earshot. "Dr. Maximar Drizdon's son and wife are safe," she whispered. "Now that they are, he's already planned the next phase of the war for our side."

"Should you be telling me this?"

Caylar nodded. "Intel has granted you appropriate clearance. And these rooms are secure from monitoring."

"From what they've seen," added Vingee, "they think you're reliable."

With Negral's demise, and Capital Galactic's quest for information before disposing of me, I didn't have a sponsor. "Do you think Intel will recruit me?"

"There'll be an offer," said Vingee.

"How many R-Techs are there in the agency?" I knew after I'd asked, it really didn't matter. Not to me.

"More than you might expect," said Caylar.

"But none quite like you," added Vingee.

"May I have the floor?" Dr. Goldsen asked through a relay next to the window. "It has direct relevance to your current debate over state of mind of the defendant."

The CGIG lawyer asked, "Who are you? And what information of relevance could you possibly add?"

Dr. Goldsen tapped the controls and a section of the window elevated. "Dr. Marjoree Goldsen, MD. I also have a PhD in neurochemistry and in psychology. I am the lead researcher in the Cranaltar Project."

"Very impressive," said the lawyer after crossing his arms. "That states who you are. Namely, a responsible party for this work of fiction."

I whispered to Vingee, "Think he passed Lawyer Arrogance 101 with flying colors?"

"If you had your set of brass knuckles," she whispered back, "I'd borrow them."

"With respect to relevance of what I have to present," said Dr. Goldsen. "Your current line of argument is based upon the fact that the defendant was in some fashion mentally defective, and that the Cranaltar IV destroyed his cognitive capacity while providing the evidence viewed in the Documentary. As such, the accuracy and the validity of the evidence presented can never be ascertained. Am I correct?"

"You appear to have the essence of the well-founded assertion."

Dr. Goldsen signaled to me. Agent Vingee helped me to my feet.

"Then, Mr. Lawyer," said Dr. Goldsen. "I think my patient has a few relevant words to say. I present to you, Security Specialist 4th Class Krakista Keesay."

I walked to the opening and met with silent stares. "*Nemo me impune lacessit*," I announced. "Tell that to Falshire Hawks."

Everyone but the intel man looked dumbfounded, and the second CGIG lawyer. He stepped forward and pointed. His jaw locked.

I yanked the .22 from my pocket, but fumbled, unfamiliar with it. The small caliber required a lucky head shot. The marine colonel hopped on his table, leapt over the front row and barreled toward the lawyer, but not fast enough. I wouldn't be either.

"Ufff," I grunted.

Vingee knocked me aside and landed on top of me as the nearby crack of MP fire sounded. It must've been Caylar.

Shouts boomed followed by barked orders.

"You're heavier than you look," I said, staring at Agent Vingee's throat. She ignored me, still scanning the room with MP pistol in hand.

"All clear," Caylar announced.

I looked over to Dr. Goldsen. She'd also taken refuge on the floor. "Recognize that smell?" I asked her.

"No," she replied. "But I can reasonably guess."

"The Cranaltar doesn't include odors?" I tried to ignore the musty acidic stench. "Experience tells me we have at least one acid-devoured body. Correct, Caylar?"

"Correct, Kra," he said. "One lawyer down."

"All's clear," I said to Vingee. "One less bad guy. One big mess."

She lifted me to my feet. "Do you recall Mr. Loams?"

"Yes," I said. "Hawks's assistant at my pretrial. Helped me escape to Io on the *Gilded Swan*."

"Well," Vingee said. "I think you just replaced him as number one on the Capital Galactic Investment Group's enemy list. Wouldn't you agree, Agent Guymin?"

Caylar nodded. "Imagine that. An R-Tech climbing so high. And you're not even off the disabled list."

"For me," I said, "making friends has been a chronic problem."

Vingee wrapped her arm around my shoulder. "Not around here."

Caylar nodded, as did Dr. Goldsen.

"Understood," I said. "We'll see. Come to think of it, Agent Vingee, don't you owe me a story?"

THE END

ABOUT THE AUTHOR

Terry W. Ervin II is an English teacher who enjoys writing Fantasy and Science Fiction. He is the author of ***Flank Hawk*** and ***Blood Sword***, the first two novels in his **First Civilization's Legacy Series**, and ***Genre Shotgun***, a collection of his previously published short stories.

When Terry isn't writing or enjoying time with his wife and daughters, he can be found in his basement raising turtles. To contact Terry, or to learn more about his writing endeavors, visit his website at www.ervin-author.com or his blog, *Up Around the Corner*, at http://uparoundthecorner.blogspot.com.

Made in the USA
Charleston, SC
05 November 2013